Masters and Masterpieces of the SHORT STORY

JOSHUA McCLENNEN
University of Michigan

HOLT, RINEHART AND WINSTON, INC. · NEW YORK

Library of Congress Catalog Card Number 57-5710

25545-0117
Printed in the United States of America
June, 1961

INTRODUCTION

THIS COLLECTION of stories has grown out of my own experience in teaching modern short stories over a period of some years, and it reflects the problems which I have encountered. Chief among these has been the impossibility, for me, of finding a single collection with a large enough number of both first-rate and teachable stories to provide material for a full semester. Differences in tastes and interests being what they are, one individual is not likely to find that much more than one half of the stories in a given collection are suited to his purposes. In this collection I have therefore included many more stories than any one teacher is likely to use, even though this has meant the omission of all such apparatus as biographical sketches and study questions.

A second problem has been the frequency with which students are unfavorably impressed by their first encounter with even an outstanding author. I find, however, that the student who dislikes Joyce or Faulkner after reading one story often comes to hold a quite different opinion when he has read several stories by the same author and has had a chance to grow familiar with a point of view or a literary method which at first seemed to him merely repellent or baffling. But if students are asked to read several stories by one author, they must either buy a number of collections of stories or do much of their reading in a library, and both of these expedients are unsatisfactory. It is for this reason and to meet what seems to me a very real need that I have included, in addition to single stories by individual authors, anywhere from two to six examples of the work of some of the more outstanding writers.

Among those who should have been represented by several selections is, of course, Ernest Hemingway. Unfortunately it has proved impossible to secure permission to include more than one of his stories.

It has also been my experience that the best kind of story for group discussion is one which has as its central focus some sort of moral or philosophical question. The advantages of such a story are twofold: in the first place it is educational in the best and broadest sense of the word; in the second, it does not as a rule yield its full meaning on a first or casual reading. This means that there is a real incentive for close and repeated readings and for the kind of analysis of character and motivation which is likely to provoke a lively discussion. Accordingly I have chosen for this collection only those stories which seem to me to give effective expression to a point of view worth knowing. At the same time I have given the preference to stories which incline toward the positive and the optimistic rather than those which are negative and pessimistic, however excellent in other respects. In an often-quoted statement William Faulkner has said that the duty of the writer is to help man prevail by lifting his heart and that the way to do this is to remind him of the old truths of the heart, pity and courage and love and endurance. Not the least of the purposes of this collection has been to demonstrate that in many instances the modern writer has done as Faulkner would have him do and has done it well.

J. McC.

December 10, 1956

CONTENTS

ELIZABETH BOWEN

A Queer Heart

MRS. CADMAN got out of the bus backwards. No amount of practice ever made her more agile; the trouble she had with her big bulk amused everyone, and herself. Gripping the handles each side of the bus door so tightly that the seams of her gloves cracked, she lowered herself cautiously, like a climber, while her feet, overlapping her smart shoes, uneasily scrabbled at each step. One or two people asked why the bus made, for one passenger, such a long, dead stop. But on the whole she was famous on this line, for she was constantly in and out of town. The conductor waited behind her, smiling, holding her basket, arms wide to catch her if she should slip.

Having got safe to the ground, Mrs. Cadman shook herself like a satisfied bird. She took back her shopping basket from the conductor and gave him a smile instead. The big kind scarlet bus once more ground into movement, off up the main road hill: it made a fading blur in the premature autumn dusk. Mrs. Cadman almost waved after it, for with it went the happy part of her day. She turned down the side road that led to her gate.

A wet wind of autumn, smelling of sodden gardens, blew in her face and tilted her hat. Leaves whirled along it, and one lime leaf, as though imploring shelter, lodged in her fur collar. Every gust did more to sadden the poor trees. This was one of those roads outside growing provincial cities that still keep the rural mystery. They seem to lead into something still not known. Traffic roars past one end, but the other end is in silence: you see a wood, a spire, a haughty manor gate, or your view ends with the turn of an old wall. Here some new raw-looking villas stood with spaces between them; in the spaces were orchards and market-gardens. A glasshouse roof reflected the wet grey light; there was a shut chapel further along. And, each standing back in half an acre of ground, there were two or three stucco houses with dark windows, sombre but at the same time ornate, built years ago in this then retired spot. Dead lime leaves showered over their grass plots and evergreens. Mrs. Cadman's house, Granville, was one of these: its name was engraved in scrolls over the porch. The solid house was not large, and Mrs. Cadman's daughter, Lucille, could look after it with a daily help.

The widow and her daughter lived here in the state of cheerless meekness Lucille considered suitable for them now. *Mr.* Cadman had liked to have everything done in style. But twelve years ago he had died, travelling on business, in a hotel up in the North. Always the gentleman, he had been glad to spare them this upset at home. He had been brought back to the Midlands for his impressive funeral, whose size showed him a popular man. How unlike Mr. Cadman was Rosa proving herself. One can be most unfriendly in one's way of dying. Ah, well, one chooses one's husband; one's sister is dealt out to one by fate.

Mrs. Cadman, thumb on the latch of her own gate, looked for a minute longer up and down the road—deeply, deeply unwilling to go in. She looked back at the corner where the bus had vanished, and an immense sigh heaved up her coat lapels and made a cotton carnation, pinned to the fur, brush a fold of her chin. Laced, hooked, buttoned so tightly into her clothes, she seemed to need to deflate herself by these sudden sighs, by yawns or by those explosions of laughter that often vexed Lucille. Through her face—embedded in fat but still very lively, as exposed, as ingenuous as a little girl's—you could see some emotional fermentation always at work in her. Her smiles were frequent, hopeful and quick. Her pitching walk was due to her tight shoes.

When she did go in, she went in with a sort of rush. She let the door bang back on the hall wall, so that the chain rattled and an outraged clatter came from the letter-box. Immediately she knew she had done wrong. Lucille, appalled, looked out of the dining-room. "*Shissssssh!* How can you, mother!" she said.

"Ever so sorry, dear," said Mrs. Cadman, cast down.

"She'd just dropped off," said Lucille. "After her bad night and everything. It really does seem hard."

Mrs. Cadman quite saw that it did. She glanced nervously up the stairs, then edged into the dining-room. It was not cheerful in here: a monkey puzzle, too close to the window, drank the last of the light up; the room still smelt of dinner; the fire smouldered resentfully, starved for coal. The big mahogany furniture lowered, with no shine. Mrs. Cadman, putting her basket down on the table, sent an uncertain smile across at Lucille, whose glasses blankly gleamed high up on her long face. She often asked herself where Lucille could have come from. *Could* this be the baby daughter she had borne, and tied pink bows on, and christened a pretty name? In the sun in this very bow window she had gurgled into the sweet-smelling creases of Lucille's neck—one summer lost in time.

"You *have* been an age," Lucille said.

"Well, the shops were quite busy. I never *saw*," she said with irrepressible pleasure, "I never *saw* so many people in town!"

Lucille, lips tighter than ever shut, was routing about, unpacking the shopping basket, handling the packages. Chemist's and grocer's parcels. Mrs. Cadman watched her with apprehension. Then Lucille pounced; she held up a small soft parcel in frivolous wrappings. "Oho," she said. "So you've been in at Babbington's?"

"Well, I missed one bus, so I had to wait for the next. So I just popped in there a minute out of the cold. And, you see, I've been wanting a little scarf—"

"Little scarf!" said Lucille. "I don't know what to make of you, mother. I don't really. How *could* you, at such a time? How you ever could have the heart!" Lucille, standing the other side of the table, leaned across it, her thin weight on her knuckles. This brought her face near her mother's. "Can't you understand?" she said. "Can't you take *anything* in? The next little scarf *you'll* need to buy will be black!"

"What a thing to say!" exclaimed Mrs. Cadman, profoundly offended. "With that poor thing upstairs now, waiting to have her tea."

"Tea? She can't take her tea. Why, since this morning she can't keep a thing down."

Mrs. Cadman blenched and began unbuttoning her coat. Lucille seemed to feel that her own prestige and Aunt Rosa's entirely hung on Aunt Rosa's approaching death. You could feel that she and her aunt had thought up this plan together. These last days had been the climax of their complicity. And there was Mrs. Cadman—as ever, as usual—put in the wrong, frowned upon, out of things. Whenever Rosa arrived to stay Mrs. Cadman had no fun in her home, and now Rosa was leaving for ever it seemed worse. A perverse kick of the heart, a flicker of naughtiness, made Mrs. Cadman say: "Oh, well, while there's life there's hope."

Lucille said: "If you won't face it, you won't. But I just say it does fall heavy on me. . . . We had the vicar round here this afternoon. He was up with Aunt for a bit, then he looked in and said he did feel I needed a prayer too. He said he thought I was wonderful. He asked where you were, and he seemed to wonder you find the heart to stay out so long. I thought from his manner he wondered a good deal."

Mrs. Cadman, with an irrepressible titter, said: "Give him something to think about! Why if I'd ha' shown up that vicar'd have popped out as fast as he popped in. Thinks I'd make a mouthful of him! Why, I've made him bolt down the street. Well, well. He's not *my* idea of a vicar. When your father and I first came here we had a rural dean. Oh, he was as pleasant as anything."

Lucille, with the air of praying for Christian patience, folded her lips. Jabbing her fingers down the inside of her waistbelt, she more tightly tucked in her tight blouse. She liked looking like Mrs. Noah—no, *Miss* Noah. "The doctor's not been again. We're to let him know of any change."

"Well, let's do the best we can," said Mrs. Cadman. "But don't keep on *talking*. You don't make things any better, keeping on going on. My opinion is one should keep bright to the last. When my time comes, oh, I would like a cheery face."

"It's well for you . . ." began Lucille. She bit the remark off and, gathering up the parcels, stalked scornfully out of the dining-room. Without comment she left exposed on the table a small carton of goodies Mrs. Cadman had bought to cheer herself up with and had concealed in the toe of the shopping bag. Soon, from the kitchen came the carefully muffled noises of Lucille putting away provisions and tearing the wrappings off the chemist's things. Mrs. Cadman, reaching out for the carton, put a peppermint into each cheek. She, oh so badly, wanted a cup of tea but dared not follow Lucille into the kitchen in order to put the kettle on.

Though, after all, Granville *was* her house. . . .

You would not think it was her house—not when Rosa was there. While Lucille and her mother were *tête à tête* Lucille's disapproval was at least fairly tacit. But as soon as Rosa arrived on one of these yearly autumn visits—always choosing the season when Mrs. Cadman felt in her least good form, the fall of the leaf—the aunt and niece got together and found everything wrong. Their two cold natures ran together. They found Mrs. Cadman lacking; they forbade the affection she would have offered them. They censured her the whole time. Mrs. Cadman could date her real alienation from Lucille from the year when Rosa's visits began. During Mr. Cadman's lifetime Rosa had never come for more than an afternoon. Mr. Cadman had been his wife's defence from her sister—a great red kind of rumbustious fortification. He had been a man who kept every chill wind out. Rosa, during those stilted afternoon visits, had adequately succeeded in conveying that she found marriage *low*. She might just have suffered a pious marriage; she openly deprecated this high living, this state of fleshly bliss. In order not to witness it too closely she lived on in lodgings in her native town. . . . But once widowhood left her sister exposed, Rosa started flapping round Granville like a doomed bird. She instituted these yearly visits, which, she made plain at the same time, gave her not much pleasure. The journey was tedious, and by breaking her habits, leaving her lodgings, Rosa was, out of duty, putting herself about. Her joyless and intimidating visits had, therefore, only one object—to protect the interests of Lucille.

Mrs. Cadman had suspected for some time that Rosa had something the matter with her. No one looks as yellow as that for nothing. But she was not sufficiently intimate with her sister to get down to the cosy subjects of insides. This time, Rosa arrived looking worse than ever, and three days afterwards had collapsed. Lucille said now she had known her aunt was poorly. Lucille said now she had always known. "But of course you wouldn't notice, mother," she said.

Mrs. Cadman sat down by the fire and, gratefully, kicked off her tight shoes. In the warmth her plump feet uncurled, relaxed, expanded like sea-anemones. She stretched her legs out, propped her heels on the fender and wiggled her toes voluptuously. They went on wiggling of their own accord: they seemed to have an independent existence. Here, in her home, where she felt so "put wrong" and chilly, they were like ten stout confidential friends. She said, out loud: "Well, *I* don't know what I've done."

The fact was: Lucille and Rosa resented her. (She'd feel better when she had had her tea.) She should *not* have talked as she had about the vicar. But it seemed so silly, Lucille having just him. She did wish Lucille had a better time. No young man so much as paused at the gate. Lucille's aunt had wrapped her own dank virginity round her, like someone sharing a mackintosh.

Mrs. Cadman had had a good time. A real good time always lasts: you have it with all your nature and all your nature stays living with it. She had been a pretty child with long, blonde hair that her sister Rosa, who was her elder sister, used to tweak when they were alone in their room. She had grown used, in that childish attic bedroom, to Rosa's malevolent silences. Then one had grown up, full of great uppish curves. Hilda Cadman could sing. She had sung at parties and sung at charity concerts, too. She had been invited from town to town, much fêted in business society. She had sung in a dress cut low at the bosom, with a rose or carnation tucked into her hair. She had drunk port wine in great red rooms blazing with chandeliers. Mr. Cadman had whisked her away from her other gentlemen friends, and not for a moment had she regretted it. Nothing had been too good for her; she had gone on singing. She had felt warm air on her bare shoulders; she still saw the kind, flushed faces crowding round. Mr. Cadman and she belonged to the jolly set. They all thought the world of her, and she thought the world of them.

Mrs. Cadman, picking up the poker, jabbed the fire into a spurt of light. It does not do any good to sit and think in the dark.

The town was not the same now. They had all died, or lost their money, or gone. But you kept on loving the town for its dear old sake. She sometimes thought: Why not move and live at the seaside, where there would be a promenade and a band? But she knew her nature clung to the old scenes; where you had lived, you lived—your nature clung like a cat. While there was *something* to look at she was not one to repine. It kept you going to keep out and about. Things went, but then new things came in their place. You can't cure yourself of the habit of loving life. So she drank up the new pleasures—the big cafés, the barging buses, the cinemas, the shops dripping with colour, almost all built of glass. She could be perfectly happy all alone in a café, digging into a cream bun with a fork, the band playing, smiling faces all round. The old faces had not gone: they had dissolved, diluted into the ruddy blur through which she saw everything.

Meanwhile, Lucille was hard put to it, living her mother down. Mother looked ridiculous, always round town like that.

Mrs. Cadman heard Lucille come out of the kitchen and go upstairs with something rattling on a tray. She waited a minute more, then sidled into the kitchen, where she cautiously started to make tea. The gas-ring, as though it were a spy of Lucille's, popped loudly when she applied the match.

"Mother, she's asking for you."

"Oh, dear—do you mean she's—?"

"She's much more herself this evening," Lucille said implacably.

Mrs. Cadman, at the kitchen table, had been stirring sugar into her third cup. She pushed her chair back, brushed crumbs from her bosom and followed Lucille like a big unhappy lamb. The light was on in the hall, but the stairs led up into shadow: she had one more start of reluctance at their foot. Autumn draughts ran about in the top story: up there the powers of darkness all seemed to mobilize. Mrs. Cadman put her hand on the banister knob. "Are you sure she *does* want to see me? Oughtn't she to stay quiet?"

"You should go when she's asking. You never know. . . ."

Breathless, breathing unevenly on the top landing, Mrs. Cadman pushed open the spare-room—that was the sick-room—door. In there—in here—the air was dead, and at first it seemed very dark. On the ceiling an oil-stove printed its flower-pattern; a hooded lamp, low down, was turned away from the bed. On that dark side of the lamp she could just distinguish Rosa, propped up, with the sheet drawn to her chin.

"Rosa?"

"Oh, it's you?"

"Yes; it's me, dear. Feeling better this evening?"

"Seemed funny, you not coming near me."

"They said for you to keep quiet."

"My own sister. . . . You never liked sickness, did you? Well, I'm going. I shan't trouble you long."

"Oh, don't talk like that!"

"I'm glad to be going. Keeping on lying here. . . . We all come to it. Oh, give over crying, Hilda. Doesn't do any good."

Mrs. Cadman sat down, to steady herself. She fumbled in her lap with her handkerchief, perpetually, clumsily knocking her elbows against the arms of the wicker chair. "It's such a shame," she said. "It's such a pity. You and me, after all . . ."

"Well, it's late for all that now. Each took our own ways." Rosa's voice went up in a sort of ghostly sharpness. "There were things that couldn't be otherwise. I've tried to do right by Lucille. Lucille's a good girl, Hilda. You should ask yourself if you've done right by her."

"Oh, for shame, Rosa," said Mrs. Cadman, turning her face through the dark towards that disembodied voice. "For shame, Rosa, even if you *are* going. You know best what's come between her and me. It's been you and her, you and her. I don't know where to turn sometimes—"

Rosa said: "You've got such a shallow heart."

"How should you know? Why, you've kept at a distance from me ever since we were tots. Oh, I know I'm a great silly, always after my fun, but I never took what was yours; I never did harm to you. I don't see what call we have got to judge each other. You didn't want my life that I've had."

Rosa's chin moved: she was lying looking up at her sister's big rippling shadow, splodged up there by the light of the low lamp. It is frightening, having your shadow watched. Mrs. Cadman said: "But what did I do to you?"

"I *could* have had a wicked heart," said Rosa. "A vain, silly heart like yours. I could have fretted, seeing you take everything. One thing, then another. But I was shown. God taught me to pity you. God taught me my lesson. . . . You wouldn't even remember that Christmas tree."

"What Christmas tree?"

"No, you wouldn't even remember. Oh, I thought it was lovely. I could have cried when they pulled the curtains open, and there it was, all blazing away with candles and silver and everything—"

"Well, isn't that funny. I—"

"No; you've had all that pleasure since. All of us older children couldn't take it in, hardly, for quite a minute or two. It didn't look real. Then I looked up, and there was a fairy doll fixed on the top, right on the top spike, fixed on to a star. I set my heart on her. She had wings and long fair hair, and she was shining away. I couldn't take my eyes off her. They cut the presents down; but she wasn't for anyone. In my childish blindness I kept praying to God. If I am not to have her, I prayed, let her stay there."

"And what did God do?" Hilda said eagerly.

"Oh, He taught me and saved me. You were a little thing in a blue sash; you piped up and asked might you have the doll."

"Fancy me! Aren't children awful!" said Mrs. Cadman. "Asking like that."

"They said: 'Make her sing for it.' They were taken with you. So you piped up again, singing. You got her, all right. I went off where they kept the coats. I've thanked God ever since for what I had to go through! I turned my face from vanity that very night. I had been shown."

"Oh, what a shame!" said Hilda. "Oh, I think it was cruel; you poor little mite."

"No, I used to see that doll all draggled about the house till no one could bear the sight of it. I said to myself: that's how those things end. Why, I'd learnt more in one evening than you've ever learnt in your life. Oh, yes, I've watched you, Hilda. Yes, and I've pitied you."

"Well, you showed me no pity."

"You asked for no pity—all vain and set up."

"No wonder you've been against me. Fancy me not knowing. I didn't *mean* any harm—why, I was quite a little thing. I don't even remember."

"Well, you'll remember one day. When you lie as I'm lying you'll find that everything comes back. And you'll see what it adds up to."

"Well, if I do?" said Hilda. "I haven't been such a baby; I've seen things out in my own way; I've had my ups and downs. It hasn't been all jam." She got herself out of the arm-chair and came and stood uncertainly by the foot of the bed. She had a great wish to reach out and turn the hooded lamp round, so that its light could fall on her sister's face. She felt she should *see* her sister, perhaps for the first time. Inside the flat, still form did implacable disappointment, then, stay locked? She wished she could give Rosa some little present. Too late to give Rosa anything pretty now: she looked back—it had always, then, been too late? She thought: you poor queer heart; you queer heart, eating yourself out, thanking God for the pain. She thought: I did that to her; then what have I done to Lucille?

She said: "You're ever so like me, Rosa, really, aren't you? Setting our hearts on things. When you've got them you don't notice. No wonder you wanted Lucille. . . . You did ought to have had that fairy doll."

ANTON CHEKHOV

The Lament

IT IS TWILIGHT. A thick wet snow is slowly twirling around the newly lighted street lamps, and lying in soft thin layers on roofs, on horses' backs, on people's shoulders and hats. The cabdriver Iona Potapov is quite white, and looks like a phantom; he is bent double as far as a human body can bend double; he is seated on his box; he never makes a move. If a whole snowdrift fell on him, it seems as if he would not find it necessary to shake it off. His little horse is also quite white, and remains motionless; its immobility, its angularity, and its straight wooden-looking legs, even close by, give it the appearance of a gingerbread horse worth a *kopek.* It is, no doubt, plunged in deep thought. If you were snatched from the plow, from your usual gray surroundings, and were thrown into this slough full of monstrous lights, unceasing noise, and hurrying people, you too would find it difficult not to think.

Iona and his little horse have not moved from their place for a long while. They left their yard before dinner, and up to now, not a fare. The evening mist is descending over the town, the white lights of the lamps replacing brighter rays, and the hubbub of the street getting louder. "Cabby for Viborg way!" suddenly hears Iona. "Cabby!"

Iona jumps, and through his snow-covered eyelashes sees an officer in a greatcoat, with his hood over his head.

"Viborg way!" the officer repeats. "Are you asleep, eh? Viborg way!"

With a nod of assent Iona picks up the reins, in consequence of which layers of snow slip off the horse's back and neck. The officer seats himself in the sleigh, the cabdriver smacks his lips to encourage his horse, stretches out his neck like a swan, sits up, and, more from habit than necessity, brandishes his whip. The little horse also stretches its neck, bends its wooden-looking legs, and makes a move undecidedly.

"What are you doing, werewolf!" is the exclamation Iona hears from the dark mass moving to and fro, as soon as they have started.

"Where the devil are you going? To the r-r-right!"

"You do not know how to drive. Keep to the right!" calls the officer angrily.

A coachman from a private carriage swears at him; a passerby, who has run across the road and rubbed his shoulder against the horse's nose, looks at him furiously as he sweeps the snow from his sleeve. Iona shifts about on his seat as if he were on needles, moves his elbows as if he were trying to keep his equilibrium, and gapes about like someone suffocating, who does not understand why and wherefore he is there.

"What scoundrels they all are!" jokes the officer; "one would think they had all entered into an agreement to jostle you or fall under your horse."

Iona looks round at the officer, and moves his lips. He evidently wants to say something, but the only sound that issues is a snuffle.

"What?" asks the officer.

Iona twists his mouth into a smile, and with an effort says hoarsely:

"My son, *barin,* died this week."

"Hm! What did he die of?"

Iona turns with his whole body toward his fare, and says:

"And who knows! They say high fever. He was three days in the hospital, and then died. . . . God's will be done."

"Turn round! The devil!" sounds from the darkness. "Have you popped off, old doggie, eh? Use your eyes!"

"Go on, go on," says the officer, "otherwise we shall not get there by tomorrow. Hurry up a bit!"

The cabdriver again stretches his neck, sits up, and, with a bad grace, brandishes his whip. Several times again he turns to look at his fare, but the latter has closed his eyes, and apparently is not disposed to listen. Having deposited the officer in the Viborg, he stops by the tavern, doubles himself up on his seat, and again remains motionless, while the snow once more begins to cover him and his horse. An hour, and another. . . . Then, along the footpath, with a squeak of galoshes, and quarreling, come three young men, two of them tall and lanky, the third one short and humpbacked.

"Cabby, to the Police Bridge!" in a cracked voice calls the humpback. "The three of us for two *griveniks!*"

Iona picks up his reins, and smacks his lips. Two *griveniks* is not a fair price, but he does not mind whether it is a *rouble* or five *kopeks*—to him it is all the same now, so long as they are fares. The young men, jostling each other and using bad language, approach the sleigh, and all three at once try to get onto the seat; then begins a discussion as to which two shall sit and who shall be the one to stand. After wrangling, abusing each other, and much petulance, it is at last decided that the humpback shall stand, as he is the smallest.

"Now then, hurry up!" says the humpback in a twanging voice, as he takes his place and breathes in Iona's neck.

"Old furry! Here, mate, what a cap you have! There is not a worse one to be found in all Petersburg! . . ."

"He-he!—he-he!" giggles Iona. "Such a . . ."

"Now you, 'such a,' hurry up, are you going the whole way at this pace? Are you? . . . Do you want it in the neck?"

"My head feels like bursting," says one of the lanky ones. "Last night at the Donkmasovs, Vaska and I drank the whole of four bottles of cognac."

"I don't understand what you lie for," says the other lanky one angrily; "you lie like a brute."

"God strike me, it's the truth!"

"It's as much the truth as that a louse coughs!"

"He, he," grins Iona, "what gay young gentlemen!"

"Pshaw, go to the devil!" says the humpback indignantly.

"Are you going to get on or not, you old pest? Is that the way to drive! Use the whip a bit! Go on, devil, go on, give it to him well!"

Iona feels at his back the little man wriggling, and the tremble in his voice. He listens to the insults hurled at him, sees the people, and little by little the feeling of loneliness leaves him. The humpback goes on swearing until he gets mixed up in some elaborate six-foot oath, or chokes with coughing. The lankies begin to talk about a certain Nadejda Petrovna. Iona looks round at them several times; he waits for a temporary silence, then, turning round again, he murmurs:

"My son . . . died this week."

"We must all die," sighs the humpback, wiping his lips after an attack of coughing. "Now, hurry up, hurry up! Gentlemen, I really cannot go any farther like this! When will he get us there?"

"Well, just you stimulate him a little in the neck!"

"You old pest, do you hear, I'll bone your neck for you! If one treated the like of you with ceremony one would have to go on foot! Do you hear, old serpent Gorinytch! Or do you not care a spit?"

Iona hears rather than feels the blows they deal him.

"He, he," he laughs. "They are gay young gentlemen, God bless 'em!"

"Cabby, are you married?" asks a lanky one.

"I? He, he, gay young gentlemen! Now I have only a wife and the moist ground. . . . he, ho, ho . . . that is to say, the grave. My son has died, and I am alive. . . . A wonderful thing, death mistook the door . . . instead of coming to me, it went to my son. . . ."

Iona turns round to tell them how his son died, but at this moment, the humpback, giving a little sigh, announces, "Thank God, we have at last reached our destination," and Iona watches them disappear through the dark entrance. Once more he is alone, and again surrounded by silence. . . . His grief, which has abated for a short while, returns and rends his heart with greater force. With an anxious and hurried look, he searches among the crowds passing on either side of the street to find whether there may be just one person who will listen to him. But the crowds hurry by without noticing him or his trouble. Yet it is such an immense, illimitable grief. Should his heart break and the grief pour out, it would flow over the whole earth, so it seems, and yet no one sees it. It has managed to conceal itself in such an insignificant shell that no one can see it even by day and with a light.

Iona sees a hall porter with some sacking, and decides to talk to him.

"Friend, what sort of time is it?" he asks.

"Past nine. What are you standing here for? Move on."

Iona moves on a few steps, doubles himself up, and abandons himself to his grief. He sees it is useless to turn to people for help. In less than five minutes he straightens himself, holds up his head as if he felt some sharp pain, and gives a tug at the reins; he can bear it no longer. "The stables," he thinks, and the little horse, as if it understands, starts off at a trot.

About an hour and a half later Iona is seated by a large dirty stove. Around the stove, on the floor, on the benches, people are snoring; the air is thick and suffocatingly hot. Iona looks at the sleepers, scratches himself, and regrets having returned so early.

"I have not even earned my fodder," he thinks. "That's what's my trouble. A man who knows his job, who has had enough to eat, and his horse too, can always sleep peacefully."

A young cabdriver in one of the corners half gets up, grunts sleepily, and stretches towards a bucket of water.

"Do you want a drink?" Iona asks him.

"Don't I want a drink?"

"That's so? Your good health! But listen, mate—you know, my son is dead. . . . Did you hear? This week, in the hospital. . . . It's a long story."

Iona looks to see what effect his words have, but sees none—the young man has hidden his face and is fast asleep again. The old man sighs, and scratches his head. Just as much as the young one wants to drink, the old man wants to talk. It will soon be a week since his son died, and he has not been able to speak about it properly to anyone. One must tell it slowly and carefully; how his son fell ill, how he suffered, what he said before he died, how he died. One must describe every detail of the funeral, and the journey to the hospital to fetch the dead son's clothes. His daughter Anissia has remained in the village—one must talk about her too. Is it nothing he has to tell? Surely the listener would gasp and sigh, and sympathize with him? It is better, too, to talk to women; although they are stupid, two words are enough to make them sob.

"I'll go and look after my horse," thinks Iona; "there's always time to sleep. No fear of that!"

He puts on his coat, and goes to the stables to his horse; he thinks of the corn, the hay, the weather. When he is alone, he dares not think of his son; he can speak about him to anyone, but to think of him, and picture him to himself, is unbearably painful.

"Are you tucking in?" Iona asks his horse, looking at its bright eyes; "go on, tuck in, though we've not earned our corn, we can eat hay. Yes! I am too old to drive—my son could have, not I. He was a first-rate cabdriver. If only he had lived!"

Iona is silent for a moment, then continues:

"That's how it is, my old horse. There's no more Kuzma Ionitch. He has left us to live, and he went off pop. Now let's say, you had a foal, you were the foal's mother, and suddenly, let's say, that foal went and left you to live after him. It would be sad, wouldn't it?"

The little horse munches, listens, and breathes over its master's hand. . . .

Iona's feelings are too much for him, and he tells the little horse the whole story.

A. E. COPPARD

Arabesque: The Mouse

IN THE main street amongst tall establishments of mart and worship was a high narrow house pressed between a coffee factory and a bootmaker's. It had four flights of long dim echoing stairs, and at the top, in a room that was full of the smell of dried apples and mice, a man in the middle age of life had sat reading Russian novels until he thought he was mad. Late was the hour, the night outside black and freezing, the pavements below empty and undistinguishable when he closed his book and sat motionless in front of the glowing but flameless fire. He felt he was very tired, yet he could not rest. He stared at a picture on the wall until he wanted to cry; it was a colour-print by Utamaro of a suckling child caressing its mother's breasts as she sits in front of a blackbound mirror. Very chaste and decorative it was, in spite of its curious anatomy. The man gazed, empty of sight though not of mind, until the sighing of the gas-jet maddened him. He got up, put out the light, and sat down again in the darkness trying to compose his mind before the comfort of the fire. And he was just about to begin a conversation with himself when a mouse crept from a hole in the skirting near the fireplace and scurried into the fender. The man had the crude dislike for such sly nocturnal things, but this mouse was so small and bright, its antics so pretty, that he drew his feet carefully from the fender and sat watching it almost with amusement. The mouse moved along the shadows of the fender, out upon the hearth, and sat before the glow, rubbing its head, ears, and tiny belly with its paws as if it were bathing itself with the warmth, until, sharp and sudden, the fire sank, an ember fell, and the mouse flashed into its hole.

The man reached forward to the mantel-piece and put his hand upon a pocket lamp. Turning on the beam, he opened the door of a cupboard beside the fireplace. Upon one of the shelves there was a small trap baited with cheese, a trap made with a wire spring, one of those that smashed down to break the back of ingenuous and unwary mice.

"Mean—so mean," he mused, "to appeal to the hunger of any living thing just in order to destroy it."

He picked up the empty trap as if to throw it in the fire.

"I suppose I had better leave it though—the place swarms with them." He still hesitated. "I hope that little beastie won't go and do anything foolish." He put the trap back quite carefully, closed the door of the cupboard, sat down again and extinguished the lamp.

Was there anyone else in the world so squeamish and foolish about such things! Even his mother, mother so bright and beautiful, even she had laughed at his childish horrors. He recalled how once in his childhood, not long after his sister Yosine was born, a friendly neighbor had sent him home with a bundle of dead larks tied by the feet "for supper." The pitiful inanimity of the birds had brought a gush of tears; he had run weeping home and into the kitchen, and there he had found the strange thing doing. It was dusk; his mother was kneeling before the fire. He dropped the larks.

"Mother!" he exclaimed softly.

She looked at his tearful face.

"What's the matter, Filip?" she asked, smiling too at his astonishment.

"Mother! What are you doing?"

Her bodice was open and she was squeezing her breasts; long thin streams of milk spurted into the fire with a plunging noise.

"Weaning your little sister," laughed Mother. She took his inquisitive face and pressed it against the delicate warmth of her bosom, and he forgot the dead birds behind him.

"Let me do it, Mother," he cried, and doing so he discovered the throb of the heart in his mother's breast. Wonderful it was for him to experience it, although she could not explain it to him.

"Why does it do that?"

"If it did not beat, little son, I should die and the Holy Father would take me from you."

"God?"

She nodded. He put his hand upon his own breast. "Oh, feel it, Mother!" he cried. Mother unbuttoned his little coat and felt the gentle *tick tick* with her warm palm.

"Beautiful!" she said.

"Is it a good one?"

She kissed his smiling lips. "It is good if it beats truly. Let it always beat truly, Filip; let it always beat truly."

There was the echo of a sigh in her voice, and he had divined some grief, for he was very wise. He kissed her bosom in his tiny ecstasy and whispered soothingly: "Little mother! little mother!" In such joys he forgot his horror of the dead larks; indeed he helped Mother to pluck them and spit them for supper.

It was a black day that succeeded, and full of tragedy for the child. A great bay horse with a tawny mane had knocked down his mother in the lane, and a heavy cart had passed over her, crushing both her hands. She was borne away moaning with anguish to the surgeon who cut off the two hands. She died in the night. For years the child's dreams were filled with the horror of the stumps of arms, bleeding unendingly. Yet he had never seen them, for he was sleeping when she died.

While this old woe was come vividly before him he again became aware of the mouse. His nerves stretched upon him in repulsion, but he soon relaxed to a tolerant interest, for it was really a most engaging little mouse. It moved with curious staccato scurries, stopping to rub its head or flicker with its ears; they seemed almost transparent ears. It spied a red cinder and skipped innocently up to it . . . sniffing . . . sniffing . . . until it jumped back scorched. It would crouch as a cat does, blinking in the warmth, or scamper madly as if dancing, and then roll upon its side rubbing its head with those pliant paws. The melancholy man watched it until it came at last to rest and squatted meditatively upon its haunches, hunched up, looking curiously wise, a pennyworth of philosophy; then once more the coals sank with a rattle and again the mouse was gone.

The man sat on before the fire and his mind filled again with unaccountable sadness. He had grown into manhood with a burning generosity of spirit and rifts of rebellion in him that proved too exacting for his fellows and seemed mere wantonness to men of casual rectitudes. "Justice and Sin," he would cry, "Property and Virtue—incompatibilities! There can be no sin in a world of justice, no property in a world of virtue!" With an engaging extravagance and a certain clear-eyed honesty of mind he had put his two and two together and seemed then to rejoice, as in some topsy-turvy dream, in having rendered unto Caesar, as you might say, the things that were due to Napoleon! But this kind of thing could not pass unexpiated in a world of men having an infinite regard for Property and a pride in their traditions of Virtue and Justice. They could indeed forgive him his sins, but they could not forgive him his compassions. So he had to go seek for more melodious-minded men and fair unambiguous women. But rebuffs can deal more deadly blows than daggers; he became timid—a timidity not of fear but of pride—and grew with the years into misanthropy, susceptible to trivial griefs and despairs, a vessel of emotion that emptied as easily as it filled, until he came at last to know that his griefs were half deliberate, his despairs half unreal, and to live but for beauty—which is tranquillity—to put her wooing hand upon him.

Now, while the mouse hunts in the cupboard, one fair recollection stirs in the man's mind—of Cassia and the harmony of their only meeting, Cassia who had such rich red hair, and eyes, yes, her eyes were full of starry inquiry like the eyes of mice. It was so long ago that he had forgotten how he came to be in it, that unaccustomed orbit of vain vivid things—a village festival, all oranges and houp-la. He could not remember how he came to be there, but at night, in the court hall, he had danced with Cassia—fair and unambiguous indeed!—who had come like the wind from among the roses and swept into his heart.

"It is easy to guess," he had said to her, "what you like most in the world."

She laughed. "To dance? Yes, and you . . .?"

"To find a friend."

"I know, I know," she cried, caressing him with recognitions. "Ah, at times I quite love my friends—until I begin to wonder how much they hate me!"

He had loved at once that cool pale face, the abundance of her hair as light as the autumn's clustered bronze, her lilac dress and all the sweetness about her like a bush of lilies. How they had laughed at the two old peasants whom they had overheard gabbling of trifles like sickness and appetite!

"There's a lot of nature in a parsnip," said one, a fat person of the kind that swells grossly when stung by a bee, "a lot of nature when it's young, but when it's old it's like everything else."

"True it is."

"And I'm very fond of vegetables, yes, and I'm very fond of bread."

"Come out with me," whispered Cassia to Filip, and they walked out in the blackness of midnight into what must have been a garden.

"Cool it is here," she said, "and quiet, but too dark even to see your face—can you see mine?"

"The moon will not rise until after dawn," said he, "it will be white in the sky when the starlings whistle in your chimney."

They walked silently and warily about until they felt the chill of the air. A dull echo of the music came to them through the walls, then stopped, and they heard the bark of a fox away in the woods.

"You are cold," he whispered, touching her bare neck with timid fingers. "Quite, quite cold," drawing his hand tenderly over the curves of her chin and face. "Let us go in," he said, moving with discretion from the rapture he desired.

"We will come out again," said Cassia.

But within the room the ball was just at an end, the musicians were packing up their instruments and the dancers were flocking out and homewards, or to the buffet which was on a platform at one end of the room. The two old peasants were there, munching hugely.

"I tell you," said one of them, "there's nothing in the world for it but the grease of an owl's liver. That's it, that's it! Take something on your stomach now, just to offset the chill of the dawn!"

Filip and Cassia were beside them, but there were so many people crowding the platform that Filip had to jump down. He stood then looking up adoringly at Cassia, who had pulled a purple cloak about her.

"For Filip, Filip, Filip," she said, pushing the last bite of her sandwich into his mouth and pressing upon him her glass of Loupiac. Quickly he drank it with a great gesture, and flinging the glass to the wall, took Cassia into his arms, shouting: "I'll carry you home, the whole way home, yes, I'll carry you!"

"Put me down!" she cried, beating his head and pulling his ear, as they passed among the departing dancers. "Put me down, you wild thing!"

Dark, dark was the lane outside, and the night an obsidian net, into which he walked carrying the girl. But her arms were looped around him; she discovered paths for him, clinging more tightly as he staggered against a wall, stumbled upon a gulley, or when her sweet hair was caught in the boughs of a little lime tree.

"Do not loose me, Filip, will you? Do not loose me," Cassia said, putting her lips against his temple.

His brain seemed bursting, his heart rocked within him, but he adored the rich grace of her limbs against his breast. "Here it is," she murmured, and he carried her into a path that led to her home in a little lawned garden where the smell of ripe apples upon the branches and the heavy lustre of roses stole upon the air. Roses and apples! Roses and apples! He carried her right into the porch before she slid down and stood close to him with her hands still upon his shoulders. He could breathe happily at the release, standing silent and looking round at the sky sprayed with wondrous stars but without a moon.

"You are stronger than I thought you, stronger than you look; you are really very strong," she whispered, nodding her head to him. Opening the buttons of his coat, she put her palm against his breast.

"Oh, how your heart does beat! Does it beat truly—and for whom?"

He had seized her wrists in a little fury of love, crying: "Little mother, little mother!"

"What are you saying?" asked the girl; but before he could continue there came a footstep sounding behind the door, and the clack of a bolt. . . .

What was that? Was that really a bolt or was it . . . was it . . . the snap of the trap? The man sat up in his room intently listening, with nerves quivering again, waiting for the trap to kill the little philosopher. When he felt it was all over he reached guardedly in the darkness for the lantern, turned on the beam, and opened the door of the cupboard. Focussing the light upon the trap, he was amazed to see the mouse sitting on its haunches before it, uncaught. Its head was bowed, but its bead-like eyes were full of brightness, and it sat blinking, it did not flee.

"Shoosh!" said the man, but the mouse did not move. "Why doesn't it go? Shoosh!" he said again, and suddenly the reason of the mouse's strange behavior was made clear. The trap had not caught it completely, but it had broken off both its forefeet, and the thing crouched there holding out its two bleeding stumps humanly, too stricken to stir.

Horror flooded the man, and conquering his repugnance he plucked the mouse up quickly by the neck. Immediately the thing fastened its teeth in his finger; the touch was no more than the slight prick of a pin. The man's impulse then exhausted itself. What should he do with it? He put his hand behind him, he dared not look, but there was nothing to be done except kill it at once, quickly, quickly. Oh, how should he do it? He bent towards the fire as if to drop the mouse into its quenching glow; but he paused and shuddered, he would hear its cries, he would have to listen. Should he crush it with finger and thumb? A glance towards the window decided him. He opened the sash with one hand and flung the wounded mouse far into the dark street. Closing the window with a crash, he sank into a chair, limp with pity too deep for tears.

So he sat for two minutes, five minutes, ten minutes. Anxiety and shame filled him with heat. He opened the window again, and the freezing air poured in and cooled him. Seizing his lantern, he ran down the echoing stairs into the dark empty street, searching long and vainly for the little philosopher until he had to desist and return to his room, shivering, frozen to his very bones.

When he had recovered some warmth he took the trap from its shelf. The two feet dropped into his hand; he cast them into the fire. Then he once more set the trap and put it back carefully into the cupboard.

E. M. FORSTER

The Celestial Omnibus

THE BOY who resided at Agathox Lodge, 28, Buckingham Park Road, Surbiton, had often been puzzled by the old sign-post that stood almost opposite. He asked his mother about it, and she replied that it was a joke, and not a very nice one, which had been made many years back by some naughty young men, and that the police ought to remove it. For there were two strange things about this sign-post; first, it pointed up a blank alley, and, secondly, it had painted on it, in faded characters, the words, "To Heaven."

"What kind of young men were they?" he asked.

"I think your father told me that one of them wrote verses, and was expelled from the University and came to grief in other ways. Still, it was a long time ago. You must ask your father about it. He will say the same as I do, that it was put up as a joke."

"So it doesn't mean anything at all?"

She sent him upstairs to put on his best things, for the Bonses were coming to tea, and he was to hand the cakestand.

It struck him, as he wrenched on his tightening trousers, that he might do worse than ask Mr. Bons about the sign-post. His father, though very kind, always laughed at him—shrieked with laughter whenever he or any other child asked a question or spoke. But Mr. Bons was serious as well as kind. He had a beautiful house and lent one books, he was a churchwarden, and a candidate for the County Council; he had donated to the Free Library enormously, he presided over the Literary Society, and had Members of Parliament to stop with him—in short, he was probably the wisest person alive.

Yet even Mr. Bons could only say that the sign-post was a joke—the joke of a person named Shelley.

"Of course!" cried the mother; "I told you so, dear. That was the name."

"Had you never heard of Shelley?" asked Mr. Bons.

"No," said the boy, and hung his head.

"But is there no Shelley in the house?"

"Why, yes!" exclaimed the lady, in much agitation. "Dear Mr. Bons, we aren't such Philistines as that. Two at the least. One a wedding present, and the other, smaller print, in one of the spare rooms."

"I believe we have seven Shelleys," said Mr. Bons, with a slow smile. Then he brushed the cake crumbs off his stomach, and, together with his daughter, rose to go.

The boy, obeying a wink from his mother, saw them all the way to the garden gate, and when they had gone he did not at once return to the house, but gazed for a little up and down Buckingham Park Road.

His parents lived at the right end of it. After No. 39 the quality of the houses dropped very suddenly, and 64 had not even a separate servants' entrance. But at the present moment the whole road looked rather pretty, for the sun had just set in splendour, and the inequalities of rent were drowned in a saffron afterglow. Small birds twittered, and the breadwinners' train shrieked musically down through the cutting—that wonderful cutting which has drawn to itself the whole beauty out of Surbiton, and clad itself, like any Alpine valley, with the glory of the fir and the silver birch and the primrose. It was this cutting that had first stirred desires within the boy—desires for something just a little different, he knew not what, desires that would return whenever things were sunlit, as they were this evening, running up and down inside him, up and down, up and down, till he would feel quite unusual all over, and as likely as not would want to cry. This evening he was even sillier, for he slipped across the road towards the sign-post and began to run up the blank alley.

The alley runs between high walls—the walls of the gardens of "Ivanhoe" and "Bella Vista," respectively. It smells a little all the way, and is scarcely twenty yards long, including the turn at the end. So not unnaturally the boy soon came to a standstill. "I'd like to kick that Shelley," he exclaimed, and glanced idly at a piece of paper which was pasted on the wall. Rather an odd piece of paper, and he read it carefully before he turned back. This is what he read:

S. AND C.R.C.C.

ALTERATION IN SERVICE

Owing to lack of patronage the Company are regretfully compelled to suspend the hourly service, and to retain only the

Sunrise and Sunset Omnibuses,

which will run as usual. It is to be hoped that the public will patronize an arrangement which is intended for their convenience. As an extra inducement, the Company will, for the first time, now issue

Return Tickets!

(available one day only), which may be obtained of the driver. Passengers are again reminded that *no tickets are issued at the other end,* and that no complaints in this connection will receive consideration from the Company. Nor will the Company be responsible for any negligence or stupidity on the part of Passengers, nor for Hailstorms, Lightning, Loss of Tickets, nor for any Act of God.

For the Direction.

Now he had never seen this notice before, nor could he imagine where the omnibus went to. S. of course was for Surbiton, and R.C.C. meant Road Car Company. But what was the meaning of the other C.? Coombe and Malden, perhaps, or possibly "City." Yet it could not hope to compete with the South-Western. The whole thing, the boy reflected, was run on hopelessly unbusinesslike lines. Why no tickets from the other end? And what an hour to start! Then he realized that unless the notice was a hoax, an omnibus must have been starting just as he was wishing the Bonses good-bye. He peered at the ground through the gathering dusk, and there he saw what might or might not be the marks of wheels. Yet nothing had come out of the alley. And he had never seen an omnibus at any time in the Buckingham Park Road. No: it must be a hoax, like the sign-post, like the fairy tales, like the dreams upon which he would wake suddenly in the night. And with a sigh he stepped from the alley—right into the arms of his father.

Oh, how his father laughed! "Poor, poor Popsey!" he cried, "Diddums! Diddums! Diddums think he'd walky-palky up to Evvink!" And his mother, also convulsed with laughter, appeared on the steps of Agathox Lodge.

"Don't Bob!" she gasped. "Don't be so naughty! Oh, you'll kill me! Oh, leave the boy alone!"

But all that evening the joke was kept up. The father implored to be taken too. Was it a very tiring walk? Need one wipe one's shoes on the door-mat? And the boy went to bed feeling faint and sore, and thankful for only one thing—that he had not said a word about the omnibus. It was a hoax, yet through his dreams it grew more and more real, and the streets of Surbiton, through which he saw it driving, seemed instead to become hoaxes and shadows. And very early in the morning he woke with a cry, for he had a glimpse of its destination.

He struck a match, and its light fell not only on his watch but also on his calendar, so that he knew it to be half-an-hour to sunrise. It was pitch dark, for the fog had come down from London in the night, and all Surbiton was wrapped in its embraces. Yet he sprang out and dressed himself, for he was determined to settle once for all which was real: the omnibus or the streets. "I shall be a fool one way or the other," he thought, "until I know." Soon he was shivering in the road under the gas lamp that guarded the entrance to the alley.

To enter the alley itself required some courage. Not only was it horribly dark, but he now realized that it was an impossible terminus for an omnibus. If it had not been for a policeman, whom he heard approaching through the fog, he would never have made the attempt. The next moment he had made the attempt and failed. Nothing. Nothing but a blank alley and a very silly boy gaping at its dirty floor. It *was* a hoax. "I'll tell papa and mamma," he decided. "I deserve it. I deserve that they should know. I am too silly to be alive." And he went back to the gate of Agathox Lodge.

There he remembered that his watch was fast. The sun was not risen; it would not rise for two minutes. "Give the bus every chance," he thought cynically, and returned into the alley.

But the omnibus was there.

II

It had two horses, whose sides were still smoking from their journey, and its two great lamps shone through the fog against the alley's walls, changing their cobwebs and moss into tissues of fairyland. The driver was huddled up in a cape. He faced the blank wall, and how he had managed to drive in so neatly and so silently was one of the many things that the boy never discovered. Nor could he imagine how ever he would drive out.

"Please," his voice quavered through the foul brown air, "please, is that an omnibus?"

"Omnibus est," said the driver, without turning round, There was a moment's silence. The policeman passed, coughing, by the entrance of the alley. The boy crouched in the shadow, for he did not want to be found out. He was pretty sure, too, that it was a Pirate; nothing else, he reasoned, would go from such odd places and at such odd hours.

"About when do you start?" He tried to sound nonchalant.

"At sunrise."

"How far do you go?"

"The whole way."

"And can I have a return ticket which will bring me all the way back?"

"You can."

"Do you know, I half think I'll come." The driver made no answer. The sun must have risen, for he unhitched the brake. And scarcely had the boy jumped in before the omnibus was off.

How? Did it turn? There was no room. Did it go forward? There was a blank wall. Yet it was moving—

moving at a stately pace through the fog, which had turned from brown to yellow. The thought of warm bed and warmer breakfast made the boy feel faint. He wished he had not come. His parents would not have approved. He would have gone back to them if the weather had not made it impossible. The solitude was terrible; he was the only passenger. And the omnibus, though well-built, was cold and somewhat musty. He drew his coat round him, and in so doing chanced to feel his pocket. It was empty. He had forgotten his purse.

"Stop!" he shouted. "Stop!" And then, being of a polite disposition, he glanced up at the painted notice-board so that he might call the driver by name. "Mr. Browne! stop; oh, do please stop!"

Mr. Browne did not stop, but he opened a little window and looked in at the boy. His face was a surprise, so kind it was and modest.

"Mr. Browne, I've left my purse behind. I've not got a penny. I can't pay for the ticket. Will you take my watch, please? I am in the most awful hole."

"Tickets on this line," said the driver, "whether single or return, can be purchased by coinage from no terrene mint. And a chronometer, though it had solaced the vigils of Charlemagne, or measured the slumbers of Laura, can acquire by no mutation the double-cake that charms the fangless Cerberus of Heaven!" So saying, he handed in the necessary ticket, and, while the boy said "Thank you," continued, "Titular pretensions, I know it well, are vanity. Yet they merit no censure when uttered on a laughing lip, and in an homonymous world are in some sort useful, since they do serve to distinguish one Jack from his fellow. Remember me, therefore, as Sir Thomas Browne."

"Are you a Sir? Oh, sorry!" He had heard of these gentlemen drivers. "It *is* good of you about the ticket. But if you go on at this rate, however does your bus pay?"

"It does not pay. It was not intended to pay. Many are the faults of my equipage; it is compounded too curiously of foreign woods; its cushions tickle erudition rather than promote repose; and my horses are nourished not on the evergreen pastures of the moment, but on the dried bents and clovers of Latinity. But that it pays!—that error at all events was never intended and never attained."

"Sorry again," said the boy rather hopelessly. Sir Thomas looked sad, fearing that, even for a moment, he had been the cause of sadness. He invited the boy to come up and sit beside him on the box, and together they journeyed on through the fog, which was now changing from yellow to white. There were no houses by the road; so it must be either Putney Heath or Wimbledon Common.

"Have you been a driver always?"

"I was a physician once."

"But why did you stop? Weren't you good?"

"As a healer of bodies I had scant success, and several score of my patients preceded me. But as a healer of the spirit I have succeeded beyond my hopes and my deserts. For though my draughts were not better nor subtler than those of other men, yet, by reason of the cunning goblets wherein I offered them, the queasy soul was ofttimes tempted to sip and be refreshed."

"The queasy soul," the boy murmured; "if the sun sets with trees in front of it, and you suddenly come strange all over, is that a queasy soul?"

"Have you felt that?"

"Why, yes."

After a pause he told the boy a little, a very little, about the journey's end. But they did not chatter much, for the boy, when he liked a person, would as soon sit silent in his company as speak, and this, he discovered, was also the mind of Sir Thomas Browne and of many others with whom he was to be acquainted. He heard, however, about the young man Shelley, who was now quite a famous person, with a carriage of his own, and about some of the other drivers who are in the service of the Company. Meanwhile the light grew stronger, though the fog did not disperse. It was now more like mist than fog, and at times would travel quickly across them, as if it was part of a cloud. They had been ascending too, in a most puzzling way; for over two hours the horses had been pulling against the collar, and even if it were Richmond Hill they ought to have been at the top long ago. Perhaps it was Epsom, or even the North Downs; yet the air seemed keener than that which blows on either. And as to the name of their destination, Sir Thomas Browne, was silent.

Crash!

"Thunder, by Jove!" said the boy, "and not so far off either. Listen to the echoes! It's more like mountains."

He thought, not very vividly, of his father and mother. He saw them sitting down to sausages and listening to the storm. He saw his own empty place. Then there would be questions, alarms, theories, jokes, consolations. They would expect him back at lunch. To lunch he would not come, nor to tea, but he would be in for dinner, and so his day's truancy would be over. If he had had his purse he would have bought them presents—not that he should have known what to get them.

Crash!

The peal and the lightning came together. The cloud quivered as if it were alive, and torn streamers of mist rushed past. "Are you afraid?" asked Sir Thomas Browne.

"What is there to be afraid of? Is it much farther?"

The horses of the omnibus stopped just as a ball of fire burst up and exploded with a ringing noise that was deafening but clear, like the noise of a blacksmith's forge. All the cloud was shattered.

"Oh, listen, Sir Thomas Browne! No, I mean look; we shall get a view at last. No, I mean listen; that sounds like a rainbow!"

The noise had died into the faintest murmur, beneath which another murmur grew, spreading stealthily, steadily, in a curve that widened but did not vary. And in widening curves a rainbow was spreading from the horses' feet into the dissolving mists.

"But how beautiful! What colours! Where will it stop? It is more like the rainbows you can tread on. More like dreams."

The colour and the sound grew together. The rainbow spanned an enormous gulf. Clouds rushed under it and were pierced by it, and still it grew, reaching forward, conquering the darkness, until it touched something that seemed more solid than a cloud.

The boy stood up. "What is that out there?" he called. "What does it rest on, out at that other end?"

In the morning sunshine a precipice shone forth beyond the gulf. A precipice—or was it a castle? The horses moved. They set their feet upon the rainbow.

"Oh, look!" the boy shouted. "Oh, listen! Those caves—or are they gateways? Oh, look between those cliffs at those ledges. I see people! I see trees!"

"Look also below," whispered Sir Thomas. "Neglect not the diviner Acheron."

The boy looked below, past the flames of the rainbow that licked against their wheels. The gulf also had cleared, and in its depths there flowed an everlasting river. One sunbeam entered and struck a green pool, and as they passed over he saw three maidens rise to the surface of the pool, singing, and playing with something that glistened like a ring.

"You down in the water—" he called.

They answered, "You up on the bridge—" There was a burst of music. "You up on the bridge, good luck to you. Truth in the depth, truth on the height."

"You down in the water, what are you doing?"

Sir Thomas Browne replied: "They sport in the mancipiary possession of their gold"; and the omnibus arrived.

III

The boy was in disgrace. He sat locked up in the nursery of Agathox Lodge, learning poetry for a punishment. His father had said, "My boy! I can pardon anything but untruthfulness," and had caned him, saying at each stroke, "There is *no* omnibus, *no* driver, *no* bridge, *no* mountain; you are a *truant,* a *guttersnipe,* a *liar.*" His father could be very stern at times. His mother had begged him to say he was sorry. But he could not say that. It was the greatest day of his life, in spite of the caning and the poetry at the end of it.

He had returned punctually at sunset—driven not by Sir Thomas Browne, but by a maiden lady who was full of quiet fun. They had talked of omnibuses and also of barouche landaus. How far away her gentle voice seemed now! Yet it was scarcely three hours since he had left her up the alley.

His mother called through the door. "Dear, you are to come down and to bring your poetry with you."

He came down, and found that Mr. Bons was in the smoking-room with his father. It had been a dinner party.

"Here is the great traveller!" said his father grimly. "Here is the young gentleman who drives in an omnibus over rainbows, while young ladies sing to him." Pleased with his wit, he laughed.

"After all," said Mr. Bons, smiling, "there is something a little like it in Wagner. It is odd how, in quite illiterate minds, you will find glimmers of Artistic Truth. The case interests me. Let me plead for the culprit. We have all romanced in our time, haven't we?"

"Hear how kind Mr. Bons is," said his mother, while his father said, "Very well. Let him say his Poem, and that will do. He is going away to my sister on Tuesday, and *she* will cure him of this alley-slopering." (Laughter.) "Say your Poem."

The boy began. " 'Standing aloof in giant ignorance.' "

His father laughed again—roared. "One for you, my son! 'Standing aloof in giant ignorance!' I never knew these poets talked sense. Just describes you. Here, Bons, you go in for poetry. Put him through it, will you, while I fetch up the whisky?"

"Yes, give me the Keats," said Mr. Bons. "Let him say his Keats to me."

So for a few moments the wise man and the ignorant boy were left alone in the smoking-room.

" 'Standing aloof in giant ignorance, of thee I dream and of the Cyclades, as one who sits ashore and longs perchance to visit—' "

"Quite right. To visit what?"

" 'To visit dolphin coral in deep seas,' " said the boy, and burst into tears.

"Come, come! why do you cry?"

"Because—because all these words that only rhymed before, now that I've come back they're me."

Mr. Bons laid the Keats down. The case was more interesting than he had expected. "*You?*" he exclaimed. "This sonnet, *you?*"

"Yes—and look further on: 'Aye, on the shores of darkness there is light, and precipices show untrodden green.' It *is* so, sir. All these things are true."

"I never doubted it," said Mr. Bons, with closed eyes.

"You—then you believe me? You believe in the omnibus and the driver and the storm and that return ticket I got for nothing and—"

"Tut, tut! No more of your yarns, my boy. I meant that I never doubted the essential truth of Poetry. Some day, when you have read more, you will understand what I mean."

"But, Mr. Bons, it *is* so. There *is* light upon the shores of darkness. I have seen it coming. Light and a wind."

"Nonsense," said Mr. Bons.

"If I had stopped! They tempted me. They told me to give up my ticket—for you cannot come back if you lose your ticket. They called from the river for it, and indeed

I was tempted, for I have never been so happy as among those precipices. But I thought of my mother and father, and that I must fetch them. Yet they will not come, though the road starts opposite our house. It has all happened as the people up there warned me, and Mr. Bons has disbelieved me like everyone else. I have been caned. I shall never see that mountain again."

"What's that about me?" said Mr. Bons, sitting up in his chair very suddenly.

"I told them about you, and how clever you were, and how many books you had, and they said, 'Mr. Bons will certainly disbelieve you.' "

"Stuff and nonsense, my young friend. You grow impertinent. I—well—I will settle the matter. Not a word to your father. I will cure you. Tomorrow evening I will myself call here to take you for a walk, and at sunset we will go up this alley opposite and hunt for your omnibus, you silly little boy."

His face grew serious, for the boy was not disconcerted, but leapt about the room singing, "Joy! joy! I told them you would believe me. We will drive together over the rainbow. I told them that you would come." After all, could there be anything in the story? Wagner? Keats? Shelley? Sir Thomas Browne? Certainly the case was interesting.

And on the morrow evening, though it was pouring with rain, Mr. Bons did not omit to call at Agathox Lodge.

The boy was ready, bubbling with excitement, and skipping about in a way that rather vexed the President of the Literary Society. They took a turn down Buckingham Park Road, and then—having seen that no one was watching them—slipped up the alley. Naturally enough (for the sun was setting) they ran straight against the omnibus.

"Good heavens!" exclaimed Mr. Bons. "Good gracious heavens!"

It was not the omnibus in which the boy had driven first, nor yet that in which he had returned. There were three horses—black, gray, and white, the gray being the finest. The driver, who turned round at the mention of goodness and of heaven, was a sallow man with terrifying jaws and sunken eyes. Mr. Bons, on seeing him, gave a cry as if of recognition, and began to tremble violently.

The boy jumped in.

"Is it possible?" cried Mr. Bons. "Is the impossible possible?"

"Sir; come in, sir. It is such a fine omnibus. Oh, here is his name—Dan someone."

Mr. Bons sprang in too. A blast of wind immediately slammed the omnibus door, and the shock jerked down all the omnibus blinds, which were very weak on their springs.

"Dan . . . Show me. Good gracious heavens! We're moving."

"Hooray!" said the boy.

Mr. Bons became flustered. He had not intended to be kidnapped. He could not find the door-handle nor push up the blinds. The omnibus was quite dark, and by the time he had struck a match, night had come on outside also. They were moving rapidly.

"A strange, a memorable adventure," he said, surveying the interior of the omnibus, which was large, roomy, and constructed with extreme regularity, every part exactly answering to every other part. Over the door (the handle of which was outside) was written, "Lasciate ogni baldanza voi che entrate"—at least, that was what was written, but Mr. Bons said that it was Lashy arty something, and that baldanza was a mistake for speranza. His voice sounded as if he was in church. Meanwhile, the boy called to the cadaverous driver for two return tickets. They were handed in without a word. Mr. Bons covered his face with his hand and again trembled. "Do you know who that is!" he whispered, when the little window had shut upon them. "It is the impossible."

"Well, I don't like him as much as Sir Thomas Browne, though I shouldn't be surprised if he had even more in him."

"More in him?" He stamped irritably. "By accident you have made the greatest discovery of the century, and all you can say is that there is more in this man. Do you remember those vellum books in my library, stamped with red lilies? This—sit still, I bring you stupendous news!—*this is the man who wrote them.*"

The boy sat quite still. "I wonder if we shall see Mrs. Gamp?" he asked, after a civil pause.

"Mrs.—?"

"Mrs. Gamp and Mrs. Harris. I like Mrs. Harris. I came upon them quite suddenly. Mrs. Gamp's bandboxes have moved over the rainbow so badly. All the bottoms have fallen out, and two of the pippins off her bedstead tumbled into the stream."

"Out there sits the man who wrote my vellum books!" thundered Mr. Bons, "and you talk to me of Dickens and of Mrs. Gamp?"

"I know Mrs. Gamp so well," he apologized. "I could not help being glad to see her. I recognized her voice. She was telling Mrs. Harris about Mrs. Prig."

"Did you spend the whole day in her elevating company?"

"Oh, no. I raced. I met a man who took me out beyond to a race-course. You run, and there are dolphins out at sea."

"Indeed. Do you remember the man's name?"

"Achilles. No; he was later. Tom Jones."

Mr. Bons sighed heavily. "Well, my lad, you have made a miserable mess of it. Think of a cultured person with your opportunities! A cultured person would have known all these characters and known what to have said to each. He would not have wasted his time with a Mrs. Gamp or a Tom Jones. The creations of Homer, of Shakespeare, and of Him who drives us now, would alone have contented him. He would not have raced. He would have asked intelligent questions."

"But, Mr. Bons," said the boy humbly, "you will be a cultured person. I told them so."

"True, true, and I beg you not to disgrace me when we arrive. No gossiping. No running. Keep close to my side, and never speak to these Immortals unless they speak to you. Yes, and give me the return tickets. You will be losing them."

The boy surrendered the tickets, but felt a little sore. After all, he had found the way to this place. It was hard first to be disbelieved and then to be lectured. Meanwhile, the rain had stopped, and moonlight crept into the omnibus through the cracks in the blinds.

"But how is there to be a rainbow?" cried the boy.

"You distract me," snapped Mr. Bons. "I wish to meditate on beauty. I wish to goodness I was with a reverent and sympathetic person."

The lad bit his lip. He made a hundred good resolutions. He would imitate Mr. Bons all the visit. He would not laugh, or run, or sing, or do any of the vulgar things that must have disgusted his new friends last time. He would be very careful to pronounce their names properly, and to remember who knew whom. Achilles did not know Tom Jones—at least, so Mr. Bons said. The Duchess of Malfi was older than Mrs. Gamp—at least, so Mr. Bons said. He would be self-conscious, reticent, and prim. He would never say he liked anyone. Yet, when the blind flew up at a chance touch of his head, all these good resolutions went to the winds, for the omnibus had reached the summit of a moonlit hill, and there was the chasm, and there, across it, stood the old precipices, dreaming, with their feet in the everlasting river. He exclaimed, "The mountain! Listen to the new tune in the water! Look at the camp fires in the ravines," and Mr. Bons, after a hasty glance, retorted, "Water? Camp fires? Ridiculous rubbish. Hold your tongue. There is nothing at all."

Yet, under his eyes, a rainbow formed, compounded not of sunlight and storm, but of moonlight and the spray of the river. The three horses put their feet upon it. He thought it the finest rainbow he had seen, but did not dare to say so, since Mr. Bons said that nothing was there. He leant out—the window had opened—and sang the tune that rose from the sleeping waters.

"The prelude of Rhinegold?" said Mr. Bons suddenly. "Who taught you these *leit motifs?*" He, too, looked out of the window. Then he behaved very oddly. He gave a choking cry and fell back onto the omnibus floor. He writhed and kicked. His face was green.

"Does the bridge make you dizzy?" the boy asked.

"Dizzy!" gasped Mr. Bons. "I want to go back. Tell the driver."

But the driver shook his head.

"We are nearly there," said the boy. "They are asleep. Shall I call? They will be so pleased to see you, for I have prepared them."

Mr. Bons moaned. They moved over the lunar rainbow, which ever and ever broke away behind their wheels. How still the night was! Who would be sentry at the Gate?

"I am coming," he shouted, again forgetting the hundred resolutions. "I am returning—I, the boy."

"The boy is returning," cried a voice to other voices, who repeated, "The boy is returning."

"I am bringing Mr. Bons with me."

Silence.

"I should have said Mr. Bons is bringing me with him."

Profound silence.

"Who stands sentry?"

"Achilles."

And on the rocky causeway, close to the springing of the rainbow bridge, he saw a young man who carried a wonderful shield.

"Mr. Bons, it is Achilles, armed."

"I want to go back," said Mr. Bons.

The last fragment of the rainbow melted, the wheels sang upon the living rock, the door of the omnibus burst open. Out leapt the boy—he could not resist—and sprang to meet the warrior, who, stooping suddenly, caught him on his shield.

"Achilles!" he cried, "let me get down, for I am ignorant and vulgar, and I must wait for that Mr. Bons of whom I told you yesterday."

But Achilles raised him aloft. He crouched on the wonderful shield, on heroes and burning cities, on vineyards graven in gold, on every dear passion, every joy, on the entire image of the Mountain that he had discovered, encircled, like it, with an everlasting stream. "No, no," he protested, "I am not worthy. It is Mr. Bons who must be up here."

But Mr. Bons was whimpering, and Achilles trumpeted and cried, "Stand upright upon my shield!"

"Sir, I did not mean to stand! something made me stand. Sir, why do you delay? Here is only the great Achilles, whom you knew."

Mr. Bons screamed, "I see no one. I see nothing. I want to go back." Then he cried to the driver, "Save me! Let me stop in your chariot. I have honoured you. I have quoted you. I have bound you in vellum. Take me back to my world."

The driver replied, "I am the means and not the end. I am the food and not the life. Stand by yourself, as that boy has stood. I cannot save you. For poetry is a spirit; and they that would worship it must worship in spirit and in truth."

Mr. Bons—he could not resist—crawled out of the beautiful omnibus. His face appeared, gaping horribly. His hands followed, one gripping the step, the other beating the air. Now his shoulders emerged, his chest, his stomach. With a shriek of "I see London," he fell—fell against the hard, moonlit rock, fell into it as if it were water, fell through it, vanished, and was seen by the boy no more.

"Where have you fallen to, Mr. Bons? Here is a procession arriving to honour you with music and torches. Here come the men and women whose names you know. The mountain is awake, the river is awake, over the race-course the sea is awakening those dolphins, and it is all for you. They want you—"

There was the touch of fresh leaves on his forehead. Someone had crowned him.

ΤΕΛΟΣ

◆

From the *Kingston Gazette, Surbiton Times,* and *Raynes Park Observer.*

The body of Mr. Septimus Bons has been found in a shockingly mutilated condition in the vicinity of the Bermondsey gas-works. The deceased's pockets contained a sovereign-purse, a silver cigar-case, a bijou pronouncing dictionary, and a couple of omnibus tickets. The unfortunate gentleman had apparently been hurled from a considerable height. Foul play is suspected, and a thorough investigation is pending by the authorities.

CAROLINE GORDON

Old Red

WHEN THE door had closed behind his daughter, Mister Maury went to the window and stood a few moments looking out. The roses that had grown in a riot all along that side of the fence had died or been cleared away, but the sun lay across the garden in the same level lances of light that he remembered. He turned back into the room. The shadows had gathered until it was nearly all in gloom. The top of his minnow bucket just emerging from the duffel bag glinted in the last rays of the sun. He stood looking down at his traps all gathered neatly in a heap at the foot of the bed. He would leave them like that. Even if they came in here sweeping and cleaning up—it was only in hotels that a man was master of his own room—even if they came in here cleaning up, he would tell them to leave all his things exactly as they were. It was reassuring to see them all there together, ready to be taken up in the hand, to be carried down and put into a car, to be driven off to some railroad station at a moment's notice.

As he moved toward the door, he spoke aloud, a habit that was growing on him:

"Anyhow, I won't stay but a week. . . . I ain't going to stay but a week, no matter what they say. . . ."

Downstairs in the dining room they were already gathered at the supper table, his white-haired, shrunken mother-in-law, his tall sister-in-law who had the proud carriage of the head, the aquiline nose, but not the spirit of his dead wife, his lean, blond new son-in-law, his black-eyed daughter who, but that she was thin, looked so much like him, all of them gathered there waiting for him, Alexander Maury. It occurred to him that this was the first time he had sat down in the bosom of the family for some years. They were always writing saying that he must make a visit this summer or certainly next fall. ". . . all had a happy Christmas together but missed you. . . ." They had even made the pretext that he ought to come up to inspect his new son-in-law. As if he hadn't always known exactly the kind of young man Sarah would marry! What was the boy's name? Stephen, yes, Stephen. He must be sure and remember that.

He sat down, and shaking out his napkin spread it over his capacious paunch and tucked it well up under his chin in the way his wife had never allowed him to do. He let his eyes rove over the table and released a long sigh.

"Hot batter bread," he said, "and ham. Merry Point ham. I sure am glad to taste them one more time before I die."

The old lady was sending the little Negro girl scurrying back to the kitchen for a hot plate of batter bread. He pushed aside the cold plate and waited. She had bridled when he spoke of the batter bread and a faint flush had dawned on her withered cheeks. Vain she had always been as a peacock, of her housekeeping, her children, the animals on her place, anything that belonged to her. And she went on, even at her advanced age, making her batter bread, smoking her hams according to that old recipe she was so proud of; but who came here now to this old house to eat or to praise?

He helped himself to a generous slice of batter bread, buttered it, took the first mouthful and chewed it slowly. He shook his head.

"There ain't anything like it," he said. "There ain't anything else like it in this world."

His dark eye roving the table fell on his son-in-law. "You like batter bread?" he inquired.

Stephen nodded, smiling. Mister Maury, still masticating slowly, regarded his face, measured the space between the eyes—his favorite test for man, horse, or dog. Yes, there was room enough for sense between the eyes. But how young the boy looked! And infected already with the fatal germ, the *cacoëthes scribendi.* Well, their children would probably escape. It was like certain diseases of the eye, skipped every other generation. His own father had had it badly all his life. He could see him now sitting at the head of the table spouting his own poetry—or Shakespeare's—while the children watched the preserve dish to see if it was going around. He, Aleck Maury, had been lucky to be born in the generation he had. He had escaped that at least. A few translations from Heine in his courting days, a few fragments from the Greek, but no, he had kept clear of that on the whole. . . .

The eyes of his sister-in-law were fixed on him. She was smiling faintly. "You don't look much like dying, Aleck. Florida must agree with you."

The old lady spoke from the head of the table. "I can't see what you do with yourself all winter long. Doesn't time hang heavy on your hands?"

Time, he thought, time! They were always mouthing the word and what did they know about it? Nothing in God's world! He saw time suddenly, a dull, leaden-colored fabric depending from the old lady's hands, from the hands of all of them, a blanket that they pulled about, now this way, now that, trying to cover up their nakedness. Or they would cast it on the ground and creep in among the folds, finding one day a little more tightly rolled than another, but all of it everywhere the same dull gray substance. But time was a banner that whipped before him always in the wind. He stood on tiptoe to catch at the bright folds, to strain them to his bosom. They were bright and glittering. But they whipped by so fast and were whipping always ever faster. The tears came into his eyes. Where, for instance, had this year gone? He could swear he had not wasted a minute of it, for no man living, he thought, knew better how to make each day a pleasure to him. Not a minute wasted and yet here it was already May! If he lived to the Biblical three score and ten, which was all he ever allowed himself in his calculations, he had before him only nine more Mays. Only nine more Mays out of all eternity, and they wanted him to waste one of them sitting on the front porch at Merry Point!

The butter plate which had seemed to swim in a glittering mist was coming solidly to rest upon the white tablecloth. He winked his eyes rapidly and laying down his knife and fork squared himself about in his chair to address his mother-in-law:

"Well, ma'am, you know I'm a man that always likes to be learning something. Now this year I learned how to smell out fish." He glanced around the table, holding his head high and allowing his well-cut nostrils to flutter slightly with his indrawn breaths. "Yes, sir," he said, "I'm probably the only white man in this country knows how to smell out feesh."

There was a discreet smile on the faces of the others. Sarah was laughing outright. "Did you have to learn how or did it just come to you?" she asked.

"I learned it from an old nigger woman," her father said. He shook his head reminiscently. "It's wonderful how much you can learn from niggers. But you have to know how to handle them. I was half the winter wooing that old Fanny. . . ."

He waited until their laughter had died down. "We used to start off every morning from the same little cove and we'd drift in there together at night. I noticed how she always brought in a good string, so I says to her, 'Fanny, you just lemme go 'long with you.' But she wouldn't have nothing to do with me. I saw she was going to be a hard nut to crack, but I kept right on. Finally I began giving her presents. . . ."

Laura was regarding him fixedly, a queer look on her face.

"What sort of presents did you give her, Aleck?"

He made his tones hearty in answer. "I gave her a fine string of fish one day and I gave her fifty cents. And finally I made her a present of a Barlow knife. That was when she broke down. She took me with her that morning. . . ."

"Could she really smell fish?" the old lady asked curiously.

"You ought to 'a' seen her," Mister Maury said. "She'd sail over that lake like a hound on the scent. She'd row right along and then all of a sudden she'd stop rowing." He bent over, wrinkling his nose and peering into the depths of imaginary water. " 'Thar they are, White Folks, thar they are. Cain't you smell 'em?' "

Stephen was leaning forward, eyeing his father-in-law intently. "Could you?" he asked.

"I got so I could smell feesh," Mister Maury told him. "I could smell out the feesh, but I couldn't tell which kind they were. Now Fanny could row over a bed and tell just by the smell whether it was bass or bream. But she'd been at it all her life." He paused, sighing. "You can't just pick these things up. You have to give yourself to them. Who was it said 'Genius is an infinite capacity for taking pains'?"

Sarah was rising briskly. Her eyes sought her husband's across the table. She was still laughing. "Sir Izaak Walton," she said, "we'd better go in the other room. Mandy wants to clear the table."

The two older ladies remained in the dining room. Mister Maury walked across the hall to the sitting room, accompanied by Steve and Sarah. He lowered himself cautiously into the most solid-looking of the rocking chairs that were drawn up around the fire. Steve was standing on the hearthrug, back to the fire, gazing abstractedly off across the room.

Mister Maury glanced up at him curiously. "What are you thinking about, feller?" he asked.

Steve looked down. He smiled, but his gaze was still contemplative. "I was thinking about the sonnet," he said, "in the form in which it first came to England."

Mister Maury shook his head, "Wyatt and Surrey," he said. "Hey, nonny, nonny. . . . You'll have hardening of the liver long before you're my age." He looked past Steve's shoulder at the picture that hung over the mantel shelf: Cupid and Psyche holding between them a fluttering veil and running along a rocky path toward the beholder. "Old Merry Point," he said; "it don't change much, does it?"

He settled himself more solidly in his chair. His mind veered from the old house to his own wanderings in brighter places. He regarded his daughter and son-in-law affably.

"Yes, sir," he said, "this winter in Florida was valuable to me just for the acquaintances I made. Take my friend, Jim Barbee. Just to live in the same hotel with that man is an education." He paused, smiling reminiscently into the fire. "I'll never forget the first time I saw him. He came up to me there in the lobby of the hotel. 'Professor Maury!' he says, 'You been hearin' about me for twenty years and I been hearin' about you for twenty years. And now we've done met!' "

Sarah had sat down in the little rocking chair by the fire. She leaned toward him now, laughing. "They ought to have put down a cloth of gold for the meeting," she said.

Mister Maury shook his head. "Nature does that in Florida," he said. "I knew right off the reel it was him. There were half a dozen men standing around. I made 'em witness. 'Jim Barbee,' I says, 'Jim Barbee of Maysville or I'll eat my hat!' "

"Why is he so famous?" Sarah asked.

Mister Maury took out his knife and cut a slice from a plug of tobacco. When he had offered a slice to his son-in-law and it had been refused, he put the plug back in his pocket. "He's a man of imagination," he said slowly. "There ain't many in this world."

He took a small tin box out of his pocket and set it on the little table that held the lamp. Removing the top he tilted the box so that they could see its contents: an artificial lure, a bug with a dark body and a red, bulbous head, a hook protruding from what might be considered its vitals.

"Look at her," he said, "ain't she a killer?"

Sarah leaned forward to look and Steve, still standing on the hearthrug, bent above them. The three heads ringed the light.

Mister Maury disregarded Sarah and addressed himself to Steve. "She takes nine strips of rind," he said, "nine strips just thick enough." He marked off the width of the strips with his two fingers on the table, then picking up the lure and cupping it in his palm he moved it back and forth quickly so that the painted eyes caught the light.

"Look at her," he said, "look at the wicked way she sets forward."

Sarah was poking at the lure with the tip of her finger. "Wanton," she said, "simply wanton. What does he call her?"

"This is his Devil Bug," Mister Maury said. "He's the only man in this country makes it. I myself had the idea thirty years ago and let it slip by me the way I do with so many of my ideas." He sighed, then elevating his tremendous bulk slightly above the table level and continuing to hold Steve with his gaze he produced from his coat pocket the oilskin book that held his flies. He spread it open on the table and began to turn the pages. His eyes sought his son-in-law's as his hand paused before a gray, rather draggled-looking lure.

"Old Speck," he said. "I've had that fly for twenty years. I reckon she's taken five hundred pounds of fish in her day. . . ."

The fire burned lower. A fiery coal rolled from the grate and fell onto the hearthrug. Sarah scooped it up with a shovel and threw it among the ashes. In the circle of the lamplight the two men still bent over the table looking at the flies. Steve was absorbed in them but he spoke seldom. It was her father's voice that rising and falling filled the room. He talked a great deal, but he had a beautiful speaking voice. He was telling Steve now about Little West Fork, the first stream ever he put a fly in. "My first love," he kept calling it. It sounded rather pretty, she thought, in his mellow voice. "My first love . . ."

II

When Mister Maury came downstairs the next morning the dining room was empty except for his daughter, Sarah, who sat dawdling over a cup of coffee and a cigarette. Mister Maury sat down opposite her. To the little Negro girl who presented herself at his elbow he outlined his wants briefly. "A cup of coffee and some hot batter bread just like we had last night." He turned to his daughter. "Where's Steve?"

"He's working," she said, "he was up at eight and he's been working ever since."

Mister Maury accepted the cup of coffee from the little girl, poured half of it into his saucer, set it aside to cool. "Ain't it wonderful," he said, "the way a man can sit down and work day after day? When I think of all the work I've done in my time. . . . Can he work *every* morning?"

"He sits down at his desk every morning," she said, "but of course he gets more done some mornings than others."

Mister Maury picked up the saucer, found the coffee cool enough for his taste. He sipped it slowly, looking out of the window. His mind was already busy with his day's program. No water—no running water—nearer than West Fork three miles away. He couldn't drive a car and Steve was going to be busy writing all morning. There was nothing for it but a pond. The Willow Sink. It was not much but it was better than nothing. He pushed his chair back and rose.

"Well," he said, "I'd better be starting."

When he came downstairs with his rod a few minutes later the hall was still full of the sound of measured typing. Sarah sat in the dining room in the same position in which he had left her, smoking. Mister Maury paused in the doorway while he slung his canvas bag over his shoulders. "How you ever going to get anything done if you don't take advantage of the morning hours?" he asked. He glanced at the door opposite as if it had been the entrance to a sick chamber.

"What's he writing about?" he inquired in a whisper.

"It's an essay on John Skelton."

Mister Maury looked out at the new green leaves framed in the doorway. "John Skelton," he said. "God Almighty!"

He went through the hall and stepped down off the porch onto the ground that was still moist with spring rains. As he crossed the lower yard he looked up into the branches of the maples. Yes, the leaves were full grown already even on the late trees. The year, how swiftly, how steadily it advanced! He had come to the far corner of the yard. Grown up it was in pokeberry shoots and honeysuckle, but there was a place to get through. The top strand of wire had been pulled down and fastened to the others with a ragged piece of rope. He rested his weight on his good leg and swung himself over onto the game one. It gave him a good, sharp twinge when he came down on it. It was getting worse all the time, that leg, but on the other hand he was learning better all the time how to handle it. His mind flew back to a dark, startled moment, that day when the cramp first came on him. He had been sitting still in the boat all day long and that evening when he had stood up to get out his leg had failed him utterly. He had pitched forward among the reeds, had lain there a second, face downwards, before it came to him what had happened. With the realization came a sharp picture of his faraway youth: Uncle Quent lowering himself ponderously out of the saddle after a hard day's hunting had fallen forward in exactly the same way, into a knot of yowling little Negroes. He had got up and cursed them all out of the lot. It had scared the old boy to death, coming down like that. The black dog he had had on his shoulder all that fall. But he himself had never lost one day's fishing on account of his leg. He had known from the start how to handle it. It meant simply that he was slowed down that much. It hadn't really made much difference in fishing. He didn't do as much wading but he got around just about as well on the whole. Hunting, of course, had had to go. You couldn't walk all day shooting birds, dragging a game leg. He had just given it up right off the reel, though it was a shame when a man was as good a shot as he was. That day he was out with Tom Kensington last November, the only day he got out during the season. Nine shots he'd had and he'd bagged nine birds. Yes, it was a shame. But a man couldn't do everything. He had to limit himself. . . .

He was up over the little rise now. The field slanted straight down before him to where the pond lay, silver in the morning sun. A Negro cabin was perched halfway up the opposite slope. A woman was hanging out washing on a line stretched between two trees. From the open doorway little Negroes spilled down the path toward the pond. Mister Maury surveyed the scene, spoke aloud:

"Ain't it funny now? Niggers always live in the good places."

He stopped under a wild cherry tree to light his pipe. It had been hot crossing the field, but the sunlight here was agreeably tempered by the branches. And that pond down there was fringed with willows. His eyes sought the bright disk of the water, then rose to where the smoke from the cabin chimney lay in a soft plume along the crest of the hill.

When he stooped to pick up his rod again it was with a feeling of sudden, keen elation. An image had risen in his memory, an image that was familiar but came to him infrequently of late and that only in moments of elation: the wide field in front of his uncle's old house in Albemarle, on one side the dark line of undergrowth that marked the Rivanna River, on the other the blue of Peters' Mountain. They would be waiting there in that broad plain when they had the first sight of the fox. On that little rise by the river, loping steadily, not yet alarmed. The sun would glint on his bright coat, on his quick-turning head as he dove into the dark of the woods. There would be hullabaloo after that and shouting and riding. Sometimes there was the tailing of the fox—that time old Whisky was brought home on a mattress! All of that to come afterward, but none of it ever like that first sight of the fox there on the broad plain between the river and the mountain.

There was one fox, they grew to know him in time, to call him affectionately by name. Old Red it was who showed himself always like that there on the crest of the hill. "There he goes, the damn' impudent scoundrel!" . . . Uncle Quent would shout and slap his thigh and yell himself hoarse at Whisky and Mag and the pups, but they would have already settled to their work. They knew his course, every turn of it by heart. Through the woods and then down across the fields again to the river. Their hope was always to cut him off before he could circle back to the mountain. If he got in there among those old field pines it was all up. But he always made it. Lost 'em every time and then dodged through to his hole in Pinnacle Rock. . . . A smart fox, Old Red. . . .

He descended the slope and paused in the shade of a clump of willows. The little Negroes who squatted, dabbling in the water, watched him out of round eyes as he unslung his canvas bag and laid it on a stump. He looked down at them gravely.

"D'you ever see a white man that could conjure?" he asked.

The oldest boy laid the brick he was fashioning out of mud down on a plank. He ran the tip of his tongue over his lower lip to moisten it before he spoke. "Naw suh."

"I'm the man," Mister Maury told him. "You chillun better quit that playin' and dig me some worms."

He drew his rod out of the case, jointed it up and laid it down on a stump. Taking out his book of flies he turned the pages, considering. "Silver Spinner," he said aloud. "They ought to take that . . . in May. Naw, I'll just give Old Speck a chance. It's a long time now since we had her out."

The little Negroes had risen and were stepping quietly off along the path toward the cabin, the two little boys hand in hand, the little girl following, the baby astride her hip. They were pausing now before a dilapidated building that might long ago have been a hen-house. Mister Maury shouted at them. "Look under them old boards. That's the place for worms." The biggest boy was turning around. His treble "Yassuh" quavered over the water. Then their voices died away. There was no sound except the light turning of the willow boughs in the wind.

Mister Maury walked along the bank, rod in hand, humming: "Bangum's gone to the wild boar's den . . . *Bangum's* gone to the wild boar's den . . ." He stopped where a white, peeled log protruded six or seven feet into the water. The pond made a little turn here. Two lines of willows curving in framed the whole surface of the water. He stepped out squarely upon the log, still humming. The line rose smoothly, soared against the blue and curved sweetly back upon the still water. His quick ear caught the little whish that the fly made when it clove the surface, his eye followed the tiny ripples of its flight. He cast again, leaning a little backward as he did sometimes when the mood was on him. Again and again his line soared out over the water. His eye rested now and then on his wrist. He noted with detachment the expert play of the muscles, admired each time the accuracy of his aim. It occurred to him that it was four days now since he had wet a line. Four days. One whole day packing up, parts of two days on the train and yesterday wasted sitting there on that front porch with the family. But the abstinence had done him good. He had never cast better than he was casting this morning.

There was a rustling along the bank, a glimpse of blue through the trees. Mister Maury leaned forward and peered around the clump of willows. A hundred yards away Steve, hatless, in an old blue shirt and khaki pants, stood jointing up a rod.

Mister Maury backed off his log and advanced along the path. He called out cheerfully, "Well, feller, do any good?"

Steve looked up. His face had lightened for a moment, but the abstracted expression stole over it again when he spoke. "Oh, I fiddled with it," he said, "all morning, but I didn't do much good."

Mister Maury nodded sympathetically. *"Minerva invita erat,"* he said; "you can do nothing unless Minerva perches on the rooftree. Why, I been castin' here all morning and not a strike. But there's a boat tied up over on the other side. What say we get in it and just drift around?" He paused, looked at the rod Steve had finished jointing up. "I brought another rod along," he said. "You want to use it?"

Steve shook his head. "I'm used to this one."

An expression of relief came over Mister Maury's face. "That's right," he said, "a man always does better with his own rod."

The boat was only a quarter full of water. They heaved her over and dumped it out, then dragged her down to the bank. The little Negroes had come up, bringing a can of worms. Mister Maury threw them each a nickel and set the can in the bottom of the boat. "I always like to have a few worms handy," he told Steve, "ever since I was a boy." He lowered himself ponderously into the bow and Steve pushed off and dropped down behind him.

The little Negroes still stood on the bank staring. When the boat was a little distance out on the water the boldest of them spoke: "Yo reckon 'at ole jawnboat going to hold you up, Cap'm?"

Mistery Maury turned his head to call over his shoulder. "Go 'way, boy, ain't I done tole you I's a conjure?"

The boat dipped ominously. Steve changed his position a little and she settled to the water. Sitting well forward Mister Maury made graceful casts, now to this side, now to that. Steve, in the stern, made occasional casts, but he laid his rod down every now and then to paddle, though there was really no use in it. The boat drifted well enough with the wind. At the end of half an hour seven sizable bass lay on the bottom of the boat. Mister Maury had caught five of them. He reflected that perhaps he really ought to change places with Steve. The man in the bow certainly had the best chance at the fish. "But no," he thought, "it don't make any difference. He don't hardly know where he is now."

He stole a glance over his shoulder at the young man's serious, abstracted face. It was like that of a person submerged. Steve seemed to float up to the surface every now and then, his expression would lighten, he would make some observation that showed he knew where he was, then he would sink again. If you asked him a question he answered punctiliously, two minutes later. Poor boy, dead to the world and would probably be that way the rest of his life! A pang of pity shot through Mister Maury, and on the heels of it a gust of that black fear that occasionally shook him. It was he, not Steve, that was the queer one! The world was full of people like this boy, all of them walking around with their heads so full of this and that they hardly knew where they were going. There was hardly anybody—there was *nobody* really in the whole world like him. . . .

Steve, coming out of his abstraction, spoke politely. He had heard that Mister Maury was a fine shot. Did he like to fish better than hunt?

Mister Maury reflected. "Well," he said, "they's something about a covey of birds rising up in front of you . . . they's something. And a good dog. Now they ain't anything in this world that I like better than a good bird dog." He stopped and sighed. "A man has got to come to himself early in life if he's going to amount to anything. Now I was smart, even as a boy. I could look around me and see all the men of my family, Uncle Jeems, Uncle Quent, my father, every one of 'em weighed two hundred by the time he was fifty. You get as heavy on your feet as all that and you can't do any good shooting. But a man can fish as long as he lives. . . . Why, one place I stayed last summer there was an old man ninety years old had himself carried down to the river every morning. . . . Yes, sir, a man can fish as long as he can get down to the water's edge. . . ."

There was a little plop to the right. He turned just in time to see the fish flash out of the water. He watched Steve take it off the hook and drop it on top of the pile in the bottom of the boat. Eight bass that made and two bream. The old lady would be pleased. "Aleck always catches me fish," she'd say.

The boat glided on over the still water. There was no wind at all now. The willows that fringed the bank might have been cut out of paper. The plume of smoke hung perfectly horizontal over the roof of the Negro cabin. Mister Maury watched it stream out in little eddies and disappear into the bright blue.

He spoke softly: "Ain't it wonderful . . . ain't it wonderful now that a man of my gifts can content himself a whole morning on this here little old pond?"

III

Mister Maury woke with a start. He realized that he had been sleeping on his left side again. A bad idea. It always gave him palpitations of the heart. It must be that that had waked him up. He had gone to sleep almost immediately after his head hit the pillow. He rolled over, cautiously, as he always did since that bed in Leesburg had given down with him, and lying flat on his back stared at the opposite wall.

The moon rose late. It must be at its height now. That patch of light was so brilliant he could almost discern the pattern of the wall paper. It hung there, wavering, bitten by the shadows into a semblance of a human figure, a man striding with bent head and swinging arms. All the shadows in the room seemed to be moving toward him. The protruding corner of the washstand was an arrow aimed at his heart, the clumsy old-fashioned dresser was a giant towering above him.

They had put him to sleep in this same room the night after his wife died. In the summer it had been, too, in June, and there must have been a full moon, for the same giant shadows had struggled there with the same towering monsters. It would be like that here on this wall every full moon, for the pieces of furniture would never change their position, had never been changed, probably, since the house was built.

He turned back on his side. The wall before him was dark, but he knew every flower in the pattern of the wall paper, interlacing pink roses with thrusting up between every third cluster the enormous, spreading fronds of ferns. The wall paper in the room across the hall was like that too. The old lady slept there, and in the room next to his own, Laura, his sister-in-law, and in the east bedroom downstairs the young couple. He and Mary had slept there when they were first married, when they were the young couple in the house.

He tried to remember Mary as she must have looked the day he first saw her, the day he arrived from Virginia to open his school in the old office that used to stand there in the corner of the yard. He could see Mister Allard plainly, sitting there under the sugar tree with his chair tilted back, could discern the old lady—young she had been then!—hospitably poised in the doorway, could hear her voice: "Well, here are two of your pupils to start with. . . ." He remembered Laura, a shy child of nine hiding her face in her mother's skirts, but Mary was only a shadow in the dark hall. He could not even remember how her voice had sounded. "Professor Maury," she would have said and her mother would have corrected her with "Cousin Aleck. . . ."

That day a year later when she was getting off her horse at the stile blocks. . . . She had turned as she walked across the lawn to look back at him. Her white sunbonnet had fallen back on her shoulders, her eyes meeting his had been wide and startled. He had gone on and had hitched both the horses before he leaped over the stile to join her. But he had known in that moment that she was the woman he was going to have. He could not remember all the rest of it, only that moment stood out. He had won her. She had become his wife, but the woman he had won was not the woman he had sought. It was as if he had had her only in that moment there on the lawn. As if she had paused there only for that one moment, and was ever after retreating before him down a devious, a dark way that he would never have chosen.

The death of the first baby had been the start of it, of course. It had been a relief when she took so definitely to religion. Before that there had been those sudden, unaccountable forays out of some dark lurking place that she had. Guerrilla warfare and trying to the nerves, but that had been only at the first. For many years they had been two enemies contending in the open. . . . Toward the last she had taken mightily to prayer. He would wake often to find her kneeling by the side of the bed in the dark. It had gone on for years. She had never given up hope. . . .

Ah, a stout-hearted one, Mary! She had never given up hope of changing him, of making him over into the man she thought he ought to be. Time and again she almost had him. And there were long periods, of course, during which he had been worn down by the conflict, one spring when he himself said, when she had told all the neighbors that he was too old now to go fishing any more. . . . But he had made a comeback. She had had to resort to stratagem. His lips curved in a smile, remembering the trick.

It had come over him suddenly, a general lassitude, an odd faintness in the mornings, the time when his spirits ordinarily were always at their highest. He had sat there looking out of the window at the woods glistening with spring rain; he had not even taken his gun down to shoot a squirrel.

Remembering Uncle Quent's last days, he had been alarmed, had decided finally that he must tell her so that they might begin preparations for the future—he had shuddered at the thought of eventual confinement, perhaps in some institution. She had looked up from her sewing, unable to repress a smile.

"You think it's your mind, Aleck. . . . It's coffee. . . . I've been giving you a coffee substitute every morning. . . ."

They had laughed together over her cleverness. He had not gone back to coffee, but the lassitude had worn off. She had gone back to the attack with redoubled vigor. In the afternoons she would stand on the porch calling after him as he slipped down to the creek, "Now, don't stay long enough to get that cramp. You remember how you suffered last time. . . ." He would have forgotten all about the cramp until that moment, but it would hang over him then through the whole afternoon's sport, and it would descend upon him inevitably when he left the river and started for the house.

Yes, he thought with pride. She was wearing him down—he didn't believe there was a man living who could withstand her a lifetime!—she was wearing him down and would have had him in another few months, another year certainly. But she had been struck down just as victory was in her grasp. The paralysis had come on her in the night. It was as if a curtain had descended, dividing their life sharply into two parts. In the bewildered year and a half that followed he had found himself forlornly trying to reconstruct the Mary he had known. The pressure she had so constantly exerted upon him had become for him a part of her personality. This new, calm Mary was not the woman he had loved all these years. She had lain there—heroically they all said—waiting for death. And lying there, waiting, all her faculties engaged now in defensive warfare, she had raised as it were her lifelong siege; she had lost interest in his comings and goings, had once even encouraged him to go out for an afternoon's sport. He felt a rush of warm pity. Poor Mary! She must have realized toward the last that she had wasted herself in conflict; she had spent her arms and her strength against an inglorious foe when all the time the real, the invincible adversary waited. . . .

He turned over on his back again. The moonlight was waning, the contending shadows paler now and retreating toward the door. From across the hall came the sound of long, sibilant breaths, ending each one on a little upward groan. The old lady . . . she would maintain till her dying day that she did not snore. He fancied that he could hear from the next room Laura's light, regular breathing, and downstairs were the young couple asleep in each other's arms. . . .

All of them quiet and relaxed now, but they had been lively enough at dinner time! It had started with the talk about Aunt Sally Crenfew's funeral Tuesday. Living as he had for some years away from women of his family he had forgotten the need to be cautious. He had spoken up before he thought:

"But that's the day Steve and I were going to Barker's Mill. . . ."

Sarah had cried out at the idea. "Barker's Mill!" she had said, "right on the Crenfew land . . . well, if not on the very farm in the very next field." It would be a scandal if he, Professor Maury, known by everybody to be in the neighborhood, could not spare one afternoon, one insignificant summer afternoon from his fishing long enough to attend the funeral of his cousin, the cousin of all of them, the oldest lady in the whole family connection. . . .

She had got him rattled; he had fallen back upon technicalities:

"I'm not a Crenfew. I'm a Maury. Aunt Sally Crenfew is no more kin to me than a catfish. . . ."

An unlucky crack, that about the catfish. Glancing around the table he had caught the same look in every eye. He had felt a gust of the same fright that had shaken him there on the pond. That look! Sooner or later you met it in every human eye. The thing was to be up and ready, ready to run for your life at a moment's notice. Yes, it had always been like that. It always would be. His fear of them was shot through suddenly with contempt. It was as if Mary was there laughing at them with him. *She* knew that none of them could have survived what he had survived, could have paid the price for freedom that he had paid. . . .

Sarah had come to a full stop. He had to say something. He shook his head:

"You think we just go fishing to have a good time. The boy and I hold high converse on that pond. . . . I'm starved for intellectual companionship, I tell you. In Florida I never see anybody but niggers. . . ."

They had all laughed out at that. "As if you didn't *prefer* the society of niggers," Sarah said scornfully.

The old lady had been moved to anecdote:

"I remember when Aleck first came out here from Virginia, Cousin Sophy said: 'Professor Maury is so well educated. Now Cousin Cave Maynor is dead, who is there in this neighborhood for him to associate with?' 'Well,' I said, 'I don't know about that. He seems perfectly satisfied now with Ben Hooser. They're off to the creek together every evening soon as school is out.' "

Ben Hooser. . . . He could see now the wrinkled face, overlaid with that ashy pallor of the aged Negro, the shrewd, smiling eyes, the pendulous lower lip that dropping away showed always some of the rotten teeth. A fine nigger, Ben, and on to a lot of tricks, the only man really that he'd ever cared to take fishing with him. . . .

But the first real friend of his bosom had been old Uncle Teague, back in Virginia. Once a week, or more likely every ten days, he fed the hounds on the carcass of a calf that had had time to get pretty high. They would drive the spring wagon out into the lot, he, a boy of ten, beside Uncle Teague on the driver's seat. The hounds would come in a great rush and rear their slobbering jowls against the wagon wheels. Uncle Teague would wield his whip, chuckling while he threw the first hunk of meat to Old Mag, his favorite.

"Dey goin' run on dis," he'd say, "dey goin' run like a shadow. . . ."

He shifted his position again, cautiously. People, he thought . . . people . . . so bone ignorant, all of them. Not one person in a thousand realized that a fox hound remains at heart a wild beast and must kill and gorge, and then when he is ravenous kill and gorge again. . . . Or that the channel cat is a night feeder. . . . Or . . . his daughter had told him once that he ought to set all his knowledges down in a book. "Why?" he had asked. "So everybody else can know as much as I do?"

If he allowed his mind to get active, really active, he would never get any sleep. He was fighting an inclination now to get up and find a cigarette. He relaxed again upon his pillows, deliberately summoned pictures up before his mind's eye. Landscapes—and streams. He observed their outlines, watched one flow into another. The Black River into West Fork, that in turn into Spring Creek and Spring Creek into the Withlicoochee. Then they were all flowing together, merging into one broad plain. He watched it take form slowly: the wide field in front of Hawkwood, the Rivanna River on one side, on the other Peters' Mountain. They would be waiting there till the fox showed himself on that little rise by the river. The young men would hold back till Uncle Quent had wheeled Old Filly, then they would all be off pell-mell across the plain. He himself would be mounted on Jonesboro. Blind as a bat, but she would take anything you put her at. That first thicket on the edge of the woods. They would break there, one half of them going around, the other half streaking it through the woods. He was always of those going around to try to cut the fox off on the other side. No, he was down off his horse. He was coursing with the fox. He could hear the sharp, pointed feet padding on the dead leaves, see the quick head turned now and then over the shoulder.

The trees kept flashing by, one black trunk after another. And now it was a ragged mountain field and the sage grass running before them in waves to where a narrow stream curved in between the ridges. The fox's feet were light in the water. He ran steadily, head down. The hounds' baying was louder now. Old Mag knew the trick. She had stopped to give tongue by the big rock, and now they had all leaped the gulch and were scrambling up through the pines. But the fox's feet were already hard on the mountain path. He ran slowly now, past the big boulder, past the blasted pine to where the shadow of the Pinnacle Rock was black across the path. He ran on and the shadow rose and swayed to meet him. Its cool touch was on his hot tongue, his heaving flanks. He had slipped in under it. He was sinking down, panting, in black dark, on moist earth while the hounds' baying filled the bowl of the valley and reverberated from the mountainside.

ERNEST HEMINGWAY

The Capital of the World

MADRID is full of boys named Paco, which is the diminutive of the name Francisco, and there is a Madrid joke about a father who came to Madrid and inserted an advertisement in the personal columns of *El Liberal* which said: PACO MEET ME AT HOTEL MONTANA NOON TUESDAY ALL IS FORGIVEN PAPA and how a squadron of Guardia Civil had to be called out to disperse the eight hundred young men who answered the advertisement. But this Paco, who waited on table at the Pension Luarca, had no father to forgive him nor anything for the father to forgive. He had two older sisters who were chambermaids at the Luarca, who had gotten their place through coming from the same small village as a former Luarca chambermaid who had proven hardworking and honest and hence given her village and its products a good name; and these sisters had paid his way on the auto-bus to Madrid and gotten him his job as an apprentice waiter. He came from a village in a part of Extramadura where conditions were incredibly primitive, food scarce, and comforts unknown and he had worked hard ever since he could remember.

He was a well built boy with very black, rather curly hair, good teeth and a skin that his sisters envied, and he had a ready and unpuzzled smile. He was fast on his feet and did his work well and he loved his sisters, who seemed beautiful and sophisticated; he loved Madrid, which was still an unbelievable place, and he loved his work, which, done under bright lights, with clean linen, the wearing of evening clothes, and abundant food in the kitchen, seemed romantically beautiful.

There were from eight to a dozen other people who lived at the Luarca and ate in the dining room but for Paco, the youngest of the three waiters who served at table, the only ones who really existed were the bull fighters.

Second-rate matadors lived at the pension because the address in the Calle San Jeronimo was good, the food was excellent and the room and board was cheap. It is necessary for a bull fighter to give the appearance, if not of prosperity, at least of respectability, since decorum and dignity rank above courage as the virtues most highly prized in Spain, and bull fighters stayed at the Luarca until their last pesetas were gone. There is no record of any bull fighter having left the Luarca for a better or more expensive hotel; second-rate bull fighters never became first rate; but the descent from the Luarca was swift since any one could stay there who was making anything at all and a bill was never presented to a guest unasked until the woman who ran the place knew that the case was hopeless.

At this time there were three full matadors living at the Luarca as well as two very good picadors, and one excellent banderillero. The Luarca was luxury for the picadors and the banderilleros who, with their families in Seville, required lodging in Madrid during the Spring season; but they were well paid and in the fixed employ of fighters who were heavily contracted during the coming season and the three of these subalterns would probably make much more apiece than any of the three matadors. Of the three matadors one was ill and trying to conceal it; one had passed his short vogue as a novelty; and the third was a coward.

The coward had at one time, until he had received a peculiarly atrocious horn wound in the lower abdomen at the start of his first season as a full matador, been exceptionally brave and remarkably skilful and he still had many of the hearty mannerisms of his days of success. He was jovial to excess and laughed constantly with and without provocation. He had, when successful, been very addicted to practical jokes but he had given them up now. They took an assurance that he did not feel. This matador had an intelligent, very open face and he carried himself with much style.

The matador who was ill was careful never to show it and was meticulous about eating a little of all the dishes that were presented at the table. He had a great many handkerchiefs which he laundered himself in his room and, lately, he had been selling his fighting suits. He had sold one, cheaply, before Christmas and another in the first week of April. They had been very expensive suits, had always been well kept and he had one more. Before he had become ill he had been a very promising, even a sensational, fighter and, while he himself could not read, he had clippings which said that in his debut in Madrid he had been better than Belmonte. He ate alone at a small table and looked up very little.

The matador who had once been a novelty was very short and brown and very dignified. He also ate alone at a separate table and he smiled very rarely and never laughed. He came from Valladolid, where the people are extremely serious, and he was a capable matador; but his style had become old-fashioned before he had ever succeeded in endearing himself to the public through his virtues, which were courage and a calm capability, and his name on a poster would draw no one to a bull ring. His novelty had been that he was so short that he could barely see over the bull's withers, but there were other short fighters, and he had never succeeded in imposing himself on the public's fancy.

Of the picadors one was a thin, hawk-faced, gray-haired man, lightly built but with legs and arms like iron, who always wore cattle-men's boots under his trousers, drank too much every evening and gazed amorously at any woman in the pension. The other was huge, dark, brown-faced, good-looking, with black hair like an Indian and enormous hands. Both were great picadors although the first was reputed to have lost much of his ability through drink and dissipation, and the second was said to be too headstrong and quarrelsome to stay with any matador more than a single season.

The banderillero was middle-aged, gray, cat-quick in spite of his years and, sitting at the table he looked a moderately prosperous business man. His legs were still good for this season, and when they should go he was intelligent and experienced enough to keep regularly employed for a long time. The difference would be that when his speed of foot would be gone he would always be frightened where now he was assured and calm in the ring and out of it.

On this evening every one had left the dining room except the hawk-faced picador who drank too much, the birthmarked-faced auctioneer of watches at the fairs and festivals of Spain, who also drank too much, and two priests from Galicia who were sitting at a corner table and drinking if not too much certainly enough. At that time wine was included in the price of the room and board at the Luarca and the waiters had just brought fresh bottles of Valdepeñas to the tables of the auctioneer, then to the picador and, finally, to the two priests.

The three waiters stood at the end of the room. It was the rule of the house that they should all remain on duty until the diners whose tables they were responsible for should all have left, but the one who served the table of the two priests had an appointment to go to an Anarcho-Syndicalist meeting and Paco had agreed to take over his table for him.

Upstairs the matador who was ill was lying face down on his bed alone. The matador who was no longer a novelty was sitting looking out of his window preparatory to walking out to the café. The matador who was a coward had the older sister of Paco in his room with him and was trying to get her to do something which she was laughingly refusing to do. This matador was saying, "Come on, little savage."

"No," said the sister. "Why should I?"

"For a favor."

"You've eaten and now you want me for dessert."

"Just once. What harm can it do?"

"Leave me alone. Leave me alone, I tell you."

"It is a very little thing to do."

"Leave me alone, I tell you."

Down in the dining room the tallest of the waiters, who was overdue at the meeting, said "Look at those black pigs drink."

"That's no way to speak," said the second waiter. "They are decent clients. They do not drink too much."

"For me it is a good way to speak," said the tall one. "There are the two curses of Spain, the bulls and the priests."

"Certainly not the individual bull and the individual priest," said the second waiter.

"Yes," said the tall waiter. "Only through the individual can you attack the class. It is necessary to kill the individual bull and the individual priest. All of them. Then there are no more."

"Save it for the meeting," said the other waiter.

"Look at the barbarity of Madrid," said the tall waiter. "It is now half-past eleven o'clock and these are still guzzling."

"They only started to eat at ten," said the other waiter. "As you know there are many dishes. That wine is cheap and these have paid for it. It is not a strong wine."

"How can there be solidarity of workers with fools like you?" asked the tall waiter.

"Look," said the second waiter who was a man of fifty. "I have worked all my life. In all that remains of my life I must work. I have no complaints against work. To work is normal."

"Yes, but the lack of work kills."

"I have always worked," said the older waiter. "Go on to the meeting. There is no necessity to stay."

"You are a good comrade," said the tall waiter. "But you lack all ideology."

"*Mejor si me falta eso que el otro*," said the older waiter (meaning it is better to lack that than work). "Go on to the *mitin*."

Paco had said nothing. He did not yet understand politics but it always gave him a thrill to hear the tall waiter speak of the necessity for killing the priests and the Guardia Civil. The tall waiter represented to him revolution and revolution also was romantic. He himself would like to be a good Catholic, a revolutionary, and have a steady job like this, while, at the same time, being a bull fighter.

"Go on to the meeting, Ignacio," he said. "I will respond for your work."

"The two of us," said the older waiter.

"There isn't enough for one," said Paco. "Go on to the meeting."

"*Pues, me voy*," said the tall waiter. "And thanks."

In the meantime, upstairs, the sister of Paco had gotten out of the embrace of the matador as skilfully as a wrestler breaking a hold and said, now angry. "These are the hungry people. A failed bullfighter. With your ton-load of fear. If you have so much of that, use it in the ring."

"That is the way a whore talks."

"A whore is also a woman, but I am not a whore."

"You'll be one."

"Not through you."

"Leave me," said the matador who, now, repulsed and refused, felt the nakedness of his cowardice returning.

"Leave you? What hasn't left you?" said the sister. "Don't you want me to make up the bed? I'm paid to do that."

"Leave me," said the matador, his broad good-looking face wrinkled into a contortion that was like crying. "You whore. You dirty little whore."

"Matador," she said, shutting the door. "My matador."

Inside the room the matador sat on the bed. His face still had the contortion which, in the ring, he made into a constant smile which frightened those people in the first rows of seats who knew what they were watching. "And this," he was saying aloud. "And this. And this."

He could remember when he had been good and it had only been three years before. He could remember the weight of the heavy gold-brocaded fighting jacket on his shoulders on that hot afternoon in May when his voice had still been the same in the ring as in the café, and how he sighted along the point-dipping blade at the place in the top of the shoulders where it was dusty in the short-haired black hump of muscle above the wide, wood-knocking, splintered-tipped horns that lowered as he went in to kill, and how the sword pushed in as easy as into a mound of stiff butter with the palm of his hand pushing the pommel, his left arm crossed low, his left shoulder forward, his weight on his left leg, and then his weight wasn't on his leg. His weight was on his lower belly and as the bull raised his head the horn was out of sight in him and he swung over on it twice before they pulled him off it. So now when he went in to kill, and it was seldom, he could not look at the horns and what did any whore know about what he went through before he fought? And what had they been through that laughed at him? They were all whores and they knew what they could do with it.

Down in the dining room the picador sat looking at the priests. If there were women in the room he stared at them. If there were no women he would stare with enjoyment at a foreigner, *un inglés,* but lacking women or strangers, he now stared with enjoyment and insolence at the two priests. While he stared the birthmarked auctioneer rose and folding his napkin went out, leaving over half the wine in the last bottle he had ordered. If his accounts had been paid up at the Luarca he would have finished the bottle.

The two priests did not stare back at the picador. One of them was saying, "It is ten days since I have been here waiting to see him and all day I sit in the ante-chamber and he will not receive me."

"What is there to do?"

"Nothing. What can one do? One cannot go against authority."

"I have been here for two weeks and nothing. I wait and they will not see me."

"We are from the abandoned country. When the money runs out we can return."

"To the abandoned country. What does Madrid care about Galicia? We are a poor province."

"One understands the action of our brother Basilio."

"Still I have no real confidence in the integrity of Basilio Alvarez."

"Madrid is where one learns to understand. Madrid kills Spain."

"If they would simply see one and refuse."

"No. You must be broken and worn out by waiting."

"Well, we shall see. I can wait as well as another."

At this moment the picador got to his feet, walked over to the priests' table and stood, gray-headed and hawk-faced, staring at them and smiling.

"A torero," said one priest to the other.

"And a good one," said the picador and walked out of the dining room, gray-jacketed, trim-waisted, bow-legged, in tight breeches over his high-heeled cattleman's boots that clicked on the floor as he swaggered quite steadily, smiling to himself. He lived in a small, tight, professional world of personal efficiency, nightly alcoholic triumph, and insolence. Now he lit a cigar and tilting his hat at an angle in the hallway went out to the café.

The priests left immediately after the picador, hurriedly conscious of being the last people in the dining room, and there was no one in the room now but Paco and the middle-aged waiter. They cleared the tables and carried the bottles into the kitchen.

In the kitchen was the boy who washed the dishes. He was three years older than Paco and was very cynical and bitter.

"Take this," the middle-aged waiter said, and poured out a glass of the Valdepeñas and handed it to him.

"Why not?" the boy took the glass.

"Tu, Paco?" the older waiter asked.

"Thank you," said Paco. The three of them drank.

"I will be going," said the middle-aged waiter.

"Good night," they told him.

He went out and they were alone. Paco took a napkin one of the priests had used and standing straight, his heels planted, lowered the napkin and with head following the movement, swung his arms in the motion of a slow sweeping veronica. He turned and advancing his right foot slightly, made the second pass, gained a little terrain on the imaginary bull and made a third pass, slow, perfectly timed and suave, then gathered the napkin to his waist and swung his hips away from the bull in a media-veronica.

The dishwasher, whose name was Enrique, watched

him critically and sneeringly.

"How is the bull?" he said.

"Very brave," said Paco. "Look."

Standing slim and straight he made four more perfect passes, smooth, elegant and graceful.

"And the bull?" asked Enrique standing against the sink, holding his wine glass and wearing his apron.

"Still has lots of gas," said Paco.

"You make me sick," said Enrique.

"Why?"

"Look."

Enrique removed his apron and citing the imaginary bull he sculptured four perfect, languid gypsy veronicas and ended up with a rebolera that made the apron swing in a stiff arc past the bull's nose as he walked away from him.

"Look at that," he said. "And I wash dishes."

"Why?"

"Fear," said Enrique. "*Miedo.* The same fear you would have in a ring with a bull."

"No," said Paco. "I wouldn't be afraid."

"*Leche!*" said Enrique. "Every one is afraid. But a torero can control his fear so that he can work the bull. I went in an amateur fight and I was so afraid I couldn't keep from running. Every one thought it was very funny. So would you be afraid. If it wasn't for fear every bootblack in Spain would be a bull fighter. You, a country boy, would be frightened worse than I was."

"No," said Paco.

He had done it too many times in his imagination. Too many times he had seen the horns, seen the bull's wet muzzle, the ear twitching, then the head go down and the charge, the hoofs thudding and the hot bull pass him as he swung the cape, to re-charge as he swung the cape again, then again, and again, and again, to end winding the bull around him in his great media-veronica, and walk swingingly away, with bull hairs caught in the gold ornaments of his jacket from the close passes; the bull standing hypnotized and the crowd applauding. No, he would not be afraid. Others, yes. Not he. He knew he would not be afraid. Even if he ever was afraid he knew that he could do it anyway. He had confidence. "I wouldn't be afraid," he said.

Enrique said, "*Leche,*" again.

Then he said, "If we should try it?"

"How?"

"Look," said Enrique. "You think of the bull but you do not think of the horns. The bull has such force that the horns rip like a knife, they stab like a bayonet, and they kill like a club. Look," he opened a table drawer and took out two meat knives. "I will bind these to the legs of a chair. Then I will play bull for you with the chair held before my head. The knives are the horns. If you make those passes then they mean something."

"Lend me your apron," said Paco. "We'll do it in the dining room."

"No," said Enrique, suddenly not bitter. "Don't do it, Paco."

"Yes," said Paco. "I'm not afraid."

"You will be when you see the knives come."

"We'll see," said Paco. "Give me the apron."

At this time, while Enrique was binding the two heavy-bladed razor-sharp meat knives fast to the legs of the chair with two soiled napkins holding the half of each knife, wrapping them tight and then knotting them, the two chambermaids, Paco's sisters, were on their way to the cinema to see Greta Garbo in "Anna Christie." Of the two priests, one was sitting in his underwear reading his breviary and the other was wearing a nightshirt and saying the rosary. All the bullfighters except the one who was ill had made their evening appearance at the Café Fornos, where the big, dark-haired picador was playing billiards, the short, serious matador was sitting at a crowded table before a coffee and milk, along with the middle-aged banderillero and other serious workmen.

The drinking, gray-headed picador was sitting with a glass of cazalas brandy before him staring with pleasure at a table where the matador whose courage was gone sat with another matador who had renounced the sword to become a banderillero again, and two very houseworn-looking prostitutes.

The auctioneer stood on the street corner talking with friends. The tall waiter was at the Anarcho-Syndicalist meeting waiting for an opportunity to speak. The middle-aged waiter was seated on the terrace of the Café Alvarez drinking a small beer. The woman who owned the Luarca was already asleep in her bed, where she lay on her back with the bolster between her legs; big, fat, clean, easy-going, very religious and never having ceased to miss or pray daily for her husband, dead, now, twenty years. In his room, alone, the matador who was ill lay face down on his bed with his mouth against a handkerchief.

Now, in the deserted dining room, Enrique tied the last knot in the napkins that bound the knives to the chair legs and lifted the chair. He pointed the legs with the knives on them forward and held the chair over his head with the two knives pointing straight ahead, one on each side of his head.

"It's heavy," he said, "Look, Paco. It is very dangerous. Don't do it." He was sweating.

Paco stood facing him, holding the apron spread, holding a fold of it bunched in each hand, thumbs up, first finger down, spread to catch the eye of the bull.

"Charge straight," he said. "Turn like a bull. Charge as many times as you want."

"How will you know when to cut the pass?" asked Enrique. "It's better to do three and then a media."

"All right," said Paco. "But come straight. Huh, torito! Come on, little bull!"

Running with head down Enrique came toward him and Paco swung the apron just ahead of the knife blade as it passed close in front of his belly and as it went by it was, to him, the real horn, white-tipped, black, smooth, and as Enrique passed him and turned to rush again it was the hot, blood-flanked mass of the bull that thudded by, then turned like a cat and came again as he swung the cape slowly. Then the bull turned and came again and, as he watched the onrushing point, he stepped his left foot two inches too far forward and the knife did not pass, but had slipped in as easily as into a wineskin and there was a hot scalding rush above and around the sudden inner rigidity of steel and Enrique shouting. "Ay! Ay! Let me get it out! Let me get it out!" and Paco slipped forward on the chair, the apron cape still held, Enrique pulling on the chair as the knife turned in him, in him, Paco.

The knife was out now and he sat on the floor in the widening warm pool.

"Put the napkin over it. Hold it!" said Enrique. "Hold it tight. I will run for the doctor. You must hold in the hemorrhage."

"There should be a rubber cup," said Paco. He had seen that used in the ring.

"I came straight," said Enrique, crying. "All I wanted was to show the danger."

"Don't worry." said Paco, his voice sounding far away. "But bring the doctor."

In the ring they lifted you and carried you, running with you, to the operating room. If the femoral artery emptied itself before you reached there they called the priest.

"Advise one of the priests," said Paco, holding the napkin tight against his lower abdomen. He could not believe that this had happened to him.

But Enrique was running down the Carrera San Jeromino to the all-night first-aid station and Paco was alone, first sitting up, then huddled over, then slumped on the floor, until it was over, feeling his life go out of him as dirty water empties from a bathtub when the plug is drawn. He was frightened and he felt faint and he tried to say an act of contrition and he remembered how it started but before he had said, as fast as he could, "Oh, my God, I am heartily sorry for having offended Thee who art worthy of all my love and I firmly resolve . . . ," he felt too faint and he was lying face down on the floor and it was over very quickly. A severed femoral artery empties itself faster than you can believe.

As the doctor from the first-aid station came up the stairs accompanied by a policeman who held on to Enrique by the arm, the two sisters of Paco were still in the moving-picture palace of the Gran Via, where they were intensely disappointed in the Garbo film, which showed the great star in miserable low surroundings when they had been accustomed to see her surrounded by great luxury and brilliance. The audience disliked the film thoroughly and were protesting by whistling and stamping their feet. All the other people from the hotel were doing almost what they had been doing when the accident happened, except that the two priests had finished their devotions and were preparing for sleep, and the gray-haired picador had moved his drink over to the table with the two house-worn prostitutes. A little later he went out of the café with one of them. It was the one for whom the matador who had lost his nerve had been buying drinks.

The boy Paco had never known about any of this nor about what all these people would be doing on the next day and on other days to come. He had no idea how they really lived nor how they ended. He did not even realize they ended. He died, as the Spanish phrase has it, full of illusions. He had not had time in his life to lose any of them, nor even, at the end, to complete an act of contrition.

He had not even had time to be disappointed in the Garbo picture which disappointed all Madrid for a week.

SHIRLEY JACKSON

The Lottery

THE MORNING of June 27th was clear and sunny, with the fresh warmth of a full-summer day; the flowers were blossoming profusely and the grass was richly green. The people of the village began to gather in the square, between the post office and the bank, around ten o'clock; in some towns there were so many people that the lottery took two days and had to be started on June 26th, but in this village, where there were only about three hundred people, the whole lottery took less than two hours, so it could begin at ten o'clock in the morning and still be through in time to allow the villagers to get home for noon dinner.

The children assembled first, of course. School was recently over for the summer, and the feeling of liberty sat uneasily on most of them; they tended to gather together quietly for a while before they broke into boisterous play, and their talk was still of the classroom and the teacher, of books and reprimands. Bobby Martin had already stuffed his pockets full of stones, and the other boys soon followed his example, selecting the smoothest and roundest stones; Bobby and Harry Jones and Dickie Delacroix—the villagers pronounced this name "Dellacroy"—eventually made a great pile of stones in one corner of the square and guarded it against the raids of the other boys. The girls stood aside, talking among themselves, looking over their shoulders at the boys, and the very small children rolled in the dust or clung to the hands of their older brothers or sisters.

Soon the men began to gather, surveying their own children, speaking of planting and rain, tractors and taxes. They stood together, away from the pile of stones in the corner, and their jokes were quiet and they smiled rather than laughed. The women, wearing faded house dresses and sweaters, came shortly after their menfolk. They greeted one another and exchanged bits of gossip as they went to join their husbands. Soon the women, standing by their husbands, began to call to their children, and the children came reluctantly, having to be called four or five times. Bobby Martin ducked under his mother's grasping hand and ran, laughing, back to the pile of stones. His father spoke up sharply, and Bobby came quickly and took his place between his father and his oldest brother.

The lottery was conducted—as were the square dances, the teen-age club, the Halloween program—by Mr. Summers, who had time and energy to devote to civic activities. He was a round-faced, jovial man and he ran the coal business, and people were sorry for him, because he had no children and his wife was a scold. When he arrived in the square, carrying the black wooden box, there was a murmur of conversation among the villagers, and he waved and called, "Little late today, folks." The postmaster, Mr. Graves, followed him, carrying a three-legged stool, and the stool was put in the center of the square and Mr. Summers set the black box down on it. The villagers kept their distance, leaving a space between themselves and the stool, and when Mr. Summers said, "Some of you fellows want to give me a hand?" there was a hesitation before two men, Mr. Martin and his oldest son, Baxter, came forward to hold the box steady on the stool while Mr. Summers stirred up the papers inside it.

The original paraphernalia for the lottery had been lost long ago, and the black box now resting on the stool had been put into use even before Old Man Warner, the oldest man in town, was born. Mr. Summers spoke frequently to the villagers about making a new box, but no one liked to upset even as much tradition as was represented by the black box. There was a story that the present box had been made with some pieces of the box that had preceded it, the one that had been constructed when the first people settled down to make a village here. Every year, after the lottery, Mr. Summers began talking again about a new box, but every year the subject was allowed to fade off without anything's being done. The black box grew shabbier each year; by now it was no longer completely black but splintered badly along one side to show the original wood color, and in some places faded or stained.

Mr. Martin and his oldest son, Baxter, held the black box securely on the stool until Mr. Summers had stirred the papers thoroughly with his hand. Because so much of the ritual had been forgotten or discarded, Mr. Summers had been successful in having slips of paper substituted for the chips of wood that had been used for generations. Chips of wood, Mr. Summers had argued, had been all very well when the village was tiny, but now that the population was more than three hundred and likely to keep on growing, it was necessary to use something that would fit more easily into the black box. The night before the lottery, Mr. Summers and Mr. Graves made up the slips of paper and put them in the box, and it was then taken to the safe of Mr. Summers' coal company and locked up until Mr. Summers was ready to take it to the square next morning. The rest of the year, the box was put away, sometimes one place, sometimes another; it had spent one year in Mr. Graves's barn and another year underfoot in the post office, and sometimes it was set on a shelf in the Martin grocery and left there.

There was a great deal of fussing to be done before Mr. Summers declared the lottery open. There were the lists to make up—of heads of families, heads of households in each family, members of each household in each family. There was the proper swearing-in of Mr. Summers by the postmaster, as the official of the lottery; at one time, some people remembered, there had been a recital of some sort, performed by the official of the lottery, a perfunctory, tuneless chant that had been rattled off duly each year; some people believed that the official of the lottery used to stand just so when he said or sang it, others believed that he was supposed to walk among the people, but years and years ago this part of the ritual had been allowed to lapse. There had been, also, a ritual salute, which the official of the lottery had had to use in addressing each person who came up to draw from the box, but this also had changed with time, until now it was felt necessary only for the official to speak to each person approaching. Mr. Summers was very good at all this; in his clean white shirt and blue jeans, with one hand resting carelessly on the black box, he seemed very proper and important as he talked interminably to Mr. Graves and the Martins.

Just as Mr. Summers finally left off talking and turned to the assembled villagers, Mrs. Hutchinson came hurriedly along the path to the square, her sweater thrown over her shoulders, and slid into place in the back of the crowd. "Clean forgot what day it was," she said to Mrs. Delacroix, who stood next to her, and they both laughed softly. "Thought my old man was out back stacking wood," Mrs. Hutchinson went on, "and then I looked out the window and the kids were gone, and then I remembered it was the twenty-seventh and came a-running." She dried her hands on her apron, and Mrs. Delacroix said, "You're in time, though. They're still talking away up there."

Mrs. Hutchinson craned her neck to see through the crowd and found her husband and children standing near the front. She tapped Mrs. Delacroix on the arm as a farewell and began to make her way through the crowd. The people separated good-humoredly to let her through; two or three people said, in voices just loud enough to be heard across the crowd, "Here comes your Missus, Hutchinson," and "Bill, she made it after all." Mrs. Hutchinson reached her husband, and Mr. Summers, who had been waiting, said cheerfully, "Thought we were going to have to get on without you, Tessie." Mrs. Hutchinson said, grinning. "Wouldn't have me leave m'dishes in the sink, now, would you, Joe?," and soft laughter ran through the crowd as the people stirred back into position after Mrs. Hutchinson's arrival.

"Well, now," Mr. Summers said soberly, "guess we better get started, get this over with, so's we can go back to work. Anybody ain't here?"

"Dunbar," several people said. "Dunbar, Dunbar."

Mr. Summers consulted his list. "Clyde Dunbar," he said. "That's right. He's broke his leg, hasn't he? Who's drawing for him?"

"Me, I guess," a woman said, and Mr. Summers turned to look at her. "Wife draws for her husband," Mr. Summers said. "Don't you have a grown boy to do it for you, Janey?" Although Mr. Summers and everyone else in the village knew the answer perfectly well, it was the business of the official of the lottery to ask such questions formally. Mr. Summers waited with an expression of polite interest while Mrs. Dunbar answered.

"Horace's not but sixteen yet," Mrs. Dunbar said regretfully. "Guess I gotta fill in for the old man this year."

"Right," Mr. Summers said. He made a note on the list he was holding. Then he asked, "Watson boy drawing this year?"

A tall boy in the crowd raised his hand. "Here," he said. "I'm drawing for m'mother and me." He blinked his eyes nervously and ducked his head as several voices in the crowd said things like "Good fellow, Jack," and "Glad to see your mother's got a man to do it."

"Well," Mr. Summers said, "guess that's everyone. Old Man Warner make it?"

"Here," a voice said, and Mr. Summers nodded.

A sudden hush fell on the crowd as Mr. Summers cleared his throat and looked at the list. "All ready?" he called. "Now, I'll read the names—heads of families first—and the men come up and take a paper out of the box. Keep the paper folded in your hand without looking at it until everyone has had a turn. Everything clear?"

The people had done it so many times that they only half listened to the directions; most of them were quiet, wetting their lips, not looking around. Then Mr. Summers raised one hand high and said, "Adams." A man disengaged himself from the crowd and came forward. "Hi, Steve," Mr. Summers said, and Mr. Adams said, "Hi Joe." They grinned at one another humorlessly and nervously. Then Mr. Adams reached into the black box and took out a folded paper. He held it firmly by one corner as he turned and went hastily back to his place in the crowd, where he stood a little apart from his family, not looking down at his hand.

"Allen," Mr. Summers said. "Andrews. . . . Bentham."

"Seems like there's no time at all between lotteries any more," Mrs. Delacroix said to Mrs. Graves in the back row. "Seems like we got through with the last one only last week."

"Time sure goes fast," Mrs. Graves said.

"Clark. . . . Delacroix."

"There goes my old man," Mrs. Delacroix said. She held her breath while her husband went forward.

"Dunbar," Mr. Summers said, and Mrs. Dunbar went steadily to the box while one of the women said, "Go on, Janey," and another said, "There she goes."

"We're next," Mrs. Graves said. She watched while Mr. Graves came around from the side of the box, greeted Mr. Summers gravely, and selected a slip of paper from the box. By now, all through the crowd there were men holding the small folded papers in their large hands, turning them over and over nervously. Mrs. Dunbar and her two sons stood together, Mrs. Dunbar holding the slip of paper.

"Harburt. . . . Hutchinson."

"Get up there, Bill," Mrs. Hutchinson said, and the people near her laughed.

"Jones."

"They do say," Mr. Adams said to Old Man Warner, who stood next to him, "that over in the north village they're talking of giving up the lottery."

Old man Warner snorted. "Pack of crazy fools," he said. "Listening to the young folks, nothing's good enough for *them.* Next thing you know, they'll be wanting to go back to living in caves, nobody work any more, live *that* way for a while. Used to be a saying about 'Lottery in June, corn be heavy soon.' First thing you know, we'd all be eating stewed chickweed and acorns. There's *always* been a lottery," he added petulantly. "Bad enough to see young Joe Summers up there joking with everybody."

"Some places have already quit lotteries," Mrs. Adams said.

"Nothing but trouble in *that,*" Old Man Warner said stoutly. "Pack of young fools."

"Martin." And Bobby Martin watched his father go forward. "Overdyke. . . . Percy."

"I wish they'd hurry," Mrs. Dunbar said to her older son. "I wish they'd hurry."

"They're almost through," her son said.

"You get ready to run tell Dad," Mrs. Dunbar said.

Mr. Summers called his own name and then stepped forward precisely and selected a slip from the box. Then he called, "Warner."

"Seventy-seventh year I been in the lottery," Old Man Warner said as he went through the crowd. "Seventy-seventh time."

"Watson." The tall boy came awkwardly through the crowd. Someone said, "Don't be nervous, Jack," and Mr. Summers said, "Take your time, son."

"Zanini."

After that, there was a long pause, a breathless pause, until Mr. Summers, holding his slip of paper in the air, said, "All right, fellows." For a minute, no one moved, and then all the slips of paper were opened. Suddenly, all the women began to speak at once, saying, "Who is it?," "who's got it?," "Is it the Dunbars?," "Is it the Watsons?" Then the voices began to say, "It's Hutchinson. It's Bill." "Bill Hutchinson got it."

"Go tell your father," Mrs. Dunbar said to her older son.

People began to look around to see the Hutchinsons. Bill Hutchinson standing quiet, staring down at the paper in his hand. Suddenly, Tessie Hutchinson shouted to Mr. Summers, "You didn't give him time enough to take any paper he wanted. I saw you. It wasn't fair."

"Be a good sport, Tessie," Mrs. Delacroix called, and Mrs. Graves said, "All of us took the same chance."

"Shut up, Tessie," Bill Hutchinson said.

"Well, everyone," Mr. Summers said, "that was done pretty fast, and now we've got to be hurrying a little more to get done in time." He consulted his next list. "Bill," he said, "you draw for the Hutchinson family. You got any other households in the Hutchinsons?"

"There's Don and Eva," Mrs. Hutchinson yelled. "Make *them* take their chance!"

"Daughters draw with their husbands' families, Tessie," Mr. Summers said gently. "You know that as well as anyone else."

"It wasn't *fair,*" Tessie said.

"I guess not, Joe," Bill Hutchinson said regretfully. "My daughter draws with her husband's family, that's only fair. And I've got no other family except the kids."

"Then as far as drawing for families is concerned, it's you," Mr. Summers said in explanation, "and as far as drawing for households is concerned, that's you, too. Right?"

"Right," Bill Hutchinson said.

"How many kids, Bill?" Mr. Summers asked formally.

"Three," Bill Hutchinson said. "There's Bill, Jr., and Nancy, and little Dave. And Tessie and me."

"All right, then," Mr. Summers said. "Harry, you got their tickets back?"

Mr. Graves nodded and held up the slips of paper. "Put them in the box, then," Mr. Summers directed. "Take Bill's and put it in."

"I think we ought to start over," Mrs. Hutchinson said, as quietly as she could. "I tell you it wasn't *fair.* You didn't give him time enough to choose. *Every*body saw that."

Mr. Graves had selected the five slips and put them in the box, and he dropped all the papers but those onto the ground, where the breeze caught them and lifted them off.

"Listen, everybody," Mrs. Hutchinson was saying to the people around her.

"Ready, Bill?" Mr. Summers asked, and Bill Hutchinson, with one quick glance around at his wife and children, nodded.

"Remember," Mr. Summers said, "take the slips and keep them folded until each person has taken one. Harry, you help little Dave." Mr. Graves took the hand of the little boy, who came willingly with him up to the box. "Take a paper out of the box, Davy," Mr. Summers said. Davy put his hand into the box and laughed. "Take just *one* paper," Mr. Summers said. "Harry, you hold it for him." Mr. Graves took the child's hand and removed the folded paper from the tight fist and held it while little Dave stood next to him and looked up at him wonderingly.

"Nancy next," Mr. Summers said. Nancy was twelve, and her school friends breathed heavily as she went forward, switching her skirt, and took a slip daintily from the box. "Bill, Jr.," Mr. Summers said, and Billy, his face red and his feet over-large, nearly knocked the box over as he got a paper out. "Tessie," Mr. Summers said. She hesitated for a minute, looking around defiantly, and then set her lips and went up to the box. She snatched a paper out and held it behind her.

"Bill," Mr. Summers said, and Bill Hutchinson reached into the box and felt around, bringing his hand out at last with the slip of paper in it.

The crowd was quiet. A girl whispered, "I hope it's not Nancy," and the sound of the whisper reached the edges of the crowd.

"It's not the way it used to be," Old Man Warner said clearly. "People ain't the way they used to be."

"All right," Mr. Summers said. "Open the papers. Harry, you open little Dave's."

Mr. Graves opened the slip of paper and there was a general sigh through the crowd as he held it up and everyone could see that it was blank. Nancy and Bill, Jr., opened theirs at the same time, and both beamed and laughed, turning around to the crowd and holding their slips of paper above their heads.

"Tessie," Mr. Summers said. There was a pause, and then Mr. Summers looked at Bill Hutchinson, and Bill unfolded his paper and showed it. It was blank.

"It's Tessie," Mr. Summers said, and his voice was hushed. "Show us her paper, Bill."

Bill Hutchinson went over to his wife and forced the slip of paper out of her hand. It had a black spot on it, the black spot Mr. Summers had made the night before with the heavy pencil in the coal-company office. Bill Hutchinson held it up, and there was a stir in the crowd.

"All right, folks," Mr. Summers said, "Let's finish quickly."

Although the villagers had forgotten the ritual and lost the original black box, they still remembered to use stones. The pile of stones the boys had made earlier was ready; there were stones on the ground with the blowing scraps of paper that had come out of the box. Mrs. Delacroix selected a stone so large she had to pick it up with both hands and turned to Mrs. Dunbar. "Come on," she said. "Hurry up."

Mrs. Dunbar had small stones in both hands, and she said, gasping for breath, "I can't run at all. You'll have to go ahead and I'll catch up with you."

The children had stones already, and someone gave little Davy Hutchinson a few pebbles.

Tessie Hutchinson was in the center of a cleared space by now, and she held her hands out desperately as the villagers moved in on her. "It isn't fair," she said. A stone hit her on the side of the head.

Old Man Warner was saying, "Come on, come on, everyone." Steve Adams was in the front of the crowd of villagers, with Mrs. Graves beside him.

"It isn't fair, it isn't right," Mrs. Hutchinson screamed, and then they were upon her.

D. H. LAWRENCE

The Rocking-Horse Winner

THERE was a woman who was beautiful, who started with all the advantages, yet she had no luck. She married for love, and the love turned to dust. She had bonny children, yet she felt they had been thrust upon her, and she could not love them. They looked at her coldly, as if they were finding fault with her. And hurriedly she felt she must cover up some fault in herself. Yet what it was that she must cover up she never knew. Nevertheless, when her children were present, she always felt the centre of her heart go hard. This troubled her, and in her manner she was all the more gentle and anxious for her children, as if she loved them very much. Only she herself knew that at the centre of her heart was a hard little place that could not feel love, no, not for anybody. Everybody else said of her: "She is such a good mother. She adores her children." Only she herself, and her children themselves, knew it was not so. They read it in each other's eyes.

There were a boy and two little girls. They lived in a pleasant house, with a garden, and they had discreet servants and felt themselves superior to anyone in the neighbourhood.

Although they lived in style, they felt always an anxiety in the house. There was never enough money. The mother had a small income, and the father had a small income, but not nearly enough for the social position which they had to keep up. The father went into town to some office. But though he had good prospects, these prospects never materialized. There was always the grinding sense of the shortage of money, though the style was always kept up.

At last the mother said: "I will see if I can't make something." But she did not know where to begin. She racked her brains, and tried this thing and the other, but could not find anything successful. The failure made deep lines come into her face. Her children were growing up, they would have to go to school. There must be more money, there must be more money. The father, who was always very handsome and expensive in his tastes, seemed as if he never would be able to do anything worth doing. And the mother, who had a great belief in herself, did not succeed any better, and her tastes were just as expensive.

And so the house came to be haunted by the unspoken

phrase: There must be more money! There must be more money! The children could hear it all the time, though nobody said it aloud. They heard it at Christmas, when the expensive and splendid toys filled the nursery. Behind the shining modern rocking-horse, behind the smart doll's-house, a voice would start whispering: "There must be more money! There must be more money!" And the children would stop playing, to listen for a moment. They would look into each other's eyes, to see if they had all heard. And each one saw in the eyes of the other two that they too had heard. "There must be more money! There must be more money!"

It came whispering from the springs of the still-swaying rocking-horse, and even the horse, bending his wooden, champing head, heard it. The big doll, sitting so pink and smirking in her new pram, could hear it quite plainly, and seemed to be smirking all the more self-consciously because of it. The foolish puppy, too, that took the place of the teddy-bear, he was looking so extraordinarily foolish for no other reason but that he heard the secret whisper all over the house: "There must be more money!"

Yet nobody ever said it aloud. The whisper was everywhere, and therefore no one spoke it. Just as no one ever says: "We are breathing!" in spite of the fact that breath is coming and going all the time.

"Mother," said the boy Paul one day, "why don't we keep a car of our own? Why do we always use uncle's, or else a taxi?"

"Because we're the poor members of the family," said the mother.

"But why are we, mother?"

"Well—I suppose," she said slowly and bitterly, "it's because your father has no luck."

The boy was silent for some time.

"Is luck money, mother?" he asked, rather timidly.

"No, Paul. Not quite. It's what causes you to have money."

"Oh!" said Paul vaguely. "I thought when Uncle Oscar said filthy lucker, it meant money."

"Filthy lucre does mean money," said the mother. "But it's lucre, not luck."

"Oh!" said the boy. "Then what is luck, mother?"

"It's what causes you to have money. If you're lucky you have money. That's why it's better to be born lucky than rich. If you're rich, you may lose your money. But if you're lucky, you will always get more money."

"Oh! Will you? And is father not lucky?"

"Very unlucky, I should say," she said bitterly.

The boy watched her with unsure eyes.

"Why?" he asked.

"I don't know. Nobody ever knows why one person is lucky and another unlucky."

"Don't they? Nobody at all? Does nobody know?"

"Perhaps God. But He never tells."

"He ought to, then. And aren't you lucky either, mother?"

"I can't be, if I married an unlucky husband."

"But by yourself, aren't you?"

"I used to think I was, before I married. Now I think I am very unlucky indeed."

"Why?"

"Well—never mind! Perhaps I'm not really," she said.

The child looked at her, to see if she meant it. But he saw by the lines of her mouth, that she was only trying to hide something from him.

"Well, anyhow," he said stoutly, "I'm a lucky person."

"Why?" said his mother, with a sudden laugh.

He stared at her. He didn't even know why he had said it.

"God told me," he asserted, brazening it out.

"I hope He did, dear!" she said, again with a laugh, but rather bitter.

"He did, mother!"

"Excellent!" said the mother, using one of her husband's exclamations.

The boy saw she did not believe him; or, rather, that she paid no attention to his assertion. This angered him somewhat, and made him want to compel her attention.

He went off by himself, vaguely, in a childish way, seeking for the clue to "luck." Absorbed, taking no heed of other people, he went about with a sort of stealth, seeking inwardly for luck. He wanted luck, he wanted it, he wanted it. When the two girls were playing dolls in the nursery, he would sit on his big rocking-horse, charging madly into space, with a frenzy that made the little girls peer at him uneasily. Wildly the horse careered, the waving dark hair of the boy tossed, his eyes had a strange glare in them. The little girls dared not speak to him.

When he had ridden to the end of his mad little journey, he climbed down and stood in front of his rocking-horse, staring fixedly into its lowered face. Its red mouth was slightly open, its big eye was wide and glassy-bright.

"Now!" he would silently command the snorting steed. "Now, take me to where there is luck! Now take me!"

And he would slash the horse on the neck with the little whip he had asked Uncle Oscar for. He knew the horse could take him to where there was luck, if only he forced it. So he would mount again, and start on his furious ride, hoping at last to get there. He knew he could get there.

"You'll break your horse, Paul!" said the nurse.

"He's always riding like that! I wish he'd leave off!" said his elder sister Joan.

But he only glared down on them in silence. Nurse gave him up. She could make nothing of him. Anyhow he was growing beyond her.

One day his mother and his Uncle Oscar came in

when he was on one of his furious rides. He did not speak to them.

"Hallo, you young jockey! Riding a winner?" said his uncle.

"Aren't you growing too big for a rocking-horse? You're not a very little boy any longer, you know," said his mother.

But Paul only gave a blue glare from his big, rather close-set eyes. He would speak to nobody when he was in full tilt. His mother watched him with an anxious expression on her face.

At last he suddenly stopped forcing his horse into the mechanical gallop, and slid down.

"Well, I got there!" he announced fiercely, his blue eyes still flaring, and his sturdy long legs straddling apart.

"Where did you get to?" asked his mother.

"Where I wanted to go," he flared back at her.

"That's right, son!" said Uncle Oscar. "Don't you stop till you get there. What's the horse's name?"

"He doesn't have a name," said the boy.

"Gets on without all right?" asked the uncle.

"Well, he has different names. He was called Sansovino last week."

"Sansovino, eh? Won the Ascot. How did you know his name?"

"He always talks about horse-races with Bassett," said Joan.

The uncle was delighted to find that his small nephew was posted with all the racing news. Bassett, the young gardener, who had been wounded in the left foot in the war and had got his present job through Oscar Cresswell, whose batman he had been, was a perfect blade of the "turf." He lived in the racing events, and the small boy lived with him.

Oscar Cresswell got it all from Bassett.

"Master Paul comes and asks me, so I can't do more than tell him, sir," said Bassett, his face terribly serious, as if he were speaking of religious matters.

"And does he ever put anything on a horse he fancies?"

"Well—I don't want to give him away—he's a young sport, a fine sport, sir. Would you mind asking him yourself? He sort of takes a pleasure in it, and perhaps he'd feel I was giving him away, sir, if you don't mind."

Bassett was serious as a church.

The uncle went back to his nephew, and took him off for a ride in the car.

"Say, Paul, old man, do you ever put anything on a horse?" the uncle asked.

The boy watched the handsome man closely.

"Why, do you think I oughtn't to?" he parried.

"Not a bit of it! I thought perhaps you might give me a tip for the Lincoln."

The car sped on into the country, going down to Uncle Oscar's place in Hampshire.

"Honour bright?" said the nephew.

"Honour bright, son!" said the uncle.

"Well, then, Daffodil."

"Daffodil! I doubt it, sonny. What about Mirza?"

"I only know the winner," said the boy. "That's Daffodil."

"Daffodil, eh?"

There was a pause. Daffodil was an obscure horse comparatively.

"Uncle!"

"Yes, son?"

"You won't let it go any further, will you? I promised Bassett."

"Bassett be damned, old man! What's he got to do with it?"

"We're partners. We've been partners from the first. Uncle, he lent me my first five shillings, which I lost. I promised him, honour bright, it was only between me and him; only you gave me that ten-shilling note I started winning with, so I thought you were lucky. You won't let it go any further, will you?"

The boy gazed at his uncle from those big, hot, blue eyes, set rather close together. The uncle stirred and laughed uneasily.

"Right you are, son! I'll keep your tip private. Daffodil, eh? How much are you putting on him?"

"All except twenty pounds," said the boy. "I keep that in reserve."

The uncle thought it a good joke.

"You keep twenty pounds in reserve, do you, you young romancer? What are you betting, then?"

"I'm betting three hundred," said the boy gravely. "But it's between you and me, Uncle Oscar! Honour bright?"

The uncle burst into a roar of laughter.

"It's between you and me all right, you young Nat Gould," he said, laughing. "But where's your three hundred?"

"Bassett keeps it for me. We're partners."

"You are, are you! And what is Bassett putting on Daffodil?"

"He won't go quite as high as I do, I expect. Perhaps he'll go a hundred and fifty."

"What, pennies?" laughed the uncle.

"Pounds," said the child, with a surprised look at his uncle. "Bassett keeps a bigger reserve than I do."

Between wonder and amusement Uncle Oscar was silent. He pursued the matter no further, but he determined to take his nephew with him to the Lincoln races.

"Now, son," he said, "I'm putting twenty on Mirza, and I'll put five for you on any horse you fancy. What's your pick?"

"Daffodil, uncle."

"No, not the fiver on Daffodil!"

"I should if it was my own fiver," said the child.

"Good! Good! Right you are! A fiver for me and a

fiver for you on Daffodil."

The child had never been to a race-meeting before, and his eyes were blue fire. He pursed his mouth tight, and watched. A Frenchman just in front had put his money on Lancelot. Wild with excitement, he flayed his arms up and down, yelling "Lancelot! Lancelot!" in his French accent.

Daffodil came in first, Lancelot second, Mirza third. The child, flushed and with eyes blazing, was curiously serene. His uncle brought him four five-pound notes, four to one.

"What am I to do with these?" he cried, waving them before the boy's eyes.

"I suppose we'll talk to Bassett," said the boy. "I expect I have fifteen hundred now; and twenty in reserve; and this twenty."

His uncle studied him for some moments.

"Look here, son!" he said. "You're not serious about Bassett and that fifteen hundred, are you?"

"Yes, I am. But it's between you and me, uncle. Honour bright!"

"Honour bright all right, son! But I must talk to Bassett."

"If you'd like to be a partner, uncle, with Bassett and me, we could all be partners. Only, you'd have to promise, honour bright, uncle, not to let it go beyond us three. Bassett and I are lucky, and you must be lucky, because it was your ten shillings I started winning with. . . ."

Uncle Oscar took both Bassett and Paul into Richmond Park for an afternoon, and there they talked.

"It's like this, you see, sir," Bassett said. "Master Paul would get me talking about racing events, spinning yarns, you know, sir. And he was always keen on knowing if I'd made or if I'd lost. It's about a year since, now, that I put five shillings on Blush of Dawn for him—and we lost. Then the luck turned, with that ten shillings he had from you, that we put on Singhalese. And since that time, it's been pretty steady, all things considering. What do you say, Master Paul?"

"We're all right when we're sure," said Paul. "It's when we're not quite sure that we go down."

"Oh, but we're careful then," said Bassett.

"But when are you sure?" smiled Uncle Oscar.

"It's Master Paul, sir," said Bassett, in a secret, religious voice. "It's as if he had it from heaven. Like Daffodil, now, for the Lincoln. That was as sure as eggs."

"Did you put anything on Daffodil?" asked Oscar Cresswell.

"Yes, sir. I made my bit."

"And my nephew?"

Bassett was obstinately silent, looking at Paul.

"I made twelve hundred, didn't I, Bassett? I told uncle I was putting three hundred on Daffodil."

"That's right," said Bassett, nodding.

"But where's the money?" asked the uncle.

"I keep it safe locked up, sir. Master Paul he can have it any minute he likes to ask for it."

"What, fifteen hundred pounds?"

"And twenty! And forty, that is, with the twenty he made on the course."

"It's amazing!" said the uncle.

"If Master Paul offers you to be partners, sir, I would, if I were you; if you'll excuse me," said Bassett.

Oscar Cresswell thought about it.

"I'll see the money," he said.

They drove home again, and sure enough, Bassett came round to the garden-house with fifteen hundred pounds in notes. The twenty pounds reserve was left with Joe Glee, in the Turf Commission deposit.

"You see, it's all right, uncle, when I'm sure! Then we go strong, for all we're worth. Don't we, Bassett?"

"We do that, Master Paul."

"And when are you sure?" said the uncle, laughing.

"Oh, well, sometimes I'm absolutely sure, like about Daffodil," said the boy; "and sometimes I have an idea; and sometimes I haven't even an idea, have I, Bassett? Then we're careful, because we mostly go down."

"You do, do you! And when you're sure, like about Daffodil, what makes you sure, sonny?"

"Oh, well, I don't know," said the boy uneasily. "I'm sure, you know, uncle; that's all."

"It's as if he had it from heaven, sir," Bassett reiterated.

"I should say so!" said the uncle.

But he became a partner. And when the Leger was coming on, Paul was "sure" about Lively Spark, which was a quite inconsiderable horse. The boy insisted on putting a thousand on the horse, Bassett went for five hundred, and Oscar Cresswell two hundred. Lively Spark came in first, and the betting had been ten to one against him. Paul had made ten thousand.

"You see," he said, "I was absolutely sure of him."

Even Oscar Cresswell had cleared two thousand.

"Look here, son," he said, "this sort of thing makes me nervous."

"It needn't, uncle! Perhaps I shan't be sure again for a long time."

"But what are you going to do with your money?" asked the uncle.

"Of course," said the boy, "I started it for mother. She said she had no luck, because father is unlucky, so I thought if I was lucky, it might stop whispering."

"What might stop whispering?"

"Our house. I hate our house for whispering."

"What does it whisper?"

"Why—why"—the boy fidgeted—"why, I don't know. But it's always short of money, you know, uncle."

"I know it, son, I know it."

"You know people send mother writs, don't you, uncle?"

"I'm afraid I do," said the uncle.

"And then the house whispers, like people laughing at you behind your back. It's awful, that is! I thought if I was lucky . . ."

"You might stop it," added the uncle.

The boy watched him with big blue eyes that had an uncanny cold fire in them, and he said never a word.

"Well, then!" said the uncle. "What are we doing?"

"I shouldn't like mother to know I was lucky," said the boy.

"Why not, son?"

"She'd stop me."

"I don't think she would."

"Oh!"—and the boy writhed in an odd way—"I don't want her to know, uncle."

"All right, son! We'll manage it without her knowing."

They managed it very easily. Paul, at the other's suggestion, handed over five thousand pounds to his uncle, who deposited it with the family lawyer, who was then to inform Paul's mother that a relative had put five thousand pounds into his hands, which sum was to be paid out a thousand pounds at a time, on the mother's birthday, for the next five years.

"So she'll have a birthday present of a thousand pounds for five successive years," said Uncle Oscar. "I hope it won't make it all the harder for her later."

Paul's mother had her birthday in November. The house had been "whispering" worse than ever lately, and, even in spite of his luck, Paul could not bear up against it. He was very anxious to see the effect of the birthday letter, telling his mother about the thousand pounds.

When there were no visitors, Paul now took his meals with his parents, as he was beyond the nursery control. His mother went into town nearly every day. She had discovered that she had an odd knack of sketching furs and dress materials, so she worked secretly in the studio of a friend who was the chief "artist" for the leading drapers. She drew the figures of ladies in furs and ladies in silk and sequins for the newspaper advertisements. This young woman artist earned several thousand pounds a year, but Paul's mother only made several hundreds, and she was again dissatisfied. She so wanted to be first in something, and she did not succeed, even in making sketches for drapery advertisements.

She was down to breakfast on the morning of her birthday. Paul watched her face as she read her letters. He knew the lawyer's letter. As his mother read it, her face hardened and became more expressionless. Then a cold determined look came on her mouth. She hid the letter under the pile of others, and said not a word about it.

"Didn't you have anything nice in the post for your birthday, mother?" said Paul.

"Quite moderately nice," she said, her voice cold and absent.

She went away to town without saying more.

But in the afternoon Uncle Oscar appeared. He said Paul's mother had had a long interview with the lawyer, asking if the whole five thousand could be advanced at once, as she was in debt.

"What do you think, uncle?" said the boy.

"I leave it to you, son."

"Oh, let her have it, then! We can get some more with the other," said the boy.

"A bird in the hand is worth two in the bush, laddie!" said Uncle Oscar.

"But I'm sure to know for the Grand National; or the Lincolnshire; or else the Derby. I'm sure to know for one of them," said Paul.

So Uncle Oscar signed the agreement, and Paul's mother touched the whole five thousand. Then something very curious happened. The voices in the house suddenly went mad, like a chorus of frogs on a spring evening. There were certain new furnishings, and Paul had a tutor. He was really going to Eton, his father's school, in the following autumn. There were flowers in the winter, and a blossoming of the luxury Paul's mother had been used to. And yet the voices in the house, behind the sprays of mimosa and almond blossom, and from under the piles of iridescent cushions, simply trilled and screamed in a sort of ecstasy: "There must be more money! Oh-h-h, there must be more money. Oh, now now-w! Now-w-w—there must be more money!—more than ever! More than ever!"

It frightened Paul terribly. He studied away at his Latin and Greek with his tutor. But his intense hours were spent with Bassett. The Grand National had gone by: he had not "known," and had lost a hundred pounds. Summer was at hand. He was in agony for the Lincoln. But even for the Lincoln he didn't "know" and he lost fifty pounds. He became wild-eyed and strange, as if something were going to explode in him.

"Let it alone, son! Don't you bother about it!" urged Uncle Oscar. But it was as if the boy couldn't really hear what his uncle was saying.

"I've got to know for the Derby! I've got to know for the Derby!" the child reiterated, his big blue eyes blazing with a sort of madness.

His mother noticed how overwrought he was.

"You'd better go to the seaside. Wouldn't you like to go now to the seaside, instead of waiting? I think you'd better," she said, looking down at him anxiously, her heart curiously heavy because of him.

But the child lifted his uncanny blue eyes.

"I couldn't possibly go before the Derby, mother!" he said. "I couldn't possibly!"

"Why not?" she said, her voice becoming heavy when she was opposed. "Why not? You can still go from the seaside to see the Derby with your Uncle Oscar, if that's what you wish. No need for you to wait here. Besides, I think you care too much about these races. It's a bad sign.

My family has been a gambling family, and you won't know till you grow up how much damage it has done. But it has done damage. I shall have to send Bassett away, and ask Uncle Oscar not to talk racing to you, unless you promise to be reasonable about it; go away to the seaside and forget it. You're all nerves!"

"I'll do what you like, mother, so long as you don't send me away till after the Derby," the boy said.

"Send you away from where? Just from this house?"

"Yes," he said, gazing at her.

"Why, you curious child, what makes you care about this house so much, suddenly? I never knew you loved it."

He gazed at her without speaking. He had a secret within a secret, something he had not divulged, even to Bassett or to his Uncle Oscar.

But his mother, after standing undecided and a little bit sullen for some moments, said:

"Very well, then! Don't go to the seaside till after the Derby, if you don't wish it. But promise me you won't let your nerves go to pieces. Promise you won't think so much about horse-racing and events, as you call them!"

"Oh, no," said the boy casually. "I won't think much about them, mother. You needn't worry. I wouldn't worry, mother, if I were you."

"If you were me and I were you," said his mother, "I wonder what we should do!"

"But you know you needn't worry, mother, don't you?" the boy repeated.

"I should be awfully glad to know it," she said wearily.

"Oh, well, you can, you know. I mean, you ought to know you needn't worry," he insisted.

"Ought I? Then I'll see about it," she said.

Paul's secret of secrets was his wooden horse, that which had no name. Since he was emancipated from a nurse and a nursery-governess, he had had his rocking-horse removed to his own bedroom at the top of the house.

"Surely, you're too big for a rocking-horse!" his mother had remonstrated.

"Well, you see, mother, till I can have a real horse, I like to have some sort of animal about," had been his quaint answer.

"Do you feel he keeps you company?" she laughed.

"Oh, yes! He's very good, he always keeps me company, when I'm there," said Paul.

So the horse, rather shabby, stood in an arrested prance in the boy's bedroom.

The Derby was drawing near, and the boy grew more and more tense. He hardly heard what was spoken to him, he was very frail, and his eyes were really uncanny. His mother had sudden seizures of uneasiness about him. Sometimes, for half-an-hour, she would feel a sudden anxiety about him that was almost anguish. She wanted to rush to him at once, and know he was safe.

Two nights before the Derby, she was at a big party in town, when one of her rushes of anxiety about her boy, her first-born, gripped her heart till she could hardly speak. She fought with the feeling, might and main, for she believed in common sense. But it was too strong. She had to leave the dance and go downstairs to telephone to the country. The children's nursery-governess was terribly surprised and startled at being rung up in the night.

"Are the children all right, Miss Wilmot?"

"Oh yes, they are quite all right."

"Master Paul? Is he all right?"

"He went to bed as right as a trivet. Shall I run up and look at him?"

"No," said Paul's mother reluctantly. "No! Don't trouble. It's all right. Don't sit up. We shall be home fairly soon." She did not want her son's privacy intruded upon.

"Very good," said the governess.

It was about one o'clock when Paul's mother and father drove up to their house. All was still. Paul's mother went to her room and slipped off her white fur cloak. She had told her maid not to wait up for her. She heard her husband downstairs, mixing a whisky-and-soda.

And then, because of the strange anxiety at her heart, she stole upstairs to her son's room. Noiselessly she went along the upper corridor. Was there a faint noise? What was it?

She stood, with arrested muscles, outside his door, listening. There was a strange, heavy, and yet not loud noise. Her heart stood still. It was a soundless noise, yet rushing and powerful. Something huge, in violent, hushed motion. What was it? What in God's name was it? She ought to know. She felt that she knew the noise. She knew what it was.

Yet she could not place it. She couldn't say what it was. And on and on it went, like a madness.

Softly, frozen with anxiety and fear, she turned the doorhandle.

The room was dark. Yet in the space near the window, she heard and saw something plunging to and fro. She gazed in fear and amazement.

Then suddenly she switched on the light, and saw her son, in his green pajamas, madly surging on the rocking-horse. The blaze of light suddenly lit him up, as he urged the wooden horse, and lit her up, as she stood, blonde, in her dress of pale green and crystal, in the doorway.

"Paul!" she cried. "Whatever are you doing?"

"It's Malabar!" he screamed, in a powerful, strange voice. "It's Malabar."

His eyes blazed at her for one strange and senseless second, as he ceased urging his wooden horse. Then he fell with a crash to the ground, and she, all her tormented motherhood flooding upon her, rushed to gather him up.

But he was unconscious, and unconscious he remained, with some brain-fever. He talked and tossed, and his mother sat stonily by his side.

"Malabar! It's Malabar! Bassett, Bassett, I know! It's Malabar!"

So the child cried, trying to get up and urge the rocking-horse that gave him his inspiration.

"What does he mean by Malabar?" asked the heart-frozen mother.

"I don't know," said the father stonily.

"What does he mean by Malabar?" she asked her brother Oscar.

"It's one of the horses running for the Derby," was the answer.

And, in spite of himself, Oscar Cresswell spoke to Bassett, and himself put a thousand on Malabar: at fourteen to one.

The third day of the illness was critical: they were waiting for a change. The boy, with his rather long, curly hair, was tossing ceaselessly on the pillow. He neither slept nor regained consciousness, and his eyes were like blue stones. His mother sat, feeling her heart had gone, turned actually into a stone.

In the evening, Oscar Cresswell did not come, but Bassett sent a message, saying could he come up for one moment, just one moment? Paul's mother was very angry at the intrusion, but on second thought she agreed. The boy was the same. Perhaps Bassett might bring him to consciousness.

The gardener, a shortish fellow with a little brown mustache, and sharp little brown eyes, tiptoed into the room, touched his imaginary cap to Paul's mother, and stole to the bedside, staring with glittering, smallish eyes, at the tossing, dying child.

"Master Paul!" he whispered. "Master Paul! Malabar come in first all right, a clean win. I did as you told me. You've made over seventy thousand pounds, you have; you've got over eighty thousand. Malabar came in all right, Master Paul."

"Malabar! Malabar! Did I say Malabar, mother? Did I say Malabar? Do you think I'm lucky, mother? I knew Malabar, didn't I? Over eighty thousand pounds! I call that lucky, don't you, mother? Over eighty thousand pounds! I knew, didn't I know I knew? Malabar came in all right. If I ride my horse till I'm sure, then I tell you, Bassett, you can go as high as you like. Did you go for all you were worth, Bassett?"

"I went a thousand on it, Master Paul."

"I never told you, mother, that if I can ride my horse, and get there, then I'm absolutely sure—oh, absolutely! Mother, did I ever tell you? I am lucky."

"No, you never did," said the mother.

But the boy died in the night.

And even as he lay dead, his mother heard her brother's voice saying to her: "My God, Hester, you're eighty-odd thousand to the good and a poor devil of a son to the bad. But, poor devil, poor devil, he's best gone out of a life where he rides his rocking-horse to find a winner."

ROBERT McLAUGHLIN

A Short Wait Between Trains

THEY CAME into Forrest Junction at eleven-thirty in the morning. Seen from the window of their coach, it wasn't much of a town. First there were the long rows of freight cars on sidings with green-painted locomotives of the Southern Railway nosing strings of them back and forth. Then they went past the sheds of cotton ginners abutting on the tracks. There were small frame houses with weed-choked lawns enclosed by broken picket fences, a block of frame stores with dingy windows and dark interiors, a small brick-and-concrete bank, and beyond that the angled roof and thin smokestacks of a textile mill.

The station was bigger than you would expect; it was of dirty brick and had a rolling, bungalow-type roof adorned with cupolas and a sort of desperate scrollwork. The grime of thousands of trains and fifty years gave it a patina suggesting such great age that it seemed to antedate the town.

Corporal Randolph, a big sad Negro, said, "Here we is."

Private Brown, his pink-palmed hand closed over a

comic book, looked out the window. "How long we here?" he asked.

"Until one o'clock," said Randolph, getting up. "Our train west is at one o'clock."

The two other privates—Butterfield and Jerdon—were taking down their barracks bags from the rack. Other passengers bunched in the aisles—two young colored girls in slacks; a fat, bespectacled mother and her brood, with the big-eyed child in her arms staring fixedly at the soldiers; tall, spare, colored farmers in blue overalls.

As they waited for the line to move, Jerdon said, "Who dat?"

Grinning, Brown answered, "Who dat say 'Who dat?' "

Jerdon replied in a nervous quaver, "Who dat say 'Who dat?' when I say 'Who dat?' "

They both began to laugh and some of the passengers looked at them with half-smiles and uncertain eyes.

Butterfield said, "Even the kid thinks you're nuts."

The child in the fat woman's arms looked at him sharply as he spoke, then her eyes went back to Jerdon and Brown.

"You think I'm nuts, baby?" asked Jerdon. "Is it like the man say?"

The line of passengers began to move.

"That baby don't think I'm nuts," said Jerdon. "That baby is sure a smart baby."

Their coach was up by the engine, and they descended to the platform into a cloud of released steam, with the sharp pant of the engine seemingly at their shoulders. A motor-driven baggage truck, operated by a colored man wearing an engineer's cap, plowed through them. The three privates, with their bags slung over their shoulders, stood watching the corporal. He was checking through the papers in a large manila envelope marked "War Department, Official Business." It contained their railway tickets and their orders to report to a camp in Arizona.

"Man," said Brown, "you better not lose anything. We don't want to stay in this place."

"This don't look like any town to me, either," said Jerdon.

Butterfield, slim, somewhat lighter in complexion, and a year or two older than the others, looked around him. "Hey," he said, "look what's up there."

The others turned. Down the platform they could see two white soldiers armed with carbines and what appeared to be a group of other white soldiers in fatigues. A crowd was forming around them.

"They're prisoners of war," said Butterfield. "You want to see some Germans, Brown? You say you're going to kill a lot of them; you want to see what they look like?"

Brown said, "That what they are?"

"Sure," said Butterfield. "See what they've got on their backs? 'P.W.' That means 'prisoner of war.' "

The four soldiers moved forward. They stood on the fringe of the crowd, which was mostly white, looking at the Nazi prisoners with wide-eyed curiosity. There were twenty Germans standing in a compact group, acting rather exaggeratedly unconscious of the staring crowd. A small mound of barracks bags was in the centre of the group, and the eyes of the prisoners looked above and through the crowd in quick glances at the station, the train, the seedy town beyond. They were very reserved, very quiet, and their silence put a silence on the crowd.

One of the guards spoke to a prisoner in German, and the prisoner gave an order to his fellows. They formed up in a rough double column and moved off.

Little boys in the crowd ran off after them and the knot of watchers broke up.

When the four soldiers were alone again, Brown said, "They don't look like much. They don't look no different."

"What did you think they'd look like?" Butterfield asked.

"I don't know," said Brown.

"Man, you just don't know nothing," said Jerdon. "You're just plain ignorant."

"Well, what did *you* think they'd look like?" Butterfield asked Jerdon.

Jerdon shifted his feet and didn't look at Butterfield or answer him directly. "That Brown, he just don't know nothing," he repeated. He and Brown began to laugh; they were always dissolving in laughter at obscure jokes of their own.

A trainman got up on the steps of one of the coaches, moved his arm in a wide arc, the pant of the locomotive changed to a short puffing, and the train jerked forward.

The colored baggageman came trundling back in his empty truck, and Corporal Randolph said to him, "They any place we can leave these bags?"

The baggageman halted. "You taking the one o'clock?"

"That's right."

"Dump them on the truck. I'll keep them for you."

Randolph said, "Any place we can eat around here?"

"No, they ain't."

"Where we have to go?"

"They ain't no place," the baggageman said, looking at them as though curious to see how they'd take it.

"Man," said Jerdon, "we're hungry. We got to eat."

"Maybe you get a handout someplace," said the baggageman, "but they sure no place for colored around here."

Butterfield said sourly, "We'll just go to the U.S.O."

"Oh, man, that's rich," Brown said, and he and Jerdon laughed.

"They got a U.S.O. in this here town?" Jerdon asked the baggageman.

"Not for you they ain't," said the baggageman.

"Man, ain't that the truth," replied Jerdon.

Randolph said stubbornly, "We got to get something to eat."

The baggageman said, "You want to walk to Rivertown you get something. That the only place, though."

"Where's Rivertown?" Butterfield asked.

"Take the main road down past the mill. It's about three, four miles."

"Hell, man," said Jerdon, "I'm hungry now. I don't have to walk no four miles to get hungry."

"You stay hungry then," said the baggageman, and went off.

"Well, ain't this just dandy?" said Brown.

The men all looked at Corporal Randolph, who transferred the manila envelope from one hand to the other, his heavy face wearing an expression of indecision.

Butterfield said, "There's a lunchroom in the station. You go tell them they've got to feed us."

Randolph said angrily, "You heard the man. You heard him say there's no place to eat."

"You're in charge of us," Butterfield said. "You've got to find us a place to eat."

"I can't find nothing that ain't there."

"You're just afraid to go talk to them," said Butterfield. "That's all that's the matter with you."

Brown said, "Corporal, you just let Mr. Butterfield handle this. He'll make them give us something to eat." He and Jerdon began to laugh.

"O.K." said Butterfield. "I'll do it."

Brown and Jerdon looked at Randolph.

"My God," said Butterfield, "you even afraid to come with me while I ask them?"

"You're awful loud-talking—" Randolph began, angrily but defensively.

"You coming with me or not?" Butterfield asked.

"We're coming with you," Randolph said.

The four soldiers went into the colored section of the station and walked through it and into the passage that led to the main entrance. The lunchroom was right next to the white waiting room. The four men moved up to the door, bunching a little as though they were soldiers under fire for the first time.

Butterfield opened the screen door of the lunchroom and they followed him in. There were five or six tables and a lunch counter and, although it was around twelve, only a few diners. A cashier's desk and cigarette counter was by the door, and seated behind it was a gray-haired woman, stout and firm-chinned and wearing glasses.

Butterfield went up to her, rested his hands on the edge of the counter, and then hastily removed them.

She looked up.

Butterfield said quickly, "Is there any place we could get something to eat, Ma'am?"

She looked at him steadily, then her eyes shifted to the others, who were looking elaborately and with desperation at their shoes.

"This all of you?" asked the woman.

"Yes, Ma'am, there's just us four."

"All right," she said. "Go out to the kitchen. They'll feed you."

"Thank you, Ma'am."

Butterfield, trailed by the others, started back toward the kitchen.

"Just a minute," said the woman. "Go out and around to the back."

They turned, bumping each other a little and went back out the door.

Brown said, when they were outside, "Mr. Butterfield, he sure do it."

"That's right," said Jerdon. "You want to look out, Corporal. That Butterfield, he'll be getting your stripes."

Butterfield and Randolph didn't answer, didn't look at each other.

In the kitchen they found a thin, aged colored man in a white apron and a young, thick-bodied colored girl who was washing dishes.

"What you want?" asked the cook.

"Something to eat."

"Man, we're hungry," Jerdon told him. "We ain't put nothing inside us since before sunup. Ain't that right, Brown?"

"Since before sunup *yesterday,*" said Brown.

"The lady say you come back here?" asked the cook.

"That right."

The cook took their orders and, as he worked, asked them what camp they were from, where they were going, how long they'd been in the Army. He told them about his two sons who were in the Engineers at Fort Belvoir.

"Labor troops," said Butterfield. "A bunch of ditch-diggers and road menders."

The cook stared at him. "What the matter with you, man?"

Butterfield didn't answer. He lit a cigarette and walked to the serving window, looking out at the woman at the cashier's desk.

Brown and Jerdon went over to the girl washing dishes, and Corporal Randolph, his manila envelope under his arm, listened mournfully to the cook.

Suddenly Butterfield threw away his half-smoked cigarette and called to the others, "Come here and look at this."

"What?" said Randolph.

"You come here and see this."

They all came over, the cook, the girl, the three other soldiers.

Sitting down at the tables in the lunchroom were the twenty German prisoners. One of their guards was at the door with his carbine slung over his shoulder, the other was talking to the cashier. The other diners were staring at the Nazis in fascination. The prisoners sat relaxed and easy at the tables, lighting cigarettes, drinking water, taking rolls from the baskets on their tables, and munching them unbuttered, their eyes incurious, their attitudes casual.

"God damn! Look at that," said Butterfield. "We don't

amount to as much here as the men we're supposed to fight. Look at them, sitting there like kings, and we can't get a scrap to eat in this place without bending our knee and sneaking out to the kitchen like dogs or something."

The cook said severely, "Where you from, boy?"

"He from Trenton, New Jersey," said Brown.

Butterfield stared around at them and saw that only Randolph and the cook even knew what he was talking about and that they were both looking at him with troubled disapproval. Brown and Jerdon and the girl just didn't care. He turned and crossed the kitchen and went out the back door.

The cook said to Randolph, "I'll wrap some sandwiches for him and you give them to him on the train." He shook his head. "All the white folks around here is talking about all the nigger killing they going to do after the war. That boy, he sure to be one of them."

Randolph cracked his big knuckles unhappily. "We all sure to be one of them," he said. "The Lord better have mercy on us all."

W. SOMERSET MAUGHAM

Rain

IT WAS nearly bed-time and when they awoke next morning land would be in sight. Dr. Macphail lit his pipe and, leaning over the rail, searched the heavens for the Southern Cross. After two years at the front and a wound that had taken longer to heal than it should, he was glad to settle down quietly at Apia for twelve months at least, and he felt already better for the journey. Since some of the passengers were leaving the ship next day at Pago-Pago they had had a little dance that evening and in his ears hammered still the harsh notes of the mechanical piano. But the deck was quiet at last. A little way off he saw his wife in a long chair talking with the Davidsons, and he strolled over to her. When he sat down under the light and took off his hat you saw that he had very red hair, with a bald patch on the crown, and the red, freckled skin which accompanies red hair; he was a man of forty, thin, with a pinched face, precise and rather pedantic; and he spoke with a Scots accent in a very low, quiet voice.

Between the Macphails and the Davidsons, who were missionaries, there had arisen the intimacy of shipboard, which is due to propinquity rather than to any community of taste. Their chief tie was the disapproval they shared of the men who spent their days and nights in the smoking-room playing poker or bridge and drinking. Mrs. Macphail was not a little flattered to think that she and her husband were the only people on board with whom the Davidsons were willing to associate, and even the doctor, shy but no fool, half unconsciously acknowledged the compliment. It was only because he was of an argumentative mind that in their cabin at night he permitted himself to carp.

"Mrs. Davidson was saying she didn't know how they'd have got through the journey if it hadn't been for us," said Mrs. Macphail, as she neatly brushed out her transformation. "She said we were really the only people on the ship they cared to know."

"I shouldn't have thought a missionary was such a big bug that he could afford to put on frills."

"It's not frills. I quite understand what she means. It wouldn't have been very nice for the Davidsons to have to mix with all that rough lot in the smoking-room."

"The founder of their religion wasn't so exclusive," said Dr. Macphail with a chuckle.

"I've asked you over and over again not to joke about religion," answered his wife. "I shouldn't like to have a nature like yours, Alec. You never look for the best in people."

He gave her a sidelong glance with his pale, blue eyes, but did not reply. After many years of married life he had learned that it was more conducive to peace to leave his wife with the last word. He was undressed before she was, and climbing into the upper bunk he settled down to read himself to sleep.

When he came on deck next morning they were close to land. He looked at it with greedy eyes. There was a thin strip of silver beach rising quickly to hills covered to the top with luxuriant vegetation. The coconut trees, thick and green, came nearly to the water's edge, and among them you saw the grass houses of the Samoans; and here and there, gleaming white, a little church. Mrs. Davidson came and stood beside him. She was dressed in black and wore round her neck a gold chain, from which dangled a small cross. She was a little woman, with brown, dull hair very elaborately arranged, and she had prominent blue eyes behind invisible *pince-nez*. Her face was long, like a sheep's, but she gave no impression of foolishness, rather of extreme alertness; she had the quick movements of a bird. The most remarkable thing about her was her voice, high, metallic, and without inflection; it fell on the ear with a hard monotony, irritating to the nerves like the pitiless clamour of the pneumatic drill.

"This must seem like home to you," said Dr. Macphail, with his thin, difficult smile.

"Ours are low islands, you know, not like these. Coral. These are volcanic. We've got another ten days' journey to reach them."

"In these parts that's almost like being in the next street at home," said Dr. Macphail facetiously.

"Well, that's rather an exaggerated way of putting it, but one does look at distances differently in the South Seas. So far you're right."

Dr. Macphail sighed faintly.

"I'm glad we're not stationed here," she went on. "They say this is a terribly difficult place to work in. The steamers' touching makes the people unsettled; and then there's the naval station; that's bad for the natives. In our district we don't have difficulties like that to contend with. There are one or two traders, of course, but we take care to make them behave, and if they don't we make the place so hot for them they're glad to go."

Fixing the glasses on her nose she looked at the green island with a ruthless stare.

"It's almost a hopeless task for the missionaries here. I can never be sufficiently thankful to God that we are at least spared that."

Davidson's district consisted of a group of islands to the North of Samoa; they were widely separated and he had frequently to go long distances by canoe. At these times his wife remained at their headquarters and managed the mission. Dr. Macphail felt his heart sink when he considered the efficiency with which she certainly managed it. She spoke of the depravity of the natives in a voice which nothing could hush, but with a vehemently unctuous horror. Her sense of delicacy was singular. Early in their acquaintance she had said to him:

"You know, their marriage customs when we first settled in the islands were so shocking that I couldn't possibly describe them to you. But I'll tell Mrs. Macphail and she'll tell you."

Then he had seen his wife and Mrs. Davidson, their deck-chairs close together, in earnest conversation for about two hours. As he walked past them backwards and forwards for the sake of exercise, he had heard Mrs. Davidson's agitated whisper, like the distant flow of a mountain torrent, and he saw by his wife's open mouth and pale face that she was enjoying an alarming experience. At night in their cabin she repeated to him with bated breath all she had heard.

"Well, what did I say to you?" cried Mrs. Davidson, exultant, next morning. "Did you ever hear anything more dreadful? You don't wonder that I couldn't tell you myself, do you? Even though you are a doctor."

Mrs. Davidson scanned his face. She had a dramatic eagerness to see that she had achieved the desired effect.

"Can you wonder that when we first went there our hearts sank? You'll hardly believe me when I tell you it was impossible to find a single good girl in any of the villages."

She used the word *good* in a severely technical manner.

"Mr. Davidson and I talked it over, and we made up our minds the first thing to do was to put down the dancing. The natives were crazy about dancing."

"I was not averse to it myself when I was a young man," said Dr. Macphail.

"I guessed as much when I heard you ask Mrs. Macphail to have a turn with you last night. I don't think there's any real harm if a man dances with his wife, but I was relieved that she wouldn't. Under the circumstances I thought it better that we should keep ourselves to ourselves."

"Under what circumstances?"

Mrs. Davidson gave him a quick look through her *pince-nez,* but did not answer his question.

"But among white people it's not quite the same," she went on, "though I must say I agree with Mr. Davidson, who says he can't understand how a husband can stand by and see his wife in another man's arms, and as far as I'm concerned I've never danced a step since I married. But the native dancing is quite another matter. It's not only immoral in itself, but it distinctly leads to immorality. However, I'm thankful to God that we stamped it out, and I don't think I'm wrong in saying that no one has danced in our district for eight years."

But now they came to the mouth of the harbour and Mrs. Macphail joined them. The ship turned sharply and steamed slowly in. It was a great landlocked harbour big enough to hold a fleet of battleships; and all around it rose, high and steep, the green hills. Near the entrance, getting such breeze as blew from the sea, stood the governor's house in a garden. The Stars and Stripes dangled languidly from a flagstaff. They passed two or three trim bungalows, and a tennis court, and then they came to the quay with its warehouses. Mrs. Davidson pointed out the schooner, moored two or three hundred yards from the side, which was to take them to Apia. There was a crowd of eager, noisy, and good-humoured natives come from all parts of the island, some from curiosity, others to barter with the travellers on their way to Sydney; and they brought pineapples and huge bunches of bananas, *tapa* cloths, necklaces of shells or sharks' teeth, *kava-*

bowls, and models of war canoes. American sailors, neat and trim, clean-shaven and frank of face, sauntered among them, and there was a little group of officials. While their luggage was being landed the Macphails and Mrs. Davidson watched the crowd. Dr. Macphail looked at the yaws from which most of the children and the young boys seemed to suffer, disfiguring sores like torpid ulcers, and his professional eyes glistened when he saw for the first time in his experience cases of elephantiasis, men going about with a huge, heavy arm or dragging along a grossly disfigured leg. Men and women wore the *lava-lava.*

"It's a very indecent costume," said Mrs. Davidson. "Mr. Davidson thinks it should be prohibited by law. How can you expect people to be moral when they wear nothing but a strip of red cotton round their loins?"

"It's suitable enough to the climate," said the doctor, wiping the sweat off his head.

Now that they were on land the heat, though it was so early in the morning, was already oppressive. Closed in by its hills, not a breath of air came in to Pago-Pago.

"In our islands," Mrs. Davidson went on in her high-pitched tones, "we've practically eradicated the *lava-lava.* A few old men still continue to wear it, but that's all. The women have all taken to the Mother Hubbard, and the men wear trousers and singlets. At the very beginning of our stay Mr. Davidson said in one of his reports: the inhabitants of these islands will never be thoroughly Christianized till every boy of more than ten years is made to wear a pair of trousers."

But Mrs. Davidson had given two or three of her bird-like glances at heavy grey clouds that came floating over the mouth of the harbour. A few drops began to fall.

"We'd better take shelter," she said.

They made their way with all the crowd to a great shed of corrugated iron, and the rain began to fall in torrents. They stood there for some time and then were joined by Mr. Davidson. He had been polite enough to the Macphails during the journey, but he had not his wife's sociability, and had spent much of his time reading. He was a silent, rather sullen man, and you felt that his affability was a duty that he imposed upon himself Christianly; he was by nature reserved and even morose. His appearance was singular. He was very tall and thin, with long limbs loosely jointed; hollow cheeks and curiously high cheek bones; he had so cadaverous an air that it surprised you to notice how full and sensual were his lips. He wore his hair very long. His dark eyes, set deep in their sockets, were large and tragic; and his hands with their big, long fingers, were finely shaped; they gave him a look of great strength. But the most striking thing about him was the feeling he gave you of suppressed fire. It was impressive and vaguely troubling. He was not a man with whom any intimacy was possible.

He brought now unwelcome news. There was an epidemic of measles, a serious and often fatal disease among the Kanakas, on the island, and a case had developed among the crew of the schooner which was to take them on their journey. The sick man had been brought ashore and put in hospital on the quarantine station, but telegraphic instructions had been sent from Apia to say that the schooner would not be allowed to enter the harbour till it was certain no other member of the crew was affected.

"It means we shall have to stay here for ten days at least."

"But I'm urgently needed at Apia," said Dr. Macphail.

"That can't be helped. If no more cases develop on board, the schooner will be allowed to sail with white passengers, but all native traffic is prohibited for three months."

"Is there a hotel here?" asked Mrs. Macphail.

Davidson gave a low chuckle.

"There's not."

"What shall we do then?"

"I've been talking to the governor. There's a trader along the front who has rooms that he rents, and my proposition is that as soon as the rain lets up we should go along there and see what we can do. Don't expect comfort. You've just got to be thankful if we get a bed to sleep on and a roof over our heads."

But the rain showed no sign of stopping, and at length with umbrellas and waterproofs they set out. There was no town, but merely a group of official buildings, a store or two, and at the back, among the coconut trees and plantains, a few native dwellings. The house they sought was about five minutes' walk from the wharf. It was a frame house of two stories, with broad verandahs on both floors and a roof of corrugated iron. The owner was a half-caste named Horn, with a native wife surrounded by little brown children, and on the ground-floor he had a store where he sold canned goods and cottons. The rooms he showed them were almost bare of furniture. In the Macphails' there was nothing but a poor, worn bed with a ragged mosquito net, a rickety chair, and a washstand. They looked round with dismay. The rain poured down without ceasing.

"I'm not going to unpack more than we actually need," said Mrs. Macphail.

Mrs. Davidson came into the room as she was unlocking a portmanteau. She was very brisk and alert. The cheerless surroundings had no effect on her.

"If you'll take my advice you'll get a needle and cotton and start right in to mend the mosquito net," she said, "or you'll not be able to get a wink of sleep to-night."

"Will they be very bad?" asked Dr. Macphail.

"This is the season for them. When you're asked to a party at Government House at Apia you'll notice that all the ladies are given a pillowslip to put their—their lower extremities in."

"I wish the rain would stop for a moment," said Mrs.

Macphail. "I could try to make the place comfortable with more heart if the sun were shining."

"Oh, if you wait for that, you'll wait a long time, Pago-Pago is about the rainiest place in the Pacific. You see, the hills, and that bay, they attract the water, and one expects rain at this time of year anyway."

She looked from Macphail to his wife, standing helplessly in different parts of the room, like lost souls, and she pursed her lips. She saw that she must take them in hand. Feckless people like that made her impatient, but her hands itched to put everything in the order which came so naturally to her.

"Here, you give me a needle and cotton and I'll mend that net of yours, while you go on with your unpacking. Dinner's at one. Dr. Macphail, you'd better go down to the wharf and see that your heavy luggage has been put in a dry place. You know what these natives are, they're capable of storing it where the rain will beat in on it all the time.

The doctor put on his waterproof again and went downstairs. At the door Mr. Horn was standing in conversation with the quartermaster of the ship they had just arrived in and a second-class passenger whom Dr. Macphail had seen several times on board. The quartermaster, a little, shrivelled man, extremely dirty, nodded to him as he passed.

"This is a bad job about the measles, doc," he said. "I see you've fixed yourself up already."

Dr. Macphail thought he was rather familiar, but he was a timid man and he did not take offence easily.

"Yes, we've got a room upstairs."

"Miss Thompson was sailing with you to Apia, so I've brought her along here."

The quartermaster pointed with his thumb to the woman standing by his side. She was twenty-seven perhaps, plump, and in a coarse fashion pretty. She wore a white dress and a large white hat. Her fat calves in white cotton stockings bulged over the top of long white boots in glacé kid. She gave Macphail an ingratiating smile.

"The feller's tryin' to soak me a dollar and a half a day for the meanest sized room," she said in a hoarse voice.

"I tell you she's a friend of mine, Jo," said the quartermaster. "She can't pay more than a dollar, and you've sure got to take her for that."

The trader was fat and smooth and quietly smiling.

"Well, if you put it like that, Mr. Swan, I'll see what I can do about it. I'll talk to Mrs. Horn and if we think we can make a reduction we will."

"Don't try to pull that stuff with me," said Miss Thompson. "We'll settle this right now. You get a dollar a day for the room and not one bean more."

Dr. Macphail smiled. He admired the effrontery with which she bargained. He was the sort of man who always paid what he was asked. He preferred to be over-charged than to haggle. The trader sighed.

"Well, to oblige Mr. Swan I'll take it."

"That's the goods," said Miss Thompson. "Come right in and have a shot of hooch. I've got some real good rye in that grip if you'll bring it along, Mr. Swan. You come along too, doctor."

"Oh, I don't think I will, thank you," he answered. "I'm just going down to see that our luggage is all right."

He stepped out into the rain. It swept in from the opening of the harbour in sheets and the opposite shore was all blurred. He passed two or three natives clad in nothing but the *lava-lava,* with huge umbrellas over them. They walked finely, with leisurely movements, very upright; and they smiled and greeted him in a strange tongue as they went by.

It was nearly dinner-time when he got back, and their meal was laid in the trader's parlour. It was a room designed not to live in but for purposes of prestige, and it had a musty, melancholy air. A suite of stamped plush was arranged neatly round the walls, and from the middle of the ceiling, protected from the flies by yellow tissue paper, hung a gilt chandelier. Davidson did not come.

"I know he went to call on the governor," said Mrs. Davidson, "and I guess he's kept him to dinner."

A little native girl brought them a dish of Hamburger steak, and after a while the trader came up to see that they had everything they wanted.

"I see we have a fellow lodger, Mr. Horn," said Dr. Macphail.

"She's taken a room, that's all," answered the trader. "She's getting her own board."

He looked at the two ladies with an obsequious air.

"I put her downstairs so she shouldn't be in the way. She won't be any trouble to you."

"Is it someone who was on the boat?" asked Mrs. Macphail.

"Yes, ma'am, she was in the second cabin. She was going to Apia. She has a position as cashier waiting for her."

"Oh!"

When the trader was gone Macphail said:

"I shouldn't think she'd find it exactly cheerful having her meals in her room."

"If she was in the second cabin I guess she'd rather," answered Mrs. Davidson. "I don't exactly know who it can be."

"I happened to be there when the quartermaster brought her along. Her name's Thompson."

"It's not the woman who was dancing with the quartermaster last night?" asked Mrs. Davidson.

"That's who it must be," said Mrs. Macphail. "I wondered at the time what she was. She looked rather fast to me."

"Not good style at all," said Mrs. Davidson.

They began to talk of other things, and after dinner,

tired with their early rise, they separated and slept. When they awoke, though the sky was still grey and the clouds hung low, it was not raining and they went for a walk on the high road which the Americans had built along the bay.

On their return they found that Davidson had just come in.

"We may be here for a fortnight," he said irritably. "I've argued it out with the governor, but he says there is nothing to be done."

"Mr. Davidson's just longing to get back to his work," said his wife, with an anxious glance at him.

"We've been away for a year," he said, walking up and down the verandah. "The mission has been in charge of native missionaries and I'm terribly nervous that they've let things slide. They're good men, I'm not saying a word against them, God-fearing, devout, and truly Christian men—their Christianity would put many so-called Christians at home to the blush—but they're pitifully lacking in energy. They can make a stand once, they can make a stand twice, but they can't make a stand all the time. If you leave a mission in charge of a native missionary, no matter how trustworthy he seems, in course of time you'll find he's let abuses creep in."

Mr. Davidson stood still. With his tall, spare form, and his great eyes flashing out of his pale face, he was an impressive figure. His sincerity was obvious in the fire of his gestures and in his deep, ringing voice.

"I expect to have my work cut out for me. I shall act and I shall act promptly. If the tree is rotten it shall be cut down and cast into the flames."

And in the evening after the high tea which was their last meal, while they sat in the stiff parlour, the ladies working and Dr. Macphail smoking his pipe, the missionary told them of his work in the islands.

"When we went there they had no sense of sin at all," he said. "They broke the commandments one after the other and never knew they were doing wrong. And I think that was the most difficult part of my work, to instill into the natives the sense of sin."

The Macphails knew already that Davidson had worked in the Solomons for five years before he met his wife. She had been a missionary in China, and they had become acquainted in Boston, where they were both spending part of their leave to attend a missionary congress. On their marriage they had been appointed to the islands in which they had laboured ever since.

In the course of all the conversations they had had with Mr. Davidson one thing had shone out clearly and that was the man's unflinching courage. He was a medical missionary, and he was liable to be called at any time to one or other of the islands in the group. Even the whaleboat is not so very safe a conveyance in the stormy Pacific of the wet season, but often he would be sent for in a canoe, and then the danger was great. In cases of illness or accident he never hesitated. A dozen times he had spent the whole night baling for his life, and more than once Mrs. Davidson had given him up for lost.

"I'd beg him not to go sometimes," she said, "or at least to wait till the weather was more settled, but he'd never listen. He's obstinate, and when he's once made up his mind, nothing can move him."

"How can I ask the natives to put their trust in the Lord if I am afraid to do so myself?" cried Davidson. "And I'm not, I'm not. They know that if they send for me in their trouble I'll come if it's humanly possible. And do you think the Lord is going to abandon me when I am on his business? The wind blows at his bidding and the waves toss and rage at his word."

Dr. Macphail was a timid man. He had never been able to get used to the hurtling of the shells over the trenches, and when he was operating in an advanced dressing-station the sweat poured from his brow and dimmed his spectacles in the effort he made to control his unsteady hand. He shuddered a little as he looked at the missionary.

"I wish I could say that I've never been afraid," he said.

"I wish you could say that you believed in God," retorted the other.

But for some reason, that evening the missionary's thoughts travelled back to the early days he and his wife had spent on the islands.

"Sometimes Mrs. Davidson and I would look at one another and the tears would stream down our cheeks. We worked without ceasing, day and night, and we seemed to make no progress. I don't know what I should have done without her then. When I felt my heart sink, when I was very near despair, she gave me courage and hope."

Mrs. Davidson looked down at her work, and a slight colour rose to her thin cheeks. Her hands trembled a little. She did not trust herself to speak.

"We had no one to help us. We were alone, thousands of miles from any of our own people, surrounded by darkness. When I was broken and weary she would put her work aside and take the Bible and read to me till peace came and settled upon me like sleep upon the eyelids of a child, and when at last she closed the book she'd say: 'We'll save them in spite of themselves.' And I felt strong again in the Lord, and I answered: 'Yes, with God's help I'll save them. I must save them.' "

He came over to the table and stood in front of it as though it were a lectern.

"You see, they were so naturally depraved that they couldn't be brought to see their wickedness. We had to make sins out of what they thought were natural actions. We had to make it a sin, not only to commit adultery and to lie and thieve, but to expose their bodies, and to dance and not to come to church. I made it a sin for a girl to show her bosom and a sin for a man not to wear trousers."

"How?" asked Dr. Macphail, not without surprise.

"I instituted fines. Obviously the only way to make people realise that an action is sinful is to punish them if they commit it. I fined them if they didn't come to church, and I fined them if they danced. I fined them if they were improperly dressed. I had a tariff, and every sin had to be paid for either in money or work. And at last I made them understand."

"But did they never refuse to pay?"

"How could they?" asked the missionary.

"It would be a brave man who tried to stand up against Mr. Davidson," said his wife, tightening her lips.

Dr. Macphail looked at Davidson with troubled eyes. What he heard shocked him, but he hesitated to express his disapproval.

"You must remember that in the last resort I could expel them from their church membership."

"Did they mind that?"

Davidson smiled a little and gently rubbed his hands.

"They couldn't sell their copra. When the men fished they got no share of the catch. It meant something very like starvation. Yes, they minded quite a lot."

"Tell him about Fred Ohlson," said Mrs. Davidson.

The missionary fixed his fiery eyes on Dr. Macphail.

"Fred Ohlson was a Danish trader who had been in the islands a good many years. He was a pretty rich man as traders go and he wasn't very pleased when we came. You see, he'd had things very much his own way. He paid the natives what he liked for their copra, and he paid in goods and whiskey. He had a native wife, but he was flagrantly unfaithful to her. He was a drunkard. I gave him a chance to mend his ways, but he wouldn't take it. He laughed at me."

Davidson's voice fell to a deep bass as he said the last words, and he was silent for a minute or two. The silence was heavy with menace.

"In two years he was a ruined man. He'd lost everything he'd saved in a quarter of a century. I broke him, and at last he was forced to come to me like a beggar and beseech me to give him a passage back to Sydney."

"I wish you could have seen him when he came to see Mr. Davidson," said the missionary's wife. "He had been a fine, powerful man, with a lot of fat on him, and he had a great big voice, but now he was half the size, and he was shaking all over. He'd suddenly become an old man."

With abstracted gaze Davidson looked out into the night. The rain was falling again.

Suddenly from below came a sound, and Davidson turned and looked questioningly at his wife. It was the sound of a gramophone, harsh and loud, wheezing out a syncopated tune.

"What's that?" he asked.

Mrs. Davidson fixed her *pince-nez* more firmly on her nose.

"One of the second-class passengers has a room in the house. I guess it comes from there."

They listened in silence, and presently they heard the sound of dancing. Then the music stopped, and they heard the popping of corks and voices raised in animated conversation.

"I daresay she's giving a farewell party to her friends on board," said Dr. Macphail. "The ship sails at twelve, doesn't it?"

Davidson made no remark, but he looked at his watch.

"Are you ready?" he asked his wife.

She got up and folded her work.

"Yes, I guess I am," she answered.

"It's early to go to bed yet, isn't it?" said the doctor.

"We have a good deal of reading to do," explained Mrs. Davidson. "Wherever we are, we read a chapter of the Bible before retiring for the night and we study it with the commentaries, you know, and discuss it thoroughly. It's a wonderful training for the mind."

The two couples bade one another good night. Dr. and Mrs. Macphail were left alone. For two or three minutes they did not speak.

"I think I'll go and fetch the cards," the doctor said at last.

Mrs. Macphail looked at him doubtfully. Her conversation with the Davidsons had left her a little uneasy, but she did not like to say that she thought they had better not play cards when the Davidsons might come in at any moment. Dr. Macphail brought them and she watched him, though with a vague sense of guilt, while he laid out his patience. Below the sound of revelry continued.

It was fine enough next day, and the Macphails, condemned to spend a fortnight of idleness at Pago-Pago, set about making the best of things. They went down to the quay and got out of their boxes a number of books. The doctor called on the chief surgeon of the naval hospital and went round the beds with him. They left cards on the governor. They passed Miss Thompson on the road. The doctor took off his hat, and she gave him a "Good morning, doc," in a loud, cheerful voice. She was dressed as on the day before, in a white frock, and her shiny white boots with their high heels, her fat legs bulging over the tops of them, were strange things on that exotic scene.

"I don't think she's very suitably dressed, I must say," said Mrs. Macphail. "She looks extremely common to me."

When they got back to their house, she was on the verandah playing with one of the trader's dark children.

"Say a word to her," Dr. Macphail whispered to his wife. "She's all alone here, and it seems rather unkind to ignore her."

Mrs Macphail was shy, but she was in the habit of doing what her husband bade her.

"I think we're fellow lodgers here," she said, rather foolishly.

"Terrible, ain't it, bein' cooped up in a one-horse

burg like this?" answered Miss Thompson. "And they tell me I'm lucky to have gotten a room. I don' see myself livin' in a native house, and that's what some have to do. I don't know why they don't have a hotel."

They exchanged a few more words. Miss Thompson, loud-voiced and garrulous, was evidently quite willing to gossip, but Mrs. Macphail had a poor stock of small talk and presently she said:

"Well, I think we must go upstairs."

In the evening when they sat down to their high-tea Davidson on coming in said:

"I see that woman downstairs has a couple of sailors sitting there. I wonder how she's gotten acquainted with them."

"She can't be very particular," said Mrs. Davidson.

They were all rather tired after the idle, aimless day.

"If there's going to be a fortnight of this I don't know what we shall feel like at the end of it," said Dr. Macphail.

"The only thing to do is to portion out the day to different activities," answered the missionary. "I shall set aside a certain number of hours to study and a certain number to exercise, rain or shine—in the wet season you can't afford to pay any attention to the rain—and a certain number to recreation."

Dr. Macphail looked at his companion with misgiving. Davidson's programme oppressed him. They were eating Hamburger steak again. It seemed the only dish the cook knew how to make. Then below the gramophone began. Davidson started nervously when he heard it, but said nothing. Men's voices floated up. Miss Thompson's guests were joining in a well-known song and presently they heard her voice too, hoarse and loud. There was a good deal of shouting and laughing. The four people upstairs, trying to make conversation, listened despite themselves to the clink of glasses and the scrape of chairs. More people had evidently come. Miss Thompson was giving a party.

"I wonder how she gets them all in," said Mrs. Macphail, suddenly breaking into a medical conversation between the missionary and her husband.

It showed whither her thoughts were wandering. The twitch of Davidson's face proved that, though he spoke of scientific things, his mind was busy in the same direction. Suddenly, while the doctor was giving some experience of practice on the Flanders front, rather prosily, he sprang to his feet with a cry.

"What's the matter, Alfred?" asked Mrs. Davidson.

"Of course! It never occurred to me. She's out of Iwelei."

"She can't be."

"She came on board at Honolulu. It's obvious. And she's carrying on her trade here. Here."

He uttered the last word with a passion of indignation.

"What's Iwelei?" asked Mrs. Macphail.

He turned his gloomy eyes on her and his voice trembled with horror.

"The plague spot of Honolulu. The Red Light district. It was a blot on our civilisation."

Iwelei was on the edge of the city. You went down side streets by the harbour, in the darkness, across a rickety bridge, till you came to a deserted road, all ruts and holes, and then suddenly you came out into the light. There was parking room for motors on each side of the road, and there were saloons, tawdry and bright, each one noisy with its mechanical piano, and there were barbers' shops and tobacconists. There was a stir in the air and a sense of expectant gaiety. You turned down a narrow alley, either to the right or to the left, for the road divided Iwelei into two parts, and you found yourself in the district. There were rows of little bungalows, trim and neatly painted in green, and the pathway between them was broad and straight. It was laid out like a garden-city. In its respectable regularity, its order and spruceness, it gave an impression of sardonic horror; for never can the search for love have been so systematised and ordered. The pathways were lit by a rare lamp, but they would have been dark except for the lights that came from the open windows of the bungalows. Men wandered about, looking at the women who sat at their windows, reading or sewing, for the most part taking no notice of the passers-by; and like the women they were of all nationalities. There were Americans, sailors from the ships in port, enlisted men off the gunboats, sombrely drunk, and soldiers from the regiments, white and black, quartered on the island; there were Japanese, walking in twos and threes; Hawaiians, Chinese in long robes, and Filipinos in preposterous hats. They were silent and as it were oppressed. Desire is sad.

"It was the most crying scandal of the Pacific," exclaimed Davidson vehemently. "The missionaries had been agitating against it for years, and at last the local press took it up. The police refused to stir. You know their argument. They say that vice is inevitable and consequently the best thing is to localise and control it. The truth is, they were paid. Paid. They were paid by the saloon-keepers, paid by the bullies, paid by the women themselves. At last they were forced to move."

"I read about it in the papers that came on board in Honolulu," said Dr. Macphail.

"Iwelei, with its sin and shame, ceased to exist on the very day we arrived. The whole population was brought before the justices. I don't know why I didn't understand at once what that woman was."

"Now you come to speak of it," said Mrs. Macphail, "I remember seeing her come on board only a few minutes before the boat sailed. I remember thinking at the time she was cutting it rather fine."

"How dare she come here!" cried Davidson indignantly. "I'm not going to allow it."

He strode towards the door.

"What are you going to do?" asked Macphail.

"What do you expect me to do? I'm going to stop it. I'm not going to have this house turned into—into . . ."

He sought for a word that should not offend the ladies' ears. His eyes were flashing and his pale face was paler still in his emotion.

"It sounds as though there were three or four men down there," said the doctor. "Don't you think it's rather rash to go in just now?"

The missionary gave him a contemptuous look and without a word flung out of the room.

"You know Mr. Davidson very little if you think the fear of personal danger can stop him in the performance of his duty," said his wife.

She sat with her hands nervously clasped, a spot of colour on her high cheek bones, listening to what was about to happen below. They all listened. They heard him clatter down the wooden stairs and throw open the door. The singing stopped suddenly, but the gramophone continued to bray out its vulgar tune. They heard Davidson's voice and then the noise of something heavy falling. The music stopped. He had hurled the gramophone on the floor. Then again they heard Davidson's voice, they could not make out the words, then Miss Thompson's, loud and shrill, then a confused clamour as though several people were shouting together at the top of their lungs. Mrs. Davidson gave a little gasp, and she clenched her hands more tightly. Dr. Macphail looked uncertainly from her to his wife. He did not want to go down, but he wondered if they expected him to. Then there was something that sounded like a scuffle. The noise now was more distinct. It might be that Davidson was being thrown out of the room. The door was slammed. There was a moment's silence and they heard Davidson come up the stairs again. He went to his room.

"I think I'll go to him," said Mrs. Davidson.

She got up and went out.

"If you want me, just call," said Mrs. Macphail, and then when the other was gone: "I hope he isn't hurt."

"Why couldn't he mind his own business?" said Dr. Macphail.

They sat in silence for a minute or two and then they both started, for the gramophone began to play once more, defiantly, and mocking voices shouted hoarsely the words of an obscene song.

Next day Mrs. Davidson was pale and tired. She complained of headache, and she looked old and wizened. She told Mrs. Macphail that the missionary had not slept at all; he had passed the night in a state of frightful agitation and at five had got up and gone out. A glass of beer had been thrown over him and his clothes were stained and stinking. But a sombre fire glowed in Mrs. Davidson's eyes when she spoke of Miss Thompson.

"She'll bitterly rue the day when she flouted Mr. Davidson," she said. "Mr. Davidson has a wonderful heart and no one who is in trouble has ever gone to him without being comforted, but he has no mercy for sin, and when his righteous wrath is excited he's terrible."

"Why, what will he do?" asked Mrs. Macphail.

"I don't know, but I wouldn't stand in that creature's shoes for anything in the world."

Mrs. Macphail shuddered. There was something positively alarming in the triumphant assurance of the little woman's manner. They were going out together that morning, and they went down the stairs side by side. Miss Thompson's door was open, and they saw her in a bedraggled dressing-gown, cooking something in a chafing-dish.

"Good morning," she called. "Is Mr. Davidson better this morning?"

They passed her in silence, with their noses in the air, as if she did not exist. They flushed, however, when she burst into a shout of derisive laughter. Mrs. Davidson turned on her suddenly.

"Don't you dare to speak to me," she screamed. "If you insult me I shall have you turned out of here."

"Say, did I ask Mr. Davidson to visit with me?"

"Don't answer her," whispered Mrs. Macphail hurriedly.

They walked on till they were out of earshot.

"She's brazen, brazen," burst from Mrs. Davidson. Her anger almost suffocated her.

And on their way home they met her strolling towards the quay. She had all her finery on. Her great white hat with its vulgar, showy flowers was an affront. She called out cheerily to them as she went by, and a couple of American sailors who were standing there grinned as the ladies set their faces to an icy stare. They got in just before the rain began to fall again.

"I guess she'll get her fine clothes spoilt," said Mrs. Davidson with a bitter sneer.

Davidson did not come in till they were half way through dinner. He was wet through, but he would not change. He sat, morose and silent, refusing to eat more than a mouthful, and he stared at the slanting rain. When Mrs. Davidson told him of their two encounters with Miss Thompson he did not answer. His deepening frown alone showed that he had heard.

Don't you think we ought to make Mr. Horn turn her out of here?" asked Mrs. Davidson. "We can't allow her to insult us."

"There doesn't seem to be any other place for her to go," said Macphail.

"She can live with one of the natives."

"In weather like this a native hut must be a rather uncomfortable place to live in."

"I lived in one for years," said the missionary.

When the little native girl brought in the fried bananas which formed the sweet they had every day, Davidson turned to her.

"Ask Miss Thompson when it would be convenient for me to see her," he said.

The girl nodded shyly and went out.

"What do you want to see her for, Alfred?" asked his wife.

"It's my duty to see her. I won't act till I've given her every chance."

"You don't know what she is. She'll insult you."

"Let her insult me. Let her spit on me. She has an immortal soul, and I must do all that is in my power to save it."

Mrs. Davidson's ears rang still with the harlot's mocking laughter.

"She's gone too far."

"Too far for the mercy of God?" His eyes lit up suddenly and his voice grew mellow and soft. "Never. The sinner may be deeper in sin than the depth of hell itself, but the love of the Lord Jesus can reach him still."

The girl came back with the message.

"Miss Thompson's compliments and as long as Rev. Davidson don't come in business hours she'll be glad to see him any time."

The party received it in stony silence, and Dr. Macphail quickly effaced from his lips the smile which had come upon them. He knew his wife would be vexed with him if he found Miss Thompson's effrontery amusing.

They finished the meal in silence. When it was over the two ladies got up and took their work. Mrs. Macphail was making another of the innumerable comforters which she had turned out since the beginning of the war, and the doctor lit his pipe. But Davidson remained in his chair and with abstracted eyes stared at the table. At last he got up and without a word went out of the room. They heard him go down and they heard Miss Thompson's defiant "come in" when he knocked at the door. He remained with her for an hour. And Dr. Macphail watched the rain. It was beginning to get on his nerves. It was not like our soft English rain that drops gently on the earth; it was unmerciful and somehow terrible; you felt in it the malignancy of the primitive powers of nature. It did not pour, it flowed. It was like a deluge from heaven, and it rattled on the roof of corrugated iron with a steady persistence that was maddening. It seemed to have a fury of its own. And sometimes you felt that you must scream if it did not stop, and then suddenly you felt powerless, as though your bones had suddenly become soft; and you were miserable and hopeless.

Macphail turned his head when the missionary came back. The two women looked up.

"I've given her every chance. I have exhorted her to repent. She is an evil woman."

He paused, and Dr. Macphail saw his eyes darken and his pale face grow hard and stern.

"Now I shall take the whips with which the Lord Jesus drove the usurers and the money changers out of the Temple of the Most High."

He walked up and down the room. His mouth was close set, and his black brows were frowning.

"If she fled to the uttermost parts of the earth I should pursue her."

With a sudden movement he turned round and strode out of the room. They heard him go downstairs again.

"What is he going to do?" asked Mrs. Macphail.

"I don't know." Mrs. Davidson took off her *pince-nez* and wiped them. "When he is on the Lord's work I never ask him questions."

She sighed a little.

"What is the matter?"

"He'll wear himself out. He doesn't know what it is to spare himself."

Dr. Macphail learnt the first results of the missionary's activity from the half-caste trader in whose house they lodged. He stopped the doctor when he passed the store and came out to speak to him on the stoop. His fat face was worried.

"The Rev. Davidson has been at me for letting Miss Thompson have a room here," he said, "but I didn't know what she was when I rented it to her. When people come and ask if I can rent them a room all I want to know is if they've the money to pay for it. And she paid me for hers a week in advance."

Dr. Macphail did not want to commit himself.

"When all's said and done it's your house. We're very much obliged to you for taking us in at all."

Horn looked at him doubtfully. He was not certain yet how definitely Macphail stood on the missionary's side.

"The missionaries are in with one another," he said, hesitatingly. "If they get it in for a trader he may just as well shut up his store and quit."

"Did he want you to turn her out?"

"No, he said so long as she behaved herself he couldn't ask me to do that. He said he wanted to be just to me. I promised she shouldn't have no more visitors. I've just been and told her."

"How did she take it?"

"She gave me Hell."

The trader squirmed in his old ducks. He had found Miss Thompson a rough customer.

"Oh, well, I daresay she'll get out. I don't suppose she wants to stay here if she can't have anyone in."

"There's nowhere she can go, only a native house, and no native'll take her now, not now that the missionaries have got their knife in her."

Dr. Macphail looked at the falling rain.

"Well, I don't suppose it's any good waiting for it to clear up."

In the evening when they sat in the parlour Davidson talked to them of his early days at college. He had had no means and had worked his way through by doing odd jobs during the vacations. There was silence downstairs. Miss Thompson was sitting in her little room alone. But suddenly the gramophone began to play. She had set it on in defiance, to cheat her loneliness, but there was no one to sing, and it had a melancholy note. It was like a cry for help. Davidson took no notice. He was in the middle of a long anecdote and without change of expression went on. The gramophone continued. Miss Thompson put on one reel after another. It looked as though the silence of the night were getting on her nerves. It was breathless and sultry. When the Macphails went to bed they could not sleep. They lay side by side with their eyes wide open, listening to the cruel singing of the mosquitoes outside their curtain.

"What's that?" whispered Mrs. Macphail at last.

They heard a voice, Davidson's voice, through the wooden partition. It went on with a monotonous, earnest insistence. He was praying aloud. He was praying for the soul of Miss Thompson.

Two or three days went by. Now when they passed Miss Thompson on the road she did not greet them with ironic cordiality or smile; she passed with her nose in the air, a sulky look on her painted face, frowning, as though she did not see them. The trader told Macphail that she had tried to get lodging elsewhere, but had failed. In the evening she played through the various reels of her gramophone, but the pretence of mirth was obvious now. The ragtime had a cracked, heart-broken rhythm as though it were a one-step of despair. When she began to play on Sunday Davidson sent Horn to beg her to stop at once since it was the Lord's day. The reel was taken off and the house was silent except for the steady pattering of the rain on the iron roof.

"I think she's getting a bit worked up," said the trader next day to Macphail. "She don't know what Mr. Davidson's up to and it makes her scared."

Macphail had caught a glimpse of her that morning and it struck him that her arrogant expression had changed. There was in her face a hunted look. The half-caste gave him a side-long glance.

"I suppose you don't know what Mr. Davidson is doing about it?" he hazarded.

"No, I don't."

It was singular that Horn should ask him that question, for he also had the idea that the missionary was mysteriously at work. He had an impression that he was weaving a net around the woman, carefully, systematically, and suddenly, when everything was ready would pull the strings tight.

"He told me to tell her," said the trader, "that if at any time she wanted him she only had to send and he'd come."

"What did she say when you told her that?"

"She didn't say nothing. I didn't stop. I just said what he said I was to and then I beat it. I thought she might be going to start weepin'."

"I have no doubt the loneliness is getting on her nerves," said the doctor. "And the rain—that's enough to make anyone jumpy," he continued irritably. "Doesn't it ever stop in this confounded place?"

"It goes on pretty steady in the rainy season. We have three hundred inches in the year. You see, it's the shape of the bay. It seems to attract the rain from all over the Pacific."

"Damn the shape of the bay," said the doctor.

He scratched his mosquito bites. He felt very short-tempered. When the rain stopped and the sun shone, it was like a hothouse, seething, humid, sultry, breathless, and you had a strange feeling that everything was growing with a savage violence. The natives, blithe and child-like by reputation, seemed then, with their tattooing and their dyed hair, to have something sinister in their appearance; and when they pattered along at your heels with their naked feet you looked back instinctively. You felt they might at any moment come behind you swiftly and thrust a long knife between your shoulder blades. You could not tell what dark thoughts lurked behind their wide-set eyes. They had a little the look of ancient Egyptians painted on a temple wall, and there was about them the terror of what is immeasurably old.

The missionary came and went. He was busy, but the Macphails did not know what he was doing. Horn told the doctor that he saw the governor every day, and once Davidson mentioned him.

"He looks as if he had plenty of determination," he said, "but when you come down to brass tacks he has no backbone."

"I suppose that means he won't do exactly what you want," suggested the doctor facetiously.

The missionary did not smile.

"I want him to do what's right. It shouldn't be necessary to persuade a man to do that."

"But there may be differences of opinion about what is right."

"If a man had a gangrenous foot would you have patience with anyone who hesitated to amputate it?"

"Gangrene is a matter of fact."

"And Evil?"

What Davidson had done soon appeared. The four of them had just finished their midday meal, and they had not yet separated for the siesta which the heat imposed on the ladies and on the doctor. Davidson had little patience with the slothful habit. The door was suddenly flung open and Miss Thompson came in. She looked round the room and then went up to Davidson.

"You low-down skunk, what have you been saying about me to the governor?"

She was spluttering with rage. There was a moment's pause. Then the missionary drew forward a chair.

"Won't you be seated, Miss Thompson? I've been hoping to have another talk with you."

"You poor low-life bastard."

She burst into a torrent of insult, foul and insolent. Davidson kept his grave eyes on her.

"I'm indifferent to the abuse you think fit to heap on me, Miss Thompson," he said, "but I must beg you to remember that ladies are present."

Tears by now were struggling with her anger. Her face was red and swollen as though she were choking.

"What has happened?" asked Dr. Macphail.

"A feller's just been in here and he says I gotter beat it on the next boat."

Was there a gleam in the missionary's eyes? His face remained impassive.

"You could hardly expect the governor to let you stay here under the circumstances."

"You done it," she shrieked. "You can't kid me. You done it."

"I don't want to deceive you. I urged the governor to take the only possible step consistent with his obligations."

"Why couldn't you leave me be? I wasn't doin' you no harm."

"You may be sure that if you had I should be the last man to resent it."

"Do you think I want to stay on in this poor imitation of a burg? I don't look no busher, do I?"

"In that case I don't see what cause of complaint you have," he answered.

She gave an inarticulate cry of rage and flung out of the room. There was a short silence.

"It's a relief to know that the governor has acted at last," said Davidson finally. "He's a weak man and he shilly-shallied. He said she was only here for a fortnight anyway, and if she went on to Apia that was under British jurisdiction and had nothing to do with him."

The missionary sprang to his feet and strode across the room.

"It's terrible the way the men who are in authority seek to evade their responsibility. They speak as though evil that was out of sight ceased to be evil. The very existence of that woman is a scandal and it does not help matters to shift it to another of the islands. In the end I had to speak straight from the shoulder."

Davidson's brow lowered, and he protruded his firm chin. He looked fierce and determined.

"What do you mean by that?"

"Our mission is not entirely without influence at Washington. I pointed out to the governor that it wouldn't do him any good if there was a complaint about the way he managed things here."

"When has she got to go?" asked the doctor, after a pause.

"The San Francisco boat is due here from Sydney next Tuesday. She's to sail on that."

That was in five days' time. It was next day, when he was coming back from the hospital where for want of something better to do Macphail spent most of his mornings, that the half-caste stopped him as he was going upstairs.

"Excuse me, Dr. Macphail, Miss Thompson's sick. Will you have a look at her?"

"Certainly."

Horn led him to her room. She was sitting in a chair idly, neither reading nor sewing, staring in front of her. She wore her white dress and the large hat with the flowers on it. Macphail noticed that her skin was yellow and muddy under her powder, and her eyes were heavy.

"I'm sorry to hear you're not well," he said.

"Oh, I ain't sick really. I just said that, because I just had to see you. I've got to clear on a boat that's going to 'Frisco."

She looked at him and he saw that her eyes were suddenly startled. She opened and clenched her hands spasmodically. The trader stood at the door, listening.

"So I understand," said the doctor.

She gave a little gulp.

"I guess it ain't very convenient for me to go to 'Frisco just now. I went to see the governor yesterday afternoon, but I couldn't get to him. I saw the secretary, and he told me I'd got to take that boat and that was all there was to it. I just had to see the governor, so I waited outside his house this morning, and when he come out I spoke to him. He didn't want to speak to me, I'll say, but I wouldn't let him shake me off, and at last he said he hadn't no objection to my staying here till the next boat to Sydney if the Rev. Davidson will stand for it."

She stopped and looked at Dr. Macphail anxiously.

"I don't know exactly what I can do," he said.

"Well, I thought maybe you wouldn't mind asking him. I swear to God I won't start anything here if he'll just only let me stay. I won't go out of the house if that'll suit him. It's no more'n a fortnight."

"I'll ask him."

"He won't stand for it," said Horn. "He'll have you out on Tuesday, so you may as well make up your mind to it."

"Tell him I can get work in Sydney, straight stuff, I mean. 'Taint asking very much."

"I'll do what I can."

"And come and tell me right away, will you? I can't set down to a thing till I get the dope one way or the other."

It was not an errand that much pleased the doctor, and, characteristically perhaps, he went about it indirectly. He told his wife what Miss Thompson had said to him and asked her to speak to Mrs. Davidson. The missionary's attitude seemed rather arbitrary and it could do no harm if the girl were allowed to stay in Pago-Pago another fortnight. But he was not prepared for the result of his diplomacy. The missionary came to him straightway.

"Mrs. Davidson tells me that Thompson has been speaking to you."

Dr. Macphail, thus directly tackled, had the shy man's resentment at being forced out into the open. He felt his temper rising, and he flushed.

"I don't see that it can make any difference if she goes to Sydney rather than to San Francisco, and so long as she promises to behave while she's here it's dashed hard to persecute her."

The missionary fixed him with his stern eyes.

"Why is she unwilling to go back to San Francisco?"

"I didn't enquire," answered the doctor with some asperity. "And I think one does better to mind one's own business."

Perhaps it was not a very tactful answer.

"The governor has ordered her to be deported by the first boat that leaves the island. He's only done his duty and I will not interfere. Her presence is a peril here."

"I think you're very harsh and tyrannical."

The two ladies looked up at the doctor with some alarm, but they need not have feared a quarrel, for the missionary smiled gently.

"I'm terribly sorry you should think that of me, Dr. Macphail. Believe me, my heart bleeds for that unfortunate woman, but I'm only trying to do my duty."

The doctor made no answer. He looked out of the window sullenly. For once it was not raining and across the bay you saw nestling among the trees the huts of a native village.

"I think I'll take advantage of the rain stopping to go out," he said.

"Please don't bear me malice because I can't accede to your wish," said Davidson, with a melancholy smile. "I respect you very much, doctor, and I should be sorry if you thought ill of me."

"I have no doubt you have a sufficiently good opinion of yourself to bear mine with equanimity," he retorted.

"That's one on me," chuckled Davidson.

When Dr. Macphail, vexed with himself because he had been uncivil to no purpose, went downstairs, Miss Thompson was waiting for him with her door ajar.

"Well," she said, "have you spoken to him?"

"Yes, I'm sorry, he won't do anything," he answered, not looking at her in his embarrassment.

But then he gave her a quick glance, for a sob broke from her. He saw that her face was white with fear. It gave him a shock of dismay. And suddenly he had an idea.

"But don't give up hope yet. I think it's a shame the way they're treating you and I'm going to see the governor myself."

"Now?"

He nodded. Her face brightened.

"Say, that's real good of you. I'm sure he'll let me stay if you speak for me. I just won't do a thing I didn't ought all the time I'm here."

Dr. Macphail hardly knew why he had made up his mind to appeal to the governor. He was perfectly indifferent to Miss Thompson's affairs, but the missionary had irritated him, and with him temper was a smouldering thing. He found the governor at home. He was a large, handsome man, a sailor, with a grey toothbrush moustache; and he wore a spotless uniform of white drill.

"I've come to see you about a woman who's lodging in the same house as we are," he said. "Her name's Thompson."

"I guess I've heard nearly enough about her, Dr. Macphail," said the governor, smiling. "I've given her the order to get out next Tuesday and that's all I can do."

"I wanted to ask you if you couldn't stretch a point and let her stay here till the boat comes in from San Francisco so that she can go to Sydney. I will guarantee her good behavior."

The governor continued to smile, but his eyes grew small and serious.

"I'd be very glad to oblige you, Dr. Macphail, but I've given the order and it must stand."

The doctor put the case as reasonably as he could, but now the governor ceased to smile at all. He listened sullenly, with averted gaze. Macphail saw that he was making no impression.

"I'm sorry to cause any lady inconvenience, but she'll have to sail on Tuesday and that's all there is to it."

"But what difference can it make?"

"Pardon me, doctor, but I don't feel called upon to explain my official actions except to the proper authorities."

Macphail looked at him shrewdly. He remembered Davidson's hint that he had used threats, and in the governor's attitude he read a singular embarrassment.

"Davidson's a damned busybody," he said hotly.

"Between ourselves, Dr. Macphail, I don't say that I have formed a very favorable opinion of Mr. Davidson, but I am bound to confess that he was within his rights in pointing out to me the danger that the presence of a woman of Miss Thompson's character was to a place like this where a number of enlisted men are stationed among a native population."

He got up and Dr. Macphail was obliged to do so too.

"I must ask you to excuse me. I have an engagement. Please give my respects to Mrs. Macphail."

The doctor left him crest-fallen. He knew that Miss Thompson would be waiting for him, and unwilling to tell her himself that he had failed, he went into the house by the back door and sneaked up the stairs as though he had something to hide.

At supper he was silent and ill-at-ease, but the missionary was jovial and animated. Dr. Macphail thought his eyes rested on him now and then with triumphant good-humour. It struck him suddenly that Davidson knew of his visit to the governor and of its ill success. But how on earth could he have heard of it? There was something sinister about the power of that man. After supper he saw Horn on the verandah and, as though to have a casual word with him, went out.

"She wants to know if you've seen the governor," the trader whispered.

"Yes. He wouldn't do anything. I'm awfully sorry, I can't do anything more."

"I knew he wouldn't. They daren't go against the missionaries."

"What are you talking about?" said Davidson affably, coming out to join them.

"I was just saying there was no chance of your getting over to Apia for at least another week," said the trader glibly.

He left them, and the two men returned into the parlour. Mr. Davidson devoted one hour after each meal to recreation. Presently a timid knock was heard at the door.

"Come in," said Mrs. Davidson, in her sharp voice.

The door was not opened. She got up and opened it. They saw Miss Thompson standing at the threshold. But the change in her appearance was extraordinary. This was no longer the flaunting hussy who had jeered at them in the road, but a broken, frightened woman. Her hair, as a rule so elaborately arranged, was tumbling untidily over her neck. She wore bedroom slippers and a skirt and blouse. They were unfresh and bedraggled. She stood at the door with the tears streaming down her face and did not dare to enter.

"What do you want?" said Mrs. Davidson harshly.

"May I speak to Mr. Davidson?" she said in a choking voice.

The missionary rose and went towards her.

"Come right in, Miss Thompson," he said in cordial tones. "What can I do for you?"

She entered the room.

"Say, I'm sorry for what I said to you the other day an' for—for everythin' else. I guess I was a bit lit up. I beg pardon."

"Oh, it was nothing. I guess my back's broad enough to bear a few hard words."

She stepped towards him with a movement that was horribly cringing.

"You've got me beat. I'm all in. You won't make me go back to 'Frisco?"

His genial manner vanished and his voice grew on a sudden hard and stern.

"Why don't you want to go back there?"

She cowered before him.

"I guess my people live there. I don't want them to see me like this. I'll go anywhere else you say."

"Why don't you want to go back to San Francisco?"

"I've told you."

He leaned forward, staring at her, and his great, shining eyes seemed to try to bore into her soul. He gave a sudden gasp.

"The penitentiary."

She screamed, and then she fell at his feet, clasping his legs.

"Don't send me back there. I swear to you before God I'll be a good woman. I'll give all this up."

She burst into a torrent of confused supplication and the tears coursed down her painted cheeks. He leaned over her and, lifting her face, forced her to look at him.

"Is that it, the penitentiary?"

"I beat it before they could get me," she gasped. "If the bulls grab me it's three years for mine."

He let go his hold of her and she fell in a heap on the floor, sobbing bitterly. Dr. Macphail stood up.

"This alters the whole thing," he said. "You can't make her go back when you know this. Give her another chance. She wants to turn over a new leaf."

"I'm going to give her the finest chance she's ever had. If she repents let her accept her punishment."

She misunderstood the words and looked up. There was a gleam of hope in her heavy eyes.

"You'll let me go?"

"No. You shall sail for San Francisco on Tuesday."

She gave a groan of horror and then burst into low, hoarse shrieks which sounded hardly human, and she beat her head passionately on the ground. Dr. Macphail sprang to her and lifted her up.

"Come on, you mustn't do that. You'd better go to your room and lie down. I'll get you something."

He raised her to her feet and partly dragging her, partly carrying her, got her downstairs. He was furious with Mrs. Davidson and with his wife because they made no effort to help. The half-caste was standing on the landing and with his assistance he managed to get her on the bed. She was moaning and crying. She was almost insensible. He gave her a hypodermic injection. He was hot and exhausted when he went upstairs again.

"I've got her to lie down."

The two women and Davidson were in the same positions as when he had left them. They could not have moved or spoken since he went.

"I was waiting for you," said Davidson, in a strange, distant voice. "I want you all to pray with me for the soul of our erring sister."

He took the Bible off a shelf, and sat down at the table at which they had supped. It had not been cleared, and he pushed the tea-pot out of the way. In a powerful voice, resonant and deep, he read to them the chapter in which is narrated the meeting of Jesus Christ with the woman taken in adultery.

"Now kneel with me and let us pray for the soul of our dear sister, Sadie Thompson."

He burst into a long, passionate prayer in which he implored God to have mercy on the sinful woman. Mrs.

Macphail and Mrs. Davidson knelt with covered eyes. The doctor, taken by surprise, awkward and sheepish, knelt too. The missionary's prayer had a savage eloquence. He was extraordinarily moved, and as he spoke the tears ran down his cheeks. Outside, the pitiless rain fell, fell steadily, with a fierce malignity that was all too human.

At last he stopped. He paused for a moment and said:

"We will now repeat the Lord's prayer."

They said it and then, following him, they rose from their knees. Mrs. Davidson's face was pale and restful. She was comforted and at peace, but the Macphails felt suddenly bashful. They did not know which way to look.

"I'll just go down and see how she is," said Dr. Macphail.

When he knocked at her door it was opened for him by Horn. Miss Thompson was in a rocking-chair, sobbing quietly.

"What are you doing there?" exclaimed Macphail. "I told you to lie down."

"I can't lie down. I want to see Mr. Davidson."

"My poor child, what do you think is the good of it? You'll never move him."

"He said he'd come if I sent for him."

Macphail motioned to the trader.

"Go and fetch him."

He waited with her in silence while the trader went upstairs. Davidson came in.

"Excuse me for asking you to come here," she said, looking at him sombrely.

"I was expecting you to send for me. I knew the Lord would answer my prayer."

They stared at one another for a moment and then she looked away. She kept her eyes averted when she spoke.

"I've been a bad women. I want to repent."

"Thank God! thank God! He has heard our prayers."

He turned to the two men.

"Leave me alone with her. Tell Mrs. Davidson that our prayers have been answered."

They went out and closed the door behind them.

"Gee whizz," said the trader.

That night Dr. Macphail could not get to sleep till late, and when he heard the missionary come upstairs he looked at his watch. It was two o'clock. But even then he did not go to bed at once, for through the wooden partition that separated their rooms he heard him praying aloud, till he himself, exhausted, fell asleep.

When he saw him next morning he was surprised at his appearance. He was paler than ever, tired, but his eyes shone with an inhuman fire. It looked as though he were filled with an overwhelming joy.

"I want you to go down presently and see Sadie," he said, "I can't hope that her body is better, but her soul—her soul is transformed."

The doctor was feeling wan and nervous.

"You were with her very late last night," he said.

"Yes, she couldn't bear to have me leave her."

"You look as pleased as Punch," the doctor said irritably.

Davidson's eyes shone with ecstasy.

"A great mercy has been vouchsafed me. Last night I was privileged to bring a lost soul to the loving arms of Jesus."

Miss Thompson was again in the rocking-chair. The bed had not been made. The room was in disorder. She had not troubled to dress herself, but wore a dirty dressing-gown, and her hair was tied in a sluttish knot. She had given her face a dab with a wet towel, but it was all swollen and creased with crying. She looked a drab.

She raised her eyes dully when the doctor came in. She was cowed and broken.

"Where's Mr. Davidson?" she asked.

"He'll come presently if you want him," answered Macphail acidly. "I came here to see how you were."

"Oh, I guess I'm O.K. You needn't worry about that."

"Have you had anything to eat?"

"Horn brought me some coffee."

She looked anxiously at the door.

"D'you think he'll come down soon? I feel as if it wasn't so terrible when he's with me."

"Are you still going on Tuesday?"

"Yes, he says I've got to go. Please tell him to come right along. You can't do me any good. He's the only one as can help me now."

"Very well," said Dr. Macphail.

During the next three days the missionary spent almost all his time with Sadie Thompson. He joined the others only to have his meals. Dr. Macphail noticed that he hardly ate.

"He's wearing himself out," said Mrs. Davidson pitifully. "He'll have a breakdown if he doesn't take care, but he won't spare himself."

She herself was white and pale. She told Mrs. Macphail that she had no sleep. When the missionary came upstairs from Miss Thompson he prayed till he was exhausted, but even then he did not sleep for long. After an hour or two he got up and dressed himself, and went for a tramp along the bay. He had strange dreams.

"This morning he told me that he'd been dreaming about the mountains of Nebraska," said Mrs. Davidson.

"That's curious," said Dr. Macphail.

He remembered seeing them from the windows of the train when he crossed America. They were like huge molehills, rounded and smooth, and they rose from the plain abruptly. Dr. Macphail remembered how it struck him that they were like a woman's breasts.

Davidson's restlessness was intolerable even to himself. But he was buoyed up by a wonderful exhilaration. He was tearing out by the roots the last vestiges of sin that lurked in the hidden corners of that poor woman's heart. He read with her and prayed with her.

"It's wonderful," he said to them one day at supper. "It's a true rebirth. Her soul, which was black as night, is now pure and white like the new-fallen snow. I am humble and afraid. Her remorse for all her sins is beautiful. I am not worthy to touch the hem of her garment."

"Have you the heart to send her back to San Francisco?" said the doctor. "Three years in an American prison. I should have thought you might have saved her from that?"

"Ah, but don't you see? It's necessary. Do you think my heart doesn't bleed for her? I love her as I love my wife and my sister. All the time that she is in prison I shall suffer all the pain that she suffers."

"Bunkum," cried the doctor impatiently.

"You don't understand because you're blind. She's sinned, and she must suffer. I know what she'll endure. She'll be starved and tortured and humiliated. I want her to accept the punishment of man as a sacrifice to God. I want her to accept it joyfully. She has an opportunity which is offered to very few of us. God is very good and very merciful."

Davidson's voice trembled with excitement. He could hardly articulate the words that tumbled passionately from his lips.

"All day I pray with her and when I leave her I pray again, I pray with all my might and main, so that Jesus may grant her this great mercy. I want to put in her heart the passionate desire to be punished so that at the end, even if I offered to let her go, she would refuse. I want her to feel that the bitter punishment of prison is the thank-offering that she places at the feet of our Blessed Lord, who gave his life for her."

The days passed slowly. The whole household, intent on the wretched, tortured woman downstairs, lived in a state of unnatural excitement. She was like a victim that was being prepared for the savage rites of a bloody idolatry. Her terror numbed her. She could not bear to let Davidson out of her sight; it was only when he was with her that she had courage, and she hung upon him with a slavish dependence. She cried a great deal, and she read the Bible, and prayed. Sometimes she was exhausted and apathetic. Then she did indeed look forward to her ordeal, for it seemed to offer an escape, direct and concrete, from the anguish she was enduring. She could not bear much longer the vague terrors which now assailed her. With her sins she had put aside all personal vanity, and she slopped about her room, unkempt and dishevelled, in her tawdry dressing-gown. She had not taken off her night-dress for four days, nor put on stockings. Her room was littered and untidy. Meanwhile the rain fell with a cruel persistence. You felt that the heavens must at last be empty of water, but still it poured down, straight and heavy, with a maddening iteration, on the iron roof. Everything was damp and clammy. There was mildew on the walls and on the boots that stood on the floor. Through the sleepless nights the mosquitoes droned their angry chant.

"If it would only stop raining for a single day it wouldn't be so bad," said Dr. Macphail.

They all looked forward to the Tuesday when the boat for San Francisco was to arrive from Sydney. The strain was intolerable. So far as Dr. Macphail was concerned, his pity and his resentment were alike extinguished by his desire to be rid of the unfortunate woman. The inevitable must be accepted. He felt he would breathe more freely when the ship had sailed. Sadie Thompson was to be escorted on board by a clerk in the governor's office. This person called on the Monday evening and told Miss Thompson to be prepared at eleven in the morning. Davidson was with her.

"I'll see that everything is ready. I mean to come on board with her myself."

Miss Thompson did not speak.

When Dr. Macphail blew out his candle and crawled cautiously under his mosquito curtains, he gave a sigh of relief.

"Well, thank God that's over. By this time to-morrow she'll be gone."

"Mrs. Davidson will be glad too. She says he's wearing himself to a shadow," said Mrs. Macphail. "She's a different woman."

"Who?"

"Sadie. I should never have thought it possible. It makes one humble."

Dr. Macphail did not answer, and presently he fell asleep. He was tired out, and he slept more soundly than usual.

He was awakened in the morning by a hand placed on his arm, and, starting up, saw Horn by the side of his bed. The trader put his finger on his mouth to prevent any exclamation from Dr. Macphail and beckoned to him to come. As a rule he wore shabby ducks, but now he was barefoot and wore only the *lava-lava* of the natives. He looked suddenly savage, and Dr. Macphail, getting out of bed, saw that he was heavily tattooed. Horn made him a sign to come on to the verandah. Dr. Macphail got out of bed and followed the trader out.

"Don't make a noise," he whispered. "You're wanted. Put on a coat and some shoes. Quick."

Dr. Macphail's first thought was that something had happened to Miss Thompson.

"What is it? Shall I bring my instruments?"

"Hurry, please, hurry."

Dr. Macphail crept back into the bedroom, put on a waterproof over his pyjamas, and a pair of rubber-soled shoes. He rejoined the trader, and together they tiptoed down the stairs. The door leading out to the road was open and at it were standing half a dozen natives.

"What is it?" repeated the doctor.

"Come along with me," said Horn.

He walked out and the doctor followed him. The natives came after them in a little bunch. They crossed the road and came on to the beach. The doctor saw a group of natives standing round some object at the water's edge. They hurried along, a couple of dozen yards perhaps, and the natives opened out as the doctor came up. The trader pushed him forward. Then he saw, lying half in the water and half out, a dreadful object, the body of Davidson. Dr. Macphail bent down—he was not a man to lose his head in an emergency—and turned the body over. The throat was cut from ear to ear, and in the right hand was still the razor with which the deed was done.

"He's quite cold," said the doctor. "He must have been dead some time."

"One of the boys saw him lying there on his way to work just now and came and told me. Do you think he did it himself?"

"Yes. Someone ought to go for the police."

Horn said something in the native tongue, and two youths started off.

"We must leave him here till they come," said the doctor.

"They mustn't take him into my house. I won't have him in my house."

"You'll do what the authorities say," replied the doctor sharply. "In point of fact I expect they'll take him to the mortuary."

They stood waiting where they were. The trader took a cigarette from a fold in his *lava-lava* and gave one to Dr. Macphail. They smoked while they stared at the corpse. Dr. Macphail could not understand.

"Why do you think he did it?" asked Horn.

The doctor shrugged his shoulders. In a little while native police came along, under the charge of a marine, with a stretcher, and immediately afterwards a couple of naval officers and a naval doctor. They managed everything in a businesslike manner.

"What about the wife?" said one of the officers.

"Now that you've come I'll go back in the house and get some things on. I'll see that it's broken to her. She'd better not see him till he's been fixed up a little."

"I guess that's right," said the naval doctor.

When Dr. Macphail went back he found his wife nearly dressed.

"Mrs. Davidson's in a dreadful state about her husband," she said to him as soon as he appeared. "He hasn't been to bed all night. She heard him leave Miss Thompson's room at two, but he went out. If he's been walking about since then he'll be absolutely dead."

Dr. Macphail told her what had happened and asked her to break the news to Mrs. Davidson.

"But why did he do it?" she asked, horror-stricken.

"I don't know."

"But I can't. I can't."

"You must."

She gave him a frightened look and went out. He heard her go into Mrs. Davidson's room. He waited a minute to gather himself together and then began to shave and wash. When he was dressed he sat down on the bed and waited for his wife. At last she came.

"She wants to see him," she said.

"They've taken him to the mortuary. We'd better go down with her. How did she take it?"

"I think she's stunned. She didn't cry. But she's trembling like a leaf."

"We'd better go at once."

When they knocked at her door Mrs. Davidson came out. She was very pale, but dry-eyed. To the doctor she seemed unnaturally composed. No word was exchanged, and they set out in silence down the road. When they arrived at the mortuary. Mrs. Davidson spoke.

"Let me go in and see him alone."

They stood aside. A native opened a door for her and closed it behind her. They sat down and waited. One or two white men came and talked to them in undertones. Dr. Macphail told them again what he knew of the tragedy. At last the door was quietly opened and Mrs. Davidson came out. Silence fell upon them.

"I'm ready to go back now," she said.

Her voice was hard and steady. Dr. Macphail could not understand the look in her eyes. Her pale face was very stern. They walked back slowly, never saying a word, and at last they came round the bend on the other side of which stood their house. Mrs. Davidson gave a gasp, and for a moment they stopped still. An incredible sound assaulted their ears. The gramophone which had been silent for so long was playing, playing ragtime loud and harsh.

"What's that?" cried Mrs. Macphail with horror.

"Let's go on," said Mrs. Davidson.

They walked up the steps and entered the hall. Miss Thompson was standing at her door, chatting with a sailor. A sudden change had taken place in her. She was no longer the cowed drudge of the last days. She was dressed in all her finery, in her white dress, with the high shiny boots over which her fat legs bulged in their cotton stockings; her hair was elaborately arranged; and she wore that enormous hat covered with gaudy flowers. Her face was painted, her eyebrows were boldly black, and her lips were scarlet. She held herself erect. She was the flaunting quean that they had known at first. As they came in she broke into a loud, jeering laugh; and then, when Mrs. Davidson involuntarily stopped, she collected the spittle in her mouth and spat. Mrs. Davidson cowered back, and two red spots rose suddenly to her cheeks. Then, covering her face with her hands, she broke away and ran quickly up the stairs. Dr. Macphail was outraged. He pushed past the woman into her room.

"What the devil are you doing?" he cried. "Stop that

damned machine."

He went up to it and tore the record off. She turned on him.

"Say, doc, you can that stuff with me. What the hell are you doin' in my room?"

"What do you mean?" he cried. "What d'you mean?"

She gathered herself together. No one could describe the scorn of her expression or the contemptuous hatred she put into her answer.

"You men! You filthy, dirty pigs! You're all the same, all of you. Pigs! Pigs!"

Dr. Macphail gasped. He understood.

FRANK O'CONNOR

The Majesty of the Law

OLD Dan Bride was breaking brosna for the fire when he heard a step on the path. He paused, a bundle of saplings on his knee.

Dan had looked after his mother while the life was in her, and after her death no other woman had crossed his threshold. Signs on it, his house had that look. Almost everything in it he had made with his own hands in his own way. The seats of the chairs were only slices of log, rough and round and thick as the saw had left them, and with the rings still plainly visible through the grime and polish that coarse trouser-bottoms had in the course of long years imparted. Into these Dan had rammed stout knotted ash-boughs that served alike for legs and back. The deal table, bought in a shop, was an inheritance from his mother and a great pride and joy to him though it rocked whenever he touched it. On the wall, unglazed and fly-spotted, hung in mysterious isolation a Marcus Stone print, and beside the door was a calendar with a picture of a racehorse. Over the door hung an old gun, old but good, and in excellent condition, and before the fire was stretched an old setter who raised his head expectantly whenever Dan rose or even stirred.

He raised it now as the steps came nearer and when Dan, laying down the bundle of saplings, cleaned his hands thoughtfully on the seat of his trousers, he gave a loud bark, but this expressed no more than a desire to show off his own watchfulness. He was half human and knew people thought he was old and past his prime.

A man's shadow fell across the oblong of dusty light thrown over the half-door before Dan looked round.

"Are you alone, Dan?" asked an apologetic voice.

"Oh, come in, come in, sergeant, come in and welcome," exclaimed the old man, hurrying on rather uncertain feet to the door which the tall policeman opened and pushed in. He stood there, half in sunlight, half in shadow, and seeing him so, you would have realized how dark the interior of the house really was. One side of his red face was turned so as to catch the light, and behind it an ash tree raised its boughs of airy green against the sky. Green fields, broken here and there by clumps of red-brown rock, flowed downhill, and beyond them, stretched all across the horizon, was the sea, flooded and almost transparent with light. The sergeant's face was fat and fresh, the old man's face, emerging from the twilight of the kitchen, had the colour of wind and sun, while the features had been so shaped by the struggle with time and the elements that they might as easily have been found impressed upon the surface of a rock.

"Begor, Dan," said the sergeant, " 'tis younger you're getting."

"Middling I am, sergeant, middling," agreed the old man in a voice which seemed to accept the remark as a compliment of which politeness would not allow him to take too much advantage. "No complaints."

"Begor, 'tis as well because no one would believe them. And the old dog doesn't look a day older."

The dog gave a low growl as though to show the sergeant that he would remember this unmannerly reference to his age, but indeed he growled every time he was mentioned, under the impression that people had nothing but ill to say of him.

"And how's yourself, sergeant?"

"Well, now, like the most of us, Dan, neither too good nor too bad. We have our own little worries, but, thanks be to God, we have our compensations."

"And the wife and family?"

"Good, praise be to God, good. They were away from me for a month, the lot of them, at the mother-in-law's place in Clare."

"In Clare, do you tell me?"

"In Clare. I had a fine quiet time."

The old man looked about him and then retired to the bedroom, from which he returned a moment later with an old shirt. With this he solemnly wiped the seat and back of the log-chair nearest the fire.

"Sit down now, sergeant. You must be tired after the journey. 'Tis a long old road. How did you come?"

"Teigue Leary gave me the lift. Wisha now, Dan, don't be putting yourself out. I won't be stopping. I promised them I'd be back inside an hour."

"What hurry is on you?" asked Dan. "Look, your foot was only on the path when I made up the fire."

"Arrah, Dan, you're not making tea for me?"

"I am not making it for you, indeed; I'm making it for myself, and I'll take it very bad of you if you won't have a cup."

"Dan, Dan, that I mightn't stir, but 'tisn't an hour since I had it at the barracks!"

"Ah, whisht, now, whisht! Whisht, will you! I have something here to give you an appetite."

The old man swung the heavy kettle onto the chain over the open fire, and the dog sat up, shaking his ears with an expression of the deepest interest. The policeman unbuttoned his tunic, opened his belt, took a pipe and a plug of tobacco from his breast pocket, and crossing his legs in an easy posture, began to cut the tobacco slowly and carefully with his pocket knife. The old man went to the dresser and took down two handsomely decorated cups, the only cups he had, which, though chipped and handleless, were used at all only on very rare occasions; for himself he preferred his tea from a basin. Happening to glance into them, he noticed that they bore signs of disuse and had collected a lot of the fine white turf-dust that always circulated in the little smoky cottage. Again he thought of the shirt, and, rolling up his sleeves with a stately gesture, he wiped them inside and out till they shone. Then he bent and opened the cupboard. Inside was a quart bottle of pale liquid, obviously untouched. He removed the cork and smelt the contents, pausing for a moment in the act as though to recollect where exactly he had noticed that particular smoky smell before. Then, reassured, he stood up and poured out with a liberal hand.

"Try that now, sergeant," he said with quiet pride.

The sergeant, concealing whatever qualms he might have felt at the idea of drinking illegal whisky, looked carefully into the cup, sniffed, and glanced up at old Dan.

"It looks good," he commented.

"It should be good," replied Dan with no mock modesty.

"It tastes good too," said the sergeant.

"Ah, sha," said Dan, not wishing to praise his own hospitality in his own house, " 'tis of no great excellence."

"You'd be a good judge, I'd say," said the sergeant without irony.

"Ever since things became what they are," said Dan, carefully guarding himself against a too-direct reference to the peculiarities of the law administered by his guest, "liquor isn't what it used to be."

"I've heard that remark made before now, Dan," said the sergeant thoughtfully. "I've heard it said by men of wide experience that it used to be better in the old days."

"Liquor," said the old man, "is a thing that takes time. There was never a good job done in a hurry."

" 'Tis an art in itself."

"Just so."

"And an art takes time."

"And knowledge," added Dan with emphasis. "Every art has its secrets, and the secrets of distilling are being lost the way the old songs were lost. When I was a boy there wasn't a man in the barony but had a hundred songs in his head, but with people running here, there and everywhere, the songs were lost. . . . Ever since things became what they are," he repeated on the same guarded note, "there's so much running about the secrets are lost."

"There must have been a power of them."

"There was. Ask any man today that makes whisky do he know how to make it out of heather."

"And was it made of heather?" asked the policeman.

"It was."

"You never drank it yourself?"

"I didn't, but I knew old men that did, and they told me that no whisky that's made nowadays could compare with it."

"Musha, Dan, I think sometimes 'twas a great mistake of the law to set its hand against it."

Dan shook his head. His eyes answered for him, but it was not in nature for a man to criticize the occupation of a guest in his own home.

"Maybe so, maybe not," he said noncommittally.

"But sure, what else have the poor people?"

"Them that makes the laws have their own good reasons."

"All the same, Dan, all the same, 'tis a hard law."

The sergeant would not be outdone in generosity. Politeness required him not to yield to the old man's defence of his superiors and their mysterious ways.

"It is the secrets I'd be sorry for," said Dan, summing up. "Men die and men are born, and where one man drained another will plough, but a secret lost is lost forever."

"True," said the sergeant mournfully. "Lost forever."

Dan took his cup, rinsed it in a bucket of clear water by the door and cleaned it again with the shirt. Then he placed it carefully at the sergeant's elbow. From the dresser he took a jug of milk and a blue bag containing sugar; this he followed up with a slab of country butter and—a sure sign that he had been expecting a visitor—a round cake of homemade bread, fresh and uncut. The kettle sang and spat and the dog, shaking his ears, barked at it angrily.

"Go away, you brute!" growled Dan, kicking him out of his way.

He made the tea and filled the two cups. The sergeant cut himself a large slice of bread and buttered it thickly.

"It is just like medicines," said the old man, resuming his theme with the imperturbability of age. "Every secret there was is lost. And leave no one tell me that a doctor is as good a man as one that had the secrets of old times."

"How could he be?" asked the sergeant with his mouth full.

"The proof of that was seen when there were doctors and wise people there together."

"It wasn't to the doctors the people went, I'll engage?"

"It was not. And why?" With a sweeping gesture the old man took in the whole world outside his cabin. "Out there on the hillsides is the sure cure for every disease. Because it is written"—he tapped the table with his thumb—"it is written by the poets 'wherever you find the disease you will find the cure.' But people walk up the hills and down the hills and all they see is flowers. Flowers! As if God Almighty—honour and praise to Him!—had nothing better to do with His time than be making old flowers!"

"Things no doctor could cure the wise people cured," agreed the sergeant.

"Ah, musha, 'tis I know it," said Dan bitterly. "I know it, not in my mind but in my own four bones."

"Have you the rheumatics at you still?" the sergeant asked in a shocked tone.

"I have. Ah, if you were alive, Kitty O'Hara, or you, Nora Malley of the Glen, 'tisn't I'd be dreading the mountain wind or the sea wind; 'tisn't I'd be creeping down with my misfortunate red ticket for the blue and pink and yellow dribble-drabble of their ignorant dispensary."

"Why then indeed," said the sergeant, "I'll get you a bottle for that."

"Ah, there's no bottle ever made will cure it."

"That's where you're wrong, Dan. Don't talk now till you try it. It cured my own uncle when he was that bad he was shouting for the carpenter to cut the two legs off him with a handsaw."

"I'd give fifty pounds to get rid of it," said Dan magniloquently. "I would and five hundred."

The sergeant finished his tea in a gulp, blessed himself and struck a match which he then allowed to go out as he answered some question of the old man. He did the same with a second and third, as though titillating his appetite with delay. Finally he succeeded in getting his pipe alight and the two men pulled round their chairs, placed their toes side by side in the ashes, and in deep puffs, lively bursts of conversation, and long, long silences, enjoyed their smoke.

"I hope I'm not keeping you?" said the sergeant, as though struck by the length of his visit.

"Ah, what would you keep me from?"

"Tell me if I am. The last thing I'd like to do is waste another man's time."

"Begor, you wouldn't waste my time if you stopped all night."

"I like a little chat myself," confessed the policeman.

And again they became lost in conversation. The light grew thick and coloured and, wheeling about the kitchen before it disappeared, became tinged with gold; the kitchen itself sank into cool greyness with cold light on the cups and basins and plates of the dresser. From the ash tree a thrush began to sing. The open hearth gathered brightness till its light was a warm, even splash of crimson in the twilight.

Twilight was also descending outside when the sergeant rose to go. He fastened his belt and tunic and carefully brushed his clothes. Then he put on his cap, tilted a little to side and back.

"Well, that was a great talk," he said.

" 'Tis a pleasure," said Dan, "a real pleasure."

"And I won't forget the bottle for you."

"Heavy handling from God to you!"

"Good-bye now, Dan."

"Good-bye, sergeant, and good luck."

Dan didn't offer to accompany the sergeant beyond the door. He sat in his old place by the fire, took out his pipe once more, blew through it thoughtfully, and just as he leaned forward for a twig to kindle it, heard the steps returning. It was the sergeant. He put his head a little way over the half-door.

"Oh, Dan!" he called softly.

"Ay, sergeant?" replied Dan, looking round, but with one hand still reaching for the twig. He couldn't see the sergeant's face, only hear his voice.

"I suppose you're not thinking of paying that little fine, Dan?"

There was a brief silence. Dan pulled out the lighted twig, rose slowly and shambled towards the door, stuffing it down in the almost empty bowl of the pipe. He leaned over the half door while the sergeant with hands in the pockets of his trousers gazed rather in the direction of the laneway, yet taking in a considerable portion of the sea line.

"The way it is with me, sergeant," replied Dan unemotionally, "I am not."

"I was thinking that, Dan; I was thinking you wouldn't."

There was a long silence during which the voice of the thrush grew shriller and merrier. The sunken sun lit up rafts of purple cloud moored high above the wind.

"In a way," said the sergeant, "that was what brought me."

"I was just thinking so, sergeant, it only struck me and you going out the door."

"If 'twas only the money, Dan, I'm sure there's many would be glad to oblige you."

"I know that, sergeant. No, 'tisn't the money so much as giving that fellow the satisfaction of paying. Because he angered me, sergeant."

The sergeant made no comment on this and another long silence ensued.

"They gave me the warrant," the sergeant said at last, in a tone which dissociated him from all connection with such an unneighbourly document.

"Did they so?" exclaimed Dan, as if he was shocked by the thoughtlessness of the authorities.

"So whenever 'twould be convenient for you—"

"Well, now you mention it," said Dan, by way of throwing out a suggestion for debate, "I could go with you now."

"Ah, sha, what do you want going at this hour for?" protested the sergeant with a wave of his hand, dismissing the notion as the tone required.

"Or I could go tomorrow," added Dan, warming to the issue.

"Would it be suitable for you now?" asked the sergeant, scaling up his voice accordingly.

"But, as a matter of fact," said the old man emphatically, "the day that would be most convenient to me would be Friday after dinner, because I have some messages to do in town, and I wouldn't have the journey for nothing."

"Friday will do grand," said the sergeant with relief that this delicate matter was now practically disposed of. "If it doesn't they can damn well wait. You could walk in there yourself when it suits you and tell them I sent you."

"I'd rather have yourself there, sergeant, if it would be no inconvenience. As it is, I'd feel a bit shy."

"Why then, you needn't feel shy at all. There's a man from my own parish there, a warder; one Whelan. Ask for him; I'll tell him you're coming, and I'll guarantee when he knows you're a friend of mine he'll make you as comfortable as if you were at home."

"I'd like that fine," Dan said with profound satisfaction. "I'd like to be with friends, sergeant."

"You will be, never fear. Good-bye again now, Dan. I'll have to hurry."

"Wait now, wait till I see you to the road."

Together the two men strolled down the laneway while Dan explained how it was that he, a respectable old man, had had the grave misfortune to open the head of another old man in such a way as to require his removal to hospital, and why it was that he couldn't give the old man in question the satisfaction of paying in cash for an injury brought about through the victim's own unmannerly method of argument.

"You see, sergeant," Dan said, looking at another little cottage up the hill, "the way it is, he's there now, and he's looking at us as sure as there's a glimmer of sight in his weak, wandering, watery eyes, and nothing would give him more gratification than for me to pay. But I'll punish him. I'll lie on bare boards for him. I'll suffer for him, sergeant, so that neither he nor any of his children after him will be able to raise their heads for the shame of it."

On the following Friday he made ready his donkey and butt and set out. On his way he collected a number of neighbours who wished to bid him farewell. At the top of the hill he stopped to send them back. An old man, sitting in the sunlight, hastily made his way indoors, and a moment later the door of his cottage was quietly closed.

Having shaken all his friends by the hand, Dan lashed the old donkey, shouted: "Hup there!" and set out alone along the road to prison.

J. F. POWERS

The Valiant Woman

THEY had come to the dessert in a dinner that was a shambles. "Well, John," Father Nulty said, turning away from Mrs. Stoner and to Father Firman, long gone silent at his own table. "You've got the bishop coming for confirmations next week."

"Yes," Mrs. Stoner cut in, "and for dinner. And if he don't eat any more than he did last year—"

Father Firman, in a rare moment, faced it. "Mrs. Stoner, the bishop is not well. You know that."

"And after I fixed that fine dinner and all." Mrs. Stoner pouted in Father Nulty's direction.

"I wouldn't feel bad about it, Mrs. Stoner," Father Nulty said. "He never eats much anywhere."

"It's funny. And that new Mrs. Allers said he ate just

fine when he was there," Mrs. Stoner argued, and then spit out, "But she's a damned liar!"

Father Nulty, unsettled but trying not to show it, said, "Who's Mrs. Allers?"

"She's at Holy Cross," Mrs. Stoner said.

"She's the housekeeper," Father Firman added, thinking Mrs. Stoner made it sound as though Mrs. Allers was the pastor there.

"I swear I don't know what to do about the dinner this year," Mrs. Stoner said.

Father Firman moaned. "Just do as you've always done, Mrs. Stoner."

"Huh! And have it all to throw out! Is that any way to do?"

"Is there any dessert?" Father Firman asked coldly.

Mrs. Stoner leaped up from the table and bolted into the kitchen, mumbling. She came back with a birthday cake. She plunged it in the center of the table. She found a big wooden match in her apron pocket and thrust it at Father Firman.

"I don't like this bishop," she said. "I never did. And the way he went and cut poor Ellen Kennedy out of Father Doolin's will!"

She went back into the kitchen.

"Didn't they talk a lot of filth about Doolin and the housekeeper?" Father Nulty asked.

"I should think they did," Father Firman said. "All because he took her to the movies on Sunday night. After he died and the bishop cut her out of the will, though I hear he gives her a pension privately, they talked about the bishop."

"I don't like this bishop at all," Mrs. Stoner said, appearing with a cake knife. "Bishop Doran—there was the man!"

"We know," Father Firman said. "All man and all priest."

"He did know real estate," Father Nulty said.

Father Firman struck the match.

"Not on the chair!" Mrs. Stoner cried, too late.

Father Firman set the candle burning—it was suspiciously large and yellow, like a blessed one, but he could not be sure. They watched the fluttering flame.

"I'm forgetting the lights!" Mrs. Stoner said, and got up to turn them off. She went into the kitchen again.

The priests had a moment of silence in the candlelight.

"Happy birthday, John," Father Nulty said softly. "Is it fifty-nine you are?"

"As if you didn't know, Frank," Father Firman said, "and you the same but one."

Father Nulty smiled, the old gold of his incisors shining in the flickering light, his collar whiter in the dark, and raised his glass of water, which would have been wine or better in the bygone days, and toasted Father Firman.

"Many of 'em, John."

"Blow it out," Mrs. Stoner said, returning to the room. She waited by the light switch for Father Firman to blow out the candle.

Mrs. Stoner, who ate no desserts, began to clear the dishes into the kitchen, and the priests, finishing their cake and coffee in a hurry, went to sit in the study.

Father Nulty offered a cigar.

"John?"

"My ulcers, Frank."

"Ah, well, you're better off." Father Nulty lit the cigar and crossed his long black legs." Fish Frawley has got him a Filipino, John. Did you hear?"

Father Firman leaned forward, interested. "He got rid of the woman he had?"

"He did. It seems she snooped."

"Snooped, eh?"

"She did. And gossiped. Fish introduced two town boys to her, said: 'Would you think these boys were my nephews?' That's all, and the next week the paper had it that his two nephews were visiting him from Erie. After that, he let her believe he was going East to see his parents, though both are dead. The paper carried the story. Fish returned and made a sermon out of it. Then he got the Filipino."

Father Firman squirmed with pleasure in his chair. "That's like Fish, Frank. He can do that." He stared at the tips of his fingers bleakly. "You could never get a Filipino to come to a place like this."

"Probably not," Father Nulty said. "Fish is pretty close to Minneapolis. Ah, say, do you remember the trick he played on us all in Marmion Hall!"

"That I'll not forget!" Father Firman's eyes remembered. "Getting up New Year's morning and finding the toilet seats all painted!"

"*HAPPY CIRCUMCISION!* Hah!" Father Nulty had a coughing fit.

When he had got himself together again, a mosquito came and sat on his wrist. He watched it a moment before bringing his heavy hand down. He raised his hand slowly, viewed the dead mosquito, and sent it spinning with a plunk of his middle finger.

"Only the female bites," he said.

"I didn't know that," Father Firman said.

"Ah, yes . . ."

Mrs. Stoner entered the study and sat down with some sewing—Father Firman's black socks.

She smiled pleasantly at Father Nulty. "And what do you think of the atom bomb, Father?"

"Not much," Father Nulty said.

Mrs. Stoner had stopped smiling. Father Firman yawned.

Mrs. Stoner served up another: "Did you read about this communist convert, Father?"

"He's been in the Church before," Father Nulty said, "and so it's not a conversion, Mrs. Stoner."

"No? Well, I already got him down on my list of Monsignor's converts."

"It's better than a conversion, Mrs. Stoner, for there is more rejoicing in heaven over the return of . . . uh, he that was lost, Mrs. Stoner, is found."

"And that congresswoman, Father?"

"Yes. A convert—she."

"And Henry Ford's grandson, Father. I got him down."

"Yes, to be sure."

Father Firman yawned, this time audibly, and held his jaw.

"But he's one only by marriage, Father," Mrs. Stoner said. "I always say you got to watch those kind."

"Indeed you do, but a convert nonetheless, Mrs. Stoner. Remember, Cardinal Newman himself was one."

Mrs. Stoner was unimpressed. "I see where Henry Ford's making steering-wheels out of soybeans, Father."

"I didn't see that."

"I read it in the *Reader's Digest* or some place."

"Yes, well . . ." Father Nulty rose and held his hand out to Father Firman. "John," he said. "It's been good."

"I heard Hirohito's next," Mrs. Stoner said, returning to converts.

"Let's wait and see, Mrs. Stoner," Father Nulty said.

The priests walked to the door.

"You know where I live, John."

"Yes. Come again, Frank. Good night."

Father Firman watched Father Nulty go down the walk to his car at the curb. He hooked the screen door and turned off the porch light. He hesitated at the foot of the stairs, suddenly moved to go to bed. But he went back into the study.

"Phew!" Mrs. Stoner said. "I thought he'd never go. Here it is after eight o'clock."

Father Firman sat down in his rocking-chair. "I don't see him often," he said.

"I give up!" Mrs. Stoner exclaimed, flinging the holey socks upon the horsehair sofa. "I'd swear you had a nail in your shoe."

"I told you I looked."

"Well, you ought to look again. And cut your toenails, why don't you? Haven't I got enough to do?"

Father Firman scratched in his coat pocket for a pill, found one, swallowed it. He let his head sink back against the chair and closed his eyes. He could hear her moving about the room, making the preparations; and how he knew them—the fumbling in the drawer for a pencil with a point, the rip of the page from his daily calendar, and finally the leg of the cardtable sliding up against his leg.

He opened his eyes. She yanked the floor lamp alongside the table, setting the bead fringe tinkling on the shade, and pulled up her chair on the other side. She sat down and smiled at him for the first time that day. Now she was happy.

She swept up the cards and began to shuffle with the abandoned virtuosity of an old river-boat gambler, standing them on end, fanning them out, whirling them through her fingers, dancing them half-way up her arms, cracking the whip over them. At last they lay before him tamed into a neat deck.

"Cut?"

"Go ahead," he said. She liked to go first.

She gave him her faint, avenging smile and drew a card, cast it aside for another which he thought must be an ace from the way she clutched it face down.

She was getting all the cards, as usual, and would have been invincible if she had possessed his restraint and if her cunning had been of a higher order. He knew a few things about leading and lying back that she would never learn. Her strategy was attack, forever attack, with one baffling departure: she might sacrifice certain tricks as expendable if only she could have the last ones, the heartbreaking ones, if she could slap them down one after another, shatteringly.

She played for blood, no bones about it, but for her there was no other way; it was her nature, as it was the lion's, and for this reason he found her ferocity pardonable, more a defect of the flesh, venial, while his own trouble was all in the will, mortal. He did not sweat and pray over each card as she must, but he did keep an eye out for reneging and demanded a cut now and then just to aggravate her, and he was always secretly hoping for aces.

With one card left in her hand, the telltale trick coming next, she delayed playing it, showing him first the smile, the preview of defeat. She laid it on the table—so! She held one more trump than he had reasoned possible. Had she palmed it from somewhere? No, she would not go that far; that would not be fair, was worse than reneging, which so easily and often happened accidentally, and she believed in being fair. Besides he had been watching her.

God smote the vines with hail, the sycamore trees with frost, and offered up the flocks to the lightning—but Mrs. Stoner! What a cross Father Firman had from God in Mrs. Stoner! There were other housekeepers as bad, no doubt, walking the rectories of the world, yes, but . . . yes. He could name one and maybe two priests who were worse off. One, maybe two. Cronin. His scraggly blonde of sixty—take her, with her everlasting banging on the grand piano, the gift of the pastor; her proud talk about the goiter operation at the Mayo Brothers', also a gift; her honking the parish Buick at passing strange priests because they were all in the game together. She was worse. She was something to keep the home fires burning. Yes sir. And Cronin said she was not a bad person really, but what was he? He was quite a freak himself.

For that matter, could anyone say that Mrs. Stoner was a bad person? No. He could not say it himself, and he was no freak. She had her points, Mrs. Stoner. She was clean. And though she cooked poorly, could not play the organ, would not take up the collection in an emergency, and went to card-parties, and told all—even so, she was clean. She washed everything. Sometimes her underwear hung down beneath her dress like a paratrooper's pants, but it and everything she touched was clean. She washed constantly. She was clean.

She had her other points, to be sure—her faults, you might say. She snooped—no mistake about it—but it was not snooping for snooping's sake; she had a reason. She did other things, always with a reason. She overcharged on rosaries and prayer books, but that was for the sake of the poor. She censored the pamphlet rack, but that was to prevent scandal. She pried into the baptismal and matrimonial records, but there was no other way if Father was out, and in this way she once had uncovered a bastard and flushed him out of the rectory, but that was the perverted decency of the times. She held her nose over bad marriages in the presence of the victims, but that was her sorrow and came from having her husband buried in a mine. And he had caught her telling a bewildered young couple that there was only one good reason for their wanting to enter into a mixed marriage—the child had to have a name, and that—that was what?

She hid his books, kept him from smoking, picked his friends (usually the pastors of her colleagues), bawled out people for calling after dark, had no humor, except at cards, and then it was grim, very grim, and she sat hatchet-faced every morning at Mass. But she went to Mass, which was all that kept the church from being empty some mornings. She did annoying things all day long. She said annoying things into the night. She said she had given him the best years of her life. Had she? Perhaps—for the miner had her only a year. It was too bad, sinfully bad, when he thought of it like that. But all talk of best years and life was nonsense. He had to consider the heart of the matter, the essence. The essence was that housekeepers were hard to get, harder to get than ushers, than willing workers, than organists, than secretaries—yes, harder to get than assistants or vocations.

And she was a *saver*—saved money, saved electricity, saved string, bags, sugar, saved—him. That's what she did. That's what she said she did, and she was right, in a way. In a way, she was usually right. In fact, she was always right—in a way. And you could never get a Filipino to come way out here and live. Not a young one anyway, and he had never seen an old one. Not a Filipino. They liked to dress up and live.

Should he let it drop about Fish having one, just to throw a scare into her, let her know he was doing some thinking? No. It would be a perfect cue for the one about a man needing a woman to look after him. He was not up to that again, not tonight.

Now she was doing what she liked most of all. She was making a grand slam, playing it out card for card, though it was in the bag, prolonging what would have been cut short out of mercy in gentle company. Father Firman knew the agony of losing.

She slashed down the last card, a miserable deuce trump, and did in the hapless king of hearts he had been saving.

"Skunked you!"

She was awful in victory. Here was the bitter end of their long day together, the final murderous hour in which all they wanted to say—all he wouldn't and all she couldn't—came out in the cards. Whoever won at honeymoon won the day, slept on the other's scalp, and God alone had to help the loser.

"We've been at it long enough, Mrs. Stoner," he said, seeing her assembling the cards for another round.

"Had enough, huh!"

Father Firman grumbled something.

"No?"

"Yes."

She pulled the table away and left it against the wall for the next time. She went out of the study carrying the socks, content and clucking. He closed his eyes after her and began to get under way in the rocking-chair, the nightly trip to nowhere. He could hear her brewing a cup of tea in the kitchen and conversing with the cat. She made her way up the stairs, carrying the tea, followed by the cat, purring.

He waited, rocking out to sea, until she would be sure to be through in the bathroom. Then he got up and locked the front door (she looked after the back door) and loosened his collar going upstairs.

In the bathroom he mixed a glass of antiseptic, always afraid of pyorrhœa, and gargled to ward off pharyngitis.

When he turned on the light in his room, the moths and beetles began to batter against the screens, the lighter insects humming. . . .

Yes, and she had the guest room. How did she come to get that? Why wasn't she in the back room, in her proper place? He knew, if he cared to remember. The screen in the back room—it let in mosquitoes, and if it didn't do that she'd love to sleep back there, Father, looking out at the steeple and the blessed cross on top, Father, if it just weren't for the screen, Father. Very well, Mrs. Stoner, I'll get it fixed or fix it myself. Oh, could you now, Father? I could, Mrs. Stoner, and I will. In the meantime you take the guest room. Yes, Father, and thank you, Father, the house ringing with amenities then. Years ago, all that. She was a pie-faced girl then, not really a girl perhaps, but not too old to marry again. But she never had. In fact, he could not remember that she had even tried for a husband since coming to the rectory, but, of course, he could be wrong, not knowing how they went about it. God! God save us! Had she got her wires crossed and mistaken him all these years for *that? that!* Him! Suffering God! No. That was going too far. That was getting morbid. No. He must not think of that again, ever. No.

But just the same she had got the guest room and she had it yet. Well, did it matter? Nobody ever came to see him any more, nobody to stay overnight anyway, nobody to stay very long . . . not any more. He knew how they laughed at him. He had heard Frank humming all right —before he saw how serious and sad the situation was and took pity—humming "Wedding Bells are Breaking Up that Old Gang of Mine." But then they'd always laughed at him for something—for not being an athlete, for wearing glasses, for having kidney trouble . . . and mail coming addressed to Rev. and Mrs. Stoner.

Removing his shirt, he bent over the table to read the volume left open from last night. He read, translating easily: "Eisdem licet cum illis . . . Clerics are allowed to reside only with women about whom there can be no suspicion, either because of a natural bond (as mother, sister, aunt) or of advanced age, combined in both cases with good repute."

Last night he had read it, and many nights before, each time as though this time to find what was missing, to find what obviously was not in the paragraph, his problem considered, a way out. She was not mother, not sister, not aunt, and *advanced age* was a relative term (why, she was younger than he was) and so, eureka, she did not meet the letter of the law—but, alas, how she fulfilled the spirit! And besides it would be a slimy way of handling it after all her years of service. He could not afford to pension her off, either.

He slammed the book shut. He slapped himself fiercely on the back, missing the wily mosquito, and whirled to find it. He took a magazine and folded it into a swatter. Then he saw it—oh, the preternatural cunning of it!—poised in the beard of St. Joseph on the book-case. He could not hit it there. He teased it away, wanting it to light on the wall, but it knew his thoughts and flew high away. He swung wildly, hoping to stun it, missed, swung back, catching St. Joseph across the neck. The statue fell to the floor and broke.

Mrs. Stoner was panting in the hall outside his door.

"What is it!"

"Mosquitoes!"

"What is it, Father? Are you hurt?"

"Mosquitoes—damn it! And only the female bites!"

Mrs. Stoner, after a moment, said: "Shame on you, Father. She needs the blood for her eggs."

He dropped the magazine and lunged at the mosquito with his bare hand.

She went back to her room, saying: "Pshaw, I thought it was burglars murdering you in your bed."

He lunged again.

FRANK ROONEY

Cyclists' Raid

JOEL BLEEKER, owner and operator of the Pendleton Hotel, was adjusting the old redwood clock in the lobby when he heard the sound of the motors. At first he thought it might be one of those four-engine planes on the flights from Los Angeles to San Francisco which occasionally got far enough off course to be heard in the valley. And for a moment, braced against the steadily approaching vibrations of the sound, he had the fantastic notion that the plane was going to strike the hotel. He even glanced at his daughter, Cathy, standing a few feet to his right and staring curiously at the street.

Then with his fingers still on the hour hand of the clock he realized that the sound was not something coming down from the air but the high, sputtering racket of many vehicles moving along the ground. Cathy and Bret Timmons, who owned one of the two drugstores in the town, went out onto the veranda but Bleeker stayed by the clock, consulting the railroad watch he pulled from his vest pocket and moving the hour hand on the clock forward a minute and a half. He stepped back deliberately, shut the glass case and looked at the huge brass numbers and the two ornate brass pointers. It was eight minutes after seven, approximately twenty-two minutes until sundown. He put the railroad watch back in his pocket and walked slowly and incuriously through the open doors of the lobby. He was methodical and orderly and the small things he did every day—like setting the clock—were important to him. He was not to be hurried—especially by something as elusively irritating as a sound, however unusual.

There were only three people on the veranda when Bleeker came out of the lobby—his daughter Cathy, Timmons, and Francis LaSalle, co-owner of LaSalle and Fleet, Hardware. They stood together quietly, looking without appearing to stare, at a long stern column of red motorcycles coming from the south, filling the single main street of the town with the noise of a multitude of pistons and the crackling of exhaust pipes. They could see now that the column was led by a single white motorcycle which when it came abreast of the hotel turned abruptly right and stopped. They saw too that the column without seeming to slow down or to execute any elaborate movement had divided itself into two single files. At the approximate second, having received a signal from their leader, they also turned right and stopped.

The whole flanking action, singularly neat and quite like the various vehicular formations he remembered in the Army, was distasteful to Bleeker. It recalled a little too readily his tenure as a lieutenant colonel overseas in England, France, and finally Germany.

"Mr. Bleeker?"

Bleeker realized the whole troop—no one in the town either then or after that night was ever agreed on the exact number of men in the troop—had dismounted and that the leader was addressing him.

"I'm Bleeker." Although he hadn't intended to, he stepped forward when he spoke, much as he had stepped forward in the years when he commanded a battalion.

"I'm Gar Simpson and this is Troop B of the Angeleno Motorcycle Club," the leader said. He was a tall, spare man and his voice was coldly courteous to the point of mockery. "We expect to bivouac outside your town tonight and we wondered if we might use the facilities of your hotel. Of course, sir, we'll pay."

"There's a washroom downstairs. If you can put up with that—"

"That will be fine, sir. Is the dining room still open?"

"It is."

"Could you take care of twenty men?"

"What about the others?"

"They can be accommodated elsewhere, sir."

Simpson saluted casually and, turning to the men assembled stiffly in front of the hotel, issued a few quiet orders. Quickly and efficiently, the men in the troop parked their motorcycles at the curb. About a third of the group detached itself and came deferentially but steadily up the hotel steps. They passed Bleeker who found himself maneuvered aside and went into the lobby. As they passed him, Bleeker could see the slight converted movement of their faces—though not their eyes, which were covered by large green goggles—toward his daughter Cathy. Bleeker frowned after them but before he could think of anything to say, Simpson, standing now at his left, touched his arm.

"I've divided the others into two groups," he said quietly. "One group will eat at the diner and the other at the Desert Hotel."

"Very good," Bleeker said. "You evidently know the town like a book. The people too. Have you ever been here before?"

"We have a map of all the towns in this part of California, sir. And of course we know the names of all the principal hotels and their proprietors. Personally, I could use a drink. Would you join me?"

"After you," Bleeker said.

He stood watching Simpson stride into the lobby and without any hesitation go directly to the bar. Then he turned to Cathy, seeing Timmons and LaSalle lounging on the railing behind her, their faces already indistinct in the plummeting California twilight.

"You go help in the kitchen, Cathy," Bleeker said. "I think it'd be better if you didn't wait on tables."

"I wonder what they look like behind those goggles," Cathy said.

"Like anybody else," Timmons said. He was about thirty, somewhat coarse and intolerant and a little embarrassed at being in love with a girl as young as Cathy. "Where did you think they came from? Mars?"

"What did they say the name of their club was?" Cathy said.

"Angeleno," LaSalle said.

"They must be from Los Angeles. Heigh-ho. Shall I wear my very best gingham, citizen colonel?"

"Remember now—you stay in the kitchen," Bleeker said.

He watched her walk into the lobby, a tall slender girl of seventeen, pretty and enigmatic, with something of the brittle independence of her mother. Bleeker remembered suddenly, although he tried not to, the way her mother had walked away from him that frosty January morning two years ago saying, "I'm going for a ride." And then the two-day search in the mountains after the horse had come back alone and the finding of her body—the neck broken—in the stream at the foot of the cliff. During the war he had never really believed that he would live to get back to Cathy's mother and after the war he hadn't really believed he would be separated from her—not again—not twice in so short a time.

Shaking his head—as if by that motion he could shed his memories as easily as a dog sheds water—Bleeker went in to join Gar Simpson who was sitting at a table in the barroom. Simpson stood politely when Bleeker took the opposite chair.

"How long do you fellows plan to stay?" Bleeker asked. He took the first sip of his drink, looked up and stared at Simpson.

"Tonight and tomorrow morning," Simpson said.

Like all the others he was dressed in a brown windbreaker, khaki shirt, khaki pants, and as Bleeker had previously observed wore dark calf-length boots. A cloth and leather helmet lay on the table beside Simpson's drink, but he hadn't removed his flat green goggles, an accouterment giving him and the men in his troop the appearance of some tropical tribe with enormous semi-precious eyes, lidless and immovable. That was Bleeker's first impression and, absurd as it was, it didn't seem an exaggeration of fancy but of truth.

"Where do you go after this?"

"North." Simpson took a rolled map from a binocular case slung over his shoulder and spread it on the table. "Roughly we're following the arc of an ellipse with its southern tip based on Los Angeles and its northern end touching Fresno."

"Pretty ambitious for a motorcycle club."

"We have a month," Simpson said. "This is our first week but we're in no hurry and we're out to see plenty of country."

"What are you interested in mainly?"

"Roads. Naturally, being a motorcycle club—you'd be surprised at the rate we're expanding—we'd like to have as much of California as possible opened up to us."

"I see."

"Keeps the boys fit too. The youth of America. Our hope for the future." Simpson pulled sternly at his drink and Bleeker had the impression that Simpson was repressing, openly, and with pride, a vast sparkling ecstasy.

Bleeker sat and watched the young men in the troop file upstairs from the public washroom and stroll casually but nevertheless with discipline into the dining room. They had removed their helmets and strapped them to their belts, each helmet in a prescribed position to the left of the belt-buckle but—like Simpson—they had retained their goggles. Bleeker wondered if they ever removed the goggles long enough to wash under them and, if they did, what the flesh under them looked like.

"I think I'd better help out at the tables." Bleeker said. He stood up and Simpson stood with him. "You say you're from Troop B? Is that right?"

"Correct. We're forming Troop G now. Someday—"

"You'll be up to Z," Bleeker said.

"And not only in California."

"Where else for instance?"

"Nevada—Arizona—Colorado—Wyoming."

Simpson smiled and Bleeker, turning away from him abruptly, went into the dining room where he began to help the two waitresses at the tables. He filled water glasses, set out extra forks, and brought steins of beer from the bar. As he served the troop, their polite thank yous, ornate and insincere, irritated him. It reminded him of tricks taught to animals, the animals only being allowed to perform under certain obvious conditions of security. And he didn't like the cool way they stared at the two waitresses, both older women and fixtures in the town and then leaned their heads together as if every individual thought had to be pooled and divided equally among them. He admitted, after some covert study, that the twenty men were really only variations of one, the variations, with few exceptions, being too subtle for him to recognize and differentiate. It was the goggles, he decided, covering that part of the face which is most noteworthy and most needful for identification—the eyes and the mask around the eyes.

Bleeker went into the kitchen, pretending to help but really to be near Cathy. The protective father, he thought ironically, watching his daughter cut pie and lay the various colored wedges on the white blue-bordered plates.

"Well, Daddy, what's the verdict?" Cathy looked extremely grave but he could see that she was amused.

"They're a fine body of men."

"Uh-huh. Have you called the police yet?"

He laughed. "It's a good thing you don't play poker."

"Child's play." She slid the last piece of blueberry pie on a plate. "I saw you through the door. You looked like you were ready to crack the Siegfried line—single-handed."

"That man Simpson."

"What about him?"

"Why don't you go upstairs and read a book or something?"

"Now, Daddy—you're the only professional here. They're just acting like little tin soldiers out on a spree."

"I wish to God they were made of tin."

"All right. I'll keep away from them. I promise." She made a gesture of crossing her throat with the thin edge of a knife. He leaned over and kissed her forehead, his hand feeling awkward and stern on her back.

After dinner the troop went into the bar, moving with a strange co-ordinated fluency that was both casual and military and sat jealously together in one corner of the room. Bleeker served them pitchers of beer and for the most part they talked quietly together, Simpson at their center, their voices guarded and urgent as if they possessed information which couldn't be disseminated safely among the public.

Bleeker left them after a while and went upstairs to his daughter's room. He wasn't used to being severe with Cathy and he was a little embarrassed by what he had said to her in the kitchen. She was turning the collars of some of his old shirts, using a portable sewing machine he had bought her as a present on her last birthday. As he came in she held one of the shirts comically to the floor lamp and he could see how thin and transparent the material was. Her mother's economy in small things, almost absurd when compared to her limitless generosity in matters of importance, had been one of the family jokes. It gave him an extraordinary sense of pleasure, so pure it was like a sudden inhalation of oxygen, to see that his daughter had not only inherited this tradition but had considered it meaningful enough to carry on. He went down the hall to his own room without saying anything further to her. Cathy was what he himself was in terms which could mean absolutely nothing to anyone else.

He had been in his room for perhaps an hour, working on the hotel accounts and thinking obliquely of the man Simpson, when he heard, faintly and apparently coming from no one direction, the sound of singing. He got up and walked to the windows overlooking the street. Standing there, he thought he could fix the sound farther up the block toward Cunningham's bar. Except for something harsh and mature in the voices it was the kind of singing that might be heard around a Boy Scout campfire, more rhythmic than melodic and more stirring than tuneful. And then he could hear it almost under his feet, coming out of the hotel lobby and making three or four people on the street turn and smile foolishly toward the doors of the veranda.

Oppressed by something sternly joyous in the voices, Bleeker went downstairs to the bar, hearing as he approached the singing become louder and fuller. Outside of Simpson and the twenty men in the troop there were only three townsmen—including LaSalle—in the bar. Simpson, seeing Bleeker in the door, got up and walked over to him, moving him out into the lobby where they could talk.

"I hope the boys aren't disturbing you," he said.

"It's early," Bleeker said.

"In an organization as large and selective as ours it's absolutely necessary to insist on a measure of discipline. And it's equally necessary to allow a certain amount of relaxation."

"The key word is selective, I suppose."

"We have our standards," Simpson said primly.

"May I ask just what the hell your standards are?"

Simpson smiled. "I don't quite understand your irritation, Mr. Bleeker."

"This is an all-year-round thing, isn't it? This club of yours?"

"Yes."

"And you have an all-year-round job with the club?"

"Of course."

"That's my objection, Simpson. Briefly and simply stated, what you're running is a private army." Bleeker tapped the case slung over Simpson's shoulder. "Complete with maps, all sorts of local information, and of course a lobby in Sacramento."

"For a man who has traveled as widely as you have, Mr. Bleeker, you display an uncommon talent for exaggeration."

"As long as you behave yourselves I don't care what you do. This is a small town and we don't have many means of entertainment. We go to bed at a decent hour and I suggest you take that into consideration. However, have your fun. Nobody here has any objections to that."

"And of course we spend our money."

"Yes," Bleeker said. "You spend your money."

He walked away from Simpson and went out onto the veranda. The singing was now both in front and in back of him. Bleeker stood for a moment on the top steps of the veranda looking at the moon, hung like a slightly soiled but luminous pennant in the sky. He was embarrassed by his outburst to Simpson and he couldn't think why he had said such things. Private army. Perhaps, as Simpson had said, he was exaggerating. He was a small-town man and he had always hated the way men surrendered their individuality to attain perfection as a unit. It had been necessary during the war but it wasn't necessary now. Kid stuff—with an element of growing pains.

He walked down the steps and went up the sidewalk toward Cunningham's bar. They were singing there too and he stood outside the big plate-glass window peering in at them and listening to the harsh, pounding voices colored here and there with the sentimentalism of strong beer. Without thinking further he went into the bar. It was dim and cool and alien to his eyes and at first he didn't notice the boy sitting by himself in a booth near the front. When he did, he was surprised—more than surprised, shocked—to see that the boy wasn't wearing his goggles but had placed them on the table by a bottle of Coca-Cola. Impulsively, he walked over to the booth and sat across from the boy.

"This seat taken?"

He had to shout over the noise of the singing. The boy leaned forward over the table and smiled.

"Hope we're not disturbing you."

Bleeker caught the word "disturbing" and shook his head negatively. He pointed to his mouth, then to the boy and to the rest of the group. The boy too shook his head. Bleeker could see that he was young, possibly twenty-five, and that he had dark straight hair cut short and parted neatly at the side. The face was square but delicate, the nose short, the mouth wide. The best thing about the boy, Bleeker decided, were his eyes, brown perhaps or dark gray, set in two distorted ovals of white flesh which contrasted sharply with the heavily tanned skin on the cheeks, forehead and jaws. With his goggles on he would have looked like the rest. Without them he was a pleasant young man, altogether human and approachable.

Bleeker pointed to the Coca-Cola bottle. "You're not drinking."

"Beer makes me sick."

Bleeker got the word "beer" and the humorous ulping motion the boy made. They sat exchanging words and sometimes phrases, illustrated always with a series of clumsy, groping gestures until the singing became less coherent and spirited and ended finally in a few isolated coughs. The men in the troop were moving about individually now, some leaning over the bar and talking in hoarse whispers to the bartender, others walking unsteadily from group to group and detaching themselves immediately to go over to another group, the groups usually two or three men constantly edging away from themselves and colliding with and being held briefly by others. Some simply stood in the center of the room and brayed dolorously at the ceiling.

Several of the troop walked out of the bar and Bleeker could see them standing on the wide sidewalk looking up and down the street—as contemptuous of one another's company as they had been glad of it earlier. Or not so much contemptuous as unwilling to be coerced too easily by any authority outside themselves. Bleeker smiled as he thought of Simpson and the man's talk of discipline.

"They're looking for women," the boy said. Bleeker had forgotten the boy temporarily and the sudden words spoken in a normal voice startled and confused him. He thought quickly of Cathy—but then Cathy was safe in her room—probably in bed. He took the watch from his vest pocket and looked at it carefully.

"Five minutes after ten," he said.

"Why do they do that?" the boy demanded. "Why do they have to be so damned indecent about things like that? They haven't got the nerve to do anything but stare at waitresses. And then they get a few beers in them and go around pinching and slapping—they—"

Bleeker shivered with embarrassment. He was looking directly into the boy's eyes and seeing the color run under the tears and the jerky pinching movement of the lids as against something injurious and baleful. It was an emotion too rawly infantile to be seen without being hurt by it and he felt both pity and contempt for a man who would allow himself to display such a feeling—without any provocation—so nakedly to a stranger.

"Sorry," the boy said.

He picked up the green goggles and fitted them awkwardly over his eyes. Bleeker stood up and looked toward the center of the room. Several of the men turned their eyes and then moved their heads away without seeming to notice the boy in the booth. Bleeker understood them. This was the one who could be approached. The reason for that was clear too. He didn't belong. Why and wherefore he would probably never know.

He walked out of the bar and started down the street toward the hotel. The night was clear and cool and smelled faintly of the desert, of sand, of heated rock, of the sweetly-sour plants growing without water and even of the sun which burned itself into the earth and never completely withdrew. There were only a few townsmen on the sidewalk wandering up and down, lured by the presence of something unusual in the town and masking, Bleeker thought, a ruthless and menacing curiosity behind a tolerant grin. He shrugged his shoulders distastefully. He was like a cat staring into a shadow the shape of its fears.

He was no more than a hundred feet from the hotel when he heard—or thought he heard—the sound of automatic firing. It was a well-remembered sound but always new and frightening.

Then he saw the motorcycle moving down the middle of the street, the exhaust sputtering loudly against the human resonance of laughter, catcalls, and epithets. He exhaled gently, the pain in his lungs subsiding with his breath. Another motorcycle speeded after the first and he could see four or five machines being wheeled out and the figures of their riders leaping into the air and bringing their weight down on the starting pedals. He was aware too that the lead motorcycles, having traversed the length of the street had turned and were speeding back to the hotel. He had the sensation of moving—even when he stood still—in relation to the objects heading toward each other. He heard the high unendurable sound of metal squeezing metal and saw the front wheel of a motorcycle twist and wobble and its rider roll along the asphalt toward the gutter where he sat up finally and moved his goggled head feebly from side to side.

As Bleeker looked around him he saw the third group of men which had divided earlier from the other two coming out of a bar across the street from Cunningham's, waving their arms in recognizable motions of cheering. The boy who had been thrown from the motorcycle vomited quietly into the gutter. Bleeker walked very fast toward the hotel. When he reached the top step of the veranda, he was caught and jostled by some five or six cyclists running out of the lobby, one of whom fell and was kicked rudely down the steps. Bleeker staggered against one of the pillars and broke a fingernail catching it. He stood there for a moment, fighting his temper, and then went into the lobby.

A table had been overthrown and lay on its top, the wooden legs stiffly and foolishly exposed, its magazines scattered around it, some with their pages spread face down so that the bindings rose along the back. He stepped on glass and realized one of the panes in the lobby door had been smashed. One of the troop walked stupidly out of the bar, his body sagging against the impetus propelling him forward until without actually falling he lay stretched on the floor, beer gushing from his mouth and nose and making a green and yellow pool before it sank into the carpet.

As Bleeker walked toward the bar, thinking of Simpson and of what he could say to him, he saw two men going up the stairs toward the second floor. He ran over to intercept them. Recognizing the authority in his voice, they came obediently down the stairs and walked across the lobby to the veranda, one of them saying over his shoulder, "Okay, pop, okay—keep your lid on." The smile they exchanged enraged him. After they were out of sight he ran swiftly up the stairs, panting a little, and along the hall to his daughter's room.

It was quiet and there was no strip of light beneath

the door. He stood listening for a moment with his ear to the panels and then turned back toward the stairs.

A man or boy, any of twenty or forty or sixty identical figures, goggled and in khaki, came around the corner of the second-floor corridor and put his hand on the knob of the door nearest the stairs. He squeezed the knob gently and then moved on to the next door, apparently unaware of Bleeker. Bleeker, remembering not to run or shout or knock the man down, walked over to him, took his arm and led him down the stairs, the arm unresisting, even flaccid, in his grip.

Bleeker stood indecisively at the foot of the stairs, watching the man walk automatically away from him. He thought he should go back upstairs and search the hall. And he thought too he had to reach Simpson. Over the noise of the motorcycles moving rapidly up and down the street he heard a crash in the bar, a series of drunken elongated curses, ending abruptly in a small sound like a man's hand laid flatly and sharply on a table.

His head was beginning to ache badly and his stomach to sour under the impact of a slow and steady anger. He walked into the bar and stood staring at Francis LaSalle —LaSalle and Fleet, Hardware—who lay sprawled on the floor, his shoulder touching the brass rail under the bar and his head turned so that his cheek rubbed the black polished wood above the rail. The bartender had his hands below the top of the bar and he was watching Simpson and a half a dozen men arranged in a loose semi-circle above and beyond LaSalle.

Bleeker lifted LaSalle, who was a little dazed but not really hurt, and set him on a chair. After he was sure LaSalle was all right he walked up to Simpson.

"Get your men together," he said. "And get them out of here."

Simpson took out a long yellow wallet folded like a book and laid some money on the bar.

"That should take care of the damages," he said. His tongue was a little thick and his mouth didn't quite shut after the words were spoken but Bleeker didn't think he was drunk. Bleeker saw too—or thought he saw—the little cold eyes behind the glasses as bright and as sterile as a painted floor. Bleeker raised his arm slightly and lifted his heels off the floor but Simpson turned abruptly and walked away from him, the men in the troop swaying at his heels like a pack of lolling hounds. Bleeker stood looking foolishly after them. He had expected a fight and his body was still poised for one. He grunted heavily.

"Who hit him?" Bleeker motioned toward LaSalle.

"Damned if I know," the bartender said. "They all look alike to me."

That was true of course. He went back into the lobby, hearing LaSalle say, weakly and tearfully, "Goddam them —the bastards." He met Campbell, the deputy sheriff, a tall man with the arms and shoulders of a child beneath a foggy, bloated face.

"Can you do anything?" Bleeker asked. The motorcycles were racing up and down the street, alternately whining and backfiring and one had jumped the curb and was cruising on the sidewalk.

"What do you want me to do?" Campbell demanded. "Put 'em all in jail?"

The motorcycle on the sidewalk speeded up and skidded obliquely into a plate-glass window, the front wheel bucking and climbing the brick base beneath the window. A single large section of glass slipped edge-down to the sidewalk and fell slowly toward the cyclist who, with his feet spread and kicking at the cement, backed clumsily away from it. Bleeker could feel the crash in his teeth.

Now there were other motorcycles on the sidewalk. One of them hit a parked car at the edge of the walk. The rider standing astride his machine beat the window out of the car with his gloved fists. Campbell started down the steps toward him but was driven back by a motocycle coming from his left. Bleeker could hear the squeal of the tires against the wooden riser at the base of the steps. Campbell's hand was on his gun when Bleeker reached him.

"That's no good," he yelled. "Get the state police. Ask for a half dozen squad cars."

Campbell, angry but somewhat relieved, went up the steps and into the lobby. Bleeker couldn't know how long he stood on the veranda watching the mounting devastation on the street—the cyclist racing past store windows and hurling, presumably, beer bottles at the glass fronts; the two, working as a team, knocking down weighing machines and the signs in front of the motion picture theater; the innumerable mounted men running the angry townspeople, alerted and aroused by the awful sounds of damage to their property, back into their suddenly lighted homes again or up the steps of his hotel or into niches along the main street, into doorways, and occasionally into the ledges and bays of glassless windows.

He saw Simpson—or rather a figure on the white motorcycle, helmeted and goggled—stationed calmly in the middle of the street under a hanging lamp. Presumably, he had been there for some time but Bleeker hadn't seen him, the many rapid movements on the street making any static object unimportant and even, in a sense, invisible. Bleeker saw him now and he felt again that spasm of anger which was like another life inside his body. He could have strangled Simpson then, slowly and with infinite pride. He knew without any effort of reason that Simpson was making no attempt to control his men but waiting rather for that moment when their minds, subdued but never actually helpless, would again take possession of their bodies.

Bleeker turned suddenly and went back into the lobby as if by that gesture of moving away he could pin his thoughts to Simpson, who, hereafter, would be responsible for them. He walked over to the desk where Timmons and Campbell, the deputy, were talking.

"You've got the authority," Timmons was saying angrily. "Fire over their heads. And if that doesn't stop them—"

Campbell looked uneasily at Bleeker. "Maybe if we could get their leader—"

"Did you get the police?" Bleeker asked.

"They're on their way," Campbell said. He avoided looking at Timmons and continued to stare hopefully and miserably at Bleeker.

"You've had your say," Timmons said abruptly. "Now I'll have mine."

He started for the lobby door but Campbell, suddenly incensed, grabbed his arm.

"You leave this to me," he said. "You start firing a gun—"

Campbell's mouth dropped and Bleeker, turning his head, saw the two motorcycles coming through the lobby doors. They circled leisurely around for a moment and then one of them shot suddenly toward them, the goggled rider looming enormously above the wide handlebars. They scattered, Bleeker diving behind a pillar and Campbell and Timmons jumping behind the desk. The noise of the two machines assaulted them with as much effect as the sight of the speeding metal itself.

Bleeker didn't know why in course of watching the two riders he looked into the hall toward the foot of the stairway. Nor did it seem at all unreasonable that when he looked he should see Cathy standing there. Deeply, underneath the outward preoccupation of his mind, he must have been thinking of her. Now there she was. She wore the familiar green robe, belted and pulled in at the waist and beneath its hem he could see the white slippers and the pink edge of her nightgown. Her hair was down and he had the impression her eyes were not quite open although, obviously, they were. She looked, he thought, as if she had waked, frowned at the clock, and come downstairs to scold him for staying up too late. He had no idea what time it was.

He saw—and of course Cathy saw—the motorcycle speeding toward her. He was aware that he screamed at her too. She did take a slight backward step and raise her arms in a pathetic warding gesture toward the inhuman figure on the motorcycle but neither could have changed —in that dwarfed period of time and in that short, unmaneuverable space—the course of their actions.

She lay finally across the lower steps, her body clinging to and equally arching away from the base of the newel post. And there was the sudden, shocking exposure of her flesh, the robe and the gown torn away from the leg as if pushed aside by the blood welling from her thigh. When he reached her there was blood in her hair too and someone—not Cathy—was screaming into his ears.

After a while the doctor came and Cathy, her head bandaged and her leg in splints, could be carried into his office and laid on the couch. Bleeker sat on the edge of the couch, his hand over Cathy's watching the still white face whose eyes were closed and would not, he knew, open again. The doctor, after his first examination, had looked up quickly and since Bleeker too had been bent over Cathy, their heads had been very close together for a moment. The doctor had assumed, almost immediately, his expression of professional austerity but Bleeker had seen him in that moment when he had been thinking as a man, fortified of course by a doctor's knowledge, and Bleeker had known then that Cathy would die but that there would be also this interval of time.

Bleeker turned from watching Cathy and saw Timmons standing across the room. The man was—or had been—crying but his face wasn't set for it and the tears, points of colorless, sparkling water on his jaws, were unexpectedly delicate against the coarse texture of his skin. Timmons waved a bandaged hand awkwardly and Bleeker remembered, abruptly and jarringly, seeing Timmons diving for the motorcycle which had reversed itself, along with the other, and raced out of the lobby.

There was no sound now either from the street or the lobby. It was incredible, thinking of the racket a moment ago, that there should be this utter quietude, not only the lack of noise but the lack of the vibration of movement. The doctor came and went, coming to bend over Cathy and then going away again. Timmons stayed. Beyond shifting his feet occasionally he didn't move at all but stood patiently across the room, his face toward Cathy and Bleeker but not, Bleeker thought once when he looked up, actually seeing them.

"The police," Bleeker said sometime later.

"They're gone," Timmons said in a hoarse whisper. And then after a while, "They'll get 'em—don't worry."

Bleeker saw that the man blushed helplessly and looked away from him. The police were no good. They would catch Simpson. Simpson would pay damages. And that would be the end of it. Who could identify Cathy's assailant? Not himself, certainly—nor Timmons nor Campbell. They were all alike. They were standardized figurines, seeking in each other a willful loss of identity, dividing themselves equally among one another until there was only a single mythical figure, unspeakably sterile and furnishing the norm for hundreds of others. He could not accuse something which didn't actually exist.

He wasn't sure of the exact moment when Cathy died. It might have been when he heard the motorcycle, unbelievably solitary in the quiet night, approaching the town. He knew only that the doctor came for the last time and that there was now a coarse, heavy blanket laid mercifully over Cathy. He stood looking down at the blanket for a moment, whatever he was feeling repressed and delayed inside him, and then went back to the lobby and out onto the veranda. There were a dozen men standing there looking up the street toward the sound of the motorcycle steadily but slowly coming nearer. He saw that when they glanced at each other their faces were hard and angry but when they looked at him they were respectful and a little abashed.

Bleeker could see from the veranda a number of people moving among the smashed store-fronts, moving, stopping, bending over and then straightening up to move somewhere else, all dressed somewhat extemporaneously and therefore seeming without purpose. What they picked up they put down. What they put down they stared at grimly and then picked up again. They were like a dispossessed minority brutally but lawfully discriminated against. When the motorcycle appeared at the north end of the street they looked at it and then looked away again, dully and seemingly without resentment.

It was only after some moments that they looked up again, this time purposefully, and began to move slowly toward the hotel where the motorcycle had now stopped, the rider standing on the sidewalk, his face raised to the veranda.

No one on the veranda moved until Bleeker, after a visible effort, walked down the steps and stood facing the rider. It was the boy Bleeker had talked to in the bar. The goggles and helmet were hanging at his belt.

"I couldn't stand it any longer," the boy said. "I had to come back."

He looked at Bleeker as if he didn't dare look anywhere else. His face was adolescently shiny and damp, the marks, Bleeker thought, of a proud and articulate fear. He should have been heroic in his willingness to come back to the town after what had been done to it but to Bleeker he was only a dirty little boy returning to a back fence his friends had defaced with pornographic writing and calling attention to the fact that he was afraid to erase the writing but was determined nevertheless to do it. Bleeker was revolted. He hated the boy far more than he could have hated Simpson for bringing this to his attention when he did not want to think of anything or anyone but Cathy.

"I wasn't one of them," the boy said. "You remember, Mr. Bleeker. I wasn't drinking."

This declaration of innocence—this willingness to take blame for acts which he hadn't committed—enraged Bleeker.

"You were one of them," he said.

"Yes. But after tonight—"

"Why didn't you stop them?" Bleeker demanded loudly. He felt the murmur of the townspeople at his back and someone breathed harshly on his neck. "You were one of them. You could have done something. Why in God's name didn't you do it?"

"What could I do?" the boy said. He spread his hands and stepped back as if to appeal to the men beyond Bleeker.

Bleeker couldn't remember, either shortly after or much later, exactly what he did then. If the boy hadn't stepped back like that—if he hadn't raised his hand. . . . Bleeker was in the middle of a group of bodies and he was striking with his fist and being struck. And then he was kneeling on the sidewalk, holding the boy's head in his lap and trying to protect him from the heavy shoes of the men around him. He was crying out, protesting, exhorting, and after a time the men moved away from him and someone helped him carry the boy up the steps and lay him on the veranda. When he looked up finally only Timmons and the doctor were there. Up and down the street there were now only shadows and the diminishing sounds of invisible bodies. The night was still again as abruptly as it had been confounded with noise.

Some time later Timmons and the doctor carried the boy, alive but terribly hurt, into the hotel. Bleeker sat on the top step of the veranda, staring at the moon which had shifted in the sky and was now nearer the mountains in the west. It was not in any sense romantic or inflamed but coldly clear and sane. And the light it sent was cold and sane and lit in himself what he would have liked to hide.

He could have said that having lost Cathy he was not afraid any longer of losing himself. No one would blame him. Cathy's death was his excuse for striking the boy, hammering him to the sidewalk, and stamping on him as he had never believed he could have stamped on any living thing. No one would say he should have lost Cathy lightly—without anger and without that appalling desire to avenge her. It was utterly natural—as natural as a man drinking a few beers and riding a motorcycle insanely through a town like this. Bleeker shuddered. It might have been all right for a man like Timmons who was and would always be incapable of thinking what he—Joel Bleeker—was thinking. It was not—and would never be—all right for him.

Bleeker got up and stood for a moment on the top step of the veranda. He wanted, abruptly and madly, to scream his agony into the night with no more restraint than that of an animal seeing his guts beneath him on the ground. He wanted to smash something—anything—glass, wood, stone—his own body. He could feel his fists going into the boy's flesh. And there was that bloody but living thing on the sidewalk and himself stooping over to shield it.

After a while, aware that he was leaning against one of the wooden pillars supporting the porch and aware too that his flesh was numb from being pressed against it, he straightened up slowly and turned to go back into the hotel.

There would always be time to make his peace with the dead. There was little if any time to make his peace with the living.

IRWIN SHAW

The Dry Rock

"WE'RE LATE," Helen said, as the cab stopped at a light. "We're twenty minutes late." She looked at her husband accusingly.

"All right," Fitzsimmons said. "I couldn't help it. The work was on the desk and it had to . . ."

"This is the one dinner party of the year I didn't want to be late for," Helen said. "So naturally . . ."

The cab started and was halfway across the street when the Ford sedan roared into it, twisting, with a crashing and scraping of metal, a high mournful scream of brakes, the tinkling of glass. The cab shook a little, then subsided.

The cabby, a little gray man, turned and looked back, worriedly. "Everybody is all right?" he asked nervously.

"Everybody is fine," Helen said bitterly, pulling at her cape to get it straight again after the jolting.

"No damage done," said Fitzsimmons, smiling reassuringly at the cabby, who looked very frightened.

"I am happy to hear that," the cabby said. He got out of his car and stood looking sadly at his fender, now thoroughly crumpled, and his headlight, now without a lens. The door of the Ford opened and its driver sprang out. He was a large young man with a light gray hat. He glanced hurriedly at the cab.

"Why don't yuh watch where the hell yer goin'?" he asked harshly.

"The light was in my favor," said the cabby. He was a small man of fifty, in a cap and a ragged coat, and he spoke with a heavy accent. "It turned green and I started across. I would like your license, Mister."

"What for?" the man in the gray hat shouted. "Yer load's all right. Get on yer way. No harm done." He started back to his car.

The cabby gently put his hand on the young man's arm. "Excuse me, friend," he said. "It is a five-dollar job, at least. I would like to see your license."

The young man pulled his arm away, glared at the cabby. "Aaah," he said and swung. His fist made a loud surprising noise against the cabby's nose. The old man sat down slowly on the running board of his cab, holding his head wearily in his hands. The young man in the gray hat stood over him, bent over, fists still clenched. "Didn't I tell yuh no harm was done?" he shouted. "Why didn't yuh lissen t'me? I got a good mind to . . ."

"Now, see here," Fitzsimmons said, opening the rear door and stepping out.

"What d'*you* want?" The young man turned and snarled at Fitzsimmons, his fists held higher. "Who asked for *you?*"

"I saw the whole thing," Fitzsimmons began, "and I don't think you . . ."

"Aaah," snarled the young man. "Dry up."

"Claude," Helen called. "Claude, keep out of this."

"Claude," the young man repeated balefully. "Dry up, Claude."

"Are you all right?" Fitzsimmons asked, bending over the cabby, who still sat reflectively on the running board, his head down, his old and swollen cap hiding his face, blood trickling down his clothes.

"I'm all right," the cabby said wearily. He stood up, looked wonderingly at the young man. "Now, my friend, you force me to make trouble. Police!" he called, loudly. *"Police!"*

"Say lissen," the man in the gray hat shouted. "What the hell do yuh need to call the cops for? Hey, cut it out!"

"Police!" the old cabby shouted calmly, but with fervor deep in his voice. "Police!"

"I ought to give it to yuh good." The young man shook his fist under the cabby's nose. He jumped around nervously. "This is a small matter," he shouted, "nobody needs the cops!"

"Police!" called the cabby.

"Claude." Helen put her head out the window, "Let's get out of here and let the two gentlemen settle this any way they please."

"I apologize!" The young man held the cabby by his lapels with both large hands, shook him, to emphasize his apology. "Excuse me. I'm sorry. Stop yelling police, for God's sake!"

"I'm going to have you locked up," the cabby said. He stood there, slowly drying the blood off his shabby coat with his cap. His hair was gray, but long and full, like a musician's. He had a big head for his little shoulders, and a sad, lined little face and he looked older than fifty, to Fitzsimmons, and very poor, neglected, badly nourished. "You have committed a crime," the cabby said, "and there is a punishment for it."

"Will yuh talk to him?" The young man turned savagely to Fitzsimmons. "Will yuh tell him I'm sorry?"

"It's entirely up to him," Fitzsimmons said.

"We're a half hour late," Helen announced bitterly. "The perfect dinner guest."

"It's not enough to be sorry," said the cab driver. *"Police . . ."*

"Say, lissen, Bud," the young man said, his voice quick and confidential, "what's yer name?"

"Leopold Tarloff," the cabby said. "I have been driving a cab on the streets of New York for twenty years and everybody thinks just because you're a cab driver they can do whatever they want to you."

"Lissen, Leopold," the young man pushed his light gray hat far back on his head. "Let's be sensible. I hit yer cab. All right. I hit you. All right."

"What's all right about it?" Tarloff asked.

"What I mean is, I admit it, I confess I did it, that's what I mean. All right." The young man grabbed Tarloff's short ragged arms as he spoke intensely. "Why the fuss? It happens every day. Police are unnecessary. I'll tell yuh what I'll do with yuh, Leopold. Five dollars, yuh say, for the fender. All right. And for the bloody nose, another pound. What do yuh say? Everybody is satisfied. Yuh've made yerself a fiver on the transaction; these good people go to their party without no more delay."

Tarloff shook his arms free from the huge hands of the man in the gray hat. He put his head back and ran his fingers through his thick hair and spoke coldly. "I don't want to hear another word. I have never been so insulted in my whole life."

The young man stepped back, his arms wide, palms up wonderingly. "I insult him!" He turned to Fitzsimmons. "Did you hear me insult this party?" he asked.

"Claude!" Helen called. "Are we going to sit here all night?"

"A man steps up and hits me in the nose," Tarloff said. "He thinks he makes everything all right with five dollars. He is mistaken. Not with five hundred dollars."

"How much d'yuh think a clap in the puss is worth?" the young man growled. "Who d'yuh think y'are—Joe Louis?"

"Not ten thousand dollars," Tarloff said, on the surface calm, but quivering underneath. "Not for twenty thousand dollars. My dignity."

"His dignity!" the young man whispered. "For Christ's sake!"

"What do you want to do?" Fitzsimmons asked, conscious of Helen glooming in the rear seat of the cab.

"I would like to take him to the station house and make a complaint," Tarloff said. "You would have to come with me, if you'd be so kind. What is your opinion on the matter?"

"Will yuh tell him the cops are not a necessity!" the young man said hoarsely. "Will yuh tell the bastidd?"

"Claude!" called Helen.

"It's up to you," Fitzsimmons said, looking with what he hoped was an impartial, judicious expression at Tarloff, hoping he wouldn't have to waste any more time. "You do what you think you ought to do."

Tarloff smiled, showing three yellow teeth in the front of his small and childlike mouth, curved and red and surprising in the lined and weatherbeaten old hackie's face. "Thank you very much," he said "I am glad to see you agree with me."

Fitzsimmons sighed.

"Yer drivin' me crazy!" the young man shouted at Tarloff. "Yer makin' life impossible!"

"To you," Tarloff said with dignity, "I talk from now on only in a court of law. That's my last word."

The young man stood there, breathing heavily, his fists clenching and unclenching, his pale gray hat shining in the light of a street lamp. A policeman turned the corner, walking in a leisurely and abstracted manner, his eyes on the legs of a girl across the street.

Fitzsimmons went over to him. "Officer," he said, "there's a little job for you over here." The policeman regretfully took his eyes off the girl's legs and sighed and walked slowly over to where the two cars were still nestling against each other.

"What are yuh?" the young man was asking Tarloff, when Fitzsimmons came up with the policeman. "Yuh don't act like an American citizen. What are yuh?"

"I'm a Russian," Tarloff said. "But I'm in the country twenty-five years now, I know what the rights of an individual are."

"Yeah," said the young man hopelessly. "Yeah . . ."

The Fitzsimmonses drove silently to the police station in the cab, with Tarloff driving slowly and carefully, though with hands that shook on the wheel. The policeman drove with the young man in the young man's Ford. Fitzsimmons saw the Ford stop at a cigar store and the young man jump out and go into the store, into a telephone booth.

"For three months," Helen said, as they drove, "I've been trying to get Adele Lowrie to invite us to dinner. Now we've finally managed it. Perhaps we ought to call her and invite the whole party down to night court."

"It isn't night court," Fitzsimmons said patiently "It's a police station. And I think you might take it a little better. After all, the poor old man has no one else to speak up for him."

"Leopold Tarloff," Helen said. "It sounds impossible. Leopold Tarloff. Leopold Tarloff."

They sat in silence until Tarloff stopped the cab in front of the police station and opened the door for them.

The Ford with the policeman and the young man drove up right behind them and they all went in together.

There were some people up in front of the desk lieutenant, a dejected-looking man with long mustaches and a loud, blonde woman who kept saying that the man had threatened her with a baseball bat three times that evening. Two Negroes with bloody bandages around their heads were waiting, too.

"It will take some time," said the policeman. "There are two cases ahead of you. My name is Kraus."

"Oh, my," said Helen.

"You'd better call Adele," Fitzsimmons said. "Tell her not to hold dinner for us."

Helen held her hand out gloomily for nickels.

"I'm sorry," Tarloff said anxiously, "to interrupt your plans for the evening."

"Perfectly all right," Fitzsimmons said, trying to screen his wife's face from Tarloff by bending over to search for the nickels in his pocket.

Helen went off, disdainfully holding her long formal skirt up with her hand, as she walked down the spit- and butt-marked corridor of the police station toward a pay telephone. Fitzsimmons reflectively watched her elegant back retreat down the hallway.

"I am tired," Tarloff said. "I think I will have to sit down, if you will excuse me." He sat on the floor, looking up with a frail apologetic smile on his red face worn by wind and rain and traffic-policemen. Fitzsimmons suddenly felt like crying, watching the old man sitting there among the spit and cigarette butts, on the floor against the wall, with his cap off and his great bush of musician's gray hair giving the lie to the tired, weathered face below it.

Four men threw open the outside doors and walked into the police station with certainty and authority. They all wore the same light-gray hats with the huge flat brims. The young man who had hit Tarloff greeted them guardedly. "I'm glad you're here, Pidgear," he said to the man who, by some subtle mixture of stance and clothing, of lift of eyebrow and droop of mouth, announced himself as leader.

They talked swiftly and quietly in a corner.

"A Russian!" Pidgear's voice rang out angrily. "There are 10,000 cab drivers in the metropolitan area, you have to pick a Russian to punch in the nose!"

"I'm excitable!" the young man yelled. "Can I help it if I'm excitable? My father was the same way; it's a family characteristic."

"Go tell that to the Russian," Pidgear said. He went over to one of the three men who had come in with him, a large man who needed a shave and whose collar was open at the throat, as though no collar could be bought large enough to go all the way around that neck. The large man nodded, went over to Tarloff, still sitting patiently against the wall.

"You speak Russian?" the man with the open collar said to Tarloff.

"Yes, sir," Tarloff said.

The large man sat down slowly beside him, gripped Tarloff's knee confidentially in his tremendous hairy hand, spoke excitedly, winningly, in Russian.

Pidgear and the young man who had hit Tarloff came over to Fitzsimmons, leaving the two other men in the gray hats, small, dark men with shining eyes, who just stood at the door and looked hotly on.

"My name is Pidgear," the man said to Fitzsimmons, who by now was impressed with the beautiful efficiency of the system that had been put into motion by the young driver of the Ford—an obviously legal mind like Pidgear, a man who spoke Russian, and two intense men with gray hats standing on call just to see justice done, and all collected in the space of fifteen minutes. "Alton Pidgear," the man said, smiling professionally at Fitzsimmons. "I represent Mr. Rusk."

"Yeah," said the young man.

"My name is Fitzsimmons."

"Frankly, Mr. Fitzsimmons," Pidgear said, "I would like to see you get Mr. Tarloff to call this whole thing off. It's an embarrassing affair for all concerned; nobody stands to gain anything by pressing it."

Helen came back and Fitzsimmons saw by the expression on her face that she wasn't happy. "They're at the soup by now," she said loudly to Fitzsimmons. "Adele said for us to take all the time we want, they're getting along fine."

"Mr. Rusk is willing to make a handsome offer," Pidgear said. "Five dollars for the car, five dollars for the nose . . ."

"Go out to dinner with your husband," Helen muttered, "and you wind up in a telephone booth in a police station. 'Excuse me for being late, darling, but I'm calling from the 8th precinct, this is our night for street-fighting.' "

"Sssh, Helen, please," Fitzsimmons said. He hadn't eaten since nine that morning and his stomach was growling with hunger.

"It was all a mistake," Pidgear said smoothly. "A natural mistake. Why should the man be stubborn? He is being reimbursed for everything, isn't he? I wish you would talk to him, Mr. Fitzsimmons; we don't want to keep you from your social engagements. Undoubtedly," Pidgear said, eyeing their evening clothes respectfully, "you and the madam were going to an important dinner party. It would be too bad to spoil an important dinner party for a little thing like this. Why, this whole affair is niggling," he said, waving his hand in front of Fitzsimmons' face. "Absolutely niggling."

Fitzsimmons looked over to where Tarloff and the other Russian were sitting on the floor. From Tarloff's face and gestures, even though he was talking in deepest Russian, Fitzsimmons could tell Tarloff was still as firm as ever. Fitzsimmons looked closely at Rusk, who was standing looking at Tarloff through narrow, baleful eyes.

"Why're you so anxious?" Fitzsimmons asked.

Rusk's eyes clouded over and his throat throbbed against his collar with rage. "I don't want to appear in court!" he yelled. "I don't want the whole goddamn business to start all over again, investigation, lawyers, fingerprints . . ."

Pidgear punched him savagely in the ribs, his fist going a short distance, but with great violence.

"Why don't you buy time on the National Broadcasting System?" Pidgear asked. "Make an address, coast to coast!"

Rusk glared murderously for a moment at Pidgear, then leaned over toward Fitzsimmons, pointing a large blunt finger at him. "Do I have to put my finger in your mouth?" he whispered hoarsely.

"What does he mean by that?" Helen asked loudly. "Put his finger in your mouth? Why should he put his finger in your mouth?"

Rusk looked at her with complete hatred, turned, too full for words, and stalked away, with Pidgear after him. The two little men in the gray hats watched the room without moving.

"Claude?" Helen began.

"Obviously," Fitzsimmons said, his voice low, "Mr. Rusk isn't anxious for anyone to look at his fingerprints. He's happier this way."

"You picked a fine night!" Helen shook her head sadly. "Why can't we just pick up and get out of here?"

Rusk, with Pidgear at his side, strode back. He stopped in front of the Fitzsimmonses. "I'm a family man," he said, trying to sound like one. "I ask yuh as a favor. Talk to the Russian."

"I had to go to Bergdorf Goodman," Helen said, too deep in her own troubles to bother with Rusk, "to get a gown to spend the evening in a police station. 'Mrs. Claude Fitzsimmons was lovely last night in blue velvet and silver fox at Officer Kraus's reception at the 8th Precinct. Other guests were the well-known Leopold Tarloff, and the Messrs. Pidgear and Rusk, in gray hats. Other guests included the Russian Ambassador and two leading Italian artillerymen, also in gray hats.' "

Pidgear laughed politely. "Your wife is a very witty woman," he said.

"Yes," said Fitzsimmons, wondering why he'd married her.

"Will yuh for Christ's sake *ask?*" Rusk demanded. "Can it hurt yuh?"

"We're willing to do our part," Pidgear said. "We even brought down a Russian to talk to him and clear up any little points in his own language. No effort is too great."

Fitzsimmons' stomach growled loudly. "Haven't eaten all day," he said, embarrassed.

"That's what happens," Pidgear said. "Naturally."

"Yeah," said Rusk.

"Perhaps I should go out and get you a malted milk," Helen suggested coldly.

Fitzsimmons went over to where Tarloff was sitting with the other Russian. The others followed him.

"Are you sure, Mr. Tarloff," Fitzsimmons said, "that you still want to prosecute?"

"Yes," Tarloff said promptly.

"Ten dollars," Rusk said. "I offer yuh ten dollars. Can a man do more?"

"Money is not the object." With his cap Tarloff patted his nose which was still bleeding slowly and had swelled enormously, making Tarloff look lopsided and monstrous.

"What's the object?" Rusk asked.

"The object, Mr. Rusk, is principle."

"*You* talk to him," Rusk said to Fitzsimmons.

"All right," Officer Kraus said, "you can go up there now."

They all filed up in front of the lieutenant sitting high at his desk.

Tarloff told his story, the accident, the wanton punch in the nose.

"It's true," Pidgear said, "that there was an accident, that there was a slight scuffle after by mistake. But the man isn't hurt. A little swelling in the region of the nose. No more." He pointed dramatically to Tarloff.

"Physically," Tarloff said, clutching his cap, talking with difficulty because his nose was clogged, "physically that's true. I am not badly hurt. But in a mental sense . . ." He shrugged. "I have suffered an injury."

"Mr. Rusk is offering the amount of ten dollars." Pidgear said. "Also, he apologizes; he's sorry."

The lieutenant looked wearily down at Rusk. "Are you sorry?" he asked.

"I'm sorry," said Rusk, raising his right hand. "On the Bible, I swear I'm sorry."

"Mr. Tarloff," the lieutenant said, "if you wish to press charges, there are certain steps you will have to take. A deposition will have to be taken. Have you got witnesses?"

"Here," Tarloff said with a shy smile at the Fitzsimmonses

"They will have to be present," the lieutenant said sleepily.

"Oh, God," Helen said.

"A warrant will have to be sworn out, there must be a hearing at which the witnesses must also be present . . ."

"Oh, God," Helen said.

"Then the trial," said the lieutenant.

"Oh, God!" Helen said loudly.

"The question is, Mr. Tarloff," said the lieutenant, yawning, "are you willing to go through all that trouble?"

"The fact is," Tarloff said unhappily, "he hit me in the head without provocation. He is guilty of a crime on my person. He insulted me. He did me an injustice. The law exists for such things. One individual is not to be hit by another individual in the streets of the city without legal punishment." Tarloff was using his hands to try to get everyone, the Fitzsimmonses, the lieutenant, Pidgear, to understand. "There is a principle. The dignity of the human body. Justice. For a bad act a man suffers. It's an important thing . . ."

"I'm excitable," Rusk shouted. "If yuh want, yuh can hit me in the head."

"That is not the idea," Tarloff said.

"The man is sorry," the lieutenant said, wiping his eyes, "he is offering you the sum of ten dollars; it will be a long, hard job to bring this man to trial; it will cost a lot of the taxpayers' money; you are bothering these good people here who have other things to do. What is the sense in it, Mr. Tarloff?"

Tarloff scraped his feet slowly on the dirty floor, looked sadly, hopefully, at Fitzsimmons. Fitzsimmons looked at his wife, who was glaring at Tarloff, tapping her foot sharply again and again. Fitzsimmons looked back at Tarloff, standing there, before the high desk, small, in his ragged coat and wild gray hair, his little worn face twisted and grotesque with the swollen nose, his eyes lost and appealing. Fitzsimmons shrugged sadly. Tarloff drooped inside his old coat, shook his head wearily, shrugged, deserted once and for all before the lieutenant's desk, on the dry rock of principle.

"O.K.," he said.

"Here." Rusk brought the ten-dollar bill out with magical speed.

Tarloff pushed it away. "Get out of here," he said, without looking up.

No one talked all the way to Adele Lowrie's house. Tarloff opened the door and sat, looking straight ahead, while they got out. Helen went to the door of the house and rang. Silently, Fitzsimmons offered Tarloff the fare. Tarloff shook his head. "You have been very good," he said. "Forget it."

Fitzsimmons put the money away slowly.

"Claude!" Helen called. "The door's open."

Fitzsimmons hated his wife, suddenly, without turning to look at her. He put out his hand and Tarloff shook it wearily.

"I'm awfully sorry," Fitzsimmons said. "I wish I . . ."

Tarloff shrugged. "That's all right," he said. "I understand." His face, in the shabby light of the cab, worn and old and battered by the streets of the city, was a deep well of sorrow. "There is no time. Principle." He laughed, shrugged. "Today there is no time for anything."

He shifted gears and the taxi moved slowly off, its motor grinding noisily.

"Claude!" Helen called.

"Oh, shut up!" Fitzsimmons said as he turned and walked into Adele Lowrie's house.

THOMAS WOLFE

Dark in the Forest, Strange as Time

SOME years ago, among the people standing on one of the platforms of the Munich railway station, beside the Swiss express, which was almost ready to depart, there were a woman and a man—a woman so lovely that the memory of her would forever haunt the mind of him who saw her, and a man on whose dark face the legend of a strange and fatal meeting was already visible.

The woman was at the flawless summit of a mature and radiant beauty, packed to the last red ripeness of her lip with life and health, a miracle of loveliness in whom all the elements of beauty had combined with such exquisite proportion and so rhythmical a balance that even as one looked at her he could scarcely believe the evidence of his eyes.

Thus, although not over tall, she seemed at times to command a superb and queenly height, then to be almost demurely small and cosy as she pressed close to her companion. Again, her lovely figure seemed never to have lost the lithe slenderness of girlhood, yet it was ripe, lavish, undulant with all the voluptuous maturity of womanhood, and every movement she made was full of seductive grace.

The woman was fashionably dressed; her little toque-like hat fitted snugly down over a crown of coppery reddish hair and shaded her eyes which had a smoke-blue and depthless quality that could darken almost into black, and change with every swiftest shade of feeling that passed across her face. She was talking to the man in low and tender tones, smiling a vague voluptuous smile as she looked at him. She spoke eagerly, earnestly, gleefully to him, and from time to time burst into a little laugh that came welling low, rich, sensual, and tender from her throat.

As they walked up and down the platform talking, the woman thrust her small gloved hand through the arm of his heavy overcoat and snuggled close to him, sometimes nestling her lovely head, which was as proud and graceful as a flower, against his arm. Again they would pause, and look steadfastly at each other for a moment. Now she spoke to him with playful reproof, chided him, shook him tenderly by the arms, pulled the heavy furred lapels of his overcoat together, and wagged a small gloved finger at him warningly.

And all the time the man looked at her, saying little, but devouring her with large dark eyes that were burning steadily with the fires of death, and that seemed to feed on her physically, with an insatiate and voracious tenderness of love. He was a Jew, his figure immensely tall, cadaverous, and so wasted by disease that it was lost, engulfed, forgotten in the heavy and expensive garments that he wore.

His thin white face, which was wasted almost to a fleshless integument of bone and skin, converged to an immense hooked nose, so that his face was not so much a face as a great beak of death, lit by two blazing and voracious eyes and colored on the flanks with two burning flags of red. Yet, with all its ugliness of disease and emaciation it was a curiously memorable and moving face, a visage somehow nobly tragic with the badge of death.

But now the time had come for parting. The guards were shouting warnings to the passengers, all up and down the platform there were swift serried movements, hurried eddyings among the groups of friends. One saw people embracing, kissing, clasping hands, crying, laughing, shouting, going back for one hard swift kiss, and then mounting hastily into their compartments. And one heard in a strange tongue the vows, oaths, promises, the jests and swift allusions, that were secret and precious to each group and that sent them off at once in roars of laughter, the words of farewell that are the same the whole world over:

"Otto! Otto! . . . Have you got what I gave you? . . . Feel! Is it still there?" He felt, it was still there: fits of laughter.

"Will you see Else?"

"How's that? Can't hear"—shouting, cupping hand to ear, and turning head sideways with a puzzled look.

"I—say—will—you—see—Else?" fairly roared out between cupped palms above the tumult of the crowd.

"Yes. I think so. We expect to meet them at St. Moritz."

"Tell her she's got to write."

"Hey? I can't hear you." Same pantomime as before.

"I—say—tell—her—she's got—to write"—another roar.

"Oh, yes! Yes!" Nodding quickly, smiling, "I'll tell her."

"—or I'll be mad at her!"

"What? Can't hear you for all this noise"—same business as before.

"I—say—tell—her—I'll—be—mad—if she—doesnt'—write" roared out again deliberately at the top of his lungs.

Here, a man who had been whispering slyly to a woman, who was trembling with smothered laughter, now turned with grinning face to shout something at the departing friend, but was checked by the woman who seized him by the arm and with a face reddened by laughter, gasped hysterically.

"No! No!"

But the man, still grinning, cupped his hands around his mouth and roared:

"Tell Uncle Walter he has got to wear his——"

"How's that? Can't hear!"—cupping ear and turning head to one side as before.

"I—say," the man began to roar deliberately.

"No! No! No! Sh-h!" the woman gasped frantically, tugging at his arm.

"—to—tell—Uncle Walter—he—must—wear—his woolen——"

"No! No! No!—Heinrich! . . . Sh-h!" the woman shrieked.

"—The—heavy—ones—Aunt—Bertha embroidered with his—initials'" the man went on relentlessly.

Here the whole crowd roared, and the women screamed with laughter, shrieking protests, and saying:

"Sh-h! Sh-h!" loudly.

"Ja—I'll tell him!" the grinning passenger yelled back at him as soon as they had grown somewhat quieter. "Maybe—he hasn't—got—'em—any—more," he shouted as a happy afterthought. "Maybe—one—of—the—Fräuleins—down—there—" he gasped and choked with laughter.

"Otto!" the women shrieked. "Sh-h!"

"Maybe—one—of—the—Fräuleins—got them—away—from"—he began to gasp with laughter.

"O-o-o-t-to! . . . Shame on you—Sh-h!" the women screamed.

"Souvenir—from—old—München," roared back his fellow wit, and the whole group was convulsed again. When they had recovered somewhat, one of the men began in a wheezing and faltering tone, as he wiped at his streaming eyes:

"Tell—Else"—here his voice broke off in a feeble squeak, and he had to pause to wipe his eyes again.

"What?"—the grinning passenger yelled back at him.

"Tell—Else," he began again more strongly, "that Aunt—Bertha—oh! my God!" he groaned weakly again, faltered, wiped at his streaming eyes, and was reduced to palsied silence.

"What?—What?" shouted the grinning passenger sharply, clapping his hand to his attentive ear. "Tell Else what?"

"Tell—Else—Aunt—Bertha—is—sending—her—recipe—for—layer—cake," the man fairly screamed now as if he would get it out at any cost before his impending and total collapse. The total effect of that apparently meaningless reference to Aunt Bertha's layer cake was astonishing: nothing that had gone before could approach the spasmodic effect it had upon this little group of friends. They were instantly reduced to a shuddering paralysis of laughter, they staggered drunkenly about, clasped one another feebly for support, tears streamed in torrents from their swollen eyes, and from their wide-open mouths there came occasionally feeble wisps of sound, strangled gasps, faint screams from the women, a panting palsied fit of mirth from which they finally emerged into a kind of hiccoughing recovery.

What it was—the total implication of that apparently banal reference which had thrown them all into such a convulsive fit of merriment—no stranger could ever know, but its effect upon the other people was infectious; they looked toward the group of friends, and grinned, laughed, and shook their heads at one another. And so it went all up and down the line. Here were people grave, gay, sad, serious, young, old, calm, casual, and excited; here were people bent on business and people bent on pleasure; here people sharing by every act, word, and gesture the excitement, joy, and hope which the voyage wakened in them, and people who looked wearily and indifferently about them, settled themselves in their seats and took no further interest in the events of the departure—but everywhere it was the same.

People were speaking the universal language of departure, that varies not all the whole world over—that language which is often banal, trivial, and even useless, but on this account curiously moving, since it serves to hide a deeper emotion in the hearts of men, to fill the vacancy that is in their hearts at the thought of parting, to act as a shield, a concealing mask to their true feeling.

And because of this there was for the youth, the stranger, and the alien who saw and heard these things, a thrilling and poignant quality in the ceremony of the train's departure. As he saw and heard these familiar words and actions—words and actions that beneath the guise of an alien tongue were identical to those he had seen and known all his life, among his own people—he felt suddenly, as he had never felt before, the overwhelming loneliness of familiarity, the sense of the human identity that so strongly unites all the people in the world, and that is rooted in the structure of man's life, far below the tongue he speaks, the race of which he is a member.

But now that the time had come for parting, the woman and the dying man said nothing. Clasped arm to arm they looked at each other with a stare of burning and voracious tenderness. They embraced, her arms clasped him, her living and voluptuous body drew toward him, her red lips clung to his mouth as if she could never let him go. Finally, she fairly tore herself away from him, gave him a desperate little push with her hands, and said, "Go, go! It's time!"

Then the scarecrow turned and swiftly climbed into the train, a guard came by and brutally slammed the door behind him, the train began to move slowly out of the station. And all the time the man was leaning from a window in the corridor looking at her, and the woman was walking along beside the train, trying to keep him in sight as long as she could. Now the train gathered motion, the woman's pace slowed, she stopped, her eyes wet, her lips murmuring words no one could hear, and as he vanished from her sight she cried, "Auf Wiedersehn!" and put her hand up to her lips and kissed it to him.

For a moment longer the younger man, who was to be this specter's brief companion of the journey, stood looking out the corridor window down the platform toward the great arched station sheds, seeming to look after the group of people departing up the platform, but really seeing nothing but the tall, lovely figure of the woman as she walked slowly away, head bent, with a long, deliberate stride of incomparable grace, voluptuous undulance. Once she paused to look back again, then turned and walked on slowly as before.

Suddenly she stopped. Some one out of the throng of people on the platform had approached her. It was a young man. The woman paused in a startled manner, lifted one gloved hand in protest, started to go on, and the next moment they were locked in a savage embrace, devouring each other with passionate kisses.

When the traveller returned to his seat, the dying man who had already come into the compartment from the corridor and had fallen back into the cushions of his seat, breathing hoarsely, was growing calmer, less exhausted. For a moment the younger man looked intently at the beak-like face, the closed weary eyes, wondering if this dying man had seen that meeting on the station platform, and what knowledge such as this could now mean to him. But that mask of death was enigmatic, unrevealing; the youth found nothing there that he could read. A faint and strangely luminous smile was playing at the edges of the man's thin mouth, and his burning eyes were now open, but far and sunken and seemed to be looking from an unspeakable depth at something that was far away. In a moment, in a profound and tender tone, he said:

"Zat vas my vife. Now in ze vinter I must go alone, for zat iss best. But in ze spring ven I am better she vill come to me."

All through the wintry afternoon the great train rushed down across Bavaria. Swiftly and powerfully it gathered motion, it left the last scattered outposts of the city behind it, and swift as dreams the train was rushing out across the level plain surrounding Munich.

The day was gray, the sky impenetrable and somewhat heavy, and yet filled with a strong, clean Alpine vigor, with that odorless and yet exultant energy of cold mountain air. Within an hour the train had entered Alpine country, now there were hills, valleys, the immediate sense of soaring ranges, and the dark enchantment of the forests of Germany, those forests which are something more than trees—which are a spell, a magic, and a sorcery, filling the hearts of men, and particularly those strangers who have some racial kinship with that land, with a dark music, a haunting memory, never wholly to be captured.

It is an overwhelming feeling of immediate and impending discovery, such as men might have who come for the first time to their father's country. It is like coming to that unknown land for which our spirits long so passionately in youth, which is the dark side of our soul, the strange brother and the complement of the land we have known in our childhood. And it is revealed to us instantly the moment that we see it with a powerful emotion of perfect recognition and disbelief, with that dream-like reality of strangeness and familiarity which dreams and all enchantment have.

What is it? What is this wild fierce joy and sorrow swelling in our hearts? What is this memory that we cannot phrase, this instant recognition for which we have no words? We cannot say. We have no way to give it utterance, no ordered evidence to give it proof, and scornful pride can mock us for a superstitious folly. Yet we will know the dark land at the very moment that we come to it, and though we have no tongue, no proof, no utterance for what we feel, we have what we have, we know what we know, we are what we are.

And what are we? We are the naked men, the lost Americans. Immense and lonely skies bend over us, ten thousand men are marching in our blood. Where does it come from—the sense of strangeness, instant recognition, the dream-haunted, almost captured, memory? Where does it come from, the constant hunger and the rending lust, and the music, dark and solemn, elfish, magic, sounding through the wood? How is it that this boy, who is American, has known this strange land from the first moment that he saw it?

How is it that from his first night in a German town he has understood the tongue he never heard before, has spoken instantly, saying all he wished to say, in a strange language which he could not speak, speaking a weird argot which was neither his nor theirs, of which he was not even conscious, so much did it seem to be the spirit of a language, not the words, he spoke, and instantly, in this fashion, understood by every one with whom he talked?

No. He could not prove it, yet he knew that it was there, buried deep in the brain and blood of man, the utter knowledge of this land and of his father's people. He had felt it all, the tragic and insoluble admixture of the race. He knew the terrible fusion of the brute and of the spirit. He knew the nameless fear of the old barbaric forest, the circle of barbaric figures gathered round him in their somber and unearthly ring, the sense of drowning in the blind forest horrors of barbaric time. He carried all within himself, the slow gluttony and lust of the unsated swine, as well as the strange and powerful music of the soul.

He knew the hatred and revulsion from the never-sated beast—the beast with the swine-face and the quenchless thirst, the never-ending hunger, the thick, slow, rending hand that fumbled with a smouldering and unsated lust. And he hated the great beast with the hate of hell and murder because he felt and knew it in himself and was himself the prey of its rending, quenchless, and obscene desires. Rivers of wine to drink, whole roast oxen turning on the spit, and through the forest murk, the roaring wall of huge beast-bodies and barbaric sound about him, the lavish flesh of the great blonde women, in brutal orgy of the all-devouring, never-sated maw of the huge belly, without end or surfeit—all was mixed into his blood, his spirit, and his life.

It had been given to him somehow from the dark time-horror of the ancient forest together with all that was magical, glorious, strange and beautiful: the husky horn-notes sounding faint and elfin through the forests, the infinite strange weavings, dense mutations of the old Germanic soul of man. How cruel, baffling, strange, and sorrowful was the enigma of the race: the power and strength of the incorruptible and soaring spirit rising from the huge corrupted beast with such a radiant purity, and the powerful enchantments of grand music, noble poetry, so sorrowfully and unalterably woven and inwrought with all the blind brute hunger of the belly and the beast of man.

It was all his, and all contained in his one life. And it could, he knew, never be distilled out of him, no more than one can secrete from his flesh his father's blood, the ancient and immutable weavings of dark time. And for this reason, as he now looked out the window of the train at that lonely Alpine land of snow and dark enchanted forest he felt the sense of familiar recognition instantly, the feeling that he had always known this place, that it was home. And something dark, wild, jubilant, and strange was exulting, swelling in his spirit like a grand and haunting music heard in dreams.

And now, a friendly acquaintance having been established, the specter, with the insatiate, possessive curiosity of his race, began to ply his companion with innumerable questions concerning his life, his home, his profession, the journey he was making, the reason for that journey. The young man answered readily, and without annoyance. He knew that he was being pumped unmercifully, but the dying man's whispering voice was so persuasive, friendly, gentle, his manner so courteous, kind, and insinuating, his smile so luminous and winning, touched with a faint and yet agreeable expression of weariness, that the questions almost seemed to answer themselves.

The young man was an American, was he not? . . . Yes. And how long had he been abroad—two months? Three months? No? Almost a year! So long as that! Then he liked Europe, yes? It was his first trip? No? His fourth?—The specter lifted his eyebrows in expressive astonishment, and yet his sensitive thin mouth was touched all the time by his faint, wearily cynical smile.

Finally, the boy was pumped dry: the specter knew all about him. Then for a moment he sat staring at the youth with his faint, luminous, subtly mocking, and yet kindly smile. At last, wearily, patiently, and with the calm finality of experience and death, he said:

"You are very young. Yes. Now you vant to see it all, to haf it all—but you haf nothing. Zat iss right—yes?" he said with his persuasive smile. "Zat vill all change. Some day you vill vant only a little—maybe, den, you *haf* a little—" and he flashed his luminous, winning smile again. "Und zat iss better—Yes?" He smiled again, and then said wearily, "I know. I know. Myself I haf gone eferyvere like you. I haf tried to see eferyt'ing—und I haf had nothing. Now I go no more. Eferyvere it iss ze same," he said wearily, looking out the window, with a dismissing gesture of his thin white hand. "Fields, hills, mountains, riffers, cities, peoples—you vish to know about zem all. Vun field, vun hill, vun riffer," the man whispered, "zat iss enough!"

He closed his eyes for a moment: when he spoke again his whisper was almost inaudible—"Vun life, vun place, vun time."

Darkness came, and the lights in the compartment were turned on. Again that whisper of waning life made its insistent, gentle, and implacable demand upon the youth. This time it asked that the light in the compartment be extinguished, while the specter stretched himself out upon the seat to rest. The younger man consented willingly and even gladly: his own journey was near its end and outside the moon, which had risen early, was shining down upon the Alpine forests and snows with a strange, brilliant, and haunting magic which gave to the darkness in the compartment some of its own ghostly and mysterious light.

The specter lay quietly stretched out on the cushions of the seat, his eyes closed, his wasted face, on which the two bright flags of burning red now shone with vermilion hue, strange and ghastly in the magic light as the beak of some great bird. The man scarcely seemed to breathe: no sound or movement of life was perceptible in the compartment except the pounding of the wheels, the leathery stretching and creaking sound of the car, and all that strange-familiar and evocative symphony of sounds a train makes—that huge symphonic monotone which is itself the sound of silence and forever.

For some time held in that spell of magic light and time, the youth sat staring out the window at the enchanted world of white and black that swept grandly and strangly past in the phantasmal radiance of the moon. Finally he got up, went out into the corridor, closing the door carefully behind him, and walked back down the narrow passageway through car after car of the rocketing train until he came to the dining car.

Here all was brilliance, movement, luxury, sensual warmth and gaiety. All the life of the train now seemed to be concentrated in this place. The waiters, surefooted and deft, were moving swiftly down the aisle of the rocketing car, pausing at each table to serve people from the great platters of well-cooked food which they carried on trays. Behind them the *sommelier* was pulling corks from tall frosty bottles of Rhine wine: he would hold the bottle between his knees as he pulled, the cork would come out with an exhilarating pop, and he would drop the cork then into a little basket.

At one table a seductive and beautiful woman was eating with a jaded-looking old man. At another a huge and powerful-looking German, with a wing collar, a shaven skull, a great swine face and a forehead of noble and lonely thought, was staring with a concentrated look of bestial gluttony at the tray of meat from which the waiter served him. He was speaking in a guttural and lustful tone, saying, "Ja! . . . Gut! . . . und etwas von diesem hier auch. . . ."

The scene was one of richness, power and luxury, evoking as it did the feeling of travel in a crack European express, which is different from the feeling one has when he rides on an American train. In America, the train gives one a feeling of wild and lonely joy, a sense of the savage, unfenced, and illimitable wilderness of the country through which the train is rushing, a wordless and unutterable hope as one thinks of the enchanted city toward which he is speeding; the unknown and fabulous promise of the life he is to find there.

In Europe, the feeling of joy and pleasure is more actual, ever present. The luxurious trains, the rich furnishings, the deep maroons, dark blues, the fresh, well-groomed vivid colors of the cars, the good food and the sparkling, heady wine, and the worldly, wealthy, cosmopolitan look of the travellers—all of this fills one with a powerful sensual joy, a sense of expectancy about to be realized. In a few hours' time one goes from country to country, through centuries of history, a world of crowded culture, and whole nations swarming with people, from one famous pleasure-city to another.

And, instead of the wild joy and nameless hope one feels as he looks out the window of an American train, one feels here (in Europe) an incredible joy of realization, an immediate sensual gratification, a feeling that there is nothing on earth but wealth, power, luxury, and love, and that one can live and enjoy this life, in all the infinite varieties of pleasure, forever.

When the young man had finished eating, and paid his bill, he began to walk back again through corridor after corridor along the length of the rocketing train. When he got back to his compartment, he saw the specter lying there as he had left him, stretched out upon the seat, with the brilliant moonlight still blazing on the great beak of his face.

The man had not changed his position by an inch, and yet at once the boy was conscious of some subtle, fatal change he could not define. What was it? He took his seat again and for some time stared fixedly at the silent ghostly figure opposite him. Did he not breathe? He thought, he was almost sure, he saw the motion of his breathing, the rise and fall of the emaciated breast, and yet he was not sure. But what he plainly saw now was that a line, vermilion in its moon-dark hue, had run out of the corner of the firm set mouth and that there was a large vermilion stain upon the floor.

What should he do? What could be done? The haunted light of the fatal moon seemed to have steeped his soul in its dark sorcery, in the enchantment of a measureless and inert calmness. Already, too, the train was slackening its speed, the first lights of the town appeared, it was his journey's end.

And now the train was slowing to a halt. There were the flare of rails, the switch-lights of the yard, small, bright, and hard, green, red, and yellow, poignant in the dark, and on other tracks he could see the little goods cars and the strings of darkened trains, all empty, dark, and waiting with their strange attentiveness of recent life. Then the long station quays began to slide slowly past the windows of the train, and the sturdy goat-like porters were coming on the run, eagerly saluting, speaking, calling to the people in the train who had already begun to pass their baggage through the window.

Softly the boy took his overcoat and suit-case from the rack above his head and stepped out into the narrow corridor. Quietly he slid the door of the compartment shut behind him. Then, for a moment, still unsure, he stood there looking back. In the semi-darkness of the compartment the spectral figure of the cadaver lay upon the cushions, did not move.

Was it not well to leave all things as he had found them, in silence, at the end? Might it not be that in this great dream of time in which we live and are the moving figures, there is no greater certitude than this: that, having met, spoken, known each other for a moment, as somewhere on this earth we were hurled onward through the darkness between two points of time, it is well to be content with this, to leave each other as we met, letting each one go alone to his appointed destination, sure of this only, needing only this—that there will be silence for us all and silence only, nothing but silence, at the end?

Already the train had come to a full stop. The boy went down the corridor to the end, and in a moment feeling the bracing shock of the cold air upon his flesh, breathing the vital and snow-laden air into his lungs, he was going down the quay with a hundred other people, all moving in the same direction, some toward certitude and home, some toward a new land, hope, and hunger, the swelling prescience of joy, the promise of a shining city. He knew that he was going home again.

VIRGINIA WOOLF

The New Dress

MABEL had her first serious suspicion that something was wrong as she took her cloak off and Mrs. Barnet, while handing her the mirror and touching the brushes and thus drawing her attention, perhaps rather markedly, to all the appliances for tidying and improving hair, complexion, clothes, which existed on the dressing table, confirmed the suspicion—that it was not right, not quite right, which growing stronger as she went upstairs and springing at her with conviction as she greeted Clarissa Dalloway, she went straight to the far end of the room, to a shaded corner where a looking-glass hung and looked. No! It was not right. And at once the misery which she always tried to hide, the profound dissatisfaction—the sense she had had, ever since she was a child, of being inferior to other people—set upon her, relentlessly, remorselessly, with an intensity which she could not beat off, as she would when she woke at night at home, by reading Borrow or Scott; for, oh, these men, oh, these women, all were thinking—"What's Mabel wearing? What a fright she looks! What a hideous new dress!"—their eyelids flickering as they came up and then their lids shutting rather tight. It was her own appalling inadequacy; her cowardice; her mean, water-sprinkled blood that depressed her. And at once the whole of the room where, for ever so many hours, she had planned with the little dressmaker how it was to go, seemed sordid, repulsive; and her own drawing-room so shabby, and herself, going out, puffed up with vanity as she touched the letters on the hall table and said: "How dull!" to show off—all this now seemed unutterably silly, paltry, and provincial. All this had been absolutely destroyed, shown up, exploded, the moment she came into Mrs. Dalloway's drawing-room.

What she had thought that evening when, sitting over the teacups, Mrs. Dalloway's invitation came, was that, of course, she could not be fashionable. It was absurd to pretend to even—fashion meant cut, meant style, meant thirty guineas at least—but why not be original? Why not be herself, anyhow? And, getting up, she had taken that old fashion book of her mother's, a Paris fashion book of the time of the Empire, and had thought how much prettier, more dignified, and more womanly, they were then, and so set herself—oh, it was foolish—trying to be like them, pluming herself in fact upon being modest and old-fashioned and very charming, giving herself up, no doubt about it, to an orgy of self-love which deserved to be chastised, and so rigged herself out like this.

But she dared not look in the glass. She could not face the whole horror—the pale yellow, idiotically old-fashioned silk dress with its long skirt and its high sleeves and its waist and all the things that looked so charming in the fashion book, but not on her, not among all these ordinary people. She felt like a dressmaker's dummy standing there for young people to stick pins into.

"But, my dear, it's perfectly charming!" Rose Shaw said, looking her up and down with that little satirical pucker of the lips which she expected—Rose herself being dressed in the height of the fashion, precisely like everybody else, always.

"We are all like flies trying to crawl over the edge of the saucer," Mabel thought, and repeated the phrase as if she were crossing herself, as if she were trying to find some spell to annul this pain, to make this agony endurable. Tags of Shakespeare, lines from books she had read ages ago, suddenly came to her when she was in agony, and she repeated them over and over again. "Flies trying to crawl," she repeated. If she could say that over often enough and make herself see the flies, she would become numb, chill, frozen, dumb. Now she could see flies crawling slowly out of a saucer of milk with their wings stuck together; and she strained and strained (standing in front of the looking-glass, listening to Rose Shaw) to make herself see Rose Shaw and all the other people there as flies, trying to hoist themselves out of something, or into something, meagre, insignificant, toiling flies. But she could not see them like that, not other people. She saw herself like that—she was a fly, but the others were dragonflies, butterflies, beautiful insects, dancing, fluttering, skimming, while she alone dragged herself up out of the saucer. (Envy and spite, the most detestable of the vices, were her chief faults.)

"I feel like some dowdy, decrepit, horribly dingy old fly," she said, making Robert Haydon stop just to hear her say that, just to reassure herself by furbishing up a poor weak-kneed phrase and so showing how detached she was, how witty, that she did not feel in the least out of anything. And, of course, Robert Haydon answered something quite polite, quite insincere, which she saw through instantly, and said to herself, directly he went (again from some book), "Lies, lies, lies!" For a party makes things either much more real or much less real, she thought; she saw in a flash to the bottom of Robert Haydon's heart; she saw through everything. She saw the truth. This was true, this drawing-room, this self, and the other false. Miss Milan's little work-room was really terribly hot, stuffy, sordid. It smelt of clothes and cabbage cooking; and yet, when Miss Milan put the glass in her hand, and she looked at herself with the dress on, finished, an extraordinary bliss shot through her heart. Suffused with light, she sprang into existence. Rid of cares and wrinkles, what she had dreamed of herself was there—a beautiful woman. Just for a second (she had not dared look longer, Miss Milan wanted to know about the length of the skirt), there looked at her, framed in the scrolloping mahogany, a grey-white, mysteriously smiling, charming girl, the core of herself, the soul of herself; and it was not vanity only, not only self-love that made her think it good, tender, and true. Miss Milan said that the skirt could not well be longer; if anything the skirt, said Miss Milan, puckering her forehead, considering with all her wits about her, must be shorter; and she felt, suddenly, honestly, full of love for Miss Milan, much, much fonder of Miss Milan than of anyone in the whole world, and could have cried for pity that she should be crawling on the floor with her mouth full of pins and her face red and her eyes bulging—that one human being should be doing this for another, and she saw them all as human beings merely, and herself going off to her party, and Miss Milan pulling the cover over the canary's cage, or letting him pick a hemp-seed from between her lips, and the thought of it, of this side of human nature and its patience and its endurance and its being content with such miserable, scanty, sordid, little pleasures filled her eyes with tears.

And now the whole thing had vanished. The dress, the room, the love, the pity, the scrolloping looking-glass, and the canary's cage—all had vanished, and here she was in a corner of Mrs. Dalloway's drawing-room, suffering tortures, woken wide awake to reality.

But it was all so paltry, weak-blooded, and petty-minded to care so much at her age with two children, to be still so utterly dependent on people's opinions and not have principles or convictions, not to be able to say as other people did, "There's Shakespeare! There's death! We're all weevils in a captain's biscuit"—or whatever it was that people did say.

She faced herself straight in the glass; she pecked at her left shoulder; she issued out into the room, as if spears were thrown at her yellow dress from all sides. But instead of looking fierce or tragic, as Rose Shaw would have done —Rose would have looked like Boadicea—she looked foolish and self-conscious and simpered like a schoolgirl and slouched across the room, positively slinking, as if she were a beaten mongrel, and looked at a picture, an engraving. As if one went to a party to look at a picture! Everybody knew why she did it—it was from shame, from humiliation.

"Now the fly's in the saucer," she said to herself, "right in the middle, and can't get out, and the milk," she thought, rigidly staring at the picture, "is sticking its wings together."

"It's so old-fashioned," she said to Charles Burt, making him stop (which by itself he hated) on his way to talk to someone else.

She meant, or she tried to make herself think that she meant, that it was the picture and not her dress, that was old-fashioned. And one word of praise, one word of affection from Charles would have made all the difference to her at the moment. If he had only said, "Mabel, you're looking charming tonight!" it would have changed her life. But then she ought to have been truthful and direct. Charles said nothing of the kind, of course. He was malice itself. He always saw through one, especially if one were feeling particularly mean, paltry, or feeble-minded.

"Mabel's got a new dress!" he said, and the poor fly was absolutely shoved into the middle of the saucer. Really, he would like her to drown, she believed. He had no heart, no fundamental kindness, only a veneer of friendliness. Miss Milan was much more real, much kinder. If only one could feel that and stick to it, always. "Why," she asked herself—replying to Charles much too pertly, letting him see that she was out of temper, or "ruffled" as he called it ("Rather ruffled?" he said and went on to laugh at her with some woman over there) —"Why," she asked herself, "can't I feel one thing always, feel quite sure that Miss Milan is right, and Charles wrong and stick to it, feel sure about the canary and pity and love and not be whipped all round in a second by coming into a room full of people?" It was her odious, weak, vacillating character again, always giving at the critical moment and not being seriously interested in conchology, etymology, botany, archeology, cutting up potatoes and watching them fructify like Mary Dennis, like Violet Searle.

Then Mrs. Holman, seeing her standing there, bore down upon her. Of course a thing like a dress was beneath Mrs. Holman's notice, with her family always tumbling downstairs or having the scarlet fever. Could Mabel tell her if Elmthorpe was ever let for August and September? Oh, it was a conversation that bored her unutterably!—it made her furious to be treated like a house agent or a messenger boy, to be made use of. Not to have value, that was it, she thought, trying to grasp something hard, something real, while she tried to answer sensibly about the bathroom and the south aspect and the hot water to the top of the house; and all the time she could see little bits of her yellow dress in the round looking-glass which made them all the size of boot-buttons or tadpoles; and it was amazing to think how much humiliation and agony and self-loathing and effort and passionate ups and down of feeling were contained in a thing the size of a threepenny bit. And what was still odder, this thing, this Mabel Waring, was separate, quite disconnected; and though Mrs. Holman (the black button) was leaning forward and telling her how her eldest boy had strained his heart running, she could see her, too, quite detached in the looking-glass, and it was impossible that the black dot, leaning forward, gesticulating, should make the yellow dot, sitting solitary, self-centered, feel what the black dot was feeling, yet they pretended.

"So impossible to keep boys quiet"—that was the kind of thing one said.

And Mrs. Holman, who could never get enough sympathy and snatched what little there was greedily, as if it were her right (but she deserved much more for there was her little girl who had come down this morning with a swollen kneejoint), took this miserable offering and looked at it suspiciously, grudgingly, as if it were a half-penny when it ought to have been a pound and put it away in her purse, must put up with it, mean and miserly though it was, times being hard, so very hard; and on she went, creaking, injured Mrs. Holman, about the girl with the swollen joints. Ah, it was tragic, this greed, this clamour of human beings, like a row of cormorants, barking and flapping their wings for sympathy—it was tragic, could one have felt it and not merely pretended to feel it!

But in her yellow dress tonight she could not wring out one drop more; she wanted it all, all for herself. She knew (she kept on looking into the glass, dipping into that dreadfully showing-up blue pool) that she was condemned, despised, left like this in a backwater, because of her being like this—a feeble, vacillating creature; and it seemed to her that the yellow dress was a penance which she had deserved, and if she had been dressed like Rose Shaw, in lovely, clinging green with a ruffle of swansdown, she would have deserved that; and she thought that there was no escape for her—none whatever. But it was not her fault altogether, after all. It was being one of a family of ten; never having money enough, always skimping and paring; and her mother carrying great cans, and the linoleum worn on the stair edges, and one sordid little domestic tragedy after another—nothing catastrophic, the sheep farm failing, but not utterly; her eldest brother marrying beneath him but not very much—there was no romance, nothing extreme about them all. They petered out respectably in seaside resorts; every watering-place had one of her aunts even now asleep in some lodging with the front windows not quite facing the sea. That was so like them—they had to squint at things always. And she had done the same—she was just like her aunts. For all her dreams of living in India, married to some hero like Sir Henry Lawrence, some empire builder (still the sight of a native in a turban filled her with romance), she had failed utterly. She had married Hubert, with his safe, permanent underling's job in the Law Courts, and they managed tolerably in a smallish house, without proper maids, and hash when she was alone or just bread and butter, but now and then—Mrs. Holman was off, thinking her the most dried-up, unsympathetic twig she had ever met, absurdly dressed, too, and would tell everyone about Mabel's fantastic appearance—now and then, thought Mabel Waring, left alone on the blue sofa, punching the cushion in order to look occupied, for she would not join Charles Burt and Rose Shaw, chattering like magpies and perhaps laughing at her by the fireplace—now and then, there did come to her delicious moments, reading the other night in bed, for instance, or down by the sea on the sand in the sun, at Easter—let her recall it—a great tuft of pale sand-grass, standing all twisted like a shock of spears against the sky, which was blue like a smooth china egg, so firm, so hard, and then the melody of the waves—"Hush, hush," they said, and the children's shouts paddling—yes, it was a divine moment, and there she lay, she felt, in the hand of the Goddess who was the world; rather a hard-hearted, but very beautiful Goddess, a little lamb laid on the altar (one did think these silly things, and it didn't matter so long as one never said them). And also with Hubert sometimes she had quite unexpectedly—carving the mutton for Sunday lunch, for no reason, opening a letter, coming into a room—divine moments, when she said to herself (for she would never say this to anybody else), "This is it. This has happened. This is it!" And the other way about it was equally surprising—that is, when everything was arranged—music, weather, holidays, every reason for happiness was there—then nothing happened at all. One wasn't happy. It was flat, just flat, that was all.

Her wretched self again, no doubt! She had always been a fretful, weak, unsatisfactory mother, a wobbly wife, lolling about in a kind of twilight existence with nothing very clear or very bold, or more one thing than another, like all her brothers and sisters, except perhaps Herbert—they were all the same poor water-veined creatures who did nothing. Then in the midst of this creeping, crawling life suddenly she was on the crest of a wave. That wretched fly—where had she read the story that kept coming into her mind about the fly and the saucer?—struggled out. Yes, she had those moments. But now that she was forty, they might come more and more seldom. By degrees she would cease to struggle any more. But that was deplorable! That was not to be endured! That made her feel ashamed of herself!

She would go to the London Library tomorrow. She would find some wonderful, helpful, astonishing book, quite by chance, a book by a clergyman, by an American no one had ever heard of; or she would walk down the strand and drop, accidentally, into a hall where a miner was telling about the life in the pit, and suddenly she would become a new person. She would be absolutely transformed. She would wear a uniform; she would be called Sister Somebody; she would never give a thought to clothes again. And forever after she would be perfectly clear about Charles Burt and Miss Milan and this room and that room; and it would be always, day after day, as if she were lying in the sun or carving the mutton. It would be it!

So she got up from the blue sofa, and the yellow button in the looking-glass got up too, and she waved her hand to Charles and Rose to show them she did not depend on them one scrap, and the yellow button moved out of the looking-glass, and all the spears were gathered into her breast as she walked towards Mrs. Dalloway and said, "Good night."

"But it's too early to go," said Mrs. Dalloway, who was always so charming.

"I'm afraid I must," said Mabel Waring. "But," she added in her weak, wobbly voice which only sounded ridiculous when she tried to strengthen it, "I have enjoyed myself enormously."

"I have enjoyed myself," she said to Mr. Dalloway, whom she met on the stairs.

"Lies, lies, lies!" she said to herself, going downstairs, and "Right in the saucer!" she said to herself as she thanked Mrs. Barnet for helping her and wrapped herself, round and round and round, in the Chinese cloak she had worn these twenty years.

STEPHEN VINCENT BENÉT

The Devil and Daniel Webster

IT'S A STORY they tell in the border country, where Massachusetts joins Vermont and New Hampshire.

Yes, Dan'l Webster's dead—or, at least, they buried him. But every time there's a thunderstorm around Marshfield, they say you can hear his rolling voice in the hollows of the sky. And they say that if you go to his grave and speak loud and clear, "Dan'l Webster—Dan'l Webster!" the ground'll begin to shiver and the trees begin to shake. And after a while you'll hear a deep voice saying, "Neighbor, how stands the Union?" Then you better answer the Union stands as she stood, rock bottomed and copper sheathed, one and indivisible, or he's liable to rear right out of the ground. At least, that's what I was told when I was a youngster.

You see, for a while, he was the biggest man in the country. He never got to be President, but he was the biggest man. There were thousands that trusted in him right next to God Almighty, and they told stories about him and all the things that belonged to him that were like the stories of patriarchs and such. They said, when he stood up to speak, stars and stripes came right out in the sky, and once he spoke against a river and made it sink into the ground. They said, when he walked the woods with his fishing rod, Killall, the trout would jump out of the streams right into his pockets, for they knew it was no use putting up a fight against him; and, when he argued a case, he could turn on the harps of the blessed and the shaking of the earth underground. That was the kind of man he was, and his big farm up at Marshfield was suitable to him. The chickens he raised were all white meat down through the drumsticks, the cows were tended like children, and the big ram he called Goliath had horns with a curl like a morning-glory vine and could butt through an iron door. But Dan'l wasn't one of your gentlemen farmers; he knew all the ways of the land, and he'd be up by candlelight to see that the chores got done. A man with a mouth like a mastiff, a brow like a mountain and eyes like burning anthracite—that was Dan'l Webster in his prime. And the biggest case he argued never got written down in the books, for he argued it against the devil, nip and tuck and no holds barred. And this is the way I used to hear it told.

There was a man named Jabez Stone, lived at Cross Corners, New Hampshire. He wasn't a bad man to start with, but he was an unlucky man. If he planted corn, he got borers; if he planted potatoes, he got blight. He had good-enough land, but it didn't prosper him; he had a decent wife and children, but the more children he had, the less there was to feed them. If stones cropped up in his neighbor's field, boulders boiled up in his; if he had a horse with the spavins, he'd trade it for one with the staggers and give something extra. There's some folks bound to be like that, apparently. But one day Jabez Stone got sick of the whole business.

He'd been plowing that morning and he'd just broke the plowshare on a rock that he could have sworn hadn't been there yesterday. And, as he stood looking at the plowshare, the off horse began to cough—that ropy kind of cough that means sickness and horse doctors. There were two children down with the measles, his wife was ailing, and he had a whitlow on his thumb. It was about the last straw for Jabez Stone. "I vow," he said, and he looked around him kind of desperate, "I vow it's enough to make a man want to sell his soul to the devil! And I would, too, for two cents!"

Then he felt a kind of queerness come over him at having said what he'd said; though naturally, being a New Hampshireman, he wouldn't take it back. But, all the same, when it got to be evening and, as far as he could see, no notice had been taken, he felt relieved in his mind, for he was a religious man. But notice is always taken, sooner or later, just like the Good Book says. And, sure enough, next day, about suppertime, a soft-spoken, dark-dressed stranger drove up in a handsome buggy and asked for Jabez Stone.

Well, Jabez told his family it was a lawyer, come to see him about a legacy. But he knew who it was. He didn't like the looks of the stranger, nor the way he smiled with his teeth. They were white teeth, and plentiful—some say they were filed to a point, but I wouldn't vouch for that. And he didn't like it when the dog took one look at the stranger and ran away howling, with his tail between his legs. But having passed the word, more or less, he stuck to it, and they went out behind the barn and made their bargain. Jabez Stone had to prick his finger to sign, and the stranger lent him a silver pin. The wound healed clean, but it left a little white scar.

After that, all of a sudden, things began to pick up and prosper for Jabez Stone. His cows got fat and his horses sleek, his crops were the envy of the neighborhood, and lightning might strike all over the valley, but it wouldn't strike his barn. Pretty soon he was one of the prosperous people of the county; they asked him to stand for selectman, and he stood for it; there began to be talk of running him for state senate. All in all, you might say the Stone family was as happy and contented as cats in a dairy. And so they were, except for Jabez Stone.

He'd been contented enough the first few years. It's a great thing when bad luck turns; it drives most other things out of your head. True, every now and then, especially in rainy weather, the little white scar on his finger would give him a twinge. And once a year, punctual as clockwork, the stranger with the handsome buggy would come driving by. But the sixth year the stranger lighted, and, after that, his peace was over for Jabez Stone.

The stranger came up through the lower field, switching his boots with a cane—they were handsome black boots, but Jabez Stone never liked the look of them, particularly the toes. And, after he'd passed the time of day, he said, "Well, Mr. Stone, you're a hummer! It's a very pretty property you've got here, Mr. Stone."

"Well, some might favor it and others might not," said Jabez Stone, for he was a New Hampshireman.

"Oh, no need to decry your industry!" said the stranger, very easy, showing his teeth in a smile. "After all, we know what's been done, and it's been according to contract and specifications. So when—ahem—the mortgage falls due next year, you shouldn't have any regrets."

"Speaking of that mortagage, mister," said Jabez Stone, and he looked around for help to the earth and the sky, "I'm beginning to have one or two doubts about it."

"Doubts?" said the stranger not quite so pleasantly.

"Why, yes," said Jabez Stone. "This being the U.S.A. and me always having been a religious man." He cleared his throat and got bolder. "Yes sir," he said, "I'm beginning to have considerable doubts as to that mortgage holding in court."

"There's courts and courts," said the stranger, clicking his teeth. "Still, we might as well have a look at the original document," And he hauled out a big black pocketbook, full of papers. "Sherwin, Slater, Stevens, Stone," he muttered. " 'I, Jabez Stone, for a term of seven years—' Oh, it's quite in order, I think."

But Jabez Stone wasn't listening, for he saw something else flutter out of the black pocketbook. It was something that looked like a moth, but it wasn't a moth. And as Jabez Stone stared at it, it seemed to speak to him in a small sort of piping voice, terrible small and thin, but terrible human. "Neighbor Stone!" it squeaked. "Neighbor Stone! Help me! For God's sake, help me!"

But before Jabez Stone could stir hand or foot, the stranger whipped out a big bandanna handkerchief, caught the creature in it, just like a butterfly, and started tying up the ends of the bandanna.

"Sorry for the interruption," he said. "As I was saying—"

But Jabez Stone was shaking all over like a scared horse.

"That's Miser Stevens' voice!" he said in a croak. "And you've got him in your handkerchief!"

The stranger looked a little embarrassed.

"Yes, I really should have transferred him to the collecting box," he said with a simper, "but there were some rather unusual specimens there and I don't want them crowded. Well, well, these little contretemps will occur."

"I don't know what you mean by contertan," said Jabez Stone, "but that was Miser Stevens' voice! And he ain't dead! You can't tell me he is! He was just as spry and mean as a woodchuck Tuesday!"

"In the midst of life . . ." said the stranger, kind of pious. "Listen!" Then a bell began to toll in the valley and Jabez Stone listened, with the sweat running down his face. For he knew it was tolled for Miser Stevens and that he was dead.

"These long-standing accounts," said the stranger with a sigh; "one really hates to close them. But business is business."

He still had the bandanna in his hand, and Jabez Stone felt sick as he saw the cloth struggle and flutter.

"Are they all as small as that?" he asked hoarsely.

"Small?" said the stranger. "Oh, I see what you mean. Why, they vary." He measured Jabez Stone with his eyes, and his teeth showed. "Don't worry, Mr. Stone," he said. "You'll go with a very good grade. I wouldn't trust you outside the collecting box. Now, a man like Dan'l Webster, of course—well, we'd have to build a special box for him, and even at that, I imagine the wing spread would astonish you. He'd certainly be a prize. I wish we could see our way clear to him. But, in your case, as I was saying—"

"Put that handkerchief away!" said Jabez Stone, and he began to beg and to pray. But the best he could get at the end was a three years' extension, with conditions.

But till you make a bargain like that, you've got no idea of how fast four years can run. By the last months of those years Jabez Stone's known all over the state and there's talk of running him for governor—and it's dust and ashes in his mouth. For every day, when he gets up, he thinks, "There's one more night gone," and every night, when he lies down, he thinks of the black pocketbook and the soul of Miser Stevens, and it makes him sick at heart. Till finally, he can't bear it any longer, and, in the last days of the last year, he hitches up his horse and drives off to seek Dan'l Webster. For Dan'l was born in New Hampshire, only a few miles from Cross Corners, and it's well known that he has a particular soft spot for old neighbors.

It was early in the morning when he got to Marshfield, but Dan'l was up already, talking Latin to the farm hands and wrestling with the ram, Goliath, and trying out a new trotter and working up speeches to make against John C. Calhoun. But when he heard a New Hampshireman had come to see him, he dropped everything else he was doing, for that was Dan'l's way. He gave Jabez Stone a breakfast that five men couldn't eat, went into the living history of every man and woman in Cross Corners, and finally asked him how he could serve him.

Jabez Stone allowed that it was a kind of mortgage case.

"Well, I haven't pleaded a mortgage case in a long time, and I don't generally plead now, except before the Supreme Court," said Dan'l, "but if I can, I'll help you."

"Then I've got hope for the first time in ten years," said Jabez Stone and told him the details.

Dan'l walked up and down as he listened, hands behind his back, now and then asking a question, now and then plunging his eyes at the floor, as if they'd bore through it like gimlets. When Jabez Stone had finished, Dan'l puffed out his cheeks and blew. Then he turned to Jabez Stone and a smile broke over his face like the sunrise over Monadnock.

"You've certainly given yourself the devil's own row to hoe, Neighbor Stone," he said, "but I'll take your case."

"You'll take it?" said Jabez Stone, hardly daring to believe.

"Yes," said Dan'l Webster. "I've got about seventy-five other things to do and the Missouri Compromise to straighten out, but I'll take your case. For if two New Hampshiremen aren't a match for the devil, we might as well give the country back to the Indians."

Then he shook Jabez Stone by the hand and said, "Did you come down here in a hurry?"

"Well, I admit I made time," said Jabez Stone.

"You'll go back faster," said Dan'l Webster, and he told 'em to hitch up Constitution and Constellation to the carriage. They were matched grays with one white forefoot, and they stepped like greased lightning.

Well, I won't describe how excited and pleased the whole Stone family was to have the great Dan'l Webster for a guest, when they finally got there. Jabez Stone had lost his hat on the way, blown off when they overtook a wind, but he didn't take much account of that. But after supper he sent the family off to bed, for he had most particular business with Mr. Webster. Mrs. Stone wanted him to sit in the front parlor, but Dan'l Webster knew front parlors and said he preferred the kitchen. So it was there they sat, waiting for the stranger, with a jug on the table between them and a bright fire on the hearth—the stranger being scheduled to show up on the stroke of midnight, according to specification.

Well, most men wouldn't have asked for better company than Dan'l Webster and a jug. But with every tick of the clock Jabez Stone got sadder and sadder. His eyes roved round, and though he sampled the jug you could see he couldn't taste it. Finally, on the stroke of 11:30 he reached over and grabbed Dan'l Webster by the arm.

"Mr. Webster, Mr. Webster!" he said, and his voice was shaking with fear and a desperate courage. "For God's sake, Mr. Webster, harness your horses and get away from this place while you can!"

"You've brought me a long way, neighbor, to tell me you don't like my company," said Dan'l Webster, quite peaceable, pulling at the jug.

"Miserable wretch that I am!" groaned Jabez Stone. "I've brought you a devilish way, and now I see my folly. Let him take me if he wills. I don't hanker after it, I must say, but I can stand it. But you're the Union's stay and New Hampshire's pride! He mustn't get you, Mr. Webster! He mustn't get you!"

Dan'l Webster looked at the distracted man, all gray and shaking in the firelight, and laid a hand on his shoulder.

"I'm obliged to you, Neighbor Stone," he said gently. "It's kindly thought of. But there's a jug on the table and a case in hand. And I never left a jug or a case half finished in my life."

And just at that moment there was a sharp rap on the door.

"Ah," said Dan'l Webster very coolly, "I thought your clock was a trifle slow, Neighbor Stone." He stepped to the door and opened it. "Come in!" he said.

The stranger came in—very dark and tall he looked in the firelight. He was carrying a box under his arm—a black japanned box with little air holes in the lid. At the sight of the box Jabez Stone gave a low cry and shrank into a corner of the room.

"Mr. Webster, I presume," said the stranger, very polite, but with his eyes glowing like a fox's deep in the woods.

"Attorney of record for Jabez Stone," said Dan'l Webster, but his eyes were glowing too. "Might I ask your name?"

"I've gone by a good many," said the stranger carelessly. "Perhaps Scratch will do for the evening. I'm often called that in these regions."

Then he sat down at the table and poured himself a drink from the jug. The liquor was cold in the jug, but it came steaming into the glass.

"And now," said the stranger, smiling and showing his teeth, "I shall call upon you, as a law-abiding citizen, to assist me in taking possession of my property."

Well, with that the argument began—and it went hot and heavy. At first Jabez Stone had a flicker of hope, but when he saw Dan'l Webster being forced back at point after point, he just sat scrunched in his corner, with his eyes on that japanned box. For there wasn't any doubt as to the deed or the signature—that was the worst of it. Dan'l Webster twisted and turned and thumped his fist on the table, but he couldn't get away from that. He offered to compromise the case; the stranger wouldn't hear of it. He pointed out the property had increased in value, and state senators ought to be worth more; the stranger stuck to the letter of the law. He was a great lawyer, Dan'l Webster, but we know who's the King of Lawyers, as the Good Book tells us, and it seemed as if, for the first time, Dan'l Webster had met his match.

Finally, the stranger yawned a little. "Your spirited efforts on behalf of your client do you credit, Mr. Webster," he said, "but if you have no more arguments to adduce, I'm rather pressed for time . . ." and Jabez Stone shuddered.

Dan'l Webster's brow looked dark as a thundercloud.

"Pressed or not, you shall not have this man!" he thundered. "Mr. Stone is an American citizen, and no American citizen may be forced into the service of a foreign prince. We fought England for that in '12 and we'll fight all hell for it again!"

"Foreign?" said the stranger. "And who calls me a foreigner?"

"Well, I never yet heard of the dev—of your claiming American citizenship," said Dan'l Webster with surprise.

"And who with better right?" said the stranger with one of his terrible smiles. "When the first wrong was done to the first Indian, I was there. When the first slaver put out for the Congo, I stood on her deck. Am I not in your books and stories and beliefs, from the first settlements on? Am I not spoken of still in every church in New England? 'Tis true the North claims me for a Southerner and the South for a Northerner, but I am neither. I am merely an honest American like yourself—and of the best descent—for, to tell the truth, Mr. Webster, though I don't like to boast of it, my name is older in this country than yours."

"Aha!" said Dan'l Webster with the veins standing out in his forehead. "Then I stand on the Constitution! I demand a trial for my client!"

"The case is hardly one for an ordinary court," said the stranger, his eyes flickering. "And, indeed, the lateness of the hour—"

"Let it be any court you choose, so it is an American judge and an American jury!" said Dan'l Webster in his pride. "Let it be the quick or the dead; I'll abide the issue!"

"You have said it," said the stranger, and pointed his finger at the door. And with that, and all of a sudden, there was a rushing of wind outside and a noise of footsteps. They came, clear and distinct, through the night. And yet they were not like the footsteps of living men.

"In God's name, who comes by so late?" cried Jabez Stone in an ague of fear.

"The jury Mr. Webster demands," said the stranger, sipping at his boiling glass. "You must pardon the rough appearance of one or two; they will have come a long way."

And with that the fire burned blue and the door blew open and twelve men entered, one by one.

If Jabez Stone had been sick with terror before, he was blind with terror now. For there was Walter Butler, the loyalist, who spread fire and horror through the Mohawk Valley in the times of the Revolution; and there was Simon Girty, the renegade, who saw white men burned at the stake and whooped with the Indians to see them burn. His eyes were green, like a catamount's, and the stains on his hunting shirt did not come from the blood of the deer. King Philip was there, wild and proud as he had been in life, with the great gash in his head that gave him his death wound, and cruel Governor Dale, who broke men on the wheel. There was Morton of Merry Mount, who so vexed the Plymouth Colony, with his flushed, loose, handsome face and his hate of the godly. There was Teach, the bloody pirate, with his black beard curling on his breast. The Reverend John Smeet, with his strangler's hands and his Geneva gown, walked as daintily as he had to the gallows. The red print of the rope was still around his neck, but he carried a perfumed handkerchief in one hand. One and all, they came into the room with the fires of hell still upon them, and the stranger named their names and their deeds as they came, till the tale of twelve was told. Yet the stranger had told the truth—they had all played a part in America.

"Are you satisfied with the jury, Mr. Webster?" said the stranger mockingly, when they had taken their places.

The sweat stood upon Dan'l Webster's brow, but his voice was clear.

"Quite satisfied," he said. "Though I miss General Arnold from the company."

"Benedict Arnold is engaged upon other business," said the stranger with a glower. "Ah, you asked for a justice, I believe."

He pointed his finger once more, and a tall man, soberly clad in Puritan garb, with the burning gaze of the fanatic, stalked into the room and took his judge's place.

"Justice Hathorne is a jurist of experience," said the stranger. "He presided at certain witch trials once held in Salem. There were others who repented of the business later, but not he."

"Repent of such notable wonders and undertakings?" said the stern old justice. "Nay, hang them—hang them all!" And he muttered to himself in a way that struck ice into the soul of Jabez Stone.

Then the trial began, and, as you might expect, it didn't look anyways good for the defense. And Jabez Stone didn't make much of a witness in his own behalf.

He took one look at Simon Girty and screeched, and they had to put him back in his corner in a kind of swoon.

It didn't halt the trial though; the trial went on, as trials do. Dan'l Webster had faced some hard juries and hanging judges in his time, but this was the hardest he'd ever faced, and he knew it. They sat there with a kind of glitter in their eyes, and the stranger's smooth voice went on and on. Every time he'd raise an objection, it'd be "Objection sustained," but whenever Dan'l objected, it'd be "Objection denied." Well, you couldn't expect fair play from a fellow like this Mr. Scratch.

It got to Dan'l in the end, and be began to heat, like iron in the forge. When he got up to speak he was going to flay that stranger with every trick known to the law, and the judge and jury too. He didn't care if it was contempt of court or what would happen to him for it. He didn't care any more what happened to Jabez Stone. He just got madder and madder, thinking of what he'd say. And yet, curiously enough, the more he thought about it, the less he was able to arrange his speech in his mind.

Till, finally, it was time for him to get up on his feet, and he did so, all ready to bust out with lightnings and denunciations. But before he started he looked over the judge and jury for a moment, such being his custom. And he noticed the glitter in their eyes was twice as strong as before, and they all leaned forward. Like hounds just before they get the fox, they looked, and the blue mist of evil in the room thickened as he watched them. Then he saw what he'd been about to do, and he wiped his forehead, as a man might who's just escaped falling into a pit in the dark.

For it was him they'd come for, not only Jabez Stone. He read it in the glitter of their eyes and in the way the stranger hid his mouth with one hand. And if he fought them with their own weapons, he'd fall into their power; he knew that, though he couldn't have told you how. It was his own anger and horror that burned in their eyes; and he'd have to wipe that out or the case was lost. He stood there for a moment, his black eyes burning like anthracite. And then he began to speak.

He started off in a low voice, though you could hear every word. They say he could call on the harps of the blessed when he chose. And this was just as simple and easy as a man could talk. But he didn't start out by condemning or reviling. He was talking about the things that make a country a country and a man a man.

And he began with the simple things that everybody's known and felt—the freshness of a fine morning when you're young, and the taste of food when you're hungry, and the new day that's every day when you're a child. He took them up and he turned them in his hands. They were good things for any man. But without freedom they sickened. And when he talked of those enslaved, and the sorrows of slavery, his voice got like a big bell. He talked of the early days of America and the men who had made those days. It wasn't a spread-eagle speech, but he made you see it. He admitted all the wrong that had ever been done. But he showed how, out of the wrong and the right, the suffering and the starvations, something new had come. And everybody had played a part in it, even the traitors.

Then he turned to Jabez Stone and showed him as he was—an ordinary man who'd had hard luck and wanted to change it. And, because he'd wanted to change it, now he was going to be punished for all eternity. And yet there was good in Jabez Stone, and he showed that good. He was hard and mean, in some ways, but he was a man. There was sadness in being a man, but it was a proud thing too. And he showed what the pride of it was till you couldn't help feeling it. Yes, even in hell, if a man was a man, you'd know it. And he wasn't pleading for any one person any more, though his voice rang like an organ. He was telling the story and the failures and the endless journey of mankind. They got tricked and trapped and bamboozled, but it was a great journey. And no demon that was ever foaled could know the inwardness of it—it took a man to do that.

The fire began to die on the hearth and the wind before morning to blow. The light was getting gray in the room when Dan'l Webster finished. And his words came back at the end to New Hampshire ground, and the one spot of land that each man loves and clings to. He painted a picture of that, and to each one of that jury he spoke of things long forgotten. For his voice could search the heart, and that was his gift and his strength. And to one his voice was like the forest and its secrecy, and to another like the sea and the storms of the sea; and one heard the cry of his lost nation in it, and another saw a little harmless scene he hadn't remembered for years. But each saw something. And when Dan'l Webster finished he didn't know whether or not he'd saved Jabez Stone. But he knew he'd done a miracle. For the glitter was gone from the eyes of judge and jury, and, for the moment, they were men again, and knew they were men.

"The defense rests," said Dan'l Webster and stood there like a mountain. His ears were still ringing with his speech, and he didn't hear anything else till he heard Judge Hathorne say, "The jury will retire to consider its verdict."

Walter Butler rose in his place and his face had a dark, gay pride on it. "The jury has considered its verdict," he said and looked the stranger full in the eye. "We find for the defendant, Jabez Stone."

With that, the smile left the stranger's face, but Walter Butler did not flinch. "Perhaps 'tis not strictly in accordance with the evidence," he said, "but even the damned may salute the eloquence of Mr. Webster."

With that, the long crow of a rooster split the gray morning sky, and judge and jury were gone from the room like a puff of smoke and as if they had never been there. The stranger turned to Dan'l Webster, smiling wryly.

"Major Butler was always a bold man," he said. "I had not thought him quite so bold. Nevertheless, my congratulations, as between two gentlemen."

"I'll have that paper first, if you please," said Dan'l Webster, and he took it and tore it into four pieces. It was queerly warm to the touch. "And now," he said, "I'll have you!" and his hand came down like a bear trap on the stranger's arm. For he knew that once you bested anybody like Mr. Scratch in fair fight, his power on you was gone. And he could see that Mr. Scratch knew it too.

The stranger twisted and wriggled, but he couldn't get out of that grip. "Come, come, Mr. Webster," he said, smiling palely. "This sort of thing is ridic—ouch!—is ridiculous. If you're worried about the costs of the case, naturally, I'd be glad to pay——"

"And so you shall!" said Dan'l Webster, shaking him till his teeth rattled. "For you'll sit right down at that table and draw up a document, promising never to bother Jabez Stone nor his heirs or assigns nor any other New Hampshireman till doomsday! For any hades we want to raise in this state, we can raise ourselves, without assistance from strangers."

"Ouch!" said the stranger. "Ouch! Well, they never did run very big to the barrel, but—ouch!—I agree!"

So he sat down and drew up the document. But Dan'l Webster kept his hand on his coat collar all the time.

"And now may I go?" said the stranger, quite humble, when Dan'l'd seen the documents in proper and legal form.

"Go?" said Dan'l, giving him another shake. "I'm still trying to figure out what I'll do with you. For you've settled the costs of the case, but you haven't settled with me. I think I'll take you back to Marshfield," he said, kind of reflective. "I've got a ram there named Goliath that can butt through an iron door. I'd kind of like to turn you loose in his field and see what he'd do."

Well, with that the stranger began to beg and to plead. And he begged and he pled so humble that finally Dan'l, who was naturally kindhearted, agreed to let him go. The stranger seemed terrible grateful for that and said, just to show they were friends, he'd tell Dan'l's fortune before leaving. So Dan'l agreed to that, though he didn't take much stock in fortune-tellers ordinarily. But, naturally, the stranger was a little different.

Well, he pried and he peered at the lines in Dan'l's hands. And he told him one thing and another that was quite remarkable. But they were all in the past.

"Yes, all that's true, and it happened," said Dan'l Webster. "But what's to come in the future?"

The stranger grinned, kind of happily, and shook his head.

"The future's not as you think it," he said. "It's dark. You have a great ambition, Mr. Webster."

"I have," said Dan'l firmly, for everybody knew he wanted to be President.

"It seems almost within your grasp," said the stranger, "but you will not attain it. Lesser men will be made President and you will be passed over."

"And, if I am, I'll still be Daniel Webster," said Dan'l. "Say on."

"You have two strong sons," said the stranger, shaking his head. "You look to found a line. But each will die in war and neither reach greatness."

"Live or die, they are still my sons," said Dan'l Webster. "Say on."

"You have made great speeches," said the stranger. "You will make more."

"Ah," said Dan'l Webster.

"But the last great speech you make will turn many of your own against you," said the stranger. "They will call you Ichabod; they will call you by other names. Even in New England some will say you have turned your coat and sold your country, and their voices will be loud against you till you die."

"So it is an honest speech, it does not matter what men say," said Dan'l Webster. Then he looked at the stranger and their glances locked.

"One question," he said. "I have fought for the Union all my life. Will I see that fight won against those who would tear it apart?"

"Not while you live," said the stranger grimly, "but it will be won. And after you are dead, there are thousands who will fight for your cause, because of words that you spoke."

"Why, then, you long-barreled, slab-sided, lantern-jawed, fortune-telling note shaver," said Dan'l Webster with a great roar of laughter, "be off with you to your own place before I put my mark on you! For, by the thirteen original colonies, I'd go to the Pit itself to save the Union!"

And with that he drew back his foot for a kick that would have stunned a horse. It was only the tip of his shoe that caught the stranger, but he went flying out of the door with his collecting box under his arm.

"And now," said Dan'l Webster, seeing Jabez Stone beginning to rouse from his swoon, "let's see what's left in the jug, for it's dry work talking all night. I hope there's pie for breakfast, Neighbor Stone."

But they say that whenever the devil comes near Marshfield, even now, he gives it a wide berth. And he hasn't been seen in the state of New Hampshire from that day to this.

I'm not talking about Massachusetts or Vermont.

STEPHEN VINCENT BENÉT

Jacob and the Indians

IT GOES back to the early days—may God profit all who lived then—and the ancestors.

Well, America, you understand, in those days was different. It was a nice place, but you wouldn't believe it if you saw it today. Without busses, without trains, without states, without Presidents, nothing!

With nothing but colonists and Indians and wild woods all over the country and wild animals to live in the wild woods. Imagine such a place! In these days, you children don't even think about it; you read about it in the schoolbooks, but what is that? And I put in a call to my daughter, in California, and in three minutes I am saying "Hello Rosie," and there it is Rosie and she is telling me about the weather, as if I wanted to know! But things were not always that way. I remember my own days, and they were different. And in the times of my grandfather's grandfather, they were different still. Listen to the story.

My grandfather's grandfather was Jacob Stein, and he came from Rettelsheim, in Germany. To Philadelphia he came, an orphan in a sailing ship, but not a common man. He had learning—he had been to the *chedar*—he could have been a scholar among the scholars. Well, that is the way things happen in this bad world. There was a plague and a new grand duke—things are always so. He would say little of it afterward—they had left his teeth in his mouth, but he would say little of it. He did not have to say—we are children of the Dispersion—we know a black day when it comes.

Yet imagine—a young man with fine dreams and learning, a scholar with a pale face and narrow shoulders, set down in those early days in such a new country. Well, he must work, and he did. It was very fine, his learning, but it did not fill his mouth. He must carry a pack on his back and go from door to door with it. That was no disgrace; it was so that many began. But it was not expounding the Law, and at first he was very homesick. He would sit in his room at night, with the one candle, and read the preacher Koheleth, till the bitterness of the preacher rose in his mouth. Myself, I am sure that Koheleth was a great preacher, but if he had had a good wife he would have been a more cheerful man. They had too many wives in those old days—it confused them. But Jacob was young.

As for the new country where he had come, it was to him a place of exile, large and frightening. He was glad to be out of the ship, but, at first, that was all. And when he saw his first real Indian in the street—well, that was a day! But the Indian, a tame one, bought a ribbon from him by signs, and after that he felt better. Nevertheless, it seemed to him at times that the straps of the pack cut into his very soul, and he longed for the smell of the *chedar* and the quiet streets of Rettelsheim and the good smoked goose-breast pious housewives keep for the scholar. But there is no going back—there is never any going back.

All the same, he was a polite young man, and a hardworking. And soon he had a stroke of luck—or at first it seemed so. It was from Simon Ettelsohn that he got the trinkets for his pack, and one day he found Simon Ettelsohn arguing a point of the Law with a friend, for Simon was a pious man and well thought of in the Congregation Mikveh Israel. Our grandfather's grandfather stood by very modestly at first—he had come to replenish his pack and Simon was his employer. But finally his heart moved within him, for both men were wrong, and he spoke and told them where they erred. For half an hour he spoke, with his pack still upon his shoulders, and never has a text been expounded with more complexity, not even by the great Reb Samuel. Till, in the end, Simon Ettelsohn threw up his hands and called him a young David and a candle of learning. Also, he allowed him a more profitable route of trade. But, best of all, he invited young Jacob to his house, and there Jacob ate well for the first time since he had come to Philadelphia. Also he laid eyes upon Miriam Ettelsohn for the first time, and she was Simon's youngest daughter and a rose of Sharon.

After that, things went better for Jacob, for the protection of the strong is like a rock and a well. But yet things did not go altogether as he wished. For, at first, Simon Ettlesohn made much of him, and there was stuffed fish and raisin wine for the young scholar, though he was a peddler. But there is a look in a man's eyes that says "H'm? Son-in-law?" and that look Jacob did not see. He was modest—he did not expect to win the maiden overnight, though he longed for her. But gradually it was borne in upon him what he was in the Ettlesohn house—a young scholar to be shown before Simon's friends, but a scholar whose learning did not fill his mouth. He did not blame Simon for it, but it was not what he had intended. He began to wonder if he would ever get on in the world at all, and that is not good for any man.

Nevertheless, he could have borne it, and the aches and pains of his love, had it not been for Meyer Kappelhuist. Now, there was a pushing man! I speak no ill of anyone, not even of your Aunt Cora, and she can keep the De Groot silver if she finds it in her heart to do so; who lies down in the straw with a dog, gets up with fleas. But this Meyer Kappelhuist! A big, red-faced fellow from Holland with shoulders the size of a barn door and red hair on the backs of his hands. A big mouth for eating and drinking and telling schnorrer stories—and he talked about the Kappelhuists, in Holland, till you'd think they were made of gold. The crane says, "I am really a peaocock—at least on my mother's side." And yet, a thriving man—that could not be denied. He had started with a pack, like our grandfather's grandfather, and now he was trading with the Indians and making money hand over fist. It seemed to Jacob that he could never go to the Ettelsohn house without meeting Meyer and hearing about those Indians. And it dried the words in Jacob's mouth and made his heart burn.

For, no sooner would our grandfather's grandfather begin to expound a text or a proverb, than he would see Meyer Kappelhuist looking at the maiden. And when Jacob had finished his expounding, and there should have been a silence, Meyer Kappelhuist would take it upon himself to thank him, but always in a tone that said: "The Law is the Law and the Prophets are the Prophets, but prime beaver is also prime beaver, my little scholar!" It took the pleasure from Jacob's learning and the joy of the maiden from his heart. Then he would sit silent and burning, while Meyer told a great tale of Indians, slapping his hands on his knees. And in the end he was always careful to ask Jacob how many needles and pins he had sold that day; and when Jacob told him, he would smile and say very smoothly that all things had small beginnings, till the maiden herself could not keep from a little smile. Then, desperately, Jacob would rack his brains for more interesting matter. He would tell of the wars of the Maccabees and the glory of the Temple. But even as he told them, he felt they were far away. Whereas Meyer and his accursed Indians were there, and the maiden's eyes shone at his words.

Finally he took his courage in both hands and went to Simon Ettelsohn. It took much for him to do it, for he had not been brought up to strive with men, but with words. But it seemed to him now that everywhere he went he heard of nothing but Meyer Kappelhuist and his trading with the Indians, till he thought it would drive him mad. So he went to Simon Ettelsohn in his shop.

"I am weary of this narrow trading in pins and needles," he said, without more words.

Simon Ettlesohn looked at him keenly; for while he was an ambitious man, he was kindly as well.

"*Nu,*" he said. "A nice little trade you have and the people like you. I myself started in with less. What would you have more?"

"I would have much more," said our grandfather's grandfather stiffly. "I would have a wife and a home in this new country. But how shall I keep a wife? On needles and pins?"

"*Nu,* it has been done," said Simon Ettelsohn, smiling a little, "You are a good boy, Jacob, and we take an interest in you. Now, if it is a question of marriage, there are many worthy maidens. Asher Levy, the baker, has a daughter. It is true that she squints a little, but her heart is of gold." He folded his hands and smiled.

"It is not of Asher Levy's daughter I am thinking," said Jacob, taken aback. Simon Ettelsohn nodded his head and his face grew grave.

"*Nu,* Jacob," he said. "I see what is in your heart. Well, you are a good boy, Jacob, and a fine scholar. And if it were in the old country, I am not saying. But here, I have one daughter married to a Seixas and one to a Da Silva. You must see that makes a difference," And he smiled the smile of a man well pleased with his world.

"And if I were such a one as Meyer Kappelhuist?" said Jacob bitterly.

"Now—well, that is a little different," said Simon Ettelsohn sensibly. "For Meyer trades with the Indians. It it true, he is a little rough. But he will die a rich man."

"I will trade with the Indians too," said Jacob, and trembled.

Simon Ettelsohn looked at him as if he had gone out of his mind. He looked at his narrow shoulders and his scholar's hands.

"Now Jacob," he said soothingly, "do not be foolish. A scholar you are, and learned, not an Indian trader. Perhaps in a store you would do better. I can speak to Aaron Copras. And sooner or later we will find you a nice maiden. But to trade with Indians—well, that takes a different sort of man. Leave that to Meyer Kappelhuist."

"And your daughter, that rose of Sharon? Shall I leave her, too, to Meyer Kappelhuist?" cried Jacob.

Simon Ettelsohn looked uncomfortable.

"*Nu,* Jacob," he said. "Well, it is not settled, of course. But—"

"I will go forth against him as David went against Goliath," said our grandfather's grandfather wildly. "I will go forth into the wilderness. And God should judge the better man!"

Then he flung his pack on the floor and strode from the shop. Simon Ettelsohn called out after him, but he did not stop for that. Nor was it in his heart to go and seek the maiden. Instead, when he was in the street, he counted the money he had. It was not much. He had meant to buy his trading goods on credit from Simon Ettelsohn, but now he could not do that. He stood in the sunlit street of Philadelphia, like a man bereft of hope.

Nevertheless, he was stubborn—though how stubborn he did not yet know. And though he was bereft of hope, he found his feet taking him to the house of Raphael Sanchez.

Now, Raphael Sanchez could have bought and sold Simon Ettelsohn twice over. An arrogant old man he was, with fierce black eyes and a beard that was whiter than snow. He lived apart, in his big house with his granddaughter, and men said he was very learned, but also very disdainful, and that to him a Jew was not a Jew who did not come of the pure sephardic strain.

Jacob had seen him, in the Congregation Mikveh Israel, and to Jacob he had looked like an eagle, and fierce as an eagle. Yet now, in his need, he found himself knocking at that man's door.

It was Raphael Sanchez himself who opened. "And what is for sale today, peddler?" he said, looking scornfully at Jacob's jacket where the pack straps had worn it.

"A scholar of the Law is for sale," said Jacob in his bitterness, and he did not speak in the tongue he had learned in this country, but in Hebrew.

The old man stared at him a moment.

"Now am I rebuked," he said. "For you have the tongue. Enter, my guest," and Jacob touched the scroll by the doorpost and went in.

They shared the noon meal at Raphael Sanchez's table. It was made of dark, glowing mahogany, and the light sank into it as sunlight sinks into a pool. There were many precious things in that room, but Jacob had no eyes for them. When the meal was over and the blessing said, he opened his heart and spoke, and Raphael Sanchez listened, stroking his beard with one hand. When the young man had finished, he spoke.

"So Scholar," he said, though mildly, "you have crossed an ocean that you might live and not die, and yet all you see is a girl's face."

"Did not Jacob serve seven years for Rachel?" said our grandfather's grandfather.

"Twice seven, Scholar," said Raphael Sanchez dryly, "but that was in the blessed days." He stroked his beard again. "Do you know why I came to this country?" he said.

"No," said Jacob Stein.

"It was not for the trading," said Raphael Sanchez. "My house has lent money to kings. A little fish, a few furs—what are they to my house? No, it was for the promise—the promise of Penn—that this land should be an habitation and a refuge, not only for the Gentiles. Well, we know Christian promises. But so far, it has been kept. Are you spat upon in the street here, Scholar of the Law?"

"No," said Jacob. "They call me Jew, now and then. But the Friends, though Gentile, are kind."

"It is not so in all countries," said Raphael Sanchez, with a terrible smile.

"No," said Jacob quietly, "it is not."

The old man nodded. "Yes, one does not forget that," he said. "The spittle wipes off the cloth, but one does not forget. One does not forget the persecutor or the persecuted. That is why they think me mad, in the Congregation Mikveh Israel, when I speak what is in my mind. For, look you"—and he pulled a map from a drawer—"here is what we know of these colonies, and here and here our people make a new beginning, in another air. But here is New France—see it?—and down the great river come the French traders and their Indians.

"Well?" said Jacob in puzzlement.

"Well?" said Raphael Sanchez. "Are you blind? I do not trust the King of France—the king before him drove out the Huguenots, and who knows what he may do? And if they hold the great rivers against us, we shall never go westward."

"We?" said Jacob in bewilderment.

"We," said Raphael Sanchez. He struck his hand on the map. "Oh, they cannot see it in Europe—not even their lords in parliament and their ministers of state," he said. "They think this is a mine, to be worked as the Spaniards worked Potosi, but it is not a mine. It is something beginning to live, and it is faceless and nameless yet. But it is our lot to be part of it—remember that in the wilderness, my young scholar of the Law. You think you are going there for a girl's face, and that is well enough. But you may find something there you did not expect to find."

He paused and his eyes had a different look.

"You see, it is the trader first," he said. "Always the trader before the settled man. The Gentiles will forget that, and some of our own folk too. But one pays for the land of Canaan; one pays in blood and sweat."

Then he told Jacob what he would do for him and dismissed him, and Jacob went home to his room with his head buzzing strangely. For at times it seemed to him that the Congregation Mikveh Israel was right in thinking Raphael Sanchez half mad. And at other times it seemed to him that the old man's words were a veil, and behind them moved and stirred some huge and unguessed shape. But chiefly he thought of the rosy cheeks of Miriam Ettelsohn.

It was with the Scotchman, McCampbell, that Jacob made his first trading journey. A strange man was McCampbell, with grim features and cold blue eyes, but strong and kindly, though silent, except when he talked of the Ten Lost Tribes of Israel. For it was his contention that they were the Indians beyond the Western Mountains, and on this subject he would talk endlessly.

Indeed, they had much profitable conversation, McCampbell quoting the doctrines of a rabbi called John Calvin, and our grandfather's grandfather replying with Talmud and Torah till McCampbell would almost weep that such a honey-mouthed scholar should be destined to eternal damnation. Yet he did not treat our grandfather's grandfather as one destined to eternal damnation, but as a man, and he, too, spoke of cities of refuge as a man speaks of realities, for his people had also been persecuted.

First they left the city behind them, and then the outlying towns and, soon enough, they were in the wilderness. It was very strange to Jacob Stein. At first he would wake at night and lie awake listening, while his heart pounded, and each rustle in the forest was the step of a wild Indian, and each screech of an owl in the forest the whoop before the attack. But gradually this passed. He began to notice how silently the big man, McCampbell, moved in the woods; he began to imitate him. He began to learn many things that even a scholar of the Law, for all his wisdom, does not know—the girthing of a packsaddle and the making of fires, the look of dawn in the forest and the look of evening. It was all very new to him, and sometimes he thought he would die of it, for his flesh weakened. Yet always he kept on.

When he saw his first Indians—in the woods, not in the town—his knees knocked together. They were there as he had dreamt of them in dreams, and he thought of the spirit, Iggereth-beth-Mathlan, and her seventy-eight dancing demons, for they were painted and in skins. But he could not let his knees knock together, before heathens and a Gentile, and the first fear passed. Then he found they were grave men, very ceremonious and silent at first, and then when the silence had been broken, full of curiosity. They knew McCampbell, but him they did not know, and they discussed him and his garments with the frankness of children, till Jacob felt naked before them, and yet not afraid. One of them pointed to the bag that hung at Jacob's neck—the bag in which, for safety's sake, he carried his phylactery—then McCampbell said something and the brown hand dropped quickly, but there was a buzz of talk.

Later on, McCampbell explained to him that they, too, wore little bags of deerskin and inside them sacred objects—and they thought, seeing his, that he must be a person of some note. It made him wonder. It made him wonder more to eat deer meat with them, by a fire.

It was a green world and a dark one that he had fallen in—dark with the shadow of the forest, green with its green. Through it ran trails and paths that were not yet roads or highways—that did not have the dust and smell of the cities of men, but another scent, another look. These paths Jacob noted carefully, making a map, for that was one of the instructions of Raphael Sanchez. It seemed a great labor and difficult and for no purpose; yet, as he had promised, so he did. And as they sank deeper and deeper into the depths of the forest, and he saw pleasant streams and wide glades, untenanted but by the deer, strange thoughts came over him. It seemed to him that the Germany he had left was very small and crowded together; it seemed to him that he had not known there was so much width to the world.

Now and then he would dream back—dream back to the quiet fields around Rettelsheim and the red-brick houses of Philadelphia, to the stuffed fish and the raisin wine, the chanting in the *chedar* and the white twisted loaves of the calm Sabbath, under the white cloth. They would seem very close for the moment, then they would seem very far away. He was eating deer's meat in a forest and sleeping beside embers in the open night. It was so that Israel must have slept in the wilderness. He had not thought of it as so, but it was so.

Now and then he would look at his hands—they seemed tougher and very brown, as if they did not belong to him anymore. Now and then he would catch a glimpse of his own face, as he drank at a stream. He had a beard, but it was not the beard of a scholar—it was wild and black. Moreover, he was dressed in skins, now; it seemed strange to be dressed in skins at first, and then not strange.

Now all this time, when he went to sleep at night, he would think of Miriam Ettelsohn. But, queerly enough, the harder he tried to summon up her face in his thoughts, the vaguer it became.

He lost track of time—there was only his map and the trading and the journey. Now it seemed to him that they should surely turn back, for their packs were full. He spoke of it to McCampbell, but McCampbell shook his head. There was a light in the Scotsman's eyes now—a light that seemed strange to our grandfather's grandfather—and he would pray long at night, sometimes too loudly. So they came to the banks of the great river, brown and great, and saw it, and the country beyond it, like a view across Jordan. There was no end to that country—it stretched to the limits of the sky and Jacob saw it with his eyes. He was almost afraid at first, and then he was not afraid.

It was there that the strong man, McCampbell, fell sick, and there that he died and was buried. Jacob buried him on a bluff overlooking the river and faced the grave to the west. In his death sickness, McCampbell raved of the Ten Lost Tribes again and swore they were just across the river and he would go to them. It took all of Jacob's strength to hold him—if it had been at the beginning of the journey, he would not have had the strength. Then he turned back, for he, too, had seen a Promised Land, not for his seed only, but for nations yet to come.

Nevertheless, he was taken by the Shawnees, in a season

of bitter cold, with his last horse dead. At first, when misfortune began to fall upon him, he had wept for the loss of the horses and the good beaver. But, when the Shawnees took him, he no longer wept; for it seemed to him that he was no longer himself, but a man he did not know.

He was not concerned when they tied him to the stake and piled the wood around him, for it seemed to him still that it must be happening to another man. Nevertheless he prayed, as was fitting, chanting loudly; for Zion in the wilderness he prayed. He could smell the smell of the *chedar* and hear the voices that he knew—Reb Moses and Reb Nathan, and through them the curious voice of Raphael Sanchez, speaking in riddles. Then the smoke took him and he coughed. His throat was hot. He called for drink, and though they could not understand his words, all men know the sign of thirst, and they brought him a bowl filled. He put it to his lips eagerly and drank, but the stuff in the bowl was scorching hot and burned his mouth. Very angry then was our grandfather's grandfather, and without so much as a cry he took the bowl in both hands and flung it straight in the face of the man who had brought it, scalding him. Then there was a cry and a murmur from the Shawnees and, after some moments, he felt himself unbound and knew that he lived.

It was flinging the bowl at the man while yet he stood at the stake that saved him, for there is an etiquette about such matters. One does not burn a madman, among the Indians; and to the Shawnees, Jacob's flinging the bowl proved that he was mad, for a sane man would not have done so. Or so it was explained to him later, though he was never quite sure that they had not been playing cat-and-mouse with him, to test him. Also they were much concerned by his chanting his death song in an unknown tongue and by the phylactery that he had taken from its bag and bound upon brow and arm for his death hour, for these they thought strong medicine and uncertain. But in any case they released him, though they would not give him back his beaver, and that winter he passed in the lodges of the Shawnees, treated sometimes like a servant and sometimes like a guest, but always on the edge of peril. For he was strange to them, and they could not quite make up their minds about him, though the man with the scalded face had his own opinion, as Jacob could see.

Yet when the winter was milder and the hunting better than it had been in some seasons, it was he who got the credit of it, and the holy phylactery also; and by the end of the winter he was talking to them of trade, though diffidently at first. Ah, our grandfather's grandfather, *selig,* what woes he had! And yet it was not all woe, for he learned much woodcraft from the Shawnees and began to speak in their tongue.

Yet he did not trust them entirely; and when spring came and he could travel, he escaped. He was no longer a scholar then, but a hunter. He tried to think what day it was by the calendar, but he could only remember the Bee Moon and the Berry Moon. Yet when he thought of a feast he tried to keep it and always he prayed for Zion. But when he thought of Zion, it was not as he had thought of it before—a white city set on a hill—but a great and open landscape, ready for nations. He could not have said why his thought had changed, but it had.

I shall not tell all, for who knows all? I shall not tell of the trading post he found deserted and the hundred and forty French louis in the dead man's journey belt. I shall not tell of the half-grown boy, McGillvray, that he found on the fringes of settlement—the boy who was to be his partner in the days to come—and how they traded again with the Shawnees and got much beaver. Only this remains to be told, for this is true.

It was a long time since he had even thought of Meyer Kappelhuist—the big pushing man with red hairs on the backs of his hands. But now they were turning back toward Philadelphia, he and McGillvray, their packhorses and their beavers; and as the paths began to grow familiar, old thoughts came into his mind. Moreover, he would hear now and then, in the outposts of the wilderness, of a red-haired trader. So when he met the man himself, not thirty miles from Lancaster, he was not surprised.

Now, Meyer Kappelhuist had always seemed a big man to our grandfather's grandfather. But he did not seem such a big man, met in the wilderness by chance, and at that Jacob was amazed. Yet the greater surprise was Meyer Kappelhuist's, for he stared at our grandfather's grandfather long and puzzledly before he cried out, "But it's the little scholar!" and clapped his hand on his knee. Then they greeted each other civilly and Meyer Kappelhuist drank liquor because of the meeting, but Jacob drank nothing. For, all the time they were talking, he could see Meyer Kappelhuist's eyes fixed greedily upon his packs of beaver, and he did not like that. Nor did he like the looks of the three tame Indians who traveled with Meyer Kappelhuist and, though he was a man of peace, he kept his hand on his arms, and the boy, McGillvray, did the same.

Meyer Kappelhuist was anxious that they should travel on together, but Jacob refused, for, as I say, he did not like the look in the red-haired man's eyes. So he said he was taking another road and left it at that.

"And the news you have of Simon Ettelsohn and his family—it is good, no doubt, for I know you are close to them," said Jacob, before they parted.

"Close to them?" said Meyer Kappelhuist, and he looked black as thunder. Then he laughed a forced laugh. "Oh, I see them no more," he said. "The old rascal has promised his daughter to a cousin of the Seixas, a greeny, just come over, but rich, they say. But to tell you the truth, I think we are well out of it, Scholar—she was always a little too skinny for my taste," and he laughed coarsely.

"She was a rose of Sharon and a lily of the valley," said Jacob respectfully, and yet not with the pang he would have expected at such news, though it made him more determined than ever not to travel with Meyer Kappelhuist. And with that they parted and Meyer Kappelhuist went his way. Then Jacob took a fork in the trail that McGillvray knew of and that was as well for him. For when he got to Lancaster, there was news of the killing of a trader by the Indians who traveled with him; and when Jacob asked for details, they showed him something dried on a willow hoop. Jacob looked at the thing and saw the hairs upon it were red.

"Sculped all right, but we got it back," said the frontiersman, with satisfaction. "The red devil had it on him when we caught him. Should have buried it, too, I guess, but we'd buried him already and it didn't seem feasible. Thought I might take it to Philadelphy, sometime —might make an impression on the governor. Say, if you're going there, you might—after all, that's where he came from. Be a sort of memento to his folks."

"And it might have been mine, if I had traveled with him," said Jacob. He stared at the thing again, and his heart rose against touching it. Yet it was well the city people should know what happened to men in the wilderness, and the price of blood. "Yes, I will take it," he said.

Jacob stood before the door of Raphael Sanchez, in Philadelphia. He knocked at the door with his knuckles, and the old man himself peered out at him.

"And what is your business with me, Frontiersman?" said the old man, peering.

"The price of blood for a country," said Jacob Stein. He did not raise his voice, but there was a note in it that had not been there when he first knocked at Raphael Sanchez's door.

The old man stared at him soberly. "Enter, my son," he said at last, and Jacob touched the scroll by the doorpost and went in.

He walked through the halls as a man walks in a dream. At last he was sitting by the dark mahogany table. There was nothing changed in the room—he wondered greatly that nothing in it had changed.

"And what have you seen, my son?" said Raphael Sanchez.

"I have seen the land of Canaan, flowing with milk and honey," said Jacob, Scholar of the Law. "I have brought back grapes from Eshcol, and other things that are terrible to behold," he cried, and even as he cried he felt the sob rise in his throat. He choked it down. "Also there are eighteen packs of prime beaver at the warehouse and a boy named McGillvray, a Gentile, but very trusty," he said. "The beaver is very good and the boy under my protection. And McCampbell died by the great river, but he had seen the land and I think he rests well. The map is not made as I would have it, but it shows new things. And we must trade with the Shawnees. There are three posts to be established—I have marked them on the map —and later, more. And beyond the great river there is country that stretches to the end of the world. That is where my friend McCampbell lies, with his face turned west. But what is the use of talking? You would not understand."

He put his head on his arms, for the room was too quiet and peaceful, and he was very tired. Raphael Sanchez moved around the table and touched him on the shoulder.

"Did I not say, my son, that there was more than a girl's face to be found in the wilderness?" he said.

"A girl's face?" said Jacob. "Why, she is to be married and, I hope, will be happy, for she was a rose of Sharon. But what are girls' faces beside this?" and he flung something on the table. It rattled dryly on the table, like a cast snakeskin, but the hairs upon it were red.

"It was Meyer Kappelhuist," said Jacob childishly, "and he was a strong man. And I am not strong, but a scholar. But I have seen what I have seen. And we must say Kaddish for him."

"Yes, yes," said Raphael Sanchez. "It will be done. I will see to it."

"But you do not understand," said Jacob. "I have eaten deer's meat in the wilderness and forgotten the month and the year. I have been a servant to the heathen and held the scalp of my enemy in my hand. I will never be the same man."

"Oh, you will be the same," said Sanchez. "And no worse a scholar, perhaps. But this is a new country."

"It must be for all," said Jacob. "For my friend McCampbell died also, and he was a Gentile."

"Let us hope," said Raphael Sanchez and touched him again upon the shoulder. Then Jacob lifted his head and he saw that the light had declined and the evening was upon him. And even as he looked, Raphael Sanchez's granddaughter came in to light the candles for Sabbath. And Jacob looked upon her, and she was a dove, with dove's eyes.

STEPHEN VINCENT BENÉT

Too Early Spring

I'M WRITING this down because I don't ever want to forget the way it was. It doesn't seem as if I could, now, but they all tell you things change. And I guess they're right. Older people must have forgotten or they couldn't be the way they are. And that goes for even the best ones, like Dad and Mr. Grant. They try to understand but they don't seem to know how. And the others make you feel dirty or else they make you feel like a goof. Till, pretty soon, you begin to forget yourself—you begin to think, "Well, maybe they're right and it was that way." And that's the end of everything. So I've got to write this down. Because they smashed it forever—but it wasn't the way they said it.

Mr. Grant always says in comp. class, "Begin at the beginning." Only I don't know quite where the beginning was. We had a good summer at Big Lake but it was just the same summer. I worked pretty hard at the practice basket I rigged up in the barn, and I learned how to do the back jackknife. I'll never dive like Kerry but you want to be as all-round as you can. And, when I took my measurements, at the end of the summer, I was 5 ft. 9¾ and I'd gained 12 lbs. 6 oz. That wasn't bad for going on sixteen and the old chest expansion was O.K. You don't want to get too heavy, because basketball's a fast game, but the year before when I got my height, and I was so skinny, I got tired. But this year, Kerry helped me practice, a couple of times, and he seemed to think I had a good chance for the team. So I felt pretty set up—they'd never had a Sophomore on it before. And Kerry's a natural athlete, so that means a lot from him. He's a pretty good brother, too. Most Juniors at State wouldn't bother with a fellow in High.

It sounds as if I were trying to run away from what I have to write down, but I'm not. I want to remember that summer, too, because it's the last happy one I'll ever have. Oh, when I'm an old man—thirty or forty—things may be all right again. But that's a long time to wait and it won't be the same.

And yet, that summer was different, too, in a way. So it must have started then, though I didn't know it. I went around with the gang as usual and we had a good time. But, every now, and then, it would strike me we were acting like awful kids. They thought I was getting the big head, but I wasn't. It just wasn't much fun—even going to the cave. It was like going on shooting marbles when you're in High.

I had sense enough not to try to tag after Kerry and his crowd. You can't do that. But when they all got out on the lake in canoes, warm evenings, and somebody brought a phonograph along, I used to go down to the Point, all by myself, and listen and listen. Maybe they'd be talking or maybe they'd be singing, but it all sounded mysterious across the water. I wasn't trying to hear what they said, you know. That's the kind of thing Tot Pickens does. I'd just listen, with my arms around my knees—and somehow it would hurt me to listen—and yet I'd rather do that than be with the gang.

I was sitting under the four pines, one night, right down by the edge of the water. There was a big moon and they were singing. It's funny how you can be unhappy and nobody knows it but yourself.

I was thinking about Sheila Coe. She's Kerry's girl. They fight but they get along. She's awfully pretty and she can swim like a fool. Once Kerry sent me over with her tennis racket and we had quite a conversation. She was fine. And she didn't pull any of this big sister stuff, either, the way some girls will with a fellow's kid brother.

And when the canoe came along, by the edge of the lake, I thought for a moment it was her. I thought maybe she was looking for Kerry and maybe she'd stop and maybe she'd feel like talking to me again. I don't know why I thought that—I didn't have any reason. Then I saw it was just the Sharon kid, with a new kind of bob that made her look grown-up, and I felt sore. She didn't have any business out on the lake at her age. She was just a Sophomore in High, the same as me.

I chunked a stone in the water and it splashed right by the canoe, but she didn't squeal. She just said, "Fish," and chuckled. It struck me it was a kid's trick, trying to scare a kid.

"Hello, Helen," I said. "Where did you swipe the gunboat?"

"They don't know I've got it," she said. "Oh, hello, Chuck Peters. How's Big Lake?"

"All right," I said. "How was camp?"

"It was peachy," she said. "We had a peachy counselor, Miss Morgan. She was on the Wellesley field-hockey team."

"Well," I said, "we missed your society." Of course we hadn't, because they're across the lake and don't swim at our raft. But you ought to be polite.

"Thanks," she said. "Did you do the special reading for English? I thought it was dumb."

"It's always dumb," I said. "What canoe is that?"

"It's the old one," she said. "I'm not supposed to have it out at night. But you won't tell anybody, will you?"

"Be your age," I said. I felt generous. "I'll paddle a while, if you want," I said.

"All right," she said, so she brought it in and I got aboard. She went back in the bow and I took the paddle. I'm not strong on carting kids around, as a rule. But it was better than sitting there by myself.

"Where do you want to go?" I said.

"Oh, back towards the house," she said in a shy kind of voice. "I ought to, really. I just wanted to hear the singing."

"K.O.," I said. I didn't paddle fast, just let her slip. There was a lot of moon on the water. We kept around the edge so they wouldn't notice us. The singing sounded as if it came from a different country, a long way off.

She was a sensible kid, she didn't ask fool questions or giggle about nothing at all. Even when we went by Petters' Cove. That's where the lads from the bungalow colony go and it's pretty well populated on a warm night. You can hear them talking in low voices and now and then a laugh. Once Tot Pickens and a gang went over there with a flashlight, and a big Bohunk chased them for half a mile.

I felt funny, going by there with her. But I said, "Well, it's certainly Old Home Week"—in an offhand tone, because, after all, you've got to be sophisticated. And she said, "People are funny," in just the right sort of way. I took quite a shine to her after that and we talked. The Sharons have only been in town three years and somehow I'd never really noticed her before. Mrs. Sharon's awfully good-looking but she and Mr. Sharon fight. That's hard on a kid. And she was a quiet kid. She had a small kind of face and her eyes were sort of like a kitten's. You could see she got a great kick out of pretending to be grown-up—and yet it wasn't all pretending. A couple of times, I felt just as if I were talking to Sheila Coe. Only more comfortable, because, after all, we were the same age.

Do you know, after we put the canoe up, I walked all the way back home, around the lake? And most of the way, I ran. I felt swell, too. I felt as if I could run forever and not stop. It was like finding something. I hadn't imagined anybody could ever feel the way I did about some things. And here was another person, even if it was a girl.

Kerry's door was open when I went by and he stuck his head out and grinned.

"Well, kid," he said. "Stepping out?"

"Sure. With Greta Garbo," I said, and grinned back to show I didn't mean it. I felt sort of lightheaded, with the run and everything.

"Look here, kid—" he said, as if he was going to say something. Then he stopped. But there was a funny look on his face.

And yet I didn't see her again till we were both back in High. Mr. Sharon's uncle died, back East, and they closed the cottage suddenly. But all the rest of the time at Big Lake, I kept remembering that night and her little face. If I'd seen her in daylight, first, it might have been different. No, it wouldn't have been.

All the same, I wasn't even thinking of her when we bumped into each other, the first day of school. It was raining and she had on a green slicker and her hair was curly under her hat. We grinned and said hello and had to run. But something happened to us, I guess.

I'll say this now—it wasn't like Tot Pickens and Mabel Palmer. It wasn't like Junior David and Betty Page—though they've been going together ever since kindergarten. It wasn't like any of those things. We didn't get sticky and sloppy. It wasn't like going with a girl.

Gosh, there'd be days and days when we'd hardly see each other, except in class. I had basketball practice almost every afternoon and sometimes evenings and she was taking music lessons four times a week. But you don't have to be always twos-ing with a person, if you feel that way about them. You seem to know the way they're thinking and feeling, the way you know yourself.

Now let me describe her. She had that little face and the eyes like a kitten's. When it rained, her hair curled all over the back of her neck. She wasn't a tall girl but she wasn't chunky—just light and well made and quick. She was awfully alive without being nervous—she never bit her finger-nails or chewed the end of her pencil, but she'd answer quicker than anyone in the class. Nearly everybody liked her, but she wasn't best friends with any particular girl, the mushy way they get. The teachers all thought a lot of her, even Miss Eagles. Well, I had to spoil that.

If we'd been like Tot and Mabel, we could have had a lot more time together, I guess. But Helen isn't a liar and I'm not a snake. It wasn't easy, going over to her house, because Mr. and Mrs. Sharon would be polite to each other in front of you and yet there'd be something wrong. And she'd have to be fair to both of them and they were always pulling at her. But we'd look at each other across the table and then it would be all right.

I don't know when it was that we knew we'd get married to each other, some time. We just started talking about it, one day, as if we always had. We thought maybe when we were eighteen. That was two years but we knew we had to be educated. You don't get as good a job, if you aren't. Or that's what people say.

We weren't mushy either, like some people. We got to kissing each other good-by sometimes, because that's what you do when you're in love. It was cool, the way she kissed you, it was like leaves. But lots of the times we wouldn't even talk about getting married, we'd just play checkers or go over the old Latin, or once in a while go to the movies with the gang. It was really a wonderful winter. I played every game after the first one and she'd sit in the gallery and watch and I'd know she was there. You could see her little green hat or her yellow hair. Those are the class colors, green and gold.

And it's a queer thing, but everybody seemed to be pleased. That's what I can't get over. They liked to see us together. The grown people, I mean. Oh, of course, we got kidded too. And old Mrs. Withers would ask me about "my little sweetheart," in that awful damp voice of hers. But, mostly, they were all right. Even Mother was all right, though she didn't like Mrs. Sharon. I did hear her say to Father, once, "Really, George, how long is this going to last? Sometimes I feel as if I just couldn't stand it."

Then Father chuckled and said to her, "Now, Mary last year you were worried about him because he didn't take any interest in girls at all."

"Well," she said, "he still doesn't. Oh, Helen's a nice child—no credit to Eva Sharon—and thank heaven she doesn't giggle. Well, Charles is mature for *his* age too. But he acts so solemn about her. It isn't natural."

"Oh, let Charlie alone," said Father. "The boy's all right. He's just got a one-track mind."

But it wasn't so nice for us after the spring came.

In our part of the state, it comes pretty late, as a rule. But it was early this year. The little kids were out with scooters when usually they'd still be having snowfights and, all of a sudden, the radiators in the classrooms smelt dry. You'd got used to that smell for months—and then, there was a day when you hated it again and everybody kept asking to open the windows. The monitors had a tough time, that first week—they always do when spring starts—but this year it was worse than ever because it came when you didn't expect it.

Usually, basketball's over by the time spring really breaks, but this year it hit us while we still had three games to play. And it certainly played hell with us as a team. After Bladesburg nearly licked us, Mr. Grant called off all practice until the day before the St. Matthew's game. He knew we were stale—and they've been state champions two years. They'd have walked all over us, the way we were going.

The first thing I did was telephone Helen. Because that meant there were six extra afternoons we could have, if she could get rid of her music lesson any way. Well, she said, wasn't it wonderful, her music teacher had a cold? And that seemed just like Fate.

Well, that was a great week and we were so happy. We went to the movies five times and once Mrs. Sharon let us take her little car. She knew I didn't have a driving license but of course I've driven ever since I was thirteen and she said it was all right. She was funny—sometimes she'd be awfully kind and friendly to you and sometimes she'd be like a piece of dry ice. She was that way with Mr. Sharon too. But it was a wonderful ride. We got stuff out of the kitchen—the cook's awfully sold on Helen—and drove way out in the country. And we found an old house, with the windows gone, on top of a hill, and parked the car and took the stuff up to the house and ate it there. There weren't any chairs or tables but we pretended there were.

We pretended it was our house, after we were married. I'll never forget that. She'd even brought paper napkins and paper plates and she set two places on the floor.

"Well, Charles," she said, sitting opposite me with her feet tucked under, "I don't suppose you remember the days we were both in school."

"Sure," I said—she was always much quicker pretending things than I was—"I remember them all right. That was before Tot Pickens got to be President." And we both laughed.

"It seems very distant in the past to me—we've been married so long," she said, as if she really believed it. She looked at me.

"Would you mind turning off the radio, dear?" she said. "This modern music always gets on my nerves."

"Have we got a radio?" I said.

"Of course, Chuck."

"With television?"

"Of course, Chuck."

"Gee, I'm glad," I said. I went and turned it off.

"Of course, if you *want* to listen to the late market reports—" she said just like Mrs. Sharon.

"Nope," I said. "The market—uh—closed firm today. Up twenty-six points."

"That's quite a long way up, isn't it?"

"Well, the country's perfectly sound at heart, in spite of this damfool Congress," I said, like Father.

She lowered her eyes a minute, just like her mother, and pushed away her plate.

"I'm not very hungry tonight," she said. "You won't mind if I go upstairs?"

"Aw, don't be like that," I said. It was too much like her mother.

"I was just seeing if I could," she said. "But I never will, Chuck."

"I'll never tell you you're nervous, either," I said. "I—oh, gosh!"

She grinned and it was all right. "Mr. Ashland and I

have never had a serious dispute in our wedded lives," she said—and everybody knows who runs *that* family. "We just talk things over calmly and reach a satisfactory conclusion, usually mine."

"Say, what kind of a house have we got?"

"It's a lovely house," she said. "We've got radios in every room and lots of servants. We've got a regular movie projector and a library full of good classics and there's always something in the icebox. I've got a shoe closet."

"A what?"

"A shoe closet. All my shoes are on tipped shelves, like Mother's. And all my dresses are on those padded hangers. And I say to the maid, 'Elsie, Madam will wear the new French model today.' "

"What are my clothes on?" I said. "Christmas trees?"

"Well," she said. "You've got lots of clothes and dogs. You smell of pipes and the open and something called Harrisburg tweed."

"I do not," I said. "I wish I had a dog. It's a long time since Jack."

"Oh, Chuck, I'm sorry," she said.

"Oh, that's all right," I said. "He was getting old and his ear was always bothering him. But he was a good pooch. Go ahead."

"Well," she said, "of course we give parties—"

"Cut the parties," I said.

"Chuck! They're grand ones!"

"I'm a home body," I said. "Give me—er—my wife and my little family and—say, how many kids have we got, anyway?"

She counted on her fingers. "Seven."

"Good Lord," I said.

"Well, I always wanted seven. You can make it three, if you like."

"Oh, seven's all right, I suppose," I said. "But don't they get awfully in the way?"

"No," she said. "We have governesses and tutors and send them to boarding school."

"O.K.," I said. "But it's a strain on the old man's pocketbook, just the same."

"Chuck, will you ever talk like that? Chuck, this is when we're rich." Then suddenly, she looked sad. "Oh, Chuck, do you suppose we ever will?" she said.

"Why, sure," I said.

"I wouldn't mind if it was only a dump," she said. "I could cook for you. I keep asking Hilda how she makes things."

I felt awfully funny. I felt as if I were going to cry.

"We'll do it," I said. "Don't you worry."

"Oh, Chuck, you're a comfort," she said.

I held her for a while. It was like holding something awfully precious. It wasn't mushy or that way. I know what that's like too.

"It takes so long to get old," she said. "I wish I could grow up tomorrow. I wish we both could."

"Don't you worry," I said. "It's going to be all right."

We didn't say much, going back in the car, but we were happy enough. I thought we passed Miss Eagles at the turn. That worried me a little because of the driving license. But, after all, Mrs. Sharon had said we could take the car.

We wanted to go back again, after that, but it was too far to walk and that was the only time we had the car. Mrs. Sharon was awfully nice about it but she said, thinking it over, maybe we'd better wait till I got a license. Well, Father didn't want me to get one till I was seventeen but I thought he might come around. I didn't want to do anything that would get Helen in a jam with her family. That shows how careful I was of her. Or thought I was.

All the same, we decided we'd do something to celebrate if the team won the St. Matthew's game. We thought it would be fun if we could get a steak and cook supper out somewhere—something like that. Of course we could have done it easily enough with a gang, but we didn't want a gang. We wanted to be alone together, the way we'd been at the house. That was all we wanted. I don't see what's wrong about that. We even took paper plates, so as not to litter things up.

Boy, that was a game! We beat them 36-34 and it took an extra period and I thought it would never end. That two-goal lead they had looked as big as the Rocky Mountains all the first half. And they gave me the full school cheer with nine Peters when we tied them up. You don't forget things like that.

Afterwards, Mr. Grant had a kind of spread for the team at his house and a lot of people came in. Kerry had driven down from State to see the game and that made me feel pretty swell. And what made me feel better yet was his taking me aside and saying, "Listen, kid. I don't want you to get the swelled head, but you did a good job. Well, just remember this. Don't let anybody kid you out of going to State. You'll like it up there." And Mr. Grant heard him and laughed and said, "Well, Peters, I'm not proselytizing. But your brother might think about some of the Eastern colleges." It was all like the kind of dream you have when you can do anything. It was wonderful.

Only Helen wasn't there because the only girls were older girls. I'd seen her for a minute. I wanted to tell her about that big St. Matthew's forward—and—oh, everything. Well, you like to talk things over with your girl.

Father and Mother were swell but they had to go on to some big shindy at the country club. And Kerry was going there with Sheila Coe. But Mr. Grant said he'd run me back to the house in his car and he did. He's a great guy. He made jokes about my being the infant phenomenon of basketball, and they were good jokes too. I didn't mind them. But, all the same, when I'd said good night to him and gone into the house, I felt sort of let down.

I knew I'd be tired the next day but I didn't feel sleepy yet. I was too excited. I wanted to talk to somebody. I wandered around downstairs and wondered if Ida was still up. Well, she wasn't, but she'd left half a chocolate cake, covered over, on the kitchen table, and a note on top of it, "Congratulations to Mister Charles Peters." Well, that was awfully nice of her and I ate some. Then I turned the radio on and got the time signal—eleven—and some snappy music. But still I didn't feel like hitting the hay.

So I thought I'd call up Helen and then I thought—probably she's asleep and Hilda or Mrs. Sharon will answer the phone and be sore. And then I thought—well, anyhow, I could go over and walk around the block and look at her house. I'd get some fresh air out of it, anyway, and it would be a little like seeing her.

So I did—and it was a swell night—cool and a lot of stars—and I felt like a king, walking over. All the lower part of the Sharon house was dark but a window upstairs was lit. I knew it was her window. I went around back of the driveway and whistled once—the whistle we made up. I never expected her to hear.

But she did, and there she was at the window, smiling. She made motions that she'd come down to the side door.

Honestly, it took my breath away when I saw her. She had on a kind of yellow thing over her night clothes and she looked so pretty. Her feet were so pretty in those slippers. You almost expected her to be carrying one of those animals that kids like—she looked young enough. I know I oughtn't to have gone into the house. But we didn't think anything about it—we were just glad to see each other. We hadn't had any sort of chance to talk over the game.

We sat in front of the fire in the living room and she went out to the kitchen and got us cookies and milk. I wasn't really hungry, but it was like that time at the house, eating with her. Mr. and Mrs. Sharon were at the country club, too, so we weren't disturbing them or anything. We turned off the lights because there was plenty of light from the fire and Mr. Sharon's one of those people who can't stand having extra lights burning. Dad's that way about saving string.

It was quiet and lovely and the firelight made shadows on the ceiling. We talked a lot and then we just sat, each of us knowing the other was there. And the room got quieter and quieter and I'd told her about the game and I didn't feel excited or jumpy any more—just rested and happy. And then I knew by her breathing that she was asleep and I put my arm around her for just a minute. Because it was wonderful to hear that quiet breathing and know it was hers. I was going to wake her in a minute. I didn't realize how tired I was myself.

And then we were back in that house in the country and it was our home and we ought to have been happy. But something was wrong because there still wasn't any glass in the windows and a wind kept blowing through them and we tried to shut the doors but they wouldn't shut. It drove Helen distracted and we were both running through the house, trying to shut the doors, and we were cold and afraid. Then the sun rose outside the windows, burning and yellow and so big it covered the sky. And with the sun was a horrible, weeping voice. It was Mrs. Sharon's saying, "Oh, my God, oh, my God."

I didn't know what had happened, for a minute, when I woke. And then I did and it was awful. Mrs. Sharon was saying, "Oh, Helen—I trusted you . . ." and looking as if she were going to faint. And Mr. Sharon looked at her for a minute and his face was horrible and he said, "Bred in the bone," and she looked as if he'd hit her. Then he said to Helen—

I don't want to think of what they said. I don't want to think of any of the things they said. Mr. Sharon is a bad man. And she is a bad woman, even if she is Helen's mother. All the same, I could stand the things he said better than hers.

I don't want to think of any of it. And it is all spoiled now. Everything is spoiled. Miss Eagles saw us going to that house in the country and she said horrible things. They made Helen sick and she hasn't been back at school. There isn't any way I can see her. And if I could, it would be spoiled. We'd be thinking about the things they said.

I don't know how many of the people know, at school. But Tot Pickens passed me a note. And, that afternoon, I caught him behind his house. I'd have broken his nose if they hadn't pulled me off. I meant to. Mother cried when she heard about it and Dad took me into his room and talked to me. He said you can't lick the whole town. But I will anybody like Tot Pickens. Dad and Mother have been all right. But they say things about Helen and that's almost worse. They're for me because I'm their son. But they don't understand.

I thought I could talk to Kerry but I can't. He was nice but he looked at me such a funny way. I don't know—sort of impressed. It wasn't the way I wanted him to look. But he's been decent. He comes down almost every weekend and we play catch in the yard.

You see, I just go to school and back now. They want me to go with the gang, the way I did, but I can't do that. Not after Tot. Of course my marks are a lot better because I've got more time to study now. But it's lucky I haven't got Miss Eagles though Dad made her apologize. I couldn't recite to her.

I think Mr. Grant knows because he asked me to his house once and we had a conversation. Not about that, though I was terribly afraid he would. He showed me a lot of his old college things and the gold football he wears on his watch chain. He's got a lot of interesting things.

Then we got talking, somehow, about history and things like that and how times had changed. Why, there were kings and queens who got married younger than Helen and me. Only now we lived longer and had a lot more to learn. So it couldn't happen now. "It's civilization," he said. "And all civilization's against nature. But I suppose we've got to have it. Only sometimes it isn't easy." Well, somehow or other, that made me feel less lonely. Before I'd been feeling that I was the only person on earth who'd ever felt that way.

I'm going to Colorado, this summer, to a ranch, and next year, I'll go East to school. Mr. Grant says he thinks I can make the basketball team, if I work hard enough, though it isn't as big a game in the East as it is with us. Well, I'd like to show them something. It would be some satisfaction. He says not to be too fresh at first, but I won't be that.

It's a boys' school and there aren't even women teachers. And, maybe, afterwards, I could be a professional basketball player or something, where you don't have to see women at all. Kerry says I'll get over that; but I won't. They all sound like Mrs. Sharon to me now, when they laugh.

They're going to send Helen to a convent—I found out that. Maybe they'll let me see her before she goes. But, if we do, it will be all wrong and in front of people and everybody pretending. I sort of wish they don't—though I want to, terribly. When her mother took her upstairs that night—she wasn't the same Helen. She looked at me as if she was afraid of me. And no matter what they do for us now, they can't fix that.

WILLIAM FAULKNER

The Bear

HE WAS ten. But it had already begun, long before that day when at last he wrote his age in two figures and he saw for the first time the camp where his father and Major de Spain and old General Compson and the others spent two weeks each November and two weeks again each June. He had already inherited then, without ever having seen it, the tremendous bear with one trap-ruined foot which, in an area almost a hundred miles deep, had earned itself a name, a definite designation like a living man.

He had listened to it for years: the long legend of corncribs rifled, of shotes and grown pigs and even calves carried bodily into the woods and devoured, of traps and deadfalls overthrown and dogs mangled and slain, and shotgun and even rifle charges delivered at point-blank range and with no more effect than so many peas blown through a tube by a boy—a corridor of wreckage and destruction beginning back before he was born, through which sped, not fast but rather with the ruthless and irresistible deliberation of a locomotive, the shaggy tremendous shape.

It ran in his knowledge before he ever saw it. It looked and towered in his dreams before he even saw the unaxed woods where it left its crooked print, shaggy, huge, red-eyed, not malevolent but just big—too big for the dogs which tried to bay it, for the horses which tried to ride it down, for the men and the bullets they fired into it, too big for the very country which was its constricting scope. He seemed to see it entire with a child's complete divination before he ever laid eyes on either—the doomed wilderness whose edges were being constantly and punily gnawed at by men with axes and plows who feared it because it was wilderness, men myriad and nameless even to one another in the land where the old bear had earned a name, through which ran not even a mortal animal but an anachronism, indomitable and invincible, out of an old dead time, a phantom, epitome and apotheosis of the old wild life at which the puny humans swarmed and hacked in a fury of abhorrence and fear, like pygmies about the ankles of a drowsing elephant: the old bear solitary, indomitable and alone, widowered, childless, and absolved of mortality—old Priam reft of his old wife and having outlived all his sons.

Until he was ten, each November he would watch the wagon containing the dogs and the bedding and food and guns and his father and Tennie's Jim, the Negro, and Sam Fathers, the Indian, son of a slave woman and a Chickasaw chief, depart on the road to town, to Jefferson, where Major de Spain and the others would join them. To the boy, at seven, eight, and nine, they were not going into the Big Bottom to hunt bear and deer, but to keep yearly rendezvous with the bear which they did not even intend to kill. Two weeks later they would return, with no trophy, no head and skin. He had not expected it. He had not even been afraid it would be in the wagon. He believed that even after he was ten and his father would let him go too, for those two weeks in November, he would merely make another one, along with his father and Major de Spain and General Compson and the others, the dogs which feared to bay it and the rifles and shotguns which failed even to bleed it, in the yearly pageant of the old bear's furious immortality.

Then he heard the dogs. It was in the second week of his first time in the camp. He stood with Sam Fathers against a big oak beside the faint crossing where they had stood each dawn for nine days now, hearing the dogs. He had heard them once before, one morning last week—a murmur, sourceless, echoing through the wet woods, swelling presently into separate voices which he could recognize and call by name. He had raised and cocked the gun as Sam told him and stood motionless again while the uproar, the invisible course, swept up and past and faded; it seemed to him that he could actually see the deer, the buck, blond, smoke-colored, elongated with speed, fleeing, vanishing, the woods, the gray solitude, still ringing even when the cries of the dogs had died away.

"Now let the hammers down," Sam said.

"You knew they were not coming here too," he said.

"Yes," Sam said. "I want you to learn how to do when you didn't shoot. It's after the chance for the bear or the deer has done already come and gone that men and dogs get killed."

"Anyway," he said, "it was just a deer."

Then on the tenth morning he heard the dogs again. And he readied the too-long, too-heavy gun as Sam had taught him, before Sam even spoke. But this time it was no deer, no ringing chorus of dogs running strong on a free scent, but a moiling yapping an octave too high, with something more than indecision and even abjectness in it, not even moving very fast, taking a long time to pass completely out of hearing, leaving then somewhere in the air that echo, thin, slightly hysterical, abject, almost grieving, with no sense of a fleeing, unseen, smoke-colored, grass-eating shape ahead of it, and Sam, who had taught him first of all to cock the gun and take position where he could see everywhere and then never move again, had himself moved up beside him; he could hear Sam breathing at his shoulder, and he could see the arched curve of the old man's inhaling nostrils.

"Hah," Sam said. "Not even running. Walking."

"Old Ben!" the boy said. "But up here!" he cried. "Way up here!"

"He do it every year," Sam said. "Once. Maybe to see who in camp this time, if he can shoot or not. Whether we got the dog yet that can bay and hold him. He'll take them to the river, then he'll send them back home. We may as well go back too; see how they look when they come back to camp."

When they reached the camp the hounds were already there, ten of them crouching back under the kitchen, the boy and Sam squatting to peer back into the obscurity where they had huddled, quiet, the eyes luminous, glowing at them and vanishing, and no sound, only that effluvium of something more than dog, stronger than dog and not just animal, just beast, because still there had been nothing in front of that abject and almost painful yapping save the solitude, the wilderness, so that when the eleventh hound came in at noon and with all the others watching—even old Uncle Ash, who called himself first a cook—Sam daubed the tattered ear and the raked shoulder with turpentine and axle grease, to the boy it was still no living creature, but the wilderness which, leaning for the moment down, had patted lightly once the hound's temerity.

"Just like a man," Sam said. "Just like folks. Put off as long as she could having to be brave, knowing all the time that sooner or later she would have to be brave to keep on living with herself, and knowing all the time beforehand what was going to happen to her when she done it."

That afternoon, himself on the one-eyed wagon mule which did not mind the smell of blood nor, as they told him, of bear, and with Sam on the other one, they rode for more than three hours through the rapid, shortening winter day. They followed no path, no trail even that he could see; almost at once they were in a country which he had never seen before. Then he knew why Sam had made him ride the mule which would not spook. The sound one stopped short and tried to whirl and bolt even as Sam got down, blowing its breath, jerking and wrenching at the rein, while Sam held it, coaxing it forward with his voice, since he could not risk tying it, drawing it forward while the boy got down from the marred one.

Then, standing beside Sam in the gloom of the dying afternoon, he looked down at the rotted over-turned log, gutted and scored with claw marks and, in the wet earth beside it, the print of the enormous warped two-toed foot. He knew now what he had smelled when he peered under the kitchen where the dogs huddled. He realized for the first time that the bear which had run in his listening and loomed in his dreams since before he could remember to the contrary, and which, therefore, must have existed in the listening and dreams of his father and Major de Spain and even old General Compson, too, before they began to remember in their turn, was a mortal animal, and that if they had departed for the camp each November without any actual hope of bringing its trophy back, it was not because it could not be slain, but because so far they had

had no actual hope to.

"Tomorrow," he said.

"We'll try tomorrow," Sam said. "We ain't got the dog yet."

"We've got eleven. They ran him this morning."

"It won't need but one," Sam said. "He ain't here. Maybe he ain't nowhere. The only other way will be for him to run by accident over somebody that has a gun."

"That wouldn't be me," the boy said. "It will be Walter or Major or—"

"It might," Sam said. "You watch close in the morning. Because he's smart. That's how come he has lived this long. If he gets hemmed up and has to pick out somebody to run over, he will pick out you."

"How?" the boy said. "How will he know—" He ceased. "You mean he already knows me, that I ain't never been here before, ain't had time to find out yet whether I—" He ceased again, looking at Sam, the old man whose face revealed nothing until it smiled. He said humbly, not even amazed, "It was me he was watching. I don't reckon he did need to come but once."

The next morning they left the camp three hours before daylight. They rode this time because it was too far to walk, even the dogs in the wagon; again the first gray light found him in a place which he had never seen before, where Sam had placed him and told him to stay and then departed. With the gun which was too big for him, which did not even belong to him, but to Major de Spain, and which he had fired only once—at a stump on the first day, to learn the recoil and how to reload it—he stood against a gum tree beside a little bayou whose black still water crept without movement out of a canebrake and crossed a small clearing and into cane again, where, invisible, a bird—the big woodpecker called Lord-to-God by Negroes—clattered at a dead limb.

It was a stand like any other, dissimilar only in incidentals to the one where he had stood each morning for ten days; a territory new to him, yet no less familiar than that other one which, after almost two weeks, he had come to believe he knew a little—the same solitude, the same loneliness through which human beings had merely passed without altering it, leaving no mark, no scar, which looked exactly as it must have looked when the first ancestor of Sam Fathers' Chickasaw predecessors crept into it and looked about, club or stone ax or bone arrow drawn and poised; different only because, squatting at the edge of the kitchen, he smelled the hounds huddled and cringing beneath it and saw the raked ear and shoulder of the one who, Sam said, had had to be brave once in order to live with herself, and saw yesterday in the earth beside the gutted log the print of the living foot.

He heard no dogs at all. He never did hear them. He only heard the drumming of the woodpecker stop short off and knew that the bear was looking at him. He never saw it. He did not know whether it was in front of him or behind him. He did not move, holding the useless gun, which he had not even had warning to cock and which even now he did not cock, tasting in his saliva that taint as of brass which he knew now because he had smelled it when he peered under the kitchen at the huddled dogs.

Then it was gone. As abruptly as it had ceased, the woodpecker's dry, monotonous clatter set up again, and after a while he even believed he could hear the dogs—a murmur, scarce a sound even, which he had probably been hearing for some time before he even remarked it, drifting into hearing and then out again, dying away. They came nowhere near him. If it was a bear they ran, it was another bear. It was Sam himself who came out of the cane and crossed the bayou, followed by the injured bitch of yesterday. She was almost at heel, like a bird dog, making no sound. She came and crouched against his leg, trembling, staring off into the cane.

"I didn't see him," he said. "I didn't Sam!"

"I know it," Sam said. "He done the looking. You didn't hear him neither, did you?"

"No," the boy said. "I—"

"He's smart," Sam said. "Too smart." He looked down at the hound, trembling faintly and steadily against the boy's knee. From the raked shoulder a few drops of fresh blood oozed and clung. "Too big. We ain't got the dog yet. But maybe someday. Maybe not next time. But someday."

So I must see him, he thought. *I must look at him.* Otherwise, it seemed to him that it would go on like this forever, as it had gone on with his father and Major de Spain, who was older than his father, and even with old General Compson, who had been old enough to be a brigade commander in 1865. Otherwise, it would go on so forever, next time and next time, after and after and after. It seemed to him that he could never see the two of them, himself and the bear, shadowy in the limbo from which time emerged, becoming time; the old bear absolved of mortality and himself partaking, sharing a little of it, enough of it. And he knew now what he had smelled in the huddled dogs and tasted in his saliva. He recognized fear. *So I will have to see him,* he thought, without dread or even hope. *I will have to look at him.*

It was in June of the next year. He was eleven. They were in camp again, celebrating Major de Spain's and General Compson's birthdays. Although the one had been born in September and the other in the depth of winter and in another decade, they had met for two weeeks to fish and shoot squirrels and turkey and run coons and wildcats with the dogs at night. That is, he and Boon Hoggenbeck and the Negroes fished and shot squirrels and ran the coons and cats, because the proved hunters, not only Major de Spain and old General Compson, who spent those two weeks sitting in a rocking chair before a tremendous iron pot of Brunswick stew, stirring and tasting, with old Ash to quarrel with about how he was making it and Tennie's Jim to pour whiskey from the demijohn into the tin dipper from which he drank it, but even the boy's father and Walter Ewell, who were still young enough, scorned such, other than shooting the wild gobblers with pistols for wagers on their marksmanship.

Or, that is, his father and the others believed he was hunting squirrels. Until the third day, he thought that Sam Fathers believed that too. Each morning he would leave the camp right after breakfast. He had his own gun now, a Christmas present. He went back to the tree beside the bayou where he had stood that morning. Using the compass which old General Compson had given him, he ranged from that point; he was teaching himself to be a better-than-fair woodsman without knowing he was doing it. On the second day he even found the gutted log where he had first seen the crooked print. It was almost completely crumbled now, healing with unbelievable speed, a passionate and almost visible relinquishment, back into the earth from which the tree had grown.

He ranged the summer woods now, green with gloom; if anything, actually dimmer than in November's gray dissolution, where, even at noon, the sun fell only in intermittent dappling upon the earth, which never completely dried out and which crawled with snakes—moccasins and water snakes and rattlers, themselves the color of the dappling gloom, so that he would not always see them until they moved, returning later and later, first day, second day, passing in the twilight of the third evening the little log pen enclosing the log stable where Sam was putting up the horses for the night.

"You ain't looked right yet," Sam said.

He stopped. For a moment he didn't answer. Then he said peacefully, in a peaceful rushing burst as when a boy's miniature dam in a little brook gives way, "All right. But how? I went to the bayou. I even found that log again. I—"

"I reckon that was all right. Likely he's been watching you. You never saw his foot?"

"I," the boy said—"I didn't—I never thought—"

"It's the gun," Sam said. He stood beside the fence motionless—the old man, the Indian, in the battered faded overalls and the five-cent straw hat which in the Negro's race had been the badge of his enslavement and was now the regalia of his freedom. The camp—the clearing, the house, the barn and its tiny lot with which Major de Spain in his turn had scratched punily and evanescently at the wilderness—faded in the dusk, back into the immemorial darkness of the woods. *The gun,* the boy thought. *The gun.*

"Be scared," Sam said. "You can't help that. But don't be afraid. Ain't nothing in the woods going to hurt you unless you corner it, or it smells that you are afraid. A bear or a deer, too, has got to be scared of a coward the same as a brave man has got to be."

The gun, the boy thought.

"You will have to choose," Sam said.

He left the camp before daylight, long before Uncle Ash would wake in his quilts on the kitchen floor and start the fire for breakfast. He had only the compass and a stick for snakes. He could go almost a mile before he would begin to need the compass. He sat on a log, the invisible compass in his invisible hand, while the secret night sounds, fallen still at his movements, scurried again and then ceased for good, and the owls ceased and gave over to the waking of day birds, and he could see the compass. Then he went fast yet still quietly; he was becoming better and better as a woodsman, still without having yet realized it.

He jumped a doe and a fawn at sunrise, walked them out of the bed, close enough to see them—the crash of undergrowth, the white scut, the fawn scudding behind her faster than he had believed it could run. He was hunting right, upwind, as Sam had taught him; not that it mattered now. He had left the gun; of his own will and relinquishment he had accepted not a gambit, not a choice, but a condition in which not only the bear's heretofore inviolable anonymity but all the old rules and balances of hunter and hunted had been abrogated. He would not even be afraid, not even in the moment when the fear would take him completely—blood, skin, bowels, bones, memory from the long time before it became his memory—all save that thin, clear, immortal lucidity which alone differed him from this bear and from all the other bear and deer he would ever kill in the humility and pride of his skill and endurance, to which Sam had spoken when he leaned in the twilight on the lot fence yesterday.

By noon he was far beyond the little bayou, farther into the new and alien country than he had ever been. He was traveling now only by the old, heavy, biscuit-thick silver watch which had belonged to his grandfather. When he stopped at last, it was for the first time since he had risen from the log at dawn when he could see the compass. It was far enough. He had left the camp nine hours ago; nine hours from now, dark would have already been an hour old. But he didn't think that. He thought, *All right. Yes. But what?* and stood for a moment, alien and small in the green and topless solitude, answering his own question before it had formed and ceased. It was the watch, the compass, the stick—the three lifeless mechanicals with which for nine hours he had fended the wilderness off; he hung the watch and compass carefully on a bush and leaned the stick beside them and relinquished completely to it.

He had not been going very fast for the last two or three hours. He went no faster now, since distance would not matter even if he could have gone fast. And he was trying to keep a bearing on the tree where he had left the compass, trying to complete a circle which would bring him back to it or at least intersect itself, since direction would not matter now either. But the tree was not there, and he did as Sam had schooled him—made the next circle in the opposite direction, so that the two patterns would bisect somewhere, but crossing no print of his own feet, finding the tree at last, but in the wrong place—no bush, no compass, no watch—and the tree not even the tree, because there was a down log beside it and he did what Sam Fathers had told him was the next thing and the last.

As he sat down on the log he saw the crooked print—the warped, tremendous, two-toed indentation which, even as he watched it, filled with water. As he looked up, the wilderness coalesced, solidified—the glade, the tree he sought, the bush, the watch and the compass glinting where a ray of sunshine touched them. Then he saw the bear. It did not emerge, appear; it was just there, immobile, solid, fixed in the hot dappling of the green and windless noon, not as big as he had dreamed it, but as big as he had expected it, bigger, dimensionless, against the dappled obscurity, looking at him where he sat quietly on the log and looked back at it.

Then it moved. It made no sound. It did not hurry. It crossed the glade, walking for an instant into the full glare of the sun; when it reached the other side it stopped again and looked back at him across one shoulder while his quiet breathing inhaled and exhaled three times.

Then it was gone. It didn't walk into the woods, the undergrowth. It faded, sank back into the wilderness as he had watched a fish, a huge old bass, sink and vanish into the dark depths of its pool without even any movement of its fins.

He thought, *It will be next fall.* But it was not next fall, nor the next nor the next. He was fourteen then. He had killed his buck, and Sam Fathers had marked his face with the hot blood, and in the next year he killed a bear. But even before that accolade he had become as competent in the woods as many grown men with the same experience; by his fourteenth year he was a better woodsman than most grown men with more. There was no territory within thirty miles of the camp that he did not know—bayou, ridge, brake, landmark, tree and path. He could have led anyone to any point in it without deviation, and brought them out again. He knew the game trails that even Sam Fathers did not know; in his thirteenth year he found a buck's bedding place, and unbeknown to his father he borrowed Walter Ewell's rifle and lay in wait at dawn and killed the buck when it walked back to the bed, as Sam had told him how the old Chickasaw fathers did.

But not the old bear, although by now he knew its footprints better than he did his own, and not only the crooked one. He could see any one of the three sound ones and distinguish it from any other, and not only by its size. There were other bears within these thirty miles which left tracks almost as large, but this was more than that. If Sam Fathers had been his mentor and the back-yard rabbits and squirrels at home his kindergarten, then the wilderness the old bear ran was his college, the old male bear itself, so long unwifed and childless as to have become its own ungendered progenitor, was his alma mater. But he never saw it.

He could find the crooked print now almost whenever he liked, fifteen or ten or five miles, or sometimes nearer the camp than that. Twice while on stand during the three years he heard the dogs strike its trail by accident; on the second time they jumped it seemingly, the voices high, abject, almost human in hysteria, as on that first morning two years ago. But not the bear itself. He would remember that noon three years ago, the glade, himself and the bear fixed during that moment in the windless and dappled blaze, and it would seem to him that it had never happened, that he had dreamed that too. But it had happened. They had looked at each other, they had emerged from the wilderness old as earth, synchronized to the instant by something more than the blood that moved the flesh and bones which bore them, and touched, pledged something, affirmed, something more lasting than the frail web of bones and flesh which any accident could obliterate.

Then he saw it again. Because of the very fact that he thought of nothing else, he had forgotten to look for it. He was still hunting with Walter Ewell's rifle. He saw it cross the end of a long blow-down, a corridor where a tornado had swept, rushing through rather than over the tangle of trunks and branches as a locomotive would have, faster than he had ever believed it could move, almost as fast as a deer even, because a deer would have spent most of that time in the air, faster than he could bring the rifle sights up with it. And now he knew what had been wrong during all the three years. He sat on a log, shaking and trembling as if he had never seen the woods before nor anything that ran them, wondering with incredulous amazement how he could have forgotton the very thing which Sam Fathers had told him and which the bear itself had proved the next day and had now returned after three years to reaffirm.

And now he knew what Sam Fathers had meant about the right dog, a dog in which size would mean less than nothing. So when he returned alone in April—school was out then, so that the sons of farmers could help with the land's planting, and at last his father had granted him permission, on his promise to be back in four days—he had the dog. It was his own, a mongrel of the sort called by Negroes a fyce, a ratter, itself not much bigger than a rat and possessing that bravery which had long since stopped being courage and had become foolhardiness.

It did not take four days. Alone again, he found the trail on the first morning. It was not a stalk; it was an ambush. He timed the meeting almost as if it were an appointment with a human being. Himself holding the fyce muffled in a feed sack and Sam Fathers with two of the hounds on a piece of a plowline rope, they lay down wind of the trail at dawn of the second morning. They were so close that the bear turned without even running, as if in surprised amazement at the shrill and frantic uproar of the released fyce, turning at bay against the trunk of a tree, on its hind feet; it seemed to the boy that it would never stop rising, taller and taller, and even the two hounds seemed to take a desperate and despairing courage from the fyce, following it as it went in.

Then he realized that the fyce was actually not going to stop. He flung, threw the gun away, and ran; when he overtook and grasped the frantically pin-wheeling little dog, it seemed to him that he was directly under the bear.

He could smell it, strong and hot and rank. Sprawling, he looked up to where it loomed and towered over him like a cloudburst and colored like a thunderclap, quite familiar, peacefully and even lucidly familiar, until he remembered: This was the way he had used to dream about it. Then it was gone. He didn't see it go. He knelt, holding the frantic fyce with both hands, hearing the abashed wailing of the hounds drawing farther and farther away, until Sam came up. He carried the gun. He laid it down quietly beside the boy and stood looking down at him.

"You've done seed him twice now with a gun in your hands," he said. "This time you couldn't have missed him."

The boy rose. He still held the fyce. Even in his arms and clear of the ground, it yapped frantically, straining and surging after the fading uproar of the two hounds like a tangle of wire springs. He was panting a little, but he was neither shaking nor trembling now.

"Neither could you!" he said. "You had the gun! Neither did you!"

"And you didn't shoot," his father said. "How close were you?"

"I don't know, sir," he said. "There was a big wood tick inside his right leg. I saw that. But I didn't have the gun then."

"But you didn't shoot when you had the gun," his father said. "Why?"

But he didn't answer, and his father didn't wait for him to, rising and crossing the room, across the pelt of the bear which the boy had killed two years ago and the larger one which his father had killed before he was born, to the bookcase beneath the mounted head of the boy's first buck. It was the room which his father called the office, from which all the plantation business was transacted; in it for the fourteen years of his life he had heard the best of all talking. Major de Spain would be there and sometimes old General Compson, and Walter Ewell and Boon Hoggenbeck and Sam Fathers and Tennie's Jim, too, were hunters, knew the woods and what ran them.

He would hear it, not talking himself but listening—the wilderness, the big woods, bigger and older than any recorded document of white man fatuous enough to believe he had bought any fragment of it or Indian ruthless enough to pretend that any fragment of it had been his to convey. It was of the men, not white nor black nor red, but men, hunters with the will and hardihood to endure and the humility and skill to survive, and the dogs and the bear and deer juxtaposed and reliefed against it, ordered and compelled by and within the wilderness in the ancient and unremitting contest by the ancient and immitigable rules which voided all regrets and brooked no quarter, the voices quiet and weighty and deliberate for retrospection and recollection and exact remembering, while he squatted in the blazing firelight as Tennie's Jim squatted, who stirred only to put more wood on the fire and to pass the bottle from one glass to another. Because the bottle was always present, so that after a while it seemed to him that those fierce instants of heart and brain and courage and wiliness and speed were concentrated and distilled into that brown liquor which not women, not boys and children, but only hunters drank, drinking not of the blood they had spilled but some condensation of the wild immortal spirit, drinking it moderately, humbly even, not with the pagan's base hope of acquiring the virtues of cunning and strength and speed, but in salute to them.

His father returned with the book and sat down again and opened it. "Listen," he said. He read the five stanzas aloud, his voice quiet and deliberate in the room where there was no fire now because it was already spring. Then he looked up. The boy watched him. "All right," his father said. "Listen." He read again, but only the second stanza this time, to the end of it, the last two lines, and closed the book and put it on the table beside him. "She cannot fade, though thou hast not thy bliss, forever wilt thou love, and she be fair," he said.

"He's talking about a girl," the boy said.

"He had to talk about something," his father said. Then he said, "He was talking about truth. Truth doesn't change. Truth is one thing. It covers all things which touch the heart—honor and pride and pity and justice and courage and love. Do you see now?"

He didn't know. Somehow it was simpler than that. There was an old bear, fierce and ruthless, not merely just to stay alive, but with the fierce pride of liberty and freedom, proud enough of the liberty and freedom to see it threatened without fear or even alarm; nay, who at times even seemed deliberately to put that freedom and liberty in jeopardy in order to savor them, to remind his old strong bones and flesh to keep supple and quick to defend and preserve them. There was an old man, son of a Negro slave and an Indian king, inheritor on the one side of the long chronicle of a people who had learned humility through suffering, and pride through the endurance which survived the suffering and injustice, and on the other side, the chronicle of a people even longer in the land than the first, yet who no longer existed in the land at all save in the solitary brotherhood of an old Negro's alien blood and the wild and invincible spirit of an old bear. There was a boy who wished to learn humility and pride in order to become skillful and worthy in the woods, who suddenly found himself becoming so skillful so rapidly that he feared he would never become worthy because he had not learned humility and pride, although he had tried to, until one day and as suddenly he discovered that an old man who could not have defined either had led him, as though by the hand, to that point where an old bear and a little mongrel of a dog showed him that, by possessing one thing other, he would possess them both.

And a little dog, nameless and mongrel and many-fathered, grown, yet weighing less than six pounds, saying as if to itself, "I can't be dangerous, because there's nothing much smaller than I am; I can't be fierce, because they would call it just a noise; I can't be humble, because I'm already too close to the ground to genuflect; I can't be proud, because I wouldn't be near enough to it for anyone to know who was casting the shadow, and I don't even know that I'm not going to heaven, because they have already decided that I don't possess an immortal soul. So all I can be is brave. But it's all right. I can be that, even if they still call it just noise."

That was all. It was simple, much simpler than somebody talking in a book about youth and a girl he would never need to grieve over, because he could never approach any nearer her and would never have to get any farther away. He had heard about a bear, and finally got big enough to trail it, and he trailed it four years and at last met it with a gun in his hands and he didn't shoot. Because a little dog— But he could have shot long before the little dog covered the twenty yards to where the bear waited, and Sam Fathers could have shot at any time during that interminable minute while Old Ben stood on his hind feet over them. He stopped. His father was watching him gravely across the spring-rife twilight of the room; when he spoke, his words were as quiet as the twilight, too, not loud, because they did not need to be because they would last. "Courage, and honor, and pride," his father said, "and pity, and love of justice and of liberty. They all touch the heart, and what the heart holds to becomes truth, as far as we know the truth. Do you see now?"

Sam, and Old Ben, and Nip, he thought. And himself too. He had been all right too. His father had said so. "Yes, sir," he said.

WILLIAM FAULKNER

Mule in the Yard

IT WAS a gray day in late January, though not cold because of the fog. Old Het, just walked in from the poorhouse, ran down the hall toward the kitchen, shouting in a strong, bright, happy voice. She was about seventy probably, though by her own counting, calculated from the ages of various housewives in the town from brides to grandmothers whom she claimed to have nursed in infancy, she would have to be around a hundred and at least triplets. Tall, lean, fog-beaded, in tennis shoes and a long rat-colored cloak, trimmed with what forty or fifty years ago had been fur, a modish though not new purple toque set upon her headrag and carrying (time was when she made her weekly rounds from kitchen to kitchen carrying a brocaded carpetbag though since the advent of the ten-cent stores the carpetbag became an endless succession of the convenient paper receptacles with which they supply their customers for a few cents) the shopping-bag, she ran into the kitchen and shouted with strong and childlike pleasure: "Miss Mannie! Mule in de yard!"

Mrs. Hait, stooping to the stove, in the act of drawing from it a scuttle of live ashes, jerked upright; clutching the scuttle, she glared at old Het, then she too spoke at once, strong too, immediate. "Them sons of bitches," she said. She left the kitchen, not running exactly, yet with a kind of outraged celerity, carrying the scuttle—a compact woman of forty-odd, with an air of indomitable yet relieved bereavement, as though that which had relicted her had been a woman and a not particularly valuable one at that. She wore a calico wrapper and a sweater coat, and a man's felt hat which they in the town knew had belonged to her ten years' dead husband. But the man's shoes had not belonged to him. They were high shoes which buttoned, with toes like small tulip bulbs, and in the town they knew that she had bought them new for herself. She and old Het ran down the kitchen steps and into the fog. That's why it was not cold: as though there lay supine and prisoned between earth and mist the long winter night's suspiration of the sleeping town in dark, close rooms—the slumber and the rousing; the stale waking thermostatic, by re-heating heat-engendered: it lay like a scum of cold grease upon the steps and the wooden entrance to the basement and upon the narrow plank walk which led to a shed building in the corner of the yard: upon these planks, running and still carrying the scuttle of live ashes, Mrs. Hait skated viciously.

"Watch out!" old Het, footed securely by her rubber soles, cried happily. "Dey in de front!" Mrs. Hait did not fall. She did not even pause. She took in the immediate scene with one cold glare and was running again when there appeared at the corner of the house and apparently having been born before their eyes of the fog itself, a mule. It looked taller than a giraffe. Long-headed, with a flying halter about its scissorlike ears, it rushed down upon them with violent and apparitionlike suddenness.

"Dar hit!" old Het cried, waving the shopping-bag. "Hoo!" Mrs. Hait whirled. Again she skidded savagely on the greasy planks as she and the mule rushed parallel with one another toward the shed building, from whose open doorway there now projected the static and astonished face of a cow. To the cow the fog-born mule doubtless looked taller and more incredibly sudden than a giraffe even, and apparently bent upon charging right through the shed as though it were made of straw or were purely and simply mirage. The cow's head likewise had a quality transient and abrupt and unmundane. It vanished, sucked into invisibility like a match flame, though the mind knew and the reason insisted that she had withdrawn into the shed, from which, as proof's burden, there came an indescribable sound of shock and alarm by shed and beast engendered, analogous to a single note from a profoundly struck lyre or harp. Toward this sound Mrs. Hait sprang, immediately, as if by pure reflex, as though in invulnerable compact of female with female against a world of mule and man. She and the mule converged upon the shed at top speed, the heavy scuttle poised lightly in her hand to hurl. Of course it did not take this long, and likewise it was the mule which refused the gambit. Old Het was still shouting "Dar hit! Dar hit!" when it swerved and rushed at her where she stood tall as a stove pipe, holding the shopping-bag which she swung at the beast as it rushed past her and vanished beyond the other corner of the house as though sucked back into the fog which had produced it, profound and instantaneous and without any sound.

With that unhasteful celerity Mrs. Hait turned and set the scuttle down on the brick coping of the cellar entrance and she and old Het turned the corner of the house in time to see the now wraithlike mule at the moment when its course converged with that of a choleric-looking rooster and eight Rhode Island Red hens emerging from beneath the house. Then for an instant its progress assumed the appearance and trappings of an apotheosis: hell-born and hell-returning, in the act of dissolving completely into the fog, it seemed to rise vanishing into a sunless and dimensionless medium borne upon and enclosed by small winged goblins.

"Dey's mo in de front!" old Het cried.

"Them sons of bitches," Mrs. Hait said, again in that grim, prescient voice without rancor or heat. It was not the mules to which she referred; it was not even the owner of them. It was her whole town-dwelling history as dated from that April dawn ten years ago when what was left of Hait had been gathered from the mangled remains of five mules and several feet of new Manila rope on a blind curve of the railroad just out of town; the geographical hap of her very home; the very components of her bereavement—the mules, the defunct husband, and the owner of them. His name was Snopes; in the town they knew about him too—how he bought his stock at the Memphis market and brought it to Jefferson and sold it to farmers and widows and orphans black and white, for whatever he could contrive—down to a certain figure; and about how (usually in the dead season of winter) teams and even small droves of his stock would escape from the fenced pasture where he kept them and, tied one to another with sometimes quite new hemp rope (and which item Snopes included in the subsequent claim), would be annihilated by freight trains on the same blind curve which was to be the scene of Hait's exit from this world; once a town wag sent him through the mail a printed train schedule for the division. A squat, pasty man perennially tieless and with a strained, harried expression, at stated intervals he passed athwart the peaceful and somnolent life of the town in dust and uproar, his advent heralded by shouts and cries, his passing marked by a yellow cloud filled with tossing jug-shaped heads and clattering hooves and the same forlorn and earnest cries of the drovers; and last of all and well back out of the dust, Snopes himself moving at a harried and panting trot, since it was said in the town that he was deathly afraid of the very beasts in which he cleverly dealt.

The path which he must follow from the railroad station to his pasture crossed the edge of town near Hait's home; Hait and Mrs. Hait had not been in the house a week before they waked one morning to find it surrounded by galloping mules and the air filled with the shouts and cries of the drovers. But it was not until that April dawn some years later, when those who reached the scene first found what might be termed foreign matter among the mangled mules and the savage fragments of new rope, that the town suspected that Hait stood in any closer relationship to Snopes and the mules than that of helping at periodical intervals to drive them out of his front yard. After that they believed that they knew; in a three days' recess of interest, surprise, and curiosity they watched to see if Snopes would try to collect on Hait also.

But they learned only that the adjuster appeared and called upon Mrs. Hait and that a few days later she cashed a check for eight thousand five hundred dollars, since this was back in the old halcyon days when even the companies considered their southern branches and divisions the legitimate prey of all who dwelt beside them. She took the cash: she stood in her sweater coat and the hat which Hait had been wearing on the fatal morning a week ago and listened in cold, grim silence while the teller counted the money and the president and the cashier tried to explain to her the virtues of a bond, then of a savings account, then of a checking account, and departed with the money in a salt sack under her apron; after a time she painted her house: that serviceable and time-defying color which the railroad station was painted, as though out of sentiment or (as some said) gratitude.

The adjuster also summoned Snopes into conference, from which he emerged not only more harried-looking than ever, but with his face stamped with a bewildered dismay which it was to wear from then on, and that was the last time his pasture fence was ever to give inexplicably away at dead of night upon mules coupled in threes and fours by adequate rope even though not always new. And then it seemed as though the mules themselves knew this, as if, even while haltered at the Memphis block at his bid, they sensed it somehow as they sensed that he was afraid of them. Now, three or four times a year and as though by fiendish concord and as soon as they were freed of the box car, the entire uproar—the dust cloud filled with shouts earnest, harried, and dismayed, with plunging demoniac shapes—would become translated in a single burst of perverse and uncontrollable violence, without any intervening contact with time, space, or earth, across the peaceful and astonished town and into Mrs. Hait's yard, where, in a certain hapless despair which abrogated for the moment even physical fear, Snopes ducked and dodged among the thundering shapes about the house (for whose very impervious paint the town believed that he felt he had paid and whose inmate lived within it a life of idle and queenlike ease on money which he considered at least partly his own) while gradually that section and neighborhood gathered to look on from behind adjacent window curtains and porches screened and not, and from the sidewalks and even from halted wagons and cars in the street—housewives in the wrappers and boudoir caps of morning, children on the way to school, casual Negroes and casual whites in static and entertained repose.

They were all there when, followed by old Het and carrying the stub of a worn-out broom, Mrs. Hait ran around the next corner and onto the handkerchief-sized plot of earth which she called her front yard. It was small; any creature with a running stride of three feet could have spanned it in two paces, yet at the moment, due perhaps to the myopic and distortive quality of the fog, it seemed to be as incredibly full of mad life as a drop of water beneath the microscope. Yet again she did not falter. With the broom clutched in her hand and apparently with a kind of sublime faith in her own invulnerability, she rushed on after the haltered mule which was still in that arrested and wraithlike process of vanishing furiously into the fog, its wake indicated by the tossing and dispersing shapes of the nine chickens like so many jagged scraps of paper in the dying air blast of an automobile, and the madly dodging figure of a man. The man was Snopes; beaded too with moisture, his wild face gaped with hoarse shouting and the two heavy lines of shaven beard descending from the corners of it as though in alluvial retrospect of years of tobacco, he screamed at her: "Fore God, Miz Hait! I done everything I could!" She didn't even look at him.

"Ketch that big un with the bridle on," she said in her cold, panting voice. "Git that big un outen here."

"Sho!" Snopes shrieked. "Just let um take their time. Jest don't git um excited now."

"Watch out!" old Het shouted. "He headin fer de back again!"

"Git the rope," Mrs. Hait said, running again. Snopes glared back at old Het.

"Fore God, where is ere rope?" he shouted.

"In de cellar fo God!" old Het shouted, also without pausing. "Go roun de udder way en head um." Again she and Mrs. Hait turned the corner in time to see again the still-vanishing mule with the halter once more in the act of floating lightly onward in its cloud of chickens with which, they being able to pass under the house and so on the chord of a circle while it had to go around on the arc, it had once more coincided. When they turned the next corner they were in the back yard again.

"Fo God!" old Het cried. "He fixin to misuse de cow!" For they had gained on the mule now, since it had stopped. In fact, they came around the corner on a tableau. The cow now stood in the centre of the yard. She and the mule faced one another a few feet apart. Motionless, with lowered heads and braced forelegs, they looked like two book ends from two distinct pairs of a general pattern which some one of amateurly bucolic leanings might have purchased, and which some child had salvaged, brought into idle juxtaposition and then forgotten; and, his head and shoulders projecting above the back-flung slant of the cellar entrance where the scuttle still sat, Snopes standing as though buried to the armpits for a Spanish-Indian-American suttee. Only again it did not take this long. It was less than tableau; it was one of those things which later even memory cannot quite affirm. Now and in turn, man and cow and mule vanished beyond the next corner, Snopes now in the lead, carrying the rope, the cow next with her tail rigid and raked slightly like the stern staff of a boat. Mrs. Hait and old Het ran on, passing the open cellar gaping upon its accumulation of human necessities and widowed womanyears—boxes for kindling wood, old papers and magazines, the broken and outworn furniture and utensils which no woman ever throws away; a pile of coal and another of pitch pine for priming fires—and ran on and turned the next corner to see man and cow and mule all vanishing now in the wild cloud of ubiquitous chickens which had once more crossed beneath the house and emerged. They ran on, Mrs. Hait in grim and unflagging silence, old Het with the eager and happy amazement of a child. But when they gained the front again they saw only Snopes. He lay flat on his stomach, his head and shoulders upreared by his outstretched arms, his coat tail swept forward by its own arrested momentum about his head so that from beneath it his slack-jawed face mused in wild repose like that of a burlesqued nun.

"Whar'd dey go?" old Het shouted at him. He didn't answer.

"Dey tightenin' on de curves!" she cried. "Dey already in de back again!" That's where they were. The cow made a feint at running into her shed, but deciding perhaps that her speed was too great, she whirled in a final desperation of despair-like valor. But they did not see this, nor see the mule, swerving to pass her, crash and blunder for an instant at the open cellar door before going on. When they arrived, the mule was gone. The scuttle was gone too, but they did not notice it; they saw only the cow standing in the centre of the yard as before, panting, rigid, with braced forelegs and lowered head facing nothing, as if the child had returned and removed one of the book ends for some newer purpose or game. They ran on. Mrs. Hait ran heavily now, her mouth too open, her face putty-colored and one hand pressed to her side. So slow was their progress that the mule in its third circuit of the house overtook them from behind and soared past with undiminished speed, with brief demon thunder and a keen ammonia-sweet reek of sweat sudden and sharp as a jeering cry, and was gone. Yet they ran doggedly on around the next corner in time to see it succeed at last in vanishing into the fog; they heard its hoofs, brief, staccato, and derisive, on the paved street, dying away.

"Well!" old Het said, stopping. She panted, happily. "Gentlemen, hush! Ain't we had—" Then she became stone still; slowly her head turned, high-nosed, her nostrils pulsing; perhaps for the instant she saw the open cellar door as they had last passed it, with no scuttle beside it. "Fo God I smells smoke!" she said. "Chile, run, get yo money."

That was still early, not yet ten o'clock. By noon the house had burned to the ground. There was a farmers' supply store where Snopes could be usually found; more than one had made a point of finding him there by that time. They told him about how when the fire engine and the crowd reached the scene, Mrs. Hait, followed by old Het carrying her shopping-bag in one hand and a framed portrait of Mr. Hait in the other, emerged with an umbrella and wearing a new, dun-colored, mail-order coat, in one pocket of which lay a fruit jar filled with smoothly rolled banknotes and in the other a heavy, nickel-plated pistol, and crossed the street to the house opposite, where with old Het beside her in another rocker, she had been sitting ever since on the veranda, grim, inscrutable, the two of them rocking steadily, while hoarse and tireless men hurled her dishes and furniture and bedding up and down the street.

"What are you telling me for?" Snopes said. "Hit warn't me that set that ere scuttle of live fire where the first thing that passed would knock hit into the cellar."

"It was you that opened the cellar door, though."

"Sho. And for what? To git that rope, her own rope, where she told me to git it."

"To catch your mule with, that was trespassing on her property. You can't get out of it this time, I. O. There ain't a jury in the county that won't find for her."

"Yes. I reckon not. And just because she is a woman. That's why. Because she is a durn woman. All right. Let her go to her durn jury with hit. I can talk too; I reckon hit's a few things I could tell a jury myself about—" He ceased. They were watching him.

"What? Tell a jury about what?"

"Nothing. Because hit ain't going to no jury. A jury between her and me? Me and Mannie Hait? You boys don't know her if you think she's going to make trouble over a pure acci-dent couldn't nobody help. Why, there ain't a fairer, finer woman in the county than Miz Mannie Hait. I just wisht I had a opportunity to tell her so." The opportunity came at once. Old Het was behind her, carrying the shopping-bag. Mrs. Hait looked once, quietly, about at the faces, making no response to the murmur of curious salutation, then not again. She didn't look at Snopes long either, nor talk to him long.

"I come to buy that mule," she said.

"What mule?" They looked at one another. "You'd like to own that mule?" She looked at him. "Hit'll cost you a hundred and fifty, Miz Mannie."

"You mean dollars?"

"I don't mean dimes nor nickels neither, Miz Mannie."

"Dollars," she said. "That's more than mules was in Hait's time."

"Lots of things is different since Hait's time. Including you and me."

"I reckon so," she said. Then she went away. She turned without a word, old Het following.

"Maybe one of them others you looked at this morning would suit you," Snopes said. She didn't answer. Then they were gone.

"I don't know as I would have said that last to her," one said.

"What for?" Snopes said. "If she was aiming to law something outen me about that fire, you reckon she would have come and offered to pay me money for hit?" That was about one o'clock. About four o'clock he was shouldering his way through a throng of Negroes before a cheap grocery store when one called his name. It was old Het, the now bulging shopping-bag on her arm, eating bananas from a paper sack.

"Fo God I wuz jest dis minute huntin for you," she said. She handed the banana to a woman beside her and delved and fumbled in the shopping-bag and extended a greenback. "Miz Mannie gimmie dis to give you; I wuz jest on de way to de sto whar you stay at. Here." He took the bill.

"What's this? From Miz Hait?"

"For de mule." The bill was for ten dollars. "You don't need to gimmie no receipt. I kin be de witness I give hit to you."

"Ten dollars? For that mule? I told her a hundred and fifty dollars."

"You'll have to fix dat up wid her yo'self. She jest gimme dis to give ter you when she sot out to fetch de mule."

"Set out to fetch—She went out there herself and taken my mule outen my pasture?"

"Lawd, chile," old Het said, "Miz Mannie ain't skeered of no mule. Ain't you done foun dat out?"

And then it became late, what with the yet short winter days; when she came in sight of the two gaunt chimneys against the sunset, evening was already finding itself. But she could smell the ham cooking before she came in sight of the cow shed even, though she could not see it until she came around in front where the fire burned beneath an iron skillet set on bricks and where nearby Mrs. Hait was milking the cow. "Well," old Het said, "you is settled down, ain't you?" She looked into the shed, neated and raked and swept even, and floored now with fresh hay. A clean new lantern burned on a box, beside it a pallet bed was spread neatly on the straw and turned neatly back for the night. "Why, you is fixed up," she said with pleased astonishment. Within the door was a kitchen chair. She drew it out and sat down beside the skillet and laid the bulging shopping-bag beside her.

"I'll tend dis meat whilst you milks. I'd offer to strip dat cow fer you ef I wazn't so wo out wid all dis excitement we been had." She looked around her. "I don't believe I sees yo new mule, dough." Mrs. Hait grunted, her head against the cow's flank. After a moment she said.

"Did you give him that money?"

"I give um ter him. He ack surprise at first, lak maybe he think you didn't aim to trade dat quick. I tole him to settle de details wid you later. He taken de money, dough. So I reckin dat's offen his mine en yo'n bofe." Again Mrs. Hait grunted. Old Het turned the ham in the skillet. Beside it the coffee pot bubbled and steamed. "Cawfee smell good too," she said. "I ain't had no appetite in years now. A bird couldn't live on de vittles I eats. But just lemme git a whiff er cawfee en seem lak hit always whets me a little. Now, ef you jest had nudder little piece o dis ham, now— Fo God, you got company aready." But Mrs. Hait did not even look up until she had finished. Then she turned without rising from the box on which she sat.

"I reckon you and me better have a little talk," Snopes said. "I reckon I got something that belongs to you and I hear you got something that belongs to me." He looked about, quickly, ceaselessly, while old Het watched him. He turned to her. "You go away, aunty. I don't reckon you want to set here and listen to us."

"Lawd, honey," old Het said. "Don't you mind me. I done already had so much troubles myself dat I kin set en listen to udder folks' widout hit worryin me a-tall. You gawn talk whut you come ter talk; I jest set here en tend de ham." Snopes looked at Mrs. Hait.

"Ain't you going to make her go away?" he said.

"What for?" Mrs. Hait said. "I reckon she ain't the first critter that ever come in this yard when hit wanted and went or stayed when hit liked." Snopes made a gesture, brief, fretted, restrained.

"Well," he said. "All right. So you taken the mule."

"I paid you for it. She give you the money."

"Ten dollars. For a hundred-and-fifty-dollar mule. Ten dollars."

"I don't know anything about hundred-and-fifty-dollar mules. All I know is what the railroad paid." Now Snopes looked at her for a full moment.

"What do you mean?"

"Them sixty dollars a head the railroad used to pay you for mules back when you and Hait—"

"Hush," Snopes said; he looked about again, quick, ceaseless. "All right. Even call it sixty dollars. But you just sent me ten."

"Yes, I sent you the difference." He looked at her, perfectly still. "Between that mule and what you owed Hait."

"What I owed—"

"For getting them five mules onto the tr—"

"Hush!" he cried. "Hush!" Her voice went on, cold, grim, level.

"For helping you. You paid him fifty dollars each time, and the railroad paid you sixty dollars a head for the mules. Ain't that right?" He watched her. "The last time you never paid him. So I taken that mule instead. And I sent you the ten dollars difference."

"Yes," he said in a tone of quiet, swift, profound bemusement; then he cried: "But look! Here's where I got you. Hit was our agreement that I wouldn't never owe him nothing until after the mules was—"

"I reckon you better hush yourself," Mrs. Hait said.

"—until hit was over. And this time, when over had come, I never owed nobody no money because the man hit would have been owed to wasn't nobody," he cried triumphantly. "You see?" Sitting on the box, motionless, downlooking, Mrs. Hait seemed to muse. "So you just take your ten dollars back and tell me where my mule is and we'll just go back good friends to where we started at. Fore God, I'm as sorry as ere a living man about that fire—"

"Fo God!" old Het said, "hit was a blaze, wuzn't it?"

"—but likely with all that ere railroad money you still got, you just been wanting a chance to build new, all along. So here. Take hit." He put the money into her hand. "Where's my mule?" But Mrs. Hait didn't move at once.

"You want to give it back to me?" she said.

"Sho. We been friends all the time; now we'll just go back to where we left off being. I don't hold no hard feelings and don't you hold none. Where you got the mule hid?"

"Up at the end of that ravine ditch behind Spilmer's," she said.

"Sho. I know. A good, sheltered place, since you ain't got nere barn. Only if you'd a just left hit in the pasture, hit would a saved us both trouble. But hit ain't no hard feelings though. And so I'll bid you goodnight. You're all fixed up, I see. I reckon you could save some more money by not building no house a-tall."

"I reckon I could," Mrs. Hait said. But he was gone.

"Whut did you leave de mule dar fer?" old Het said.

"I reckon that's far enough," Mrs. Hait said.

"Fer enough?" But Mrs. Hait came and looked into the skillet, and old Het said, "Wuz hit me er you dat mentioned something erbout er nudder piece o dis ham?" So they were both eating when in the not-quite-yet accomplished twilight Snopes returned. He came up quietly and stood, holding his hands to the blaze as if he were quite cold. He did not look at any one now.

"I reckon I'll take that ere ten dollars," he said.

"What ten dollars?" Mrs. Hait said. He seemed to muse upon the fire. Mrs. Hait and old Het chewed quietly, old Het alone watching him.

"You ain't going to give hit back to me?" he said.

"You was the one that said to let's go back to where we started," Mrs. Hait said.

"Fo God you wuz, en dat's de fack," old Het said. Snopes mused upon the fire; he spoke in a tone of musing and amazed despair:

"I go to the worry and the risk and the agoment for years and years and I get sixty dollars. And you, one time, without no trouble and no risk, without even knowing you are going to git it, git eighty-five hundred dollars. I never begrudged hit to you; can't nere a man say I did, even if hit did seem a little strange that you should git it all when he wasn't working for you and you never even knowed where he was at and what doing; that all you done to git it was to be married to him. And now, after all these ten years of not begrudging you hit, you taken the best mule I had and you ain't even going to pay me ten dollars for hit. Hit ain't right. Hit ain't justice."

"You got de mule back, en you ain't satisfried yit," old Het said. "Whut does you want?" Now Snopes looked at Mrs. Hait.

"For the last time I ask hit," he said. "Will you or won't you give hit back?"

"Give what back?" Mrs. Hait said. Snopes turned. He stumbled over something—it was old Het's shopping-bag—and recovered and went on. They could see him in silhouette, as though framed by the two blackened chimneys against the dying west; they saw him fling up both clenched hands in a gesture almost Gallic, of resignation and impotent despair. Then he was gone. Old Het was watching Mrs. Hait.

"Honey," she said. "Whut did you do wid de mule?" Mrs. Hait leaned forward to the fire. On her plate lay a stale biscuit. She lifted the skillet and poured over the biscuit the grease in which the ham had cooked.

"I shot it," she said.

"You which?" old Het said. Mrs. Hait began to eat the biscuit. "Well," old Het said, happily, "de mule burnt de house en you shot de mule. Dat's whut I calls justice." It was getting dark fast now, and before her was still the three-mile walk to the poorhouse. But the dark would last a long time in January, and the poorhouse too would not move at once. She sighed with weary and happy relaxation. "Gentlemen, hush! Ain't we had a day!"

WILLIAM FAULKNER

Spotted Horses

YES, SIR. Flem Snopes has filled that whole country full of spotted horses. You can hear folks running them all day and all night, whooping and hollering, and the horses running back and forth across them little wooden bridges ever now and then kind of like thunder. Here I was this morning pretty near half way to town, with the team ambling along and me setting in the buckboard about half asleep, when all of a sudden something come swurging up outen the bushes and jumped the road clean, without touching hoof to it. It flew right over my team big as a billboard and flying through the air like a hawk. It taken me thirty minutes to stop my team and untangle the harness and the buckboard and hitch them up again.

That Flem Snopes. I be dog if he ain't a case, now. One morning about ten years ago the boys was just getting settled down on Varner's porch for a little talk and tobacco, when here come Flem out from behind the counter, with his coat off and his hair all parted, like he might have been clerking for Varner for ten years already. Folks all knowed him; it was a big family of them about five miles down the bottom. That year, at least. Share-cropping. They never stayed on any place over a year. Then they would move on to another place, with the chap or maybe the twins of that year's litter. It was a regular nest of them. But Flem. The rest of them stayed tenant farmers, moving ever year, but here come Flem one day, walking out from behind Jody Varner's counter like he owned it. And he wasn't there but a year or two before folks knowed that if him and Jody was both still in that store in ten years more it would be Jody clerking for Flem Snopes. Why, that fellow could make a nickel where it wasn't but four cents to begin with. He skun me in two trades myself, and the fellow that can do that, I just hope he'll get rich before I do; that's all.

All right, So here Flem was, clerking at Varner's, making a nickel here and there and not telling nobody about it. No, sir. Folks never knowed when Flem got the better of somebody lessen the fellow he beat told it. H'd just set there in the store-chair, chewing his tobacco and keeping his own business to hisself, until about a week later we'd find out it was somebody else's business he was keeping to hisself—provided the fellow he trimmed was mad enough to tell it. That's Flem.

We give him ten years to own ever thing Jody Varner had. But he never waited no ten years. I reckon you-all know that gal of Uncle Billy Varner's, the youngest one; Eula. Jody's sister. Ever Sunday ever yellow-wheeled buggy and curried riding horse in that country would be hitched to Bill Varner's fence, and the young bucks setting on the porch, swarming around Eula like bees around a honey pot. One of these here kind of big, soft-looking gals that could giggle richer than plowed new-ground. Wouldn't none of them leave before the others, and so they would set there on the porch until time to go home, with some of them with nine and ten miles to ride and then get up tomorrow and go back to the field. So they would all leave together and they would ride in a clump down to the creek ford and hitch them curried horses and yellow-wheeled buggies and get out and fight one another. Then they would get in the buggies again and go on home.

Well, one day about a year ago, one of them yellow-wheeled buggies and one of them curried saddle-horses quit this country. We heard they was heading for Texas. The next day Uncle Billy and Eula and Flem come into town in Uncle Billy's surrey, and when they come back, Flem and Eula was married. And on the next day we heard that two more of them yellow-wheeled buggies had left the country. They mought have gone to Texas, too. It's a big place.

Anyway, about a month after the wedding, Flem and Eula went to Texas, too. They was gone pretty near a year. Then one day last month, Eula come back, with a baby. We figured up, and we decided that it was as well-growed a three-months-old baby as we ever see. It can already pull up on a chair. I reckon Texas makes big men quick, being a big place. Anyway, if it keeps on like it started, it'll be chewing tobacco and voting time it's eight years old.

And so last Friday here come Flem himself. He was on a wagon with another fellow. The other fellow had one of these two-gallon hats and a ivory-handled pistol and a box of gingersnaps sticking out of his hind pocket, and tied to the tail-gate of the wagon was about two dozen of them Texas ponies, hitched to one another with barbed wire. They was colored like parrots and they was quiet as doves, and ere a one of them would kill you quick as a rattlesnake. Nere a one of them had two eyes the same color, and nere a one of them had ever seen a bridle, I reckon; and when that Texas man got down offen the wagon and walked up to them to show how gentle they was, one of them cut his vest clean offen him, same as with a razor.

Flem had done already disappeared; he had went on to see his wife, I reckon, and to see if that ere baby had done gone on to the field to help Uncle Billy plow, maybe. It was the Texas man that taken the horses on to Mrs. Littlejohn's lot. He had a little trouble at first, when they come to the gate, because they hadn't never see a fence before, and when he finally got them in and taken a pair of wire cutters and unhitched them and got them into the barn and poured some shell corn into the trough, they durn nigh tore down the barn. I reckon they thought that shell corn was bugs, maybe. So he left them in the lot and he announced that the auction would begin at sunup tomorrow.

That night we was setting on Mrs. Littlejohn's porch. You-all mind the moon was nigh full that night, and we could watch them spotted varmints swirling along the fence and back and forth across the lot same as minnows in a pond. And then now and then they would all kind of huddle up against the barn and rest themselves by biting and kicking one another. We would hear a squeal, and then a set of hoofs would go Bam! against the barn, like a pistol. It sounded just like a fellow with a pistol, in a nest of cattymounts, taking his time.

II

It wasn't ere a man knowed yet if Flem owned them things or not. They just knowed one thing: that they wasn't never going to know for sho if Flem did or not, or if maybe he didn't just get on that wagon at the edge of town, for the ride or not. Even Eck Snopes didn't know, Flem's own cousin. But wasn't nobody surprised at that. We knowed that Flem would skin Eck quick as he would ere a one of us.

They was there by sunup next morning, some of them come twelve and sixteen miles, with seed-money tied up in tobacco sacks in their overalls, standing along the fence, when the Texas man come out of Mrs. Littlejohn's after breakfast and clumb onto the gate post with that ere white pistol butt sticking outen his hind pocket. He taken a new box of gingersnaps outen his pocket and bit the end offen it like a cigar and spit out the paper, and said the auction was open. And still they was coming up in wagons and a horse- and mule-back and hitching the teams across the road and coming to the fence. Flem wasn't nowhere in sight.

But he couldn't get them started. He begun to work on Eck, because Eck holp him last night to get them into the barn and feed them that shell corn. Eck got out just in time. He come outen that barn like a chip on the crest of a busted dam of water, and clumb into the wagon just in time.

He was working on Eck when Henry Armstid come up in his wagon. Eck was saying he was skeered to bid on one of them, because he might get it, and the Texas man says, 'Them ponies? Them little horses?' He clumb down offen the gate post and went toward the horses. They broke and run, and him following them, kind of chirping to them, with his hand out like he was fixing to catch a fly, until he got three or four of them cornered. Then he jumped into them, and then we couldn't see nothing for a while because of the dust. It was a big cloud of it, and them blare-eyed, spotted things swoaring outen it twenty foot to a jump, in forty directions without counting up. Then the dust settled and there they was, that Texas man and the horse. He had its head twisted clean around like a owl's head. Its legs was braced and it was trembling like a new bride and groaning like a saw mill, and him holding its head wrung clean around on its neck so it was snuffing sky. 'Look it over,' he says, with his heels dug too and that white pistol sticking outen his pocket and his neck swole up like a spreading adder's until you could just tell what he was saying, cussing the horse and talking to us all at once: 'Look him over, the fiddle-headed son of fourteen fathers. Try him, buy him; you will get the best—' Then it was all dust again, and we couldn't see nothing but spotted hide and mane, and that ere Texas man's boot-heels like a couple of walnuts on two strings, and after a while that two-gallon hat come sailing out like a fat old hen crossing a fence.

When the dust settled again, he was just getting outen the far fence corner, brushing himself off. He come and got his hat and brushed it off and come and clumb onto the gate post again. He was breathing hard. The hammer-head horse was still running round and round the lot like a merry-go-round at a fair. That was when Henry Armstid come shoving up to the gate in them patched overalls and one of them dangle-armed shirts of hisn. Hadn't nobody noticed him until then. We was all watching the Texas man and the horse. Even Mrs. Littlejohn; she had done come out and built a fire under the wash-pot in her back yard, and she would stand at the fence a while and then go back into the house and come out again with a arm full of wash and stand at the fence again. Well, here come Henry shoving up, and then we see Mrs. Armstid right behind him, in that ere faded wrapper and sunbonnet and them tennis shoes. 'Get on back to that wagon,' Henry says.

'Henry,' she says.

'Here, boys,' the Texas man says; 'make room for

missus to get up and see. Come on Henry,' he says; 'here's your chance to buy that saddle-horse missus has been wanting. What about ten dollars, Henry?'

'Henry,' Mrs. Armstid says. She put her hand on Henry's arm. Henry knocked her hand down.

'Git on back to that wagon, like I told you,' he says.

Mrs. Armstid never moved. She stood behind Henry, with her hands rolled into her dress, not looking at nothing. 'He hain't no more despair than to buy one of them things,' she says. 'And us not five dollars ahead of the pore house, he hain't no more despair.' It was the truth, too. They ain't never made more than a bare living offen that place of theirs, and them with four chaps and the very clothes they wears she earns by weaving by the firelight at night when Henry's asleep.

'Shut your mouth and git on back to that wagon,' Henry says. 'Do you want I taken a wagon stake to you here in the big road?'

Well, that Texas man taken one look at her. Then he begun on Eck again; like Henry wasn't even there. But Eck was skeered. 'I can git me a snapping turtle or a water moccasin for nothing. I ain't going to buy none.'

So the Texas man said he would give Eck a horse. 'To start the auction, and because you holp me last night. If you'll start the bidding on the next horse,' he says, 'I'll give you that fiddle-head horse.'

I wish you could have seen them, standing there with their seed-money in their pockets, watching that Texas man give Eck Snopes a live horse, all fixed to call him a fool if he taken it or not. Finally Eck says he'll take it. 'Only I just starts the bidding,' he says. 'I don't have to buy the next one lessen I ain't overtopped.' The Texas man said all right, and Eck bid a dollar on the next one, with Henry Armstid standing there with his mouth already open, watching Eck and the Texas man like a mad-dog or something. 'A dollar,' Eck says.

The Texas man looked at Eck. His mouth was already open too, like he had started to say something and what he was going to say had up and died on him. 'A dollar? You mean, *one* dollar, Eck?'

'Durn it,' Eck says; 'two dollars, then.'

Well, sir, I wish you could a seen that Texas man. He taken out that gingersnap box and held it up and looked into it, careful, like it might have been a diamond ring in it, or a spider. Then he throwed it away and wiped his face with a bandana. 'Well,' he says. 'Well. Two dollars. Two dollars. Is your pulse all right, Eck?' he says. 'Do you have ager-sweats at night, maybe?" he says. 'Well,' he says, 'I got to take it. But are you boys going to stand there and see Eck get two horses at a dollar a head?'

That done it. I be dog if he wasn't nigh as smart as Flem Snopes. He hadn't no more than got the words outen his mouth before here was Henry Armstid, waving his hand. 'Three dollars,' Henry says. Mrs. Armstid tried to hold him again. He knocked her hand off, shoving up to the gate post.

'Mister,' Mrs. Armstid says, 'we got chaps in the house and not corn to feed the stock. We got five dollars I earned my chaps a-weaving after dark, and him snoring in the bed. And he hain't no more despair.'

'Henry bids three dollars,' the Texas man says. 'Raise him a dollar, Eck, and the horse is yours.'

'Henry,' Mrs. Armstid says.

'Raise him, Eck,' the Texas man says.

'Four dollars,' Eck says.

'Five dollars,' Henry says, shaking his fist. He shoved up right under the gate post. Mrs. Armstid was looking at the Texas man too.

'Mister,' she says, 'if you take that five dollars I earned my chaps a-weaving for one of them things, it'll be a curse onto you and yourn during all the time of man.'

But it wasn't no stopping Henry. He had shoved up, waving his fist at the Texas man. He opened it; the money was in nickels and quarters, and one dollar bill that looked like a cow's cud. 'Five dollars,' he says. 'And the man that raises it'll have to beat my head off, or I'll beat his'n.'

'All right,' the Texas man says. 'Five dollars is bid. But don't you shake your hand at me.'

III

It taken till nigh sundown before the last one was sold. He got them hotted up once and the bidding got to seven dollars and a quarter, but most of them went around three or four dollars, him setting on the gate post and picking the horses out one at a time by mouth-word, and Mrs. Littlejohn pumping up and down at the tub and stopping and coming to the fence for a while and going back to the tub again. She had done got done too, and the wash was hung on the line in the back yard, and we could smell supper cooking. Finally they was all sold; he swapped the last two and the wagon for a buckboard.

We was all kind of tired, but Henry Armstid looked more like a mad-dog than ever. When he bought, Mrs. Armstid had went back to the wagon, setting in it behind them two rabbit-sized, bone-pore mules, and the wagon itself looking like it would fall all to pieces soon as the mules moved. Henry hadn't even waited to pull it outen the road; it was still in the middle of the road and her setting in it, not looking at nothing, ever since this morning.

Henry was right up against the gate. He went up to the Texas man. "I bought a horse and I paid cash,' Henry says. 'And yet you expect me to stand around here until they are all sold before I can get my horse. I'm going to take my horse outen that lot.'

The Texas man looked at Henry. He talked like he might have been asking for a cup of coffee at the table. 'Take your horse,' he says.

Then Henry quit looking at the Texas man. He begun to swallow, holding onto the gate. 'Ain't you going to help me?" he says.

'It ain't my horse,' the Texas man says.

Henry never looked at the Texas man again, he never looked at nobody. 'Who'll help me catch my horse?" he says. Never nobody said nothing. 'Bring the plowline,' Henry says. Mrs. Armstid got outen the wagon and brought the plowline. The Texas man got down offen the post. The woman made to pass him, carrying the rope.

'Don't you go in there, missus,' the Texas man says.

Henry opened the gate. He didn't look back. 'Come on here,' he says.

'Don't go in there, missus,' the Texas man says.

Mrs. Armstid wasn't looking at nobody, neither, with her hands across her middle, holding the rope. 'I reckon I better,' she says. Her and Henry went into the lot. The horses broke and run. Henry and Mrs. Armstid followed.

'Get him into the corner,' Henry says. They got Henry's horse cornered finally, and Henry taken the rope, but Mrs. Armstid let the horse get out. They hemmed it up again, but Mrs. Armstid let it get out again, and Henry turned and hit her wth the rope. 'Why didn't you head him back?' Henry says. He hit her again. 'Why didn't you?' It was about that time I looked around and see Flem Snopes standing there.

It was the Texas man that done something. He moved fast for a big man. He caught the rope before Henry could hit the third time, and Henry whirled and made like he would jump at the Texas man. But he never jumped. The Texas man went and taken Henry's arm and led him outen the lot. Mrs. Armstid come behind them and the Texas man taken some money outen his pocket and he give it into Mrs. Armstid's hand. 'Get him into the wagon and take him on home,' the Texas man says, like he might have been telling them he enjoyed his supper.

Then here come Flem. 'What's that for Buck?' Flem says.

'Thinks he bought one of them ponies,' the Texas man says. 'Get him on away, missus.'

But Henry wouldn't go. 'Give him back that money,' he says. 'I bought that horse and I aim to have him if I have to shoot him.'

And there was Flem, standing there with his hands in his pockets, chewing, like he had just happened to be passing.

'You take your money and I take my horse,' Henry says. 'Give it back to him,' he says to Mrs. Armstid.

'You don't own no horse of mine,' the Texas man says. 'Get him home, missus.'

Then Henry seen Flem. 'You got something to do with these horses,' he says. 'I bought one. Here's the money for it.' He taken the bill outen Mrs. Armstid's hand. He offered it to Flem. 'I bought one. Ask him. Here. Here's the money,' he says, giving the bill to Flem.

When Flem taken the money, the Texas man dropped the rope he had snatched outen Henry's hand. He had done sent Eck Snopes's boy up to the store for another box of gingersnaps, and he taken the box outen his pocket and looked into it. It was empty and he dropped it on the ground. 'Mr. Snopes will have your money for you tomorrow,' he says to Mrs. Armstid. 'You can get it from him tomorrow. He don't own no horse. You get him into the wagon and get him on home.' Mrs. Armstid went back to the wagon and got in. 'Where's that ere buckboard I bought?' the Texas man says. It was after sundown then. And then Mrs. Littlejohn come out on the porch and rung the supper bell.

IV

I come on in and et supper. Mrs. Littlejohn would bring in a pan of bread or something, then she would go out to the porch a minute and come back to tell us. The Texas man had hitched his team to the buckboard he had swapped them last two horses for, and him and Flem had gone, and then she told that the rest of them that never had ropes had went back to the store with I. O. Snopes to get some ropes, and wasn't nobody at the gate but Henry Armstid, and Mrs. Armstid setting in the wagon in the road, and Eck Snopes and that boy of hisn. 'I don't care how many of them fool men gets killed by them things,' Mrs. Littlejohn says, 'but I ain't going to let Eck Snopes take that boy into that lot again.' So she went down to the gate, but she come back without the boy or Eck neither.

'It ain't no need to worry about that boy,' I says. 'He's charmed.' He was right behind Eck last night when Eck went to help feed them. The whole drove of them jumped clean over that boy's head and never touched him. It was Eck that touched him. Eck snatched him into the wagon and taken a rope and frailed the tar outen him.

So I had done et and went to my room and was undressing, long as I had a long trip to make next day; I was trying to sell a machine to Mrs. Bundren up past Whiteleaf; when Henry Armstid opened the gate and went in by hisself. They couldn't make him wait for the balance of them to get back with their ropes. Eck Snopes said he tried to make Henry wait, but Henry wouldn't do it. Eck said Henry walked right up to them and then when they broke, they run clean over Henry like a haymow breaking down. Eck said he snatched that boy of hisn out of the way just in time and that them things went through that gate like a creek flood and into the wagons and teams hitched side the road, busting wagon tongues and snapping harness like it was fishing-line, with Mrs. Armstid still setting in their wagon in the middle of it like something carved outen wood. Then they scattered, wild horses and tame mules with pieces of harness and single trees dangling offen them, both ways up and down the road.

'There goes ourn, paw!' Eck says his boy said. 'There it goes, into Mrs. Littlejohn's house.' Eck says it run right up the steps and into the house like a boarder late for supper. I reckon so. Anyway, I was in my room, in my underclothes, with one sock on and one sock in my hand, leaning out the window when the commotion busted out, when I heard something run into the melodeon in the hall; it sounded like a railroad engine. Then the door to my room come sailing in like when you throw a tin bucket top into the wind and I looked over my shoulder and see something that looked like a fourteen-foot pinwheel a-blaring its eyes at me. It had to blare them fast, because I was already done jumped out the window.

I reckon it was anxious, too. I reckon it hadn't never seen barbed wire or shell corn before, but I know it hadn't never seen underclothes before, or maybe it was a sewing-machine agent it hadn't never seen. Anyway, it whirled and turned to run back up the hall and outen the house, when it met Eck Snopes and that boy just coming in, carrying a rope. It swirled again and run down the hall and out the back door just in time to meet Mrs. Littlejohn. She had just gathered up the clothes she had washed, and she was coming onto the back porch with an armful of washing in one hand and a scrubbing-board in the other, when the horse skidded up to her, trying to stop and swirl again. It never taken Mrs. Littlejohn no time a-tall.

'Get outen here, you son,' she says. She hit it across the face with the scrubbing-board; that ere scrubbing-board split as neat as ere a axe could have done it, and when the horse swirled to run back up the hall, she hit it again with what was left of the scrubbing-board, not on the head this time. 'And stay out,' she says.

Eck and that boy was half-way down the hall by this time. I reckon that horse looked like a pinwheel to Eck too. 'Get to hell outen here. Ad!' Eck says. Only there wasn't time. Eck dropped flat on his face, but the boy never moved. The boy was about a yard tall maybe, in overalls just like Eck's; that horse swoared over his head without touching a hair. I saw that, because I was just coming back up the front step, still carrying that ere sock and still in my underclothes, when the horse come onto the porch again. It taken one look at me and swirled again and run to the end of the porch and jumped the banisters and the lot fence like a hen-hawk and lit in the lot running and went out the gate again and jumped eight or ten upsidedown wagons and went on down the road. It was a full moon then. Mrs. Armstid was still setting in the wagon like she had done been carved outen wood and left there and forgot.

That horse. It ain't never missed a lick. It was going about forty miles an hour when it come to the bridge over the creek. It would have had a clear road, but it so happened that Vernon Tull was already using the bridge when it got there. He was coming back from town; he hadn't heard about the auction; him and his wife and three daughters and Mrs. Tull's aunt, all setting in chairs in the wagon bed, and all asleep, including the mules. They waked up when the horse hit the bridge one time, but Tull said the first he knew was when the mules tried to turn the wagon around in the middle of the bridge and he seen that spotted varmint run right twixt the mules and run up the wagon tongue like a squirrel. He said he just had time to hit it across the face with his whip-stock because about that time the mules turned the wagon around on that ere one-way bridge and that horse clumb across onto the bridge again and went on, with Vernon standing up in the wagon and kicking at it.

Tull said the mules turned in the harness and clumb back into the wagon too, with Tull trying to beat them out again, with the reins wrapped around his wrist. After that he says all he seen was overturned chairs and women-folks' legs and white drawers shining in the moonlight, and his mules and that spotted horse going on up the road like a ghost.

The mules jerked Tull outen the wagon and drug him a spell on the bridge before the reins broke. They thought at first that he was dead, and while they was kneeling around him, picking the bridge splinters outen him, here come Eck and that boy, still carrying the rope. They was running and breathing a little hard. 'Where'd he go,' Eck says.

V

I went back and got my pants and shirt and shoes on just in time to go and help get Henry Armstid outen the trash in the lot. I be dog if he didn't look like he was dead, with his head hanging back and his teeth showing in the moonlight, and a little rim of white under his eye-lids. We could still hear them horses, here and there; hadn't none of them got more than four—five miles away yet, not knowing the country, I reckon. So we could hear them and folks yelling now and then: 'Whooey. Head him!'

We toted Henry into Mrs. Littlejohn's. She was in the hall; she hadn't put down the armful of clothes. She taken one look at us, and she laid down the busted scrubbing-board and taken up the lamp and opened a empty door. 'Bring him in here,' she says.

We toted him in and laid him on the bed. Mrs. Littlejohn set the lamp on the dresser, still carrying the clothes. 'I'll declare, you men,' she says. Our shadows was way up the wall, tiptoeing too; we could hear ourselves breathing. 'Better get his wife,' Mrs. Littlejohn says. She went out, carrying the clothes.

'I reckon we had,' Quick says. 'Go get her, somebody.'

'Whyn't you go?' Winterbottom says.

'Let Ernest git her,' Durley says. 'He lives neighbors with them.'

Ernest went to fetch her. I be dog if Henry didn't look

like he was dead. Mrs. Littlejohn come back, with a kettle and some towels. She went to work on Henry, and then Mrs. Armstid and Ernest come in. Mrs. Armstid come to the foot of the bed and stood there, with her hands rolled into her apron, watching what Mrs. Littlejohn was doing, I reckon.

'You men get outen the way,' Mrs. Littlejohn says. 'Git outside,' she says. 'See if you can't find something else to play with that will kill some more of you.'

'Is he dead?' Winterbottom says.

'It ain't your fault if he ain't,' Mrs. Littlejohn says. 'Go tell Will Varner to come up here. I reckon a man ain't so different from a mule, come long come short. Except maybe a mule's got more sense.'

We went to get Uncle Billy. It was a full moon. We could hear them, now and then, four miles away: 'Whooey. Head him.' The country was full of them, one on every wooden bridge in the land, running across it like thunder: 'Whooey. There he goes. Head him.'

We hadn't got far before Henry begun to scream. I reckon Mrs. Littlejohn's water had brung him to; anyway, he wasn't dead. We went on to Uncle Billy's. The house was dark. We called to him, and after a while the window opened and Uncle Billy put his head out, peart as a peckerwood, listening. 'Are they still trying to catch them durn rabbits?' he says.

He come down, with his britches on over his nightshirt and his suspenders dangling, carrying his horse-doctoring grip. 'Yes, sir,' he says, cocking his head like a woodpecker; 'they're still a-trying.'

We could hear Henry before we reached Mrs. Littlejohn's. He was going Ah-Ah-Ah. We stopped in the yard. Uncle Billy went on in. We could hear Henry. We stood in the yard hearing them on the bridges, this-a-way and that: 'Whooey. Whooey.'

'Eck Snopes ought to caught hisn,' Ernest says.

'Looks like he ought,' Winterbottom said.

Henry was going Ah-Ah-Ah steady in the house; then he begun to scream. 'Uncle Billy's started,' Quick says. We looked into the hall. We could see the light where the door was. Then Mrs. Littlejohn come out.

'Will needs some help,' she says. 'You, Ernest, You'll do.' Ernest went into the house.

'Hear them?' Quick said. 'That one was on Four Mile bridge.' We could hear them; it sounded like thunder a long way off; it didn't last long.

'Whooey.'

We could hear Henry: 'Ah-Ah-Ah-Ah-Ah.'

'They are both started now.' Winterbottom says. 'Ernest too.'

That was early in the night. Which was a good thing, because it taken a long night for folks to chase them things right and for Henry to lay there and holler, being as Uncle Billy never had none of this here chloryfoam to set Henry's leg with. So it was considerate in Flem to get them started early. And what do you reckon Flem's comment was?

That's right. Nothing. Because he wasn't there. Hadn't nobody see him since that Texas man left.

VI

That was Saturday night. I reckon Mrs. Armstid got home about daylight, to see about the chaps. I don't know where they thought her and Henry was. But lucky the oldest one was a gal, about twelve, big enough to take care of the little ones. Which she did for the next two days. Mrs. Armstid would nurse Henry all night and work in the kitchen for hern and Henry's keep, and in the afternoon she would drive home (it was about four miles) to see to the chaps. She would cook up a pot of victuals and leave it on the stove, and the gal would bar the house and keep the little ones quiet. I would hear Mrs. Littlejohn and Mrs. Armstid talking in the kitchen. 'How are the chaps making out?' Mrs. Littlejohn says.

'All right,' Mrs. Armstid says.

'Don't they git skeered at night?' Mrs. Littlejohn says.

'Ina May bars the door when I leave,' Mrs. Armstid says. 'She's got the axe in bed with her. I reckon she can make out.'

I reckon they did. And I reckon Mrs. Armstid was waiting for Flem to come back to town; hadn't nobody seen him until this morning; to get her money the Texas man said Flem was keeping for her. Sho. I reckon she was.

Anyway, I heard Mrs. Armstid and Mrs. Littlejohn talking in the kitchen this morning while I was eating breakfast. Mrs. Littlejohn had just told Mrs. Armstid that Flem was in town. 'You can ask him for that five dollars,' Mrs. Littlejohn says.

'You reckon he'll give it to me?' Mrs. Armstid says.

Mrs. Littlejohn was washing dishes, washing them like a man, like they was made out of iron. 'No,' she says. 'But asking him won't do no hurt. It might shame him. I don't reckon it will, but it might.'

'If he wouldn't give it back, it ain't no use to ask,' Mrs. Armstid says.

'Suit yourself,' Mrs. Littlejohn says. 'It's your money.'

I could hear the dishes.

'Do you reckon he might give it back to me?' Mrs. Armstid says. 'That Texas man said he would. He said I could get it from Mr. Snopes later.'

'Then go and ask him for it,' Mrs. Littlejohn says.

I could hear the dishes.

'He won't give it back to me,' Mrs. Armstid says.

'All right,' Mrs. Littlejohn says. 'Don't ask him for it, then.'

I could hear the dishes; Mrs. Armstid was helping. 'You don't reckon he would, do you?' she says. Mrs. Littlejohn never said nothing. It sounded like she was throwing the dishes at one another. 'Maybe I better go and talk to

Henry about it,' Mrs. Armstid says.

'I would,' Mrs. Littlejohn says. I be dog if it didn't sound like she had two plates in her hands, beating them together. 'Then Henry can buy another five-dollar horse with it. Maybe he'll buy one next time that will out and out kill him. If I thought that, I'd give you back the money, myself.'

'I reckon I better talk to him first,' Mrs. Armstid said. Then it sounded like Mrs. Littlejohn taken up all the dishes and throwed them at the cook-stove, and I come away.

That was this morning. I had been up to Bundren's and back, and I thought that things would have kind of settled down. So after breakfast, I went up to the store. And there was Flem, setting in the store chair and whittling, like he might not have ever moved since he come to clerk for Jody Varner. I. O. was leaning in the door, in his shirt sleeves and with his hair parted too, same as Flem was before he turned the clerking job over to I. O. It's a funny thing about them Snopes: they all look alike, yet there ain't ere a two of them that claims brothers. They're always just cousins, like Flem and Eck and Flem and I. O. Eck was there too, squatting against the wall, him and that boy, eating cheese and crackers outen a sack; they told me that Eck hadn't been home a-tall. And that Lon Quick hadn't got back to town, even. He followed his horse clean down to Samson's Bridge, with a wagon and a camp outfit. Eck finally caught one of hisn. It run into a blind lane at Freeman's and Eck and the boy taken and tied their rope across the end of the lane, about three foot high. The horse come to the end of the lane and whirled and run back without ever stopping. Eck says it never seen the rope a-tall. He says it looked just like one of these here Christmas pinwheels. 'Didn't it try to run again?' I says.

'No,' Eck says, eating a bite of cheese offen his knife blade. 'Just kicked some.'

'Kicked some?' I says.

'It broke its neck,' Eck says.

Well, they was squatting there, about six of them, talking, talking at Flem; never nobody knowed yet if Flem had ere a interest in them horses or not. So finally I come right out and asked him. 'Flem's done skun all of us so much,' I says, 'that we're proud of him. Come on, Flem,' I says, 'how much did you and that Texas man make offen them horses? You can tell us. Ain't nobody here but Eck that bought one of them; the others ain't got back to town yet, and Eck's your own cousin; he'll be proud to hear, too. How much did you-all make?'

They was all whittling, not looking at Flem, making like they was studying. But you could a heard a pin drop. And I. O. He had been rubbing his back up and down on the door, but he stopped now, watching Flem like a pointing dog. Flem finished cutting the sliver offen his stick. He spit across the porch, into the road. 'Twarn't none of my horses,' he says.

I. O. cackled, like a hen, slapping his legs with both hands. 'You boys might just as well quit trying to get ahead of Flem,' he said.

Well, about that time I see Mrs. Armstid come outen Mrs. Littlejohn's gate, coming up the road. I never said nothing. I says: 'Well, if a man can't take care of himself in a trade, he can't blame the man that trims him.'

Flem never said nothing, trimming at the stick. He hadn't seen Mrs. Armstid. 'Yes, sir,' I says. 'A fellow like Henry Armstid ain't got nobody but hisself to blame.'

'Course he ain't,' I. O. says. He ain't seen her, either. 'Henry Armstid's a born fool. Always is been. If Flem hadn't a got his money, somebody else would.'

We looked at Flem. He never moved. Mrs. Armstid come on up the road.

'That's right,' I says. 'But come to think of it, Henry never bought no horse.' We looked at Flem; you could a heard a match drop. 'That Texas man told her to get that five dollars back from Flem next day. I reckon Flem's done already taken that money to Mrs. Littlejohn's and give it to Mrs. Armstid.'

We watched Flem. I. O. quit rubbing his back against the door again. After a while Flem raised his head and spit across the porch, into the dust. I. O. cackled, just like a hen. 'Ain't he a beating fellow, now?' I. O. says.

Mrs. Armstid was getting closer, so I kept on talking, watching to see if Flem would look up and see her. But he never looked up. I went on talking about Tull, about how he was going to sue Flem, and Flem setting there, whittling his stick, not saying nothing else after he said they wasn't none of his horses.

Then I. O. happened to look around. He seen Mrs. Armstid. 'Pssst!' he says. Flem looked up. 'Here she comes!' I. O. says. 'Go out the back. I'll tell her you done went in to town today.'

But Flem never moved. He just set there, whittling, and we watched Mrs. Armstid come up onto the porch, in that ere faded sunbonnet and wrapper and them tennis shoes that made a kind of hissing noise on the porch. She come onto the porch and stopped, her hands rolled into her dress in front, not looking at nothing.

'He said Saturday,' she says, 'that he wouldn't sell Henry no horse. He said I could get the money from you.'

Flem looked up. The knife never stopped. It went on trimming off a sliver same as if he was watching it. 'He taken that money off with him when he left,' Flem says.

Mrs. Armstid never looked at nothing. We never looked at her, neither, except that boy of Eck's. He had a half-et cracker in his hand, watching her, chewing.

'He said Henry hadn't bought no horse,' Mrs. Armstid says. 'He said for me to get the money from you today.'

'I reckon he forgot about it,' Flem said. 'He taken that money off with him Saturday.' He whittled again. I. O.

kept on rubbing his back, slow. He licked his lips. After a while the woman looked up the road, where it went on up the hill, toward the graveyard. She looked up that way for a while, with that boy of Eck's watching her and I. O. rubbing his back slow against the door. Then she turned back toward the steps.

'I reckon it's time to get dinner started,' she says.

'How's Henry this morning, Mrs. Armstid?' Winterbottom says.

She looked at Winterbottom; she almost stopped. 'He's resting, I thank you kindly,' she says.

Flem got up, outen the chair, putting his knife away. He spit across the porch. 'Wait a minute, Mrs. Armstid,' he says. She stopped again. She didn't look at him. Flem went on into the store, with I. O. done quit rubbing his back now, with his head craned after Flem, and Mrs. Armstid standing there with her hands rolled into her dress, not looking at nothing. A wagon come up the road and passed; it was Freeman, on the way to town. Then Flem come out again, with I. O. still watching him. Flem had one of these little striped sacks of Jody Varner's candy; I bet he still owes Jody that nickel, too. He put the sack into Mrs. Armstid's hand, like he would have put it into a hollow stump. He spit again across the porch.

'A little sweetening for the chaps,' he says.

'You're right kind,' Mrs. Armstid says. She held the sack of candy in her hand, not looking at nothing. Eck's boy was watching the sack, the half-et cracker in his hand; he wasn't chewing now. He watched Mrs. Armstid roll the sack into her apron. 'I reckon I better get on back and help with dinner,' she says. She turned and went back across the porch. Flem set down in the chair again and opened his knife. He spit across the porch again, past Mrs. Armstid where she hadn't went down the steps yet. Then she went on, in that ere sunbonnet and wrapper all the same color, back down the road toward Mrs. Littlejohn's. You couldn't see her dress move, like a natural woman walking. She looked like a old snag still standing up and moving along on a high water. We watched her turn in at Mrs. Littlejohn's and go outen sight. Flem was whittling. I. O. begun to rub his back on the door. Then he begun to cackle, just like a durn hen.

'You boys might just as well quit trying,' I. O. says. 'You can't git ahead of Flem. You can't touch him. Ain't he a sight, now?'

I be dog if he ain't. If I had brung a herd of wild cattymounts into town and sold them to my neighbors and kinfolks, they would have lynched me. Yes sir.

WILLIAM FAULKNER

That Evening Sun

MONDAY is no different from any other weekday in Jefferson now. The streets are paved now, and the telephone and electric companies are cutting down more and more of the shade trees—the water oaks, the maples and locusts and elms—to make room for iron poles bearing clusters of bloated and ghostly and bloodless grapes, and we have a city laundry which makes the rounds on Monday morning, gathering the bundles of clothes into bright-colored, specially made motorcars: the soiled wearing of a whole week now flees apparitionlike behind alert and irritable electric horns, with a long diminishing noise of rubber and asphalt like tearing silk, and even the Negro women who still take in white people's washing after the old custom, fetch and deliver it in automobiles.

But fifteen years ago, on Monday morning the quiet, dusty, shady streets would be full of Negro women with, balanced on their steady, turbaned heads, bundles of clothes tied up in sheets, almost as large as cotton bales, carried so without touch of hand between the kitchen door of the white house and the blackened washpot beside a cabin door in Negro Hollow.

Nancy would set her bundle on the top of her head, then upon the bundle in turn she would set the black straw sailor hat which she wore winter and summer. She was tall, with a high, sad face sunken a little where her teeth were missing. Sometimes we would go a part of the way down the lane and across the pasture with her, to watch the balanced bundle and the hat that never bobbed nor wavered, even when she walked down into the ditch and up the other side and stooped through the fence. She would go down on her hands and knees and crawl through the gap, her head rigid, uptilted, the bundle steady as a rock or a balloon, and rise to her feet again and go on.

Sometimes the husbands of the washing women would

fetch and deliver the clothes, but Jesus never did that for Nancy, even before Father told him to stay away from our house, even when Dilsey was sick and Nancy would come to cook for us.

And then about half the time we'd have to go down the lane to Nancy's cabin and tell her to come on and cook breakfast. We would stop at the ditch, because Father told us to not have anything to do with Jesus—he was a short black man, with a razor scar down his face—and we would throw rocks at Nancy's house until she came to the door, leaning her head around it without any clothes on.

"What yawl mean, chunking my house?" Nancy said. "What you little devils mean?"

"Father says for you to come on and get breakfast," Caddy said. "Father says it's over a half an hour now, and you've got to come this minute."

"I ain't studying no breakfast," Nancy said. "I going to get my sleep out."

"I bet you're drunk," Jason said. "Father says you're drunk. Are you drunk, Nancy?"

"Who says I is?" Nancy said. "I got to get my sleep out. I ain't studying no breakfast."

So after a while we quit chunking the cabin and went back home. When she finally came, it was too late for me to go to school. So we thought it was whiskey until that day they arrested her again and they were taking her to jail and they passed Mr. Stovall. He was the cashier in the bank and a deacon in the Baptist church, and Nancy began to say:

"When you going to pay me, white man? When you going to pay me, white man? It's been three times now since you paid me a cent—" Mr. Stovall knocked her down, but she kept on saying, "When you going to pay me, white man? It's been three times now since—" until Mr. Stovall kicked her in the mouth with his heel and the marshal caught Mr. Stovall back, and Nancy lying in the street, laughing. She turned her head and spat out some blood and teeth and said, "It's been three times now since he paid me a cent."

That was how she lost her teeth, and all that day they told about Nancy and Mr. Stovall, and all that night the ones that passed the jail could hear Nancy singing and yelling. They could see her hands holding to the window bars, and a lot of them stopped along the fence, listening to her and the jailer trying to make her stop. She didn't shut up until almost daylight, when the jailer began to hear a bumping and scraping upstairs and he went up there and found Nancy hanging from the window bar. He said that it was cocaine and not whiskey, because no nigger would try to commit suicide unless he was full of cocaine, because a nigger full of cocaine wasn't a nigger any longer.

The jailer cut her down and revived her; then he beat her, whipped her. She had hung herself with her dress. She had fixed it all right, but when they arrested her she didn't have on anything except a dress and so she didn't have anything to tie her hands with, and she couldn't make her hands let go of the window ledge. So the jailer heard the noise and ran up there and found Nancy hanging from the window, stark naked, her belly already swelling out a little, like a little balloon.

When Dilsey was sick in her cabin and Nancy was cooking for us, we could see her apron swelling out; that was before Father told Jesus to stay away from the house. Jesus was in the kitchen, sitting behind the stove, with his razor scar on his black face like a piece of dirty string. He said it was a watermelon that Nancy had under her dress.

"It never come off of your vine, though," Nancy said.

"Off of what vine?" Caddy said.

"I can cut down the vine it did come off of," Jesus said.

"What makes you want to talk like that before these chillen?" Nancy said. "Whyn't you go on to work? You done et. You want Mr. Jason to catch you hanging around his kitchen, talking that way before these chillen?"

"Talking what way?" Caddy said. "What vine?"

"I can't hang around white man's kitchen," Jesus said. "But white men can hang around mine. White man can come in my house, but I can't stop him. When white man want to come in my house, I ain't got no house. I can't stop him, but he can't kick me outen it. He can't do that."

Dilsey was still sick in her cabin. Father told Jesus to stay off our place. Dilsey was still sick. It was a long time. We were in the library after supper.

"Isn't Nancy through in the kitchen yet?" Mother said. "It seems to me that she has had plenty of time to have finished the dishes."

"Let Quentin go and see," Father said. "Go and see if Nancy is through, Quentin. Tell her she can go on home."

I went to the kitchen. Nancy was through. The dishes were put away and the fire was out. Nancy was sitting in a chair, close to the cold stove. She looked at me.

"Mother wants to know if you are through," I said.

"Yes," Nancy said, She looked at me. "I done finished." She looked at me.

"What is it?" I said. "What is it?"

"I ain't nothing but a nigger," Nancy said. "It ain't none of my fault."

She looked at me sitting in the chair before the cold stove, the sailor hat on her head. I went back to the library. It was the cold stove and all, when you think of a kitchen being warm and busy and cheerful. And with a cold stove and the dishes all put away, and nobody wanting to eat at that hour.

"Is she through?" Mother said.

"Yessum," I said.

"What is she doing?" Mother said.

"She's not doing anything. She's through."

"I'll go and see," Father said.

"Maybe she's waiting for Jesus to come and take her home," Caddy said.

"Jesus is gone," I said. Nancy told us how one morning she woke up and Jesus was gone.

"He quit me," Nancy said. "Done gone to Memphis, I reckon. Dodging them city *po*-lice for a while, I reckon."

"And a good riddance," Father said. "I hope he stays there."

"Nancy's scaired of the dark," Jason said.

"So are you," Caddy said.

"I'm not," Jason said.

"Scairy cat," Caddy said.

"I'm not," Jason said.

"You, Candace!" Mother said, Father came back.

"I am going to walk down the lane with Nancy," he said. "She says that Jesus is back."

"Has she seen him?" Mother said.

"No. Some Negro sent her word that he was back in town. I won't be long."

"You'll leave me alone, to take Nancy home?" Mother said. "Is her safety more precious to you than mine?"

"I won't be long," Father said.

"You'll leave these children unprotected, with that Negro about?"

"I'm going too," Caddy said. "Let me go, Father."

"What would he do with them if he were unfortunate enough to have them?" Father said.

"I want to go, too," Jason said.

"Jason!" Mother said. She was speaking to Father. You could tell that by the way she said the name. Like she believed that all day Father had been trying to think of doing the thing she wouldn't like the most, and that she knew all the time that after a while he would think of it. I stayed quiet, because Father and I both knew that Mother would want him to make me stay with her if she just thought of it in time. So Father didn't look at me. I was the oldest. I was nine and Caddy was seven and Jason was five.

"Nonsense," Father said. "We won't be long."

Nancy had her hat on. We came to the lane. "Jesus always been good to me," Nancy said. "Whenever he had two dollars, one of them was mine." We walked in the lane. "If I can just get through the lane," Nancy said, "I be all right then."

The lane was always dark. "This is where Jason got scaired on Hallowe'en," Caddy said.

"I didn't," Jason said.

"Can't Aunt Rachel do anything with him?" Father said. Aunt Rachel was old. She lived in a cabin beyond Nancy's by herself. She had white hair and she smoked a pipe in the door, all day long; she didn't work any more. They said she was Jesus' mother. Sometimes she said she was and sometimes she said she wasn't any kin to Jesus.

"Yes you did," Caddy said. "You were scairder than Frony. You were scairder than T.P. even. Scaider than niggers."

"Can't nobody do nothing with him," Nancy said. "He say I done woke up the devil in him and ain't but one thing going to lay it down again."

"Well, he's gone now," Father said. "There's nothing for you to be afraid of now. And if you'd just let white men alone."

"Let what white men alone?" Caddy said. "How let them alone?"

"He ain't gone nowhere," Nancy said. "I can feel him. I can feel him now, in this lane. He hearing us talk, every word, hid somewhere, waiting. I ain't seen him, and I ain't going to see him again but once more, with that razor in his mouth. That razor on that string down his back, inside his shirt. And then I ain't going to be even surprised."

"I wasn't scaired," Jason said.

"If you'd behave yourself, you'd have kept out of this," Father said. "But it's all right now. He's probably in Saint Louis now. Probably got another wife by now and forgot all about you."

"If he has, I better not find out about it," Nancy said. "I'd stand there right over them, and every time he wropped her, I'd cut that arm off. I'd cut his head off and I'd slit her belly and I'd shove—"

"Hush," Father said.

"Slit whose belly, Nancy?" Caddy said.

"I wasn't scaired," Jason said. "I'd walk right down this lane by myself."

"Yah," Caddy said. "You wouldn't dare to put your foot down in it if we were not here too."

II

Dilsey was still sick, so we took Nancy home every night until Mother said, "How much longer is this going on? I to be left alone in this big house while you take home a frightened Negro?"

We fixed a pallet in the kitchen for Nancy. One night we waked up, hearing the sound. It was not singing and it was not crying, coming up the dark stairs. There was a light in Mother's room and we heard Father going down the hall, down the back stairs, and Caddy and I went into the hall. The floor was cold. Our toes curled away from it while we listened to the sound. It was like singing and it wasn't like singing, like the sound that Negroes make.

Then it stopped and we heard Father going down the back stairs, and we went to the head of the stairs. Then the sound began again, in the stairway, not loud, and we could see Nancy's eyes halfway up the stairs, against the wall. They looked like cat's eyes do, like a big cat against the wall, watching us. When we came down the steps to where she was, she quit making the sound again, and we stood there until Father came back up from the kitchen, with his pistol in his hand. He went back down with Nancy and they came back with Nancy's pallet.

We spread the pallet in our room. After the light in Mother's room went off, we could see Nancy's eyes again. "Nancy," Caddy whispered, "are you asleep, Nancy?"

Nancy whispered something. It was oh or no, I don't know which. Like nobody had made it, like it came from nowhere and went nowhere, until it was like Nancy was not there at all; that I had looked so hard at her eyes on the stairs that they had got printed on my eyeballs, like the sun does when you have closed your eyes and there is no sun. "Jesus," Nancy whispered. "Jesus."

"Was it Jesus?" Caddy said. "Did he try to come into the kitchen?"

"Jesus," Nancy said. Like this: Jeeeeeeeeeeeeesus, until the sound went out, like a match or a candle does.

"It's the other Jesus she means," I said.

"Can you see us, Nancy?" Caddy whispered. "Can you see our eyes too?"

"I ain't nothing but a nigger," Nancy said. "God knows. God knows."

"What did you see down there in the kitchen?" Caddy whispered. "What tried to get in?"

"God knows," Nancy said. We could see her eyes. "God knows."

Dilsey got well. She cooked dinner. "You'd better stay in bed a day or two longer," Father said.

"What for?" Dilsey said. "If I had been a day later, this place would be to rack and ruin. Get on out of here now, and let me get my kitchen straight again."

Dilsey cooked supper too. And that night, just before dark, Nancy came into the kitchen.

"How do you know he's back?" Dilsey said. "You ain't seen him."

"Jesus is a nigger," Jason said.

"I can feel him," Nancy said. "I can feel him laying yonder in the ditch."

"Tonight?" Dilsey said. "Is he there tonight?"

"Dilsey's a nigger too," Jason said.

"You try to eat something," Dilsey said.

"I don't want nothing," Nancy said.

"I ain't a nigger," Jason said.

"Drink some coffee," Dilsey said. She poured a cup of coffee for Nancy. "Do you know he's out there tonight? How come you know it's tonight?"

"I know," Nancy said. "He's there waiting. I know. I done lived with him too long. I know what he is fixing to do fore he know it himself."

"Drink some coffee," Dilsey said. Nancy held the cup to her mouth and blew into the cup. Her mouth pursed out like a spreading adder's, like a rubber mouth, like she had blown all the color out of her lips with blowing the coffee.

"I ain't a nigger," Jason said. "Are you a nigger, Nancy?"

"I hellborn, child," Nancy said. "I won't be nothing soon. I going back where I come from soon."

III

She began to drink the coffee. While she was drinking, holding the cup in both hands, she began to make the sound again. She made the sound into the cup and the coffee sploshed out onto her hands and her dress. Her eyes looked at us and she sat there, her elbows on her knees, holding the cup in both hands, looking at us across the wet cup, making the sound.

"Look at Nancy," Jason said. "Nancy can't cook for us now. Dilsey's got well now."

"You hush up," Dilsey said. Nancy held the cup in both hands, looking at us, making the sound, like there were two of them: one looking at us and the other making the sound. "Whyn't you let Mr. Jason telefoam the marshall?" Dilsey said. Nancy stopped then, holding the cup in her long brown hands. She tried to drink some coffee again, but it sploshed out of the cup, onto her hands and her dress, and she put the cup down. Jason watched her.

"I can't swallow it," Nancy said. "I swallows but it won't go down me."

"You go down to the cabin," Dilsey said. "Frony will fix you a pallet and I'll be there soon."

"Won't no nigger stop him," Nancy said.

"I ain't a nigger," Jason said. "Am I, Dilsey?"

"I reckon not," Dilsey said. She looked at Nancy. "I don't reckon so. What you going to do, then?"

Nancy looked at us. Her eyes went fast, like she was afraid there wasn't time to look, without hardly moving at all. She looked at us, at all three of us at one time. "You member that night I stayed in yawls' room?" she said. She told about how we waked up early the next morning, and played. We had to play quiet, on her pallet, until Father woke up and it was time to get breakfast. "Go and ask your maw to let me stay here tonight," Nancy said. "I won't need no pallet. We can play some more."

Caddy asked Mother. Jason went too. "I can't have Negroes sleeping in the bedrooms," Mother said. Jason cried. He cried until Mother said he couldn't have any dessert for three days if he didn't stop. Then Jason said he would stop if Dilsey would make a chocolate cake. Father was there.

"Why don't you do something about it?" Mother said. "What do we have officers for?"

"Why is Nancy afraid of Jesus?" Caddy said. "Are you afraid of Father, Mother?"

"What could the officers do?" Father said. "If Nancy hasn't seen him, how could the officers find him?"

"Then why is she afraid?" Mother said.

"She says he is there. She says she knows he is there

tonight."

"Yet we pay taxes," Mother said. "I must wait here alone in this big house while you take a Negro woman home."

"You know that I am not lying outside with a razor," Father said.

"I'll stop if Dilsey will make a chocolate cake," Jason said. Mother told us to go out and Father said he didn't know if Jason would get a chocolate cake or not, but he knew what Jason was going to get in about a minute. We went back to the kitchen and told Nancy.

"Father said for you to go home and lock the door, and you'll be all right," Caddy said. "All right from what, Nancy? Is Jesus mad at you?" Nancy was holding the coffee cup in her hands again, her elbows on her knees and her hands holding the cup between her knees. She was looking into the cup. "What have you done that made Jesus mad?" Caddy said. Nancy let the cup go. It didn't break on the floor, but the coffee spilled out, and Nancy sat there with her hands still making the shape of the cup. She began to make the sound again, not loud. Not singing and not unsinging. We watched her.

"Here," Dilsey said. "You quit that, now. You get aholt of yourself. You wait here. I going to get Versh to walk home with you." Dilsey went out.

We looked at Nancy. Her shoulders kept shaking, but she quit making the sound. We stood and watched her.

"What's Jesus going to do to you?" Caddy said. "He went away."

Nancy looked at us. "We had fun that night I stayed in yawls' room, didn't we?"

"I didn't," Jason said. "I didn't have any fun."

"You were asleep in Mother's room," Caddy said. "You were not there."

"Let's go down to my house and have some more fun," Nancy said.

"Mother won't let us," I said. "It's too late now."

"Don't bother her," Nancy said. "We can tell her in the morning. She won't mind."

"She wouldn't let us," I said.

"Don't ask her now," Nancy said. "Don't bother her now."

"She didn't say we couldn't go," Caddy said.

"We didn't ask," I said.

"If you go, I'll tell," Jason said.

"We'll have fun," Nancy said. "They won't mind, just to my house. I been working for yawl a long time. They won't mind."

"I'm not afraid to go," Caddy said. "Jason is the one that's afraid. He'll tell."

"I'm not," Jason said.

"Yes, you are," Caddy said. "You'll tell."

"I won't tell," Jason said. "I'm not afraid."

"Jason ain't afraid to go with me," Nancy said. "Is you, Jason?"

"Jason is going to tell," Caddy said. The lane was dark. We passed the pasture gate. "I bet if something was to jump out from behind that gate, Jason would holler."

"I wouldn't," Jason said. We walked down the lane. Nancy was talking loud.

"What are you talking so loud for, Nancy?" Caddy said.

"Who; me?" Nancy said. "Listen at Quentin and Caddy and Jason saying I'm talking loud."

"You talk like there was five of us here," Caddy said. "You talk like Father was here too."

"Who; me talking loud, Mr. Jason?" Nancy said.

"Nancy called Jason 'Mister,'" Caddy said.

"Listen how Caddy and Quentin and Jason talk," Nancy said.

"We're not talking loud," Caddy said. "You're the one that's talking like Father—"

"Hush," Nancy said: "hush, Mr. Jason."

"Nancy called Jason 'Mister' aguh—"

"Hush," Nancy said. She was talking loud when we crossed the ditch and stooped through the fence where she used to stoop through with the clothes on her head. Then we came to her house. We were going fast then. She opened the door. The smell of the house was like the lamp and the smell of Nancy was like the wick, like they were waiting for one another to begin to smell. She lit the lamp and closed the door and put the bar up. Then she quit talking loud, looking at us.

"What're we going to do?" Caddy said.

"What do yawl want to do?" Nancy said.

"You said we would have some fun," Caddy said.

There was something about Nancy's house; something you could smell besides Nancy and the house. Jason smelled it, even. "I don't want to stay here," he said. "I want to go home."

"Go home, then," Caddy said.

"I don't want to go by myself," Jason said.

"We're going to have some fun," Nancy said.

"How?" Caddy said.

Nancy stood by the door. She was looking at us, only it was like she had emptied her eyes, like she had quit using them. "What do you want to do?" she said.

"Tell us a story," Caddy said. "Can you tell a story?"

"Yes," Nancy said.

"Tell it," Caddy said. We looked at Nancy. "You don't know any stories."

"Yes," Nancy said. "Yes I do."

She came and sat in a chair before the hearth. There was a little fire there. Nancy built it up, when it was already hot inside. She built a good blaze. She told a story. She talked like her eyes looked, like her eyes watching us and her voice talking to us did not belong to her. Like she was living somewhere else, waiting somewhere else. She was outside the cabin. Her voice was inside and the shape of her, that Nancy that could stoop under a barbed wire fence with a bundle of clothes balanced on her head as though without weight, like a balloon, was there. But that was all. "And so this here queen come walking up to the ditch, where that bad man was hiding. She was walking up to the ditch, and she say, 'If I can just get past this here ditch,' was what she say . . ."

"What ditch?" Caddy said. "A ditch like that one out there? Why did a queen want to go into a ditch?"

"To get to her house," Nancy said. She looked at us. "She had to cross the ditch to get into her house quick and bar the door."

"Why did she want to go home and bar the door?" Caddy said.

IV

Nancy looked at us. She quit talking. She looked at us. Jason's legs stuck straight out of his pants where he sat on Nancy's lap. "I don't think that's a good story," he said. "I want to go home."

"Maybe we had better," Caddy said. She got up from the floor. "I bet they are looking for us right now." She went toward the door.

"No," Nancy said. "Don't open it." She got up quick and passed Caddy. She didn't touch the door, the wooden bar.

"Why not?" Caddy said.

"Come back to the lamp," Nancy said. "We'll have fun. You don't have to go."

"We ought to go," Caddy said. "Unless we have a lot of fun." She and Nancy came back to the fire, the lamp.

"I want to go home," Jason said. "I'm going to tell."

"I know another story," Nancy said. She stood close to the lamp. She looked at Caddy, like when your eyes look up at a stick balanced on your nose. She had to look down to see Caddy, but her eyes looked like that, like when you are balancing a stick.

"I won't listen to it," Jason said. "I'll bang on the floor."

"It's a good one," Nancy said. "It's better than the other one."

"What's it about?" Caddy said. Nancy was standing by the lamp. Her hand was on the lamp, against the light, long and brown.

"Your hand is on that hot globe," Caddy said. "Don't it feel hot to your hand?"

Nancy looked at her hand on the lamp chimney. She took her hand away, slow. She stood there, looking at Caddy, wringing her long hand as though it were tied to her wrist with a string.

"Let's do something else," Caddy said.

"I want to go home," Jason said.

"I got some popcorn," Nancy said. She looked at Caddy and then at Jason and then at me and then at Caddy again. "I got some popcorn."

"I don't like popcorn," Jason said. "I'd rather have candy."

Nancy looked at Jason. "You can hold the popper.' She was still wringing her hand; it was long and limp and brown.

"All right," Jason said. "I'll stay a while if I can do that. Caddy can't hold it. I'll want to go home again if Caddy holds the popper."

Nancy built up the fire. "Look at Nancy putting her hands in the fire," Caddy said. "What the matter with you, Nancy?"

"I got popcorn," Nancy said. "I got some." She took the popper from under the bed. It was broken. Jason began to cry.

"Now we can't have any popcorn," he said.

"We ought to go home anyway," Caddy said. "Come on, Quentin."

"Wait," Nancy said: "wait. I can fix it. Don't you want to help me fix it?"

"I don't think I want any," Caddy said. "It's too late now."

"You help me, Jason," Nancy said. "Don't you want to help me?"

"No," Jason said. "I want to go home."

"Hush," Nancy said; "hush. Watch. Watch me. I can fix it so Jason can hold it and pop the corn." She got a piece of wire and fixed the popper.

"It won't hold good," Caddy said.

"Yes it will," Nancy said. "Yawl watch. Yawl help me shell some corn."

The popcorn was under the bed too. We shelled it into the popper and Nancy helped Jason hold the popper over the fire.

"It's not popping," Jason said. "I want to go home."

"You wait," Nancy said. "It'll begin to pop. We'll have fun then."

She was sitting close to the fire. The lamp was turned up so high it was beginning to smoke. "Why don't you turn it down some?" I said.

"It's all right," Nancy said. "I'll clean it. Yawl wait. The popcorn will start in a minute."

"I don't believe it's going to start," Caddy said. "We ought to start home, anyway. They'll be worried."

"No," Nancy said. "It's going to pop. Dilsey will tell um yawl with me. I been working for yawl long time. They won't mind if yawl at my house. You wait, now. It'll start popping any minute now."

Then Jason got some smoke in his eyes and he began to cry. He dropped the popper into the fire. Nancy got a wet rag and wiped Jason's face, but he didn't stop crying.

"Hush," she said. "Hush." But he didn't hush. Caddy took the popper out of the fire.

"It's burned up," she said. "You'll have to get some more popcorn, Nancy."

"Did you put all of it in?" Nancy said.

"Yes," Caddy said. Nancy looked at Caddy. Then she took the popper and opened it and poured the cinders into her apron and began to sort the grains, her hands long and brown, and we watched her.

"Haven't you got any more?" Caddy said.

"Yes," Nancy said; "yes. Look. This here ain't burnt. All we need to do is—"

"I want to go home," Jason said. "I'm going to tell."

"Hush," Caddy said. We all listened. Nancy's head was already turned toward the barred door, her eyes filled with red lamplight. "Somebody is coming," Caddy said.

Then Nancy began to make that sound again, not loud, sitting there above the fire, her long hands dangling between her knees; all of a sudden water began to come out on her face in big drops, running down her face, carrying in each one a little turning ball of firelight like a spark until it dropped off her chin. "She's not crying," I said.

"I ain't crying," Nancy said. Her eyes were closed. "I ain't crying. Who is it?"

"I don't know," Caddy said. She went to the door and looked out. "We've got to go now," she said. "Here comes Father."

"I'm going to tell," Jason said. "Yawl made me come."

The water still ran down Nancy's face. She turned in her chair. "Listen. Tell him. Tell him we going to have fun. Tell him I take good care of yawl until in the morning. Tell him to let me come home with yawl and sleep on the floor. Tell him I won't need no pallet. We'll have fun. You member last time how we had so much fun?"

"I didn't have fun," Jason said. "You hurt me. You put smoke in my eyes. I'm going to tell."

V

Father came in. He looked at us. Nancy did not get up.

"Tell him," she said.

"Caddy made us come down here," Jason said. "I didn't want to."

Father came to the fire. Nancy looked up at him. "Can't you go to Aunt Rachel's and stay?" he said. Nancy looked up at Father, her hands between her knees. "He's not here," Father said. "I would have seen him. There's not a soul in sight."

"He in the ditch," Nancy said. "He waiting in the ditch yonder."

"Nonsense," Father said. He looked at Nancy. "Do you know he's there?"

"I got the sign," Nancy said.

"What sign?"

"I got it. It was on the table when I come in. It was a hogbone, with blood meat still on it, laying by the lamp. He's out there. When yawl walk out that door, I gone."

"Gone where Nancy?" Caddy said.

"I'm not a tattletale," Jason said.

"Nonsense," Father said.

"He out there," Nancy said. "He looking through that window this minute, waiting for yawl to go. Then I gone."

"Nonsense," Father said. "Lock up your house and we'll take you on to Aunt Rachel's."

"'Twon't do no good," Nancy said. She didn't look at Father now, but he looked down at her, at her long, limp, moving hands. "Putting it off won't do no good."

"Then what do you want to do?" Father said.

"I don't know," Nancy said. "I can't do nothing. Just put it off. And that don't do no good. I reckon it belong to me. I reckon what I going to get ain't no more than mine."

"Get what?" Caddy said. "What's yours?"

"Nothing," Father said. "You all must get to bed."

"Caddy made me come," Jason said.

"Go on to Aunt Rachel's," Father said.

"It won't do no good," Nancy said. She sat before the fire, her elbows on her knees, her long hands between her knees. "When even your own kitchen wouldn't do no good. When even if I was sleeping on the floor in the room with your chillen, and the next morning there I am, and blood—"

"Hush," Father said. "Lock the door and put out the lamp and go to bed."

"I scaired of the dark," Nancy said. "I scaired for it to happen in the dark."

"You mean you're going to sit right here with the lamp lighted?" Father said. Then Nancy began to make the sound again, sitting before the fire, her long hands between her knees. "Ah damnation," Father said. "Come along chillen. It's past bedtime."

"When yawl go home, I gone," Nancy said. She talked quieter now, and her face looked quiet, like her hands. "Anyway, I got my coffin money saved up with Mr. Lovelady." Mr. Lovelady was a short dirty man who collected the Negro insurance, coming around to the cabins or the kitchens every Saturday morning, to collect fifteen cents. He and his wife lived at the hotel. One morning his wife committed suicide. They had a child, a little girl. He and the child went away. After a week or two he came back alone. We would see him going along the lanes and the back streets on Saturday mornings.

"Nonsense," Father said. "You'll be the first thing I'll see in the kitchen tomorrow morning."

"You'll see what you'll see, I reckon," Nancy said. "But it will take the Lord to say what that will be."

VI

We left her sitting before the fire.

"Come and put the bar up," Father said. But she didn't move. She didn't look at us again, sitting quietly there between the lamp and the fire. From some distance down the lane we could look back and see her through the open door.

"What, Father?" Caddy said. "What's going to happen?"

"Nothing," Father said. Jason was on Father's back, so Jason was the tallest of all of us. We went down into the ditch. I looked at it, quiet. I couldn't see much where the moonlight and the shadows tangled.

"If Jesus *is* hid here, he can see us, can't he?" Caddy said.

"He's not there," Father said. "He went away a long time ago."

"You made me come," Jason said, high; against the sky it looked like Father had two heads, a little one and a big one. "I didn't want to."

We went up out of the ditch. We could still see Nancy's house and the open door, but we couldn't see Nancy now, sitting before the fire with the door open, because she was tired. "I just done got tired," she said. "I just a nigger. It ain't no fault of mine."

But we could hear her, because she began just after we came up out of the ditch, the sound that was not singing and not unsinging. "Who will do our washing now, Father?" I said.

"I'm not a nigger," Jason said, high and close above Father's head.

"You're worse," Caddy said, "you are a tattletale. If something was to jump out, you'd be scairder than a nigger."

"I wouldn't," Jason said.

"You'd cry," Caddy said.

"Caddy," Father said.

"I wouldn't!" Jason said.

"Scairy cat," Caddy said.

"Candace!" Father said.

WILLIAM FAULKNER

Wash

SUTPEN stood above the pallet bed on which the mother and child lay. Between the shrunken planking of the wall the early sunlight fell in long pencil strokes, breaking upon his straddled legs and upon the riding whip in his hand, and lay across the still shape of the mother, who lay looking up at him from still, inscrutable, sullen eyes, the child at her side wrapped in a piece of dingy though clean cloth. Behind them an old Negro woman squatted beside the rough hearth where a meager fire smoldered.

"Well, Milly," Sutpen said, "too bad you're not a mare. Then I could give you a decent stall in the stable."

Still the girl on the pallet did not move. She merely continued to look up at him without expression, with a young, sullen, inscrutable face still pale from recent travail. Sutpen moved, bringing into the splintered pencils of sunlight the face of a man of sixty. He said quietly to the squatting Negress, "Griselda foaled this morning."

"Horse or mare?" the Negress said.

"A horse. A damned fine colt. . . . What's this?" He indicated the pallet with the hand which held the whip. "That un's a mare, I reckon."

"Hah," Sutpen said. "A damned fine colt. Going to be the spit and image of old Rob Roy when I rode him North in '61. Do you remember?"

"Yes, Marster."

"Hah." He glanced back towards the pallet. None could have said if the girl still watched him or not. Again his whip hand indicated the pallet. "Do whatever they need with whatever we've got to do it with." He went out, passing out the crazy doorway and stepping down into the rank weeds (there yet leaned rusting against the corner of the porch the scythe which Wash had borrowed from him three months ago to cut them with) where his horse waited, where Wash stood holding the reins.

When Colonel Sutpen rode away to fight the Yankees, Wash did not go. "I'm looking after the Kernel's place and niggers," he would tell all who asked him and some who had not asked—a gaunt, malaria-ridden man with pale, questioning eyes, who looked about thirty-five, though it was known that he had not only a daughter but an eight-year-old granddaughter as well. This was a lie, as most of them—the few remaining men between eighteen and fifty—to whom he told it, knew, though there were some who believed that he himself really believed it, though even these believed that he had better sense than to put it to the test with Mrs. Sutpen or the Sutpen slaves. Knew better or was just too lazy and shiftless to try it, they said, knowing that his sole connection with the Sutpen plantation lay in the fact that for years now Colonel Sutpen had allowed him to squat in a crazy shack on a slough in the river bottom on the Sutpen place, which Sutpen had built for a fishing lodge in his bachelor days and which had since fallen in dilapidation from disuse, so that now it looked like an aged or sick wild beast crawled terrifically there to drink in the act of dying.

The Sutpen slaves themselves heard of his statement. They laughed. It was not the first time they had laughed at him, calling him white trash behind his back. They began to ask him themselves, in groups, meeting him in the faint road which led up from the slough and the old fish camp, "Why ain't you at de war, white man?"

Pausing, he would look about the ring of black faces and white eyes and teeth behind which derision lurked. "Because I got a daughter and family to keep," he said. "Git out of my road, niggers."

"Niggers?" they repeated; "niggers?" laughing now. "Who him, calling us niggers?"

"Yes," he said. "I ain't got no niggers to look after my folks if I was gone."

"Nor nothing else but dat shack down yon dat Cunnel wouldn't *let* none of us live in."

Now he cursed them; sometimes he rushed at them, snatching up a stick from the ground while they scattered before him, yet seeming to surround him still with that black laughing, derisive, evasive, inescapable, leaving him panting and impotent and raging. Once it happened in the very back yard of the big house itself. This was after bitter news had come down from the Tennessee mountains and from Vicksburg, and Sherman had passed through the plantation, and most of the Negroes had followed him. Almost everything else had gone with the Federal troops, and Mrs. Sutpen had sent word to Wash that he could have the scuppernongs ripening in the arbor in the back yard. This time it was a house servant, one of the few Negroes who remained; this time the Negress had to retreat up the kitchen steps, where she turned, "Stop right dar, white man. Stop right whar you is. You ain't never crossed dese steps whilst Cunnel here, and you ain't ghy' do hit now."

This was true. But there was this of a kind of pride: he had never tried to enter the big house, even though he believed that if he had, Sutpen would have received him, permitted him. "But I ain't going to give no black nigger the chance to tell me I can't go nowhere," he said to himself. "I ain't even going to give Kernel the chance to have to cuss a nigger on my account." This, though he and Sutpen had spent more than one afternoon together on those rare Sundays when there would be no company in the house. Perhaps his mind knew that it was because Sutpen had nothing else to do, being a man who could not bear his own company. Yet the fact remained that the two of them would spend whole afternoons in the scuppernong arbor, Sutpen in the hammock and Wash squatting against a post, a pail of cistern water between them, taking drink for drink from the same demijohn. Meanwhile on weekdays he would see the fine figure of the man—they were the same age almost to a day, though neither of them (perhaps because Wash had a grandchild while Sutpen's son was a youth in school) ever thought of himself as being so—on the fine figure of the black stallion, galloping about the plantation. For that moment his heart would be quiet and proud. It would seem to him that that world in which Negroes, whom the Bible told him had been created and cursed by God to be brute and vassal to all men of white skin, were better found and housed and even clothed than he and his; that world in which he sensed always about him mocking echoes of black laughter was but a dream and an illusion, and that the actual world was this one across which his own lonely apotheosis seemed to gallop on the black thoroughbred, thinking how the Book said also that all men were created in the image of God and hence all men made the same image in God's eyes at least; so that he could say, as though speaking of himself, "A fine proud man. If God Himself was to come down and ride the natural earth, that's what He would aim to look like."

Sutpen returned in 1865, on the black stallion. He seemed to have aged ten years. His son had been killed in action the same winter in which his wife had died. He returned with his citation for gallantry from the hand of General Lee to a ruined plantation, where for a year now his daughter had subsisted partially on the meager bounty of the man to whom fifteen years ago he had granted permission to live in that tumbledown fishing camp whose very existence he had at the time forgotten. Wash was there to meet him, unchanged: still gaunt, still ageless, with his pale, questioning gaze, his air diffident, a little servile, a little familiar. "Well Kernel," Wash said, "they kilt us but they ain't whupped us yit, air they?"

That was the tenor of their conversation for the next five years. It was inferior whisky which they drank now together from a stoneware jug, and it was not in the scuppernong arbor. It was in the rear of the little store which Sutpen managed to set up on the highroad: a frame shelved room where, with Wash for clerk and porter, he dispensed kerosene and staple foodstuffs and stale gaudy candy and cheap beads and ribbons to Negroes or poor whites of Wash's own kind, who came afoot or on gaunt mules to haggle tediously for dimes and quarters with a man who at one time could gallop (the black stallion was still alive; the stable in which his jealous get lived was in better repair than the house where the master himself lived) for ten miles across his own fertile land and who had led troops gallantly in battle; until Sutpen in fury would empty the store, close and lock the doors from the inside. Then he and Wash would repair to the rear and the jug. But the talk would not be quiet now, as when Sutpen lay in the hammock, delivering an arrogant monologue while Wash squatted guffawing against his post. They both sat now, though Sutpen had the single chair while Wash used whatever box or keg was handy, and even this for just a little while, because soon Sutpen would reach that stage of impotent and furious undefeat in which he would rise, swaying and plunging, and declare again that he would take his pistol and the black stallion and ride single-handed into Washington and kill Lincoln, dead now, and Sherman, now a private citizen. "Kill them!" he would shout. "Shoot them down like the dogs they are—"

"Sho, Kernel; sho, Kernel," Wash would say, catching Sutpen as he fell. Then he would commandeer the first passing wagon or, lacking that, he would walk the mile to the nearest neighbor and borrow one and return and carry Sutpen home. He entered the house now. He had been doing so for a long time, taking Sutpen home in whatever borrowed wagon might be, talking him into locomotion with cajoling murmurs as though he were a horse, a stallion himself. The daughter would meet them and hold open the door without a word. He would carry his burden through the once white formal entrance, surmounted by a fanlight imported piece by piece from Europe and with a board now nailed over a missing pane, across a velvet carpet from which all nap was now gone, and up a formal stairs, now but a fading ghost of bare boards between two strips of fading paint, and into the bedroom. It would be dusk by now, and he would let his burden sprawl onto the bed and undress it and then he would sit quietly in a chair beside. After a time the daughter would come to the door. "We're all right now," he would tell her. "Don't you worry none, Miss Judith."

Then it would become dark, and after a while he would lie down on the floor beside the bed, though not to sleep, because after a time—sometimes before midnight—the man on the bed would stir and groan and then speak. "Wash?"

"Hyer I am, Kernel. You go back to sleep. We ain't whupped yit, air we? Me and you kin do hit."

Even then he had already seen the ribbon about his granddaughter's waist. She was now fifteen, already mature, after the early way of her kind. He knew where the ribbon came from; he had been seeing it and its kind daily for three years, even if she had lied about where she got it, which she did not, at once bold, sullen, and fearful. "Sho now," he said. "Ef Kernel wants to give hit to you, I hope you minded to thank him."

His heart was quiet, even when he saw the dress, watching her secret, defiant, frightened face when she told him that Miss Judith, the daughter, had helped her to make it. But he was quite grave when he approached Sutpen after they closed the store that afternoon, following the other to the rear.

"Get the jug," Sutpen directed.

"Wait," Wash said. "Not yit for a minute."

Neither did Sutpen deny the dress. "What about it?" he said.

But Wash met his arrogant stare; he spoke quietly. "I've knowed you for going on twenty years. I ain't never yit denied to do what you told me to do. And I'm a man nigh sixty. And she ain't nothing but a fifteen-year-old gal."

"Meaning that I'd harm a girl? I, a man as old as you are?"

"If you was ara other man, I'd say you was as old as me. And old or no old, I wouldn't let her keep that dress nor nothing else that come from your hand. But you are different."

"How different?" But Wash merely looked at him with his pale, questioning, sober eyes. "So that's why you are afraid of me?"

Now Wash's gaze no longer questioned. It was tranquil, serene. "I ain't afraid. Because you air brave. It ain't that you were a brave man at one minute or day of your life and got a paper to show hit from General Lee. But you air brave, the same as you air alive and breathing. That's where hit's different. Hit don't need no ticket from nobody to tell me that. And I know that whatever you handle or tech, whether hit's a regiment of men or a ignorant gal or just a hound dog, that you will make hit right."

Now it was Sutpen who looked away, turning suddenly, brusquely. "Get the jug," he said sharply.

"Sho, Kernel," Wash said.

So on that Sunday dawn two years later, having watched the Negro midwife, which he had walked three miles to fetch, enter the crazy door beyond which his granddaughter lay wailing, his heart was still quiet though concerned. He knew what they had been saying—the Negroes in cabins about the land, the white men who loafed all day long about the store, watching quietly the three of them: Sutpen, himself, his granddaughter with her air of brazen and shrinking defiance as her condition became daily more and more obvious, like three actors that came and went upon a stage. "I know what they say to one another," he thought. "I can almost hyear them: *Wash Jones has fixed old Sutpen at last. Hit taken him twenty years, but he has done hit at last.*"

It would be dawn after a while, though not yet. From the house, where the lamp shone dim beyond the warped doorframe, his granddaughter's voice came steadily as though run by a clock, while thinking went slowly and terrifically, fumbling, involved somehow with a sound of galloping hooves, until there broke suddenly free in mid-gallop the fine proud figure of the man on the fine proud stallion, galloping; and then that at which thinking fumbled, broke free too and quite clear, not in justification nor even explanation, but as the apotheosis, lonely, explicable, beyond all fouling by human touch: "He is bigger than all them Yankees that kilt his son and his wife and taken his niggers and ruined his land, bigger than this hyer durn country that he fit for and that has denied him into keeping a little country store; bigger than the denial which hit helt to his lips like the bitter cup in the Book. And how could I have lived this nigh to him for twenty years without being teched and changed by him? Maybe I ain't as big as him and maybe I ain't done none of the galloping. But at least I done been drug along. Me and him kin do hit, if so be he will show me what he aims for me to do."

Then it was dawn. Suddenly he could see the house, and the old Negress in the door looking at him. Then he realized that his granddaughter's voice had ceased. "It's a girl," the Negress said. "You can go tell him if you want to." She reëntered the house.

"A girl," he repeated; "a girl"; in astonishment, hearing the galloping hooves, seeing the proud galloping figure emerge again. He seemed to watch it pass, galloping through avatars which marked the accumulation of years, time, to the climax where it galloped beneath a brandished saber and a shot-torn flag rushing down a sky in color like thunderous sulphur, thinking for the first time in his life that perhaps Sutpen was an old man like himself. "Gittin a gal," he thought in that astonishment; then he thought with the pleased surprise of a child: "Yes, sir. Be dawg if I ain't lived to be a great-grandpaw after all."

He entered the house. He moved clumsily, on tiptoe, as if he no longer lived there, as if the infant which had just drawn breath and cried in light had dispossessed him, be it of his own blood too though it might. But even above the pallet he could see little save the blur of his granddaughter's exhausted face. Then the Negress squatting at the hearth spoke, "You better gawn tell him if you going to. Hit's daylight now."

But this was not necessary. He had no more than turned the corner of the porch where the scythe leaned which he had borrowed three months ago to clear away the weeds through which he walked, when Sutpen himself rode up on the old stallion. He did not wonder how Sutpen had got the word. He took it for granted that this was what had brought the other out at this hour on Sunday morning, and he stood while the other dismounted, and he took the reins from Sutpen's hand, an expression on his gaunt face almost imbecile with a kind of weary triumph, saying, "Hit's a gal, Kernel. I be dawg if you ain't as old as I am—" until Sutpen passed him and entered the house. He stood there with the reins in his hand and heard Sutpen cross the floor to the pallet. He heard what Sutpen said, and something seemed to stop dead in him before going on.

The sun was now up, the swift sun of Mississippi latitudes, and it seemed to him that he stood beneath a strange sky, in a strange scene, familiar only as things are familiar in dreams, like the dreams of falling to one who has never climbed. "I kain't have heard what I thought I heard," he thought quietly. "I know I kain't." Yet the voice, the familiar voice which had said the words was still speaking, talking now to the old Negress about a colt foaled that morning. "That's why he was up so early," he thought. "That was hit. Hit ain't me and mine. Hit ain't even hisn that got him outen bed."

Sutpen emerged. He descended into the weeds, moving with that heavy deliberation which would have been haste when he was younger. He had not yet looked full at Wash. He said, "Dicey will stay and tend to her. You better—" Then he seemed to see Wash facing him and paused. "What?" he said.

"You said—" To his own ears Wash's voice sounded flat and ducklike, like a deaf man's. "You said if she was a mare, you could give her a good stall in the stable."

"Well?" Sutpen said. His eyes widened and narrowed, almost like a man's fists flexing and shutting, as Wash began to advance towards him, stooping a little. Very astonishment kept Sutpen still for the moment, watching that man whom in twenty years he had no more known to make any motion save at command than he had the horse which he rode. Again his eyes narrowed and widened; without moving he seemed to rear suddenly upright. "Stand back," he said suddenly and sharply. "Don't you touch me."

"I'm going to tech you, Kernel," Wash said in that flat, quiet, almost soft voice, advancing.

Sutpen raised the hand which held the riding whip; the old Negress peered around the crazy door with her black gargoyle face of a worn gnome. "Stand back, Wash," Sutpen said. Then he struck. The old Negress leaped down into the weeds with the agility of a goat and fled. Sutpen slashed Wash again across the face with the whip, striking him to his knees. When Wash rose and advanced once more he held in his hands the scythe which he had borrowed from Sutpen three months ago and which Sutpen would never need again.

When he reëntered the house his granddaughter stirred on the pallet bed and called his name fretfully. "What was that?" she said.

"What was what, honey?"

"That ere racket out there."

" 'Twarn't nothing," he said gently. He knelt and touched her hot forehead clumsily. "Do you want ara thing?"

"I want a sup of water," she said querulously. "I been laying here wanting a sup of water a long time, but don't nobody care enough to pay me no mind."

"Sho now," he said soothingly. He rose stiffly and fetched the dipper of water and raised her head to drink and laid her back and watched her turn to the child with an absolutely stonelike face. But a moment later he saw that she was crying quietly. "Now, now," he said, "I wouldn't do that. Old Dicey says hit's a right fine gal. Hit's all right now. Hit's all over now. Hit ain't no need to cry now."

But she continued to cry quietly, almost sullenly, and he rose again and stood uncomfortably above the pallet for a time, thinking as he had thought when his own wife lay so and then his daughter in turn: "Women. Hit's a mystry to me. They seem to want em, and yit when they git em they cry about hit. Hit's a mystry to me. To ara man." Then he moved away and drew a chair up to the window and sat down.

Through all that long, bright, sunny forenoon he sat at the window, waiting. Now and then he rose and tiptoed to the pallet. But his granddaughter slept now, her face sullen and calm and weary, the child in the crook of her arm. Then he returned to the chair and sat again, waiting, wondering why it took them so long, until he remembered that it was Sunday. He was sitting there at mid-afternoon when a half-grown white boy came around the corner of the house upon the body and gave a choked cry and looked up and glared for a mesmerized instant at Wash in the window before he turned and fled. Then Wash rose and tiptoed again to the pallet.

The granddaughter was awake now, wakened perhaps by the boy's cry without hearing it. "Milly," he said, "air you hungry?" She didn't answer, turning her face away. He built up the fire on the hearth and cooked the food which he had brought home the day before: fatback it was, and cold corn pone; he poured water into the stale coffee pot and heated it. But she would not eat when he carried the plate to her, so he ate himself, quietly, alone, and left the dishes as they were and returned to the window.

Now he seemed to sense, feel, the men who would be gathering with horses and guns and dogs—the curious, and the vengeful: men of Sutpen's own kind, who had made the company about Sutpen's table in the time when Wash himself had yet to approach nearer to the house than the scuppernong arbor—men who had also shown the lesser ones how to fight in battle, who maybe also had signed papers from the generals saying that they were among the first of the brave; who had also galloped in the old days arrogant and proud on the fine horses across the fine plantations—symbols also of admiration and hope; instruments too of despair and grief.

That was whom they would expect him to run from. It seemed to him that he had no more to run from than he had to run to. If he ran, he would merely be fleeing one set of bragging and evil shadows for another just like them, since they were all of a kind throughout all the earth which he knew, and he was old, too old to flee far even if he were to flee. He could never escape them, no matter how much or how far he ran: a man going on sixty could not run that far. Not far enough to escape beyond the boundaries of earth where such men lived, set the order and the rule of living. It seemed to him that he now saw for the first time, after five years, how it was that Yankees or any other living armies had managed to whip them: the gallant, the proud, the brave; the acknowledged and chosen best among them all to carry courage and honor and pride. Maybe if he had gone to the war with them he would have discovered them sooner. But if he had discovered them sooner, what would he have done with his life since? How could he have borne to remember for five years what his life had been before?

Now it was getting toward sunset. The child had been crying; when he went to the pallet he saw his granddaughter nursing it, her face still bemused, sullen, inscrutable. "Air you hungry yit?" he said.

"I don't want nothing."

"You ought to eat."

This time she did not answer at all, looking down at the child. He returned to his chair and found that the sun had set. "Hit kain't be much longer," he thought. He could feel them quite near now, the curious and the vengeful. He could even seem to hear what they were saying about him, the undercurrent of believing beyond the immediate fury: *Old Wash Jones he come a tumble at last. He thought he had Sutpen, but Sutpen fooled him. He thought he had Kernel where he would have to marry the gal or pay up. And Kernel refused.* "But I never expected that, Kernel!" he cried aloud, catching himself at the sound of his own voice, glancing quickly back to find his granddaughter watching him.

"Who you talking to now?" she said.

"Hit ain't nothing. I was just thinking and talked out before I knowed hit."

Her face was becoming indistinct again, again a sullen blur in the twilight. "I reckon so. I reckon you'll have to holler louder than that before he'll hear you, up yonder at that house. And I reckon you'll need to do more than holler before you get him down here too."

"Sho now," he said. "Don't you worry none." But already thinking was going smoothly on: "You know I never. You know how I ain't never expected or asked nothing from ara living man but what I expected from you. And I never asked that. I didn't think hit would need. I said, *I don't need to. What need has a fellow like Wash Jones to question or doubt the man that General Lee himself says in a handwrote ticket that he was brave?* Brave," he thought. "Better if nara one of them had never rid back home in '65"; thinking *Better if his kind and mine too had never drawn the breath of life on this earth. Better that all who remain of us be blasted from the face of earth than that another Wash Jones should see his whole life shredded from him and shrivel away like a dried shuck thrown onto the fire.*

He ceased, became still. He heard the horses, suddenly and plainly; presently he saw the lantern and the movement of men, the glint of gun barrels, in its moving light. Yet he did not stir. It was quite dark now, and he listened to the voices and the sounds of underbrush as they surrounded the house. The lantern itself came on; its light fell upon the quiet body in the weeds and stopped, the horses tall and shadowy. A man descended and stooped in the lantern light, above the body. He held a pistol; he rose and faced the house. "Jones," he said.

"I'm here," Wash said quietly from the window. "That you, Major?"

"Come out."

"Sho," he said quietly. "I just want to see to my granddaughter."

"We'll see to her. Come on out."

"Sho, Major. Just a minute."

"Show a light. Light your lamp."

"Sho. In just a minute." They could hear his voice retreat into the house, though they could not see him as he went swiftly to the crack in the chimney where he kept the butcher knife: the one thing in his slovenly life and house in which he took pride, since it was razor sharp. He approached the pallet, his granddaughter's voice:

"Who is it? Light the lamp, grandpaw."

"Hit won't need no light, honey. Hit won't take but a minute," he said, kneeling, fumbling toward her voice, whispering now. "Where air you?"

"Right here," she said fretfully. "Where would I be? What is . . ." His hand touched her face. "What is . . . Grandpaw! Grand. . . ."

"Jones!" the sheriff said. "Come out of there!"

"In just a minute, Major," he said. Now he rose and moved swiftly. He knew where in the dark the can of kerosene was, just as he knew that it was full, since it was not two days ago that he had filled it at the store and held it there until he got a ride home with it, since the five gallons were heavy. There were still coals on the hearth; besides, the crazy building itself was like tinder: the coals, the hearth, the walls exploding in a single blue glare. Against it the waiting men saw him in a wild instant springing toward them with the lifted scythe before the horses reared and whirled. They checked the horses and turned them back toward the glare, yet still in wild relief against it the gaunt figure ran toward them with the lifted scythe.

"Jones!" the sheriff shouted; "stop! Stop, or I'll shoot. Jones! *Jones!*" Yet still the gaunt, furious figure came on against the glare and roar of the flames. With the scythe lifted, it bore down upon them, upon the wild glaring eyes of the horses and the swinging glints of gun barrels, without any cry, any sound.

JAMES JOYCE

Araby

NORTH RICHMOND STREET, being blind, was a quiet street except at the hour when the Christian Brothers' School set the boys free. An uninhabited house of two storeys stood at the blind end, detached from its neighbours in a square ground. The other houses of the street, conscious of decent lives within them, gazed at one another with brown imperturbable faces.

The former tenant of our house, a priest, had died in the back drawing-room. Air, musty from having been long enclosed, hung in all the rooms, and the waste room behind the kitchen was littered with old useless papers. Among these I found a few paper-covered books, the pages of which were curled and damp: *The Abbot,* by Walter Scott, *The Devout Communicant* and *The Memoirs of Vidocq.* I liked the last best because its leaves were yellow. The wild garden behind the house contained a central apple-tree and a few straggling bushes under one of which I found the late tenant's rusty bicycle-pump. He had been a very charitable priest; in his will he had left all his money to institutions and the furniture of his house to his sister.

When the short days of winter came dusk fell before we had well eaten our dinners. When we met in the street the houses had grown sombre. The space of sky above us was the colour of everchanging violet and towards it the lamps of the street lifted their feeble lanterns. The cold air stung us and we played till our bodies glowed. Our shouts echoed in the silent street. The career of our play brought us through the dark muddy lanes behind the houses where we ran the gauntlet of the rough tribes from the cottages, to the back doors of the dark dripping gardens where odours arose from the ashpits, to the dark odorous stables where a coachman smoothed and combed the horse or shook music from the buckled harness. When we returned to the street light from the kitchen windows had filled the areas. If my uncle was seen turning the corner we hid in the shadow until we had seen him safely housed. Or if Mangan's sister came out on the doorstep to call her brother in to his tea we watched her from our shadow peer up and down the street. We waited to see whether she would remain or go in and, if she remained, we left our shadow and walked up to Mangan's steps resignedly. She was waiting for us, her figure defined by the light from the half-opened door. Her brother always teased her before he obeyed and I stood by the railings looking at her. Her dress swung as she moved her body and the soft rope of her hair tossed from side to side.

Every morning I lay on the floor in the front parlour watching her door. The blind was pulled down to within an inch of the sash so that I could not be seen. When she came out on the doorstep my heart leaped. I ran to the hall, seized my books and followed her. I kept her brown figure always in my eye and, when we came near the point at which our ways diverged, I quickened my pace and passed her. This happened morning after morning. I had never spoken to her, except for a few casual words, and yet her name was like a summons to all my foolish blood.

Her image accompanied me even in places the most hostile to romance. On Saturday evenings when my aunt went marketing I had to go to carry some of the parcels. We walked through the flaring streets, jostled by drunken men and bargaining women, amid the curses of labourers, the shrill litanies of shop-boys who stood on guard by the barrels of pigs' cheeks, the nasal chanting of street-singers, who sang a *come-all-you* about O'Donovan Rossa, or a ballad about the troubles in our native land. These noises converged in a single sensation of life for me: I imagined that I bore my chalice safely through a throng of foes. Her name sprang to my lips at moments in strange prayers and praises which I myself did not understand. My eyes were often full of tears (I could not tell why) and at times a flood from my heart seemed to pour itself out into my bosom. I thought little of the future. I did not know whether I would ever speak to her or not or, if I spoke to her, how I could tell her of my confused adoration. But my body was like a harp and her words and gestures were like fingers running upon the wires.

One evening I went into the back drawing-room in which the priest had died. It was a dark rainy evening and there was no sound in the house. Through one of the broken panes I heard the rain impinge upon the earth, the fine incessant needles of water playing in the sodden beds. Some distant lamp or lighted window gleamed below me. I was thankful that I could see so little. All my senses seemed to desire to veil themselves and, feeling that I was about to slip from them, I pressed the palms of my hands together until they trembled, murmuring: "*O love! O love!*" many times.

At last she spoke to me. When she addressed the first words to me I was so confused that I did not know what to answer. She asked me was I going to *Araby*. I forgot whether I answered yes or no. It would be a splendid bazaar, she said she would love to go.

"And why can't you?" I asked.

While she spoke she turned a silver bracelet round and round her wrist. She could not go, she said, because there would be a retreat that week in her convent. Her brother and two other boys were fighting for their caps and I was alone at the railings. She held one of the spikes, bowing her head towards me. The light from the lamp opposite our door caught the white curve of her neck, lit up her hair that rested there and, falling, lit up the hand upon the railing. It fell over one side of her dress and caught the white border of a petticoat, just visible as she stood at ease.

"It's well for you," she said.

"If I go," I said, "I will bring you something."

What innumerable follies laid waste my waking and sleeping thoughts after that evening! I wished to annihilate the tedious intervening days. I chafed against the work of school. At night in my bedroom and by day in the classroom her image came between me and the page I strove to read. The syllables of the word *Araby* were called to me through the silence in which my soul luxuriated and cast an Eastern enchantment over me. I asked for leave to go to the bazaar on Saturday night. My aunt was surprised and hoped it was not some Freemason affair. I answered few questions in class. I watched my master's face pass from amiability to sternness; he hoped I was not beginning to idle. I could not call my wandering thoughts together. I had hardly any patience with the serious work of life which, now that it stood between me and my desire, seemed to me child's play, ugly monotonous child's play.

On Saturday morning I reminded my uncle that I wished to go to the bazaar in the evening. He was fussing at the hallstand, looking for the hat-brush, and answered me curtly:

"Yes, boy, I know."

As he was in the hall I could not go into the front parlour and lie at the window. I left the house in bad humour and walked slowly towards the school. The air was pitilessly raw and already my heart misgave me.

When I came home to dinner my uncle had not yet been home. Still it was early. I sat staring at the clock for some time and, when its ticking began to irritate me, I left the room. I mounted the staircase and gained the upper part of the house. The high cold empty gloomy rooms liberated me and I went from room to room singing. From the front window I saw my companions playing below in the street. Their cries reached me weakened and indistinct and, leaning my forehead against the cool glass, I looked over at the dark house where she lived. I may have stood there for an hour, seeing nothing but the brown-clad figure cast by my imagination, touched discreetly by the lamplight at the curved neck, at the hand upon the railings and at the border below the dress.

When I came downstairs again I found Mrs. Mercer sitting at the fire. She was an old garrulous woman, a pawnbroker's widow, who collected used stamps for some pious purpose. I had to endure the gossip of the tea-table. The meal was prolonged beyond an hour and still my uncle did not come. Mrs. Mercer stood up to go: she was sorry she couldn't wait any longer, but it was after eight o'clock and she did not like to be out late, as the night air was bad for her. When she had gone I began to walk up and down the room, clenching my fists. My aunt said:

"I'm afraid you may put off your bazaar for this night of Our Lord."

At nine o'clock I heard my uncle's latchkey in the halldoor. I heard him talking to himself and heard the hallstand rocking when it had received the weight of his overcoat. I could interpret these signs. When he was midway through his dinner I asked him to give me the money to go to the bazaar. He had forgotten.

"The people are in bed and after their first sleep now," he said.

I did not smile. My aunt said to him energetically: "Can't you give him the money and let him go? You've kept him late enough as it is."

My uncle said he was very sorry he had forgotten. He said he believed in the old saying: "All work and no play makes Jack a dull boy." He asked me where I was going and, when I had told him a second time he asked me did I know *The Arab's Farewell to his Steed.* When I left the kitchen he was about to recite the opening lines of the piece to my aunt.

I held a florin tightly in my hand as I strode down Buckingham Street towards the station. The sight of the streets thronged with buyers and glaring with gas recalled to me the purpose of my journey. I took my seat in a third-class carriage of a deserted train. After an intolerable delay the train moved out of the station slowly. It crept onward among ruinous houses and over the twinkling river. At Westland Row Station a crowd of people pressed to the carriage doors; but the porters moved them back, saying that it was a special train for the bazaar. I remained alone in the bare carriage. In a few minutes the train drew up beside an improvised wooden platform. I passed out on to the road and saw by the lighted dial of a clock that it was ten minutes to ten. In front of me was a large building which displayed the magical name.

I could not find any sixpenny entrance and, fearing that the bazaar would be closed, I passed in quickly through a turnstile, handing a shilling to a weary-looking man. I found myself in a big hall girdled at half its height by a gallery. Nearly all the stalls were closed and the greater part of the hall was in darkness. I recognized a silence like that which pervades a church after a service. I walked into the centre of the bazaar timidly. A few people were gathered about the stalls which were still open. Before a curtain, over which the words *Café Chantant* were written in coloured lamps, two men were counting money on a salver. I listened to the fall of the coins.

Remembering with difficulty why I had come I went over to one of the stalls and examined porcelain vases and flowered tea-sets. At the door of the stall a young lady was talking and laughing with two young gentlemen. I remarked their English accents and listened vaguely to their conversation.

"O, I never said such a thing!"

"O, but you did!"

"O, but I didn't!"

"Didn't she say that?"

"Yes. I heard her."

"O, there's a . . . fib!"

Observing me the young lady came over and asked me did I wish to buy anything. The tone of her voice was not encouraging; she seemed to have spoken to me out of a sense of duty. I looked humbly at the great jars that stood like eastern guards at either side of the dark entrance to the stall and murmured:

"No, thank you."

The young lady changed the position of one of the vases and went back to the two young men. They began to talk of the same subject. Once or twice the young lady glanced at me over her shoulder.

I lingered before her stall, though I knew my stay was useless, to make my interest in her wares seem the more real. Then I turned away slowly and walked down the middle of the bazaar. I allowed the two pennies to fall against the sixpence in my pocket. I heard a voice call from one end of the gallery that the light was out. The upper part of the hall was now completely dark.

Gazing up into the darkness I saw myself as a creature driven and derided by vanity; and my eyes burned with anguish and anger.

JAMES JOYCE

Clay

THE matron had given her leave to go out as soon as the women's tea was over and Maria looked forward to her evening out. The kitchen was spick and span: the cook said you could see yourself in the big copper boilers. The fire was nice and bright and on one of the side-tables were four very big barmbracks. These barmbracks seemed uncut; but if you went closer you would see that they had been cut into long thick even slices and were ready to be handed round at tea. Maria had cut them herself.

Maria was a very, very small person indeed but she had a very long nose and a very long chin. She talked a little through her nose, always soothingly: *"Yes, my dear,"* and *"No, my dear."* She was always sent for when the women quarrelled over their tubs and always succeeded in making peace. One day the matron had said to her:

"Maria, you are a veritable peace-maker!"

And the sub-matron and two of the Board ladies had heard the compliment. And Ginger Mooney was always saying what she wouldn't do to the dummy who had charge of the irons if it wasn't for Maria. Everyone was so fond of Maria.

The women would have their tea at six o'clock and she would be able to get away before seven. From Ballsbridge to the Pillar, twenty minutes; from the Pillar to Drumcondra, twenty minutes; and twenty minutes to buy the things. She would be there before eight. She took out her purse with the silver clasps and read again the words *A Present from Belfast.* She was very fond of that purse because Joe had brought it to her five years before when he and Alphy had gone to Belfast on a Whit-Monday trip. In the purse were two half-crowns and some coppers. She would have five shillings clear after paying tram fare. What a nice evening they would have, all the children singing! Only she hoped that Joe wouldn't come in drunk. He was so different when he took any drink.

Often he had wanted her to go and live with them; but she would have felt herself in the way (though Joe's wife was ever so nice with her) and she had become accustomed to the life of the laundry. Joe was a good fellow. She had nursed him and Alphy too; and Joe used often say:

"Mamma is mamma but Maria is my proper mother."

After the break-up at home the boys had got her that position in the *Dublin by Lamplight* laundry, and she liked it. She used to have such a bad opinion of Protestants but now she thought they were very nice people, a little quiet and serious, but still very nice people to live with. Then she had her plants in the conservatory and she liked looking after them. She had lovely ferns and wax-plants and, whenever anyone came to visit her, she always gave the visitor one or two slips from her conservatory. There was one thing she didn't like and that was the tracts on the walls; but the matron was such a nice person to deal with, so genteel.

When the cook told her everything was ready she went into the women's room and began to pull the big bell. In a few minutes the women began to come in by twos and threes, wiping their steaming hands in their petticoats and pulling down the sleeves of their blouses over their red steaming arms. They settled down before their huge mugs which the cook and the dummy filled up with hot tea, already mixed with milk and sugar in huge tin cans. Maria superintended the distribution of the barmbrack and saw that every woman got her four slices. There was a great deal of laughing and joking during the meal. Lizzie Fleming said Maria was sure to get the ring and, though Fleming had said that for so many Hallow Eves, Maria had to laugh and say she didn't want any ring or man either; and when she laughed her grey-green eyes sparkled with disappointed shyness and the tip of her nose nearly met the tip of her chin. Then Ginger Mooney lifted up her mug of tea and proposed Maria's health while all the other women clattered with their mugs on the table, and said she was sorry she hadn't a sup of porter to drink in it. And Maria laughed again till the tip of her nose nearly met the tip of her chin and till her minute body nearly shook itself asunder because she knew that Mooney meant well though, of course, she had the notions of a common woman.

But wasn't Maria glad when the women had finished their tea and the cook and the dummy had begun to clear away the tea-things! She went into her little bedroom and, remembering that the next morning was a mass morning, changed the hand of the alarm from seven to six. Then she took off her working skirt and her house-boots and laid her best skirt out on the bed and her tiny dress-boots beside the foot of the bed. She changed her blouse too and, as she stood before the mirror, she thought of how she used to dress for mass on Sunday morning when she was a young girl; and she looked with quaint affection at the diminutive body which she had so often adorned. In spite of its years she found it a nice tidy little body.

When she got outside the streets were shining with rain and she was glad of her old brown waterproof. The tram was full and she had to sit on the little stool at the end of the car, facing all the people, with her toes barely touching the floor. She arranged in her mind all she was going to do and thought how much better it was to be independent and to have your own money in your pocket. She hoped they would have a nice evening. She was sure they would but she could not help thinking what a pity it was Alphy and Joe were not speaking. They were always falling out now but when they were boys together they used to be the best of friends: but such was life.

She got out of her tram at the Pillar and ferreted her way quickly among the crowds. She went into Downes's cake-shop but the shop was so full of people that it was a long time before she could get herself attended to. She bought a dozen of mixed penny cakes, and at last came out of the shop laden with a big bag. Then she thought what else would she buy: she wanted to buy something really nice. They would be sure to have plenty of apples and nuts. It was hard to know what to buy and all she could think of was cake. She decided to buy some plumcake but Downes's plumcake had not enough almond icing on top of it so she went over to a shop in Henry Street. Here she was a long time in suiting herself and the stylish young lady behind the counter, who was evidently a little annoyed by her, asked her was it wedding-cake she wanted to buy. That made Maria blush and smile at the young lady; but the young lady took it all very seriously and finally cut a thick slice of plumcake, parcelled it up and said:

"Two-and-four, please."

She thought she would have to stand in the Drumcondra tram because none of the young men seemed to notice her but an elderly gentleman made room for her. He was a stout gentleman and he wore a brown hard hat; he had a square red face and a greyish moustache. Maria thought he was a colonel-looking gentleman and she reflected how much more polite he was than the young men who simply stared straight before them. The gentleman began to chat with her about Hallow Eve and the rainy weather. He supposed the bag was full of good things for the little ones and said it was only right that the youngsters should enjoy themselves while they were young. Maria agreed with him and favoured him with demure nods and hems. He was very nice with her, and when she was getting out at the Canal Bridge she thanked him and bowed, and he bowed to her and raised his hat and smiled agreeably; and while she was going up along the terrace, bending her tiny head under the rain, she thought how easy it was to know a gentleman even when he has a drop taken.

Everybody said: *"O, here's Maria!"* when she came to Joe's house. Joe was there, having come home from business, and all the children had their Sunday dresses on. There were two big girls in from next door and games were going on. Maria gave the bag of cakes to the eldest boy, Alphy, to divide and Mrs. Donnelly said it was too good of her to bring such a big bag of cakes and made the children say:

"Thanks, Maria."

But Maria said she had brought something special for papa and mamma, something they would be sure to like, and she began to look for her plumcake. She tried in Downes's bag and then in the pockets of her waterproof and then on the hallstand but nowhere could she find it. Then she asked all the children had any of them eaten it—by mistake, of course—but the children all said no and looked as if they did not like to eat cakes if they were to be accused of stealing. Everybody had a solution for the mystery and Mrs. Donnelly said it was plain that Maria had left it behind her in the tram. Maria, remembering how confused the gentleman with the greyish moustache had made her, coloured with shame and vexation and disappointment. At the thought of the failure of her little surprise and of the two and four-pence she had thrown away for nothing she nearly cried outright.

But Joe said it didn't matter and made her sit down by the fire. He was very nice with her. He told her all that went on in his office, repeating for her a smart answer which he had made to the manager. Maria did not understand why Joe laughed so much over the answer he had made but she said that the manager must have been a very overbearing person to deal with. Joe said he wasn't so bad when you knew how to take him, that he was a decent sort so long as you didn't rub him the wrong way. Mrs. Donnelly played the piano for the children and they danced and sang. Then the two next-door girls handed round the nuts. Nobody could find the nutcrackers and Joe was nearly getting cross over it and asked how did they expect Maria to crack nuts without a nutcracker. But Maria said she didn't like nuts and that they weren't to bother about her. Then Joe asked would she take a bottle of stout and Mrs. Donnelly said there was port wine too in the house if she would prefer that. Maria said she would rather they didn't ask her to take anything: but Joe insisted.

So Maria let him have his way and they sat by the fire talking over old times and Maria thought she would put in a good word for Alphy. But Joe cried that God might strike him stone dead if ever he spoke a word to his brother again and Maria said she was sorry she had mentioned the matter. Mrs. Donnelly told her husband it was a great shame for him to speak that way of his own flesh and blood but Joe said that Alphy was no brother of his and there was nearly being a row on the head of it. But Joe said he would not lose his temper on account of the night it was and asked his wife to open some more stout. The two next-door girls had arranged some Hallow Eve games and soon everything was merry again. Maria was delighted to see the children so merry and Joe and his wife in such good spirits. The next-door girls put some saucers on the table and then led the children up to the table, blindfold. One got the prayer-book and the other three got the water; and when one of the next-door girls got the ring Mrs. Donnelly shook her finger at the blushing girl as much as to say: *O, I know all about it!* They insisted then on blindfolding Maria and leading her up to the table to see what she would get; and, while they were putting on the bandage, Maria laughed and laughed again till the tip of her nose nearly met the tip of her chin.

They led her up to the table amid laughing and joking and she put her hand out in the air as she was told to do. She moved her hand about here and there in the air and descended on one of the saucers. She felt a soft wet substance with her fingers and was surprised that nobody spoke or took off her bandage. There was a pause for a few seconds; and then a great deal of scuffling and whispering. Somebody said something about the garden, and at last Mrs. Donnelly said something very cross to one of the next-door girls and told her to throw it out at once: that was no play. Maria understood that it was wrong that time and so she had to do it over again: and this time she got the prayer-book.

After that Mrs. Donnelly played Miss McCloud's Reel for the children and Joe made Maria take a glass of wine. Soon they were all quite merry again and Mrs. Donnelly said Maria would enter a convent before the year was out because she had got the prayer-book. Maria had never seen Joe so nice to her as he was that night, so full of pleasant talk and reminiscences. She said they were all very good to her.

At last the children grew tired and sleepy and Joe asked Maria would she not sing some little song before she went, one of the old songs. Mrs. Donnelly said *"Do, please, Maria!"* and so Maria had to get up and stand beside the piano. Mrs. Donnelly bade the children be quiet and listen to Maria's song. Then she played the prelude and said *"Now, Maria!"* and Maria, blushing very much, began to sing in a tiny quavering voice. She sang *I Dreamt that I Dwelt,* and when she came to the second verse she sang again:

"I dreamt that I dwelt in marble halls
With vassals and serfs at my side
And of all who assembled within those walls
That I was the hope and the pride.

"I had riches too great to count, could boast
Of a high ancestral name,
But I also dreamt, which pleased me most,
That you loved me still the same."

But no one tried to show her her mistake; and when she had ended her song Joe was very much moved. He said that there was no time like the long ago and no music for him like poor old Balfe, whatever other people might say; and his eyes filled up so much with tears that he could not find what he was looking for and in the end he had to ask his wife to tell him where the corkscrew was.

JAMES JOYCE

The Dead

LILY, the caretaker's daughter, was literally run off her feet. Hardly had she brought one gentleman into the little pantry behind the office on the ground floor and helped him off with his overcoat than the wheezy hall-door bell clanged again and she had to scamper along the bare hallway to let in another guest. It was well for her she had not to attend to the ladies also. But Miss Kate and Miss Julia had thought of that and had converted the bathroom upstairs into a ladies' dressing-room. Miss Kate and Miss Julia were there, gossiping and laughing and fussing, walking after each other to the head of the stairs, peering down over the banisters and calling down to Lily to ask her who had come.

It was always a great affair, the Misses Morkan's annual dance. Everybody who knew them came to it, members of the family, old friends of the family, the members of Julia's choir, any of Kate's pupils that were grown up enough, and even some of Mary Jane's pupils too. Never once had it fallen flat. For years and years it had gone off in splendid style, as long as anyone could remember; ever since Kate and Julia, after the death of their brother Pat, had left the house in Stoney Batter and taken Mary Jane, their only niece, to live with them in the dark, gaunt house on Usher's Island, the upper part of which they had rented from Mr. Fulham, the corn-factor on the ground floor. That was a good thirty years ago if it was a day. Mary Jane, who was then a little girl in short clothes, was now the main prop of the household, for she had the organ in Haddington Road. She had been through the Academy and gave a pupils' concert every year in the upper room of the Antient Concert Rooms. Many of her pupils belonged to the better-class families on the Kingstown and Dalkey line. Old as they were, her aunts also did their share. Julia, though she was quite grey, was still the leading soprano in Adam and Eve's, and Kate, being too feeble to go about much, gave music lessons to beginners on the old square piano in the back room. Lily, the caretaker's daughter, did housemaid's work for them. Though their life was modest, they believed in eating well; the best of everything: diamond-bone sirloins, three-shilling tea and the best bottled stout. But Lily seldom made a mistake in the orders, so that she got on well with her three mistresses. They were fussy, that was all. But the only thing they would not stand was back answers.

Of course, they had good reason to be fussy on such a night. And then it was long after ten o'clock and yet there was no sign of Gabriel and his wife. Besides they were dreadfully afraid that Freddy Malins might turn up screwed. They would not wish for worlds that any of Mary Jane's pupils should see him under the influence; and when he was like that it was sometimes very hard to manage him. Freddy Malins always came late, but they wondered what could be keeping Gabriel: and that was what brought them every two minutes to the banisters to ask Lily had Gabriel or Freddy come.

"O, Mr. Conroy," said Lily to Gabriel when she opened the door for him, "Miss Kate and Miss Julia thought you were never coming. Goodnight, Mrs. Conroy."

"I'll engage they did," said Gabriel, "but they forget that my wife here takes three mortal hours to dress herself."

He stood on the mat, scraping the snow from his goloshes, while Lily led his wife to the foot of the stairs and called out:

"Miss Kate, here's Mrs. Conroy."

Kate and Julia came toddling down the dark stairs at once. Both of them kissed Gabriel's wife, said she must be perished alive, and asked was Gabriel with her.

"Here I am as right as the mail, Aunt Kate! Go on up. I'll follow," called out Gabriel from the dark.

He continued scraping his feet vigorously while the three women went upstairs, laughing, to the ladies' dressing-room. A light fringe of snow lay like a cape on the shoulders of his overcoat and like toecaps on the toes of his goloshes; and, as the buttons of his overcoat slipped with a squeaking noise through the snow-stiffened frieze, a cold, fragrant air from out-of-doors escaped from crevices and folds.

"Is it snowing again, Mr. Conroy?" asked Lily.

She had preceded him into the pantry to help him off with his overcoat. Gabriel smiled at the three syllables she had given his surname and glanced at her. She was a slim, growing girl, pale in complexion and with hay-coloured hair. The gas in the pantry made her look still paler. Gabriel had known her when she was a child and used to sit on the lowest step nursing a rag doll.

"Yes, Lily," he answered, "and I think we're in for a night of it."

He looked up at the pantry ceiling, which was shaking with the stamping and shuffling of feet on the floor above, listened for a moment to the piano and then glanced at the girl, who was folding his overcoat carefully at the end of a shelf.

"Tell me, Lily," he said in a friendly tone, "do you still go to school?"

"O no, sir," she answered. "I'm done schooling this year and more."

"O, then," said Gabriel gaily, "I suppose we'll be going to your wedding one of these fine days with your young man, eh?"

The girl glanced back at him over her shoulder and said with great bitterness:

"The men that is now is only all palaver and what they can get out of you."

She just wasn't being courted

Gabriel coloured, as if he felt he had made a mistake and, without looking at her, kicked off his goloshes and flicked actively with his muffler at his patent-leather shoes.

He was a stout, tallish young man. The high colour of his cheeks pushed upwards even to his forehead, where it scattered itself in a few formless patches of pale red; and on his hairless face there scintillated restlessly the polished lenses and the bright gilt rims of the glasses which screened his delicate and restless eyes. His glossy black hair was parted in the middle and brushed in a long curve behind his ears where it curled slightly beneath the groove left by his hat.

When he had flicked lustre into his shoes he stood up and pulled his waistcoat down more tightly on his plump body. Then he took a coin rapidly from his pocket.

"O Lily," he said, thrusting it into her hands, "it's Christmas-time, isn't it? Just . . . here's a little. . . ."

He walked rapidly towards the door.

"O no, sir!" cried the girl, following him. "Really, sir, I wouldn't take it."

"Christmas-time! Christmas-time!" said Gabriel, almost trotting to the stairs and waving his hand to her in deprecation.

The girl, seeing that he had gained the stairs, called out after him:

"Well, thank you sir."

He waited outside the drawing-room door until the waltz should finish, listening to the skirts that swept against it and to the shuffling of feet. He was still discomposed by the girl's bitter and sudden retort. It had cast a gloom over him which he tried to dispel by arranging his cuffs and the bows of his tie. He then took from his waistcoat pocket a little paper and glanced at the headings he had made for his speech. He was undecided about the lines from Robert Browning, for he feared they would be above the heads of his hearers. Some quotation that they would recognise from Shakespeare or from the Melodies would be better. The indelicate clacking of the men's heels and the shuffling of their soles reminded him that their grade of culture differed from his. He would only make himself ridiculous by quoting poetry to them which they could not understand. They would think that he was airing his superior education. He would fail with them just as he had failed with the girl in the pantry. He had taken up a wrong tone. His whole speech was a mistake from the first to last, an utter failure.

Just then his aunts and his wife came out of the ladies' dressing-room. His aunts were two small, plainly dressed old women. Aunt Julia was an inch or so the taller. Her hair, drawn low over the tops of her ears, was grey; and grey also, with darker shadows, was her large flaccid face. Though she was stout in build and stood erect, her slow eyes and parted lips gave her the appearance of a woman who did not know where she was or where she was going. Aunt Kate was more vivacious. Her face, healthier than her sister's, was all puckers and creases, like a shrivelled red apple, and her hair, braided in the same old-fashioned way, had not lost its ripe nut colour.

They both kissed Gabriel frankly. He was their favourite nephew, the son of their dead elder sister, Ellen, who had married T. J. Conroy of the Port and Docks.

"Gretta tells me you're not going to take a cab back to Monkstown to-night, Gabriel," said Aunt Kate.

"No," said Gabriel, turning to his wife, "we had quite enough of that last year, hadn't we? Don't you remember, Aunt Kate, what a cold Gretta got out of it? Cab windows rattling all the way, and the east wind blowing in after we passed Merion. Very jolly it was. Gretta caught a dreadful cold."

Aunt Kate frowned severely and nodded her head at every word.

"Quite right, Gabriel, quite right," she said. "You can't be too careful."

"But as for Gretta there," said Gabriel, "she'd walk home in the snow if she were let."

Mrs. Conroy laughed.

"Don't mind him, Aunt Kate," she said. "He's really an awful bother, what with green shades for Tom's eyes at night and making him do the dumb-bells, and forcing Eva to eat the stirabout. The poor child! And she simply hates the sight of it! . . . O, but you'll never guess what he makes me wear now!"

She broke out into a peal of laughter and glanced at her husband, whose admiring and happy eyes had been wandering from her dress to her face and hair. The two aunts laughed heartily, too, for Gabriel's solicitude was a standing joke with them.

"Goloshes!" said Mrs. Conroy. "That's the latest. Whenever it's wet underfoot I must put on my goloshes. To-night even, he wanted me to put them on, but I wouldn't. The next thing he'll buy me will be a diving suit."

Gabriel laughed nervously and patted his tie reassuringly, while Aunt Kate nearly doubled herself, so heartily did she enjoy the joke. The smile soon faded from Aunt Julia's face and her mirthless eyes were directed towards her nephew's face. After a pause she asked:

"And what are goloshes, Gabriel?"

"Goloshes, Julia!" exclaimed her sister. "Goodness me, don't you know what goloshes are? You wear them over your . . . over your boots, Gretta, isn't it?"

"Yes," said Mrs. Conroy. "Guttapercha things. We both have a pair now. Gabriel says everyone wears them on the continent."

"O, on the continent," murmured Aunt Julia, nodding her head slowly.

Gabriel knitted his brows and said, as if he were slightly angered:

"It's nothing very wonderful, but Gretta thinks it very funny because she says the word reminds her of Christy Minstrels."

"But tell me, Gabriel," said Aunt Kate, with brisk tact. "Of course, you've seen about the room. Gretta was saying . . ."

"O, the room is all right," replied Gabriel. "I've taken one in the Gresham."

"To be sure," said Aunt Kate, "by far the best thing to do. And the children, Gretta, you're not anxious about them?"

"O, for one night," said Mrs. Conroy. "Besides, Bessie will look after them."

"To be sure," said Aunt Kate again. "What a comfort it is to have a girl like that, one you can depend on! There's that Lily, I'm sure I don't know what has come over her lately. She's not the girl she was at all."

Gabriel was about to ask his aunt some questions on

this point, but she broke off suddenly to gaze after her sister, who had wandered down the stairs and was craning her neck over the banisters.

"Now, I ask you," she said almost testily, "where is Julia going? Julia! Julia! Where are you going?"

Julia, who had gone half way down one flight, came back and announced blandly:

"Here's Freddy."

At the same moment a clapping of hands and a final flourish of the pianist told that the waltz had ended. The drawing-room door was opened from within and some couples came out. Aunt Kate drew Gabriel aside hurriedly and whispered into his ear:

"Slip down, Gabriel, like a good fellow and see if he's all right, and don't let him up if he's screwed. I'm sure he's screwed. I'm sure he is."

Gabriel went to the stairs and listened over the banisters. He could hear two persons talking in the pantry. Then he recognised Freddy Malins' laugh. He went down the stairs noisily.

"It's such a relief," said Aunt Kate to Mrs. Conroy, "that Gabriel is here. I always feel easier in my mind when he's here. . . . Julia, there's Miss Daly and Miss Power will take some refreshment. Thanks for your beautiful waltz, Miss Daly. It made lovely time."

A tall wizen-faced man, with a stiff grizzled moustache and swarthy skin, who was passing out with his partner, said:

"And may we have some refreshment, too, Miss Morkan?"

"Julia," said Aunt Kate summarily, "and here's Mr. Browne and Miss Furlong. Take them in, Julia, with Miss Daly and Miss Power."

"I'm the man for the ladies," said Mr. Browne, pursing his lips until his moustache bristled and smiling in all his wrinkles. "You know, Miss Morkan, the reason they are so fond of me is—"

He did not finish his sentence, but, seeing that Aunt Kate was out of earshot, at once led the three young ladies into the backroom. The middle of the room was occupied by two square tables placed end to end, and on these Aunt Julia and the caretaker were straightening and smoothing a large cloth. On the sideboard were arrayed dishes and plates, and glasses and bundles of knives and forks and spoons. The top of the closed square piano served also as a sideboard for viands and sweets. At a smaller sideboard in one corner two young men were standing, drinking hop-bitters.

Mr. Browne led his charges thither and invited them all, in jest, to some ladies' punch, hot, strong and sweet. As they said they never took anything strong, he opened three bottles of lemonade for them. Then he asked one of the young men to move aside, and, taking hold of the decanter, filled out for himself a goodly measure of whisky. The young men eyed him respectfully while he took a trial sip.

"God help me," he said, smiling, "it's the doctor's orders."

His wizened face broke into a broader smile, and the three young ladies laughed in musical echo to his pleasantry, swaying their bodies to and fro, with nervous jerks of their shoulders. The boldest said:

"O, now, Mr. Browne, I'm sure the doctor never ordered anything of the kind."

Mr. Browne took another sip of his whisky and said, with sidling mimicry:

"Well, you see, I'm like the famous Mrs. Cassidy, who is reported to have said: 'Now, Mary Grimes, if I don't take it, make me take it, for I feel I want it.' "

His hot face had leaned forward a little too confidentially and he had assumed a very low Dublin accent so that the young ladies, with one instinct, received his speech in silence. Miss Furlong, who was one of Mary Jane's pupils, asked Miss Daly what was the name of the pretty waltz she had played; and Mr. Browne, seeing that he was ignored, turned promptly to the two young men who were more appreciative.

A red-faced young woman, dressed in pansy, came into the room, excitedly clapping her hands and crying:

"Quadrilles! Quadrilles!"

Close on her heels came Aunt Kate, crying:

"Two gentlemen and three ladies, Mary Jane!"

"O, here's Mr. Bergin and Mr. Kerrigan," said Mary Jane. "Mr. Kerrigan, will you take Miss Power? Miss Furlong, may I get you a partner, Mr. Bergin. O, that'll just do now."

"Three ladies, Mary Jane," said Aunt Kate.

The two young gentlemen asked the ladies if they might have the pleasure, and Mary Jane turned to Miss Daly.

"O, Miss Daly, you're really awfully good, after playing for the last two dances, but really we're so short of ladies to-night."

"I don't mind in the least, Miss Morkan."

"But I've a nice partner for you, Mr. Bartell D'Arcy, the tenor. I'll get him to sing later on. All Dublin is raving about him."

"Lovely voice, lovely voice!" said Aunt Kate.

As the piano had twice begun the prelude to the first figure Mary Jane led her recruits quickly from the room. They had hardly gone when Aunt Julia wandered slowly into the room, looking behind her at something.

"What is the matter, Julia?" asked Aunt Kate anxiously. "Who is it?"

Julia, who was carrying in a column of table-napkins turned to her sister and said, simply, as if the question had surprised her:

"It's only Freddy, Kate, and Gabriel with him."

In fact right behind her Gabriel could be seen piloting Freddy Malins across the landing. The latter, a young man of about forty, was of Gabriel's size and build, with very round shoulders. His face was fleshy and pallid, touched with colour only at the thick hanging lobes of his ears and at the wide wings of his nose. He had coarse features, a blunt nose, a convex and receding brow, tumid and protruded lips. His heavy-lidded eyes and the disorder of his scanty hair made him look sleepy. He was laughing heartily in a high key at a story which he had been telling Gabriel on the stairs and at the same time rubbing the knuckles of his left fist backwards and forwards into his left eye.

"Good-evening, Freddy," said Aunt Julia.

Freddy Malins bade the Misses Morkan good-evening in what seemed an offhand fashion by reason of the habitual catch in his voice and then, seeing that Mr. Browne was grinning at him from the sideboard, crossed the room on rather shaky legs and began to repeat in an undertone the story he had just told to Gabriel.

"He's not so bad, is he?" said Aunt Kate to Gabriel.

Gabriel's brows were dark but he raised them quickly and answered:

"O, no, hardly noticeable."

"Now, isn't he a terrible fellow!" she said. "And his poor mother made him take the pledge on New Year's Eve. But come on, Gabriel, into the drawing-room."

Before leaving the room with Gabriel she signalled to Mr. Browne by frowning and shaking her forefinger in warning to and fro. Mr. Browne nodded in answer and, when she had gone, said to Freddy Malins:

"Now, then, Teddy, I'm going to fill you out a good glass of lemonade just to buck you up."

Freddy Malins, who was nearing the climax of his story, waved the offer aside impatiently but Mr. Browne, having first called Freddy Malins' attention to a disarray in his dress, filled out and handed him a full glass of lemonade. Freddy Malins' left hand accepted the glass mechanically, his right hand being engaged in the mechanical readjustment of his dress. Mr. Browne, whose face was once more wrinkling with mirth, poured out for himself a glass of whiskey while Freddy Malins exploded, before he had well reached the climax of his story, in a kink of high-pitched bronchitic laughter and, setting down his untasted and overflowing glass, began to rub the knuckles of his left fist backwards and forwards into his left eye, repeating words of his last phrase as well as his fit of laughter would allow him.

. . . .

Gabriel could not listen while Mary Jane was playing her Academy piece, full of runs and difficult passages, to the hushed drawing-room. He liked music but the piece she was playing had no melody for him and he doubted whether it had any melody for the other listeners, though they had begged Mary Jane to play something. Four young men, who had come from the refreshment-room to stand in the doorway at the sound of the piano, had gone away quietly in couples after a few minutes. The only persons who seemed to follow the music were Mary Jane herself, her hands racing along the key-board or lifted from it at the pauses like those of a priestess in momentary imprecation, and Aunt Kate standing at her elbow to turn the page.

Gabriel's eyes, irritated by the floor, which glittered with beeswax under the heavy chandelier, wandered to the wall above the piano. A picture of the balcony scene in *Romeo and Juliet* hung there and beside it was a picture of the two murdered princes in the Tower which Aunt Julia had worked in red, blue and brown wools when she was a girl. Probably in the school they had gone to as girls that kind of work had been taught for one year. His mother had worked for him as a birthday present a waistcoat of purple tabinet, with little foxes' heads upon it, lined with brown satin and having round mulberry buttons. It was strange that his mother had had no musical talent though Aunt Kate used to call her the brains carrier of the Morkan family. Both she and Julia had always seemed a little proud of their serious and matronly sister. Her photograph stood before the pier-glass. She held an open book on her knees and was point-out something in it to Constantine who, dressed in a man-o'-war suit, lay at her feet. It was she who had chosen the names of her sons for she was very sensible of the dignity of family life. Thanks to her, Constantine was now senior curate in Balbriggan and, thanks to her, Gabriel himself had taken his degree in the Royal University. A shadow passed over his face as he remembered her sullen opposition to his marriage. Some slighting phrases she had used still rankled in his memory; she had once spoken of Gretta as being country cute and that was not true of Gretta at all. It was Gretta who had nursed her during all her last long illness in their house at Monkstown.

He knew that Mary Jane must be near the end of her piece for she was playing again the opening melody with runs of scales after every bar and while he waited for the end the resentment died down in his heart. The piece ended with a trill of octaves in the treble and a final deep octave in the bass. Great applause greeted Mary Jane as, blushing and rolling up her music nervously, she escaped from the room. The most vigorous clapping came from the four young men in the doorway who had gone away to the refreshment-room at the beginning of the piece but had come back when the piano stopped.

Lancers were arranged. Gabriel found himself partnered with Miss Ivors. She was a frank-mannered talkative young lady, with a freckled face and prominent brown eyes. She did not wear a low-cut bodice and the large brooch which was fixed in the front of her collar bore on it an Irish device and motto.

When they had taken their places she said abruptly: "I have a crow to pluck with you."

"With me?" said Gabriel.

She nodded her head gravely.

"What is it?" asked Gabriel, smiling at her solemn manner.

"Who is G. C.?" answered Miss Ivors, turning her eyes upon him.

Gabriel coloured and was about to knit his brows, as if he did not understand, when she said bluntly:

"O, innocent Amy! I have found out that you write for *The Daily Express.* Now, aren't you ashamed of yourself?"

"Why should I be ashamed of myself?" asked Gabriel, blinking his eyes and trying to smile.

"Well, I'm ashamed of you," said Miss Ivors frankly. "To say you'd write for a paper like that. I didn't think you were a West Briton."

A look of perplexity appeared on Gabriel's face. It was true that he wrote a literary column every Wednesday in *The Daily Express,* for which he was paid fifteen shillings. But that did not make him a West Briton surely. The books he received for review were almost more welcome than the paltry cheque. He loved to feel the covers and turn over the pages of newly printed books. Nearly every day when his teaching in the college was ended he used to wander down the quays to the second-hand booksellers, to Hickey's on Bachelor's Walk, to Webb's or Massey's on Aston's Quay, or to O'Clohissey's in the by-street. He did not know how to meet her charge. He wanted to say that literature was above politics. But they were friends of many years' standing and their careers had been parallel, first at the University and then as teachers: he could not risk a grandiose phrase with her. He continued blinking his eyes and trying to smile and murmured lamely that he saw nothing political in writing reviews of books.

When their turn to cross had come he was still perplexed and inattentive. Miss Ivors promptly took his hand in a warm grasp and said in a soft friendly tone:

"Of course, I was only joking. Come, we cross now."

When they were together again she spoke of the University question and Gabriel felt more at ease. A friend of hers had shown her his review of Brownings' poems. That was how she had found out the secret: but she liked the review immensely. Then she said suddenly:

"O, Mr. Conroy, will you come for an excursion to the Aran Isles this summer? We're going to stay there a whole month. It will be splendid out in the Atlantic. You ought to come. Mr. Clancy is coming, and Mr. Kilkelly and Kathleen Kearney. It would be splendid for Gretta too if she'd come. She's from Connacht, isn't she?"

"Her people are," said Gabriel shortly.

"But you will come, won't you?" said Miss Ivors, laying her warm hand eagerly on his arm.

"The fact is," said Gabriel, "I have just arranged to go——"

"Go where?" asked Miss Ivors.

"Well, you know, every year I go for a cycling tour with some fellows and so——"

"But where?" asked Miss Ivors.

"Well, we usually go to France or Belgium or perhaps Germany," said Gabriel awkwardly.

"And why do you go to France and Belgium," said Miss Ivors, "instead of visiting your own land?"

"Well," said Gabriel, "it's partly to keep in touch with the languages and partly for a change."

"And haven't you your own language to keep in touch with—Irish?" asked Miss Ivors.

"Well," said Gabriel, "if it comes to that, you know, Irish is not my language."

Their neighbours had turned to listen to the cross-examination. Gabriel glanced right and left nervously and tried to keep his good humour under the ordeal which was making a blush invade his forehead.

"And haven't you your own land to visit," continued Miss Ivors, "that you know nothing of, your own people, and your own country?"

"O, to tell you the truth," retorted Gabriel suddenly, "I'm sick of my own country, sick of it!"

"Why?" asked Miss Ivors.

Gabriel did not answer for his retort had heated him.

"Why?" repeated Miss Ivors.

They had to go visiting together and, as he had not answered her, Miss Ivors said warmly:

"Of course, you've no answer."

Gabriel tried to cover his agitation by taking part in the dance with great energy. He avoided her eyes for he had seen a sour expression on her face. But when they met in the long chain he was surprised to feel his hand firmly pressed. She looked at him from under her brows for a moment quizzically until he smiled. Then, just as the chain was about to start again, she stood on tiptoe and whispered into his ear:

"West Briton!" (traitor to Ireland)

When the lancers were over Gabriel went away to a remote corner of the room where Freddy Malins' mother was sitting. She was a stout feeble old woman with white hair. Her voice had a catch in it like her son's and she stuttered slightly. She had been told that Freddy had come and that he was nearly all right. Gabriel asked her whether she had had a good crossing. She lived with her married daughter in Glasgow and came to Dublin on a visit once a year. She answered placidly that she had had a beautiful crossing and that the captain had been most attentive to her. She spoke also of the beautiful house her daughter kept in Glasgow, and of all the friends they had there. While her tongue rambled on Gabriel tried to banish from his mind all memory of the unpleasant incident with Miss Ivors. Of course the girl or woman, or whatever she was, was an enthusiast but there was a time for all things. Perhaps he ought not to have answered her like that. But she had no right to call him a West Briton before people, even in joke. She had tried to make him ridiculous before people, heckling him and staring at him with her rabbit's eyes.

He saw his wife making her way towards him through the waltzing couples. When she reached him she said into his ear:

"Gabriel, Aunt Kate wants to know won't you carve the goose as usual. Miss Daly will carve the ham and I'll do the pudding."

"All right," said Gabriel.

"She's sending in the younger ones first as soon as this waltz is over so that we'll have the table to ourselves."

"Were you dancing?" asked Gabriel.

"Of course I was. Didn't you see me? What row had you with Molly Ivors?"

"No row. Why? Did she say so?"

"Something like that. I'm trying to get that Mr. D'Arcy to sing. He's full of conceit, I think."

"There was no row," said Gabriel moodily, "only she wanted me to go for a trip to the west of Ireland and I said I wouldn't."

His wife clasped her hands excitedly and gave a little jump.

"O, do go, Gabriel," she cried. "I'd love to see Galway again."

"You can go if you like," said Gabriel coldly.

She looked at him for a moment, then turned to Mrs. Malins and said:

"There's a nice husband for you, Mrs. Malins."

While she was threading her way back across the room Mrs. Malins, without adverting to the interruption, went on to tell Gabriel what beautiful places there were in Scotland and beautiful scenery. Her son-in-law brought them every year to the lakes and they used to go fishing. Her son-in-law was a splendid fisher. One day he caught a beautiful big fish and the man in the hotel cooked it for their dinner.

Gabriel hardly heard what she said. Now that supper was coming near he began to think again about his speech and about the quotation. When he saw Freddy Malins coming across the room to visit his mother Gabriel left the chair free for him and retired into the embrasure of the window. The room had already cleared and from the back room came the clatter of plates and knives. Those who still remained in the drawing-room seemed tired of dancing and were conversing quietly in little groups. Gabriel's warm trembling fingers tapped the cold pane of the window. How cool it must be outside! How pleasant it would be to walk out alone, first along by the river and then through the park! The snow would be lying on the branches of the trees and forming a bright cap on the top of the Wellington Monument. How much more pleasant it would be there than at the supper-table!

He ran over the headings of his speech: Irish hospitality, sad memories, the Three Graces, Paris, the quotation from Browning. He repeated to himself a phrase he had written in his review: "One feels that one is listening to a thought-tormented music." Miss Ivors had praised the review. Was she sincere? Had she really any life of her own behind all her propagandism? There had never been any ill-feeling between them until that night. It unnerved him to think that she would be at the supper-table, looking up at him while he spoke with her critical quizzing eyes. Perhaps she would not be sorry to see him fail in his speech. An idea came into his mind and gave him courage. He would say, alluding to Aunt Kate and Aunt Julia: "Ladies and Gentlemen, the generation which is now on the wane among us may have had its faults but for my part I think it had certain qualities of hospitality, of humour, of humanity, which the new and very serious and hypereducated generation that is growing up around us seems to me to lack." Very good: that was one for Miss Ivors. What did he care that his aunts were only two ignorant old women?

A murmur in the room attracted his attention. Mr. Browne was advancing from the door, gallantly escorting Aunt Julia, who leaned upon his arm, smiling and hanging her head. An irregular musketry of applause escorted her also as far as the piano and then, as Mary Jane seated herself on the stool, and Aunt Julia, no longer smiling, half turned so as to pitch her voice fairly into the room, gradually ceased. Gabriel recognized the prelude. It was that of an old song of Aunt Julia's—*Arrayed for the Bridal*. Her voice, strong and clear in tone, attacked with great spirit the runs which embellish the air and though she sang very rapidly she did not miss even the smallest of the grace notes. To follow the voice, without looking at the singer's face, was to feel and share the excitement of swift and secure flight. Gabriel applauded loudly with all the others at the close of the song and loud applause was borne in from the invisible supper-table. It sounded so genuine that a little colour struggled into Aunt Julia's face as she bent to replace in the music-stand the old leather-bound song-book that had her initials on the cover. Freddy Malins, who had listened with his head perched sideways to hear her better, was still applauding when everyone else had ceased and talking animatedly to his mother who nodded her head gravely and slowly in acquiescence. At last, when he could clap no more, he stood up suddenly and hurried across the room to Aunt Julia whose hand he seized and held in both his hands, shaking it when words failed him or the catch in his voice proved too much for him.

"I was just telling my mother," he said, "I never heard you sing so well, never. No, I never heard your voice so good as it is to-night. Now! Would you believe that now? That's the truth. Upon my word and honour that's the truth. I never heard your voice sound so fresh and so . . . so clear and fresh, never."

Aunt Julia smiled broadly and murmured something about compliments as she released her hand from his grasp. Mr. Browne extended his open hand towards her and said to those who were near him in the manner of a showman introducing a prodigy to an audience:

"Miss Julia Morkan, my latest discovery!"

He was laughing very heartily at this himself when Freddy Malins turned to him and said:

"Well, Browne, if you're serious you might make a worse discovery. All I can say is I never heard her sing half so well as long as I am coming here. And that's the honest truth."

"Neither did I," said Mr. Browne. "I think her voice has greatly improved."

Aunt Julia shrugged her shoulders and said with meek pride:

"Thirty years ago I hadn't a bad voice as voices go."

"I often told Julia," said Aunt Kate emphatically, "that she was simply thrown away in that choir. But she never would be said by me."

She turned as if to appeal to the good sense of the others against a refractory child while Aunt Julia gazed in front of her, a vague smile of reminiscence playing on her face.

"No," continued Aunt Kate, "she wouldn't be said or led by anyone, slaving there in that choir night and day, night and day. Six o'clock on Christmas morning! And all for what?"

"Well, isn't it for the honour of God, Aunt Kate?" asked Mary Jane, twisting round on the piano-stool and smiling.

Aunt Kate turned fiercely on her niece and said:

"I know all about the honour of God, Mary Jane, but I think it's not at all honourable for the pope to turn out the women out of the choirs that have slaved there all their lives and put little whipper-snappers of boys over their heads. I suppose it is for the good of the Church if the pope does it. But it's not just, Mary Jane, and it's not right."

She had worked herself into a passion and would have continued in defence of her sister for it was a sore subject with her but Mary Jane, seeing that all the dancers had come back, intervened pacifically:

"Now, Aunt Kate, you're giving scandal to Mr. Browne who is of the other persuasion."

Aunt Kate turned to Mr. Browne, who was grinning at this allusion to his religion, and said hastily:

"O, I don't question the pope's being right. I'm only a stupid old woman and I wouldn't presume to do such a thing. But there's such a thing as common everyday politeness and gratitude. And if I were in Julia's place I'd tell that Father Healey straight up to his face . . ."

"And besides, Aunt Kate," said Mary Jane, "we really are all hungry and when we are hungry we are all very quarrelsome."

"And when we are thirsty we are also quarrelsome," added Mr. Browne.

"So that we had better go to supper," said Mary Jane, "and finish the discussion afterwards."

On the landing outside the drawing-room Gabriel found his wife and Mary Jane trying to persuade Miss Ivors to stay for supper. But Miss Ivors, who had put on her hat and was buttoning her cloak, would not stay. She did not feel in the least hungry and she had already overstayed her time.

"But only for ten minutes, Molly," said Mrs. Conroy. "That won't delay you."

"To take a pick itself," said Mary Jane, "after all your dancing."

"I really couldn't," said Miss Ivors.

"I am afraid you didn't enjoy yourself at all," said Mary Jane hopelessly.

"Ever so much, I assure you," said Miss Ivors, "but you really must let me run off now."

"But how can you get home?" asked Mrs. Conroy.

"O, it's only two steps up the quay."

Gabriel hesitated a moment and said:

"If you will allow me, Miss Ivors, I'll see you home if you are really obliged to go."

But Miss Ivors broke away from them.

"I won't hear of it," she cried. "For goodness' sake go in to your suppers and don't mind me. I'm quite well able to take care of myself."

"Well, you're the comical girl, Molly," said Mrs. Conroy frankly.

"Beannacht libh," cried Miss Ivors, with a laugh, as she ran down the staircase.

Mary Jane gazed after her, a moody puzzled expression on her face, while Mrs. Conroy leaned over the banisters to listen for the hall-door. Gabriel asked himself was he the cause of her abrupt departure. But she did not seem to be in ill humour: she had gone away laughing. He stared blankly down the staircase.

At the moment Aunt Kate came toddling out of the supper-room, almost wringing her hands in despair.

"Where is Gabriel?" she cried. "Where on earth is Gabriel? There's everyone waiting in there, stage to let, and nobody to carve the goose!"

"Here I am, Aunt Kate!" cried Gabriel, with sudden animation, "ready to carve a flock of geese, if necessary."

A fat brown goose lay at one end of the table and at the other end, on a bed of creased paper strewn with sprigs of parsley, lay a great ham, stripped of its outer skin and peppered over with crust crumbs, a neat paper frill round its shin and beside this was a round of spiced beef. Between these rival ends ran parallel lines of side-dishes: two little ministers of jelly, red and yellow; a shallow dish full of blocks of blancmange and red jam, a large green leaf-shaped dish with a stalk-shaped handle, on which lay bunches of purple raisins and peeled almonds, a companion dish on which lay a solid rectangle of Smyrna figs, a dish of custard topped with grated nutmeg, a small bowl full of chocolates and sweets wrapped in gold and silver papers and a glass vase in which stood some tall celery stalks. In the centre of the table there stood, as sentries to a fruit-stand which upheld a pyramid of oranges and American apples, two squat old-fashioned decanters of cut glass, one containing port and the other dark sherry. On the closed square piano a pudding in a huge yellow dish lay in waiting and behind it were three squads of bottles of stout and ale and minerals, drawn up according to the colours of their uniforms, the first two black, with brown and red labels, the third and smallest squad white, with transverse green sashes.

Gabriel took his seat boldly at the head of the table and, having looked to the edge of the carver, plunged his fork firmly into the goose. He felt quite at ease now for he was an expert carver and liked nothing better than to find himself at the head of a well-laden table.

"Miss Furlong, what shall I send you?" he asked. "A wing or a slice of the breast?"

"Just a small slice of the breast."

"Miss Higgins, what for you?"

"O, anything at all, Mr. Conroy."

While Gabriel and Miss Daly exchanged plates of goose and plates of ham and spiced beef Lily went from guest to guest with a dish of hot floury potatoes wrapped in a white napkin. This was Mary Jane's idea and she had also suggested apple sauce for the goose but Aunt Kate had said that plain roast goose without any apple sauce had always been good enough for her and she hoped she might never eat worse. Mary Jane waited on her pupils and saw that they got the best slices and Aunt Kate and Aunt Julia opened and carried across from the piano bottles of stout and ale for the gentlemen and bottles of minerals for the ladies. There was a great deal of confusion and laughter and noise, the noise of orders and counter-orders, of knives and forks, of corks and glass-stoppers. Gabriel began to carve second helpings as soon as he had finished the first round without serving himself. Everyone protested loudly so that he compromised by taking a long draught of stout for he had found the carving hot work. Mary Jane settled down quietly to her supper but Aunt Kate and Aunt Julia were still toddling round the table, walking on each other's heels, getting in each other's way and giving each other unheeded orders. Mr. Browne begged of them to sit down and eat their suppers and so did Gabriel but they said there was time enough, so that, at last, Freddy Malins stood up and, capturing Aunt Kate, plumped her down on her chair amid general laughter.

When everyone had been well served Gabriel said, smiling:

"Now, if anyone wants a little more of what vulgar people call stuffing let him or her speak."

A chorus of voices invited him to begin his own supper and Lily came forward with three potatoes which she had reserved for him.

"Very well," said Gabriel amiably, as he took another preparatory draught, "kindly forget my existence, ladies and gentlemen, for a few minutes."

He set to his supper and took no part in the conversation with which the table covered Lily's removal of the plates. The subject of talk was the opera company which was then at the Theatre Royal. Mr. Bartell D'Arcy, the tenor, a dark-complexioned young man with a smart moustache, praised very highly the leading contralto of the company but Miss Furlong thought she had a rather vulgar style of production. Freddy Malins said there was a negro chieftain singing in the second part of the Gaiety pantomime who had one of the finest tenor voices he had ever heard.

"Have you heard him?" he asked Mr. Bartell D'Arcy across the table.

"No," answered Mr. Bartell D'Arcy carelessly.

"Because," Freddy Malins explained, "now I'd be curious to hear your opinion of him. I think he has a grand voice."

"It takes Teddy to find out the really good things," said Mr. Browne familiarly to the table.

"And why couldn't he have a voice too?" asked Freddy Malins sharply. "Is it because he's only a black?"

Nobody answered this question and Mary Jane led the table back to the legitimate opera. One of her pupils had given her a pass for *Mignon.* Of course it was very fine, she said, but it made her think of poor Georgina Burns. Mr. Browne could go back farther still, to the old Italian companies that used to come to Dublin—Tietjens, Ilma de Murzka, Campanini, the great Trebelli Giuglini, Ravelli, Aramburo. Those were the days, he said, when there was something like singing to be heard in Dublin. He told too of how the top gallery of the old Royal used to be packed night after night, of how one night an Italian tenor had sung five encores to *Let me like a Soldier fall,* introducing a high C every time, and of how the gallery boys would sometimes in their enthusiasm unyoke the horses from the carriage of some great *prima donna* and pull her themselves through the streets to her hotel. Why did they never play the grand old operas now, he asked, *Dinorah, Lucrezia Borgia?* Because they could not get the voices to sing them: that was why."

"O, well," said Mr. Bartell D'Arcy, "I presume there are as good singers to-day as there were then."

"Where are they?" asked Mr. Browne defiantly.

"In London, Paris, Milan," said Mr. Bartell D'Arcy warmly. "I suppose Caruso, for example, is quite as good, if not better than any of the men you have mentioned."

"Maybe so," said Mr. Browne. "But I may tell you I doubt it strongly."

"O, I'd give anything to hear Caruso sing," said Mary Jane.

"For me," said Aunt Kate, who had been picking a

bone, "there was only one tenor. To please me, I mean. But I suppose none of you ever heard of him."

"Who was he, Miss Morkan?" asked Mr. Bartell D'Arcy politely.

"His name," said Aunt Kate, "was Parkinson. I heard him when he was in his prime and I think he had then the purest tenor voice that was ever put into a man's throat."

"Strange," said Mr. Bartell D'Arcy. "I never even heard of him."

"Yes, yes, Miss Morkan is right," said Mr. Browne. "I remember hearing of old Parkinson but he's too far back for me."

"A beautiful, pure, sweet, mellow English tenor," said Aunt Kate with enthusiasm.

Gabriel having finished, the huge pudding was transferred to the table. The clatter of forks and spoons began again. Gabriel's wife served out spoonfuls of the pudding and passed the plates down the table. Midway down they were held up by Mary Jane, who replenished them with raspberry or orange jelly or with blancmange and jam. The pudding was of Aunt Julia's making and she received praises for it from all quarters. She herself said that it was not quite brown enough.

"Well, I hope, Miss Morkan," said Mr. Browne, "that I'm brown enough for you because, you know, I'm all brown."

All the gentlemen, except Gabriel, ate some of the pudding out of compliment to Aunt Julia. As Gabriel never ate sweets the celery had been left for him. Freddy Malins also took a stalk of celery and ate it with his pudding. He had been told that celery was a capital thing for the blood and he was just then under doctor's care. Mrs. Malins, who had been silent all through the supper, said that her son was going down to Mount Melleray in a week or so. The table then spoke of Mount Melleray, how bracing the air was down there, how hospitable the monks were and how they never asked for a penny-piece from their guests.

"And do you mean to say," asked Mr. Browne incredulously, "that a chap can go down there and put up there as if it were a hotel and live on the fat of the land and then come away without paying anything?"

"O, most people give some donation to the monastery when they leave," said Mary Jane.

"I wish we had an institution like that in our Church," said Mr. Browne candidly.

He was astonished to hear that the monks never spoke, got up at two in the morning and slept in their coffins. He asked what they did it for.

"That's the rule of the order," said Aunt Kate firmly.

"Yes, but why?" asked Mr. Browne.

Aunt Kate repeated that it was the rule, that was all. Mr. Browne still seemed not to understand. Freddy Malins explained to him, as best he could, that the monks were trying to make up for the sins committed by all the sinners in the outside world. The explanation was not very clear for Mr. Browne grinned and said:

"I like that idea very much but wouldn't a comfortable spring bed do them as well as a coffin?"

"The coffin," said Mary Jane, "is to remind them of their last end."

As the subject had grown lugubrious it was buried in a silence of the table during which Mrs. Malins could be heard saying to her neighbour in an indistinct undertone:

"They are very good men, the monks, very pious men."

The raisins and almonds and figs and apples and oranges and chocolates and sweets were now passed about the table and Aunt Julia invited all the guests to have either port or sherry. At first Mr. Bartell D'Arcy refused to take either but one of his neighbours nudged him and whispered something to him upon which he allowed his glass to be filled. Gradually as the last glasses were being filled the conversation ceased. A pause followed, broken only by the noise of the wine and by unsettlings of chairs. The Misses Morkan, all three, looked down at the tablecloth. Someone coughed once or twice and then a few gentlemen patted the table gently as a signal for silence. The silence came and Gabriel pushed back his chair and stood up.

The patting at once grew louder in encouragement and then ceased altogether. Gabriel leaned his ten trembling fingers on the tablecloth and smiled nervously at the company. Meeting a row of upturned faces he raised his eyes to the chandelier. The piano was playing a waltz tune and he could hear the skirts sweeping against the drawing-room door. People, perhaps, were standing in the snow on the quay outside, gazing up at the lighted windows and listening to the waltz music. The air was pure there. In the distance lay the park where the trees were weighted with snow. The Wellington Monument wore a gleaming cap of snow that flashed westward over the white field of Fifteen Acres.

He began:

"Ladies and Gentlemen,

"It has fallen to my lot this evening, as in years past, to perform a very pleasing task but a task for which I am afraid my poor powers as a speaker are all too inadequate."

"No, no!" said Mr. Browne.

"But, however that may be I can only ask you to-night to take the will for the deed and to lend me your attention for a few moments while I endeavour to express to you in words what my feelings are on this occasion.

"Ladies and Gentlemen, it is not the first time that we have gathered together under this hospitable roof, around this hospitable board. It is not the first time that we have been the recipients—or perhaps, I had better say, the victims—of the hospitality of certain good ladies."

He made a circle in the air with his arm and paused. Everyone laughed or smiled at Aunt Kate and Aunt

Julia and Mary Jane who all turned crimson with pleasure. Gabriel went on more boldly:

"I feel more strongly with every recurring year that our country has no tradition which does it so much honour and which it should guard so jealously as that of its hospitality. It is a tradition that is unique as far as my experience goes (and I have visited not a few places abroad) among the modern nations. Some would say, perhaps, that with us it is rather a failing than anything to be boasted of. But granted even that, it is, to my mind, a princely failing, and one that I trust will long be cultivated among us. Of one thing, at least, I am sure. As long as this one roof shelters the good ladies aforesaid—and I wish from my heart it may do so for many and many a long year to come—the tradition of genuine warm-hearted courteous Irish hospitality, which our forefathers have handed down to us and which we in turn must hand down to our descendants, is still alive among us."

A hearty murmur of assent ran round the table. It shot through Gabriel's mind that Miss Ivors was not there and that she had gone away discourteously: and he said with confidence in himself:

"Ladies and Gentlemen,

"A new generation is growing up in our midst, a generation actuated by new ideas and new principles. It is serious and enthusiastic for these new ideas and its enthusiasm, even when it is misdirected, is, I believe, in the main sincere. But we are living in a sceptical and, if I may use the phrase, a thought-tormented age; and sometimes I fear that this new generation, educated or hypereducated as it is, will lack those qualities of humanity, of hospitality, of kindly humour which belonged to an older day. Listening to-night to the names of all those great singers of the past it seemed to me, I must confess, that we were living in a less spacious age. Those days might, without exaggeration, be called spacious days: and if they are gone beyond recall let us hope, at least, that in gatherings such as this we shall still speak of them with pride and affection, still cherish in our hearts the memory of those dead and gone great ones whose fame the world will not willingly let die."

"Hear, hear!" said Mr. Browne loudly.

"But yet," continued Gabriel, his voice falling into a softer inflection, "there are always in gatherings such as this sadder thoughts that will recur to our minds: thoughts of the past, of youth, of changes, of absent faces that we miss here to-night. Our path through life is strewn with many such sad memories: and were we to brood upon them always we could not find the heart to go on bravely with our work among the living. We have all of us living duties and living affections which claim, and rightly claim, our strenuous endeavours.

"Therefore, I will not linger on the past. I will not let any gloomy moralising intrude upon us here to-night. Here we are gathered together for a brief moment from the bustle and rush of our everyday routine. We are met here as friends, in the spirit of good-fellowship, as colleagues, also to a certain extent, in the true spirit of *camaraderie,* and as the guests of—what shall I call them?—the Three Graces of the Dublin musical world."

The table burst into applause and laughter at this allusion. Aunt Julia vainly asked each of her neighbours in turn to tell her what Gabriel had said.

"He says we are the Three Graces, Aunt Julia," said Mary Jane.

Aunt Julia did not understand but she looked up, smiling, at Gabriel, who continued in the same vein:

"Ladies and Gentlemen,

"I will not attempt to play to-night the part that Paris played on another occasion. I will not attempt to choose beween them. The task would be an invidious one and one beyond my poor powers. For when I view them in turn, whether it be our chief hostess herself, whose good heart, whose too good heart, has become a byword with all who know her, or her sister, who seems to be gifted with perennial youth and whose singing must have been a surprise and a revelation to us all to-night, or, last but not least, when I consider our youngest hostess, talented, cheerful, hard-working and the best of nieces, I confess, Ladies and Gentlemen, that I do not know to which of them I should award the prize."

Gabriel glanced down at his aunts and, seeing the large smile on Aunt Julia's face and the tears which had risen to Aunt Kate's eyes, hastened to his close. He raised his glass of port gallantly, while every member of the company fingered a glass expectantly, and said loudly:

"Let us toast them all three together. Let us drink to their health, wealth, long life, happiness and prosperity and may they long continue to hold the proud and self-won position which they hold in their profession and the position of honour and affection which they hold in our hearts."

All the guests stood up, glass in hand, and turning towards the three seated ladies, sang in unison, with Mr. Browne as leader:

"For they are jolly gay fellows,
For they are jolly gay fellows,
For they are jolly gay fellows,
Which nobody can deny."

Aunt Kate was making frank use of her handkerchief and even Aunt Julia seemed moved. Freddy Malins beat time with his pudding-fork and the singers turned towards one another, as if in melodious conference, while they sang with emphasis:

"Unless he tells a lie,
Unless he tells a lie,"

Then, turning once more towards their hostesses, they sang:

"For they are jolly gay fellows,
For they are jolly gay fellows,
For they are jolly gay fellows,
Which nobody can deny."

The acclamation which followed was taken up beyond the door of the supper-room by many of the other guests and renewed time after time, Freddy Malins acting as officer with his fork on high.

. . . .

The piercing morning air came into the hall where they were standing so that Aunt Kate said:

"Close the door, somebody. Mrs. Malins will get her death of cold."

"Browne is out there, Aunt Kate," said Mary Jane.

"Browne is everywhere," said Aunt Kate, lowering her voice.

Mary Jane laughed at her tone.

"Really," she said archly, "he is very attentive."

"He has been laid on here like the gas," said Aunt Kate in the same tone, "all during the Christmas."

She laughed herself this time good-humouredly and then added quickly:

"But tell him to come in, Mary Jane, and close the door. I hope to goodness he didn't hear me."

At that moment the hall-door was opened and Mr. Browne came in from the doorstep, laughing as if his heart would break. He was dressed in a long green overcoat with mock astrakhan cuffs and collar and wore on his head an oval fur cap. He pointed down the snow-covered quay from where the sound of shrill prolonged whistling was borne in.

"Teddy will have all the cabs in Dublin out," he said.

Gabriel advanced from the little pantry behind the office, struggling into his overcoat and, looking round the hall, said:

"Gretta not down yet?"

"She's getting on her things, Gabriel," said Aunt Kate.

"Who's playing up there?" asked Gabriel.

"Nobody. They're all gone."

"O no, Aunt Kate," said Mary Jane. "Bartell D'Arcy and Miss O'Callaghan aren't gone yet."

"Someone is fooling at the piano anyhow," said Gabriel.

Mary Jane glanced at Gabriel and Mr. Browne and said with a shiver:

"It makes me feel cold to look at you two gentlemen muffled up like that. I wouldn't like to face your journey home at this hour."

"I'd like nothing better this minute," said Mr..Browne stoutly, "then a rattling fine walk in the country or a fast drive with a good spanking goer between the shafts."

"We used to have a very good horse and trap at home," said Aunt Julia sadly.

"The never-to-be-forgotten Johnny," said Mary Jane, laughing.

Aunt Kate and Gabriel laughed too.

"Why, what was wonderful about Johnny?" asked Mr. Browne.

"The late lamented Patrick Morkan, our grandfather, that is," explained Gabriel, "commonly known in his later years as the old gentleman, was a glue-boiler."

"O, now, Gabriel," said Aunt Kate, laughing, "he had a starch mill."

"Well, glue or starch," said Gabriel, "the old gentleman had a horse by the name of Johnny. And Johnny used to work in the old gentleman's mill, walking round and round in order to drive the mill. That was all very well; but now comes the tragic part about Johnny. One fine day the old gentleman thought he'd like to drive out with the quality to a military review in the park."

"The Lord have mercy on his soul," said Aunt Kate compassionately.

"Amen," said Gabriel. "So the old gentleman, as I said, harnessed Johnny and put on his very best tall hat and his very best stock collar and drove out in grand style from his ancestral mansion somewhere near Back Lane, I think."

Everyone laughed, even Mrs. Malins, at Gabriel's manner and Aunt Kate said:

"O, now, Gabriel, he didn't live in Back Lane, really. Only the mill was there."

"Out from the mansion of his forefathers," continued Gabriel, "he drove with Johnny. And everything went on beautifully until Johnny came in sight of King Billy's statue: and whether he fell in love with the horse King Billy sits on or whether he thought he was back again in the mill, anyhow he began to walk round the statue."

Gabriel paced in a circle round the hall in his goloshes amid the laughter of the others.

"Round and round he went," said Gabriel, "and the old gentleman, who was a very pompous old gentleman, was highly indignant. 'Go on, sir! What do you mean, sir? Johnny! Johnny! Most extraordinary conduct! Can't understand the horse!' "

The peal of laughter which followed Gabriel's imitation of the incident was interrupted by a resounding knock at the hall door. Mary Jane ran to open it and let in Freddy Malins. Freddy Malins, with his hat well back on his head and his shoulders humped with cold, was puffing and steaming after his exertions.

"I could only get one cab," he said.

"O, we'll find another along the quay," said Gabriel.

"Yes," said Aunt Kate. "Better not keep Mrs. Malins standing in the draught."

Mrs. Malins was helped down the front steps by her son and Mr. Browne and, after many manoeuvres, hoisted into the cab. Freddy Malins clambered in after her and spent a long time settling her on the seat, Mr. Browne helping him with advice. At last she was settled comfortably and Freddy Malins invited Mr. Browne into the cab.

There was a good deal of confused talk, and then Mr. Browne got into the cab. The cabman settled his rug over his knees, and bent down for the address. The confusion grew greater and the cabman was directed differently by Freddy Malins and Mr. Browne, each of whom had his head out through a window of the cab. The difficulty was to know where to drop Mr. Browne along the route, and Aunt Kate, Aunt Julia and Mary Jane helped the discussion from the doorstep with cross-directions and contradictions and abundance of laughter. As for Freddy Malins he was speechless with laughter. He popped his head in and out of the window every moment to the great danger of his hat, and told his mother how the discussion was progressing, till at last Mr. Browne shouted to the bewildered cabman above the din of everybody's laughter:

"Do you know Trinity College?"

"Yes, sir," said the cabman.

"Well, drive bang up against Trinity College gates," said Mr. Browne, "and then we'll tell you where to go. You understand now?"

"Yes, sir," said the cabman.

"Make like a bird for Trinity College."

"Right, sir," said the cabman.

The horse was whipped up and the cab rattled off along the quay amid a chorus of laughter and adieus.

Gabriel had not gone to the door with the others. He was in a dark part of the hall gazing up the staircase. A woman was standing near the top of the first flight, in the shadow also. He could not see her face but he could see the terracotta and salmon-pink panels of her skirt which the shadow made appear black and white. It was his wife. She was leaning on the banisters, listening to something. Gabriel was surprised at her stillness and strained his ear to listen also. But he could hear little save the noise of laughter and dispute on the front steps, a few chords struck on the piano and a few notes of a man's voice singing.

He stood still in the gloom of the hall, trying to catch the air that the voice was singing and gazing up at his wife. There was grace and mystery in her attitude as if she were a symbol of something. He asked himself what is a woman standing on the stairs in the shadow, listening to distant music, a symbol of. If he were a painter he would paint her in that attitude. Her blue felt hat would show off the bronze of her hair against the darkness and the dark panels of her skirt would show off the light ones. *Distant Music* he would call the picture if he were a painter.

The hall-door was closed; and Aunt Kate, Aunt Julia and Mary Jane came down the hall, still laughing.

"Well, isn't Freddy terrible?" said Mary Jane. "He's really terrible."

Gabriel said nothing but pointed up the stairs towards where his wife was standing. Now that the hall-door was closed the voice and the piano could be heard more clearly. Gabriel held up his hand for them to be silent. The song seemed to be in the old Irish tonality and the singer seemed uncertain both of his words and of his voice. The voice, made plaintive by distance and by the singer's hoarseness, faintly illuminated the cadence of the air with words expressing grief:

"O, the rain falls on my heavy locks
And the dew wets my skin,
My babe lies cold . . ."

"O," exclaimed Mary Jane. "It's Bartell D'Arcy singing and he wouldn't sing all the night. O, I'll get him to sing a song before he goes."

"O, do, Mary Jane," said Aunt Kate.

Mary Jane brushed past the others and ran to the staircase, but before she reached it the singing stopped and the piano was closed abruptly.

"O, what a pity" she cried. "Is he coming down, Gretta?"

Gabriel heard his wife answer yes and saw her come down towards them. A few steps behind her were Mr. Bartell D'Arcy and Miss O'Callaghan.

"O, Mr. D'Arcy," cried Mary Jane, "It's downright mean of you to break off like that when we were all in raptures listening to you."

"I have been at him all the evening," said Miss O'Callaghan, "and Mrs. Conroy, too, and he told us he had a dreadful cold and couldn't sing."

"O, Mr. D'Arcy," said Aunt Kate, "now that was a great fib to tell."

"Can't you see that I'm as hoarse as a crow?" said Mr. D'Arcy roughly.

He went into the pantry hastily and put on his overcoat. The others, taken aback by his rude speech, could find nothing to say. Aunt Kate wrinkled her brows and made signs to the others to drop the subject. Mr. D'Arcy stood swathing his neck carefully and frowning.

"It's the weather," said Aunt Julia, after a pause.

"Yes, everybody has colds," said Aunt Kate readily, "everybody."

"They say," said Mary Jane, "we haven't had snow like it for thirty years; and I read this morning in the newspapers that the snow is general all over Ireland."

"I love the look of snow," said Aunt Julia sadly.

"So do I," said Miss O'Callaghan. "I think Christmas is never really Christmas unless we have the snow on the ground."

"But poor Mr. D'Arcy doesn't like the snow," said Aunt Kate, smiling.

Mr. D'Arcy came from the pantry, fully swathed and buttoned, and in a repentant tone told them the history of his cold. Everyone gave him advice and said it was a great pity and urged him to be very careful of his throat in the night air. Gabriel watched his wife, who did not join in the conversation. She was standing right under the dusty fanlight and the flame of the gas lit up the rich bronze of her hair, which he had seen her drying at the fire a few days before. She was in the same attitude and seemed unaware of the talk about her. At last she turned towards them and Gabriel saw that there was colour on her checks and that her eyes were shining. A sudden tide of joy went leaping out of his heart.

"Mr. D'Arcy," she said, "what is the name of that song you were singing?"

"It's called *The Lass of Aughrim,*" said Mr. D'Arcy, "but I couldn't remember it properly. Why? Do you know it?"

"*The Lass of Aughrim,*" she repeated. "I couldn't think of the name."

"It's a very nice air," said Mary Jane. "I'm sorry you were not in voice to-night."

"Now, Mary Jane," said Aunt Kate, "don't annoy Mr. D'Arcy. I won't have him annoyed."

Seeing that all were ready to start she shepherded them to the door, where good-night was said:

"Well, good-night, Aunt Kate, and thanks for the pleasant evening."

"Good-night, Gabriel. Good-night, Gretta!"

"Good-night, Aunt Kate, and thanks ever so much.

"Good-night Aunt Julia."

"O, Good-night, Gretta, I didn't see you."

"Good-night, Mr. D'Arcy. Good-night, Miss O'Callaghan."

"Good-night, Miss Morkan."

"Good-night, again."

"Good-night, all. Safe home."

"Good-night. Good night."

The morning was still dark. A dull, yellow light brooded over the houses and the river; and the sky seemed to be descending. It was slushy underfoot; and only streaks and patches of snow lay on the roofs, on the parapets of the quay and on the area railings. The lamps were still burning redly in the murky air and, across the river, the palace of the Four Courts stood out menacingly against the heavy sky.

She was walking on before him with Mr. Bartell D'Arcy, her shoes in a brown parcel tucked under one arm and her hands holding her skirt up from the slush. She had no longer any grace of attitude, but Gabriel's eyes were still bright with happiness. The blood went bounding along his veins; and the thoughts went rioting through his brain, proud, joyful, tender, valorous.

She was walking on before him so lightly and so erect that he longed to run after her noiselessly, catch her by the shoulders and say something foolish and affectionate into her ear. She seemed to him so frail that he longed to defend her against something and then to be alone with her. Moments of their secret life together burst like stars upon his memory. A heliotrope envelope was lying beside his breakfast-cup and he was caressing it with his hand. Birds were twittering in the ivy and the sunny web of the curtain was shimmering along the floor: he could not eat for happiness. They were standing on the crowded platform and he was placing a ticket inside the warm palm of her glove. He was standing with her in the cold, looking in through a grated window at a man making bottles in a roaring furnace. It was very cold. Her face, fragrant in the cold air, was quite close to his; and suddenly he called out to the man at the furnace:

"Is the fire hot, sir?"

But the man could not hear with the noise of the furnace. It was just as well. He might have answered rudely.

A wave of yet more tender joy escaped from his heart and went coursing in warm flood along his arteries. Like the tender fire of stars moments of their life together, that no one knew of or would ever know of, broke upon and illumined his memory. He longed to recall to her those moments, to make her forget the years of their dull existence together and remember only their moments of ecstasy. For the years, he felt, had not quenched his soul or hers. Their children, his writing, her household cares had not quenched all their souls' tender fire. In one letter that he had written to her then he had said: "Why is it that words like these seem to me so dull and cold? Is it because there is no word tender enough to be your name?"

Like distant music these words that he had written years before were borne towards him from the past. He longed to be alone with her. When the others had gone away, when he and she were in the room in the hotel, then they would be alone together. He would call her softly:

"Gretta!"

Perhaps she would not hear at once: she would be undressing. Then something in his voice would strike her. She would turn and look at him. . . .

At the corner of Winetavern Street they met a cab. He was glad of its rattling noise as it saved him from conversation. She was looking out of the window and seemed tired. The others spoke only a few words, pointing out some building or street. The horse galloped along wearily under the murky morning sky, dragging his old rattling box after his heels, and Gabriel was again in a cab with her, galloping to catch the boat, galloping to their honeymoon.

As the cab drove across O'Connell Bridge Miss O'Callaghan said:

"They say you never cross O'Connell Bridge without seeing a white horse."

"I see a white man this time," said Gabriel.

"Where?" asked Mr. Bartell D'Arcy.

Gabriel pointed to the statue, on which lay patches of snow. Then he nodded familiarly to it and waved his hand.

"Good-night, Dan," he said gaily.

When the cab drew up before the hotel, Gabriel jumped out and, in spite of Mr. Bartell D'Arcy's protest, paid the driver. He gave the man a shilling over his fare. The man saluted and said:

"A prosperous New Year to you, sir."

"The same to you," said Gabriel cordially.

She leaned for a moment on his arm in getting out of the cab and while standing at the curbstone, bidding the others good-night. She leaned lightly on his arm, as lightly as when she had danced with him a few hours before. He had felt proud and happy then, happy that she was his, proud of her grace and wifely carriage. But now, after the kindling again of so many memories, the first touch of her body, musical and strange and perfumed, sent through him a keen pang of lust. Under cover of her silence he pressed her arm closely to his side; and, as they stood at the hotel door, he felt that they had escaped from their lives and duties, escaped from home and friends and run away together with wild and radiant hearts to a new adventure.

An old man was dozing in a great hooded chair in the hall. He lit a candle in the office and went before them to the stairs. They followed him in silence, their feet falling in soft thuds on the thickly carpeted stairs. She mounted the stairs behind the porter, her head bowed in the ascent, her frail shoulders curved as with a burden, her skirt girt tightly about her. He could have flung his arms about her hips and held her still, for his arms were trembling with desire to seize her and only the stress of his nails against the palms of his hands held the wild impulse of his body in check. The porter halted on the stairs to settle his guttering candle. They halted, too, on the steps below him. In the silence Gabriel could hear the falling of the molten wax into the tray and the thumping of his own heart against his ribs.

The porter led them along a corridor and opened a door. Then he set his unstable candle down on a toilet-table and asked at what hour they were to be called in the morning.

"Eight," said Gabriel.

The porter pointed to the tap of the electric-light and began a muttered apology, but Gabriel cut him short.

"We don't want any light. We have light enough from the street. And I say," he added, pointing to the candle, "you might remove that handsome article, like a good man."

The porter took up his candle again, but slowly, for he was surprised by such a novel idea. Then he mumbled good-night and went out. Gabriel shot the lock to.

A ghastly light from the street lamp lay in a long shaft from one window to the door. Gabriel threw his overcoat and hat on a couch and crossed the room towards the window. He looked down into the street in order that his emotion might calm a little. Then he turned and leaned against a chest of drawers with his back to the light. She had taken off her hat and cloak and was standing before a large swinging mirror, unhooking her waist. Gabriel paused for a few moments watching her, and then said:

"Gretta!"

She turned away from the mirror slowly and walked along the shaft of light towards him. Her face looked so serious and weary that the words would not pass Gabriel's lips. No, it was not the moment yet.

"You look tired," he said.

"I am a little," she answered.

"You don't feel ill or weak?"

"No, tired: that's all."

She went on to the window and stood there, looking out. Gabriel waited again and then fearing that diffidence was about to conquer him, he said abruptly:

"By the way, Gretta!"

"What is it?"

"You know that poor fellow Malins?" he said quickly.

"Yes, What about him?"

"Well, poor fellow, he's a decent sort of chap, after all," continued Gabriel in a false voice. "He gave me back that sovereign I lent him, and I didn't expect it, really. It's a pity he wouldn't keep away from that Browne, because he's not a bad fellow, really."

He was trembling now with annoyance. Why did she seem so abstracted? He did not know how he could begin. Was she annoyed, too, about something? If she would only turn to him or come to him of her own accord! To take her as she was would be brutal. No, he must see some ardour in her eyes first. He longed to be master of her strange mood.

"When did you lend him the pound?" she asked, after a pause.

Gabriel strove to restrain himself from breaking out into brutal language about the sottish Malins and his pound. He longed to cry to her from his soul, to crush her body against his, to overmaster her. But he said:

"O, at Christmas, when he opened that little Christmas-card shop in Henry Street."

He was in such a fever of rage and desire that he did not hear her come from the window. She stood before him for an instant, looking at him strangely. Then, suddenly raising herself on tip-toe and resting her hands lightly on his shoulders, she kissed him.

"You are a very generous person, Gabriel," she said.

Gabriel, trembling with delight at her sudden kiss and at the quaintness of her phrase, put his hands on her hair and began smoothing it back, scarcely touching it with his fingers. The washing had made it fine and brilliant. His heart was brimming over with happiness. Just when he was wishing for it she had come to him of her own accord. Perhaps her thoughts had been running with his. Perhaps she had felt the impetuous desire that was in him, and then the yielding mood had come upon her. Now that she had fallen to him so easily, he wondered why he had been so diffident.

He stood, holding her head between his hands. Then, slipping one arm swiftly about her body and drawing her towards him, he said softly:

"Gretta, dear, what are you thinking about?"

She did not answer nor yield wholly to his arm. He said again, softly:

"Tell me what it is, Gretta. I think I know what is the matter. Do I know?"

She did not answer at once. Then she said in an outburst of tears:

"O, I am thinking about that song, *The Lass of Aughrim.*"

She broke loose from him and ran to the bed and, throwing her arms across the bed-rail, hid her face. Gabriel stood stock-still for a moment in astonishment and then followed her. As he passed in the way of the cheval-glass he caught sight of himself in full length, his broad, well filled shirt-front, the face whose expression always puzzled him when he saw it in a mirror, and his glimmering gilt-rimmed eyeglasses. He halted a few paces from her and said:

"What about the song? Why does that make you cry?"

She raised her head from her arms and dried her eyes with the back of her hand like a child. A kinder note than he had intended went into his voice.

"Why, Gretta?" he asked.

"I am thinking about a person long ago who used to sing that song."

"And who was the person long ago?" asked Gabriel, smiling.

"It was a person I used to know in Galway when I was living with my grandmother," she said.

The smile passed away from Gabriel's face. A dull anger began to gather again at the back of his mind and the dull fires of his lust began to glow angrily in his veins.

"Someone you were in love with?" he asked ironically.

"It was a young boy I used to know," she answered, "named Michael Furey. He used to sing that song, *The Lass of Aughrim.* He was very delicate."

Gabriel was silent. He did not wish her to think that he was interested in this delicate boy.

"I can see him so plainly," she said, after a moment. "Such eyes as he had: big, dark eyes! And such an expression in them—an expression!"

"O, then, you are in love with him?" said Gabriel.

"I used to go out walking with him," she said, "when I was in Galway."

A thought flew across Gabriel's mind.

"Perhaps that was why you wanted to go to Galway with that Ivors girl?" he said coldly.

She looked at him and asked in surprise:

"What for?"

Her eyes made Gabriel feel awkward. He shrugged his shoulders and said:

"How do I know? To see him, perhaps."

She looked away from him along the shaft of light towards the window in silence.

"He is dead," she said at length. "He died when he was only seventeen. Isn't it a terrible thing to die so young as that?"

"What was he?" asked Gabriel, still ironically.

"He was in the gasworks," she said.

Gabriel felt humiliated by the failure of his irony and by the evocation of this figure from the dead, a boy in the gasworks. While he had been full of memories of their secret life together, full of tenderness and joy and desire, she had been comparing him in her mind with another. A shameful consciousness of his own person assailed him. He saw himself as a ludicrous figure, acting as a penny-boy for his aunts, a nervous, well-meaning sentimentalist, orating to vulgarians and idealising his own clownish lusts, the pitiable fatuous fellow he had caught a glimpse of in the mirror. Instinctively he turned his back more to the light lest she might see the shame that burned upon his forehead.

(errand boy)

He tried to keep up his tone of cold interrogation, but his voice when he spoke was humble and indifferent.

"I suppose you were in love with this Michael Furey, Gretta," he said.

"I was great with him at that time," she said.

Her voice was veiled and sad. Gabriel, feeling now how vain it would be to try to lead her whither he had purposed, caressed one of her hands and said, also sadly:

"And what did he die of so young, Gretta? Consumption, was it?"

"I think he died for me," she answered.

A vague terror seized Gabriel at this answer, as if, at that hour when he had hoped to triumph, some impalpable and vindictive being was coming against him, gathering forces against him in its vague world. But he shook himself free of it with an effort of reason and continued to caress her hand. He did not question her again, for he felt that she would tell him of herself. Her hand was warm and moist: it did not respond to his touch, but he continued to caress it just as he had caressed her first letter to him that spring morning.

"It was in the winter," she said, "about the beginning of the winter when I was going to leave my grandmother's and come up here to the convent. And he was ill at the time in his lodgings in Galway and wouldn't be let out, and his people in Oughterard were written to. He was in decline, they said, or something like that. I never knew rightly."

She paused for a moment and sighed.

"Poor fellow," she said. "He was very fond of me and he was such a gentle boy. We used to go out together, walking, you know, Gabriel, like the way they do in the country. He was going to study singing only for his health. He had a very good voice, poor Michael Furey."

"Well; and then?" asked Gabriel.

"And then when it came to the time for me to leave Galway and come up to the convent he was much worse and I wouldn't be let see him so I wrote him a letter saying I was going up to Dublin and would be back in the summer, and hoping he would be better then."

She paused for a moment to get her voice under control, and then went on:

"Then the night before I left, I was in my grandmother's house in Nuns' Island, packing up, and I heard gravel thrown up against the window. The window was so wet I couldn't see, so I ran downstairs as I was and slipped out the back into the garden and there was the poor fellow at the end of the garden, shivering."

"And did you not tell him to go back?" asked Gabriel.

"I implored of him to go home at once and told him he would get his death in the rain. But he said he did not want to live. I can see his eyes as well as well! He was standing at the end of the wall where there was a tree."

"And did he go home?" asked Gabriel.

"Yes, he went home. And when I was only a week in the convent he died and he was buried in Oughterard, where his people came from. O, the day I heard that, that he was dead!"

She stopped, choking with sobs, and, overcome by emotion, flung herself face downward on the bed, sobbing in the quilt. Gabriel held her hand for a moment longer, irresolutely, and then, shy of intruding on her grief, let it fall gently and walked quietly to the window.

She was fast asleep.

Gabriel, leaning on his elbow, looked for a few moments unresentfully on her tangled hair and half-open mouth, listening to her deep-drawn breath. So she had had that romance in her life: a man had died for her sake. It hardly pained him now to think how poor a part he, her husband, had played in her life. He watched her while she slept, as though he and she had never lived together as man and wife. His curious eyes rested long upon her face and on her hair: and, as he thought of what she must have been then, in that time of her first girlish beauty, a strange, friendly pity for her entered his soul. He did not like to say even to himself that her face was no longer beautiful, but he knew that it was no longer the face for which Michael Furey had braved death.

Perhaps she had not told him all the story. His eyes moved to the chair over which she had thrown some of her clothes. A petticoat string dangled to the floor. One boot stood upright, its limp upper fallen down: the fellow of it lay upon its side. He wondered at his riot of emotions of an hour before. From what had it proceeded? From his aunt's supper, from his own foolish speech, from the wine and dancing, the merrymaking when saying good-night in the hall, the pleasure of the walk along the river in the snow. Poor Aunt Julia! She, too, would soon be a shade with the shade of Patrick Morkan and his horse. He had caught that haggard look upon her face for a moment when she was singing *Arrayed for the Bridal*. Soon, perhaps, he would be sitting in that same drawing-room, dressed in black, his silk hat on his knees. The blinds would be drawn down and Aunt Kate would be sitting beside him, crying and blowing her nose and telling him how Julia had died. He would cast about in his mind for some words that might console her, and would find only lame and useless ones. Yes, yes: that would happen very soon.

The air of the room chilled his shoulders. He stretched himself cautiously along under the sheets and lay down beside his wife. One by one, they were all becoming shades. Better pass boldly into that other world, in the full glory of some passion, than fade and wither dismally with age. He thought of how she who lay beside him had locked in her heart for so many years that image of her lover's eyes when he had told her that he did not wish to live.

Generous tears filled Gabriel's eyes. He had never felt like that himself towards any woman, but he knew that such a feeling must be love. The tears gathered more thickly in his eyes and in the partial darkness he imagined he saw the form of a young man standing under a dripping tree. Other forms were near. His soul had approached that region where dwell the vast hosts of the dead. He was conscious of, but could not apprehend, their wayward and flickering existence. His own identity was fading out into a grey impalpable world: the solid world itself, which these dead had one time reared and lived in, was dissolving and dwindling.

A few light taps upon the pane made him turn to the window. It had begun to snow again. He watched sleepily the flakes, silver and dark, falling obliquely against the lamplight. The time had come for him to set out on his journey westward. Yes, the newspapers were right, snow was general all over Ireland. It was falling on every part of the dark central plain, on the treeless hills, falling softly upon the Bog of Allen and, farther westward softly falling into the dark mutinous Shannon waves. It was falling, too, upon every part of the lonely churchyard on the hill where Michael Furey lay buried. It lay thickly drifted on the crooked crosses and headstones, on the spears of the little gate, on the barren thorns. His soul swooned slowly as he heard the snow falling faintly through the universe and faintly falling, like the descent of their last end, upon all the living and the dead.

JAMES JOYCE

Eveline

SHE sat at the window watching the evening invade the avenue. Her head was leaned against the window curtains and in her nostrils was the odour of dusty cretonne. She was tired.

Few people passed. The man out of the last house passed on his way home; she heard his footsteps clacking along the concrete pavement and afterwards crunching on the cinder path before the new red houses. One time there used to be a field there in which they used to play every evening with other people's children. Then a man from Belfast bought the field and built houses in it—not like their little brown houses but bright brick houses with shining roofs. The children of the avenue used to play together in that field—the Devines, the Waters, the Dunns, little Keogh the cripple, she and her brothers and sisters. Ernest, however, never played: he was too grown up. Her father used often to hunt them in out of the field with his blackthorn stick; but usually little Keogh used to keep *nix* and call out when he saw her father coming. Still they seemed to have been rather happy then. Her father was not so bad then; and besides, her mother was alive. That was a long time ago; she and her brothers and sisters were all grown up; her mother was dead. Tizzie Dunn was dead, too, and the Waters had gone back to England. Everything changes. Now she was going to go away like the others, to leave her home.

Home! She looked round the room, reviewing all its familiar objects which she had dusted once a week for so many years, wondering where on earth all the dust came from. Perhaps she would never see again those familiar objects from which she had never dreamed of being divided. And yet during all those years she had never found out the name of the priest whose yellowing photograph hung on the wall above the broken harmonium beside the coloured print of the promises made to Blessed Margaret Mary Alacoque. He had been a school friend of her father. Whenever he showed the photograph to a visitor her father used to pass it with a casual word:

"He is in Melbourne now."

She had consented to go away, to leave her home. Was that wise? She tried to weigh each side of the question. In her home anyway she had shelter and food; she had those whom she had known all her life about her. Of course she had to work hard, both in the house and at business. What would they say of her in the Stores when they found out that she had run away with a fellow? Say she was a fool, perhaps; and her place would be filled up by advertisement. Miss Gavan would be glad. She had always had an edge on her, especially whenever there were people listening.

"Miss Hill, don't you see these ladies are waiting?"

"Look lively, Miss Hill, please."

She would not cry many tears at leaving the Stores.

But in her new home, in a distant unknown country, it would not be like that. Then she would be married—she, Eveline. People would treat her with respect then. She would not be treated as her mother had been. Even now, though she was over nineteen, she sometimes felt herself in danger of her father's violence. She knew it was that that had given her the palpitations. When they were growing up he had never gone for her, like he used to go for Harry and Ernest, because she was a girl; but latterly he had begun to threaten her and say what he would do to her only for her dead mother's sake. And now she had nobody to protect her. Ernest was dead and Harry, who was in the church decorating business, was nearly always down somewhere in the country. Besides, the invariable squabble for money on Saturday nights had begun to weary her unspeakably. She always gave her entire wages—seven shillings—and Harry always sent up what he could but the trouble was to get any money from her father. He said she used to squander the money, that she had no head, that he wasn't going to give her his hard earned money to throw about the streets, and much more, for he was usually fairly bad on Saturday night. In the end he would give her the money and ask her had she any intention of buying Sunday's dinner. Then she had to rush out as quickly as she could and do her marketing, holding her black leather purse tightly in her hand as she elbowed her way through the crowds and returning home late under her load of provisions. She had hard work to keep the house together and to see that the two young children who had been left to her charge went to school regularly and got their meals regularly. It was hard work—a hard life—but now that she was about to leave it she did not find it a wholly undesirable life.

She was about to explore another life with Frank. Frank was very kind, manly, open-hearted. She was to go away with him by the night-boat to be his wife and to live with him in Buenos Ayres where he had a home waiting for her. How well she remembered the first time she had seen him; he was lodging in a house on the main road where she used to visit. It seemed a few weeks ago. He was standing at the gate, his peaked cap pushed back on his head and his hair tumbled forward over a face of bronze. Then they had come to know each other. He used to meet her outside the Stores every evening and see her home. He took her to see *The Bohemian Girl* and she felt elated as she sat in an unaccustomed part of the theatre with him. He was awfully fond of music and sang a little. People knew that they were courting and, when he sang about the lass that loves a sailor, she always felt pleasantly confused. He used to call her Poppens out of fun. First of all it had been an excitement for her to have a fellow and then she had begun to like him. He had tales of distant countries. He had started as a deck boy at a pound a month on a ship of the Allan Line going out to Canada. He told her the names of the ships he had been on and the names of the different services. He had sailed through the Straits of Magellan and he told her stories of the terrible Patagonians. He had fallen on his feet in Buenos Ayres, he said, and had come over to the old country just for a holiday. Of course, her father had found out the affair and had forbidden her to have anything to say to him.

"I know these sailor chaps," he said.

One day he had quarrelled with Frank and after that she had to meet her lover secretly.

The evening deepened in the avenue. The white of two letters in her lap grew indistinct. One was to Harry; the other was to her father. Ernest had been her favourite but she still liked Harry, too. Her father was becoming old lately, she noticed; he would miss her. Sometimes he could be very nice. Not long before, when she had been laid up for a day, he had read her out a ghost story and made toast for her at the fire. Another day, when their mother was alive, they had all gone for a picnic to the Hill of Howth. She remembered her father putting on her mother's bonnet to make the children laugh.

Her time was running out but she continued to sit by the window, leaning her head against the window curtain, inhaling the odour of dusty cretonne. Down far in the avenue she could hear a street organ playing. She knew the air. Strange that it should come that very night to remind her of the promise to her mother, her promise to keep the home together as long as she could. She remembered the last night of her mother's illness; she was again in the close dark room at the other side of the hall and outside she heard a melancholy air of Italy. The organ-player had been ordered to go away and given sixpence. She remembered her father strutting back into the sickroom saying:

"Damned Italians! coming over here!"

As she mused the pitiful vision of her mother's life laid its spell on the very quick of her being—that life of commonplace sacrifices closing in final craziness. She trembled as she heard again her mother's voice saying constantly with foolish insistence:

"Derevaun Seraun! Derevaun Seraun!"

She stood up in a sudden impulse of terror. Escape! She must escape! Frank would save her. He would give her life, perhaps love, too. But she wanted to live. Why should she be unhappy? She had a right to happiness. Frank would take her in his arms, fold her in his arms. He would save her.

. . . .

She stood among the swaying crowd in the station at the North Wall. He held her hand and she knew that he was speaking to her, saying something about the passage over and over again. The station was full of soldiers with brown baggages. Through the wide doors of the sheds she caught a glimpse of the black mass of the boat, lying in beside the quay wall, with illumined portholes. She answered nothing. She felt her cheek pale and cold and, out of a maze of distress, she prayed to God to direct her, to show her what was her duty. The boat blew a long mournful whistle into the mist. If she went, to-morrow she would be on the sea with Frank, steaming towards Buenos Ayres. Their passage had been booked. Could she still draw back after all he had done for her? Her distress awoke a nausea in her body and she kept moving her lips in silent fervent prayer.

A bell clanged upon her heart. She felt him seize her hand:

"Come!"

All the seas of the world tumbled about her heart. He was drawing her into them: he would drown her. She gripped with both hands at the iron railing.

"Come!"

No! No! No! It was impossible. Her hands clutched the iron in frenzy. Amid the seas she sent a cry of anguish!

"Eveline! Evvy!"

He rushed beyond the barrier and called to her to follow. He was shouted at to go on but he still called to her. She set her white face to him, passive, like a helpless animal. Her eyes gave him no sign of love or farewell or recognition.

JAMES JOYCE

A Little Cloud

EIGHT years before he had seen his friend off at the North Wall and wished him godspeed. Gallaher had got on. You could tell that at once by his travelled air, his well-cut tweed suit, and fearless accent. Few fellows had talents like his and fewer still could remain unspoiled by such success. Gallaher's heart was in the right place and he had deserved to win. It was something to have a friend like that.

Little Chandler's thoughts ever since lunch-time had been of his meeting with Gallaher, of Gallaher's invitation and of the great city London where Gallaher lived. He was called Little Chandler because, though he was but slightly under the average stature, he gave one the idea of being a little man. His hands were white and small, his frame was fragile, his voice was quiet and his manners were refined. He took the greatest care of his fair silken hair and moustache and used perfume discreetly on his handkerchief. The half-moons of his nails were perfect and when he smiled you caught a glimpse of a row of childish white teeth.

As he sat at his desk in the King's Inns he thought what changes those eight years had brought. The friend whom he had known under a shabby and necessitous guise had become a brilliant figure on the London Press. He turned often from his tiresome writing to gaze out of the office window. The glow of a late autumn sunset covered the grass plots and walks. It cast a shower of kindly golden dust on the untidy nurses and decrepit old men who drowsed on the benches; it flickered upon all the moving figures—on the children who ran screaming along the gravel paths and on everyone who passed through the gardens. He watched the scene and thought of life; and (as always happened when he thought of life) he became sad. A gentle melancholy took possession of him. He felt how useless it was to struggle against fortune, this being the burden of wisdom which the ages had bequeathed to him.

He remembered the books of poetry upon his shelves at home. He had bought them in his bachelor days and many an evening, as he sat in the little room off the hall, he had been tempted to take one down from the bookshelf and read out something to his wife. But shyness had always held him back; and so the books had remained on their shelves. At times he repeated lines to himself and this consoled him.

When his hour had struck he stood up and took leave of his desk and of his fellow-clerks punctiliously. He emerged from under the feudal arch of the King's Inns, a neat modest figure, and walked swiftly down Henrietta Street. The golden sunset was waning and the air had grown sharp. A horde of grimy children populated the street. They stood or ran in the roadway or crawled up the steps before the gaping doors or squatted like mice upon the thresholds. Little Chandler gave them no thought. He picked his way deftly through all that minute vermin-like life and under the shadow of the gaunt spectral mansions in which the old nobility of Dublin had roystered. No memory of the past touched him, for his mind was full of a present joy.

He had never been in Corless's but he knew the value of the name. He knew that people went there after the theatre to eat oysters and drink liqueurs; and he had heard that the waiters there spoke French and German. Walking swiftly by at night he had seen cabs drawn up before the door and richly dressed ladies, escorted by cavaliers, alight and enter quickly. They wore noisy dresses and many wraps. Their faces were powdered and they caught up their dresses, when they touched earth, like alarmed Atalantas. He had always passed without turning his head to look. It was his habit to walk swiftly in the street even by day and whenever he found himself in the city late at night he hurried on his way apprehensively and excitedly. Sometimes, however, he courted the causes of his fear. He chose the darkest and narrowest streets and, as he walked boldly forward, the silence that was spread about his footsteps troubled him, the wandering, silent figures troubled him; and at times a sound of low fugitive laughter made him tremble like a leaf.

He turned to the right towards Capel Street. Ignatius Gallaher on the London Press! Who would have thought it possible eight years before? Still, now that he reviewed the past, Little Chandler could remember many signs of future greatness in his friend. People used to say that Ignatius Gallaher was wild. Of course, he did mix with a rakish set of fellows at that time, drank freely and borrowed money on all sides. In the end he had got mixed up in some shady affair, some money transaction: at least, that was one version of his flight. But nobody denied him talent. There was always a certain . . . something in Ignatius Gallaher that impressed you in spite of yourself. Even when he was out at elbows and at his wits' end for money he kept up a bold face. Little Chandler remembered (and the remembrance brought a slight flush of pride to his cheek) one of Ignatius Gallaher's sayings when he was in a tight corner:

"Half time now, boys," he used to say lightheartedly. "Where's my considering cap?"

That was Ignatius Gallaher all out; and, damn it, you couldn't but admire him for it.

Little Chandler quickened his pace. For the first time in his life he felt himself superior to the people he passed. For the first time his soul revolted against the dull inelegance of Capel Street. There was no doubt about it: if you wanted to succeed you had to go away. You could do nothing in Dublin. As he crossed Grattan Bridge he looked down the river towards the lower quays and pitied the poor stunted houses. They seemed to him a band of tramps, huddled together along the river-banks, their old coats covered with dust and soot, stupefied by the panorama of sunset and waiting for the first chill of night to bid them arise, shake themselves and begone. He wondered whether he could write a poem to express his idea. Perhaps Gallaher might be able to get it into some London paper for him. Could he write something original? He was not sure what idea he wished to express but the thought that a poetic moment had touched him took life within him like an infant hope. He stepped onward bravely.

Every step brought him nearer to London, farther from his own sober inartistic life. A light began to tremble on the horizon of his mind. He was not so old—thirty-two. His temperament might be said to be just at the point of maturity. There were so many different moods and impressions that he wished to express in verse. He felt them within him. He tried to weigh his soul to see if it was a poet's soul. Melancholy was the dominant note of his temperament, he thought, but it was a melancholy tempered by recurrences of faith and resignation and simple joy. If he could give expression to it in a book of poems perhaps men would listen. He would never be popular: he saw that. He could not sway the crowd but he might appeal to a little circle of kindred minds. The English critics, perhaps, would recognise him as one of the Celtic school by reason of the melancholy tone of his poems; besides that, he would put in allusions. He began to invent sentences and phrases from the notice which his book would get. *"Mr. Chandler has the gift of easy and graceful verse."* . . . *"A wistful sadness pervades these poems."* . . . *"The Celtic note."* It was a pity his name was not more Irish-looking. Perhaps it would be better to insert his mother's name before the surname: Thomas Malone Chandler, or better still: T. Malone Chandler. He would speak to Gallaher about it.

He pursued his revery so ardently that he passed his street and had to turn back. As he came near Corless's his former agitation began to overmaster him and he halted before the door in indecision. Finally he opened the door and entered.

The light and noise of the bar held him at the doorways for a few moments. He looked about him, but his sight was confused by the shining of many red and green wine-glasses. The bar seemed to him to be full of people and he felt that the people were observing him curiously. He glanced quickly to right and left (frowning slightly to make his errand appear serious), but when his sight cleared a little he saw that nobody had turned to look at him: and there, sure enough, was Ignatius Gallaher leaning with his back against the counter and his feet planted far apart.

"Hallo, Tommy, old hero, here you are! What is it to be? What will you have? I'm taking whisky: better stuff than we get across the water. Soda? Lithia? No mineral? I'm the same. Spoils the flavour. . . . Here, *garçon,* bring us two halves of malt whisky, like a good fellow. . . . Well, and how have you been pulling along since I saw you last? Dear God, how old we're getting! Do you see any signs of aging in me—eh, what? A little grey and thin on the top—what?"

Ignatius Gallaher took off his hat and displayed a large closely cropped head. His face was heavy, pale and clean-shaven. His eyes, which were of bluish slate-colour, relieved his unhealthy pallor and shone out plainly above the vivid orange tie he wore. Between these rival features the lips appeared very long and shapeless and colourless. He bent his head and felt with two sympathetic fingers the thin hair at the crown. Little Chandler shook his head as a denial. Ignatius Gallaher put on his hat again.

"It pulls you down," he said, "Press life. Always hurry and scurry, looking for copy and sometimes not finding it: and then, always to have something new in your stuff. Damn proofs and printers, I say, for a few days. I'm deuced glad, I can tell you, to get back to the old country. Does a fellow good, a bit of a holiday. I feel a ton better since I landed again in dear dirty Dublin. . . . Here you are, Tommy. Water? Say when."

Little Chandler allowed his whisky to be very much diluted.

"You don't know what's good for you, my boy," said Ignatius Gallaher. "I drink mine neat."

"I drink very little as a rule," said Little Chandler modestly. "An odd half-one or so when I meet any of the old crowd: that's all."

"Ah, well," said Ignatius Gallaher, cheerfully, "here's to us and to old times and old acquaintance."

They clinked glasses and drank the toast.

"I met some of the old gang to-day," said Ignatius Gallaher. "O'Hara seems to be in a bad way. What's he doing?"

"Nothing," said Little Chandler. "He's gone to the dogs."

"But Hogan has a good sit, hasn't he?"

"Yes; he's in the Land Commission."

"I met him one night in London and he seemed to be very flush. . . . Poor O'Hara! Boose, I suppose?"

"Other things, too," said Little Chandler shortly.

Ignatius Gallaher laughed.

"Tommy," he said, "I see you haven't changed an atom. You're the very same serious person that used to lecture me on Sunday mornings when I had a sore head and a fur on my tongue. You'd want to knock about a bit in the world. Have you never been anywhere even for a trip?"

"I've been to the Isle of Man," said Little Chandler.

Ignatius Gallaher laughed.

"The Isle of Man!" he said. "Go to London or Paris: Paris, for choice. That'd do you good."

"Have you seen Paris?"

"I should think I have! I've knocked about there a little."

"And is it really so beautiful as they say?" asked Little Chandler.

He sipped a little of his drink while Ignatius Gallaher finished his boldly.

"Beautiful?" said Ignatius Gallaher, pausing on the word and on the flavour of his drink. "It's not so beautiful, you know. Of course, it is beautiful. . . . But it's the life of Paris; that's the thing. Ah, there's no city like Paris for gaiety, movement, excitement. . . ."

Little Chandler finished his whisky and, after some trouble, succeeded in catching the barman's eye. He ordered the same again.

"I've been to the Moulin Rouge," Ignatius Gallaher continued when the barman had removed their glasses, "and I've been to all the Bohemian cafés. Hot stuff! Not for a pious chap like you, Tommy."

Little Chandler said nothing until the barman returned with two glasses: then he touched his friend's glass lightly and reciprocated the former toast. He was beginning to feel somewhat disillusioned. Gallaher's accent and way of expressing himself did not please him. There was something vulgar in his friend which he had not observed before. But perhaps it was only the result of living in London amid the bustle and competition of the Press. The old personal charm was still there under this new gaudy manner. And, after all, Gallaher had lived, he had seen the world. Little Chandler looked at his friend enviously.

"Everything in Paris is gay," said Ignatius Gallaher. "They believe in enjoying life—and don't you think they're right? If you want to enjoy yourself properly you must go to Paris. And, mind you, they've a great feeling for the Irish there. When they heard I was from Ireland they were ready to eat me, man."

Little Chandler took four or five sips from his glass.

"Tell me," he said, "is it true that Paris is so . . . immoral as they say?"

Ignatius Gallaher made a catholic gesture with his right arm.

"Every place is immoral," he said. "Of course you do find spicy bits in Paris. Go to one of the students' balls, for instance. That's lively, if you like, when the *cocottes* begin to let themselves loose. You know what they are, I suppose?"

"I've heard of them," said Little Chandler.

Ignatius Gallaher drank off his whisky and shook his head.

"Ah," he said, "you may say what you like. There's no woman like the Parisienne—for style, for go."

"Then it is an immoral city," said Little Chandler, with timid insistence—"I mean, compared with London or Dublin?"

"London!" said Ignatius Gallaher. "It's six of one and half-a-dozen of the other. You ask Hogan, my boy. I showed him a bit about London when he was over there. He'd open your eye. . . . I say, Tommy, don't make punch of that whisky: liquor up."

"No, really. . . ."

"O, come on, another one won't do you any harm. What is it? The same again, I suppose?"

"Well . . . all right."

"*François,* the same again. . . . Will you smoke, Tommy?"

Ignatius Gallaher produced his cigar-case. The two friends lit their cigars and puffed at them in silence until their drinks were served.

"I'll tell you my opinion," said Ignatius Gallaher, emerging after some time from the clouds of smoke in which he had taken refuge, "it's a rum world. Talk of immorality! I've heard of cases—what am I saying?—I've known them: cases of . . . immorality. . . ."

Ignatius Gallaher puffed thoughtfully at his cigar and then, in a calm historian's tone, he proceeded to sketch for his friend some pictures of the corruption which was rife abroad. He summarised the vices of many capitals and seemed inclined to award the palm to Berlin. Some things he could not vouch for (his friends had told him), but of others he had had personal experience. He spared neither rank nor caste. He revealed many of the secrets of religious houses on the Continent and described some of the practices which were fashionable in high society and ended by telling, with details, a story about an English duchess—a story which he knew to be true. Little

Chandler was astonished.

"Ah, well," said Ignatius Gallaher, "here we are in old jog-along Dublin where nothing is known of such things."

"How dull you must find it," said Little Chandler, "after all the other places you've seen!"

"Well," said Ignatius Gallaher, "it's a relaxation to come over here, you know. And, after all, it's the old country, as they say, isn't it? You can't help having a certain feeling for it. That's human nature. . . . But tell me something about yourself. Hogan told me you had . . . tasted the joys of connubial bliss. Two years ago, wasn't it?"

Little Chandler blushed and smiled.

"Yes," he said. "I was married last May twelve months."

"I hope it's not too late in the day to offer my best wishes," said Ignatius Gallaher. "I didn't know your address or I'd have done so at the time."

He extended his hand, which Little Chandler took.

"Well, Tommy," he said, "I wish you and yours every joy in life, old chap, and tons of money, and may you never die till I shoot you. And that's the wish of a sincere friend, an old friend. You know that?"

"I know that," said Little Chandler.

"Any youngsters?" said Ignatius Gallaher.

Little Chandler blushed again.

"We have one child," he said.

"Son or daughter?"

"A little boy."

Ignatius Gallaher slapped his friend sonorously on the back.

"Bravo," he said, "I wouldn't doubt you, Tommy."

Little Chandler smiled, looked confusedly at his glass and bit his lower lip with three childishly white front teeth.

"I hope you'll spend an evening with us," he said, "before you go back. My wife will be delighted to meet you. We can have a little music and—"

"Thanks awfully, old chap," said Ignatius Gallaher, "I'm sorry we didn't meet earlier. But I must leave to-morrow night."

"To-night, perhaps . . . ?"

"I'm awfully sorry, old man. You see I'm over here with another fellow, clever young chap he is too, and we arranged to go to a little card party. Only for that . . ."

"O, in that case. . . ."

"But who knows?" said Ignatius Gallaher considerately. "Next year I may take a little skip over here now that I've broken the ice. It's only a pleasure deferred."

"Very well," said Little Chandler, "the next time you come we must have an evening together. That's agreed now, isn't it?"

"Yes, that's agreed," said Ignatius Gallaher. "Next year if I come, *parole d'honneur*."

"And to clinch the bargain," said Little Chandler, "we'll just have one more now."

Ignatius Gallaher took out a large gold watch and looked at it.

"Is it to be the last?" he said. "Because you know, I have an a.p."

"O, yes, positively," said Little Chandler.

"Very well, then," said Ignatius Gallaher, "let us have another one as a *deoc an doruis*—that's good vernacular for a small whisky, I believe."

Little Chandler ordered the drinks. The blush which had risen to his face a few moments before was establishing itself. A trifle made him blush at any time: and now he felt warm and excited. Three small whiskies had gone to his head and Gallaher's strong cigar had confused his mind, for he was a delicate and abstinent person. The adventure of meeting Gallaher after eight years, of finding himself with Gallaher in Corless's surrounded by lights and noise, of listening to Gallaher's stories and of sharing for a brief space Gallaher's vagrant and triumphant life, upset the equipoise of his sensitive nature. He felt acutely the contrast between his own life and his friend's, and it seemed to him unjust. Gallaher was his inferior in birth and education. He was sure that he could do something better than his friend had ever done, or could ever do, something higher than mere tawdry journalism if he only got the chance. What was it that stood in his way? His unfortunate timidity! He wished to vindicate himself in some way, to assert his manhood. He saw behind Gallaher's refusal of his invitation. Gallaher was only patronising him by his friendliness just as he was patronising Ireland by his visit.

The barman brought their drinks. Little Chandler pushed one glass towards his friend and took up the other boldly.

"Who knows?" he said, as they lifted their glasses. "When you come next year I may have the pleasure of wishing long life and happiness to Mr. and Mrs. Ignatius Gallaher."

Ignatius Gallaher in the act of drinking closed one eye expressively over the rim of his glass. When he had drunk he smacked his lips decisively, set down his glass and said:

"No blooming fear of that, my boy. I'm going to have my fling first and see a bit of life and the world before I put my head in the sack—if I ever do."

"Some day you will," said Little Chandler calmly.

Ignatius Gallaher turned his orange tie and slate-blue eyes full upon his friend.

"You think so?" he said.

"You'll put your head in the sack," repeated Little Chandler stoutly, "like everyone else if you can find the girl."

He had slightly emphasised his tone and he was aware that he had betrayed himself; but, though the colour had heightened in his cheek, he did not flinch from his friend's gaze. Ignatius Gallaher watched him for a few moments and then said:

"If ever it occurs, you may bet your bottom dollar there'll be no mooning and spooning about it. I mean to marry money. She'll have a good fat account at the bank or she won't do for me."

Little Chandler shook his head.

"Why, man alive," said Ignatius Gallaher, vehemently, "do you know what it is? I've only to say the word and to-morrow I can have the woman and the cash. You don't believe it? Well, I know it. There are hundreds —what am I saying?—thousands of rich Germans and Jews, rotten with money, that'd only be too glad. . . . You wait a while, my boy. See if I don't play my cards properly. When I go about a thing I mean business, I tell you. You just wait."

He tossed his glass to his mouth, finished his drink and laughed loudly. Then he looked thoughtfully before him and said in a calmer tone:

"But I'm in no hurry. They can wait. I don't fancy tying myself to one woman, you know."

He imitated with his mouth the act of tasting and made a wry face.

"Must get a bit stale, I should think," he said.

Little Chandler sat in the room off the hall, holding a child in his arms. To save money they kept no servant but Annie's young sister Monica came for an hour or so in the morning and an hour or so in the evening to help. But Monica had gone home long ago. It was a quarter to nine. Little Chandler had come home late for tea and, moreover, he had forgotten to bring Annie home the parcel of coffee from Bewley's. Of course she was in a bad humour and gave him short answers. She said she would do without any tea but when it came near the time at which the shop at the corner closed she decided to go out herself for a quarter of a pound of tea and two pounds of sugar. She put the sleeping child deftly in his arms and said:

"Here. Don't waken him."

A little lamp with a white china shade stood upon the table and its light fell over a photograph which was enclosed in a frame of crumpled horn. It was Annie's photograph. Little Chandler looked at it, pausing at the thin tight lips. She wore the pale blue summer blouse which he had brought her home as a present one Saturday. It had cost him ten and elevenpence; but what an agony of nervousness it had cost him! How he had suffered that day, waiting at the shop door until the shop was empty, standing at the counter and trying to appear at his ease while the girl piled ladies' blouses before him, paying at the desk and forgetting to take up the odd penny of his change, being called back by the cashier, and finally, striving to hide his blushes as he left the shop by examining the parcel to see if it was securely tied. When he brought the blouse home Annie kissed him and said it was very pretty and stylish; but when she heard the price she threw the blouse on the table and said it was a regular swindle to charge ten and elevenpence for it. At first she wanted to take it back but when she tried it on she was delighted with it, especially with the make of the sleeves, and kissed him and said he was very good to think of her.

Hm! . . .

He looked coldly into the eyes of the photograph and they answered coldly. Certainly they were pretty and the face itself was pretty. But he found something mean in it. Why was it so unconscious and ladylike? The composure of the eyes irritated him. They repelled him and defied him: there was no passion in them, no rapture. He thought of what Gallaher had said about rich Jewesses. Those dark Oriental eyes, he thought, how full they are of passion, of voluptuous longing! . . . Why had he married the eyes in the photograph?

He caught himself up at the question and glanced nervously round the room. He found something mean in the pretty furniture which he had bought for his house on the hire system. Annie had chosen it herself and it reminded him of her. It too was prim and pretty. A dull resentment against his life awoke within him. Could he not escape from his little house? Was it too late for him to try to live bravely like Gallaher? Could he go to London? There was the furniture still to be paid for. If he could only write a book and get it published, that might open the way for him.

A volume of Byron's poems lay before him on the table. He opened it cautiously with his left hand lest he should waken the child and began to read the first poem in the book:

"Hushed are the winds and still the evening gloom,
Not e'en a Zephyr wanders through the grove,
Whilst I return to view my Margaret's tomb
And scatter flowers on the dust I love."

He paused. He felt the rhythm of the verse about him in the room. How melancholy it was! Could he, too, write like that, express the melancholy of his soul in verse? There were so many things he wanted to describe: his sensation of a few hours before on Grattan Bridge, for example. If he could get back again into that mood. . . .

The child awoke and began to cry. He turned from the page and tried to hush it: but it would not be hushed. He began to rock it to and fro in his arms but its wailing cry grew keener. He rocked it faster while his eyes began to read the second stanza:

"Within this narrow cell reclines her clay,
That clay where once . . ."

It was useless. He couldn't read. He couldn't do anything. The wailing of the child pierced the drum of his ear. It was useless, useless! He was a prisoner for life. His arms trembled with anger and suddenly bending to the child's face he shouted:

"Stop!"

The child stopped for an instant, had a spasm of fright and began to scream. He jumped up from his chair and walked hastily up and down the room with the child in his arms. It began to sob piteously, losing its breath for four or five seconds, and then bursting out anew. The thin walls of the room echoed the sound. He tried to soothe it but it sobbed more convulsively. He looked at the contracted and quivering face of the child and began to be alarmed. He counted seven sobs without a break between them and caught the child to his breast in fright. If it died! . . .

The door was burst open and a young woman ran in, panting.

"What is it? What is it?" she cried.

The child, hearing its mother's voice, broke out into a paroxysm of sobbing.

"It's nothing, Annie . . . it's nothing. . . . He began to cry . . ."

She flung her parcels on the floor and snatched the child from him.

"What have you done to him?" she cried, glaring into his face.

Little Chandler sustained for one moment the gaze of her eyes and his heart closed together as he met the hatred in them. He began to stammer:

"It's nothing. . . . He . . . he began to cry. . . . I couldn't . . . I didn't do anything. . . . What?"

Giving no heed to him she began to walk up and down the room, clasping the child tightly in her arms and murmuring:

"My little man! My little mannie! Was 'ou frightened, love? . . . There now, love! There now! . . . Lambabaun! Mamma's little lamb of the world! . . . There now!"

Little Chandler felt his cheeks suffused with shame and he stood back out of the lamplight. He listened while the paroxysm of the child's sobbing grew less and less; and tears of remorse started to his eyes.

JAMES JOYCE

A Painful Case

MR. JAMES DUFFY lived in Chapelizod because he wished to live as far as possible from the city of which he was a citizen and because he found all the other suburbs of Dublin mean, modern and pretentious. He lived in an old sombre house and from his windows he could look into the disused distillery or upwards along the shallow river on which Dublin is built. The lofty walls of his uncarpeted room were free from pictures. He had himself bought every article of furniture in the room: a black iron bedstead, an iron washstand, four cane chairs, a clothes-rack, a coal-scuttle, a fender and irons and a square table on which lay a double desk. A bookcase had been made in an alcove by means of shelves of white wood. The bed was clothed with white bedclothes and a black and scarlet rug covered the foot. A little hand-mirror hung above the washstand and during the day a white-shaded lamp stood as the sole ornament of the mantelpiece. The books on the white wooden shelves were arranged from below upwards according to bulk. A complete Wordsworth stood at one end of the lowest shelf and a copy of the *Maynooth Catechism,* sewn into the cloth cover of a notebook, stood at one end of the top shelf. Writing materials were always on the desk. In the desk lay a manuscript translation of Hauptmann's *Michael Kramer,* the stage directions of which were written in purple ink, and a little sheaf of papers held together by a brass pin. In these sheets a sentence was inscribed from time to time and, in an ironical moment, the headline of an advertisement for *Bile Beans* had been pasted on to the first sheet. On lifting the lid of the desk a faint fragrance escaped—the fragrance of new cedarwood pencils or of a bottle of gum or of an overripe apple which might have been left there and forgotten.

Mr. Duffy abhorred anything which betokened physical or mental disorder. A mediaeval doctor would have called him saturnine. His face, which carried the entire tale of his years, was of the brown tint of Dublin streets. On his long and rather large head grew dry black hair and a tawny moustache did not quite cover an unamiable mouth. His cheekbones also gave his face a harsh character; but there was no harshness in the eyes which, looking at the world from under their tawny eyebrows, gave the impression of a man ever alert to greet a redeeming instinct in others but often disappointed. He lived at a little distance from his body, regarding his own acts with doubtful side-glances. He had an odd autobiographical habit which led him to compose in his mind from time to time a short sentence about himself containing a subject in the third person and a predicate in the past tense. He never gave alms to beggars and walked firmly, carrying a stout hazel.

He had been for many years cashier of a private bank in Baggot Street. Every morning he came in from Chapelizod by tram. At midday he went to Dan Burke's and took his lunch—a bottle of lager beer and a small trayful of arrowroot biscuits. At four o'clock he was set free. He dined in an eating-house in George's Street where he felt himself safe from the society of Dublin's gilded youth and where there was a certain plain honesty in the bill of fare. His evenings were spent either before his landlady's piano or roaming about the outskirts of the city. His liking for Mozart's music brought him sometimes to an opera or a concert: these were the only dissipations of his life.

He had neither companions nor friends, church nor creed. He lived his spiritual life without any communion with others, visiting his relatives at Christmas and escorting them to the cemetery when they died. He performed these two social duties for old dignity's sake but conceded nothing further to the conventions which regulate the civic life. He allowed himself to think that in certain circumstances he would rob his bank but, as these circumstances never arose, his life rolled out evenly—an adventureless tale.

One evening he found himself sitting beside two ladies in the Rotunda. The house, thinly peopled and silent, gave distressing prophecy of failure. The lady who sat next him looked round at the deserted house once or twice and then said:

"What a pity there is such a poor house tonight! It's so hard on people to have to sing to empty benches."

He took the remark as an invitation to talk. He was surprised that she seemed so little awkward. While they talked he tried to fix her permanently in his memory. When he learned that the young girl besides her was her daughter he judged her to be a year or so younger than himself. Her face, which must have been handsome, had remained intelligent. It was an oval face with strongly marked features. The eyes were very dark blue and steady. Their gaze began with a defiant note but was confused by what seemed a deliberate swoon of the pupil into the iris, revealing for an instant a temperament of great sensibility. The pupil reasserted itself quickly, this half-disclosed nature fell again under the reign of prudence, and her astrakhan jacket, moulding a bosom of a certain fullness, struck the note of defiance more definitely.

He met her again a few weeks afterwards at a concert in Earlsfort Terrace and seized the moments when her daughter's attention was diverted to become intimate. She alluded once or twice to her husband but her tone was not such as to make the allusion a warning. Her name was Mrs. Sinico. Her husband's great-great-grandfather had come from Leghorn. Her husband was captain of a mercantile boat plying between Dublin and Holland; and they had one child.

Meeting her a third time by accident he found courage to make an appointment. She came. This was the first of many meetings; they met always in the evening and chose the most quiet quarters for their walks together. Mr. Duffy, however, had a distaste for underhand ways and, finding that they were compelled to meet stealthily, he forced her to ask him to her house. Captain Sinico encouraged his visits, thinking that his daughter's hand was in question. He had dismissed his wife so sincerely from his gallery of pleasures that he did not suspect that anyone else would take an interest in her. As the husband was often away and the daughter out giving music lessons Mr. Duffy had many opportunities of enjoying the lady's society. Neither he nor she had had any such adventure before and neither was conscious of any incongruity. Little by little he entangled his thoughts with hers. He lent her books, provided her with ideas, shared his intellectual life with her. She listened to all.

Sometimes in return for his theories she gave out some fact of her own life. With almost maternal solicitude she urged him to let his nature open to the full: she became his confessor. He told her that for some time he had assisted at the meetings of an Irish Socialist Party where he had felt himself a unique figure amidst a score of sober workmen in a garret lit by an inefficient oil-lamp. When the party had divided into three sections, each under its own leader and in its own garret, he had discontinued his attendances. The workmen's discussions, he said, were too timorous; the interest they took in the question of wages was inordinate. He felt that they were hard-featured realists and that they resented an exactitude which was the produce of a leisure not within their reach. No social revolution, he told her, would be likely to strike Dublin for some centuries.

She asked him why did he not write out his thoughts. For what, he asked her, with careful scorn. To compete with phrasemongers, incapable of thinking consecutively for sixty seconds? To submit himself to the criticisms of an obtuse middle class which entrusted its morality to policemen and its fine arts to impresarios?

He went often to her little cottage outside Dublin; often they spent their evenings alone. Little by little, as their thoughts entangled, they spoke of subjects less remote. Her companionship was like a warm soil about an exotic. Many times she allowed the dark to fall upon them, refraining from lighting the lamp. The dark discreet room, their isolation, the music that still vibrated in their ears united them. This union exalted him, wore away the rough edges of his character, emotionalised his mental life. Sometimes he caught himself listening to the sound of his own voice. He thought that in her eyes he would ascend to an angelical stature; and, as he attached the fervent nature of his companion more and more closely to him, he heard the strange impersonal voice which he recognised as his own, insisting on the soul's incurable loneliness. We cannot give ourselves, it said: we are our own. The end of these discourses was that one night during which she had shown every sign of unusual excitement, Mrs. Sinico caught up his hand passionately and pressed it to her cheek.

Mr. Duffy was very much surprised. Her interpretation of his words disillusioned him. He did not visit her for a week; then he wrote to her asking her to meet him. As he did not wish their last interview to be troubled by the influence of their ruined confessional they met in a little cakeshop near the Parkgate. It was cold autumn weather but in spite of the cold they wandered up and down the roads of the Park for nearly three hours. They agreed to break off their intercourse: every bond, he said, is a bond to sorrow. When they came out of the Park they walked in silence towards the tram; but here she began to tremble so violently that, fearing another collapse on her part, he bade her good-bye quickly and left her. A few days later he received a parcel containing his books and music.

Four years passed. Mr. Duffy returned to his even way of life. His room still bore witness of the orderliness of his mind. Some new pieces of music encumbered the music-stand in the lower room and on his shelves stood two volumes by Nietzsche: *Thus Spake Zarathustra* and *The Gay Science*. He wrote seldom in the sheaf of papers which lay in his desk. One of his sentences, written two months after his last interview with Mrs. Sinico, read: Love between man and man is impossible because there must not be sexual intercourse and friendship between man and woman is impossible because there must be sexual intercourse. He kept away from concerts lest he should meet her. His father died; the junior partner of the bank retired. And still every morning he went into the city by tram and every evening walked home from the city after having dined moderately in George's Street and read the evening paper for dessert.

One evening as he was about to put a morsel of corned beef and cabbage into his mouth his hand stopped. His eyes fixed themselves on a paragraph in the evening paper which he had propped against the water-carafe. He replaced the morsel of food on his plate and read the paragraph attentively. Then he drank a glass of water, pushed his plate to one side, doubled the paper down before him between his elbows and read the paragraph over and over again. The cabbage began to deposit a cold white grease on his plate. The girl came over to him to ask was his dinner not properly cooked. He said it was very good and ate a few mouthfuls of it with difficulty. Then he paid his bill and went out.

He walked along quickly through the November twilight, his stout hazel stick striking the ground regularly, the fringe of the buff *Mail* peeping out of a side-pocket of his tight reefer overcoat. On the lonely road which leads from the Parkgate to Chapelizod he slackened his pace. His stick struck the ground less emphatically and his breath, issuing irregularly, almost with a sighing sound, condensed in the wintry air. When he reached his house he went up at once to his bedroom and, taking the paper from his pocket, read the paragraph again by the failing light of the window. He read it not aloud, but moving his lips as a priest does when he reads the prayers *Secreto*. This was the paragraph:

DEATH OF A LADY AT SYDNEY PARADE

A PAINFUL CASE

To-day at the City of Dublin Hospital the Deputy Coroner (in the absence of Mr. Leverett) held an inquest on the body of Mrs. Emily Sinico, aged forty-three years, who was killed at Sydney Parade Station yesterday evening. The evidence showed that the deceased lady, while attempting to cross the line, was knocked down by the engine of the ten o'clock slow train from Kingstown, thereby sustaining injuries of the head and right side which led to her death.

James Lennon, driver of the engine, stated that he had been in the employment of the railway company for fifteen years. On hearing the guard's whistle he set the train in motion and a second or two afterwards brought it to rest in response to loud cries. The train was going slowly.

P. Dunne, railway porter, stated that as the train was about to start he observed a woman attempting to cross the lines. He ran towards her and shouted, but, before he could reach her, she was caught by the buffer of the engine and fell to the ground.

A juror. "You saw the lady fall?"

Witness. "Yes."

Police Sergeant Croly deposed that when he arrived he found the deceased lying on the platform apparently dead. He had the body taken to the waiting-room pending the arrival of the ambulance.

Constable 57E corroborated.

Dr. Halpin, assistant house surgeon of the City of Dublin Hospital, stated that the deceased had two lower ribs fractured and had sustained severe contusions of the right shoulder. The right side of the head had been injured in the fall. The injuries were not sufficient to have caused death in a normal person. Death, in his opinion, had been probably due to shock and sudden failure of the heart's action.

Mr. H. B. Patterson Finlay, on behalf of the railway company, expressed his deep regret at the accident. The company had always taken every precaution to prevent people crossing the lines except by the bridges, both by placing notices in every station and by the use of patent spring gates at level crossings. The deceased had been in the habit of crossing the lines late at night from platform to platform and, in view of certain other circumstances of the case, he did not think the railway officials were to blame.

Captain Sinico, of Leoville, Sydney Parade, husband of the deceased, also gave evidence. He stated that the deceased was his wife. He was not in Dublin at the time of the accident as he had arrived only that morning from Rotterdam. They had been married for twenty-two years and had lived happily until about two years ago when his wife began to be rather intemperate in her habits.

Miss Mary Sinico said that of late her mother had been in the habit of going out at night to buy spirits. She, witness, had often tried to reason with her mother and had induced her to join a League. She was not at home until an hour after the accident.

The jury returned a verdict in accordance with the medical evidence and exonerated Lennon from all blame.

The Deputy Coroner said it was a most painful case, and expressed great sympathy with Captain Sinico and his daughter. He urged on the railway company to take strong measures to prevent the possibility of similar accidents in the future. No blame attached to anyone.

Mr. Duffy raised his eyes from the paper and gazed out of his window on the cheerless evening landscape. The river lay quiet beside the empty distillery and from time to time a light appeared in some house on the Lucan road. What an end! The whole narrative of her death revolted him and it revolted him to think that he had ever spoken to her of what he held sacred. The threadbare phrases, the inane expressions of sympathy, the cautious words of a reporter won over to conceal the details of a commonplace vulgar death attacked his stomach. Not merely had she degraded herself; she had degraded him. He saw the squalid tract of her vice, miserable and malodorous. His soul's companion! He thought of the hobbling wretches whom he had seen carrying cans and bottles to be filled by the barman. Just God, what an end. Evidently she had been unfit to live, without any strength of purpose, an easy prey to habits, one of the wrecks on which civilisation has been reared. But that she could have sunk so low! Was it possible he had deceived himself so utterly about her? He remembered her outburst of that night and interpreted it in a harsher sense than he had ever done. He had no difficulty now in approving of the course he had taken.

As the light failed and his memory began to wander he thought her hand touched his. The shock which had first attacked his stomach was now attacking his nerves. He put on his overcoat and hat quickly and went out. The cold air met him on the threshold; it crept into the sleeves of his coat. When he came to the public-house at Chapelizod Bridge he went in and ordered a hot punch.

The proprietor served him obsequiously but did not venture to talk. There were five or six workingmen in the shop discussing the value of a gentleman's estate in County Kildare. They drank at intervals from their huge pint tumblers and smoked, spitting often on the floor and sometimes dragging the sawdust over their spits with their heavy boots. Mr. Duffy sat on his stool and gazed at them, without seeing or hearing them. After a while they went out and he called for another punch. He sat a long time over it. The shop was very quiet. The proprietor sprawled on the counter reading the *Herald* and yawning. Now and again a tram was heard swishing along the lonely road outside.

As he sat there, living over his life with her and evoking alternately the two images in which he now conceived her, he realised that she was dead, that she had ceased to exist, that she had become a memory. He began to feel ill at ease. He asked himself what else could he have done. He could not have carried on a comedy of deception with her; he could not have lived with her openly. He had done what seemed to him best. How was he to blame? Now that she was gone he understood how lonely her life must have been, sitting night after night alone in that room. His life would be lonely too until he, too, died, ceased to exist, became a memory—if anyone remembered him.

It was after nine o'clock when he left the shop. The night was cold and gloomy. He entered the Park by the first gate and walked along under the gaunt trees. He walked through the bleak alleys where they had walked four years before. She seemed to be near him in the darkness. At moments he seemed to feel her voice touch his ear, her hand touch his. He stood still to listen. Why had he withheld life from her? Why had he sentenced her to death? He felt his moral nature falling to pieces.

When he gained the crest of the Magazine Hill he halted and looked along the river towards Dublin, the lights of which burned redly and hospitably in the cold night. He looked down the slope and, at the base, in the shadow of the wall of the Park, he saw some human figures lying. Those venal and furtive loves filled him with despair. He gnawed the rectitude of his life; he felt that he had been outcast from life's feast. One human being had seemed to love him and he had denied her life and happiness: he had sentenced her to ignominy, a death of shame. He knew that the prostrate creatures down by the wall were watching him and wished him gone. No one wanted him; he was outcast from life's feast. He turned his eyes to the grey gleaming river, winding along towards Dublin. Beyond the river he saw a goods train winding out of Kingsbridge Station, like a worm with a fiery head winding through the darkness, obstinately and laboriously. It passed slowly out of sight; but still he heard in his ears the laborious drone of the engine reiterating the syllables of her name.

He turned back the way he had come, the rhythm of the engine pounding in his ears. He began to doubt the reality of what memory told him. He halted under a tree and allowed the rhythm to die away. He could not feel her near him in the darkness nor her voice touch his ear. He waited for some minutes listening. He could hear nothing: the night was perfectly silent. He listened again: perfectly silent. He felt that he was alone.

KATHERINE MANSFIELD

The Garden Party uses...

See what's happening by seeing everything through the eyes of a girl. it follows Laura's pt. of view. not a camera eye. See her impressions

AND AFTER all the weather was ideal. They could not have had a more perfect day for a garden-party if they had ordered it. Windless, warm, the sky without a cloud. Only the blue was veiled with a haze of light gold, as it is sometimes in early summer. The gardener had been up since dawn, mowing the lawns and sweeping them, until the grass and the dark flat rosettes where the daisy plants had been seemed to shine. As for the roses, you could not help feeling they understood that roses are the only flowers that impress people at garden parties; the only flowers that everybody is certain of knowing. Hundreds, yes, literally hundreds, had come out in a single night; the green bushes bowed down as though they had been visited by archangels.

Breakfast was not yet over before the men came to put up the marquee.

"Where do you want the marquee put, mother?"

"My dear child, it's no use asking me. I'm determined to leave everything to you children this year. Forget I am your mother. Treat me as an honoured guest."

But Meg could not possibly go and supervise the men. She had washed her hair before breakfast, and she sat drinking her coffee in a green turban, with a dark wet curl stamped on each cheek. Jose, the butterfly, always came down in a silk petticoat and a kimono jacket.

"You'll have to go, Laura; you're the artistic one."

Away Laura flew, still holding her piece of bread-and-butter. It's so delicious to have an excuse for eating out of doors, and besides, she loved having to arrange things; she always felt she could do it so much better than anybody else.

Four men in their shirt-sleeves stood grouped together on the garden path. They carried staves covered with rolls of canvas, and they had big toolbags slung on their backs. They looked impressive. Laura wished now that she had not got the bread-and-butter, but there was nowhere to put it, and she couldn't possibly throw it away. She blushed and tried to look severe and even a little bit short-sighted as she came up to them.

"Good Morning," she said, copying her mother's voice. But that sounded so fearfully affected that she was ashamed, and stammered like a little girl, "Oh—er—have you come—is it about the marquee?"

"That's right, miss," said the tallest of the men, a lanky, freckled fellow, and he shifted his tool-bag, knocked back his straw hat and smiled down at her. "That's about it."

His smile was so easy, so friendly that Laura recovered. What nice eyes he had, small, but such a dark blue! And now she looked at the others, they were smiling too. "Cheer up, we won't bite," their smile seemed to say. How very nice workmen were! And what a beautiful morning! She mustn't mention the morning; she must be business-like. The marquee.

"Well, what about the lily-lawn? Would that do?"

And she pointed to the lily-lawn with the hand that didn't hold the bread-and-butter. They turned, they stared in the direction. A little fat chap thrust out his under-lip, and the tall fellow frowned.

"I don't fancy it," said he. "Not conspicuous enough. You see, with a thing like a marquee," and he turned to Laura in his easy way, "you want to put it somewhere

where it'll give you a bang slap in the eye, if you follow me."

Laura's upbringing made her wonder for a moment whether it was quite respectful of a workman to talk to her of bangs slap in the eye. But she did quite follow him.

"A corner of the tennis-court," she suggested. "But the band's going to be in one corner."

"H'm, going to have a band, are you?" said another of the workmen. He was pale. He had a haggard look as his dark eyes scanned the tennis-court. What was he thinking?

"Only a very small band," said Laura gently. Perhaps he wouldn't mind so much if the band was quite small. But the tall fellow interrupted.

"Look here, miss, that's the place. Against those trees. Over there. That'll do fine."

Against the karakas. Then the karaka-trees would be hidden. And they were so lovely, with their broad, gleaming leaves, and their clusters of yellow fruit. They were like trees you imagined growing on a desert island, proud, solitary, lifting their leaves and fruits to the sun in a kind of silent splendour. Must they be hidden by a marquee?

They must. Already the men had shouldered their staves and were making for the place. Only the tall fellow was left. He bent down, pinched a sprig of lavender, put his thumb and forefinger to his nose and snuffed up the smell. When Laura saw that gesture she forgot all about the karakas in her wonder at him caring for things like that—caring for the smell of lavender. How many men that she knew would have done such a thing? Oh, how extraordinarily nice workmen were, she thought. Why couldn't she have workmen for friends rather than the silly boys she danced with and who came to Sunday night supper? She would get on much better with men like these.

It's all the fault, she decided, as the tall fellow drew something on the back of an envelope, something that was to be looped up or left to hang, of these absurd class distinctions. Well, for her part, she didn't feel them. Not a bit, not an atom. . . . And now there came the chock-chock of wooden hammers. Some one whistled, some one sang out, "Are you right there, matey?" "Matey!" The friendliness of it, the—the——Just to prove how happy she was, just to show the tall fellow how at home she felt, and how she despised stupid conventions, Laura took a big bite of her bread-and-butter as she stared at the little drawing. She felt just like a work-girl.

"Laura, Laura, where are you? Telephone, Laura!" a voice cried from the house.

"Coming!" Away she skimmed, over the lawn, up the path, up the steps, across the veranda, and into the porch. In the hall her father and Laurie were brushing their hats ready to go to the office.

"I say, Laura," said Laurie very fast, "you might just give a squiz at my coat before this afternoon. See if it wants pressing."

"I will," said she. Suddenly she couldn't stop herself. She ran at Laurie and gave him a small quick squeeze. "Oh, I do love parties, don't you?" gasped Laura.

"Ra-ther," said Laurie's warm, boyish voice, and he squeezed his sister too, and gave her a gentle push. "Dash off to the telephone, old girl."

The telephone. "Yes, yes; oh yes. Kitty? Good morning, dear. Come to lunch? Do, dear. Delighted of course. It will only be a very scratch meal—just the sandwich crusts and broken meringue-shells and what's left over. Yes, isn't it a perfect morning? Your white? Oh, I certainly should. One moment—hold the line. Mother's calling." And Laura sat back. "What, Mother? Can't hear."

Mrs. Sheridan's voice floated down the stairs. "Tell her to wear that sweet hat she had on last Sunday."

"Mother says you're to wear that *sweet* hat you had on last Sunday. Good. One o'clock. Bye-bye."

Laura put back the receiver, flung her arms over her head, took a deep breath, stretched and let them fall. "Huh," she sighed, and the moment after the sigh she sat up quickly. She was still, listening. All the doors in the house seemed to be open. The house was alive with soft, quick steps and running voices. The green baize door that led to the kitchen regions swung open and shut with a muffled thud. And now there came a long, chuckling absurd sound. It was the heavy piano being moved on its stiff castors. But the air! If you stopped to notice, was the air always like this? Little faint winds were playing chase, in at the tops of the windows, out at the doors. And there were two tiny spots of sun, one on the inkpot, one on a silver photograph frame, playing too. Darling little spots. Especially the one on the the inkpot lid. It was quite warm. A warm little silver star. She could have kissed it.

The front door bell pealed, and there sounded the rustle of Sadie's print skirt on the stairs. A man's voice murmured; Sadie answered, careless, "I'm sure I don't know. Wait. I'll ask Mrs. Sheridan."

"What is it, Sadie?" Laura came into the hall.

"It's the florist, Miss Laura."

It was, indeed. There, just inside the door, stood a wide shallow tray full of pots of pink lilies. No other kind. Nothing but lilies—canna lilies, big pink flowers, wide open, radiant, almost frighteningly alive on bright crimson stems.

"O-oh, Sadie!" said Laura, and the sound was like a little moan. She crouched down as if to warm herself at that blaze of lilies; she felt they were in her fingers, on her lips, growing in her breast.

"It's some mistake," she said faintly. "Nobody ever ordered so many. Sadie, go and find mother."

But at that moment Mrs. Sheridan joined them.

"It's quite right," she said calmly. "Yes, I ordered them.

Aren't they lovely?" She pressed Laura's arm. "I was passing the shop yesterday, and I saw them in the window. And I suddenly thought for once in my life I shall have enough canna lilies. The garden-party will be a good excuse."

"But I thought you said you didn't mean to interfere," said Laura. Sadie had gone. The florist's man was still outside at his van. She put her arm round her mother's neck and gently, very gently, she bit her mother's ear.

"My darling child, you wouldn't like a logical mother, would you? Don't do that. Here's the man."

He carried more lilies still, another whole tray.

"Bank them up, just inside the door, on both sides of the porch, please," said Mrs. Sheridan. "Don't you agree, Laura?"

"Oh, I *do,* mother."

In the drawing-room Meg, Jose and good little Hans had at last succeeded in moving the piano.

"Now, if we put this chesterfield against the wall and move everything out of the room except the chairs, don't you think?"

"Quite."

"Hans, move these tables into the smoking-room, and bring a sweeper to take these marks off the carpet and—one moment, Hans——" Jose loved giving orders to the servants, and they loved obeying her. She always made them feel they were taking part in some drama. "Tell mother and Miss Laura to come here at once."

"Very good, Miss Jose."

She turned to Meg. "I want to hear what the piano sounds like, just in case I'm asked to sing this afternoon. Let's try over 'This life is Weary.' "

Pom! Ta-ta-ta *Tee-* ta! The piano burst out so passionately that Jose's face changed. She clasped her hands. She looked mournfully and enigmatically at her mother and Laura as they came in.

This Life is *Wee*-ary,
A Tear—a Sigh.
A Love that *Chan*-ges,
This Life is *Wee*-ary,
A Tear—a Sigh.
A Love that *Chan*-ges,
And then . . . Good-bye!

But at the word "Good-bye," and although the piano sounded more desperate than ever, her face broke into a brilliant, dreadfully unsympathetic smile.

"Aren't I in good voice, mummy?" she beamed.

This Life is *Wee*-ary,
Hope comes to Die.
A Dream—a *Wa*-kening.

But now Sadie interrupted them. "What is it, Sadie?"

"If you please, m'm, cook says have you got the flags for the sandwiches?"

"The flags for the sandwiches, Sadie?" echoed Mrs. Sheridan dreamily. And the children knew by her face that she hadn't got them. "Let me see." And she said to Sadie firmly, "Tell cook I'll let her have them in ten minutes."

Sadie went.

"Now Laura," said her mother quickly. "Come with me into the smoking-room. I've got the names somewhere on the back of an envelope. You'll have to write them out for me. Meg, go upstairs this minute and take that wet thing off your head. Jose, run and finish dressing this instant. Do you hear me, children, or shall I have to tell your father when he comes home to-night? And—and, Jose, pacify cook if you do go into the kitchen, will you? I'm terrified of her this morning."

The envelope was found at last behind the dining-room clock, though how it got there Mrs. Sheridan could not imagine.

"One of you children must have stolen it out of my bag, because I remember vividly—cream cheese and lemon-curd. Have you done that?"

"Yes."

"Egg and——" Mrs. Sheridan held the envelope away from her. "It looks like mice. It can't be mice, can it?"

"Olive, pet," said Laura, looking over her shoulder.

"Yes, of course, olive. What a horrible combination it sounds. Egg and olive."

They were finished at last, and Laura took them off to the kitchen. She found Jose there pacifying the cook, who did not look at all terrifying.

"I have never seen such exquisite sandwiches," said Jose's rapturous voice. "How many kinds did you say there were, cook? Fifteen?"

"Fifteen, Miss Jose."

"Well, cook, I congratulate you."

Cook swept up crusts with a long sandwich knife, and smiled broadly.

"Godber's has come," announced Sadie, issuing out of the pantry. She had seen the man pass the window.

That meant the cream puffs had come. Godber's were famous for their cream puffs. Nobody ever thought of making them at home.

"Bring them in and put them on the table, my girl," ordered cook.

Sadie brought them in and went back to the door. Of course Laura and Jose were far too grown-up to really care about such things. All the same, they couldn't help agreeing that the puffs looked very attractive. Very. Cook began arranging them, shaking off the extra icing sugar.

"Don't they carry one back to all one's parties?" said Laura.

"I suppose they do," said practical Jose, who never liked to be carried back. "They look beautifully light and feathery, I must say."

"Have one each, my dears," said cook in her comfortable voice. "Yer ma won't know."

Oh, impossible. Fancy cream puffs so soon after breakfast. The very idea made one shudder. All the same, two minutes later Jose and Laura were licking their fingers with that absorbed inward look that only comes from whipped cream.

"Let's go into the garden, out by the back way," suggested Laura. "I want to see how the men are getting on with the marquee. They're such awfully nice men."

But the back door was blocked by cook, Sadie, Godber's man and Hans.

Something had happened.

"Tuk-tuk-tuk," clucked cook like an agitated hen. Sadie had her hand clapped to her cheek as though she had toothache. Hans's face was screwed up in the effort to understand. Only Godber's man seemed to be enjoying himself; it was his story.

"What's the matter? What's happened?"

"There's been a horrible accident," said Cook. "A man killed."

"A man killed! Where? How? When?"

But Godber's man wasn't going to have his story snatched from under his very nose.

"Know those little cottages just below here, miss?" Know them? Of course, she knew them. "Well, there's a young chap living there, name of Scott, a carter. His horse shied at a traction-engine, corner of Hawke Street this morning, and he was thrown out on the back of his head. Killed."

"Dead!" Laura stared at Godber's man.

"Dead when they picked him up," said Godber's man with relish. "They were taking the body home as I come up here." And he said to the cook, "He's left a wife and five little ones."

"Jose, come here." Laura caught hold of her sister's sleeve and dragged her through the kitchen to the other side of the green baize door. There she paused and leaned against it. "Jose!" she said, horrified, "however are we going to stop everything?"

"Stop everything, Laura!" cried Jose in astonishment. "What do you mean?"

"Stop the garden party, of course." Why did Jose pretend?

But Jose was still more amazed. "Stop the garden party? My dear Laura, don't be so absurd. Of course we can't do anything of the kind. Nobody expects us to. Don't be so extravagant."

"But we can't possibly have a garden party with a man dead just outside the front gate."

That really was extravagant, for the little cottages were in a lane to themselves at the very bottom of a steep rise that led up to the house. A broad road ran between. True, they were far too near. They were the greatest possible eyesore, and they had no right to be in that neighbourhood at all. They were little mean dwellings painted a chocolate brown. In the garden patches there was nothing but cabbage stalks, sick hens and tomato cans. The very smoke coming out of their chimneys was poverty-stricken. Little rags and shreds of smoke, so unlike the great silvery plumes that uncurled from the Sheridans' chimneys. Washer-women lived in the lane and sweeps and a cobbler, and a man whose house-front was studded all over with minute bird-cages. Children swarmed. When the Sheridans were little they were forbidden to set foot there because of the revolting language and of what they might catch. But since they were grown up, Laura and Laurie on their prowls sometimes walked through. It was disgusting and sordid. They came out with a shudder. But still one must go everywhere; one must see everything. So through they went.

"And just think of what the band would sound like to that poor woman," said Laura.

"Oh, Laura!" Jose began to be seriously annoyed. "If you're going to stop a band playing every time some one has an accident, you'll lead a very strenuous life. I'm every bit as sorry about it as you. I feel just as sympathetic." Her eyes hardened. She looked at her sister just as she used to when they were little and fighting together. "You won't bring a drunken workman back to life by being sentimental," she said softly.

"Drunk! Who said he was drunk?" Laura turned furiously on Jose. She said, just as they had used to say on those occasions, "I'm going straight up to tell mother."

"Do, dear," cooed Jose.

"Mother, can I come into your room?" Laura turned the big glass door-knob.

"Of course, child. Why, what's the matter? What's given you such a colour?" And Mrs. Sheridan turned round from her dressing-table. She was trying on a new hat.

"Mother, a man's been killed," began Laura.

"*Not* in the garden?" interrupted her mother.

"No no!"

"Oh, what a fright you gave me!" Mrs. Sheridan sighed with relief, and took off the big hat and held it on her knees.

"But listen, mother," said Laura. Breathless, half-choking, she told the dreadful story. "Of course, we can't have our party, can we?" she pleaded. "The band and everybody arriving. They'd hear us, mother; they're nearly neighbours!"

To Laura's astonishment her mother behaved just like Jose; it was harder to bear because she seemed amused. She refused to take Laura seriously.

"But, my dear child, use your common sense. It's only by accident we've heard of it. If some one had died there normally—and I can't understand how they keep alive in those poky little holes—we should still be having our party, shouldn't we?"

Laura had to say "yes" to that, but she felt it was all wrong. She sat down on her mother's sofa and pinched the cushion frill.

"Mother, isn't it really terribly heartless of us?" she asked.

"Darling!" Mrs. Sheridan got up and came over to her, carrying the hat. Before Laura could stop her she had popped it on. "My child!" said her mother, "the hat is yours. It's made for you. It's much too young for me. I have never seen you look such a picture. Look at yourself!" And she held up her hand-mirror.

"But, mother," Laura began again. She couldn't look at herself; she turned aside.

This time Mrs. Sheridan lost patience just as Jose had done.

"You are being very absurd, Laura," she said coldly. "People like that don't expect sacrifices from us. And it's not very sympathetic to spoil everybody's enjoyment as you're doing now."

"I don't understand," said Laura, and she walked quickly out of the room into her own bedroom. There, quite by chance, the first thing she saw was this charming girl in the mirror, in her black hat trimmed with gold daisies, and a long black velvet ribbon. Never had she imagined she could look like that. Is mother right? she thought. And now she hoped her mother was right. Am I being extravagant? Perhaps it was extravagant. Just for a moment she had another glimpse of that poor woman and those little children, and the body being carried into the house. But it all seemed blurred, unreal, like a picture in the newspaper. I'll remember it again after the party's over, she decided. And somehow that seemed quite the best plan. . . .

Lunch was over by half-past one. By half-past two they were all ready for the fray. The green-coated band had arrived and was established in a corner of the tennis-court.

"My dear!" trilled Kitty Maitland, "aren't they too like frogs for words? You ought to have arranged them round the pond with the conductor in the middle on a leaf."

Laurie arrived and hailed them on his way to dress. At the sight of him Laura remembered the accident again. She wanted to tell him. If Laurie agreed with the others, then it was bound to be all right. And she followed him into the hall.

"Laurie!"

"Hallo!" He was half-way upstairs, but when he turned round and saw Laura he suddenly puffed out his cheeks and goggled his eyes at her. "My word, Laura! You do look stunning," said Laurie. "What an absolutely topping hat!"

Laura said faintly "Is it?" and smiled up at Laurie, and didn't tell him after all.

Soon after that people began coming in streams. The band struck up; the hired waiters ran from the house to the marquee. Wherever you looked there were couples strolling, bending to the flowers, greeting, moving on over the lawn. They were like bright birds that had alighted in the Sheridan's garden for this one afternoon, on their way to—where? Ah, what happiness it is to be with people who all are happy, to press hands, press cheeks, smile into eyes.

"Darling Laura, how well you look!"

"What a becoming hat, child!"

"Laura, you look quite Spanish. I've never seen you look so striking."

And Laura, glowing, answered softly, "Have you had tea? Won't you have an ice? The passion-fruit ices really are rather special." She ran to her father and begged him. "Daddy darling, can't the band have something to drink?"

And the perfect afternoon slowly ripened, slowly faded, slowly its petals closed.

"Never a more delightful garden party . . ."

"The greatest success . . ." "Quite the most . . ."

Laura helped her mother with the good-byes. They stood side by side in the porch till it was all over.

"All over, all over, thank heaven," said Mrs. Sheridan. "Round up the others, Laura. Let's go and have some fresh coffee. I'm exhausted. Yes, it's been very successful. But oh, these parties, these parties! Why will you children insist on giving parties!" And they all of them sat down in the deserted marquee.

"Have a sandwich, daddy dear. I wrote the flag."

"Thanks," Mr. Sheridan took a bite and the sandwich was gone. He took another. "I suppose you didn't hear of a beastly accident that happened to-day?" he said.

"My dear," said Mrs. Sheridan, holding up her hand, "we did. It nearly ruined the party, Laura insisted we should put it off."

"Oh, mother!" Laura didn't want to be teased about it.

"It was a horrible affair all the same," said Mr. Sheridan. "The chap was married too. Lived just below in the lane, and leaves a wife and half a dozen kiddies, so they say."

An awkward little silence fell. Mrs. Sheridan fidgeted with her cup. Really, it was very tactless of father . . .

Suddenly she looked up. There on the table were all those sandwiches, cakes, puffs, all uneaten, all going to be wasted. She had one of her brilliant ideas.

"I know," she said. "Let's make up a basket. Let's send that poor creature some of this perfectly good food. At any rate, it will be the greatest treat for the children. Don't you agree? And she's sure to have neighbours calling in and so on. What a point to have it all ready prepared. Laura!" She jumped up. "Get me the big basket out of the stairs cupboard."

"But mother, do you really think it's a good idea?" said Laura.

Again, how curious, she seemed to be different from them all. To take scraps from their party. Would the poor woman really like that?

"Of course! What's the matter with you to-day? An hour or two ago you were insisting on us being sympathetic, and now——"

Oh, well! Laura ran for the basket. It was filled, it was heaped by her mother.

"Take it yourself, darling," said she. "Run down just as you are. No, wait, take the arum lilies too. People of that class are so impressed by arum lilies."

"The stems will ruin her lace frock," said practical Jose.

So they would. Just in time. "Only the basket, then. And, Laura!"—her mother followed her out of the marquee—"don't on any account——"

"What, mother?"

No, better not put such ideas into the child's head! "Nothing! Run along."

It was just growing dusky as Laura shut their garden gates. A big dog ran by like a shadow. The road gleamed white, and down below in the hollow the little cottages were in deep shade. How quiet it seemed after the afternoon. Here she was going down the hill to somewhere where a man lay dead, and she couldn't realize it. Why couldn't she? She stopped a minute. And it seemed to her that kisses, voices, tinkling spoons, laughter, the smell of crushed grass were somehow inside her. She had no room for anything else. How strange! She looked up at the pale sky, and all she thought was, "Yes, it was the most successful party."

Now the broad road was crossed. The lane began, smoky and dark. Women in shawls and men's tweed caps hurried by. Men hung over the palings; the children played in the doorways. A low hum came from the mean little cottages. In some of them there was a flicker of light, and a shadow, crab-like, moved across the window. Laura bent her head and hurried on. She wished now she had put on a coat. How her frock shone! And the big hat with the velvet streamer—if only it was another hat! Were the people looking at her? They must be. It was a mistake to have come; she knew all along it was a mistake. Should she go back even now?

No, too late. This was the house. It must be. A dark knot of people stood outside. Beside the gate an old, old woman with a crutch sat in a chair, watching. She had her feet on a newspaper. The voices stopped as Laura drew near. The group parted. It was as though she was expected, as though they had known she was coming here.

Laura was terribly nervous. Tossing the velvet ribbon over her shoulder, she said to a woman standing by, "Is this Mrs. Scott's house?" and the woman, smiling queerly, said, "It is, my lass."

Oh, to be away from this! She actually said, "Help me God," as she walked up the tiny path and knocked. To be away from those staring eyes, or to be covered up in anything, one of those women's shawls even. I'll just leave the basket and go, she decided. I shan't even wait for it to be emptied.

Then the door opened. A little woman in black showed in the gloom.

Laura said, "Are you Mrs. Scott?" But to her horror the woman answered, "Walk in please, miss," and she was shut in the passage.

"No," said Laura, "I don't want to come in. I only want to leave this basket. Mother sent——"

The little woman in the gloomy passage seemed not to have heard her. "Step this way, please, miss," she said in an oily voice, and Laura followed her.

She found herself in a wretched little low kitchen, lighted by a smoky lamp. There was a woman sitting before the fire.

"Em," said the little creature who had let her in. "Em! It's a young lady." She turned to Laura. She said meaningly, "I'm 'er sister, Miss. You'll excuse 'er, won't you?"

"Oh, but of course!" said Laura. "Please, please don't disturb her. I—I only want to leave——"

But at that moment the woman at the fire turned round. Her face, puffed up, red, with swollen eyes and swollen lips, looked terrible. She seemed as though she couldn't understand why Laura was there. What did it mean? Why was this stranger standing in the kitchen with a basket? What was it all about? And the poor face puckered up again.

"All right, my dear," said the other. "I'll thenk the young lady."

And again she began, "You'll excuse her, miss, I'm sure," and her face, swollen too, tried an oily smile.

Laura only wanted to get out, to get away. She was back in the passage. The door opened. She walked straight through into the bedroom, where the dead man was lying.

"You'd like a look at 'im, wouldn't you?" said Em's sister, and she brushed past Laura over to the bed. "Don't be afraid, my lass,—" and now her voice sounded fond and sly, and fondly she drew down the sheet—" 'e looks a picture. There's nothing to show. Come along, my dear."

Laura came.

There lay a young man, fast asleep—sleeping so soundly, so deeply, that he was far, far away from them both. Oh, so remote, so peaceful. He was dreaming. Never wake him up again. His head was sunk in the pillow, his eyes were closed; they were blind under the closed eyelids. He was given up to his dream. What did garden-parties and baskets and lace frocks matter to him? He was far from all those things. He was wonderful, beautiful. While they were laughing and while the band was playing, this marvel had come to the lane. Happy . . . happy. . . . All is well, said that sleeping face. This is just as it should be. I am content.

But all the same you had to cry, and she couldn't go out of the room without saying something to him. Laura gave a loud childish sob.

"Forgive my hat," she said.

And this time she didn't wait for Em's sister. She found her way out of the door, down the path, past all those dark people. At the corner of the lane she met Laurie.

He stepped out of the shadow. "Is that you, Laura?"

"Yes."

"Mother was getting anxious. Was it all right?"

"Yes, quite. Oh, Laurie!" She took his arm, she pressed up against him.

"I say, you're not crying, are you?" asked her brother.

Laura shook her head. She was.

Laurie put his arm round her shoulder. "Don't cry," he said in his warm, loving voice. "Was it awful?"

"No," sobbed Laura. "It was simply marvellous. But, Laurie——" She stopped, she looked at her brother. "Isn't life," she stammered, "isn't life——" But what life was she couldn't explain. No matter. He quite understood.

"*Isn't* it, darling?" said Laurie.

KATHERINE MANSFIELD

Her First Ball

Exactly when the ball began Leila would have found it hard to say. Perhaps her first real partner was the cab. It did not matter that she shared the cab with the Sheridan girls and their brother. She sat back in her own little corner of it, and the bolster on which her hand rested felt like the sleeve of an unknown young man's dress suit; and away they bowled, past waltzing lamp-posts and houses and fences and trees.

"Have you really never been to a ball before, Leila? But, my child, how too weird——" cried the Sheridan girls.

"Our nearest neighbour was fifteen miles," said Leila softly, gently opening and shutting her fan.

Oh, dear, how hard it was to be indifferent like the others! She tried not to smile too much; she tried not to care. But every single thing was so new and exciting . . . Meg's tuberoses, Jose's long loop of amber, Laura's little dark head, pushing above her white fur like a flower through snow. She would remember for ever. It even gave her a pang to see her cousin Laurie throw away the wisps of tissue paper he pulled from the fastenings of his new gloves. She would like to have kept those wisps as a keepsake, as a remembrance. Laurie leaned forward and put his hand on Laura's knee.

"Look here, darling," he said. "The third and the ninth as usual. Twig?"

Oh, how marvellous to have a brother! In her excitement Leila felt that if there had been time, if it hadn't been impossible, she couldn't have helped crying because she was an only child, and no brother had ever said "Twig?" to her; no sister would ever say, as Meg said to Jose that moment, "I've never known your hair go up more successfully than it has to-night!"

But, of course, there was no time. They were at the drill hall already; there were cabs in front of them and cabs behind. The road was bright on either side with moving fan-like lights, and on the pavement gay couples seemed to float through the air; little satin shoes chased each other like birds.

"Hold on to me, Leila; you'll get lost," said Laura.

"Come on, girls, let's make a dash for it," said Laurie.

Leila put two fingers on Laura's pink velvet cloak, and they were somehow lifted past the big golden lantern, carried along the passage, and pushed into the little room marked "Ladies." Here the crowd was so great there was hardly space to take off their things; the noise was deafening. Two benches on either side were stacked high with wraps. Two old women in white aprons ran up and down tossing fresh armfuls. And everybody was pressing forward trying to get at the little dressing-table and mirror at the far end.

A great quivering jet of gas lighted the ladies' room. It couldn't wait; it was dancing already. When the door opened again and there came a burst of tuning from the drill hall, it leaped almost to the ceiling.

Dark girls, fair girls were patting their hair, tying ribbons again, tucking handkerchiefs down the fronts of their bodices, smoothing marble-white gloves. And because they were all laughing it seemed to Leila that they were all lovely.

"Aren't there any invisible hair-pins?" cried a voice. "How most extraordinary! I can't see a single invisible hair-pin."

"Powder my back, there's a darling," cried someone else.

"But I must have a needle and cotton. I've torn simply miles and miles of the frill," wailed a third.

Then, "Pass them along, pass them along!" The straw basket of programmes was tossed from arm to arm. Darling little pink-and-silver programmes, with pink pencils and fluffy tassels. Leila's fingers shook as she took one out of the basket. She wanted to ask some one, "Am I meant to have one too?" but she had just time to read: "Waltz 3. *Two, Two in a Canoe.* Polka 4. *Making the Feathers Fly,*" when Meg cried, "Ready, Leila?" and they pressed their way through the crush in the passage towards the big double doors of the drill hall.

Dancing had not begun yet, but the band had stopped tuning, and the noise was so great it seemed that when it did begin to play it would never be heard. Leila, pressing close to Meg, looking over Meg's shoulder, felt that even the little quivering coloured flags strung across the ceiling were talking. She quite forgot to be shy; she forgot how in the middle of dressing she had sat down on the bed with one shoe off and one shoe on and begged her mother to ring up her cousins and say she couldn't go after all. And the rush of longing she had had to be sitting on the veranda of their forsaken up-country home, listening to the baby owls crying "More pork" in the moonlight, was changed to a rush of joy so sweet that it was hard to bear alone. She clutched her fan, and, gazing at the gleaming, golden floor, the azaleas, the lanterns, the stage at one end with its red carpet and gilt chairs and the band in a corner, she thought breathlessly, "How heavenly; how simply heavenly!"

All the girls stood grouped together at one side of the doors, the men at the other, and the chaperones in dark dresses, smiling rather foolishly, walked with little careful steps over the polished floor towards the stage.

"This is my little country cousin Leila. Be nice to her. Find her partners; she's under my wing," said Meg, going up to one girl after another.

Strange faces smiled at Leila—sweetly, vaguely. Strange voices answered, "Of course, my dear." But Leila felt the girls didn't really see her. They were looking towards the men. Why didn't the men begin? What were they waiting for? There they stood, smoothing their gloves, patting their glossy hair and smiling among themselves. Then, quite suddenly, as if they had only just made up their minds that that was what they had to do, the men came gliding over the parquet. There was a joyful flutter among the girls. A tall, fair man flew up to Meg, seized her programme, scribbled something; Meg passed him on to Leila. "May I have the pleasure?" He ducked and smiled. There came a dark man wearing an eyeglass, then cousin Laurie with a friend, and Laura with a little freckled fellow whose tie was crooked. Then quite an old man—fat, with a big bald patch on his head—took her programme and murmured, "Let me see, let me see!" And he was a long time comparing his programme, which looked black with names, with hers. It seemed to give him so much trouble that Leila was ashamed. "Oh, please don't bother," she said eagerly. But instead of replying the fat man wrote something, glanced at her again. "Do I remember this bright little face?" he said softly. "Is it known to me of yore?" At that moment the band began playing; the fat man disappeared. He was tossed away on a great wave of music that came flying over the gleaming floor, breaking the groups up into couples, scattering them, sending them spinning. . . .

Leila had learned to dance at boarding school. Every Saturday afternoon the boarders were hurried off to a little corrugated iron mission hall where Miss Eccles (of London) held her "select" classes. But the difference between that dusty-smelling hall—with calico texts on the walls, the poor terrified little woman in a brown velvet toque with rabbit's ears thumping the cold piano, Miss Eccles poking the girls' feet with her long white wand—and this was so tremendous that Leila was sure if her partner didn't come and she had to listen to that marvellous music and to watch the others sliding, gliding over the golden floor, she would die at least, or faint, or lift her arms and fly out of one of those dark windows that showed the stars.

"Ours, I think——" Some one bowed, smiled, and offered her his arm; she hadn't to die after all. Some one's hand pressed her waist, and she floated away like a flower that is tossed into a pool.

"Quite a good floor, isn't it?" drawled a faint voice close to her ear.

"I think it's most beautifully slippery," said Leila.

"Pardon!" The faint voice sounded surprised. Leila said it again. And there was a tiny pause before the voice echoed, "Oh, quite!" and she was swung round again.

He steered so beautifully. That was the great difference between dancing with girls and men, Leila decided. Girls banged into each other, and stamped on each other's feet; the girl who was gentleman always clutched you so.

The azaleas were separate flowers no longer; they were pink and white flags streaming by.

"Were you at the Bells' last week?" the voice came again. It sounded tired. Leila wondered whether she ought to ask him if he would like to stop.

"No, this is my first dance," said she.

Her partner gave a little gasping laugh. "Oh I say," he protested.

"Yes, it is really the first dance I've ever been to." Leila was most fervent. It was such a relief to be able to tell somebody. "You see, I've lived in the country all my life up until now. . . ."

At that moment the music stopped, and they went to sit on two chairs against the wall. Leila tucked her pink satin feet under and fanned herself, while she blissfully watched the other couples passing and disappearing through the swing doors.

"Enjoying yourself, Leila?" asked Jose, nodding her golden head.

Laura passed and gave her the faintest little wink; it made Leila wonder for a moment whether she was quite grown up after all. Certainly her partner did not say very much. He coughed, tucked his handkerchief away, pulled down his waistcoat, took a minute thread off his sleeve. But it didn't matter. Almost immediately the band started, and her second partner seemed to spring from the ceiling.

"Floor's not bad," said the new voice. Did one always begin with the floor? And then, "Were you at the Neaves' on Tuesday?" And again Leila explained. Perhaps it was a little strange that her partners were not more interested. For it was thrilling. Her first ball! She was only at the beginning of everything. It seemed to her that she had never known what the night was like before. Up till now it had been dark, silent, beautiful very often —oh, yes—but mournful somehow. Solemn. And now it would never be like that again—it had opened dazzling bright.

"Care for an ice?" said her partner. And they went through the swing doors, down the passage, to the supper room. Her cheeks burned, she was fearfully thirsty. How sweet the ices looked on little glass plates, and how cold the frosted spoon was, iced too! And when they came back to the hall there was the fat man waiting for her by the door. It gave her quite a shock again to see how old he was; he ought to have been on the stage with the fathers and mothers. And when Leila compared him with her other partners he looked shabby. His waistcoat was creased, there was a button off his glove, his coat looked as if it was dusty with French chalk.

"Come along, little lady," said the fat man. He scarcely troubled to clasp her, and they moved away so gently, it was more like walking than dancing. But he said not a word about the floor. "Your first dance, isn't it?" he murmured.

"How *did* you know?"

"Ah," said the fat man, "that's what it is to be old!" He wheezed faintly as he steered her past an awkward couple. "You see, I've been doing this kind of thing for the last thirty years."

"Thirty years?" cried Leila. Twelve years before she was born!

"It hardly bears thinking about, does it?" said the fat man gloomily. Leila looked at his bald head, and she felt quite sorry for him.

"I think it's marvellous to be still going on," she said kindly.

"Kind little lady," said the fat man, and he pressed her a little closer, and hummed a bar of the waltz. "Of course," he said, "you can't hope to last anything like as long as that. No-o," said the fat man, "long before that you'll be sitting up there on the stage, looking on, in your nice black velvet. And these pretty arms will have turned into little short fat ones, and you'll beat time with such a different kind of fan—a black bony one." The fat man seemed to shudder. "And you'll smile away like the poor old dears up there, and point to your daughter, and tell the elderly lady next to you how some dreadful man tried to kiss her at the club ball. And your heart will ache, ache"—the fat man squeezed her closer still, as if he really was sorry for that poor heart—"because no one wants to kiss you now. And you'll say how unpleasant these polished floors are to walk on, how dangerous they are. Eh, Mademoiselle Twinkletoes?" said the fat man softly.

Leila gave a light little laugh, but she did not feel like laughing. Was it—could it all be true? It sounded terribly true. Was this first ball only the beginning of her last ball after all? At that the music seemed to change; it sounded sad, sad; it rose upon a great sigh. Oh, how quickly things changed! Why didn't happiness last for ever? For ever wasn't a bit too long.

"I want to stop," she said in a breathless voice. The fat man led her to the door.

"No," she said, "I won't go outside. I won't sit down. I'll just stand here, thank you." She leaned against the wall, tapping with her foot, pulling up her gloves and trying to smile. But deep inside her a little girl threw her pinafore over her head and sobbed. Why had he spoiled it all?

"I say, you know," said the fat man, "you mustn't take me seriously, little lady."

"As if I should!" said Leila, tossing her small dark head and sucking her underlip. . . .

Again the couples paraded. The swing doors opened and shut. Now new music was given out by the bandmaster. But Leila didn't want to dance any more. She wanted to be home, or sitting on the veranda listening to those baby owls. When she looked through the dark windows at the stars, they had long beams like wings. . . .

But presently a soft, melting, ravishing tune began, and a young man with curly hair bowed before her. She would have to dance, out of politeness, until she could find Meg. Very stiffly she walked into the middle; very haughtily she put her hand on his sleeve. But in one minute, in one turn, her feet glided, glided. The lights, the azaleas, the dresses, the pink faces, the velvet chairs, all became one beautiful flying wheel. And when her next partner bumped into the fat man and he said, "Par*don,*" she smiled at him more radiantly than ever. She didn't even recognize him again.

KATHERINE MANSFIELD

Marriage à la Mode

ON HIS way to the station William remembered with a fresh pang of disappointment that he was taking nothing down to the kiddies. Poor little chaps! It was hard lines on them. Their first words always were as they ran to greet him, "What have you got for me, daddy?" and he had nothing. He would have to buy them some sweets at the station. But that was what he had done for the past four Saturdays; their faces had fallen last time when they saw the same old boxes produced again.

And Paddy had said, "I had red ribbing on mine *bee*-fore!"

And Johnny had said, "It's always pink on mine, I hate pink."

But what was William to do? The affair wasn't so easily settled. In the old days, of course, he would have taken a taxi off to a decent toyshop and chosen them something in five minutes. But nowadays they had Russian toys, French toys, Serbian toys—toys from God knows where. It was over a year since Isabel had scrapped the old donkeys and engines and so on because they were so "dreadfully sentimental" and "so appallingly bad for the babies' sense of form."

"It's so important," the new Isabel had explained, "that they should like the right things from the very beginning. It saves so much time later on. Really, if the poor pets have to spend their infant years staring at these horrors, one can imagine them growing up and asking to be taken to the Royal Academy."

And she spoke as though a visit to the Royal Academy was certain immediate death to any one. . . .

"Well, I don't know," said William slowly. "When I was their age I used to go to bed hugging an old towel with a knot in it."

The new Isabel looked at him, her eyes narrowed, her lips apart.

"*Dear* William! I'm sure you did!" She laughed in the new way.

Sweets it would have to be, however, thought William gloomily, fishing in his pocket for change for the taxi-man. And he saw the kiddies handing the boxes round—they were awfully generous little chaps—while Isabel's precious friends didn't hesitate to help themselves. . . .

What about fruit? William hovered before a stall just inside the station. What about a melon each? Would they have to share that, too? Or a pineapple for Pad, and a melon for Johnny? Isabel's friends could hardly go sneaking up to the nursery at the children's meal-times. All the same, as he bought the melon William had a horrible vision of one of Isabel's young poets lapping up a slice, for some reason, behind the nursery door.

With his two very awkward parcels he strode off to his train. The platform was crowded, the train was in. Doors banged open and shut. There came such a loud hissing from the engine that people looked dazed as they scurried to and fro. William made straight for a first-class smoker, stowed away his suit-case and parcels, and taking a huge wad of papers out of his inner pocket, he flung down in the corner and began to read.

"Our client moreover is positive. . . . We are inclined to reconsider . . . in the event of——" Ah, that was better. William pressed back his flattened hair and stretched his legs across the carriage floor. The familiar dull gnawing in his breast quietened down. "With regard to our decision——" He took out a blue pencil and scored a paragraph slowly.

Two men came in, stepped across him, and made for the farther corner. A young fellow swung his golf clubs into the rack and sat down opposite. The train gave a gentle lurch, they were off. William glanced up and saw the hot, bright station slipping away. A red-faced girl raced along by the carriages, there was something strained and almost desperate in the way she waved and called. "Hysterical!" thought William dully. Then a greasy, black-faced workman at the end of the platform grinned at the passing train. And William thought, "A filthy life!" and went back to his papers.

When he looked up again there were fields, and beasts standing for shelter under the dark trees. A wide river, with naked children splashing in the shallows, glided into sight and was gone again. The sky shone pale, and one bird drifted high like a dark fleck in a jewel.

"We have examined our client's correspondence files. . . ." The last sentence he had read echoed in his mind. "We have examined . . ." William hung on to that sentence, but it was no good; it snapped in the middle, and the fields, the sky, the sailing bird, the water, all said "Isabel." The same thing happened every Saturday afternoon. When he was on his way to meet Isabel there began those countless imaginary meetings. She was at the station, standing just a little apart from everybody else; she was sitting in the open taxi outside; she was at the garden gate; walking across the parched grass; at the door, or just inside the hall.

And her clear, light voice, "It's William," or "Hillo, William!" or "So William has come!" He touched her cool hand, her cool cheek.

The exquisite freshness of Isabel! When he had been a little boy, it was his delight to run into the garden after a shower of rain and shake the rose-bush over him. Isabel was that rose-bush, petal-soft, sparkling and cool. And he was still that little boy. But there was no running into the garden now, no laughing and shaking. The dull, persistent gnawing in his breast started again. He drew up his legs, tossed the papers aside, and shut his eyes.

"What is it, Isabel? What is it?" he said tenderly. They were in their bedroom in the new house. Isabel sat on a painted stool before the dressing-table that was strewn with little black and green boxes.

"What is what, William?" And she bent forward, and her fine light hair fell over her cheeks.

"Ah, you know!" He stood in the middle of the strange room and he felt a stranger. At that Isabel wheeled round quickly and faced him.

"Oh, William!" she cried imploringly, and she held up the hair-brush: "Please! Please don't be so dreadfully stuffy and—tragic. You're always saying or looking or hinting that I've changed. Just because I've got to know really congenial people, and go about more, and am frightfully keen on—on everything, you behave as though I'd——" Isabel tossed back her hair and laughed—"killed our love or something. It's so awfully absurd"—she bit her lip—"and it's so maddening, William. Even this new house and the servants you grudge me."

"Isabel!"

"Yes, yes, it's true in a way," said Isabel quickly. "You think they are another bad sign. Oh, I know you do. I feel it," she said softly, "every time you come up the stairs. But we couldn't have gone on living in that other poky little hole, William. Be practical, at least! Why, there wasn't enough room for the babies even."

No, it was true. Every morning when he came back from chambers it was to find the babies with Isabel in the back drawing-room. They were having rides on the leopard skin thrown over the sofa back, or they were playing shops with Isabel's desk for a counter, or Pad was sitting on the hearthrug rowing away for dear life with a little brass fire shovel, while Johnny shot at pirates with the tongs. Every evening they each had a pick-a-back up the narrow stairs to their fat old Nanny.

Yes, he supposed it was a poky little house. A little white house with blue curtains and a window-box of petunias. William met their friends at the door with "Seen our petunias? Pretty terrific for London, don't you think?"

But the imbecile thing, the absolutely extraordinary thing was that he hadn't the slightest idea that Isabel wasn't as happy as he. God, what blindness! He hadn't the remotest notion in those days that she really hated that inconvenient little house, that she thought the fat Nanny was ruining the babies, that she was desperately lonely, pining for new people and new music and pictures and so on. If they hadn't gone to that studio party at Moira Morrison's—if Moira Morrison hadn't said as they were leaving, "I'm going to rescue your wife, selfish man. She's like an exquisite little Titania"—if Isabel hadn't gone with Moira to Paris—if—if . . .

The train stopped at another station. Bettingford. Good heavens! They'd be there in ten minutes. William stuffed the papers back into his pockets; the young man opposite had long since disappeared. Now the other two got out. The late afternoon sun shone on women in cotton frocks and little sunburnt, barefoot children. It blazed on a silky yellow flower with coarse leaves which sprawled over a bank of rock. The air ruffling through the window smelled of the sea. Had Isabel the same crowd with her this week-end, wondered William?

And he remembered the holidays they used to have, the four of them, with a little farm girl, Rose, to look after the babies. Isabel wore a jersey and her hair in a plait; she looked about fourteen. Lord! how his nose used to peel! And the amount they ate, and the amount they slept in that immense feather bed with their feet locked together. . . . William couldn't help a grim smile as he thought of Isabel's horror if she knew the full extent of his sentimentality.

. . . .

"Hillo, William!" She was at the station after all, standing just as he had imagined, apart from the others, and—William's heart leapt—she was alone.

"Hallo, Isabel!" William stared. He thought she looked so beautiful that he had to say someting, "You look very cool."

"Do I?" said Isabel. "I don't feel very cool. Come along, your horrid old train is late. The taxi's outside." She put her hand lightly on his arm as they passed the ticket collector. "We've all come to meet you," she said. "But we've left Bobby Kane at the sweet shop, to be called for."

"Oh!" said William. It was all he could say for the moment.

There in the glare waited the taxi, with Bill Hunt and Dennis Green sprawling on one side, their hats tilted over their faces, while on the other, Moira Morrison, in a bonnet like a huge strawberry, jumped up and down.

"No ice! No ice! No ice!" she shouted gaily.

And Dennis chimed in from under his hat. "*Only* to be had from the fishmonger's."

And Bill Hunt, emerging, added, "With *whole* fish in it."

"Oh, what a bore!" wailed Isabel. And she explained to William how they had been chasing round the town for ice while she waited for him. "Simply everything is running down the steep cliffs into the sea, beginning with the butter."

"We shall have to anoint ourselves with the butter," said Dennis. "May thy head, William, lack not ointment."

"Look here," said William, "how are we going to sit? I'd better get up by the driver."

"No, Bobby Kane's by the driver," said Isabel. "You're to sit between Moira and me." The taxi started. "What have you got in those mysterious parcels?"

"De-cap-it-ated heads!" said Bill Hunt, shuddering beneath his hat.

"Oh, fruit!" Isabel sounded very pleased. "Wise William! A melon and a pineapple. How too nice!"

"No, wait a bit," said William, smiling. But he really was anxious. "I brought them down for the kiddies."

"Oh, my dear!" Isabel laughed, and slipped her hand through his arm. "They'd be rolling in agonies if they were to eat them. No"—she patted his hand—"you must bring them something next time. I refuse to part with my pineapple."

"Cruel Isabel! Do let me smell it!" said Moira. She flung her arms across William appealingly. "Oh!" The strawberry bonnet fell forward: she sounded quite faint.

"A Lady in Love with a Pineapple," said Dennis, as the taxi drew up before a little shop with a striped blind. Out came Bobby Kane, his arms full of little packets.

"I do hope they'll be good. I've chosen them because of the colours. There are some round things which really look too divine. And just look at this nougat," he cried ecstatically, "just look at it! It's a perfect little ballet."

But at that moment the shopman appeared. "Oh, I forgot. They're none of them paid for," said Bobby, looking frightened. Isabel gave the shopman a note, and Bobby was radiant again. "Hallo, William! I'm sitting by the driver." And bare-headed, all in white, with his sleeves rolled up to the shoulders, he leapt into his place. "Avanti!" he cried. . . .

After tea the others went off to bathe, while William stayed and made his peace with the kiddies. But Johnny and Paddy were asleep, the rose-red glow had paled, bats were flying, and still the bathers had not returned. As William wandered downstairs, the maid crossed the hall carrying a lamp. He followed her into the sitting-room. It was a long room, coloured yellow. On the wall opposite William some one had painted a young man, over life-size, with very wobbly legs, offering a wide-eyed daisy to a young woman who had one very short arm and one very long, thin one. Over the chairs and sofa there hung strips of black material, covered with big splashes like broken eggs, and everywhere one looked there seemed to be an ash-tray full of cigarette ends. William sat down in one of the arm-chairs. Nowadays, when one felt with one hand down the sides, it wasn't to come upon a sheep with three legs or a cow that had lost one horn, or a very fat dove out of the Noah's Ark. One fished up yet another little paper-covered book of smudged-looking poems. . . . He thought of the wad of papers in his pocket, but he was too hungry and tired to read. The door was open; sounds came from the kitchen. The servants were talking as if they were alone in the house. Suddenly there came a loud screech of laughter and an equally loud "Sh!" They had remembered him. William got up and went through the French windows into the garden, and as he stood there in the shadow he heard the bathers coming up the sandy road; their voices rang through the quiet.

"I think its up to Moira to use her little arts and wiles."

A tragic moan from Moira.

"We ought to have a gramophone for the week-ends that played 'The Maid of the Mountains.' "

"Oh no! Oh no!" cried Isabel's voice. "That's not fair to William. Be nice to him, my children! He's only staying until to-morrow evening."

"Leave him to me," cried Bobby Kane. "I'm awfully good at looking after people."

The gate swung open and shut. William moved on the terrace; they had seen him. "Hallo, William!" And Bobby Kane, flapping his towel, began to leap and pirouette on the parched lawn. "Pity you didn't come, William. The water was divine. And we all went to a little pub afterwards and had sloe gin."

The others had reached the house. "I say, Isabel," called Bobby, "would you like me to wear my Nijinsky dress to-night?"

"No," said Isabel, "nobody's going to dress. We're all starving. William's starving, too. Come along, *mes amis*, let's begin with sardines."

"I've found the sardines," said Moira, and she ran into the hall, holding a box high in the air.

"A Lady with a Box of Sardines," said Dennis gravely.

"Well, William, and how's London?" asked Bill Hunt, drawing the cork out of a bottle of whisky.

"Oh, London's not much changed," answered William.

"Good old London," said Bobby, very hearty, spearing a sardine.

But a moment later William was forgotten. Moira Morrison began wondering what colour one's legs really were under water.

"Mine are the palest, palest mushroom colour."

Bill and Dennis ate enormously. And Isabel filled glasses, and changed plates, and found matches, smiling blissfully. At one moment she said, "I do wish, Bill, you'd paint it."

"Paint what?" said Bill loudly, stuffing his mouth with bread.

"Us," said Isabel, "round the table. It would be so fascinating in twenty years' time."

Bill screwed up his eyes and chewed. "Light's wrong," he said rudely, "far too much yellow"; and went on eating. And that seemed to charm Isabel, too.

But after supper they were all so tired they could do nothing but yawn until it was late enough to go to bed. . . .

It was not until William was waiting for his taxi the next afternoon that he found himself alone with Isabel. When he brought his suit-case down into the hall, Isabel left the others and went over to him. She stooped down and picked up the suit-case. "What a weight!" she said, and she gave a little awkward laugh. "Let me carry it! To the gate."

"No, why should you?" said William. "Of course, not. Give it to me."

"Oh, please do let me," said Isabel. "I want to really." They walked together silently. William felt there was nothing to say now.

"There," said Isabel triumphantly, setting the suit-case down, and she looked anxiously along the sandy road. "I hardly seem to have seen you this time," she said breathlessly. "It's so short, isn't it? I feel you've only just come. Next time——" The taxi came into sight. "I hope they look after you properly in London. I'm so sorry the babies have been out all day, but Miss Neil had arranged it. They'll hate missing you. Poor William, going back to London." The taxi turned. "Good-bye!" She gave him a little hurried kiss; she was gone.

Fields, trees, hedges streamed by. They shook through the empty, blind-looking little town, ground up the steep hill to the station.

The train was in. William made straight for a first-class smoker, flung back into the corner, but this time he let the papers alone. He folded his arms against the dull, persistent gnawing, and began in his mind to write a letter to Isabel.

. . . .

The post was late as usual. They sat outside the house in long chairs under coloured parasols. Only Bobby Kane lay on the turf at Isabel's feet. It was dull, stifling; the day drooped like a flag.

"Do you think there will be Mondays in Heaven?" asked Bobby childishly.

And Dennis murmured, "Heaven will be one long Monday."

But Isabel couldn't help wondering what had happened to the salmon they had for supper last night. She had meant to have fish mayonnaise for lunch and now . . .

Moira was asleep. Sleeping was her latest discovery. "It's *so* wonderful. One simply shuts one's eyes, that's all. It's *so* delicious."

When the old ruddy postman came beating along the sandy road on his tricycle one felt the handlebars ought to have been oars.

Bill Hunt put down his book. "Letters," he said complacently, and they all waited. But, heartless postman—O malignant world! There was only one, a fat one for Isabel. Not even a paper.

"And mine's only from William," said Isabel mournfully.

"From William—already?"

"He's sending you back your marriage lines as a gentle reminder."

"Does everybody have marriage lines? I thought they were only for servants."

"Pages and pages! Look at her! A Lady reading a Letter," said Dennis.

My darling, precious Isabel. Pages and pages there were. As Isabel read on her feeling of astonishment changed to a stifled feeling. What on earth had induced William . . .? How extraordinary it was. . . . What could have made him . . .? She felt confused, more and more excited, even frightened. It was just like William. Was it? It was absurd, of course, it must be absurd, ridiculous. "Ha, ha, ha! Oh dear!" What was she to do? Isabel flung back in her chair and laughed till she couldn't stop laughing.

"Do, do tell us," said the others. "You must tell us."

"I'm longing to," gurgled Isabel. She sat up, gathered the letter and waved it at them. "Gather round," she said. "Listen, it's too marvellous. A love-letter!"

"A love-letter! But how divine!" *Darling, precious Isabel.* But she had hardly begun before their laughter interrupted her.

"Go on, Isabel, it's perfect."

"It's the most marvellous find."

"Oh, do go on, Isabel!"

God forbid, my darling, that I should be a drag on your happiness.

"Oh! oh! oh!"

"Sh! sh! sh!"

And Isabel went on. When she reached the end they were hysterical: Bobby rolled on the turf and almost sobbed.

"You must let me have it just as it is, entire, for my new book," said Dennis firmly. "I shall give it a whole chapter."

"Oh, Isabel," moaned Moira, "that wonderful bit about holding you in his arms!"

"I always thought those letters in divorce cases were made up. But they pale before this."

"Let me hold it. Let me read it, mine own self," said Bobby Kane.

But, to their surprise, Isabel crushed the letter in her hand. She was laughing no longer. She glanced quickly at them all; she looked exhausted. "No, not just now. Not just now," she stammered.

And before they could recover she had run into the house, through the hall, up the stairs into her bedroom. Down she sat on the side of the bed. "How vile, odious, abominable, vulgar," muttered Isabel. She pressed her eyes with her knuckles and rocked to and fro. And again she saw them, but not four, more like forty, laughing, sneering, jeering, stretching out their hands while she read them William's letter. Oh, what a loathsome thing to have done. How could she have done it! *God forbid, my darling, that I should be a drag on your happiness.* William! Isabel pressed her face into the pillow. But she felt that even the grave bedroom knew her for what she was, shallow, tinkling, vain. . . .

Presently from the garden below there came voices.

"Isabel, we're all going for a bathe. Do come!"

"Come thou wife of William!"

"Call her once before you go, call once yet!"

Isabel sat up. Now was the moment, now she must decide. Would she go with them, or stay here and write to William. Which, which should it be? "I must make up my mind." Oh, but how could there be any question? Of course she would stay here and write.

"Titania!" piped Moira.

"Isa-bel?"

No, it was too difficult. "I'll—I'll go with them, and write to William later. Some other time. Later. Not now. But I shall *certainly* write," thought Isabel hurriedly.

And, laughing in the new way, she ran down the stairs.

KATHERINE MANSFIELD

Miss Brill

ALTHOUGH it was so brilliantly fine—the blue sky powdered with gold and great spots of light like white wine splashed over the Jardins Publiques—Miss Brill was glad that she had decided on her fur. The air was motionless, but when you opened your mouth there was just a faint chill, like a chill from a glass of iced water before you sip, and now and again a leaf came drifting—from nowhere, from the sky. Miss Brill put up her hand and touched her fur. Dear little thing! It was nice to feel it again. She had taken it out of its box that afternoon, shaken out the moth-powder, given it a good brush, and rubbed the life back into the dim little eyes. "What has been happening to me?" said the sad little eyes. Oh, how sweet it was to see them snap at her again from the red eiderdown! . . . But the nose, which was of some black composition, wasn't at all firm. It must have had a knock, somehow. Never mind—a little dab of black sealing-wax when the time came—when it was absolutely necessary. . . . Little rogue! Yes, she really felt like that about it. Little rogue biting its tail just by her left ear. She could have taken it off and laid it on her lap and stroked it. She felt a tingling in her hands and arms, but that came from walking, she supposed. And when she breathed, something light and sad—no, not sad, exactly—something gentle seemed to move in her bosom.

There were a number of people out this afternoon, far more than last Sunday. And the band sounded louder and gayer. That was because the Season had begun. For although the band played all the year round on Sundays, out of season it was never the same. It was like some one playing with only the family to listen; it didn't care how it played if there weren't any strangers present. Wasn't the conductor wearing a new coat, too? She was sure it was new. He scraped with his foot and flapped his arms like a rooster about to crow, and the bandsmen sitting in the green rotunda blew out their cheeks and glared at the music. Now there came a little "flutey" bit—very pretty!—a little chain of bright drops. She was sure it would be repeated. It was; she lifted her head and smiled.

Only two people shared her "special" seat: a fine old man in a velvet coat, his hands clasped over a huge carved walking-stick, and a big old woman, sitting upright, with a roll of knitting on her embroidered apron. They did not speak. This was disappointing, for Miss Brill always looked forward to the conversation. She had become really quite expert, she thought, at listening as though she didn't listen, at sitting in other people's lives just for a minute while they talked round her.

She glanced, sideways, at the old couple. Perhaps they would go soon. Last Sunday, too, hadn't been as interesting as usual. An Englishman and his wife, he wearing a dreadful Panama hat and she button boots. And she'd gone on the whole time about how she ought to wear spectacles; she knew she needed them; but that it was no good getting any; they'd be sure to break and they'd never keep on. And he'd been so patient. He'd suggested everything—gold rims, the kind that curved round your ears, little pads inside the bridge. No, nothing would please her. "They'll always be sliding down my nose!" Miss Brill had wanted to shake her.

The old people sat on the bench, still as statues. Never mind, there was always the crowd to watch. To and fro, in front of the flower-beds and the band rotunda, the couples and groups paraded, stopped to talk, to greet, to buy a handful of flowers from the old beggar who had his tray fixed to the railings. Little children ran among them, swooping and laughing; little boys with big white silk bows under their chins, little girls, little French dolls, dressed up in velvet and lace. And sometimes a tiny staggerer came suddenly rocking into the open from under the trees, stopped, stared, as suddenly sat down "flop," until its small high-stepping mother, like a young hen, rushed scolding to its rescue. Other people sat on the benches and green chairs, but they were nearly always the same, Sunday after Sunday, and—Miss Brill had often noticed—there was something funny about nearly all of them. They were odd, silent, nearly all old, and from the way they stared they looked as though they'd just come from dark little rooms or even—even cupboards!

Behind the rotunda the slender trees with yellow leaves down drooping, and through them just a line of sea, and beyond the blue sky with gold-veined clouds.

Tum-tum-tum tiddle-um! tiddle-um! tum tiddley-um tum ta! blew the band.

Two young girls in red came by and two young soldiers in blue met them, and they laughed and paired and went off arm-in-arm. Two peasant women with funny straw hats passed, gravely, leading beautiful smoke-coloured donkeys. A cold, pale nun hurried by. A beautiful woman came along and dropped her bunch of violets, and a little boy ran after to hand them to her, and she took them and threw them away as if they'd been poisoned. Dear me! Miss Brill didn't know whether to admire that or not! And now an ermine toque and a gentleman in grey met just in front of her. He was tall, stiff, dignified, and she was wearing the ermine toque she'd bought when her hair was yellow. Now everything, her hair, her face, even her eyes, was the same colour as the shabby ermine, and her hand, in its cleaned glove, lifted to dab her lips, was a tiny yellowish paw. Oh, she was so pleased to see him—delighted! She rather thought they were going to meet that afternoon. She described where she'd been—everywhere, here, there, along by the sea. The day was so charming—didn't he agree? And wouldn't he, perhaps? . . . But he shook his head, lighted a cigarette, slowly breathed a great deep puff into her face, and, even while she was still talking and laughing, flicked the match away and walked on. The ermine toque was alone; she smiled more brightly than ever. But even the band seemed to know what she was feeling and played more softly, played tenderly, and the drum beat, "The Brute! The Brute!" over and over. What would she do? What was going to happen now? But as Miss Brill wondered, the ermine toque turned, raised her hand as though she'd seen some one else, much nicer, just over there, and pattered away. And the band changed again and played more quickly, more gaily than ever, and the old couple on Miss Brill's seat got up and marched away, and such a funny old man with long whiskers hobbled along in time to the music and was nearly knocked over by four girls walking abreast.

Oh, how fascinating it was! How she enjoyed it! How she loved sitting here, watching it all! It was like a play. It was exactly like a play. Who could believe the sky at the back wasn't painted? But it wasn't till a little brown dog trotted on solemn and then slowly trotted off, like a little "theatre" dog, a little dog that had been drugged, that Miss Brill discovered what it was that made it so exciting. They were all on the stage. They weren't only the audience, not only looking on; they were acting. Even she had a part and came every Sunday. No doubt somebody would have noticed if she hadn't been there; she was part of the performance after all. How strange she'd never thought of it like that before! And yet it explained why she made such a point of starting from home at just the same time each week—so as not to be late for the performance—and it also explained why she had quite a queer, shy feeling at telling her English pupils how she spent her Sunday afternoons. No wonder! Miss Brill nearly laughed out loud. She was on the stage. She thought of the old invalid gentleman to whom she read the newspaper four afternoons a week while he slept in the garden. She had got quite used to the frail head on the cotton pillow, the hollowed eyes, the open mouth and the high pinched nose. If he'd been dead she mightn't have noticed for weeks; she wouldn't have minded. But suddenly he knew he was having the paper read to him by an actress! "An actress!" The old head lifted; two points of light quivered in the old eyes. "An actress—are ye?" And Miss

Brill smoothed the newspaper as though it were the manuscript of her part and said gently: "Yes, I have been an actress for a long time."

The band had been having a rest. Now they started again. And what they played was warm, sunny, yet there was just a faint chill—a something, what was it?—not sadness—no, not sadness—a something that made you want to sing. The tune lifted, lifted, the light shone; and it seemed to Miss Brill that in another moment all of them, all the whole company, would begin singing. The young ones, the laughing ones who were moving together, they would begin, and the men's voices, very resolute and brave, would join them. And then she too, she too, and the others on the benches—they would come in with a kind of accompaniment—something low, that scarcely rose or fell, something so beautiful—moving. . . . And Miss Brill's eyes filled with tears and she looked smiling at all the other members of the company. Yes, we understand, we understand, she thought—though what they understood she didn't know.

Just at that moment a boy and a girl came and sat down where the old couple had been. They were beautifully dressed; they were in love. The hero and heroine, of course, just arrived from his father's yacht. And still soundlessly singing, still with that trembling smile, Miss Brill prepared to listen.

"No, not now," said the girl. "Not here, I can't."

"But why? Because of that stupid old thing at the end there?" asked the boy. "Why does she come here at all—who wants her? Why doesn't she keep her silly old mug at home?"

"It's her fu-fur which is so funny," giggled the girl. "It's exactly like a fried whiting."

"Ah, be off with you!" said the boy in an angry whisper. Then: "Tell me, ma petite chère——"

"No, not here," said the girl. "Not *yet*."

. . . .

On her way home she usually bought a slice of honey-cake at the baker's. It was her Sunday treat. Sometimes there was an almond in her slice, sometimes not. It made a great difference. If there was an almond it was like carrying home a tiny present—a surprise—something that might very well not have been there. She hurried on the almond Sundays and struck the match for the kettle in quite a dashing way.

But to-day she passed the baker's by, climbing the stairs, went into the little dark room—her room like a cupboard—and sat down on the red eiderdown. She sat there for a long time. The box that the fur came out of was on the bed. She unclasped the necklet quickly; quickly, without looking, laid it inside. But when she put the lid on she thought she heard something crying.

KATHERINE MANSFIELD

The Stranger

IT SEEMED to the little crowd on the wharf that she was never going to move again. There she lay, immense, motionless on the grey crinkled water, a loop of smoke above her, an immense flock of gulls screaming and diving after the galley droppings at the stern. You could just see little couples parading—little flies walking up and down the dish on the grey crinkled tablecloth. Other flies clustered and swarmed at the edge. Now there was a gleam of white on the lower deck—the cook's apron or the stewardess perhaps. Now a tiny black spider raced up the ladder on to the bridge.

In the front of the crowd a strong-looking, middle-aged man, dressed very well, very snugly in a grey overcoat, grey silk scarf, thick gloves and dark felt hat, marched up and down, twirling his folded umbrella. He seemed to be the leader of the little crowd on the wharf and at the same time to keep them together. He was something between the sheep-dog and the shepherd.

But what a fool—what a fool he had been not to bring any glasses! There wasn't a pair of glasses between the whole lot of them.

"Curious thing, Mr. Scott, that none of us thought of glasses. We might have been able to stir 'em up a bit. We might have managed a little signalling. *Don't hesitate to land. Natives harmless.* Or: *A welcome awaits you. All is forgiven.* What? Eh?"

Mr. Hammond's quick, eager glance, so nervous and yet so friendly and confiding, took in everybody on the wharf, roped in even those old chaps lounging against the gangways. They knew, every manjack of them, that Mrs. Hammond was on that boat, and he was so tremendously excited it never entered his head not to believe that this marvellous fact meant something to them too. It warmed his heart towards them. They were, he decided, as decent a crowd of people—— Those old chaps over by the gangways, too—fine, solid old chaps. What chests—by Jove! And he squared his own, plunged his thick-gloved hands into his pockets, rocked from heel to toe.

"Yes, my wife's been in Europe for the last ten months. On a visit to our eldest girl, who was married last year. I brought her up here, as far as Salisbury, myself. So I thought I'd better come and fetch her back. Yes, yes, yes." The shrewd grey eyes narrowed again and searched anxiously, quickly, the motionless liner. Again his overcoat was unbuttoned. Out came the thin, butter-yellow watch again, and for the twentieth—fiftieth—hundredth time he made the calculation.

"Let me see, now. It was two fifteen when the doctor's launch went off. Two fifteen. It is now exactly twenty-eight minutes past four. That is to say, the doctor's been gone two hours and thirteen minutes. Two hours and thirteen minutes! Wheeooh!" He gave a queer little half-whistle and snapped his watch to again. "But I think we should have been told if there was anything up—don't you Mr. Gaven?"

"Oh, yes, Mr. Hammond! I don't think there's anything to—anything to worry about," said Mr. Gaven, knocking out his pipe against the heel of his shoe. "At the same time——"

"Quite so! Quite so!" cried Mr. Hammond. "Dashed annoying!" He paced quickly up and down and came back again to his stand between Mr. and Mrs. Scott and Mr. Gaven. "It's getting quite dark, too," and he waved his folded umbrella as though the dusk at least might have had the decency to keep off for a bit. But the dusk came slowly, spreading like a slow stain over the water. Little Jean Scott dragged at her mother's hand.

"I wan' my tea, mammy!" she wailed.

"I expect you do," said Mr. Hammond. "I expect all these ladies want their tea." And his kind, flushed, almost pitiful glance roped them all in again. He wondered whether Janey was having a final cup of tea in the saloon out there. He hoped so; he thought not. It would be just like her not to leave the deck. In that case perhaps the deck steward would bring her up a cup. If he'd been there he'd have got it for her—somehow. And for a moment he was on deck, standing over her, watching her little hand fold round the cup in the way she had, while she drank the only cup of tea to be got on board. . . . But now he was back here, and the Lord only knew when that cursed Captain would stop hanging about in the stream. He took another turn, up and down, up and down. He walked as far as the cab-stand to make sure his driver hadn't disappeared; back he swerved again to the little flock huddled in the shelter of the banana crates. Little Jean Scott was still wanting her tea. Poor little beggar! He wished he had a bit of chocolate on him.

"Here, Jean!" he said. "Like a lift up?" And easily, gently, he swung the little girl on to a higher barrel. The movement of holding her, steadying her, relieved him wonderfully, lightened his heart.

"Hold on," he said, keeping an arm round her.

"Oh, don't worry about *Jean,* Mr. Hammond!" said Mrs. Scott.

"That's all right, Mrs. Scott. No trouble. It's a pleasure. Jean's a little pal of mine, aren't you, Jean?"

"Yes, Mr. Hammond," said Jean, and she ran her finger down the dent of his felt hat.

But suddenly she caught him by the ear and gave a loud scream. "Lo-ok, Mr. Hammond! She's moving! Look, she's moving in!"

By Jove! So she was. At last! She was slowly, slowly turning round. A bell sounded far over the water and a great spout of steam gushed into the air. The gulls rose; they fluttered away like bits of white paper. And whether that deep throbbing was her engines or his heart Mr. Hammond couldn't say. He had to nerve himself to bear it, whatever it was. At that moment old Captain Johnson, the harbour-master, came striding down the wharf, a leather portfolio under his arm.

"Jean'll be all right," said Mr. Scott. "I'll hold her." He was just in time. Mr. Hammond had forgotten about Jean. He sprang away to greet old Captain Johnson.

"Well, Captain," the eager, nervous voice rang out again, "you've taken pity on us at last."

"It's no good blaming me, Mr. Hammond," wheezed old Captain Johnson, staring at the liner. "You got Mrs. Hammond on board, ain't yer?"

"Yes, yes!" said Hammond, and kept by the harbour-master's side. "Mrs. Hammond's there. Hul-lo! We shan't be long now!"

With her telephone ring-ringing, the thrum of her screw filling the air, the big liner bore down on them, cutting sharp through the dark water so that big white shavings curled to either side. Hammond and the harbour-master kept in front of the rest. Hammond took off his hat; he raked the decks—they were crammed with passengers; he waved his hat and bawled a loud, strange "Hul-lo!" across the water; and then turned round and burst out laughing and said something—nothing—to old Captain Johnson.

"Seen her?" asked the harbour-master.

"No, not yet. Steady—wait a bit!" And suddenly, between two great clumsy idiots—"Get out of the way there!" he signed with his umbrella—he saw a hand raised—a white glove shaking a handkerchief. Another moment, and—thank God, thank God!—there she was.

There was Janey. There was Mrs. Hammond, yes, yes, yes—standing by the rail and smiling and nodding and waving her handkerchief.

"Well, that's first class—first class! Well, well, well!" He positively stamped. Like lightning he drew out his cigar-case and offered it to old Captain Johnson. "Have a cigar, Captain! They're pretty good. Have a couple! Here"—and he pressed all the cigars in the case on the harbour-master—"I've a couple of boxes up at the hotel."

"Thenks, Mr. Hammond!" wheezed old Captain Johnson.

Hammond stuffed the cigar-case back. His hands were shaking, but he'd got hold of himself again. He was able to face Janey. There she was, leaning on the rail, talking to some woman and at the same time watching him, ready for him. It struck him, as the gulf of water closed, how small she looked on that huge ship. His heart was wrung with such a spasm that he could have cried out. How little she looked to have come all that long way and back by herself! Just like her, though. Just like Janey. She had the courage of a ——And now the crew had come forward and parted the passengers; they had lowered the rails for the gangways.

The voices on shore and the voices on board flew to greet each other.

"All well?"

"All well."

"How's mother?"

"Much better."

"Hullo, Jean!"

"Hillo, Aun' Emily!"

"Had a good voyage?"

"Splendid!"

"Shan't be long now!"

"Not long now."

The engines stopped. Slowly she edged to the wharf-side.

"Make way there—make way—make way!" And the wharf hands brought the heavy gangways along at a sweeping run. Hammond signed to Janey to stay where she was. The old harbour-master stepped forward; he followed. As to "ladies first," or any rot like that, it never entered his head.

"After you, Captain!" he cried genially. And, treading on the old man's heels, he strode up the gangway on to the deck in a bee-line to Janey, and Janey was clasped in his arms.

"Well, well, well! Yes, yes! Here we are at last!" he stammered. It was all he could say. And Janey emerged, and her cool little voice—the only voice in the world for him—said,

"Well, darling! Have you been waiting long?"

No; not long. Or, at any rate, it didn't matter. It was over now. But the point was, he had a cab waiting at the end of the wharf. Was she ready to go off. Was her luggage ready? In that case they could cut off sharp with her cabin luggage and let the rest go hang until to-morrow. He bent over her and she looked up with her familiar half-smile. She was just the same. Not a day changed. Just as he'd always known her. She laid her small hand on his sleeve.

"How are the children, John?" she asked.

(Hang the children!) "Perfectly well. Never better in their lives."

"Haven't they sent me letters?"

"Yes, yes—of course! I've left them at the hotel for you to digest later on."

"We can't go quite so fast," said she. I've got people to say good-bye to—and then there's the Captain." As his face fell she gave his arm a small understanding squeeze. "If the Captain comes off the bridge I want you to thank him for having looked after your wife so beautifully." Well, he'd got her. If she wanted another ten minutes—— As he gave way she was surrounded. The whole first-class seemed to want to say good-bye to Janey.

"Good-bye, *dear* Mrs. Hammond! And next time you're in Sydney I'll *expect* you."

"Darling Mrs. Hammond! You won't forget to write to me, will you?"

"Well, Mrs. Hammond, what this boat would have been without you!"

It was as plain as a pikestaff that she was by far the most popular woman on board. And she took it all—just as usual. Absolutely composed. Just her little self—just Janey all over; standing there with her veil thrown back. Hammond never noticed what his wife had on. It was all the same to him whatever she wore. But to-day he did notice that she wore a black "costume"—didn't they call it?—with white frills, trimmings he supposed they were, at the neck and sleeves. All this while Janey handed him round.

"John, dear!" And then: "I want to introduce you to——"

Finally they did escape, and she led the way to her state-room. To follow Janey down the passage that she knew so well—that was so strange to him; to part the green curtains after her and to step into the cabin that had been hers gave him exquisite happiness. But—confound it!—the stewardess was there on the floor, strapping up the rugs.

"That's the last, Mrs. Hammond," said the stewardess, rising and pulling down her cuffs.

He was introduced again, and then Janey and the stewardess disappeared into the passage. He heard whisperings. She was getting the tipping business over, he supposed. He sat down on the striped sofa and took his hat off. There were the rugs she had taken with her; they looked good as new. All her luggage looked fresh, perfect. The labels were written in her beautiful little dear hand—"Mrs. John Hammond."

"Mrs. John Hammond!" He gave a long sigh of content and leaned back, crossed his arms. The strain was over. He felt he could have sat there for ever sighing his relief—the relief at being rid of that horrible tug, pull, grip on his heart. The danger was over. That was the feeling. They were on dry land again.

But at that moment Janey's head came round the corner.

"Darling—do you mind? I just want to go and say good-bye to the doctor."

Hammond started up. "I'll come with you."

"No, no!" she said. "Don't bother. I'd rather not. I'll not be a minute."

And before he could answer she was gone. He had half a mind to run after her; but instead he sat down again.

Would she really not be long? What was the time now? Out came the watch; he stared at nothing. That was rather queer of Janey, wasn't it? Why couldn't she have told the stewardess to say good-bye for her? Why did she have to go chasing after the ship's doctor? She could have sent a note from the hotel even if the affair had been urgent. Urgent? Did it—could it mean that she had been ill on the voyage—she was keeping something from him? That was it! He seized his hat. He was going off to find that fellow and to wring the truth out of him at all costs. He thought he'd noticed just something. She was just a touch too calm—too steady. From the very first moment——

The curtains rang. Janey was back. He jumped to his feet.

"Janey, have you been ill on this voyage? You have!"

"Ill?" Her airy little voice mocked him. She stepped over the rugs, and came up close, touched his breast, and looked up at him.

"Darling," she said, "don't frighten me. Of course I haven't! Whatever makes you think I have? Do I look ill?"

But Hammond didn't see her. He only felt that she was looking at him and that there was no need to worry about anything. She was here to look after things. It was all right. Everything was.

The gentle pressure of her hand was so calming that he put his over hers to hold it there. And she said:

"Stand still. I want to look at you. I haven't seen you yet. You've had your beard beautifully trimmed, and you look—younger, I think, and decidedly thinner! Bachelor life agrees with you."

"Agrees with me!" He groaned for love and caught her close again. And again, as always, he had the feeling he was holding something that never was quite his—his. Something too delicate, too precious, that would fly away once he let go.

"For God's sake let's get off to the hotel so that we can be by ourselves!" And he rang the bell hard for some one to look sharp with the luggage.

. . . .

Walking down the wharf together she took his arm. He had her on his arm again. And the difference it made to get into the cab after Janey—to throw the red-and-yellow striped blanket round them both—to tell the driver to hurry because neither of them had had any tea. No more going without his tea or pouring out his own. She was back. He turned to her, squeezed her hand, and said gently, teasingly, in the "special" voice he had for her: "Glad to be home again, dearie?" She smiled; she didn't even bother to answer, but gently she drew his hand away as they came to the brighter streets.

"We've got the best room in the hotel," he said. "I wouldn't be put off with another. And I asked the chambermaid to put in a bit of a fire in case you felt chilly. She's a nice, attentive girl. And I thought now we were here we wouldn't bother to go home to-morrow, but spend the day looking round and leave the morning after. Does that suit you? There's no hurry, is there? The children will have you soon enough. . . . I thought a day's sight-seeing might make a nice break in your journey—eh, Janey?"

"Have you taken the tickets for the day after?" she asked.

"I should think I have!" He unbuttoned his overcoat and took out his bulging pocket-book. "Here we are! I reserved a first-class carriage to Cooktown. There it is—'Mr. *and* Mrs. John Hammond.' I thought we might as well do ourselves comfortably, and we don't want other people butting in, do we? But if you'd like to stop here a bit longer——?"

"Oh, no!" said Janey quickly. "Not for the world! The day after to-morrow, then. And the children——"

But they had reached the hotel. The manager was standing in the broad, brilliantly-lighted porch. He came down to greet them. A porter ran from the hall for their boxes.

"Well, Mr. Arnold, here's Mrs. Hammond at last!"

The manager led them through the hall himself and pressed the elevator-bell. Hammond knew there were business pals of his sitting at the little hall tables having a drink before dinner. But he wasn't going to risk interruption; he looked neither to the right nor the left. They could think what they pleased. If they didn't understand, the more fools they—and he stepped out of the lift, unlocked the door of their room, and shepherded Janey in. The door shut. Now, at last, they were alone together. He turned up the light. The curtains were drawn; the fire blazed. He flung his hat on to the huge bed and went towards her.

But—would you believe it!—again they were interrupted. This time it was the porter with the luggage. He made two journeys of it, leaving the door open in between, taking his time, whistling through his teeth in the corridor. Hammond paced up and down the room, tearing off his gloves, tearing off his scarf. Finally he flung his overcoat on to the bedside.

At last the fool was gone. The door clicked. Now they *were* alone. Said Hammond: "I feel I'll never have you to myself again. These cursed people! Janey"—and he bent his flushed, eager gaze upon her—"let's have dinner up here. If we go down to the restaurant we'll be interrupted, and then there's the confounded music" (the music he'd praised so highly, applauded so loudly last night!). "We shan't be able to hear each other speak. Let's have something up here in front of the fire. It's too late for tea. I'll order a little supper, shall I? How does that idea strike you?"

"Do, darling!" said Janey. "And while you're away—the children's letters——"

"Oh, later on will do!" said Hammond.

"But then we'd get it over," said Janey. "And I'd first have time to——"

"Oh, I needn't go down!" explained Hammond. "I'll just ring and give the order . . . you don't want to send me away, do you?"

Janey shook her head and smiled.

"But you're thinking of something else. You're worrying about something," said Hammond. "What is it? Come and sit here—come and sit on my knee before the fire."

"I'll just unpin my hat," said Janey, and she went over to the dressing-table. "A-ah!" She gave a little cry.

"What is it?"

"Nothing, darling. I've just found the children's letters. That's all right! They will keep. No hurry now!" She turned to him, clasping them. She tucked them into her frilled blouse. She cried quickly, gaily: "Oh, how typical this dressing-table is of you!"

"Why? What's the matter with it?" said Hammond.

"If it were floating in eternity I should say 'John!'" laughed Janey, staring at the big bottle of hair tonic, the wicker bottle of eau-de-Cologne, the two hair-brushes, and a dozen new collars tied with pink tape. "Is this all your luggage?"

"Hang my luggage!" said Hammond; but all the same he liked being laughed at by Janey. "Let's talk. Let's get down to things. Tell me"—and as Janey perched on his knees he leaned back and drew her into the deep, ugly chair—"tell me you're really glad to be back, Janey."

"Yes, darling, I am glad," she said.

But just as when he embraced her he felt she would fly away, so Hammond never knew—never knew for dead certain that she was as glad as he was. How could he know? Would he ever know? Would he always have this craving—this pang like hunger, somehow, to make Janey so much part of him that there wasn't any of her to escape? He wanted to blot out everybody, everything. He wished now he'd turned off the light. That might have brought her nearer. And now those letters from the children rustled in her blouse. He could have chucked them into the fire.

"Janey," he whispered.

"Yes, dear?" She lay on his breast, but so lightly, so remotely. Their breathing rose and fell together.

"Janey!"

"What is it?"

"Turn to me," he whispered. A slow, deep flush flowed into his forehead. "Kiss me, Janey! You kiss me!"

It seemed to him there was a tiny pause—but long enough for him to suffer torture—before her lips touched his, firmly, lightly—kissing them as she always kissed him, as though the kiss—how could he describe it?—confirmed what they were saying, signed the contract. But that wasn't what he wanted; that wasn't at all what he thirsted for. He felt suddenly, horribly tired.

"If you knew," he said, opening his eyes, "what it's been like—waiting to-day. I thought the boat never would come in. There we were, hanging about. What kept you so long?"

She made no answer. She was looking away from him at the fire. The flames hurried—hurried over the coals, flickered, fell.

"Not asleep, are you?" said Hammond, and he jumped her up and down.

"No," she said. And then: "Don't do that, dear. No, I was thinking. As a matter of fact," she said, "one of the passengers died last night—a man. That's what held us up. We brought him in—I mean, he wasn't buried at sea. So, of course, the ship's doctor and the shore doctor——"

"What was it?" asked Hammond uneasily. He hated to hear of death. He hated this to have happened. It was, in some queer way, as though he and Janey had met a funeral on their way to the hotel.

"Oh, it wasn't anything in the least infectious!" said Janey. She was speaking scarcely above her breath. "It was *heart.*" A pause. "Poor fellow!" she said. "Quite young." And she watched the fire flicker and fall. "He died in my arms," said Janey.

The blow was so sudden that Hammond thought he would faint. He couldn't move; he couldn't breathe. He felt all his strength flowing—flowing into the big dark chair, and the big dark chair held him fast, gripped him, forced him to bear it.

"What?" he said dully. "What's that you say?"

"The end was quite peaceful," said the small voice. "He just"—and Hammond saw her lift her gentle hand—"breathed his life away at the end." And her hand fell.

"Who—else was there?" Hammond managed to ask.

"Nobody. I was alone with him."

Ah, my God, what was she saying! What was she doing to him! This would kill him! And all the while she spoke:

"I saw the change coming and I sent the steward for the doctor, but the doctor was too late. He couldn't have done anything, anyway."

"But—why *you,* why *you?*" moaned Hammond.

At that Janey turned quickly, quickly searched his face.

"You don't *mind,* John, do you?" she asked.

"You don't —— It's nothing to do with you and me."

Somehow or other he managed to shake some sort of smile at her. Somehow or other he stammered: "No—go—on, go on! I want you to tell me."

"But, John darling——"

"Tell me, Janey!"

"There's nothing to tell," she said, wondering. "He was one of the first-class passengers. I saw he was very ill when he came on board. . . . But he seemed to be so much better until yesterday. He had a severe attack in the afternoon—excitement—nervousness, I think, about arriving. And after that he never recovered."

"But why didn't the stewardess——"

"Oh, my dear—the stewardess!" said Janey "What would he have felt? And besides . . . he might have wanted to leave a message . . . to——"

"Didn't he?" muttered Hammond. "Didn't he say anything?"

"No, darling, not a word!" She shook her head softly. "All the time I was with him he was too weak . . . he was too weak even to move a finger. . . ."

Janey was silent. But her words, so light, so soft, so chill, seemed to hover in the air, to rain into his breast like snow.

The fire had gone red. Now it fell in with a sharp sound and the room was colder. Cold crept up his arms. The room was huge, immense, glittering. It filled his whole world. There was the great blind bed, with his coat flung across it like some headless man saying his prayers. There was the luggage, ready to be carried away again, anywhere, tossed into trains, carted on to boats.

. . . "He was too weak. He was too weak to move a finger." And yet he died in Janey's arms. She—who'd never—never once in all these years—never on one single solitary occasion——

No; he mustn't think of it. Madness lay in thinking of it. No, he wouldn't face it. He couldn't stand it. It was too much to bear!

And now Janey touched his tie with her fingers. She pinched the edges of the tie tighter.

"You're not—sorry I told you, John darling? It hasn't made you sad? It hasn't spoilt our evening—our being alone together?"

But at that he had to hide his face. He put his face into her bosom and his arms enfolded her.

Spoilt their evening! Spoilt their being alone together! They would never be alone together again.

KATHERINE MANSFIELD

The Young Girl

In her blue dress, with her cheeks lightly flushed, her blue, blue eyes, and her gold curls pinned up as though for the first time—pinned up to be out of the way for her flight—Mrs. Raddick's daughter might have just dropped from this radiant heaven. Mrs. Raddick's timid, faintly astonished, but deeply admiring glance looked as if she believed it, too; but the daughter didn't appear any too pleased—why should she?—to have alighted on the steps of the Casino. Indeed, she was bored—bored as though Heaven had been full of casinos with snuffy old saints for *croupiers* and crowns to play with.

"You don't mind taking Hennie?" said Mrs. Raddick. "Sure you don't? There's the car, and you'll have tea and we'll be back here on this step—right here—in an hour. You see, I want her to go in. She's not been before, and it's worth seeing. I feel it wouldn't be fair to her."

"Oh, shut up, mother," said she wearily. "Come along. Don't talk so much. And your bag's open; you'll be losing all your money again."

"I'm sorry, darling," said Mrs. Raddick.

"Oh, *do* come in! I want to make money," said the impatient voice. "It's all jolly well for you—but I'm broke!"

"Here—take fifty francs, darling, take a hundred!" I saw Mrs. Raddick pressing notes into her hand as they passed through the swing doors.

Hennie and I stood on the steps a minute, watching the people. He had a very broad, delighted smile.

"I say," he cried, "there's an English bulldog. Are they allowed to take dogs in there?"

"No, they're not."

"He's a ripping chap, isn't he? I wish I had one. They're such fun. They frighten people so, and they're never fierce with their—the people they belong to." Suddenly he squeezed my arm. "I say, *do* look at that old woman. Who is she? Why does she look like that? Is she a gambler?"

The ancient, withered creature, wearing a green satin dress, a black velvet cloak and a white hat with purple feathers, jerked slowly, slowly up the steps as though she were being drawn up on wires. She stared in front of her, she was laughing and nodding and cackling to herself; her claws clutched round what looked like a dirty boot-bag.

But just at that moment there was Mrs. Raddick again with—*her*—and another lady hovering in the background. Mrs. Raddick rushed at me. She was brightly flushed, gay, a different creature. She was like a woman who is saying "good-bye" to her friends on the station platform, with not a minute to spare before the train starts.

"Oh, you're here, still. Isn't that lucky! You've not gone. Isn't that fine! I've had the most dreadful time with—her," and she waved to her daughter, who stood absolutely still, disdainful, looking down, twiddling her foot on the step, miles away. "They won't let her in. I swore she was twenty-one. But they won't believe me. I showed the man my purse; I didn't dare to do more. But it was no use. He simply scoffed. . . . And now I've just met Mrs. MacEwen from New York, and she just won thirteen thousand in the *Salle Privée*—and she wants me to go back with her while the luck lasts. Of course I can't leave—her. But if you'd——"

At that "she" looked up; she simply withered her mother. "Why can't you leave me?" she said furiously. "What utter rot! How dare you make a scene like this? This is the last time I'll come out with you. You really are too awful for words." She looked her mother up and down. "Calm yourself," she said superbly.

Mrs. Raddick was desperate, just desperate. She was "wild" to go back with Mrs. MacEwen, but at the same time . . .

I seized my courage. "Would you—do you care to come to tea with—us?"

"Yes, yes, she'll be delighted. That's just what I wanted, isn't it, darling? Mrs. MacEwen . . . I'll be back here in an hour . . . or less . . . I'll——"

Mrs. R. dashed up the steps. I saw her bag was open again.

So we three were left. But really it wasn't my fault. Hennie looked crushed to the earth, too. When the car was there she wrapped her dark coat round her—to escape contamination. Even her little feet looked as though they scorned to carry her down the steps to us.

"I am so awfully sorry," I murmured as the car started.

"Oh, I don't *mind,*" said she. "I don't *want* to look twenty-one. Who would—if they were seventeen! It's"—and she gave a faint shudder—"the stupidity I loathe, and being stared at by old fat men. Beasts!"

Hennie gave her a quick look and then peered out of the window.

We drew up before an immense palace of pink-and-white marble with orange-trees outside the doors in gold-and-black tubs.

"Would you care to go in?" I suggested.

She hesitated, glanced, bit her lip, and resigned herself. "Oh well, there seems nowhere else," said she. "Get out, Hennie."

I went first—to find the table, of course—she followed. But the worst of it was having her little brother, who was only twelve, with us. That was the last, final straw—having that child, trailing at her heels.

There was one table. It had pink carnations and pink plates with little blue tea-napkins for sails.

"Shall we sit here?"

She put her hand wearily on the back of a white wicker chair.

"We may as well. Why not?" said she.

Hennie squeezed past her and wriggled on to a stool at the end. He felt awfully out of it. She didn't even take her gloves off. She lowered her eyes and drummed on the table. When a faint violin sounded she winced and bit her lip again. Silence.

The waitress appeared. I hardly dared to ask her. "Tea—coffee? China tea—or iced tea with lemon?"

Really she didn't mind. It was all the same to her. She didn't really want anything. Hennie whispered, "Chocolate!"

But just as the waitress turned away she cried out carelessly, "Oh, you may as well bring me a chocolate, too."

While we waited she took out a little, gold powder-box with a mirror in the lid, shook the poor little puff as though she loathed it, and dabbed her lovely nose.

"Hennie," she said, "take those flowers away." She pointed with her puff to the carnations, and I heard her murmur, "I can't bear flowers on a table." They had evidently been giving her intense pain, for she positively closed her eyes as I moved them away.

The waitress came back with the chocolate and the tea. She put the big, frothing cups before them and pushed across my clear glass. Hennie buried his nose, emerged, with, for one dreadful moment, a little trembling blob of cream on the tip. But he hastily wiped it off like a little gentleman. I wondered if I should dare draw her attention to her cup. She didn't notice it—didn't see it—until suddenly, quite by chance, she took a sip. I watched anxiously; she faintly shuddered.

"Dreadfully sweet!" said she.

A tiny boy with a head like a raisin and a chocolate body came round with a tray of pastries—row upon row of little freaks, little inspirations, little melting dreams. He offered them to her. "Oh, I'm not at all hungry. Take them away."

He offered them to Hennie. Hennie gave me a swift

look—it must have been satisfactory—for he took a chocolate cream, a coffee éclair, a meringue stuffed with chestnut and a tiny horn filled with fresh strawberries. She could hardly bear to watch him. But just as the boy swerved away she held up her plate.

"Oh well, give me *one,*" said she.

The silver tongs dropped one, two, three—and a cherry tartlet. "I don't know why you're giving me all these," she said, and nearly smiled. "I shan't eat them; I couldn't!"

I felt much more comfortable. I sipped my tea, leaned back, and even asked if I might smoke. At that she paused, the fork in her hand, opened her eyes and really did smile. "Of course," said she. "I always expect people to."

But at that moment a tragedy happened to Hennie. He speared his pastry horn too hard, and it flew in two, and one half spilled on the table. Ghastly affair! He turned crimson. Even his ears flared, and one ashamed hand crept across the table to take what was left of the body away.

"You *utter* little beast!" said she.

Good heavens! I had to fly to the rescue. I cried hastily, "Will you be abroad long?"

But she had already forgotten Hennie. I was forgotten, too. She was trying to remember something. . . . She was miles away.

"I—don't—know," she said slowly, from that far place.

I suppose you prefer it to London. It's more—more ——"

When I didn't go on she came back and looked at me, very puzzled. "More——?"

"*Enfin*—gayer," I cried, waving my cigarette.

But that took a whole cake to consider. Even then, "Oh well, that depends!" was all she could safely say.

Hennie had finished. He was still very warm.

I seized the butterfly list off the table. "I say—what about an ice, Hennie? What about tangerine and ginger? No, something cooler. What about a fresh pineapple cream?"

Hennie strongly approved. The waitress had her eye on us. The order was taken when she looked up from her crumbs.

"Did you say tangerine and ginger? I like ginger. You can bring me one." And then quickly, "I wish that orchestra wouldn't play things from the year One. We were dancing to that all last Christmas. It's too sickening!"

But it was a charming air. Now that I noticed it, it warmed me.

"I think this is rather a nice place, don't you, Hennie?" I said.

Hennie said: "Ripping!" He meant to say it very low, but it came out very high in a kind of squeak.

Nice? This place? Nice? For the first time she stared about her, trying to see what there was. . . . She blinked; her lovely eyes wondered. A very good-looking elderly man stared back at her through a monocle on a black ribbon. But him she simply couldn't see. There was a hole in the air where he was. She looked through and through him.

Finally the little flat spoons lay still on the glass plates. Hennie looked rather exhausted, but she pulled on her white gloves again. She had some trouble with her diamond wrist-watch; it got in her way. She tugged at it—tried to break the stupid little thing—it wouldn't break. Finally, she had to drag her glove over. I saw, after that, she couldn't stand this place a moment longer, and, indeed, she jumped up and turned away while I went through the vulgar act of paying for the tea.

And then we were outside again. It had grown dusky. The sky was sprinkled with small stars; the big lamps glowed. While we waited for the car to come up she stood on the step, just as before, twiddling her foot, looking down.

Hennie bounded forward to open the door and she got in and sank back with—oh—such a sigh!

"Tell him," she gasped, "to drive as fast as he can."

Hennie grinned at his friend the chauffeur. "*Allie veet!*" said he. Then he composed himself and sat on the small seat facing us.

The gold powder-box came out again. Again the poor little puff was shaken; again there was that swift, deadly-secret glance between her and the mirror.

We tore through the black-and-gold town like a pair of scissors tearing through brocade. Hennie had great difficulty not to look as though he were hanging on to something.

And when we reached the Casino, of course Mrs. Raddick wasn't there. There wasn't a sign of her on the steps—not a sign.

"Will you stay in the car while I go and look?"

But no—she wouldn't do that. Good heavens, no! Hennie could stay. She couldn't bear sitting in a car. She'd wait on the steps.

"But I scarcely like to leave you," I murmured. "I'd very much rather not leave you here."

At that she threw back her coat; she turned and faced me; her lips parted. "Good heavens—why! I—I don't mind it a bit. I—I like waiting." And suddenly her cheeks crimsoned, her eyes grew dark—for a moment I thought she was going to cry. "L—let me, please," she stammered, in a warm, eager voice. "I like it. I love waiting! Really—really I do! I'm always waiting—in all kinds of places. . . ."

Her dark coat fell open, and her white throat—all her soft young body in the blue dress—was like a flower that is just emerging from its dark bud.

KATHERINE ANNE PORTER

The Jilting of Granny Weatherall

SHE FLICKED her wrist neatly out of Doctor Harry's pudgy careful fingers and pulled the sheet up to her chin. The brat ought to be in knee breeches. Doctoring around the country with spectacles on his nose! "Get along now, take your schoolbooks and go. There's nothing wrong with me."

Doctor Harry spread a warm paw like a cushion on her forehead where the forked green vein danced and made her eyelids twitch. "Now, now, be a good girl, and we'll have you up in no time."

"That's no way to speak to a woman nearly eighty years old just because she's down. I'd have you respect your elders, young man."

"Well, Missy, excuse me." Doctor Harry patted her cheek. "But I've got to warn you, haven't I? You're a marvel, but you must be careful or you're going to be good and sorry."

"Don't tell me what I'm going to be. I'm on my feet now, morally speaking. It's Cornelia. I had to go to bed to get rid of her."

Her bones felt loose, and floated around in her skin, and Doctor Harry floated like a balloon around the foot of the bed. He floated and pulled down his waistcoat and swung his glasses on a cord. "Well, stay where you are, it certainly can't hurt you."

"Get along and doctor your sick," said Granny Weatherall. "Leave a well woman alone. I'll call for you when I want you. . . . Where were you forty years ago when I pulled through milk-leg and double pneumonia? You weren't even born. Don't let Cornelia lead you on," she shouted, because Doctor Harry appeared to float up to the ceiling and out. "I pay my own bills, and I don't throw my money away on nonsense!"

She meant to wave good-by, but it was too much trouble. Her eyes closed of themselves, it was like a dark curtain drawn around the bed. The pillow rose and floated under her, pleasant as a hammock in a light wind. She listened to the leaves rustling outside the window. No, somebody was swishing newspapers: no, Cornelia and Doctor Harry were whispering together. She leaped broad awake, thinking they whispered in her ear.

"She was never like this, *never* like this!" "Well, what can we expect?" "Yes, eighty years old. . . ."

Well, and what if she was? She still had ears. It was like Cornelia to whisper around doors. She always kept things secret in such a public way. She was always being tactful and kind. Cornelia was dutiful; that was the trouble with her. Dutiful and good: "So good and dutiful," said Granny, "that I'd like to spank her." She saw herself spanking Cornelia and making a fine job of it.

"What'd you say, Mother?"

Granny felt her face tying up in hard knots.

"Can't a body think, I'd like to know?"

"I thought you might want something."

"I do. I want a lot of things. First off, go away and don't whisper."

She lay and drowsed, hoping in her sleep that the children would keep out and let her rest a minute. It had been a long day. Not that she was tired. It was always pleasant to snatch a minute now and then. There was always so much to be done, let me see: tomorrow.

Tomorrow was far away and there was nothing to trouble about. Things were finished somehow when the time came; thank God there was always a little margin over for peace: then a person could spread out the plan of life and tuck in the edges orderly. It was good to have everything clean and folded away, with the hair brushes and tonic bottles sitting straight on the white embroidered linen: the day started without fuss and the pantry shelves laid out with rows of jelly glasses and brown jugs and white stone-china jars with blue whirligigs and words painted on them: coffee, tea, sugar, ginger, cinnamon, allspice: and the bronze clock with the lion on top nicely dusted off. The dust that lion could collect in twenty-four hours! The box in the attic with all those letters tied up, well, she'd have to go through that tomorrow. All those letters—George's letters and John's letters and her letters to them both—lying around for the children to find afterwards made her uneasy. Yes, that would be tomorrow's business. No use to let them know how silly she had been once.

While she was rummaging around she found death in her mind and it felt clammy and unfamiliar. She had spent so much time preparing for death there was no need for bringing it up again. Let it take care of itself now. When she was sixty she had felt very old, finished, and went around making farewell trips to see her children and grandchildren, with a secret in her mind: This is the very last of your mother, children! Then she made her will and came down with a long fever. That was all just a notion like a lot of other things, but it was lucky too, for she had once for all got over the idea of dying for a long time. Now she couldn't be worried. She hoped she had better sense now. Her father had lived to be one hundred and two years old and had drunk a noggin of strong hot toddy on his last birthday. He told the reporters it was his daily habit, and he owed his long life to that. He had made quite a scandal and was very pleased about it. She believed she'd just plague Cornelia a little.

"Cornelia! Cornelia!" No footsteps, but a sudden hand on her cheek. "Bless you, where have you been?"

"Here, mother."

"Well, Cornelia, I want a noggin of hot toddy."

"Are you cold, darling?"

"I'm chilly, Cornelia. Lying in bed stops the circulation. I must have told you that a thousand times."

Well, she could just hear Cornelia telling her husband that Mother was getting a little childish and they'd have to humor her. The thing that most annoyed her was that Cornelia thought she was deaf, dumb, and blind. Little hasty glances and tiny gestures tossed around her and over her head saying, "Don't cross her, let her have her way, she's eighty years old," and she sitting there as if she lived in a thin glass cage. Sometimes Granny almost made up her mind to pack up and move back to her own house where nobody could remind her every minute that she was old. Wait, wait, Cornelia, till your own children whisper behind your back!

In her day she had kept a better house and had got more work done. She wasn't too old yet for Lydia to be driving eighty miles for advice when one of the children jumped the track, and Jimmy still dropped in and talked things over: "Now, Mammy, you've a good business head, I want to know what you think of this? . . ." Old. Cornelia couldn't change the furniture around without asking. Little things, little things! They had been so sweet when they were little. Granny wished the old days were back again with the children young and everything to be done over. It had been a hard pull, but not too much for her. When she thought of all the food she had cooked, and all the clothes she had cut and sewed, and all the gardens she had made—well, the children showed it. There they were, made out of her, and they couldn't get away from that. Sometimes she wanted to see John again and point to them and say. Well, I didn't do so badly, did I? But that would have to wait. That was for tomorrow. She used to think of him as a man, but now all the children were older than their father, and he would be a child beside her if she saw him now. It seemed strange and there was something wrong in the idea. Why, he couldn't possibly recognize her. She had fenced in a hundred acres once, digging the post holes herself and clamping the wires with just a negro boy to help. That changed a woman. John would be looking for a young woman with the peaked Spanish comb in her hair and the painted fan. Digging post holes changed a woman. Riding country roads in the winter when women had their babies was another thing: sitting up nights with sick horses and sick negroes and sick children and hardly ever losing one. John, I hardly ever lost one of them! John would see that in a minute, that would be something he could understand, she wouldn't have to explain anything!

It made her feel like rolling up her sleeves and putting the whole place to rights again. No matter if Cornelia was determined to be everywhere at once, there were a great many things left undone on this place. She would start tomorrow and do them. It was good to be strong enough for everything, even if all you made melted and changed and slipped under your hands, so that by the time you finished you almost forgot what you were working for. What was it I set out to do? she asked herself intently, but she could not remember. A fog rose over the valley, she saw it marching across the creek swallowing the trees and moving up the hill like an army of ghosts. Soon it would be at the near edge of the orchard, and then it was time to go in and light the lamps. Come in, children, don't stay out in the night air.

Lighting the lamps had been beautiful. The children huddled up to her and breathed like little calves waiting at the bars in the twilight. Their eyes followed the match and watched the flame rise and settle in a blue curve, then they moved away from her. The lamp was lit, they didn't have to be scared and hang on to mother any more. Never, never, never more. God, for all my life I thank Thee. Without Thee, my God, I could never have done it. Hail, Mary, full of grace.

I want you to pick all the fruit this year and see that nothing is wasted. There's always someone who can use it. Don't let good things rot for want of using. You waste life when you waste good food. Don't let things get lost. It's bitter to lose things. Now, don't let me get to thinking, not when I am tired and taking a little nap before supper. . . .

The pillow rose about her shoulders and pressed against her heart and the memory was being squeezed out of it: oh, push down the pillow, somebody: it would smother her if she tried to hold it. Such a fresh breeze blowing and such a green day with no threats in it. But he had not come, just the same. What does a woman do when she has put on the white veil and set out the white cake for a man and he doesn't come? She tried to remember. No, I swear he never harmed me but in that. He never harmed me but in that . . . and what if he did? There was the day, the day, but a whirl of dark smoke rose and covered it, crept up and over into the bright field where everything was planted so carefully in orderly rows. That was hell, she knew hell when she saw it. For sixty years she had prayed against remembering him and against losing her soul in the deep pit of hell, and now the two things were mingled in one and the thought of him was a smoky cloud from hell that moved and crept in her head when she had just got rid of Doctor Harry and was trying to rest a minute. Wounded vanity, Ellen, said a sharp voice in the top of her mind. Don't let your wounded vanity get the upper hand of you. Plenty of girls get jilted. You were jilted, weren't you? Then stand up to it. Her eyelids wavered and let in streamers of blue-gray light like tissue paper over her eyes. She must get up and pull the shades down or she'd never sleep. She was in bed again and the shades were not down. How could that happen? Better turn over, hide from the light, sleeping in the light gave you nightmares. "Mother, how do you feel now?" and a stinging wetness on her forehead. But I don't like having my face washed in cold water!

Hapsy? George? Lydia? Jimmy? No, Cornelia, and her features were swollen and full of little puddles. "They're coming, darling, they'll all be here soon." Go wash your face, child, you look funny.

Instead of obeying, Cornelia knelt down and put her head on the pillow. She seemed to be talking but there was no sound. "Well, are you tongue-tied? Whose birthday is it? Are you going to give a party?"

Cornelia's mouth moved urgently in strange shapes. "Don't do that, you bother me, daughter."

"Oh, no, Mother. Oh, no. . . ."

Nonsense. It was strange about children. They disputed your every word. "No what, Cornelia?"

"Here's Doctor Harry."

"I won't see that boy again. He just left five minutes ago."

"That was this morning, Mother. It's night now. Here's the nurse."

"This is Doctor Harry, Mrs. Weatherall. I never saw you look so young and happy!"

"Ah, I'll never be young again—but I'd be happy if they'd let me lie in peace and get rested."

She thought she spoke up loudly, but no one answered. A warm weight on her forehead, a warm bracelet on her wrist, and a breeze went on whispering, trying to tell her something. A shuffle of leaves in the everlasting hand of God, He blew on them and they danced and rattled. "Mother, don't mind, we're going to give you a little hypodermic." "Look here, daughter, how do ants get in this bed? I saw sugar ants yesterday." Did you send for Hapsy too?

It was Hapsy she really wanted. She had to go a long way back through a great many rooms to find Hapsy standing with a baby on her arm. She seemed to herself to be Hapsy also, and the baby on Hapsy's arm was Hapsy and himself and herself, all at once, and there was no surprise in the meeting. Then Hapsy melted from within and turned flimsy as gray gauze and the baby was a gauzy shadow, and Hapsy came up close and said, "I thought you'd never come," and looked at her very searchingly and said, "You haven't changed a bit!" They leaned forward to kiss, when Cornelia began whispering from a long way off, "Oh, is there anything you want to tell me? Is there anything I can do for you?"

Yes, she had changed her mind after sixty years and she would like to see George. I want you to find George. Find him and be sure to tell him I forgot him. I want him to know I had my husband just the same and my children and my house like any other woman. A good house too and a good husband that I loved and fine children out of him. Better than I hoped for even. Tell him I was given back everything he took away and more. Oh, no, oh, God, no, there was something else besides the house and the man and the children. Oh, surely they were not all? What was it? Something not given back. . . . Her breath crowded down under her ribs and grew into a monstrous frightening shape with cutting edges; it bored up into her head, and the agony was unbelievable: Yes, John, get the doctor now, no more talk, my time has come.

When this one was born it should be the last. The last. It should have been born first, for it was the one she had truly wanted. Everything came in good time. Nothing left out, left over. She was strong, in three days she would be as well as ever. Better. A woman needed milk in her to have her full health.

"Mother, do you hear me?"

"I've been telling you—"

"Mother, Father Connolly's here."

"I went to Holy Communion only last week. Tell him I'm not so sinful as all that."

"Father just wants to speak to you."

He could speak as much as he pleased. It was like him to drop in and inquire about her soul as if it were a teething baby, and then stay on for a cup of tea and a round of cards and gossip. He always had a funny story of some sort, usually about an Irishman who made his little mistakes and confessed them, and the point lay in some absurd thing he would blurt out in the confessional showing his struggles between native piety and original sin. Granny felt easy about her soul. Cornelia, where are your manners? Give Father Connolly a chair. She had her secret comfortable understanding with a few favorite saints who cleared a straight road to God for her. All as surely signed and sealed as the papers for the new Forty Acres. Forever . . . heirs and assigns forever. Since the day the wedding cake was not cut, but thrown out and wasted. The whole bottom dropped out of the world, and there she was blind and sweating with nothing under her feet and the walls falling away. His hand had caught her under the breast, she had not fallen, there was the freshly polished floor with the green rug on it, just as before. He had cursed like a sailor's parrot and said, "I'll kill him for you." Don't lay a hand on him, for my sake leave something to God. "Now, Ellen, you must believe what I tell you. . . ."

So there was nothing, nothing to worry about any more, except sometimes in the night one of the children screamed in a nightmare, and they both hustled out shaking and hunting for the matches and calling, "There, wait a minute, here we are!" John, get the doctor now, Hapsy's time has come. But there was Hapsy standing by the bed in a white cap. "Cornelia, tell Hapsy to take off her cap. I can't see her plain."

Her eyes opened very wide and the room stood out like a picture she had seen somewhere. Dark colors with the shadows rising towards the ceiling in long angles. The tall black dresser gleamed with nothing on it but John's picture, enlarged from a little one, with John's eyes very black when they should have been blue. You never saw him, so how do you know how he looked? But the man insisted the copy was perfect, it was very rich and handsome. For a picture, yes, but it's not my husband. The table by the bed had a linen cover and a candle and a crucifix. The light was blue from Cornelia's silk lampshades. No sort of light at all, just frippery. You had to live forty years with kerosene lamps to appreciate honest electricity. She felt very strong and she saw Doctor Harry with a rosy nimbus around him.

"You look like a saint, Doctor Harry, and I vow that's as near as you'll ever come to it."

"She's saying something."

"I heard you, Cornelia. What's all this carrying-on?"

"Father Connolly's saying—"

Cornelia's voice staggered and bumped like a cart in a bad road. It rounded corners and turned back again and arrived nowhere. Granny stepped up in the cart very lightly and reached for the reins, but a man sat beside her and she knew him by his hands, driving the cart. She did not look in his face, for she knew without seeing, but looked instead down the road where the trees leaned over and bowed to each other and a thousand birds were singing a Mass. She felt like singing too, but she put her hand in the bosom of her dress and pulled out a rosary, and Father Connolly murmured Latin in a very solemn voice and tickled her feet. My God, will you stop that nonsense? I'm a married woman. What if he did run away and leave me to face the priest by myself? I found another a whole world better. I wouldn't have exchanged my husband for anybody except St. Michael himself, and you may tell him that for me with a thank you in the bargain.

Light flashed on her closed eyelids, and a deep roaring shook her. Cornelia, is that lightning? I hear thunder. There's going to be a storm. Close all the windows. Call the children in. . . . "Mother, here we are, all of us." "Is that you, Hapsy?" "Oh, no, I'm Lydia. We drove as fast as we could." Their faces drifted above her, drifted away. The rosary fell out of her hands and Lydia put it back. Jimmy tried to help, their hands fumbled together, and Granny closed two fingers around Jimmy's thumb. Beads wouldn't do, it must be something alive. She was so amazed her thoughts ran round and round. So, my dear Lord, this is my death and I wasn't even thinking about it. My children have come to see me die. But I can't, its not time. Oh, I always hated surprises. I wanted to give Cornelia the amethyst set—Cornelia, you're to have the amethyst set, but Hapsy's to wear it when she wants, and, Doctor Harry, do shut up. Nobody sent for you. Oh, my dear Lord, do wait a minute. I meant to do something about the Forty Acres, Jimmy doesn't need it and Lydia will later on, with that worthless husband of hers. I meant to finish the altar cloth and send six bottles of wine to Sister Borgia for her dyspepsia. I want to send six bottles of wine to Sister Borgia, Father Connolly, now don't let me forget.

Cornelia's voice made short turns and tilted over and crashed. "Oh, Mother, oh, Mother, oh, Mother. . . ."

"I'm not going, Cornelia. I'm taken by surprise. I can't go."

You'll see Hapsy again. What about her? "I thought you'd never come." Granny made a long journey outward, looking for Hapsy. What if I don't find her? What then? Her heart sank down, there was no bottom to death, she couldn't come to the end of it. The blue light from Cornelia's lampshade drew into a tiny point in the center of her brain, it flickered and winked like an eye, quietly it fluttered and dwindled. Granny lay curled down within herself, amazed and watchful, staring at the point of light that was herself; her body was now only a deeper mass of shadow in an endless darkness and this darkness would curl around the light and swallow it up. God, give a sign!

For the second time there was no sign. Again no bridegroom and the priest in the house. She could not remember any other sorrow because this grief wiped them all away. Oh, no, there's nothing more cruel than this—I'll never forgive it. She stretched herself with a deep breath and blew out the light.

KATHERINE ANNE PORTER

Theft

SHE HAD the purse in her hand when she came in. Standing in the middle of the floor, holding her bathrobe around her and trailing a damp towel in one hand, she surveyed the immediate past and remembered everything clearly. Yes, she had opened the flap and spread it out on the bench after she had dried the purse with her handkerchief.

She had intended to take the Elevated, and naturally she looked in her purse to make certain she had the fare, and was pleased to find forty cents in the coin envelope. She was going to pay her own fare, too, even if Camilo did have the habit of seeing her up the steps and dropping a nickel in the machine before he gave the turnstile a little push and sent her through it with a bow. Camilo by a series of compromises had managed to make effective a fairly complete set of smaller courtesies, ignoring the larger and more troublesome ones. She had walked with him to the station in a pouring rain, because she knew he was almost as poor as she was, and when he insisted on a taxi, she was firm and said, "You know it simply will not do." He was wearing a new hat of a pretty biscuit shade, for it never occurred to him to buy anything of a practical color; he had put it on for the first time and the rain was spoiling it. She kept thinking, "But this is dreadful, where will he get another?" She compared it with Eddie's hats that always seemed to be precisely seven years old and as if they had been quite purposely left out in the rain, and yet they sat with a careless and incidental rightness on Eddie. But Camilo was far different; if he wore a shabby hat it would be merely shabby on him, and he would lose his spirits over it. If she had not feared Camilo would take it badly, for he insisted on the practice of his little ceremonies up to the point he had fixed for them, she would have said to him as they left Thora's house, "Do go home. I can surely reach the station by myself."

"It is written that we must be rained upon tonight," said Camilo, "so let it be together."

At the foot of the platform stairway she staggered slightly—they were both nicely set up on Thora's cocktails—and said: "At least, Camilo, do me the favor not to climb these stairs in your present state, since for you it is only a matter of coming down again at once, and you'll certainly break your neck."

He made three quick bows, he was Spanish, and leaped off through the rainy darkness. She stood watching him, for he was a very graceful young man, thinking that tomorrow morning he would gaze soberly at his spoiled hat and soggy shoes and possibly associate her with his misery. As she watched, he stopped at the far corner and took off his hat and hid it under his overcoat. She felt she had betrayed him by seeing, because he would have been humiliated if he thought she even suspected him of trying to save his hat.

Roger's voice sounded over her shoulder above the clang of the rain falling on the stairway shed, wanting to know what she was doing out in the rain at this time of night, and did she take herself for a duck? His long, imperturbable face was streaming with water, and he tapped a bulging spot on the breast of his buttoned-up overcoat: "Hat," he said. "Come on, let's take a taxi."

She settled back against Roger's arm which he laid around her shoulders, and with the gesture they exchanged a glance full of long amiable associations, then she looked through the window at the rain changing the shapes of everything, and the colors. The taxi dodged in and out between the pillars of the Elevated, skidding slightly on every curve, and she said: "The more it skids the calmer I feel, so I really must be drunk."

"You must be," said Roger. "This bird is a homicidal maniac, and I could do with a cocktail myself this minute."

They waited on the traffic at Fortieth Street and Sixth Avenue, and three boys walked before the nose of the taxi. Under the globes of light they were cheerful scarecrows, all very thin and all wearing very seedy snappy-cut suits and gay neckties. They were not very sober either, and they stood for a moment wobbling in front of the car, and there was an argument going on among them. They leaned toward each other as if they were getting ready to sing, and the first one said: "When I get married it won't be jus' for getting married, I'm gonna marry for *love*, see?" and the second one said, "Aw, gwan and tell that stuff to *her*, why n't yuh?" and the third one gave a kind of hoot, and said, "Hell, dis guy? Wot the hell's he got?" and the first one said:

"Aaah, shurrup yuh mush, I got plenty." Then they all squealed and scrambled across the street beating the first one on the back and pushing him around.

"Nuts," commented Roger, "pure nuts."

Two girls went skittering by in short transparent raincoats, one green, one red, their heads tucked against the drive of the rain. One of them was saying to the other, "Yes, I know all about *that*. But what about me? You're always so sorry for *him* . . ." and they ran on with their little pelican legs flashing back and forth.

The taxi backed up suddenly and leaped forward again, and after a while Roger said: "I had a letter from Stella today, and she'll be home on the twenty-sixth, so I suppose she's made up her mind and it's all settled."

"I had a sort of letter today too," she said, "making up my mind for me. I think it is time for you and Stella to do something definite."

When the taxi stopped on the corner of West Fifty-third Street, Roger said, "I've just enough if you'll add ten cents," so she opened her purse and gave him a dime, and he said, "That's beautiful, that purse."

"It's a birthday present," she told him, "and I like it. How's your show coming?"

"Oh, still hanging on, I guess. I don't go near the place. Nothing sold yet. I mean to keep right on the way I'm going and they can take it or leave it. I'm through with the argument."

"It's absolutely a matter of holding out, isn't it?"

"Holding out's the tough part."

"Good night, Roger."

"Good night, you should take aspirin and push yourself into a tub of hot water, you look as though you're catching cold."

"I will."

With the purse under her arm she went upstairs, and on the first landing Bill heard her step and poked his head out with his hair tumbled and his eyes red, and he said: "For Christ's sake come in and have a drink with me. I've had some bad news."

"You're perfectly sopping," said Bill, looking at her drenched feet. They had two drinks, while Bill told how the director had thrown his play out after the cast had been picked over twice, and had gone through three rehearsals. "I said to him, 'I didn't say it was a masterpiece, I said it would make a good show.' And he said, 'It just doesn't *play*, do you see? It needs a doctor.' So I'm stuck, absolutely stuck," said Bill, on the edge of weeping again. "I've been crying," he told her, "in my cups." And he went on to ask her if she realized his wife was ruining him with her extravagance. "I send her ten dollars every week of my unhappy life, and I don't really have to. She threatens to jail me if I don't, but she can't do it. God, let her try it after the way she treated me! She's no right to alimony and she knows it. She keeps on saying she's got to have it for the baby and I keep on sending it because I can't bear to see anybody suffer. So I'm way behind on the piano and the victrola, both—"

"Well, this is a pretty rug, anyhow," she said.

Bill stared at it and blew his nose. "I got it at Ricci's for ninety-five dollars," he said. "Ricci told me it once belonged to Marie Dressler, and cost fifteen hundred dollars, but there's a burnt place on it, under the divan. Can you beat that?"

"No," she said. She was thinking about her empty purse and that she could not possibly expect a check for her latest review for another three days, and her arrangement with the basement restaurant could not last much longer if she did not pay something on account. "It's no time to speak of it," she said, "but I've been hoping you would have by now that fifty dollars you promised for my scene in the third act. Even if it doesn't play. You were to pay me for the work anyhow out of your advance."

"Weeping Jesus," said Bill, "you, too?" He gave a loud sob, or hiccough, in his moist handkerchief. "Your stuff was no better than mine, after all. Think of that."

"But you got something for it," she said. "Seven hundred dollars."

Bill said, "Do me a favor, will you? Have another drink and forget about it. I can't, you know I can't, I would if I could, but you know the fix I'm in."

"Let it go, then," she found herself saying almost in spite of herself. She had meant to be quite firm about it. They drank again without speaking, and she went to her apartment on the floor above.

There, she now remembered distinctly, she had taken the letter out of the purse before she spread the purse out to dry.

She had sat down and read the letter over again: but there were phrases that insisted on being read many times, they had a life of their own separate from the others, and when she tried to read past and around them, they moved with the movement of her eyes, and she could not escape them . . . "thinking about you more than I mean to . . . yes, I even talk about you . . . why were you so anxious to destroy . . . even if I could see you now I would not . . . not worth all this abominable . . . the end . . ."

Carefully she tore the letter into narrow strips and touched a lighted match to them in the coal grate.

Early the next morning she was in the bathtub when the janitress knocked and then came in, calling out that she wished to examine the radiators before she started the furnace going for the winter. After moving about the room for a few minutes, the janitress went out, closing the door very sharply.

She came out of the bathroom to get a cigarette from the package in the purse. The purse was gone. She dressed and made coffee, and sat by the window while she drank it. Certainly the janitress had taken the purse, and certainly it would be impossible to get it back without a great deal of ridiculous excitement. Then let it go. With this decision of her mind, there rose coincidentally in her blood a deep murderous anger. She set the cup carefully in the center of the table, and walked steadily downstairs, three long flights and a short hall and a steep short flight into the basement, where the janitress, her face streaked with coal dust, was shaking up the furnace. "Will you please give me back my purse? There isn't any money in it, It was a present, and I don't want to lose it."

The janitress turned without straightening up and peered at her with hot flickering eyes, a red light from the furnace reflected in them. "What do you mean, your purse?"

"The gold cloth purse you took from the wooden bench in my room," she said. "I must have it back."

"Before God I never laid eyes on your purse, and that's the holy truth," said the janitress.

"Oh, well then, keep it," she said, but in a very bitter voice; "keep it if you want it so much." And she walked away.

She remembered how she had never locked a door in her life, on some principle of rejection in her that made her uncomfortable in the ownership of things, and her paradoxical boast before the warnings of her friends, that she had never lost a penny by theft; and she had been pleased with the bleak humility of this concrete example designed to illustrate and justify a certain fixed, otherwise baseless and general faith which ordered the movements of her life without regard to her will in the matter.

In this moment she felt that she had been robbed of an enormous number of valuable things, whether material or intangible: things lost or broken by her own fault, things she had forgotten and left in houses when she moved: books borrowed from her and not returned, journeys she had planned and had not made, words she had waited to hear spoken to her and had not heard, and the words she had meant to answer with; bitter alternatives and intolerable substitutes worse than nothing, and yet inescapable: the long patient suffering of dying friendships and the dark inexplicable death of love—all that she had had, and all that she had missed, were lost together, and were twice lost in this landslide of remembered losses.

The janitress was following her upstairs with the purse in her hand and the same deep red fire flickering in her eyes. The janitress thrust the purse towards her while they were still a half dozen steps apart, and said: "Don't never tell on me. I musta been crazy. I get crazy in the head sometimes, I swear I do. My son can tell you."

She took the purse after a moment, and the janitress went on: "I got a niece who is going on seventeen, and she's a nice girl and I thought I'd give it to her. She needs a pretty purse. I musta been crazy; I thought maybe you wouldn't mind, you leave things around and don't seem to notice much."

She said: "I missed this because it was a present to me from someone . . ."

The janitress said: "He'd get you another if you lost this one. My niece is young and needs pretty things, we oughta give the young ones a chance. She's got young men after her maybe will want to marry her. She oughta have nice things. She needs them bad right now. You're a grown woman, you've had your chance, you ought to know how it is!"

She held the purse out to the janitress saying: "You don't know what you're talking about. Here, take it, I've changed my mind. I really don't want it."

The janitress looked up at her with hatred and said: "I don't want it either now. My niece is young and pretty, she don't need fixin' up to be pretty, she's young and pretty anyhow! I guess you need it worse than she does!"

"It wasn't really yours in the first place," she said, turning away. "You mustn't talk as if I had stolen it from you."

"It's not from me, it's from her you're stealing it," said the janitress, and went back downstairs.

She laid the purse on the table and sat down with the cup of chilled coffee, and thought: I was right not to be afraid of any thief but myself, who will end by leaving me nothing.

JOHN STEINBECK

The Chrysanthemums

THE HIGH grey-flannel fog of winter closed off the Salinas Valley from the sky and from all the rest of the world. On every side it sat like a lid on the mountains and made of the great valley a closed pot. On the broad, level land floor the gang plows bit deep and left the black earth shining like metal where the shares had cut. On the foothill ranches across the Salinas River, the yellow stubble fields seemed to be bathed in pale cold sunshine, but there was no sunshine in the valley now in December. The thick willow scrub along the river flamed with sharp and positive yellow leaves.

It was a time of quiet and of waiting. The air was cold and tender. A light wind blew up from the southwest so that the farmers were mildly hopeful of a good rain before long; but fog and rain do not go together.

Across the river, on Henry Allen's foothill ranch there was little work to be done, for the hay was cut and stored and the orchards were plowed up to receive the rain deeply when it should come. The cattle on the higher slopes were becoming shaggy and rough-coated.

Elisa Allen, working in her flower garden, looked down across the yard and saw Henry, her husband, talking to two men in business suits. The three of them stood by the tractor shed, each man with one foot on the side of the little Fordson. They smoked cigarettes and studied the machine as they talked.

Elisa watched them for a moment and then went back to her work. She was thirty-five. Her face was lean and strong and her eyes were as clear as water. Her figure looked blocked and heavy in her gardening costume, a man's black hat pulled low down over her eyes, clodhopper shoes, a figured print dress almost completely covered by a big corduroy apron with four big pockets to hold the snips, the trowel and scratcher, the seeds and the knife she worked with. She wore heavy leather gloves to protect her hands while she worked.

She was cutting down the old year's chrysanthemum stalks with a pair of short and powerful scissors. She looked down toward the men by the tractor shed now and then. Her face was eager and mature and handsome; even her work with the scissors was over-eager, overpowerful. The chrysanthemum stems seemed too small and easy for her energy.

She brushed a cloud of hair out of her eyes with the back of her glove, and left a smudge of earth on the cheek in doing it. Behind her stood the neat white farm house with red geraniums close-banked around it as high as the windows. It was a hard-swept looking little house, with hard-polished windows, and a clean mud-mat on the front steps.

Elisa cast another glance toward the tractor shed. The strangers were getting into their Ford coupe. She took off a glove and put her strong fingers down into the forest of new green chrysanthemum sprouts that were growing around the old roots. She spread the leaves and looked down among the close-growing stems. No aphids were there, no sowbugs or snails or cutworms. Her terrier fingers destroyed such pests before they could get started.

Elisa started at the sound of her husband's voice. He had come near quietly, and he leaned over the wire fence that protected her flower garden from cattle and dogs and chickens.

"At it again," he said. "You've got a strong new crop coming."

Elisa straightened her back and pulled on the gardening glove again. "Yes. They'll be strong this coming year." In her tone and on her face there was a little smugness.

"You've got a gift with things," Henry observed. "Some of those yellow chrysanthemums you had this year were ten inches across. I wish you'd work out in the orchard and raise some apples that big."

Her eyes sharpened. "Maybe I could do it, too. I've a gift with things, all right. My mother had it. She could stick anything in the ground and make it grow. She said it was having planters' hands that knew how to do it."

"Well, it sure works with flowers," he said.

"Henry, who were those men you were talking to?"

"Why, sure, that's what I came to tell you. They were from the Western Meat Company. I sold those thirty head of three-year-old steers. Got nearly my own price, too."

"Good," she said. "Good for you."

"And I thought," he continued, "I thought how it's Saturday afternoon, and we might go into Salinas for dinner at a restaurant, and then to a picture show—to celebrate, you see."

"Good," she repeated. "Oh, yes. That will be good."

Henry put on his joking tone. "There's fights tonight. How'd you like to go to the fights?"

"Oh, no," she said breathlessly. "No, I wouldn't like fights."

"Just fooling, Elisa. We'll go to a movie. Let's see. It's two now. I'm going to take Scotty and bring down those steers from the hill. It'll take us maybe two hours. We'll go in town about five and have dinner at the Cominos Hotel. Like that?"

"Of course I'll like it. It's good to eat away from home."

"All right, then. I'll go get up a couple of horses."

She said, "I'll have plenty of time to transplant some of these sets, I guess."

She heard her husband calling Scotty down by the barn. And a little later she saw the two men ride up the pale yellow hillside in search of the steers.

There was a little square sandy bed kept for rooting the chrysanthemums. With her trowel she turned the soil over and over, and smoothed it and patted it firm. Then she dug ten parallel trenches to receive the sets. Back at the chrysanthemum bed she pulled out the little crisp shoots, trimmed off the leaves of each one with her scissors and laid it on a small orderly pile.

A squeak of wheels and plod of hoofs came from the road. Elisa looked up. The country road ran along the dense bank of willows and cottonwoods that bordered the river, and up this road came a curious vehicle, curiously drawn. It was an old spring-wagon, with a round canvas top on it like the cover of a prairie schooner. It was drawn by an old bay horse and a little grey-and-white burro. A big stubble-bearded man sat between the cover flaps and drove the crawling team. Underneath the wagon, between the hind wheels, a lean and rangy mongrel dog walked sedately. Words were painted on the canvas in clumsy, crooked letters. "Pots, pans, knives, sisors, lawn mores. Fixed." Two rows of articles and the triumphantly definitive "Fixed" below. The black paint had run down in little sharp points beneath each letter.

Elisa, squatting on the ground, watched to see the crazy, loose-jointed wagon pass by. But it didn't pass. It turned into the farm road in front of her house, crooked old wheels skirling and squeaking. The rangy dog darted from between the wheels and ran ahead. Instantly the two ranch shepherds flew out at him. Then all three stopped, and with stiff and quivering tails, with taut straight legs, with ambassadorial dignity, they slowly circled, sniffing daintily. The caravan pulled up to Elisa's wire fence and stopped. Now the newcomer dog, feeling outnumbered, lowered his tail and retired under the wagon with raised hackles and bared teeth.

The man on the wagon seat called out. "That's a bad dog in a fight when he gets started."

Elisa laughed. "I see he is. How soon does he generally get started?"

The man caught up her laughter and echoed it heartily. "Sometimes not for weeks and weeks," he said. He climbed stiffly down, over the wheel. The horse and the donkey drooped like unwatered flowers.

Elisa saw that he was a very big man. Although his hair and beard were greying, he did not look old. His worn black suit was wrinkled and spotted with grease. The laughter had disappeared from his face and eyes the moment his laughing voice ceased. His eyes were dark, and they were full of the brooding that gets in the eyes of teamsters and of sailors. The calloused hands he rested on the wire fence were cracked, and every crack was a black line. He took off his battered hat.

"I'm off my general road, ma'am," he said. "Does this dirt road cut over across the river to the Los Angeles highway?"

Elisa stood up and shoved the thick scissors in her apron pocket. "Well, yes, it does, but it winds around and then fords the river. I don't think your team could pull through the sand."

He replied with some asperity, "It might surprise you what them beasts can pull through."

"When they get started?" she asked.

He smiled for a second. "Yes. When they get started."

"Well," said Elisa, "I think you'll save time if you go back to the Salinas road and pick up the highway there."

He drew a big finger down the chicken wire and made it sing. "I ain't in any hurry, ma'am. I go from Seattle to San Diego and back every year. Takes all my time. About six months each way. I aim to follow nice weather."

Elisa took off her gloves and stuffed them in the apron pocket with the scissors. She touched the under edge of her man's hat, searching for fugitive hairs. "That sounds like a nice kind of a way to live," she said.

He leaned confidentially over the fence. "Maybe you noticed the writing on my wagon. I mend pots and sharpen knives and scissors. You got any of them things to do?"

"Oh, no," she said quickly. "Nothing like that." Her eyes hardened with resistance.

"Scissors is the worst thing," he explained. "Most people just ruin scissors trying to sharpen 'em, but I know how. I got a special tool. It's a little bobbit kind of thing, and patented. But it sure does the trick."

"No. My scissors are all sharp."

"All right, then. Take a pot," he continued earnestly, "a bent pot, or a pot with a hole. I can make it like new so you don't have to buy no new ones. That's a saving for you."

"No," she said shortly. "I tell you I have nothing like that for you to do."

His face fell to an exaggerated sadness. His voice took

on a whining undertone. "I ain't had a thing to do today. Maybe I won't have no supper tonight. You see I'm off my regular road. I know folks on the highway clear from Seattle to San Diego. They save their things for me to sharpen up because they know I do it so good and save them money."

"I'm sorry," Elisa said irritably. "I haven't anything for you to do."

His eyes left her face and fell to searching the ground. They roamed about until they came to the chrysanthemum bed where she had been working. "What's them plants, ma'am?"

The irritation and resistance melted from Elisa's face. "Oh, those are chrysanthemums, giant whites and yellows. I raise them every year, bigger than anybody around here."

"Kind of a long-stemmed flower? Looks like a quick puff of colored smoke?" he asked.

"That's it. What a nice way to describe them."

"They smell kind of nasty till you get used to them," he said.

"It's a good bitter smell," she retorted, "not nasty at all."

He changed his tone quickly. "I like the smell myself."

"I had ten-inch blooms this year," she said.

The man leaned farther over the fence. "Look. I know a lady down the road a piece, has got the nicest garden you ever seen. Got nearly every kind of flower but no chrysanthemums. Last time I was mending a copper-bottom washtub for her (that's a hard job but I do it good), she said to me, 'If you ever run acrost some nice chrysanthemums I wish you'd try to get me a few seeds.' That's what she told me."

Elisa's eyes grew alert and eager. "She couldn't have known much about chrysanthemums. You can raise them from seed, but it's much easier to root the little sprouts you see there."

"Oh," he said. "I s'pose I can't take none to her, then."

"Why yes you can," Elisa cried. "I can put some in damp sand, and you can carry them right along with you. They'll take root in the pot if you keep them damp. And then she can transplant them."

"She'd sure like to have some, ma'am. You say they're nice ones?"

"Beautiful," she said. "Oh, beautiful." Her eyes shone. She tore off the battered hat and shook out her dark pretty hair. "I'll put them in a flower pot, and you can take them right with you. Come into the yard."

While the man came through the picket gate Elisa ran excitedly along the geranium-bordered path to the back of the house. And she returned carrying a big red flower pot. The gloves were forgotten now. She kneeled on the ground by the starting bed and dug up the sandy soil with her fingers and scooped it into the bright new flower pot. Then she picked up the little pile of shoots she had prepared. With her strong fingers she pressed them into the sand and tamped around them with her knuckles. The man stood over her. "I'll tell you what to do," she said. "You remember so you can tell the lady."

"Yes, I'll try to remember."

"Well, look. These will take root in about a month. Then she must set them out, about a foot apart in good rich earth like this, see?" She lifted a handful of dark soil for him to look at. "They'll grow fast and tall. Now remember this. In July tell her to cut them down, about eight inches from the ground."

"Before they bloom?" he asked.

"Yes, before they bloom." Her face was tight with eagerness. "They'll grow right up again. About the last of September the buds will start."

She stopped and seemed perplexed. "It's the budding that takes the most care," she said hesitantly. "I don't know how to tell you." She looked deep into his eyes, searchingly. Her mouth opened a little, and she seemed to be listening. "I'll try to tell you," she said. "Did you ever hear of planting hands?"

"Can't say I have, ma'am."

"Well, I can only tell you what it feels like. It's when you're picking off the buds you don't want. Everything goes right down into your finger-tips. You watch your fingers work. They do it themselves. You can feel how it is. They pick and pick the buds. They never make a mistake. They're with the plant. Do you see? Your fingers and the plant. You can feel that, right up your arm. They know. They never make a mistake. You can feel it. When you're like that you can't do anything wrong. Do you see that? Can you understand that?"

She was kneeling on the ground looking up at him. Her breast swelled passionately.

The man's eyes narrowed. He looked away self-consciously. "Maybe I know," he said. "Sometimes in the night in the wagon there——"

Elisa's voice grew husky. She broke in on him. "I've never lived as you do, but I know what you mean. When the night is dark—why, the stars are sharp-pointed, and there's quiet. Why, you rise up and up! Every pointed star gets driven into your body. It's like that. Hot and sharp and—lovely."

Kneeling there, her hand went out toward his legs in the greasy black trousers. Her hesitant fingers almost touched the cloth. Then her hand dropped to the ground. She crouched low like a fawning dog.

He said, "It's nice, just like you say. Only when you don't have no dinner, it ain't."

She stood up then, very straight, and her face was ashamed. She held the flower pot out to him and placed it gently in his arms. "Here. Put it in your wagon, on the seat, where you can watch it. Maybe I can find something for you to do."

At the back of the house she dug in the can pile and

found two old and battered aluminum saucepans. She carried them back and gave them to him. "Here, maybe you can fix these."

His manner changed. He became professional. "Good as new I can fix them." At the back of his wagon he set a little anvil, and out of an oily tool box dug a small machine hammer. Elisa came through the gate to watch him while he pounded out the dents in the kettles. His mouth grew sure and knowing. At a difficult part of the work he sucked his under-lip.

"You sleep right in the wagon?" Elisa asked.

"Right in the wagon, ma'am. Rain or shine I'm dry as a cow in there."

"It must be nice," she said. "It must be very nice. I wish women could do such things."

"It ain't the right kind of a life for a woman."

Her upper lip raised a little, showing her teeth. "How do you know? How can you tell?" she said.

"I don't know ma'am," he protested. "Of course I don't know. Now here's your kettles, done. You don't have to buy no new ones."

"How much?"

"Oh, fifty cents'll do. I keep my prices down and my work good. That's why I have all them satisfied customers up and down the highway."

Elisa brought him a fifty-cent piece from the house and dropped it in his hand. "You might be surprised to have a rival some time. I can sharpen scissors, too. And I can beat the dents out of little pots. I could show you what a woman might do."

He put his hammer back in the oily box and shoved the little anvil out of sight. "It would be a lonely life for a woman, ma'am, and a scarey life, too, with animals creeping under the wagon all night." He climbed over the single-tree, steadying himself with a hand on the burro's white rump. He settled himself in the seat, picked up the lines. "Thank you kindly, ma'am," he said. "I'll do like you told me; I'll go back and catch the Salinas road."

"Mind," she called, "if you're long in getting there, keep the sand damp."

"Sand, ma'am? . . . Sand? Oh, sure. You mean round the chrysanthemums. Sure I will." He clucked his tongue. The beasts leaned luxuriously into their collars. The mongrel dog took his place between the back wheels. The wagon turned and crawled out the entrance road and back the way it had come, along the river.

Elisa stood in front of her wire fence watching the slow progress of the caravan. Her shoulders were straight, her head thrown back, her eyes half-closed, so that the scene came vaguely into them. Her lips moved silently, forming the words "Good-bye—good-bye." Then she whispered, "That's a bright direction. There's a glowing there." The sound of her whisper startled her. She shook herself free and looked about to see whether anyone had been listening. Only the dogs had heard. They lifted their heads toward her from their sleeping in the dust, and then stretched out their chins and settled asleep again. Elisa turned and ran hurriedly into the house.

In the kitchen she reached behind the stove and felt the water tank. It was full of hot water from the noonday cooking. In the bathroom she tore off her soiled clothes and flung them into the corner. And then she scrubbed herself with a little block of pumice, legs and thighs, loins and chest and arms, until her skin was scratched and red. When she had dried herself she stood in front of a mirror in her bedroom and looked at her body. She tightened her stomach and threw out her chest. She turned and looked over her shoulder at her back.

After a while she began to dress, slowly. She put on her newest under-clothing and her nicest stockings and the dress which was the symbol of her prettiness. She worked carefully on her hair, pencilled her eyebrows and rouged her lips.

Before she was finished she heard the little thunder of hoofs and the shouts of Henry and his helper as they drove the red steers into the corral. She heard the gate bang shut and set herself for Henry's arrival.

His step sounded on the porch. He entered the house calling, "Elisa, where are you?"

"In my room, dressing. I'm not ready. There's hot water for your bath. Hurry up. It's getting late."

When she heard him splashing in the tub, Elisa laid his dark suit on the bed, and shirt and socks and tie beside it. She stood his polished shoes on the floor beside the bed. Then she went to the porch and sat primly and stiffly down. She looked toward the river road where the willow-line was still yellow with frosted leaves so that under the high grey fog they seemed a thin band of sunshine. This was the only color in the grey afternoon. She sat unmoving for a long time. Her eyes blinked rarely.

Henry came banging out of the door, shoving his tie inside his vest as he came. Elisa stiffened and her face grew tight. Henry stopped short and looked at her. "Why—why, Elisa. You look so nice!"

"Nice? You think I look nice? What do you mean by 'nice?' "

Henry blundered on. "I don't know. I mean you look different, strong and happy."

"I am strong? Yes, strong. What do you mean 'strong?' "

He looked bewildered. "You're playing some kind of a game," he said helplessly. "It's a kind of a play. You look strong enough to break a calf over your knee, happy enough to eat it like a watermelon."

For a second she lost her rigidity. "Henry! Don't talk like that. You didn't know what you said." She grew complete again. "I'm strong," she boasted. "I never knew before how strong."

Henry looked down toward the tractor shed, and when

he brought his eyes back to her, they were his own again. "I'll get out the car. You can put on your coat while I'm starting."

Elisa went into the house. She heard him drive to the gate and idle down his motor, and then she took a long time to put on her hat. She pulled it here and pressed it there. When Henry turned the motor off she slipped into her coat and went out.

The little roadster bounced along on the dirt road by the river, raising the birds and driving the rabbits into the brush. Two cranes flapped heavily over the willow-line and dropped into the river-bed.

Far ahead on the road Elisa saw a dark speck. She knew.

She tried not to look as they passed it, but her eyes would not obey. She whispered to herself sadly, "He might have thrown them off the road. That wouldn't have been much trouble, not very much. But he kept the pot," she explained. "He had to keep the pot. That's why he couldn't get them off the road "

The roadster turned a bend and she saw the caravan ahead. She swung full around toward her husband so she could not see the little covered wagon and the mismatched team as the car passed them.

In a moment it was over. The thing was done. She did not look back. She said loudly, to be heard above the motor, "It will be good, tonight, a good dinner."

"Now you're changed again," Henry complained. He took one hand from the wheel and patted her knee. "I ought to take you in to dinner oftener. It would be good for both of us. We get so heavy out on the ranch."

"Henry," she asked, "could we have wine at dinner?"

"Sure we could. Say! That will be fine."

She was silent for a while; then she said, "Henry, at those prize fights, do the men hurt each other very much?"

"Sometimes a little, not often. Why?"

"Well, I've read how they break noses, and blood runs down their chests. I've read how the fighting gloves get heavy and soggy with blood."

He looked around at her. "What's the matter, Elisa? I didn't know you read things like that." He brought the car to a stop, then turned to the right over the Salinas River bridge.

"Do any women ever go to the fights?" she asked.

"Oh, sure, some. What's the matter, Elisa? Do you want to go? I don't think you'd like it, but I'll take you if you really want to go."

She relaxed limply in the seat. "Oh, no. No. I don't want to go. I'm sure I don't." Her face was turned away from him. "It will be enough if we can have wine. It will be plenty." She turned up her coat collar so he could not see that she was crying weakly—like an old woman.

JOHN STEINBECK

Flight

ABOUT fifteen miles below Monterey, on the wild coast, the Torres family had their farm, a few sloping acres above a cliff that dropped to the brown reefs and to the hissing white waters of the ocean. Behind the farm the stone mountains stood up against the sky. The farm buildings huddled like little clinging aphids on the mountain skirts, crouched low to the ground as though the wind might blow them into the sea. The little shack, the rattling, rotting barn were grey-bitten with sea salt, beaten by the damp wind until they had taken on the color of the granite hills. Two horses, a red cow and a red calf, half a dozen pigs and a flock of lean, multicolored chickens stocked the place. A little corn was raised on the sterile slope, and it grew short and thick under the wind, and all the cobs formed on the landward sides of the stalks.

Mamma Torres, a lean, dry woman with ancient eyes, had ruled the farm for ten years, ever since her husband tripped over a stone in the field one day and fell full length on a rattlesnake. When one is bitten on the chest there is not much that can be done.

Mamma Torres had three children, two undersized black ones of twelve and fourteen, Emilio and Rosy, whom Mamma kept fishing on the rocks below the farm when the sea was kind and when the truant officer was in some distant part of Monterey County. And there was Pepé, the tall smiling son of nineteen, a gentle, affectionate boy, but very lazy. Pepé had a tall head, pointed at the top, and from its peak, coarse black hair grew down like a thatch all around. Over his smiling little eyes Mama cut a straight bang so he could see. Pepé had sharp Indian cheekbones and an eagle nose, but his mouth was as sweet and shapely as a girl's mouth, and his chin was fragile and chiseled. He was loose and gangling, all legs and feet and wrists, and he was very lazy. Mama thought him fine and brave, but she never told him so. She said, "Some lazy cow must have got into thy father's family, else how could I have a son like thee." And she said, "When I carried thee, a sneaking lazy coyote came out of the brush and looked at me one day. That must have made thee so."

Pepé smiled sheepishly and stabbed at the ground with his knife to keep the blade sharp and free from rust. It was his inheritance, that knife, his father's knife. The long heavy blade folded back into the black handle. There was a button on the handle. When Pepé pressed the button, the blade leaped out ready for use. The knife was with Pepé always, for it had been his father's knife.

One sunny morning when the sea below the cliff was glinting and blue and the white surf creamed on the reef, when even the stone mountains looked kindly, Mama Torres called out the door of the shack, "Pepé, I have a labor for thee."

There was no answer. Mama listened. From behind the barn she heard a burst of laughter. She lifted her full long skirt and walked in the direction of the noise.

Pepé was sitting on the ground with his back against a box. His white teeth glistened. On either side of him stood the two black ones, tense and expectant. Fifteen feet away a redwood post was set in the ground. Pepé's right hand lay limply in his lap, and in the palm the big black knife rested. The blade was closed back into the handle. Pepé looked smiling at the sky.

Suddenly Emilio cried, "Ya!"

Pepé's wrist flicked like the head of a snake. The blade seemed to fly open in mid-air, and with a thump the point dug into the redwood post, and the black handle quivered. The three burst into excited laughter. Rosy ran to the post and pulled out the knife and brought it back to Pepé. He closed the blade and settled the knife carefully in his listless palm again. He grinned self-consciously at the sky.

"Ya!"

The heavy knife lanced out and sunk into the post again. Mama moved forward like a ship and scattered the play.

"All day you do foolish things with the knife, like a toy-baby," she stormed. "Get up on thy huge feet that eat up shoes. Get up!" She took him by one loose shoulder and hoisted at him. Pepé grinned sheepishly and came half-heartedly to his feet. "Look!" Mama cried. "Big lazy, you must catch the horse and put on him thy father's saddle. You must ride to Monterey. The medicine bottle is empty. There is no salt. Go thou now, Peanut! Catch the horse."

A revolution took place in the relaxed figure of Pepé. "To Monterey, me? Alone? *Si,* Mama."

She scowled at him. "Do not think, big sheep, that you will buy candy. No, I will give you only enough for the medicine and salt."

Pepé smiled. "Mama, you will put the hatband on the hat?"

She relented then. "Yes, Pepé. You may wear the hatband."

His voice grew insinuating. "And the green handkerchief, Mama?"

"Yes, if you go quickly and return with no trouble, the silk green handkerchief will go. If you make sure to take off the handkerchief when you eat so no spot may fall on it. . . ."

"*Si,* Mama. I will be careful. I am a man."

"Thou? A man? Thou art a peanut."

He went into the rickety barn and brought out a rope, and he walked agilely enough up the hill to catch the horse.

When he was ready and mounted before the door, mounted on his father's saddle that was so old that the oaken frame showed through torn leather in many places, then Mama brought out the round black hat with the tooled leather band, and she reached up and knotted the green silk handkerchief about his neck. Pepé's blue denim coat was much darker than his jeans, for it had been washed much less often.

Mama handed up the big medicine bottle and the silver coins. "That for the medicine," she said, "and that for the salt. That for a candle to burn for the papa. That for *dulces* for the little ones. Our friend Mrs. Rodriguez will give you dinner and maybe a bed for the night. When you go to the church say only ten Paternosters and only twenty-five Ave Marias. Oh! I know, big coyote. You would sit there flapping your mouth over Aves all day while you looked at the candles and the holy pictures. That is not good devotion to stare at the pretty things."

The black hat, covering the high pointed head and black thatched hair of Pepé, gave him dignity and age. He sat the rangy horse well. Mama thought how handsome he was, dark and lean and tall. "I would not send thee now alone, thou little one, except for the medicine," she said softly. "It is not good to have no medicine, for who knows when the toothache will come or the sadness of the stomach. These things are."

"Adios, Mama," Pepé cried. "I will come back soon. You may send me often alone. I am a man."

"Thou art a foolish chicken."

He straightened his shoulders, flipped the reins against the horse's shoulder and rode away. He turned once and saw that they still watched him, Emilio and Rosy and Mama. Pepé grinned with pride and gladness and lifted the tough buckskin horse to a trot.

When he had dropped out of sight over a little dip in the road, Mama turned to the black ones, but she spoke to herself. "He is nearly a man now," she said. "It will be a nice thing to have a man in the house again." Her eyes sharpened on the children. "Go to the rocks now. The tide is going out. There will be abalones to be found." She put the iron hooks into their hands and saw them down the steep trail to the reefs. She brought the smooth stone *metate* to the doorway and sat grinding her corn to flour and looking occasionally at the road over which Pepé had gone. The noonday came and then the afternoon, when the little ones beat the abalones on a rock to make them tender and Mama patted the tortillas to make them thin. They ate their dinner as the red sun was plunging down toward the ocean. They sat on the doorsteps and watched the big white moon come over the mountain tops.

Mama said, "He is now at the house of our friend Mrs. Rodriguez. She will give him nice things to eat and maybe a present."

Emilio said, "Some day I too will ride to Monterey for medicine. Did Pepé come to be a man today?"

Mama said wisely, "A boy gets to be a man when a man is needed. Remember this thing. I have known boys forty years old because there was no need for a man."

Soon afterwards they retired, Mamma in her big oak bed on one side of the room, Emilio and Rosy in their boxes full of straw and sheepskins on the other side of the room.

The moon went over the sky and the surf roared on the rocks. The roosters crowed the first call. The surf subsided to a whispering surge against the reef. The moon dropped toward the sea. The roosters crowed again.

The moon was near down to the water when Pepé rode on a winded horse to his home flat. His dog bounced out and circled the horse yelping with pleasure. Pepé slid off the saddle to the ground. The weathered little shack was silver in the moonlight and the square shadow of it was black to the north and east. Against the east the piling mountains were misty with light; their tops melted into the sky.

Pepé walked wearily up the three steps and into the house. It was dark inside. There was a rustle in the corner.

Mama cried out from her bed. "Who comes? Pepé, is it thou?"

"*Si,* Mama."

"Did you get the medicine?"

"*Si,* Mama."

"Well, go to sleep, then. I thought you would be sleeping at the house of Mrs. Rodriguez." Pepé stood silently in the dark room. "Why do you stand there, Pepé? Did you drink wine?"

"*Si,* Mama."

"Well, go to bed then and sleep out the wine."

His voice was tired and patient, but very firm. "Light the candle, Mama. I must go away into the mountains."

"What is this, Pepé? You are crazy." Mama struck a sulphur match and held the little blue burr until the flame spread up the stick. She set light to the candle on the floor beside her bed. "Now, Pepé, what is this you say?" She looked anxiously into his face.

He was changed. The fragile quality seemed to have gone from his chin. His mouth was less full than it had been, the lines of the lips were straighter, but in his eyes the greatest change had taken place. There was no laughter in them any more, nor any bashfulness. They were sharp and bright and purposeful.

He told her in a tired monotone, told everything just as it had happened. A few people came into the kitchen of Mrs. Rodriguez. There was wine to drink. Pepé drank wine. The little quarrel—the man started toward Pepé and then the knife—it went almost by itself. It flew, it darted before Pepé knew it. As he talked, Mama's face grew stern, and it seemed to grow more lean. Pepé finished. "I am a man now, Mama. The man said names to me I could not allow."

Mama nodded. "Yes, thou art a man, my poor little Pepé. Thou art a man. I have seen it coming on thee. I have watched you throwing the knife into the post, and I have been afraid." For a moment her face had softened, but now it grew stern again. "Come! We must get you ready. Go. Awaken Emilio and Rosy. Go quickly."

Pepé stepped over to the corner where his brother and sister slept among the sheepskins. He leaned down and shook them gently. "Come, Rosy! Come, Emilio! The mama says you must arise."

The little black ones sat up and rubbed their eyes in the candlelight. Mama was out of bed now, her long black skirt over her nightgown. "Emilio," she cried. "Go up and catch the other horse for Pepé. Quickly, now! Quickly!" Emilio put his legs in his overalls and stumbled sleepily out the door.

"You heard no one behind you on the road?" Mama demanded.

"No, Mama. I listened carefully. No one was on the road."

Mama darted like a bird about the room. From a nail on the wall she took a canvas water bag and threw it on the floor. She stripped a blanket from her bed and rolled it into a tight tube and tied the ends with string. From a box beside the stove she lifted a flour sack half full of black stringy jerky. "Your father's black coat, Pepé. Here, put it on."

Pepé stood in the middle of the floor watching her activity. She reached behind the door and brought out the rifle, a long 38-56, worn shiny the whole length of the barrel. Pepé took it from her and held it in the crook of his elbow. Mama brought a little leather bag and counted the cartridges into his hand. "Only ten left," she warned. "You must not waste them."

Emilio put his head in the door. "*'Qui 'st 'l caballo,* Mama."

"Put on the saddle from the other horse. Tie on the blanket. Here, tie the jerky to the saddle horn."

Still Pepé stood silently watching his mother's frantic activity. His chin looked hard, and his sweet mouth was drawn and thin. His little eyes followed Mama about the room almost suspiciously.

Rosy asked softly, "Where goes Pepé?"

Mama's eyes were fierce. "Pepé goes on a journey. Pepé is a man now. He has a man's thing to do."

Pepé straightened his shoulders. His mouth changed until he looked very much like Mama.

At last the preparation was finished. The loaded horse stood outside the door. The water bag dripped a line of moisture down the bay shoulder.

The moonlight was being thinned by the dawn and the big white moon was near down to the sea. The family stood by the shack. Mama confronted Pepé. "Look, my son! Do not stop until it is dark again. Do not sleep even though you are tired. Take care of the horse in order that he may not stop of weariness. Remember to be careful with the bullets—there are only ten. Do not fill thy stomach with jerky or it will make thee sick. Eat a little jerky and fill thy stomach with grass. When thou comest to the high mountains, if thou seest any of the dark watching men, go not near to them nor try to speak to them. And forget not thy prayers." She put her lean hands on Pepé's shoulders, stood on her toes and kissed him formally on both cheeks, and Pepé kissed her on both cheeks. Then he went to Emilio and Rosy and kissed both of their cheeks.

Pepé turned back to Mama. He seemed to look for a little softness, a little weakness in her. His eyes were searching, but Mama's face remained fierce. "Go now," she said. "Do not wait to be caught like a chicken."

Pepé pulled himself into the saddle. "I am a man," he said.

It was the first dawn when he rode up the hill toward the little canyon which let a trail into the mountains. Moonlight and daylight fought with each other, and the two warring qualities made it difficult to see. Before Pepé had gone a hundred yards, the outlines of his figure were misty; and long before he entered the canyon, he had become a gray, indefinite shadow.

Mama stood stiffly in front of her doorstep, and on either side of her stood Emilio and Rosy. They cast furtive glances at Mama now and then.

When the gray shape of Pepé melted into the hillside and disappeared, Mama relaxed. She began the high, whining keen of the death wail. "Our beautiful—our brave," she cried. "Our protector, our son is gone." Emilio and Rosy moaned beside her. "Our beautiful—our brave, he is gone." It was the formal wail. It rose to a high piercing whine and subsided to a moan. Mama raised it three times and then she turned and went into the house and shut the door.

Emilio and Rosy stood wondering in the dawn. They heard Mama whimpering in the house. They went out to sit on the cliff above the ocean. They touched shoulders. "When did Pepé come to be a man?" Emilio asked.

"Last night," said Rosy. "Last night in Monterey." The ocean clouds turned red with the sun that was behind the mountains.

"We will have no breakfast," said Emilio. "Mama will not want to cook." Rosy did not answer him. "Where is Pepé gone?" he asked.

Rosy looked around at him. She drew her knowledge from the quiet air. "He has gone on a journey. He will never come back."

"Is he dead? Do you think he is dead?"

Rosy looked back at the ocean again. A little steamer drawing a line of smoke sat on the edge of the horizon. "He is not dead," Rosy explained. "Not yet."

Pepé rested the big rifle across the saddle in front of him. He let the horse walk up the hill and he didn't look back. The stony slope took on a coat of short brush so that Pepé found the entrance to a trail and entered it.

When he came to the canyon opening, he swung once in his saddle and looked back, but the houses were swallowed in the misty light. Pepé jerked forward again. The high shoulder of the canyon closed in on him. His horse stretched out its neck and sighed and settled to the trail.

It was a well-worn path, dark soft leaf-mould earth strewn with broken pieces of sandstone. The trail rounded the shoulder of the canyon and dropped steeply into the bed of the stream. In the shallows the water ran smoothly, glinting in the first morning sun. Small round stones on the bottom were as brown as rust with sun moss. In the sand along the edges of the stream the tall, rich wild mint grew, while in the water itself the cress, old and tough, had gone to heavy seed.

The path went into the stream and emerged on the other side. The horse sloshed into the water and stopped. Pepé dropped his bridle and let the beast drink of the running water.

Soon the canyon sides became steep and the first giant sentinel redwoods guarded the trail, great round red trunks bearing foliage as green and lacy as ferns. Once Pepé was among the trees, the sun was lost. A perfumed and purple light lay in the pale green of the underbrush. Gooseberry bushes and blackberries and tall ferns lined the stream, and overhead the branches of the redwoods met and cut off the sky.

Pepé drank from the water bag, and he reached into the flour sack and brought out a black string of jerky. His white teeth gnawed at the string until the tough meat parted. He chewed slowly and drank occasionally from the water bag. His little eyes were slumberous and tired, but the muscles of his face were hard set. The earth of the trail was black now. It gave up a hollow sound under the walking hoofbeats.

The stream fell more sharply. Little waterfalls splashed on the stones. Five-fingered ferns hung over the water and dripped spray from their fingertips. Pepé rode half over in his saddle, dangling one leg loosely. He picked a bay leaf from a tree beside the way and put it into his mouth for a moment to flavor the dry jerky. He held the gun loosely across the pommel.

Suddenly he squared in his saddle, swung the horse from the trail and kicked it hurriedly up behind a big redwood tree. He pulled up the reins tight against the bit to keep the horse from whinnying. His face was intent and his nostrils quivered a little.

A hollow pounding came down the trail, and a horseman rode by, a fat man with red cheeks and a white stubble beard. His horse put down its head and blubbered at the trail when it came to the place where Pepé had turned off. "Hold up!" said the man and he pulled up his horse's head.

When the last sound of the hoofs died away, Pepé came back into the trail again. He did not relax in the saddle any more. He lifted the big rifle and swung the lever to throw a shell into the chamber, and then he let down the hammer to half cock.

The trail grew very steep. Now the redwood trees were smaller and their tops were dead, bitten dead where the wind reached them. The horse plodded on; the sun went slowly overhead and started down toward the afternoon.

Where the stream came out of a side canyon, the trail left it. Pepé dismounted and watered his horse and filled up his water bag. As soon as the trail had parted from the stream, the trees were gone and only the thick brittle sage and manzanita and chaparral edged the trail. And the soft black earth was gone, too, leaving only the light tan broken rock for the trail bed. Lizards scampered away into the brush as the horse rattled over the little stones.

Pepé turned in his saddle and looked back. He was in the open now: he could be seen from a distance. As he ascended the trail the country grew more rough and terrible and dry. The way wound about the bases of great square rocks. Little gray rabbits skittered in the brush. A bird made a monotonous high creaking. Eastward the bare rock mountaintops were pale and powder-dry under the dropping sun. The horse plodded up and up the trail toward a little V in the ridge which was the pass.

Pepé looked suspiciously back every minute or so, and his eyes sought the tops of the ridges ahead. Once, on a white barren spur, he saw a black figure for a moment, but he looked quickly away, for it was one of the dark watchers. No one knew who the watchers were, nor where they lived, but it was better to ignore them and never to show interest in them. They did not bother one who stayed on the trail and minded his own business.

The air was parched and full of light dust blown by the breeze from the eroding mountains. Pepé drank sparingly from his bag and corked it tightly and hung it on the horn again. The trail moved up the dry shale hillside, avoiding rocks, dropping under clefts, climbing in and out of old water scars. When he arrived at the little pass he stopped and looked back for a long time. No dark watchers were to be seen now. The trail behind was empty. Only the high tops of the redwoods indicated where the stream flowed.

Pepé rode on through the pass. His little eyes were nearly closed with weariness, but his face was stern, relentless and manly. The high mountain wind coasted sighing through the pass and whistled on the edges of the black blocks of broken granite. In the air, a red-tailed hawk sailed over close to the ridge and screamed angrily. Pepé went slowly through the broken jagged pass and looked down on the other side.

The trail dropped quickly, staggering among broken rock. At the bottom of the slope there was a dark crease, thick with brush, and on the other side of the crease a little flat, in which a grove of oak trees grew. A scar of green grass cut across the flat. And behind the flat another mountain rose, desolate with dead rocks and starving little black bushes. Pepé drank from the bag again for the air was so dry that it encrusted his nostrils and burned his lips. He put the horse down the trail. The hooves slipped and struggled on the steep way, starting little stones that rolled off into the brush. The sun was gone behind the westward mountain now, but still it glowed brilliantly on the oaks and on the grassy flat. The rocks and hillsides still sent up waves of the heat they had gathered from the day's sun.

Pepé looked up to the top of the next dry withered ridge. He saw a dark form against the sky, a man's figure standing on top of a rock, and he glanced away quickly not to appear curious. When a moment later he looked up again, the figure was gone.

Downward the trail was quickly covered. Sometimes the horse floundered for footing, sometimes set his feet and slid a little way. They came at last to the bottom where the dark chaparral was higher than Pepé's head. He held up his rifle on one side and his arm on the other to shield his face from the sharp brittle fingers of the brush.

Up and out of the crease he rode, and up a little cliff. The grassy flat was before him, and the round comfortable oaks. For a moment he studied the trail down which he had come, but there was no movement and no sound from it. Finally he rode out over the flat, to the green streak, and at the upper end of the damp he found a little spring welling out of the earth and dropping into a dug basin before it seeped out over the flat.

Pepé filled his bag first, and then he let the thirsty horse drink out of the pool. He led the horse to the clump of oaks, and in the middle of the grove, fairly protected from sight on all sides, he took off the saddle and the bridle and laid them on the ground. The horse stretched his jaws sideways and yawned. Pepé knotted the lead rope about the horse's neck and tied him to a sapling among the oaks, where he could graze in a fairly large circle.

When the horse was gnawing hungrily at the dry grass, Pepé went to the saddle and took a black string of jerky from the sack and strolled to an oak tree on the edge of the grove, from under which he could watch the trail. He sat down in the crisp dry oak leaves and automatically felt for his big black knife to cut the jerky, but he had no knife. He leaned back on his elbow and gnawed at the tough strong meat. His face was blank, but it was a man's face.

The bright evening light washed the eastern ridge, but the valley was darkening. Doves flew down from the hills to the spring, and the quail came running out of the brush and joined them, calling clearly to one another.

Out of the corner of his eye Pepé saw a shadow grow out of the bushy crease. He turned his head slowly. A big spotted wildcat was creeping toward the spring, belly to the ground, moving like thought.

Pepé cocked his rifle and edged the muzzle slowly around. Then he looked apprehensively up the trail and dropped the hammer again. From the ground beside him he picked an oak twig and threw it toward the spring. The quail flew up with a roar and the doves whistled away. The big cat stood up; for a long moment he looked at Pepé with cold yellow eyes, and then fearlessly walked back into the gulch.

The dusk gathered quickly in the deep valley. Pepé muttered his prayers, put his head down on his arm and went instantly to sleep.

The moon came up and filled the valley with cold blue light, and the wind swept rustling down from the peaks. The owls worked up and down the slopes looking for rabbits. Down in the brush of the gulch a coyote gabbled. The oak trees whispered softly in the night breeze.

Pepé started up, listening. His horse had whinnied. The moon was just slipping behind the western ridge, leaving the valley in darkness behind it. Pepé sat tensely gripping his rifle. From far up the trail he heard an answering whinny and the crash of shod hooves on the broken rock. He jumped to his feet, ran to his horse and led it under the trees. He threw on the saddle and cinched it tight for the steep trail, caught the unwilling head and forced the bit into the mouth. He felt the saddle to make sure the water bag and the sack of jerky were there. Then he mounted and turned up the hill.

It was velvet dark. The horse found the entrance to the trail where it left the flat, and started up, stumbling and slipping on the rocks. Pepé's hand rose up to his head. His hat was gone. He had left it under the oak tree.

The horse had struggled far up the trail when the first change of dawn came into the air, a steel grayness as light mixed thoroughly with dark. Gradually the sharp snaggled edge of the ridge stood out above them, rotten granite tortured and eaten by the winds of time. Pepé had dropped his reins on the horn, leaving direction to the horse. The brush grabbed at his legs in the dark until one knee of his jeans was ripped.

Gradually the light flowed down over the ridge. The starved brush and rocks stood out in the half light, strange and lonely in high perspective. Then there came warmth into the light. Pepé drew up and looked back, but he could see nothing in the darker valley below. The sky turned blue over the coming sun. In the waste of the mountainside, the poor dry brush grew only three feet high. Here and there, big outcroppings of unrotted granite stood up like mouldering houses. Pepé relaxed a little. He drank from his water bag and bit off a piece of jerky. A single eagle flew over, high in the light.

Without warning Pepé's horse screamed and fell on its side. He was almost down before the rifle crash echoed up from the valley. From a hole behind the struggling shoulder, a stream of bright crimson blood pumped and stopped and pumped and stopped. The hooves threshed on the ground. Pepé lay half stunned beside the horse. He looked slowly down the hill. A piece of sage clipped off beside his head and another crash echoed up from side to side of the canyon. Pepé flung himself frantically behind a bush.

He crawled up the hill on his knees and one hand. His right hand held the rifle up off the ground and pushed it ahead of him. He moved with the instinctive care of an animal. Rapidly he wormed his way toward one of the big outcroppings of granite on the hill above him. Where the brush was high he doubled up and ran, but where the cover was slight he wriggled forward on his stomach, pushing the rifle ahead of him. In the last little distance there was no cover at all. Pepé poised and then he darted across the space and flashed around the corner of the rock.

He leaned panting against the stone. When his breath came easier he moved along behind the big rock until he came to a narrow slit that offered a thin section of vision down the hill. Pepé lay on his stomach and pushed the rifle barrel through the slit and waited.

The sun reddened the western ridges now. Already the buzzards were settling down toward the place where the horse lay. A small brown bird scratched in the dead sage leaves directly in front of the rifle muzzle. The coasting eagle flew back toward the rising sun.

Pepé saw a little movement in the brush far below. His grip tightened on the gun. A little brown doe stepped daintly out on the trail and crossed it and disappeared into the brush again. For a long time Pepé waited. Far below he could see the little flat and the oak trees and the slash of green. Suddenly his eyes flashed back at the trail again. A quarter of a mile down there had been a quick movement in the chaparral. The rifle swung over. The front sight nestled in the v of the rear sight. Pepé studied for a moment and than raised the rear sight a notch. The little movement in the brush came again. The sight settled on it. Pepé squeezed the trigger. The explosion crashed down the mountain and up the other side, and came rattling back. The whole side of the slope grew still. No more movement. And then a white streak cut into the granite of the slit and a bullet whined away and a crash sounded up from below. Pepé felt a sharp pain in his right hand. A sliver of granite was sticking out from between his first and second knuckles and the point protruded from his palm. Carefully he pulled out the sliver of stone. The wound bled evenly and gently. No vein or artery was cut.

Pepé looked into a little dusty cave in the rock and gathered a handful of spider web, and he pressed the mass into the cut, plastering the soft web into the blood. The flow stopped almost at once.

The rifle was on the ground. Pepé picked it up, levered a new shell into the chamber. And then he slid into the brush on his stomach. Far to the right he crawled, and then up the hill, moving slowly and carefully, crawling to cover and resting and then crawling again.

In the mountains the sun is high in its arc before it penetrates the gorges. The hot face looked over the hill and brought instant heat with it. The white light beat on the rocks and reflected from them and rose up quivering from the earth again, and the rocks and bushes seemed to quiver behind the air.

Pepé crawled in the general direction of the ridge peak, zig-zagging for cover. The deep cut between his knuckles began to throb. He crawled close to a rattlesnake before he saw it, and when it raised its dry head and made a soft beginning whirr, he backed up and took another way. The quick gray lizards flashed in front of him, raising a tiny line of dust. He found another mass of spider web and pressed it against his throbbing hand.

Pepé was pushing the rifle with his left hand now. Little drops of sweat ran to the ends of his coarse black hair and rolled down his cheeks. His lips and tongue were growing thick and heavy. His lips writhed to draw saliva into his mouth. His little dark eyes were uneasy and suspicious. Once when a gray lizzard paused in front of him on the parched ground and turned its head sideways he crushed it flat with a stone.

When the sun slid past noon he had not gone a mile. He crawled exhaustedly a last hundred yards to a patch of high sharp manzanita, crawled desperately, and when the patch was reached he wriggled in among the tough gnarly trunks and dropped his head on his left arm. There was little shade in the meager brush, but there was cover and safety. Pepé went to sleep as he lay and the sun beat on his back. A few little birds hopped close to him and peered and hopped away. Pepé squirmed in his sleep and he raised and dropped his wounded hand again and again.

The sun went down behind the peaks and the cool evening came, and then the dark. A coyote yelled from the hillside. Pepé started awake and looked about with misty eyes. His hand was swollen and heavy; a little thread of pain ran up the inside of his arm and settled in a pocket in his armpit. He peered about and then stood up, for the mountains were black and the moon had not yet risen. Pepé stood up in the dark. The coat of his father pressed on his arm. His tongue was swollen until it nearly filled his mouth. He wriggled out of the coat and dropped it in the brush, and then he struggled up the hill, falling over rocks and tearing his way through the brush. The rifle knocked against stones as he went. Little dry avalanches of gravel and shattered stone went whispering down the hill behind him.

After a while the old moon came up and showed the jagged ridge top ahead of him. By moonlight Pepé traveled more easily. He bent forward so that his throbbing arm hung away from his body. The journey uphill was made in dashes and rests, a frantic rush up a few yards and then a rest. The wind coasted down the slope rattling the dry stems of the bushes.

The moon was at meridian when Pepé came at last to the sharp backbone of the ridge top. On the last hundred yards of the rise no soil had clung under the wearing winds. The way was on solid rock. He clambered to the top and looked down on the other side. There was a draw like the last below him, misty with moonlight, brushed with dry struggling sage and chaparral. On the other side the hill rose up sharply and at the top the jagged rotten teeth of the mountain showed against the sky. At the bottom of the cut the brush was thick and dark.

Pepé stumbled down the hill. His throat was almost closed with thirst. At first he tried to run, but immediately he fell and rolled. After that he went more carefully. The moon was just disappearing behind the mountains when he came to the bottom. He crawled into the heavy brush feeling with his fingers for water. There was no water in the bed of the stream, only damp earth. Pepé laid his gun down and scooped up a handful of mud and put it in his mouth, and then he spluttered and scraped the earth from his tongue with his finger, for the mud drew at his mouth like a poultice. He dug a hole in the stream bed with his fingers, dug a little basin to catch water; but before it was very deep his head fell forward on the damp ground and he slept.

The dawn came and the heat of the day fell on the earth, and still Pepé slept. Late in the afternoon his head jerked up. He looked slowly around. His eyes were slits of wariness. Twenty feet away in the heavy brush a big tawny mountain lion stood looking at him. Its long thick tail waved gracefully, its ears were erect with interest, not laid back dangerously. The lion squatted down on its stomach and watched him.

Pepé looked at the hole he had dug in the earth. A half inch of muddy water had collected in the bottom. He tore the sleeve from his hurt arm, with his teeth ripped out a little square, soaked it in the water and put it in his mouth. Over and over he filled the cloth and sucked it.

Still the lion sat and watched him. The evening came down but there was no movement on the hills. No birds visited the dry bottom of the cut. Pepé looked occasionally at the lion. The eyes of the yellow beast drooped as though he were about to sleep. He yawned and his long thin red tongue curled out. Suddenly his head jerked around and his nostrils quivered. His big tail lashed. He stood up and slunk like a tawny shadow into the thick brush.

A moment later Pepé heard the sound, the faint far crash of horses' hooves on gravel. And he heard something else, a high whining yelp of a dog.

Pepé took his rifle in his left hand and he glided into the brush almost as quietly as the lion had. In the darkening evening he crouched up the hill toward the next ridge. Only when the dark came did he stand up. His energy was short. Once it was dark he fell over the rocks and slipped to his knees on the steep slope, but he moved on and on up the hill, climbing and scrabbling over the broken hillside.

When he was far up toward the top, he lay down and slept for a little while. The withered moon, shining on his face, awakened him. He stood up and moved up the hill. Fifty yards away he stopped and turned back, for he had forgotten his rifle. He walked heavily down and poked about in the brush, but he could not find his gun. At last he lay down to rest. The pocket of pain in his armpit had grown more sharp. His arm seemed to swell out and fall with every heartbeat. There was no position lying down where the heavy arm did not press against his armpit.

With the effort of a hurt beast, Pepé got up and moved again toward the top of the ridge. He held his swollen arm away from his body with his left hand. Up the steep hill he dragged himself, a few steps and a rest, and a few more steps. At last he was nearing the top. The moon showed the uneven sharp back of it against the sky.

Pepé's brain spun in a big spiral up and away from him. He slumped to the ground and lay still. The rock ridge top was only a hundred feet above him.

The moon moved over the sky. Pepé half turned on his back. His tongue tried to make words, but only a thick hissing came from between his lips.

When the dawn came, Pepé pulled himself up. His eyes were sane again. He drew his great puffed arm in front of him and looked at the angry wound. The black line ran up from his wrist to his armpit. Automatically he reached in his pocket for the big black knife, but it was not there. His eyes searched the ground. He picked up a sharp blade of stone and scraped at the wound, sawed at the proud flesh and then squeezed the green juice out in big drops. Instantly he threw back his head and whined like a dog. His whole right side shuddered at the pain, but the pain cleared his head.

In the gray light he struggled up the last slope of the ridge and crawled over and lay down behind a line of rocks. Below him lay a deep canyon exactly like the last, waterless and desolate. There was no flat, no oak trees, not even heavy brush in the bottom of it. And on the other side a sharp ridge stood up, thinly brushed with starving sage, littered with broken granite. Strewn over the hill there were giant outcroppings, and on the top the granite teeth stood out against the sky.

The new day was light now. The flame of the sun came over the ridge and fell on Pepé where he lay on the ground. His coarse black hair was littered with twigs and bits of spider web. His eyes had retreated back into his head. Between his lips the tip of his black tongue showed.

He sat up and dragged his great arm into his lap and nursed it, rocking his body and moaning in his throat. He threw back his head and looked up into the pale sky. A big black bird circled nearly out of sight, and far to the left another was sailing near.

He lifted his head to listen, for a familiar sound had come to him from the valley he had climbed out of; it was the crying yelp of hounds, excited and feverish, on a trail.

Pepé bowed his head quickly. He tried to speak rapid words but only a thick hiss came from his lips. He drew a shaky cross on his breast with his left hand. It was a long struggle to get to his feet. He crawled slowly and mechanically to the top of a big rock on the ridge peak. Once there, he arose slowly, swaying to his feet, and stood erect. Far below he could see the dark brush where he had slept. He braced his feet and stood there, black against the morning sky.

There came a ripping sound at his feet. A piece of stone flew up and a bullet droned off into the next gorge. The hollow crash echoed up from below. Pepé looked down for a moment and then pulled himself straight again.

His body jarred back. His left hand fluttered helplessly toward his breast. The second crash sounded from below. Pepé swung forward and toppled from the rock. His body struck and rolled over and over, starting a little avalanche. And when at last he stopped against a bush, the avalanche slid slowly down and covered up his head.

JOHN STEINBECK

The Leader of the People

ON SATURDAY afternoon Billy Buck, the ranch-hand, raked together the last of the old year's haystack and pitched small forkfuls over the wire fence to a few mildly interested cattle. High in the air small clouds like puffs of cannon smoke were driven eastward by the March wind. The wind could be heard whishing in the brush on the ridge crests, but no breath of it penetrated down into the ranch-cup.

The little boy, Jody, emerged from the house eating a thick piece of buttered bread. He saw Billy working on the last of the haystack. Jody tramped down scuffing his shoes in a way he had been told was destructive to good shoe-leather. A flock of white pigeons flew out of the black cypress tree as Jody passed, and circled the tree and landed again. A half-grown tortoise-shell cat leaped from the bunkhouse porch, galloped on stiff legs across the road, whirled and galloped back again. Jody picked up a stone to help the game along, but he was too late, for the cat was under the porch before the stone could be discharged. He threw the stone into the cypress tree and started the white pigeons on another whirling flight.

Arriving at the used-up haystack, the boy leaned against the barbed wire fence. "Will that be all of it, do you think?" he asked.

The middle-aged ranch-hand stopped his careful raking and stuck his fork into the ground. He took off his black hat and smoothed down his hair. "Nothing left of it that isn't soggy from ground moisture," he said. He replaced his hat and rubbed his dry leathery hands together.

"Ought to be plenty mice," Jody suggested.

"Lousy with them," said Billy. "Just crawling with mice."

"Well, maybe, when you get all through, I could call the dogs and hunt the mice."

"Sure, I guess you could," said Billy Buck. He lifted a forkful of the damp ground-hay and threw it into the air. Instantly three mice leaped out and burrowed frantically under the hay again.

Jody sighed with satisfaction. Those plump, sleek, arrogant mice were doomed. For eight months they had lived and multiplied in the haystack. They had been immune from cats, from traps, from poison and from Jody. They had grown smug in their security, overbearing and fat. Now the time of disaster had come; they would not survive another day.

Billy looked up at the top of the hills that surrounded the ranch. "Maybe you better ask your father before you do it, he suggested.

"Well, where is he? I'll ask him now."

"He rode up to the ridge ranch after dinner. He'll be back pretty soon."

Jody slumped gainst the fence post. "I don't think he'd care."

As Billy went back to his work he said ominously, "You'd better ask him anyway. You know how he is."

Jody did know. His father, Carl Tiflin, insisted upon giving permission for anything that was done on the ranch, whether it was important or not. Jody sagged farther against the post until he was sitting on the ground. He looked up at the little puffs of wind-driven cloud. "Is it like to rain, Billy?"

"It might. The wind's good for it, but not strong enough."

"Well, I hope it don't rain until after I kill those damn mice." He looked over his shoulder to see whether Billy had noticed the mature profanity. Billy worked on without comment.

Jody turned back and looked at the side-hill where the road from the outside world came down. The hill was washed with lean March sunshine. Silver thistles, blue lupins and a few poppies bloomed among the sage bushes. Halfway up the hill Jody could see Doubletree Mutt, the black dog, digging in a squirrel hole. He paddled for a while and then paused to kick bursts of dirt out between his hind legs, and he dug with an earnestness which belied the knowledge he must have had that no dog had ever caught a squirrel by digging in a hole.

Suddenly, while Jody watched, the black dog stiffened, and backed out of the hole and looked up the hill toward the cleft in the ridge where the road came through. Jody looked up too. For a moment Carl Tiflin on horseback stood out against the pale sky and then he moved down the road toward the house. He carried something white in his hand.

The boy started to his feet. "He's got a letter," Jody cried. He trotted away toward the ranch house, for the letter would probably be read aloud and he wanted to be there. He reached the house before his father did, and ran in. He heard Carl dismount from his creaking saddle and slap the horse on the side to send it to the barn where Billy would unsaddle it and turn it out.

Jody ran into the kitchen. "We got a letter!" he cried.

His mother looked up from a pan of beans. "Who has?"

"Father has. I saw it in his hand."

Carl strode into the kitchen then, Jody's mother asked, "Who's the letter from, Carl?"

He frowned quickly. "How did you know there was a letter?"

She nodded her head in the boy's direction. "Big-Britches Jody told me."

Jody was embarrassed.

His father looked down at him contemptuously. "He *is* getting to be a Big-Britches," Carl said. "He's minding everybody's business but his own. Got his big nose into everything."

Mrs. Tiflin relented a little. "Well, he hasn't enough to keep him busy. Who's the letter from?"

Carl still frowned on Jody. "I'll keep him busy if he isn't careful." He held out a sealed letter. "I guess it's from your father."

Mrs. Tiflin took a hairpin from her head and slit open the flap. Her lips pursed judiciously. Jody saw her eyes snap back and forth over the lines. "He says," she translated, "he says he's going to drive out Saturday to stay for a while. Why, this is Saturday. The letter must have been delayed." She looked at the postmark. "This was mailed day before yesterday. It should have been here yesterday." She looked up questioningly at her husband, and then her face darkened angrily. "Now what have you got that look on you for? He doesn't come often."

Carl turned his eyes away from her anger. He could be stern with her most of the time, but when occasionally her temper arose, he could not combat it.

"What's the matter with you?" she demanded again.

In his explanation there was a tone of apology Jody himself might have used. "It's just that he talks," Carl said lamely. "Just talks."

"Well, what of it? You talk yourself."

"Sure I do. But your father only talks about one thing."

"Indians!" Jody broke in excitedly. "Indians and crossing the plains!"

Carl turned fiercely on him. "You get out, Mr. Big-Britches! Go on, now! Get out!"

Jody went miserably out the back door and closed the screen with elaborate quietness. Under the kitchen window his shamed, downcast eyes fell upon a curiously shaped stone, a stone of such fascination that he squatted down and picked it up and turned it over in his hands.

The voices came clearly to him through the open kitchen window. "Jody's damn well right," he heard his father say. "Just Indians and crossing the plains. I've heard that story about how the horses got driven off about a thousand times. He just goes on and on, and he never changes a word in the things he tells."

When Mrs. Tiflin answered her tone was so changed that Jody, outside the window, looked up from his study of the stone. Her voice had become soft and explanatory. Jody knew how her face would have changed to match the tone. She said quietly, "Look at it this way, Carl. That was the big thing in my father's life. He led a wagon train clear across the plains to the coast, and when it was finished, his life was done. It was a big thing to do, but it didn't last long enough. Look!" she continued, "it's as though he was born to do that, and after he finished it, there wasn't anything more for him to do but think about it and talk about it. If there'd been any farther west to go, he'd have gone. He's told me so himself. But at last there was the ocean. He lives right by the ocean where he had to stop."

She had caught Carl, caught him and entangled him in her soft tone.

"I've seen him," he agreed quietly. "He goes down and stares off west over the ocean." His voice sharpened a little. "And then he goes up to the Horseshoe Club in Pacific Grove, and he tells people how the Indians drove off the horses."

She tried to catch him again. "Well, it's everything to him. You might be patient with him and pretend to listen."

Carl turned impatiently away. "Well, if it gets too bad, I can always go down to the bunkhouse and sit with Billy," he said irritably. He walked through the house and slammed the front door after him.

Jody ran to his chores. He dumped the grain to the chickens without chasing any of them. He gathered the eggs from the nests. He trotted into the house with the wood and interlaced it so carefully in the wood-box that two armloads seemed to fill it to overflowing.

His mother had finished the beans by now. She stirred up the fire and brushed off the stove-top with a turkey wing. Jody peered cautiously at her to see whether any rancor toward him remained. "Is he coming today?" Jody asked.

"That's what his letter said."

"Maybe I better walk up the road to meet him."

Mrs. Tiflin clanged the stove-lid shut. "That would be nice," she said. "He'd probably like to be met."

"I guess I'll just do it then."

Outside, Jody whistled shrilly to the dogs. "Come on up the hill," he commanded. The two dogs waved their tails and ran ahead. Along the roadside the sage had tender new tips. Jody tore off some pieces and rubbed them on his hands until the air was filled with the sharp wild smell. With a rush the dogs leaped from the road and yapped into the brush after a rabbit. That was the last Jody saw of them, for when they failed to catch the rabbit, they went back home.

Jody plodded on up the hill toward the ridge top. When he reached the little cleft where the road came through, the afternoon wind struck him and blew up his hair and ruffled his shirt. He looked down on the little hills and ridges below and then out at the huge green Salinas Valley. He could see the white town of Salinas far out in the flat and the flash of its windows under the waning sun. Directly below him, in an oak tree, a crow congress had convened. The tree was black with crows all cawing at once.

Then Jody's eyes followed the wagon road down from the ridge where he stood, and lost it behind a hill, and picked it up again on the other side. On that distant stretch he saw a cart slowly pulled by a bay horse. It disappeared behind the hill. Jody sat down on the ground and watched the place where the cart would reappear again. The wind sang on the hilltops and the puff-ball clouds hurried eastward.

Then the cart came into sight and stopped. A man dressed in black dismounted from the seat and walked to the horse's head. Although it was so far away, Jody knew he had unhooked the check-rein, for the horses's head dropped forward. The horse moved on, and the man walked slowly up the hill beside it. Jody gave a glad cry and ran down the road toward them. The squirrels bumped along off the road, and a road-runner flirted its tail and raced over the edge of the hill and sailed out like a glider.

Jody tried to leap into the middle of his shadow at every step. A stone rolled under his foot and he went down. Around a little bend he raced, and there, a short distance ahead, were his grandfather and the cart. The boy dropped from his unseemly running and approached at a dignified walk.

The horse plodded stumble-footedly up the hill and the old man walked beside it. In the lowering sun their giant shadows flickered darkly behind them. The grandfather was dressed in a black broadcloth suit and he wore kid congress gaiters and a black tie on a short, hard collar. He carried his black slouch hat in his hand. His white beard was cropped close and his white eyebrows overhung his eyes like mustaches. The blue eyes were sternly merry. About the whole face and figure there was a granite dignity, so that every motion seemed an impossible thing. Once at rest, it seemed the old man would be stone, would never move again. His steps were slow and certain. Once made, no step could ever be retraced; once headed in a direction, the path would never bend nor the pace increase nor slow.

When Jody appeared around the bend, Grandfather waved his hat slowly in welcome, and he called, "Why, Jody! Come down to meet me, have you?"

Jody sidled near and turned and matched his step to the old man's step and stiffened his body and dragged his heels a little. "Yes, sir," he said. "We got your letter only today."

"Should have been here yesterday," said Grandfather. "It certainly should. How are all the folks?"

"They're fine sir." He hesitated and then suggested shyly, "Would you like to come on a mouse hunt tomorrow, sir?"

"Mouse hunt, Jody?" Grandfather chuckled. "Have the people of this generation come down to hunting mice? They aren't very strong, the new people, but I hardly thought mice would be game for them."

"No sir. It's just play. The haystack's gone. I'm going to drive out the mice to the dogs. And you can watch, or even beat the hay a little."

The stern, merry eyes turned down on him. "I see. You don't eat them, then. You haven't come to that yet."

Jody explained, "The dogs eat them, sir. It wouldn't be much like hunting Indians, I guess."

"No, not much—but then later, when the troops were hunting Indians and shooting children and burning tepees, it wasn't much different from your mouse hunt."

They topped the rise and started down into the ranch cup, and they lost the sun from their shoulders. "You've grown," Grandfather said. "Nearly an inch, I should say."

"More," Jody boasted. "Where they mark me on the door, I'm up more than an inch since Thanksgiving even."

Grandfather's rich throaty voice said, "Maybe you're getting too much water and turning to pith and stalk. Wait until you head out, and then we'll see."

Jody looked quickly into the old man's face to see whether his feelings should be hurt, but there was no will to injure, no punishing nor putting-in-your-place light in the keen blue eyes. "We might kill a pig," Jody suggested.

"Oh, no! I couldn't let you do that. You're just humoring me. It isn't the time and you know it."

"You know Riley, the big boar, sir?"

"Yes. I remember Riley well."

"Well, Riley ate a hole into that same haystack, and it fell down on him and smothered him."

"Pigs do that when they can," said Grandfather.

"Riley was a nice pig, for a boar, sir. I rode him sometimes, and he didn't mind."

A door slammed at the house below them, and they saw Jody's mother standing on the porch waving her apron in welcome. And they saw Carl Tiflin walking up from the barn to be at the house for the arrival.

The sun had disappeared from the hills by now. The

blue smoke from the house chimney hung in flat layers in the purpling ranch-cup. The puff-ball clouds, dropped by the falling wind, hung listlessly in the sky.

Billy Buck came out of the bunkhouse and flung a wash basin of soapy water on the ground. He had been shaving in mid-week, for Billy held Grandfather in reverence, and Grandfather said that Billy was one of the few men of the new generation who had not gone soft. Although Billy was in middle age, Grandfather considered him a boy. Now Billy was hurrying toward the house too.

When Jody and Grandfather arrived, the three were waiting for them in front of the yard gate.

Carl said, "Hello, sir. We've been looking for you."

Mrs. Tiflin kissed Grandfather on the side of his beard, and stood still while his big hand patted her shoulder. Billy shook hands solemnly, grinning under his straw mustache. "I'll put up your horse," said Billy, and he led the rig away.

Grandfather watched him go, and then, turning back to the group, he said as he had said a hundred times before, "There's a good boy. I knew his father, old Mule-tail Buck. I never knew why they called him Mule-tail except he packed mules."

Mrs. Tiflin turned and led the way into the house. "How long are you going to stay, Father? Your letter didn't say."

"Well, I don't know. I thought I'd stay about two weeks. But I never stay as long as I think I'm going to."

In a short while they were sitting at the white oilcloth table eating their supper. The lamp with the tin reflector hung over the table. Outside the dining-room windows the big moths battered softly against the glass.

Grandfather cut his steak into tiny pieces and chewed slowly. "I'm hungry," he said. "Driving out here got my appetite up. It's like when we were crossing. We all got so hungry every night we could hardly wait to let the meat get done. I could eat about five pounds of buffalo meat every night."

"It's moving around does it," said Billy. "My father was a government packer. I helped him when I was a kid. Just the two of us could clean up a deer's ham."

"I knew your father, Billy," said Grandfather. "A fine man he was. They called him Mule-tail Buck. I don't know why except he packed mules."

"That was it," Billy agreed. "He packed mules."

Grandfather put down his knife and fork and looked around the table. "I remember one time we ran out of meat—" His voice dropped to a curious low sing-song, dropped into a tonal groove the story had worn for itself. "There was no buffalo, no antelope, not even rabbits. The hunters couldn't even shoot a coyote. That was the time for the leader to be on the watch. I was the leader, and I kept my eyes open. Know why? Well, just the minute the people began to get hungry they'd start slaughtering the team oxen. Do you believe that? I've heard of parties that just ate up their draft cattle. Started from the middle and worked toward the ends. Finally they'd eat the lead pair, and then the wheelers. The leader of a party had to keep them from doing that."

In some manner a big moth got into the room and circled the hanging kerosene lamp. Billy got up and tried to clap it between his hands. Carl struck with a cupped palm and caught the moth and broke it. He walked to the window and dropped it out.

"As I was saying," Grandfather began again, but Carl interrupted him. "You'd better eat some more meat. All the rest of us are ready for our pudding."

Jody saw a flash of anger in his mother's eyes. Grandfather picked up his knife and fork. "I'm pretty hungry, all right," he said. "I'll tell you about that later."

When supper was over, when the family and Billy Buck sat in front of the fireplace in the other room, Jody anxiously watched Grandfather. He saw the signs he knew. The bearded head leaned forward; the eyes lost their sternness and looked wonderingly into the fire; the big lean fingers laced themselves on the black knees. "I wonder," he began, "I just wonder whether I ever told you how those thieving Piutes drove off thirty-five of our horses."

"I think you did," Carl interrupted. "Wasn't it just before you went up into the Tahoe country?"

Grandfather turned quickly toward his son-in-law. "That's right. I guess I must have told you that story."

"Lots of times," Carl said cruelly, and he avoided his wife's eyes. But he felt the angry eyes on him, and he said, " 'Course I'd like to hear it again."

Grandfather looked back at the fire. His fingers unlaced and laced again. Jody knew how he felt, how his insides were collapsed and empty. Hadn't Jody been called a Big-Britches that very afternoon? He arose to heroism and opened himself to the term Big-Britches again. "Tell about Indians," he said softly.

Grandfather's eyes grew stern again. "Boys always want to hear about Indians. It was a job for men, but boys want to hear about it. Well, let's see. Did I ever tell you how I wanted each wagon to carry a long iron plate?"

Everyone but Jody remained silent. Jody said, "No. You didn't."

"Well, when the Indians attacked, we always put the wagons in a circle and fought from between the wheels. I thought that if every wagon carried a long plate with rifle holes, the men could stand the plates on the outside of the wheels when the wagons were in the circle and they would be protected. It would save lives and that would make up for the extra weight of the iron. But of course the party wouldn't do it. No party had done it before and they couldn't see why they should go to the expense. They lived to regret it, too."

Jody looked at his mother, and knew from her expression that she was not listening at all. Carl picked at a callus on his thumb and Billy Buck watched a spider crawling up the wall.

Grandfather's tone dropped into its narrative groove again. Jody knew in advance exactly what words would fall. The story droned on, speeded up for the attack, grew sad over the wounds, struck a dirge at the burials on the great plains. Jody sat quietly watching Grandfather. The stern blue eyes were detached. He looked as though he were not very interested in the story himself.

When it was finished, when the pause had been politely respected as the frontier of the story, Billy Buck stood up and stretched and hitched his trousers. "I guess I'll turn in," he said. Then he faced Grandfather. "I've got an old powder horn and a cap and ball pistol down to the bunkhouse. Did I ever show them to you?"

Grandfather nodded slowly. "Yes, I think you did, Billy. Reminds me of a pistol I had when I was leading the people across." Billy stood politely until the little story was done, and then he said, "Good night," and went out of the house.

Carl Tiflin tried to turn the conversation then. "How's the country between here and Monterey? I've heard it's pretty dry."

"It is dry," said Grandfather. "There's not a drop of water in the Laguna Seca. But it's a long pull from '87. The whole country was powder then, and in '61 I believe all the coyotes starved to death. We had fifteen inches of rain this year."

"Yes, but it all came too early. We could do with some now." Carl's eye fell on Jody. "Hadn't you better be getting to bed?"

Jody stood up obediently. "Can I kill the mice in the old haystack, sir?"

"Mice? Oh! Sure, kill them all off. Billy said there isn't any good hay left."

Jody exchanged a secret and satisfying look with Grandfather. "I'll kill every one tomorrow," he promised.

Jody lay in his bed and thought of the impossible world of Indians and buffaloes, a world that had ceased to be forever. He wished he could have been living in the heroic time, but he knew he was not of heroic timber. No one living now, save possibly Billy Buck, was worthy to do the things that had been done. A race of giants had lived then, fearless men, men of a staunchness unknown in this day. Jody thought of the wide plains and of the wagons moving across like centipedes. He thought of Grandfather on a huge white horse, marshaling the people. Across his mind marched the great phantoms, and they marched off the earth and they were gone.

He came back to the ranch for a moment, then. He heard the dull rushing sound that space and silence make. He heard one of the dogs, out in the doghouse, scratching a flea and bumping his elbow against the floor with every stroke. Then the wind arose again and the black cypress groaned and Jody went to sleep.

He was up half an hour before the triangle sounded for breakfast. His mother was rattling the stove to make the flames roar when Jody went through the kitchen. "You're up early," she said. "Where are you going?"

"Out to get a good stick. We're going to kill the mice today."

"Who is 'we'?"

"Why, Grandfather and I."

"So you've got him in it. You always like to have someone in with you in case there's blame to share."

"I'll be right back," said Jody. "I just want to have a good stick ready for after breakfast."

He closed the screen door after him and went out into the cool blue morning. The birds were noisy in the dawn and the ranch cats came down from the hill like blunt snakes. They had been hunting gophers in the dark, and although the four cats were full of gopher meat, they sat in a semi-circle at the back door and mewed piteously for milk. Doubletree Mutt and Smasher moved sniffing along the edge of the brush, performing the duty with rigid ceremony, but when Jody whistled, their heads jerked up and their tails waved. They plunged down to him, wriggling their skins and yawning. Jody patted their heads seriously, and moved on to the weathered scrap pile. He selected an old broom handle and a short piece of inch-square scrap wood. From his pocket he took a shoelace and tied the ends of the sticks loosely together to make a flail. He whistled his new weapon through the air and struck the ground experimentally, while the dogs leaped aside and whined with apprehension.

Jody turned and started down past the house toward the old haystack ground to look over the field of slaughter, but Billy Buck, sitting patiently on the back steps, called to him, "You better come back. It's only a couple of minutes till breakfast."

Jody changed his course and moved toward the house. He leaned his flail against the steps. "That's to drive the mice out," he said. "I'll bet they're fat. I'll bet they don't know what's going to happen to them today."

"No, nor you either," Billy remarked philosophically, "nor me, nor anyone."

Jody was staggered by this thought. He knew it was true. His imagination twitched away from the mouse hunt. Then his mother came out on the back porch and struck the triangle, and all thoughts fell in a heap.

Grandfather hadn't appeared at the table when they sat down. Billy nodded at his empty chair. "He's all right? He isn't sick?"

"He takes a long time to dress," said Mrs. Tiflin. "He combs his whiskers and rubs up his shoes and brushes his clothes."

Carl scattered sugar on his mush. "A man that's led a wagon train across the plains has got to be pretty careful how he dresses."

Mrs. Tiflin turned on him. "Don't do that, Carl! Please don't!" There was more of threat than of request in her tone. And the threat irritated Carl.

"Well, how many times do I have to listen to the story of the iron plates, and the thirty-five horses? That time's done. Why can't he forget it, now it's done?" He grew angrier while he talked, and his voice rose. "Why does he have to tell them over and over? He came across the plains. All right! Now it's finished. Nobody wants to hear about it over and over."

The door into the kitchen closed softly. The four at the table sat frozen. Carl laid his mush spoon on the table and touched his chin with his fingers.

Then the kitchen door opened and Grandfather walked in. His mouth smiled tightly and his eyes were squinted. "Good morning," he said, and he sat down and looked at his mush dish.

Carl could not leave it there. "Did—did you hear what I said?"

Grandfather jerked a little nod.

"I don't know what got into me, sir. I didn't mean it. I was just being funny."

Jody glanced in shame at his mother, and he saw that she was looking at Carl, and that she wasn't breathing. It was an awful thing that he was doing. He was tearing himself to pieces to talk like that. It was a terrible thing to him to retract a word, but to retract it in shame was infinitely worse.

Grandfather looked sidewise. "I'm trying to get right side up," he said gently. "I'm not being mad. I don't mind what you said, but it might be true, and I would mind that."

"It isn't true," said Carl. "I'm not feeling well this morning. I'm sorry I said it."

"Don't be sorry, Carl. An old man doesn't see things sometimes. Maybe you're right. The crossing is finished. Maybe it should be forgotten, now it's done."

Carl got up from the table. "I've had enough to eat. I'm going to work. Take your time, Billy!" He walked quickly out of the dining-room. Billy gulped the rest of his food and followed soon after. But Jody could not leave his chair.

"Won't you tell any more stories?" Jody asked.

"Why, sure I'll tell them, but only when—I'm sure people want to hear them."

"I like to hear them, sir."

"Oh! Of course you do, but you're a little boy. It was a job for men, but only little boys like to hear about it."

Jody got up from his place. "I'll wait outside for you, sir. I've got a good stick for those mice."

He waited by the gate until the old man came out on the porch. "Let's go down and kill the mice now," Jody called.

"I think I'll just sit in the sun, Jody. You go kill the mice."

"You can use my stick if you like."

"No, I'll just sit here a while."

Jody turned disconsolately away, and walked down toward the old haystack. He tried to whip up his enthusiasm with thoughts of the fat juicy mice. He beat the ground with his flail. The dogs coaxed and whined about him, but he could not go. Back at the house he could see Grandfather sitting on the porch, looking small and thin and black.

Jody gave up and went to sit on the steps at the old man's feet.

"Back already? Did you kill the mice?"

"No, sir. I'll kill them some other day."

The morning flies buzzed close to the ground and the ants dashed about in front of the steps. The heavy smell of sage slipped down the hill. The porch boards grew warm in the sunshine.

Jody hardly knew when Grandfather started to talk. "I shouldn't stay here, feeling the way I do." He examined his strong old hands. "I feel as though the crossing wasn't worth doing." His eyes moved up the side-hill and stopped on a motionless hawk perched on a dead limb. "I tell those old stories, but they're not what I want to tell. I only know how I want people to feel when I tell them.

"It wasn't Indians that were important, nor adventures, nor even getting out here. It was a whole bunch of people made into one big crawling beast. And I was the head. It was westering and westering. Every man wanted something for himself, but the big beast that was all of them wanted only westering. I was the leader, but if I hadn't been there, someone else would have been the head. The thing had to have a head.

"Under the little bushes the shadows were black at white noonday. When we saw the mountains at last, we cried—all of us. But it wasn't getting here that mattered, it was movement and westering.

"We carried life out here and set it down the way those ants carry eggs. And I was the leader. The westering was as big as God, and the slow steps that made the movement piled up and piled up until the continent was crossed.

"Then we came down to the sea, and it was done." He stopped and wiped his eyes until the rims were red. "That's what I should be telling instead of stories."

When Jody spoke, Grandfather started and looked down at him. "Maybe I could lead the people some day," Jody said.

The old man smiled. "There's no place to go. There's the ocean to stop you. There's a line of old men along the shore hating the ocean because it stopped them."

"In boats I might, sir."

"No place to go, Jody. Every place is taken. But that's not the worst—no, not the worst. Westering has died out of the people. Westering isn't a hunger any more. It's all done. Your father is right. It is finished." He laced his fingers on his knee and looked at them.

Jody felt very sad. "If you'd like a glass of lemonade I could make it for you."

Grandfather was about to refuse, and then he saw Jody's face. "That would be nice," he said. "Yes, it would be nice to drink a lemonade."

Jody ran into the kitchen where his mother was wiping the last of the breakfast dishes. "Can I have a lemon to make a lemonade for Grandfather?"

His mother mimicked— "And another lemon to make a lemonade for you."

"No, ma'am. I don't want one."

"Jody! You're sick!" Then she stopped suddenly. "Take a lemon out of the cooler," she said softly. "Here, I'll reach the squeezer down to you."

JOHN STEINBECK

The Promise

IN A MID-AFTERNOON of spring, the little boy Jody walked martially along the brushlined road toward his home ranch. Banging his knee against the golden lard bucket he used for school lunch, he contrived a good bass drum, while his tongue fluttered sharply against his teeth to fill in snare drums and occasional trumpets. Some time back the other members of the squad that walked so smartly from the school had turned into the various little canyons and taken the wagon roads to their own home ranches. Now Jody marched seemingly alone, with high-lifted knees and pounding feet; but behind him there was a phantom army with great flags and swords, silent but deadly.

The afternoon was green and gold with spring. Underneath the spread branches of the oaks the plants grew pale and tall, and on the hills the feed was smooth and thick. The sage-brushes shone with new silver leaves and the oaks wore hoods of golden green. Over the hills there hung such a green odor that the horses on the flats galloped madly, and then stopped, wondering; lambs, and even old sheep, jumped in the air unexpectedly and landed on stiff legs, and went on eating; young clumsy calves butted their heads together and drew back and butted again.

As the grey and silent army marched past, led by Jody, the animals stopped their feeding and their play and watched it go by.

Suddenly Jody stopped. The grey army halted, bewildered and nervous. Jody went down on his knees. The army stood in long uneasy ranks for a moment, and then, with a soft sigh of sorrow, rose up in a faint grey mist and disappeared. Jody had seen the thorny crown of a horny-toad moving under the dust of the road. His grimy hand went out and grasped the spiked halo and held firmly while the little beast struggled. Then Jody turned the horny-toad over, exposing its pale gold stomach. With a gentle forefinger he stroked the throat and chest until the horny-toad relaxed, until its eyes closed and it lay languorous and asleep.

Jody opened his lunch pail and deposited the first game inside. He moved on now, his knees bent slightly, his shoulders crouched; his bare feet were wise and silent. In his right hand there was a long grey rifle. The brush along the road stirred restively under a new and unexpected population of grey tigers and grey bears. The hunting was very good, for by the time Jody reached the fork of the road where the mail box stood on a post, he had captured two more horny-toads, four little grass lizards, a blue snake, sixteen yellow-winged grasshoppers and a brown damp newt from under a rock. This assortment scrabbled unhappily against the tin of the lunch bucket.

At the road fork the rifle evaporated and the tigers and bears melted from the hillsides. Even the moist and uncomfortable creatures in the lunch pail ceased to exist, for the little red metal flag was up on the mail box, signifying that some postal matter was inside. Jody set his pail on the ground and opened the letter box. There was a Montgomery Ward catalog and a copy of the Salinas Weekly Journal. He slammed the box, picked up his lunch pail and trotted over the ridge and down into the cup of the ranch. Past the barn he ran, and past the used-up haystack and the bunkhouse and the cypress tree. He banged through the front screen door of the ranch house calling, "Ma'am, ma'am, there's a catalog."

Mrs. Tiflin was in the kitchen spooning clabbered milk into a cotton bag. She put down her work and rinsed her hands under the tap. "Here in the kitchen, Jody. Here I am."

He ran in and clattered his lunch pail on the sink. "Here it is. Can I open the catalog, ma'am?"

Mrs. Tiflin took up the spoon again and went back to her cottage cheese. "Don't lose it, Jody. Your father will want to see it." She scraped the last of the milk into the bag. "Oh, Jody, your father wants to see you before you go to your chores." She waved a cruising fly from the cheese bag.

Jody closed the new catalog in alarm. "Ma'am?"

"Why don't you ever listen? I say your father wants to see you."

The boy laid the catalog gently on the sink board. "Do you—is it something I did?"

Mrs. Tiflin laughed. "Always a bad conscience. What did you do?"

"Nothing, ma'am," he said lamely. But he couldn't remember, and besides it was impossible to know what action might later be construed as a crime.

His mother hung the full bag on a nail where it could drip into the sink. "He just said he wanted to see you when you got home. He's somewhere down by the barn."

Jody turned and went out the back door. Hearing his mother open the lunch pail and then gasp with rage, a memory stabbed him and he trotted away toward the barn, conscientiously not hearing the angry voice that called him from the house.

Carl Tiflin and Billy Buck, the ranch hand, stood against the lower pasture fence. Each man rested one foot on the lowest bar and both elbows on the top bar. They were talking slowly and aimlessly. In the pasture half a dozen horses nibbled contentedly at the sweet grass. The mare, Nellie, stood backed up against the gate, rubbing her buttocks on the heavy post.

Jody sidled uneasily near. He dragged one foot to give an impression of great innocence and nonchalance. When he arrived beside the men he put one foot on the lowest fence rail, rested his elbows on the second bar and looked into the pasture too. The two men glanced sideways at him.

"I wanted to see you," Carl said in the stern tone he reserved for children and animals.

"Yes, sir," said Jody guiltily.

"Billy, here, says you took good care of the pony before it died."

No punishment was in the air. Jody grew bolder. "Yes, sir, I did."

"Billy says you have a good patient hand with horses."

Jody felt a sudden warm friendliness for the ranch hand.

Billy put in, "He trained that pony as good as anybody I ever seen."

Then Carl Tiflin came gradually to the point. "If you could have another horse would you work for it?"

Jody shivered. "Yes, sir."

"Well, look here, then. Billy says the best way for you to be a good hand with horses is to raise a colt."

"It's the only good way," Billy interrupted.

"Now, look here, Jody," continued Carl. "Jess Taylor, up to the ridge ranch, has a fair stallion, but it'll cost five dollars. I'll put up the money, but you'll have to work it out all summer. Will you do that?"

Jody felt that his insides were shriveling. "Yes, sir," he said softly.

"And no complaining? And no forgetting when you're told to do something?"

"Yes, sir."

"Well, all right, then. Tomorrow morning you take Nellie up to the ridge ranch and get her bred. You'll have to take care of her, too, till she throws the colt."

"Yes, sir."

"You better get to the chickens and the wood now."

Jody slid away. In passing behind Billy Buck he very nearly put out his hand to touch the blue-jeaned legs. His shoulders swayed a little with maturity and importance.

He went to his work with unprecedented seriousness. This night he did not dump the can of grain to the chickens so that they had to leap over each other and struggle to get it. No, he spread the wheat so far and so carefully that the hens couldn't find some of it at all. And in the house, after listening to his mother's despair over boys who filled their lunch pails with slimy, suffocated reptiles, and bugs, he promised never to do it again. Indeed, Jody felt that all such foolishness was lost in the past. He was far too grown up ever to put horny-toads in his lunch pail any more. He carried in so much wood and built such a high structure with it that his mother walked in fear of an avalanche of oak. When he was done, when he had gathered eggs that had remained hidden for weeks, Jody walked down again past the cypress tree, and past the bunk house toward the pasture. A fat warty toad that looked out at him from under the watering trough had no emotional effect on him at all.

Carl Tiflin and Billy Buck were not in sight, but from a metallic ringing on the other side of the barn Jody knew that Billy Buck was just starting to milk a cow.

The other horses were eating toward the upper end of the pasture, but Nellie continued to rub herself nervously against the post. Jody walked slowly near, saying, "So, girl, so-o, Nellie." The mare's ears went back naughtily and her lips drew away from her yellow teeth. She turned her head around; her eyes were glazed and mad. Jody climbed to the top of the fence and hung his feet over and looked paternally down on the mare.

The evening hovered while he sat there. Bats and night-hawks flicked about. Billy Buck, walking toward the house carrying a full milk bucket, saw Jody and stopped. "It's a long time to wait," he said gently. "You'll get awful tired waiting."

"No I won't, Billy. How long will it be?"

"Nearly a year."

"Well, I won't get tired."

The triangle at the house rang stridently. Jody climbed down from the fence and walked to supper beside Billy Buck. He even put out his hand and took hold of the milk bucket to help carry it.

The next morning after breakfast Carl Tiflin folded a five-dollar bill in a piece of newspaper and pinned the package in the bib pocket of Jody's overalls. Billy Buck haltered the mare Nellie and led her out of the pasture.

"Be careful now," he warned. "Hold her up short here so she can't bite you. She's crazy as a coot."

Jody took hold of the halter leather itself and started up the hill toward the ridge ranch with Nellie skittering and jerking behind him. In the pasturage along the road the wild oat heads were just clearing their scabbards. The warm morning sun shone on Jody's back so sweetly that he was forced to take a serious stiff-legged hop now and then in spite of his maturity. On the fences the shiny blackbirds with red epaulets clicked their dry call. The meadowlarks sang like water, and the wild doves, concealed among the bursting leaves of the oaks, made a sound of restrained grieving. In the fields the rabbits sat sunning themselves, with only their forked ears showing above the grass heads.

After an hour of steady uphill walking, Jody turned into a narrow road that led up a steeper hill to the ridge ranch. He could see the red roof of the barn sticking up above the oak trees, and he could hear a dog barking unemotionally near the house.

Suddenly Nellie jerked back and nearly freed herself. From the direction of the barn Jody heard a shrill whistling scream and a splintering of wood, and then a man's voice shouting. Nellie reared and whinnied. When Jody held to the halter rope she ran at him with bared teeth. He dropped his hold and scuttled out of the way, into the brush. The high scream came from the oaks again, and Nellie answered it. With hoofs battering the ground the stallion appeared and charged down the hill trailing a broken halter rope. His eyes glittered feverishly. His stiff, erected nostrils were as red as flame. His black, sleek hide shone in the sunlight. The stallion came on so fast that he couldn't stop when he reached the mare. Nellie's ears went back; she whirled and kicked at him as he went by. The stallion spun around and reared. He struck the mare with his front hoof, and while she staggered under the blow, his teeth raked her neck and drew an ooze of blood.

Instantly Nellie's mood changed. She became coquettishly feminine. She nibbled his arched neck with her lips. She edged around and rubbed her shoulder against his shoulder. Jody stood half-hidden in the brush and watched. He heard the step of a horse behind him, but before he could turn, a hand caught him by the overall straps and lifted him off the ground. Jess Taylor sat the boy behind him on the horse.

"You might have got killed," he said. "Sundog's a mean devil sometimes. He busted his rope and went right through a gate."

Jody sat quietly, but in a moment he cried, "He'll hurt her, he'll kill her. Get him away!"

Jess chuckled. "She'll be all right. Maybe you'd better climb off and go up to the house for a little. You could get maybe a piece of pie up there."

But Jody shook his head. "She's mine, and the colt's going to be mine. I'm going to raise it up."

Jess nodded. "Yes, that's a good thing. Carl has good sense sometimes."

In a little while the danger was over. Jess lifted Jody down and then caught the stallion by its broken halter rope. And he rode ahead, while Jody followed, leading Nellie.

It was only after he had unpinned and handed over the five dollars, and after he had eaten two pieces of pie, that Jody started for home again. And Nellie followed docilely after him. She was so quiet that Jody climbed on a stump and rode her most of the way home.

The five dollars his father had advanced reduced Jody to peonage for the whole late spring and summer. When the hay was cut he drove a rake. He led the horse that pulled on the Jackson-fork tackle, and when the baler came he drove the circling horse that put pressure on the bales. In addition, Carl Tiflin taught him to milk and put a cow under his care, so that a new chore was added night and morning.

The bay mare Nellie quickly grew complacent. As she walked about the yellowing hillsides or worked at easy tasks, her lips were curled in a perpetual fatuous smile. She moved slowly, with the calm importance of an empress. When she was put to a team, she pulled steadily and unemotionally. Jody went to see her every day. He studied her with critical eyes and saw no change whatever.

One afternoon Billy Buck leaned the many-tined manure fork against the barn wall. He loosened his belt and tucked in his shirt-tail and tightened the belt again. He picked one of the little straws from his hatband and put it in the corner of his mouth. Jody, who was helping Doubletree Mutt, the big serious dog, to dig out a gopher, straightened up as the ranch hand sauntered out of the barn.

"Let's go up and have a look at Nellie," Billy suggested.

Instantly Jody fell into step with him. Doubletree Mutt watched them over his shoulder; then he dug furiously, growled, sounded little sharp yelps to indicate that the gopher was practically caught. When he looked over his shoulder again, and saw that neither Jody nor Billy was interested, he climbed reluctantly out of the hole and followed them up the hill.

The wild oats were ripening. Every head bent sharply under its load of grain, and the grass was dry enough so that it made a swishing sound as Jody and Billy stepped through it. Halfway up the hill they could see Nellie and the iron-grey gelding, Pete, nibbling the heads from the wild oats. When they approached, Nellie looked at them and backed her ears and bobbed her head up and down rebelliously. Billy walked to her and put his hand under her mane and patted her neck, until her ears came forward again and she nibbled delicately at his shirt.

Jody asked, "Do you think she's really going to have a colt?"

Billy rolled the lids back from the mare's eyes with his thumb and forefinger. He felt the lower lip and fingered the black, leathery teats. "I wouldn't be surprised," he said.

"Well, she isn't changed at all. It's three months gone."

Billy rubbed the mare's flat forehead with his knuckle while she grunted with pleasure. "I told you you'd get tired waiting. It'll be five months more before you can even see a sign, and it'll be at least eight months more before she throws the colt, about next January."

Jody sighed deeply. "It's a long time, isn't it?"

"And then it'll be about two years more before you can ride."

Jody cried out in despair, "I'll be grown up."

"Yep, you'll be an old man," said Billy.

"What color do you think the colt'll be?"

"Why, you can't ever tell. The stud is black and the dam is bay. Colt might be black or bay or grey or dappled. You can't tell. Sometimes a black dam might have a white colt."

"Well, I hope it's black, and a stallion."

"If it's a stallion, we'll have to geld it. Your father wouldn't let you have a stallion."

"Maybe he would," Jody said. "I could train him not to be mean."

Billy pursed his lips, and the little straw that had been in the corner of his mouth rolled down to the center. "You can't ever trust a stallion," he said critically. "They're mostly fighting and making trouble. Sometimes when they're feeling funny they won't work. They make the mares uneasy and kick hell out of the geldings. Your father wouldn't let you keep a stallion."

Nellie sauntered away, nibbling the drying grass. Jody skinned the grain from a grass stem and threw the handful into the air, so that each pointed, feathered seed sailed out like a dart. "Tell me how it'll be, Billy. Is it like when the cows have calves?"

"Just about. Mares are a little more sensitive. Sometimes you have to be there to help the mare. And sometimes if it's wrong, you have to——" he paused.

"Have to what, Billy?"

"Have to tear the colt to pieces to get it out, or the mare'll die."

"But it won't be that way this time, will it Billy?"

"Oh, no. Nellie's thrown good colts."

"Can I be there, Billy? Will you be certain to call me? It's my colt."

"Sure, I'll call you. Of course I will."

"Tell me how it'll be."

"Why, you've seen the cows calving. It's almost the same. The mare starts groaning and stretching, and then, if it's a good right birth, the head and forefeet come out, and the front hoofs kick a hole just the way the calves do. And the colt starts to breathe. It's good to be there, 'cause if its feet aren't right maybe he can't break the sack, and then he might smother."

Jody whipped his leg with a bunch of grass. "We'll have to be there, then, won't we?"

"Oh, we'll be there, all right."

They turned and walked slowly down the hill toward the barn. Jody was tortured with a thing he had to say, although he didn't want to. "Billy," he began miserably, "Billy, you won't let anything happen to the colt, will you?"

And Billy knew he was thinking of the red pony, Gabilan, and of how it died of strangles. Billy knew he had been infallible before that, and now he was capable of failure. This knowledge made Billy much less sure of himself than he had been. "I can't tell," he said roughly. "All sorts of things might happen, and they wouldn't be my fault. I can't do everything." He felt badly about his lost prestige, and so he said, meanly, "I'll do everything I know, but I won't promise anything. Nellie's a good mare. She's thrown good colts before. She ought to this time." And he walked away from Jody and went into the saddle-room beside the barn, for his feelings were hurt.

Jody traveled often to the brushline behind the house. A rusty iron pipe ran a thin stream of spring water into an old green tub. Where the water spilled over and sank into the ground there was a patch of perpetually green grass. Even when the hills were brown and baked in the summer that little patch was green. The water whined softly into the trough all the year round. This place had grown to be a center-point for Jody. When he had been punished the cool green grass and the singing water soothed him. When he had been mean the biting acid of meanness left him at the brushline. When he sat in the grass and listened to the purling stream, the barriers set up in his mind by the stern day went down to ruin.

On the other hand, the black cypress tree by the bunkhouse was as repulsive as the water-tub was dear; for to this tree all the pigs came, sooner or later, to be slaughtered. Pig killing was fascinating, with the screaming and the blood, but it made Jody's heart beat so fast that it hurt him. After the pigs were scalded in the big iron tripod kettle and their skins were scraped and white, Jody had to go to the water-tub to sit in the grass until his heart grew quiet. The water-tub and the black cypress were opposites and enemies.

When Billy left him and walked angrily away, Jody turned up toward the house. He thought of Nellie as he walked, and of the little colt. Then suddenly he saw that he was under the black cypress, under the very singletree where the pigs were hung. He brushed his dry-grass hair off his forehead and hurried on. It seemed to him an unlucky thing to be thinking of his colt in the very slaughter place, especially after what Billy had said. To counteract any evil result of that bad conjunction he walked quickly past the ranch house, through the chicken yard, through the vegetable patch, until he came at last to the brushline.

He sat down in the green grass. The trilling water sounded in his ears. He looked over the farm buildings and across at the round hills, rich and yellow with grain. He could see Nellie feeding on the slope. As usual the water place eliminated time and distance. Jody saw a black, long-legged colt, butting against Nellie's flanks, demanding milk. And then he saw himself breaking a large colt to halter. All in a few moments the colt grew to be a magnificent animal, deep of chest, with a neck as high and arched as a sea-horse's neck, with a tail that tongued and rippled like black flame. This horse was terrible to everyone but Jody. In the schoolyard the boys begged rides, and Jody smilingly agreed. But no sooner were they mounted than the black demon pitched them off. Why, that was his name, Black Demon! For a moment the trilling water and the grass and the sunshine came back, and then . . .

Sometimes in the night the ranch people, safe in their beds, heard a roar of hoofs go by. They said, "It's Jody, on Demon. He's helping out the sheriff again." And then . . .

The golden dust filled the air in the arena at the Salinas Rodeo. The announcer called the roping contests. When Jody rode the black horse to the starting chute the other contestants shrugged and gave up first place, for it was well known that Jody and Demon could rope and throw and tie a steer a great deal quicker than any roping team of two men could. Jody was not a boy any more, and Demon was not a horse. The two together were one glorious individual. And then . . .

The President wrote a letter and asked them to help catch a bandit in Washington. Jody settled himself comfortably in the grass. The little stream of water whined into the mossy tub.

The year passed slowly on. Time after time Jody gave up his colt for lost. No change had taken place in Nellie. Carl Tiflin still drove her to a light cart, and she pulled on a hay rake and worked the Jackson-fork tackle when the hay was being put into the barn.

The summer passed, and the warm bright autumn. And then the frantic morning winds began to twist along the ground, and a chill came into the air, and the poison oak turned red. One morning in September, when he had finished his breakfast, Jody's mother called him into the kitchen. She was pouring boiling water into a bucket full of dry middlings and stirring the materials to a steaming paste.

"Yes, ma'am?" Jody asked.

"Watch how I do it. You'll have to do it after this every other morning."

"Well, what is it?"

"Why, it's warm mash for Nellie. It'll keep her in good shape."

Jody rubbed his forehead with a knuckle. "Is she all right?" he asked timidly.

Mrs. Tiflin put down the kettle and stirred the mash with a wooden paddle. "Of course she's all right, only you've got to take better care of her from now on. Here, take this breakfast out to her!"

Jody seized the bucket and ran, down past the bunkhouse, past the barn, with the heavy bucket banging against his knees. He found Nellie playing with the water in the trough, pushing waves and tossing her head so that the water slopped out on the ground.

Jody climbed the fence and set the bucket of steaming mash beside her. Then he stepped back to look at her. And she was changed. Her stomach was swollen. When she moved, her feet touched the ground gently. She buried her nose in the bucket and gobbled the hot breakfast. And when she had finished and had pushed the bucket around the ground with her nose a little, she stepped quietly over to Jody and rubbed her cheek against him.

Billy Buck came out of the saddle-room and walked over. "Starts fast when it starts, doesn't it?"

"Did it come all at once?"

"Oh, no, you just stopped looking for a while." He pulled her head around toward Jody. "She's goin' to be nice, too. See how nice her eyes are! Some mares get mean, but when they turn nice, they just love everything." Nellie slipped her head under Billy's arm and rubbed her neck up and down between his arm and his side. "You better treat her awful nice now," Billy said.

"How long will it be?" Jody demanded breathlessly.

The man counted in whispers on his fingers. "About three months," he said aloud. "You can't tell exactly. Sometimes it's eleven months to the day, but it might be two weeks early, or a month late, without hurting anything."

Jody looked hard at the ground. "Billy," he began

nervously, "Billy, you'll call me when it's getting born, won't you? You'll let me be there, won't you?"

Billy bit the tip of Nellie's ear with his front teeth. "Carl says he wants you to start right at the start. That's the only way to learn. Nobody can tell you anything. Like my old man did with me about the saddle blanket. He was a government packer when I was your size, and I helped him some. One day I left a wrinkle in my saddle blanket and made a saddle-sore. My old man didn't give me hell at all. But the next morning he saddled me up with a forty-pound stock saddle. I had to lead my horse and carry that saddle over a whole damn mountain in the sun. It darn near killed me, but I never left no wrinkles in a blanket again. I couldn't. I never in my life since then put on a blanket but I felt that saddle on my back."

Jody reached up a hand and took hold of Nellie's mane. "You'll tell me what to do about everything, won't you? I guess you know everything about horses, don't you?"

Billy laughed. "Why I'm half horse myself, you see," he said. "My ma died when I was born, and being my old man was a government packer in the mountains, and no cows around most of the time, why he just gave me mostly mare's milk." He continued seriously. "And horses know that. Don't you know it, Nellie?"

The mare turned her head and looked full into his eyes for a moment, and this is a thing horses practically never do. Billy was proud and sure of himself now. He boasted a little. "I'll see you get a good colt. I'll start you right. And if you do like I say, you'll have the best horse in the country."

That made Jody feel warm and proud, too; so proud that when he went back to the house he bowed his legs and swayed his shoulders as horsemen do. And he whispered, "Whoa, you Black Demon, you! Steady down there and keep your feet on the ground."

The winter fell sharply. A few preliminary gusty showers, and then a strong steady rain. The hills lost their straw color and blackened under the water, and the winter streams scrambled noisily down the canyons. The mushrooms and puffballs popped up and the new grass started before Christmas.

But this year Christmas was not the central day to Jody. Some undetermined time in January had become the axis day around which the months swung. When the rains fell, he put Nellie in a box stall and fed her warm food every morning and curried her and brushed her.

The mare was swelling so greatly that Jody became alarmed. "She'll pop wide open," he said to Billy.

Billy laid his strong square hand against Nellie's swollen abdomen. "Feel here," he said quietly. "You can feel it move. I guess it would surprise you if there were twin colts."

"You don't think so?" Jody cried. "You don't think it will be twins, do you, Billy?"

"No, I don't, but it does happen, sometimes."

During the first two weeks of January it rained steadily.

Jody spent most of his time, when he wasn't in school, in the box stall with Nellie. Twenty times a day he put his hand on her stomach to feel the colt move. Nellie became more and more gentle and friendly to him. She rubbed her nose on him. She whinnied softly when he walked into the barn.

Carl Tiflin came to the barn with Jody one day. He looked admiringly at the groomed bay coat, and he felt the firm flesh over ribs and shoulders. "You've done a good job," he said to Jody. And this was the greatest praise he knew how to give. Jody was tight with pride.

The fifteenth of January came, and the colt was not born. And the twentieth came; a lump of fear began to form in Jody's stomach. "Is it all right?" he demanded of Billy.

"Oh, sure."

And again, "Are you sure it's going to be all right?"

Billy stroked the mare's neck. She swayed her head uneasily. "I told you it wasn't always the same time, Jody. You just have to wait."

When the end of the month arrived with no birth, Jody grew frantic. Nellie was so big that her breath came heavily, and her ears were close together and straight up, as though her head ached. Jody's sleep grew restless, and his dreams confused.

On the night of the second of February he awakened crying. His mother called to him, "Jody, you're dreaming. Wake up and start over again."

But Jody was filled with terror and desolation. He lay quietly a few moments, waiting for his mother to go back to sleep, and then he slipped his clothes on, and crept out in his bare feet.

The night was black and thick. A little misting rain fell. The cypress tree and the bunkhouse loomed and then dropped back into the mist. The barn door screeched as he opened it, a thing it never did in the daytime. Jody went to the rack and found a lantern and a tin box of matches. He lighted the wick and walked down the long straw-covered aisle to Nellie's stall. She was standing up. Her whole body weaved from side to side. Jody called to her, "So, Nellie, so-o, Nellie," but she did not stop her swaying nor look around. When he stepped into the stall and touched her on the shoulder she shivered under his hand. Then Billy Buck's voice came from the hayloft right above the stall.

"Jody, what are you doing?"

Jody started back and turned miserable eyes up toward the nest where Billy was lying in the hay. "Is she all right, do you think?"

"Why sure, I think so."

"You won't let anything happen, Billy, you're sure you won't?"

Billy growled down at him, "I told you I'd call you, and I will. Now you get back to bed and stop worrying that mare. She's got enough to do without you worrying her."

Jody cringed, for he had never heard Billy speak in such a tone. "I only thought I'd come and see," he said, "I woke up."

Billy softened a little then. "Well, you get to bed. I don't want you bothering her. I told you I'd get you a good colt. Get along now."

Jody walked slowly out of the barn. He blew out the lantern and set it in the rack. The blackness of the night, and the chilled mist struck him and enfolded him. He wished he believed everything Billy said as he had before the pony died. It was a moment before his eyes, blinded by the feeble lantern-flame, could make any form of the darkness. The damp ground chilled his bare feet. At the cypress tree the roosting turkeys chattered a little in alarm, and the two good dogs responded to their duty and came charging out, barking to frighten away the coyotes they thought were prowling under the tree.

As he crept through the kitchen, Jody stumbled over a chair. Carl called from his bedroom. "Who's there? What's the matter there?"

And Mrs. Tiflin said sleepily, "What's the matter, Carl?"

The next second Carl came out of the bedroom carrying a candle, and found Jody before he could get into bed. "What are you doing out?"

Jody turned shyly away. "I was down to see the mare."

For a moment anger at being awakened fought with approval in Jody's father. "Listen," he said, finally, "there's not a man in this country that knows more about colts than Billy. You leave it to him."

Words burst out of Jody's mouth. "But the pony died——"

"Don't you go blaming that on him," Carl said sternly. "If Billy can't save a horse, it can't be saved."

Mrs. Tiflin called, "Make him clean his feet and go to bed Carl. He'll be sleepy all day tomorrow."

It seemed to Jody that he had just closed his eyes to try to go to sleep when he was shaken violently by the shoulder. Billy Buck stood beside him, holding a lantern in his hand. "Get up," he said. "Hurry up." He turned and walked quickly out of the room.

Mrs. Tiflin called, "What's the matter? Is that you, Billy?"

"Yes, ma'am."

"Is Nellie ready?"

"Yes, ma'am."

"All right, I'll get up and heat some water in case you need it."

Jody jumped into his clothes so quickly that he was out the back door before Billy's swinging lantern was halfway to the barn. There was a rim of dawn on the mountain-tops, but no light had penetrated into the cup of the ranch yet. Jody ran frantically after the lantern and caught up to Billy just as he reached the barn. Billy hung the lantern to a nail on the stall-side and took off his blue denim coat. Jody saw that he wore only a sleeveless shirt under it.

Nellie was standing rigid and stiff. While they watched, she crouched. Her whole body was wrung with a spasm. The spasm passed. But in a few moments it started all over again, and passed.

Billy muttered nervously, "There's something wrong." His bare hand disappeared. "Oh, Jesus," he said. "It's wrong."

The spasm came again, and this time Billy strained, and the muscles stood out on his arm and shoulder. He heaved strongly, his forehead beaded with perspiration. Nellie cried with pain. Billy was muttering, "It's wrong. I can't turn it. It's way wrong. It's turned all around wrong."

He glared wildly toward Jody. And then his fingers made a careful, careful diagnosis. His cheeks were growing tight and grey. He looked for a long questioning minute at Jody standing back of the stall. Then Billy stepped to the rack under the manure window and picked up a horseshoe hammer with his wet right hand.

"Go outside, Jody," he said.

The boy stood still and stared dully at him.

"Go outside, I tell you. It'll be too late."

Jody didn't move.

Then Billy walked quickly to Nellie's head. He cried, "Turn your face away, damn you, turn your face."

This time Jody obeyed. His head turned sideways. He heard Billy whispering hoarsely in the stall. And then he heard a hollow crunch of bone. Nellie chuckled shrilly. Jody looked back in time to see the hammer rise and fall again on the flat forehead. Then Nellie fell heavily to her side and quivered for a moment.

Billy jumped to the swollen stomach; his big pocket-knife was in his hand. He lifted the skin and drove the knife in. He sawed and ripped at the tough belly. The air filled with the sick odor of warm living entrails. The other horses reared back against their halter chains and squealed and kicked.

Billy dropped the knife. Both of his arms plunged into the terrible ragged hole and dragged out a big, white, dripping bundle. His teeth tore a hole in the covering. A little black head appeared through the tear, and little slick, wet ears. A gurgling breath was drawn, and then another. Billy shucked off the sac and found his knife and cut the string. For a moment he held the little black colt in his arms and looked at it. And then he walked slowly over and laid it in the straw at Jody's feet.

Billy's face and arms and chest were dripping red. His body shivered and his teeth chattered. His voice was gone;

he spoke in a throaty whisper. "There's your colt. I promised. And there it is. I had to do it—had to." He stopped and looked over his shoulder into the box stall. "Go get hot water and a sponge," he whispered. "Wash him and dry him the way his mother would. You'll have to feed him by hand. But there's your colt, the way I promised."

Jody stared stupidly at the wet, panting foal. It stretched out its chin and tried to raise its head. Its blank eyes were navy blue.

"God damn you," Billy shouted, "will you go now for the water? Will you go?"

Then Jody turned and trotted out of the barn into the dawn. He ached from his throat to his stomach. His legs were stiff and heavy. He tried to be glad because of the colt, but the bloody face, and the haunted, tired eyes of Billy Buck hung in the air ahead of him.

EUDORA WELTY

*Ida M'Toy**

FOR ONE human being to point out another as "unforgettable" seems a trifle condescending, and in the ideal world we would all keep well aware of each other, but there are nevertheless a few persons one meets who are as inescapable of notice as sky-rockets, it may be because like skyrockets they are radiant with their own substance and shower it about regardlessly. Ida M'Toy, an old Negro woman, for a long time a midwife in my little Mississippi town and for another long time a dealer in second-hand clothes in the same place, has been a sky-rocket as far back as most people remember. Or, rather, she is a kind of meteor (for she is not ephemeral, only sudden and startling). Her ways seem on a path of their own without regard to any course of ours and of a somewhat wider circuit; she will probably leave a glow behind and return in the far future on some other lap of her careening through all our duller and steadier bodies. She herself deals with the rest of us in this mighty and spacious way, calling in allegories and the elements, so it is owing to her nature that I may speak a little grandly.

The slave traders of England and New England, when they went capturing, took away the most royal of Africans along with their own slaves, and I have not much doubt that Ida has come down from a race of tall black queens. I wish I might have seen her when she was young. She has sharp clever features, light-filled black eyes, arched nostrils, and fine thin mobile lips, and her hair, gray now, springs like a kind of diadem from the widow's peak over her forehead. Her voice is indescribable but it is a constant part of her presence and is filled with invocation. She never speaks lightly of any person or thing, but she flings out her arm and points at something and begins, "O, precious, I'm telling you to look at that—*look* at it!" and then she invokes about it, and tolerates no interruptions. I have heard long chants and utterances on the origin and history and destination of the smallest thing, any article or object her eye lights on; a bit of candle stuck on the mantelpiece will set her off, as if its little fire had ignited her whole mind. She invokes what she wishes to invoke and she has in all ways something of the seer about her. She wields a control over great numbers of her race by this power, which has an integrity that I believe nothing could break, and which sets her up, aloof and triumphant, above the rest. She is inspired and they are not. Maybe off by themselves they could be inspired, but nobody else could be inspired in the same room with Ida, it would be too crowded.

Ida is not a poor old woman, she is a rich old woman. She accepts it that she is held in envy as well as respect, but it is only another kind of tribute as far as she is concerned, and she is not at all prouder of being rich or of having been married in the home of a white lady, "in her bay window," then she is of being very wise. She expects to be gaped at, but she is not vain.

Ida's life has been divided in two (it is, in many ways, eloquent of duality); but there is a thread that runs from one part into the other and to trace this connection between delivering the child and clothing the man is an interesting speculation. Moreover, it has some excuse, for Ida herself helps it along by a wild and curious kind

* Miss Welty regards "Ida M'Toy" as a sketch, not as a short story. Originally published in *Accent*. Reprinted by permission.

of talk that sashays from one part to the other and sounds to some of her customers like "ranting and raving." It is my belief that if Ida had not been a midwife she would not be the same kind of second-hand clothes dealer she is. Midwifery set her off, it gave her a hand in the mysteries, and she will never let go that flying hold merely because she is engaged in something else. An ex-alchemist would run a second-hand clothes business with extra touches—a reminiscence of glitter would cling to the garments he sold, and it is the same with Ida. So it is well when you meet her to think what she was once.

Ida's memory goes back to her beginnings, when she was, she says, the first practical nurse in Jackson at the age of twenty-one, and she makes the past sound very dark and far back. She thanks God, she says, that today Capitol Street is not just three planks to walk on and is the prettiest place on earth, but that "people white and black is too high and don't they know Ida seen them when they carried a little tin coal-lamp that wasn't any bigger than their little fingers?" Ida speaks of herself in the third person and in indirect discourse often and especially when she says something good of herself or something of herself long ago. She will intone, "Ida say that she was good to the poor white people as she was to the rich, as she made a bargain to nurse a poor white lady in obstetrical case for a peck of peas. Ida said no, she couldn't see her suffer, and therefore a peck of black-eyed peas would be sufficient." She wants all she says to be listened to with the whole attention, and declares she does wish it were all written down. "Let her keep it straight, darling, if she remember Ida's true words, the angels will know it and be waiting around the throne for her." But Ida's true words are many and strange. When she talks about the old days it is almost like a story of combat against evil. "Ida fitted a duel from twenty-one to fifty-six, and then they operated on her right side and she was never able to stoop down to the floor again. She was never like those young devils, that pace around in those white shoes and those white clothes and up and down the streets of an evening while their patient is calling for a drink of water down poor parched throat—though I wore those white shoes and those white clothes. Only, my heart was in another direction."

Ida said, "I was nursing ever since there was a big road in Jackson. There was only nine doctors, and they were the best in all the world, all nine, right here in Jackson, but they were weak in finance. There wasn't nary hospital nowhere—there wasn't nary brick in Jackson, not one brick, no brick walk, no brick store, no brick nothing-else. There wasn't no Old Ladies' Home at the end of the street, there wasn't no stopping place but the country. Town was as black as tar come night, and praise God they finally put some gas in bottles on the corners. There wasn't no such thing in the world as a nice buggy. Never heard tell of a cotton mattress, but tore up shucks and see the bed, so high, and the hay pillow stand up so beautiful! Now they got all this electric light and other electricity. Can't do nothing without the clickety-click. And bless God they fly just like buzzards up in the air, but Ida don't intend to ride till she ride to Glory."

In those early days when Jackson seems to have been a Slough of Despond with pestilence sticking out its head in the nights as black as tar, Ida was not only a midwife, she nursed all diseases. "It was the yellow fever first, and the next after that was the worst pox that there ever was in this world—it would kill you then, in my girl-days, six or seven a day. They had to stretch a rope across the road to keep the poor sick ones apart and many's the day I've et at the rope and carried the food back to the ones suffering." Ida remembers epidemics as major combats in which she was a kind of giant-killer. She nursed through influenza "six at a blow, until the doctor told me if I didn't quit nursing by sixes I would drop dead in the room." She says the doctors wrote her a recommendation as long as where she will show you up her arm, saying that when they called, it never was too cold and it never was too hot for Ida to go, and that the whole town would bow and say Amen, from the Jews on. "Bless my patients," she says, "nary one ever did die under my nursing, though plenty were sick enough to die. But laugh here," she directs. "My husband stayed sick on me twenty-one years and cost me one thousand whole dollars, but you can't nurse the heart to do no good, and in the night he fallen asleep and left me a widow, and I am a widow still."

When Ida found she could no longer stoop to the floor she stopped being a midwife and began selling clothes. She was successful at once in that too, for there is a natural flowering-ground for the second-hand clothes business in the small American community where the richest people are only a little richer than the poor people and the poorest have ways to save pride and not starve or go naked. In Jackson the most respectable matron, if she would like a little extra cash to buy a new camellia bush or take the excursion to New Orleans, can run over to Ida's with her husband's other suit and Ida will sell it to a customer as a bargain at $5 and collect 25% for herself, and everybody except the husband ("Right off my back! Perfectly good suit!") will be satisfied.

It could be a grubby enough little business in actual fact, but Ida is not a grubby person, and in her handling it has become an affair of imagination and, to my notion, an expression of a whole attitude of life as integrated as an art or a philosophy.

Ida's store is her house, a white-painted little house with a porch across the front, a picket-fence around, and the dooryard planted to capacity in big flowers. Inside, it is a phantasmagoria of garments. Every room except the kitchen is hung with dresses or suits (the sexes are segregated) three and four times around the walls, for the turnover is large and unpredictable, though not always rapid—people have to save up or wait for cotton-money. She has assumed all the ceremonies of Business and employs its practices and its terms to a point within sight of madness. She puts on a show of logic and executive order before which the customer is supposed to quail; sometimes I think her customers take on worth with her merely as witnesses of the miracles of her workings, though that is unfair. Her house turns year by year into a better labyrinth, more inescapable, and she delights in its complication of aisles and curtains and its mystery of closed doors with little signs on ruled paper, "Nobody can come in here." Some day some little colored girl is going to get lost in Ida's house. The richer she gets, the more "departments" she builds and adds on to the house, and each one is named for the color of its walls, the pink department, or the blue. Even now her side yard is filled with miscellaneous doors, glass panes, planks, and little stacks of bricks that she is accumulating for a new green department she says she will build in 1943.

Her cupboards and drawers are a progressive series of hiding places, which is her interpretation of the filing system. She hides trinkets of mysterious importance or bits of paper filled with abbreviated information; she does not hide money, however, and she tells how much she has on hand ($660.60 is the latest figure), and her life insurance policy is nailed up on the wall over the mantel. Everybody knows her to be an old woman living with only a small grandchild to guard her in a house full of cash money, and yet she has not been murdered. She never will be. I have wondered what Ida would do if she saw a burglar coming after her money. I am convinced that she has no axe or gun ready for him, but a flow of words will be unstoppered that will put the fear of God in him for life; and I think the would-be burglars have the same suspicion, and will continue to keep away, not wanting so much fear of God as that.

She keeps as strict and full a ledger of transaction as the Book of Judgment, and in as enthusiastic and exalted a spirit of accuracy as an angel book-keeper should have. The only trouble is, it is almost impossible to find in it what she is looking for—but perhaps there will be confusion on Doomsday too. The book, a great black one, which she now has little William, her grandson, to hold for her while she consults it (and he will kneel under it like a little mural figure), covers a period of 26 years, concerns hundreds of people, "white and black," and innumerable transactions, all noted down in a strange code full of flourishes, for Ida properly considers all she does confidential. "You could find anything in the world in this book," she says reverently, then slamming it shut in your face, "if you turn enough pages and go in the right direction. Nothing in here is wrong," she says. Loose slips are always flying out of the ledger like notes in the Sybil's book, and she sets William flying to chase them and get them inside again.

She writes her own descriptions of the garments brought to her to sell, and a lady giving over her finest white dress of last summer must not be surprised, if she looks over Ida's shoulder, to see her pen the words, "Rally Day, $2.00" or note down her best spring straw hat as "Tom Boy, 75¢." The customer might be right, but Ida does not ever ask the customer. After a moment of concentration Ida goes and hangs the object for sale on the wall in the room of her choice, and a tag is pinned to the sleeve, saying simply, "Mrs. So-and-So." Accuracy is a passion with Ida, and so is her belief in her own conscience, and I do not know what it must have cost her to pin a tag on one poor sagging dress that has hung there year in, year out, saying "Don't know who this is."

She bears respect to clothes in the same degree as she bears it to the people from whose backs they come; she treats them like these people, until indeed it seems that dignity is in them, shapeless and even ridiculous as they have seemed at first; she gives them the space on the wall and the room in the house that correspond to the honor in which she holds the human beings, and she even speaks in the proper tone of voice when she is in the room with them. They hang at human height from the hangers on the walls, the brighter and more important ones in front and on top. With the most serene impartiality she makes up her mind about client and clothes, and she has been known to say, "For God's sake take it back. Wouldn't a man white or black wear that suit out of here."

There is a magnificence in Ida's business, an extent and an influence at which she hints without ceasing, that undoubtedly inspire the poorest or idlest customer with almost an anxiety to buy. It is almost like an appeasement, and the one that goes off with nothing must feel mean, foolish, and naked indeed, naked to scorn. "I clothe them," she says, "from Jackson to Vicksburg, Meridian to Jackson, Big Black to 'Azoo, Memphis to New Orleans —Clinton! Bolton! Edwards! Bovina! Pocahontas! Flora! Bentonia! 'Azoo City! Everywhere. There ain't nobody hasn't come to Ida, or sooner or later will come."

If no one else had thought of the second-hand clothes business Ida would have originated it, for she did originate it as far as she is concerned; and likewise I am forced to believe that if there had never been any midwives in the world Ida would have invented midwifery, so ingenious and delicate-handed and wise she is, and sure of her natural right to take charge. She loves transformation and bringing things about, she simply cannot resist it. The Negro midwives of this state have a kind of organization these days and lesser powers, they do certain things in certain book-specified ways, and all memorize and sing at meetings a song about "First we put—Drops in their eyes," but in Ida's day a midwife was a lone person, invested with the whole charge of life; she had to draw upon her own resources and imagination. Ida's constant gestures today still involve a dramatic out-thrust of the right hand, and let any prominent names be mentioned (and she mentions them) and she will fling out her palm and cry into the conversation, "Born in this hand!" "Four hundred little white babies—or more," she says. "My God, I was bringing them all the time. I got 'em everywhere—doctors, lawyers, school teachers, and preachers, married ladies." She has been in the clothes business for twenty-six years, but she was a midwife for thirty-five.

She herself has been married, twice, and by her first husband she had one son, "The only one I ever did have and I want his name written down: Julius Knight." Her mother (before she died) and her brothers lived out in the country, and only one little grandson has lived with her for a long time. Her husband Braddie M'Toy, whom she called Toy, is remembered collecting and delivering clothes in a wagon when he was young, and was to be seen always on some street if not another, moving very slowly on account of his heart.

Now without Toy, Ida uses a telephone down the road and a kind of de luxe grapevine service to rouse up her clients and customers. Anybody who is asked to by Ida feels a duty to phone any stranger for her and "tell them for God's sake to come get their money and bring the change." Strange Negroes call people at dawn, giving news of a sale, white ladies call unknown white ladies, notes on small rolls or scraps of paper folded like doctors' "powders" are conscientiously delivered, and the whole town contrives in her own spirit of emergency to keep Ida's messages on their way. Ida takes 25% of the sales price and if she sells your dress for a dollar you have to take her a quarter when you go, or come back another time, for she will not make change for anybody. She will not violate her system of book-keeping any more than she would violate her code of ethics or her belief in God—down to the smallest thing all is absolute in Ida's sight.

Whether it is due to a savage ancestry or a philosophical turn of mind, Ida finds all Ornament a wonderful and appropriate thing, the proper materializing of the rejoicing or sorrowing soul. I believe she holds Ornament next to birth and somehow kin to it. She despises a drab color and welcomes bright clothes with a queenly and triumphant smile, as if she acknowledges the bold brave heart that chose that. Inferior color means inferior spirit, and an inferior person should not hope to get or spend more than four-bits for an outfit. She dearly loves a dress that is at once identifiable as either rich mourning or "Rally-day"—the symbolic and celebrating kind appeal to her inevitably over the warm or the serviceable, and she will ask and (by oratory) get the finest prices for rather useless but splendid garments. "Girl, you buy this spangle-dress," she says to a customer, and the girl buys it and puts it on and shines. Ida's scale of prices would make a graph showing precisely the rise from her condemnation of the subdued and nondescript to her acclaim of the bright and glorious. Her customers, poverty-bound little cooks and maids and cotton-choppers, go away feeling that they have turned into queens. Ida has put second-hand clothes on their backs and, with all the abrupt bullying of a busy fairy, wrapped them in some glowing raiment of illusion, set them in a whirl of bedazzlement; and they skitter out with shining eyes and empty hands, with every hoarded penny spent. Ida has put them in inner spangles and she has taken an actual warm moist fifty-cent piece out of their palms, and in that world both items exchanged are precious above price, fifty cents being as miraculous as glory. With something second-hand, worn, yet finer than could ever be bought new, she brings to them a perfection in her own eyes and in theirs. She dresses them up and turns them with a little ceremonial jerk towards the mirror, and a magic must hang over the green cracked glass, for (I have seen it happen a hundred times) the glances that go into its surface begin to shine with a pride that could only be a kind of enchantment. It is nice on Saturdays to pass in front of Ida's house on the edge of town and see the customers emerge. With some little flash of scarf, some extra glitter of trimming for which they have paid dearly, dressed like some visions in Ida's speculations on the world, glorious or menial as befits their birth, merit, and willingness, but all rampant and somehow fulfilled by this last touch of costume as though they have been tapped by a spirit when Ida's thimble rapped them, they float dizzily down the steps and through the flowers out the gate; and you could not help thinking of the phrase "going out into the world," as if Ida had just birthed them anew.

I used to think she must be, a little, the cross between a transcendentalist and a witch, with the happiness and kind of self-wonder that this combination must enjoy. They say that all things we write could be; and sometimes in amazement I wonder if a tiny spark of the wonderful Philosopher of Clothes, Diogenes Teufelsdröckh, could be flashing for an instant, and somewhat barbarically, in the wild and enthusiastic spirit of this old black woman. Her life like his is proudly emblematic—she herself being the first to see her place in the world. It is she literally who clothes her entire world, as far and wide as she knows—a hard-worked midwife grown old, with a memory like a mill turning through it all the lives that were born in her hand or have passed through her door.

When she stalks about, alternately clapping her hand over her forehead and flinging out her palm and muttering "Born in this hand!" as she is likely to do when some lady of the old days comes bringing a dress to sell, you cannot help believing that she sees them all, her children and her customers, in the double way, naked and clothed, young and then old, with love and with contempt, with open arms or with a push to bar the door. She is moody now, if she has not always been, and sees her customers as a procession of sweet supplicant spirits that she has birthed, who have returned to her side, and again sometimes as a bunch of scarecrows or even changelings, that she wishes were well gone out of sight. "They would steal from their own mother," she says, and while she is pinning up some purchase in a newspaper and the customer is still counting out the pennies, she will shout in a deep voice to the grandchild that flutters around like a little blackbird, "Hold the door, William."

I have never caught Ida doing anything except selling clothes or holding forth on her meditations, but she has a fine garden. "If you want to carry me something I really like," she will say, bringing up the subject first, "carry me dallion potatoes (dahlia bulbs) *first,* and old newspapers second." Ida has the green finger from her mother, and she says, "You're never going to see any flowers prettier than these right here." She adores giving flowers away; under your protest she will cut every one in the garden, every red and white rose on the trellis, which is a wooden sunset with painted rays, the blossoms with little two-inch stems the way a child cuts them, and distribute them among all present and those passing in the road. She is full of all the wild humors and extravagances of the godlike toward this entire town and its environs. Sometimes, owing to her superior wisdom, she is a little malign, but much oftener she will become excruciatingly tender, holding, as if in some responsibility toward all the little ones of the world, the entire population to her great black cameoed breast. Then she will begin to call people "It." "It's all hot and tired, it is, coming so far to see Ida. Ah, take these beautiful flowers Ida grew with her own hand, *that's* what it would like. Put 'em in its bedroom," and she presses forward all the flowers she has cut and then, not content, a bouquet dripping from a vase, one of a kind of everything, all into your arms.

She loves music too, and in her house she has one room, also hung with clothes, called the music room. "I got all the music in the world in here," she used to say, jabbing a finger at a silent radio and an old gramophone shut up tight, "but what's the use of letting those contrivances run when you can make your own music?" And ignoring the humble customers waiting she would fling down at the old pump-organ in the corner and tear into a frenzy of chords. "I make my own!" she would shout into the turmoil. She would send for little William, with a voice like a little bird's, and he knew how to sing with her, though he would give out. "Bass, William!" she would shout, and in his tiny treble he sang bass, bravely.

When Ida speaks of her mother it is in a strange kind of pity, a tender amazement. She says she knew when her mother was going to die, and with her deep feeling for events and commemorations, she gave her a fine big party. Ida would no more shrink from doing anything the grand way than she would shrink from other demands upon her greatness. "Hush now," she told me, "don't say a word while I tell you this. All that day long I was cooking dinner between niggers. I had: four turkeys, four hens, four geese, four hams, red cake, white cake, chocolate cake, caramel cake, every color cake known. The table reached from the front door to the ice box. I had all the lights burning up electricity, and all the flowers cut. I had the plates changed seven times, and three waiters from the hotel. I'd got Mama a partner. Mama was eighty years old and I got her another old lady eighty years old to march with. I had everybody come. All her children—one son, the big shot, came all the way from Detroit, riding in a train, to be at Mama's grand dinner. We had somebody play 'Silent Night' and march music to follow later. And there was Mama: look at Mama! Mama loved powder. Mama had on a little old-fashioned hat, but she wouldn't take it off—had nice hair, too. Mama did all right for the march, she marched all right, and sat down on time at the right place at the head of the table, but she wouldn't take off her hat. So the waiters, they served the chicken soup first, and Mama says, 'Where my coffee? Bring on turnip and cornbread. Didn't you make a blackberry pie?' I said, 'Mama you don't eat coffee first.' But she said, 'Where my coffee? Bring on turnip and cornbread. Didn't you make a blackberry pie? What's the matter with you?' Everything was so fine, you know. It took her two big sons, one on each side, to quiet her, that's the way Mama acted!" And Ida ended the story laughing and crying. It was plain that there was one person who had no recognition of Ida's grandeur and high place in the world, and who had never yielded at all to the glamour as others did. It was a cruelty for Ida, but perhaps all vision has lived in the house with cruelty.

Nowadays, she is carried to such heights of business and power, and its paraphernalia crowds her so, that she is overcome with herself, and suddenly gives way to the magnitude of it all. A kind of chaos comes over her. Now and then she falls down in a trance and stays "dead as that chair for three days." White doctors love her and by a little struggle take care of her. Ida bears with them. "They took my appendix," she will say. "Well, they took my teeth." She says she has a paralyzed heel, though it is hard to see how she can tell—perhaps like Achilles she feels that her end is coming by entering that way. "The doctor told me I got to rest until 1945," she declares, with a lifted hand warding you off. "Rest! Rest! Rest! I must rest." If a step is heard on the front porch she instantly cries warning from within the house, "Don't set your heels down! When you speak to me, whisper!" When a lady that was a stranger came to see her, Ida appeared, but said in haste, "Don't tell me your name, for I'm resting my mind. The doctors don't want me to have any more people in my head than I got already."

Now on Saturdays if a dusty battered car full of customers from across the cottonfields draws up, one by one all the shades in the house are yanked down. Ida wishes to see no one, she wishes to sell nothing.

Perhaps the truth is that she has expended herself to excess and now suffers with a corresponding emptiness that she does not want anyone to see. She can show you the track of the pain it gives her: her finger crosses her two breasts. She is as hard to see as a queen.

And I think she lives today the way she would rather be living, directly in symbols. People are their vestures now. Memories, the great memories of births and marriages and deaths, are nearly the same as the pieces of jewelry ("$147.65 worth") she has bought on anniversary days and wears on her person. "That's Mama's death," she says—a silver watch on a silver chain. She holds out for your admiration the yellow hands that she asserts most of this country was born in, on which now seven signet rings flash. "Don't go to church any longer," she says—"or need to go. I just sit at home and enjoy my fingers."

EUDORA WELTY

Petrified Man

"REACH in my purse and git me a cigarette without no powder in it if you kin, Mrs. Fletcher, honey," said Leota to her ten o'clock shampoo-and-set customer. "I don't like no perfumed cigarettes."

Mrs. Fletcher gladly reached over to the lavender shelf under the lavender-framed mirror, shook a hair net loose from the clasp of the patent-leather bag, and slapped her hand down quickly on a powder puff which burst out when the purse was opened.

"Why, look at the peanuts, Leota!" said Mrs. Fletcher in her marveling voice.

"Honey, them goobers has been in my purse a week if they's been in it a day. Mrs. Pike bought them peanuts."

"Who's Mrs. Pike?" asked Mrs. Fletcher, settling back. Hidden in this den of curling fluid and henna packs, separated by a lavender swing-door from the other customers, who were being gratified in other booths, she could give her curiosity its freedom. She looked expectantly at the black part in Leota's yellow curls as she bent to light the cigarette.

"Mrs. Pike is this lady from New Orleans," said Leota, puffing, and pressing into Mrs. Fletcher's scalp with strong red-nailed fingers. "A friend, not a customer. You see, like maybe I told you last time, me and Fred and Sal and Joe all had us a fuss, so Sal and Joe up and moved out, so we didn't do a thing but rent out their room. So we rented it to Mrs. Pike. And Mr. Pike." She flicked an ash into the basket of dirty towels. "Mrs. Pike is a very decided blonde. *She* bought me the peanuts."

"She must be cute," said Mrs. Fletcher.

"Honey, 'cute' ain't the word for what she is. I'm tellin' you, Mrs. Pike is attractive. She has her a good time. She's got a sharp eye out, Mrs. Pike has."

She dashed the comb through the air, and paused dramatically as a cloud of Mrs. Fletcher's hennaed hair floated out of the lavender teeth like a small storm-cloud.

"Hair fallin'."

"Aw, Leota."

"Uh-huh, commencin' to fall out," said Leota, combing again, and letting fall another cloud.

"Is it any dandruff in it?" Mrs. Fletcher was frowning, her hair-line eyebrows diving down toward her nose, and her wrinkled, beady-lashed eyelids batting with concentration.

"Nope." She combed again. "Just fallin' out."

"Bet it was that last perm'nent you gave me that did it," Mrs. Fletcher said cruelly. "Remember you cooked me fourteen minutes."

"You had fourteen minutes comin' to you," said Leota with finality.

"Bound to be somethin'," persisted Mrs. Fletcher. "Dandruff, dandruff. I couldn't have caught a thing like that from Mr. Fletcher, could I?"

"Well," Leota answered at last, "you know what I heard in here yestiddy, one of Thelma's ladies was settin' over yonder in Thelma's booth gittin' a machineless, and I don't mean to insist or insinuate or anything, Mrs. Fletcher, but Thelma's lady just happ'med to throw out—I forgotten what she was talkin' about at the time—that you was p-r-e-g., and lots of times that'll make your hair do awful funny, fall out and God knows what all. It just ain't our fault is the way I look at it."

There was a pause. The women stared at each other in the mirror.

"Who was it?" demanded Mrs. Fletcher.

"Honey, I really couldn't say," said Leota. "Not that you look it."

"Where's Thelma? I'll get it out of her," said Mrs. Fletcher.

"Now, honey I wouldn't go and git mad over a little thing like that," Leota said, combing hastily, as though to hold Mrs. Fletcher down by the hair. "I'm sure it was somebody didn't mean no harm in the world. How far gone are you?"

"Just wait," said Mrs. Fletcher, and shrieked for Thelma, who came in and took a drag from Leota's cigarette.

"Thelma, honey, throw your mind back to yestiddy if you kin," said Leota, drenching Mrs. Fletcher's hair with a thick fluid and catching the overflow in a cold wet towel at her neck.

"Well, I got my lady half wound for a spiral," said Thelma doubtfully.

"This won't take but a minute," said Leota. "Who is it you got in there, old Horse Face? Just cast your mind back and try to remember who your lady was yestiddy who happ'm to mention that my customer was pregnant, that's all. She's dead to know."

Thelma drooped her blood-red lips and looked over Mrs. Fletcher's head into the mirror. "Why, honey, I ain't got the faintest," she breathed. "I really don't recollect the faintest. But I'm sure she meant no harm. I declare, I forgot my hair finally got combed and thought it was a stranger behind me."

"Was it that Mrs. Hutchinson?" Mrs. Fletcher was tensely polite.

"Mrs. Hutchinson? Oh, Mrs. Hutchinson." Thelma batted her eyes. "Naw, precious, she come on Thursday and didn't ev'm mention your name. I doubt if she ev'm knows you're on the way."

"Thelma!" cried Leota stanchly.

"All I know is, whoever it is'll be sorry someday. Why, I just barely knew it myself!" cried Mrs. Fletcher. "Just let her wait!"

"Why? What're you gonna do to her?"

It was a child's voice, and the women looked down. A little boy was making tents with aluminum wave pinchers on the floor under the sink.

"Billy Boy, hon, mustn't bother nice ladies," Leota smiled. She slapped him brightly and behind her back waved Thelma out of the booth. "Ain't Billy Boy a sight? Only three years old and already just nuts about the beauty-parlor business."

"I never saw him here before," said Mrs. Fletcher, still unmollified.

"He ain't been here before, that's how come," said Leota. "He belongs to Mrs. Pike. She got her a job but it was Fay's Millinery. He oughtn't to try on those ladies' hats, they come down over his eyes like I don't know what. They just git to look ridiculous, that's what, an' of course he's gonna put em on: hats. They tole Mrs. Pike they didn't appreciate him hangin' around there. Here, he couldn't hurt a thing."

"Well! I don't like children that much," said Mrs. Fletcher.

"Well!" said Leota moodily.

"Well, I'm almost tempted not to have this one," said Mrs. Fletcher. "That Mrs. Hutchinson! Just looks straight through you when she sees you on the street and then spits at you behind your back."

"Mr. Fletcher would beat you on the head if you didn't have it now," said Leota reasonably. "After going this far."

Mrs. Fletcher sat up straight. "Mr. Fletcher can't do a thing with me."

"He can't!" Leota winked at herself in the mirror.

"No siree, he can't. If he so much as raises his voice against me, he knows good and well I'll have one of my sick headaches, and then I'm just not fit to live with. And if I really look that pregnant already—"

"Well, now, honey, I just want you to know—I habm't told any of my ladies and I ain't goin' to tell 'em—even that you're losin' your hair. You just get you one of those Stork-a-Lure dresses and stop worryin'. What people don't know don't hurt nobody, as Mrs. Pike says."

"Did you tell Mrs. Pike?" asked Mrs. Fletcher sulkily.

"Well, Mrs. Fletcher, look, you ain't ever goin' to lay eyes on Mrs. Pike or her lay eyes on you, so what diffunce does it make in the long run?"

"I knew it!" Mrs. Fletcher deliberately nodded her head so as to destroy a ringlet Leota was working on behind her ear. "Mrs. Pike!"

Leota sighed. "I reckon I might as well tell you. It wasn't any more Thelma's lady tole me you was pregnant than a bat."

"Not Mrs. Hutchinson?"

"Naw, Lord! It was Mrs. Pike."

"Mrs. Pike!" Mrs. Fletcher could only sputter and let curling fluid roll into her ear. "How could Mrs. Pike possibly know I was pregnant or otherwise, when she doesn't even know me? The nerve of some people!"

"Well, here's how it was. Remember Sunday?"

"Yes," said Mrs. Fletcher.

"Sunday, Mrs. Pike an' me was all by ourself. Mr. Pike and Fred had gone over to Eagle Lake, sayin' they was goin' to catch 'em some fish, but they didn't, a course. So we was sittin' in Mrs. Pike's car, is a 1939 Dodge—"

"1939, eh," said Mrs. Fletcher.

"—An' we was gettin' us a Jax beer apiece—that's the beer that Mrs. Pike says is made right in N.O., so she won't drink no other kind. So I seen you drive up to the drugstore an' run in for just a secont, leavin' I reckon Mr. Fletcher in the car, an' come runnin' out with what looked like a perscription. So I says to Mrs. Pike, just to be makin' talk, 'Right yonder's Mrs. Fletcher, and I reckon that's Mr. Fletcher—she's one of my regular customers,' I says."

"I had on a figured print," said Mrs. Fletcher tentatively.

"You sure did," agreed Leota. "So Mrs. Pike, she give you a good look—she's very observant, a good judge of character, cute as a minute, you know—and she says, 'I bet you another Jax that lady's three months on the way.' "

"What gall!" said Mrs. Fletcher. "Mrs. Pike!"

"Mrs. Pike ain't goin' to bite you," said Leota. "Mrs. Pike is a lovely girl, you'd be crazy about her, Mrs. Fletcher. But she can't sit still a minute. We went to the travelin' freak show yestiddy after work. I got through early—nine o'clock. In the vacant store next door? What, you ain't been?"

"No, I despise freaks," declared Mrs. Fletcher.

"Aw. Well, honey, talkin' about bein' pregnant an' all, you ought to see those twins in a bottle, you really owe it to yourself."

"What twins?" asked Mrs. Fletcher out of the side of her mouth.

"Well, honey, they got these two twins in a bottle, see? Born joined plumb together—dead of course." Leota dropped her voice into a soft lyrical hum. "They was about this long—pardon—must of been full time, all right, wouldn't you say?—an' they had these two heads an' two faces an' four arms an' four legs, all kind of joined *here*. See, this face looked this-a-way, and the other face looked that-a-way, over their shoulder, see. Kinda pathetic."

"Glah!" said Mrs. Fletcher disapprovingly.

"Well, ugly? Honey, I mean to tell you—their parents was first cousins and all like that. Billy Boy, git me a fresh towel from off Teeny's stack—this 'n's wringin' wet—an' quit ticklin' my ankles with that curler. I declare! He don't miss nothin'."

"Me and Mr. Fletcher aren't one speck of kin, or he could never of had me," said Mrs. Fletcher placidly.

"Of course not!" protested Leota. "Neither is me an' Fred, not that we know of. Well, honey, what Mrs. Pike liked was the pygmies. They've got these pygmies down there, too, an' Mrs. Pike was just wild about 'em. You know, the tee-niniest men in the universe? Well honey, they can rest back on their little bohunkus an' roll around an' you can't hardly tell if they're sittin or standin'. That'll give you some idea. They're about forty-two years old. Just suppose it was your husband!"

"Well, Mr. Fletcher is five foot nine and one half," said Mrs. Fletcher quickly.

"Fred's five foot ten," said Leota, "but I tell him he's still a shrimp, account of I'm so tall." She made a deep wave over Mrs. Fletcher's other temple with the comb. "Well, these pygmies are a kind of a dark brown, Mrs. Fletcher. Not bad-lookin' for what they are, you know."

"I wouldn't care for them," said Mrs. Fletcher. "What does that Mrs. Pike see in them?"

"Aw, I don't know," said Leota. "She's just cute, that's all. But they got this man, this petrified man, that ever'thing ever since he was nine years old, when it goes through his digestion, see, somehow Mrs. Pike says it goes to his joints and has been turning to stone."

"How awful!" said Mrs. Fletcher.

"He's forty-two too. That looks like a bad age."

"Who said so, that Mrs. Pike? I bet she's forty-two," said Mrs. Fletcher.

"Naw," said Leota, "Mrs. Pike's thirty-three, born in January, an Aquarian. He could move his head—like this. A course his head and mind ain't a joint, so to speak, and I guess his stomach ain't either—not yet, anyways. But see—his food, he eats it, and it goes down, see, and then he digests it"—Leota rose on her toes for an instant—"and it goes out to his joints and before you can say 'Jack Robinson,' it's stone—pure stone. He's turning to stone. How'd you like to be married to a guy like that? All he can do, he can move his head just a quarter of an inch. A course he *looks* just *terrible*."

"I should think he would," said Mrs. Fletcher frostily. "Mr. Fletcher takes bending exercises every night of the world. I make him."

"All Fred does is lay around the house like a rug. I wouldn't be surprised if he woke up someday and couldn't move. The petrified man just sat there moving his quarter of an inch though," said Leota reminiscently.

"Did Mrs. Pike like the petrified man?" asked Mrs. Fletcher.

"Not as much as she did the others," said Leota deprecatingly. "And then she likes a man to be a good dresser, and all that."

"Is Mr. Pike a good dresser?" asked Mrs. Fletcher skeptically.

"Oh, well, yeah," said Leota, "but he's twelve or fourteen years older 'n her. She ast Lady Evangeline about him."

"Who's Lady Evangeline?" asked Mrs. Fletcher.

"Well, it's this mind reader they got in the freak show," said Leota. "Was real good. Lady Evangeline is her name, and if I had another dollar I wouldn't do a thing but have my other palm read. She had what Mrs. Pike said was the 'sixth mind' but she had the worst manicure I ever saw on a living person."

"What did she tell Mrs. Pike?" asked Mrs. Fletcher.

"She told her Mr. Pike was as true to her as he could be and, besides, would come into some money."

"Humph!" said Mrs. Fletcher. "What does he do?"

"I can't tell," said Leota, "because he don't work. Lady Evangeline didn't tell me near enough about my nature or anything. And I would like to go back and find out some more about this boy. Used to go with this boy got married to this girl. Oh, shoot, that was about three and a half years ago, when you was still goin' to the Robert E. Lee Beauty Shop in Jackson. He married her for her money. Another fortune-teller tole me that at the time. So I'm not in love with him any more, anyway, besides being married to Fred, but Mrs. Pike thought, just for the hell of it, see, to ask Lady Evangeline was she happy."

"Does Mrs. Pike know everything about you already?" asked Mrs. Fletcher unbelievingly. "Mercy!"

"Oh yeah, I tole her ever'thing about ever'thing, from now on back to I don't know when—to when I first started goin' out," said Leota. "So I ast Lady Evangeline for one of my questions, was he happily married, and she says, just like she was glad I ask her, 'Honey,' she says, 'naw, he isn't. You write down this day, March 8, 1941,' she says, 'and mock it down: three years from today him and her won't be occupyin' the same bed.' There it is, up on the wall with them other dates—see, Mrs. Fletcher? And she says, 'Child, you ought to be glad you didn't git him, because he's so mercenary.' So I'm glad I married Fred. He sure ain't mercenary, money don't mean a thing to him. But I sure would like to go back and have my other palm read."

"Did Mrs. Pike believe in what the fortune-teller said?" asked Mrs. Fletcher in a superior tone of voice.

"Lord, yes, she's from New Orleans. Ever'body in New Orleans believes ever'thing spooky. One of 'em in New Orleans before it was raided says to Mrs. Pike one summer she was goin' to go from State to State and meet some gray-headed men, and, sure enough, she says she went on a beautician convention up to Chicago. . . ."

"Oh!" said Mrs. Fletcher. "Oh, is Mrs. Pike a beautician too?"

"Sure she is," protested Leota. "She's a beautician. I'm goin' to git her in here if I can. Before she married. But it don't leave you. She says sure enough, there was three men who was a very large part of making her trip what it was, and they all three had gray in their hair and they went in six States. Got Christmas cards from 'em. Billy Boy, go see if Thelma's got any dry cotton. Look how Mrs. Fletcher's a-drippin'."

"Where did Mrs. Pike meet Mr. Pike?" asked Mrs. Fletcher primly.

"On another train," said Leota.

"I met Mr. Fletcher, or rather he met me, in a rental library," said Mrs. Fletcher with dignity, as she watched the net come down over her head.

"Honey, me an' Fred, we met in a rumble seat eight months ago and we was practically on what you might call the way to the altar inside of half an hour," said Leota in a guttural voice, and bit a bobby pin open. "Course it don't last. Mrs. Pike says nothin' like that ever lasts."

"Mr. Fletcher and myself are as much in love as the day we married," said Mrs. Fletcher belligerently as Leota stuffed cotton into her ears.

"Mrs. Pike says it don't last," repeated Leota in a louder voice. "Now go git under the dryer. You can turn yourself on, can't you? I'll be back to comb you out. Durin' lunch I promised to give Mrs. Pike a facial. You know—free. Her bein' in the business, so to speak."

"I bet she needs one," said Mrs. Fletcher, letting the swing-door fly back against Leota. "Oh, pardon me."

A week later, on time for her appointment, Mrs. Fletcher sank heavily into Leota's chair after first removing a drugstore rental book, called *Life Is Like That,* from the seat. She stared in a discouraged way into the mirror.

"You can tell it when I'm sitting down, all right," she said.

Leota seemed preoccupied and stood shaking out a lavender cloth. She began to pin it around Mrs. Fletcher's neck in silence.

"I said you sure can tell it when I'm sitting straight on and coming at you this way," Mrs. Fletcher said.

"Why, honey, naw you can't," said Leota gloomily. "Why, I'd never know. If somebody was to come up to me on the street, and say, 'Mrs. Fletcher is pregnant!' I'd say, 'Heck, she don't look it to me.' "

"If a certain party hadn't found it out and spread it around, it wouldn't be too late even now," said Mrs. Fletcher frostily, but Leota was almost choking her with the cloth, pinning it so tight, and she couldn't speak clearly. She paddled her hands in the air until Leota wearily loosened her.

"Listen, honey, you're just a virgin compared to Mrs. Montjoy," Leota was going on, still absent-minded. She bent Mrs. Fletcher back in the chair and, sighing, tossed liquid from a teacup onto her head and dug both hands into her scalp. "You know Mrs. Montjoy—her husband's that premature-gray-headed fella?"

"She's in the Trojan Garden Club, is all I know," said Mrs. Fletcher.

"Well, honey," said Leota, but in a weary voice, "she come in here not the week before and not the day before she had her baby—she come in here the very selfsame day, I mean to tell you. Child, we was all plumb scared to death. There she was! Come for her shampoo an' set. Why, Mrs. Fletcher, in a hour an' twenty minutes she was layin' up there in the Babtist Hospital with a seb'm-pound son. It was that close a shave. I declare, if I hadn't been so tired I would of drank up a bottle of gin that night."

"What gall," said Mrs. Fletcher. "I never knew her at all well."

"See, her husband was waitin' outside in the car, and her bags was all packed an' in the back seat, an' she was all ready, 'cept she wanted her shampoo an' set. An' havin' one pain right after another. Her husband kep' comin' in here, scared-like, but couldn't do nothin' with her a course. She yelled bloody murder, too, but she always yelled her head off when I give her a perm'nent."

"She must of been crazy," said Mrs. Fletcher. "How did she look?"

"Shoot!" said Leota.

"Well, I can guess," said Mrs. Fletcher. "Awful."

"Just wanted to look pretty while she was havin' her baby is all," said Leota airily. "Course, we was glad to give the lady what she was after—that's our motto—but I bet an hour later she wasn't payin' no mind to them little end curls. I bet she wasn't thinkin' about she ought to have on a net. It wouldn't of done her no good if she had."

"No, I don't suppose it would," said Mrs. Fletcher.

"Yeah man! She was a-yellin'. Just like when I give her her perm'nent."

"Her husband ought to make her behave. Don't it seem that way to you?" asked Mrs. Fletcher. "He ought to put his foot down."

"Ha," said Leota. "A lot he could do. Maybe some women is soft."

"Oh, you mistake me, I don't mean for her to get soft—far from it! Women have to stand up for themselves, or there's just no telling. But now you take me—I ask Mr. Fletcher's advice now and then, and he appreciates it, especially on something important, like is it time for a permanent—not that I've told him about the baby. He says, 'Why dear, go ahead!' Just ask their *advice*."

"Huh! If I ever ast Fred's advice we'd be floatin' down the Yazoo River on a houseboat or somethin' by this time," said Leota. "I'm sick of Fred. I told him to go over to Vicksburg."

"Is he going?" demanded Mrs. Fletcher.

"Sure. See, the fortune-teller—I went back and had my other palm read, since we've got to rent the room again—said my lover was goin' to work in Vicksburg, so I don't know who she could mean, unless she meant Fred. And Fred ain't workin' here—that much is so."

"Is he going to work in Vicksburg?" asked Mrs. Fletcher. "And—"

"Sure. Lady Evangeline said so. Said the future is going to be brighter than the present. He don't want to go, but I ain't gonna put up with nothin' like that. Lays around the house an' bulls—did bull—with that good-for-nothin' Mr. Pike. He says if he goes who'll cook, but I says I never get to eat anyway—not meals. Billy Boy, take Mrs. Grover that *Screen Secrets* and leg it."

Mrs. Fletcher heard stamping feet go out the door.

"Is that that Mrs. Pike's little boy here again?" she asked, sitting up gingerly.

"Yeah, that's still him." Leota stuck out her tongue.

Mrs. Fletcher could hardly believe her eyes. "Well! How's Mrs. Pike, your attractive new friend with the sharp eyes who spreads it around town that perfect strangers are pregnant?" she asked in a sweetened tone.

"Oh, Mizziz Pike." Leota combed Mrs. Fletcher's hair with heavy strokes.

"You act like you're tired," said Mrs. Fletcher.

"Tired? Feel like it's four o'clock in the afternoon already," said Leota. "I ain't told you the awful luck we had, me and Fred? It's the worst thing you ever heard of. Maybe *you* think Mrs. Pike's got sharp eyes. Shoot, there's a limit! Well, you know, we rented out our room to this Mr. and Mrs. Pike from New Orleans when Sal an' Joe Fentress got mad at us 'cause they drank up some home-brew we had in the closet—Sal an' Joe did. So, a week ago Sat'day Mr. and Mrs. Pike moved in. Well, I kinda fixed up the room, you know—put a sofa pillow on the couch and picked some ragged robins and put in a vase, but they never did say they appreciated it. Anyway, then I put some old magazines on the table."

"I think that was lovely," said Mrs. Fletcher.

"Wait. So, come night 'fore last, Fred and this Mr. Pike, who Fred just took up with, was back from they said they was fishin', bein' as neither one of 'em has got a job to his name, and we was all settin' around in their room. So Mrs. Pike was settin' there, readin' a old *Startling G-Man Tales* that was mine, mind you, I'd bought it myself, and all of a sudden she jumps!—into the air—you'd 'a' thought she'd set on a spider—an' says, 'Canfield'—ain't that silly, that's Mr. Pike—'Canfield, my God A'mighty,' she says, 'honey,' she says, 'we're rich, and you won't have to work.' Not that he turned one hand anyway. Well, me and Fred rushes over to her, and Mr. Pike, too, and there she sets, pointin' her finger at a photo in my copy of *Startling G-Man*. 'See that man?' yells Mrs. Pike. 'Remember him, Canfield?' 'Never forget a face,' says Mr. Pike. 'It's Mr. Petrie, that we stayed with him in the apartment next to ours in Toulouse Street in N.O. for six weeks. Mr. Petrie.' 'Well,' says Mrs. Pike, like she can't hold out one secont longer, 'Mr. Petrie is wanted for five hundred dollars cash, for rapin' four women in California, and I know where he is.'"

"Mercy!" said Mrs. Fletcher. "Where was he?"

At some time Leota had washed her hair and now she yanked her up by the back locks and sat her up.

"Know where he was?"

"I certainly don't," Mrs. Fletcher said. Her scalp hurt all over.

Leota flung a towel around the top of her customer's head. "Nowhere else but in that freak show! I saw him just as plain as Mrs. Pike. *He* was the petrified man!"

"Who would ever have thought that!" cried Mrs. Fletcher sympathetically.

"So Mr. Pike says, 'Well, whatta you know about that,' an' he looks real hard at the photo, and whistles. And she starts dancin' and singin' about their good luck. She meant our bad luck! I made a point of tellin' that fortuneteller the next time I saw her. I said, 'Listen, that magazine was layin' around the house for a month, and there was five hundred dollars in it for somebody. An' there was the freak show runnin' night an' day, not two steps away from my own beauty parlor, with Mr. Petrie just settin' there waitin'. An' it had to be Mr. and Mrs. Pike, almost perfect strangers.' "

"What gall," said Mrs. Fletcher. She was only sitting there, wrapped in a turban, but she did not mind.

"Fortunetellers don't care. And Mrs. Pike, she goes around actin' like she thinks she was Mrs. God," said Leota. "So they're goin' to leave tomorrow, Mr. and Mrs. Pike. And in the meantime I got to keep that mean, bad little ole kid here, gettin' under my feet ever' minute of the day an' talkin' back too."

"Have they gotten the five hundred dollars' reward already?" asked Mrs. Fletcher.

"Well," said Leota, "at first Mr. Pike didn't want to do anything about it. Can you feature that? Said he kinda liked that ole bird and said he was real nice to 'em, lent 'em money or somethin'. But Mrs. Pike simply tole him he could just go to hell, and I can see her point. She says, 'You ain't worked a lick in six months, and here I made five hundred dollars in two seconts, and what thanks do I get for it? You go to hell, Canfield,' she says. So," Leota went on in a despondent voice, "they called up the cops and they caught the ole bird, all right, right there in the freak show where I saw him with my own eyes, thinkin' he was petrified. He's the one. Did it under his real name—Mr. Petrie. Four women in California, all in the month of August. So Mrs. Pike gits five hundred dollars. And my magazine, and right next door to my beauty parlor. I cried all night, but Fred said it wasn't a bit of use and to go to sleep, because the whole thing was just a sort of coincidence—you know: can't do nothin' about it. He says it put him clean out the notion of goin' to Vicksburg for a few days till we rent out the room again—no tellin' who we'll git this time."

"But can you imagine anybody knowing this old man, that's raped four women?" persisted Mrs. Fletcher, and she shuddered audibly. "Did Mrs. Pike *speak* to him when she met him in the freak show?"

Leota had begun to comb Mrs. Fletcher's hair. "I says to her, I says, 'I didn't notice you fallin' on his neck when he was the petrified man—don't tell me you didn't recognize your fine friend?' And she says, 'I didn't recognize him with that white powder all over his face. He just looked familiar,' Mrs. Pike says, 'and lots of people look familiar.' But she says that ole petrified man did put her in mind of somebody. She wondered who it was! Kep' her awake, which man she'd ever knew it reminded her of. So when she seen the photo, it all come to her. Like a flash. Mr. Petrie. The way he'd turn his head and look at her when she took him in his breakfast."

"Took him in his breakfast!" shrieked Mrs. Fletcher. "Listen—don't tell me. I'd 'a' felt something."

"Four women. I guess those women didn't have the faintest notion at the time they'd be worth a hundred an' twenty-five bucks a piece some day to Mrs. Pike. We ast her how old the fella was then, an' she says he musta had one foot in the grave, at least. Can you beat it?"

"Not really petrified at all, of course," said Mrs. Fletcher meditatively. She drew herself up. "I'd 'a' felt something," she said proudly.

"Shoot! I did feel somethin'," said Leota. "I tole Fred when I got home I felt so funny. I said, 'Fred, that ole petrified man sure did leave me with a funny feelin'.' He says, 'Funny-haha or funny-peculiar?' and I says, 'Funny-peculiar.' " She pointed her comb into the air emphatically.

"I'll bet you did," said Mrs. Fletcher.

They both heard a crackling noise.

Leota screamed, "Billy Boy! What you doin' in my purse?"

"Aw, I'm just eatin' these ole stale peanuts up," said Billy Boy.

"You come here to me!" screamed Leota, recklessly flinging down the comb, which scattered a whole ashtray full of bobby pins and knocked down a row of Coca-Cola bottles. "This is the last straw!"

"I caught him! I caught him!" giggled Mrs. Fletcher. "I'll hold him on my lap. You bad, bad boy, you! I guess I better learn how to spank little old bad boys," she said.

Leota's eleven o'clock customer pushed open the swing-door upon Leota paddling him heartily with the brush, while he gave angry but belittling screams which penetrated beyond the booth and filled the whole curious beauty parlor. From everywhere ladies began to gather round to watch the paddling. Billy Boy kicked both Leota and Mrs. Fletcher as hard as he could, Mrs. Fletcher with her new fixed smile.

"There, my little man!" gasped Leota. "You won't be able to set down for a week if I knew what I was doin'."

Billy Boy stomped through the group of wild-haired ladies and went out the door, but flung back the words, "If you're so smart, why ain't you rich?"

EUDORA WELTY

A Worn Path

IT WAS December—a bright frozen day in the early morning. Far out in the country there was an old Negro woman with her head tied in a red rag, coming along a path through the pinewoods. Her name was Phoenix Jackson. She was very old and small and she walked slowly in the dark pine shadows, moving a little from side to side in her steps, with the balanced heaviness and lightness of a pendulum in a grandfather clock. She carried a thin, small cane made from an umbrella, and with this she kept tapping the frozen earth in front of her. This made a grave and persistent noise in the still air, that seemed meditative, like the chirping of a solitary little bird.

She wore a dark striped dress reaching down to her shoetops, and an equally long apron of bleached sugar sacks, with a full pocket; all neat and tidy, but every time she took a step she might have fallen over her shoe-laces, which dragged from her unlaced shoes. She looked straight ahead. Her eyes were blue with age. Her skin had a pattern all its own of numberless branching wrinkles and as though a whole little tree stood in the middle of her forehead, but a golden colour ran underneath, and the two knobs of her cheeks were illuminated by a yellow burning under the dark. Under the red rag her hair came down on her neck in the frailest of ringlets, still black, and with an odor like copper.

Now and then there was a quivering in the thicket. Old Phoenix said, "Out of my way, all you foxes, owls, beetles, jack rabbits, coons, and wild animals! . . . Keep out from under these feet, little bobwhites. . . . Keep the big wild hogs out of my path. Don't let none of those come running my direction. I got a long way." Under her small black-freckled hand her cane, limber as a buggy whip, would switch at the brush as if to rouse up any hiding things.

On she went. The woods were deep and still. The sun made the pine needles almost too bright to look at, up where the wind rocked. The cones dropped as light as feathers. Down in the hollow was the mourning dove—it was not too late for him.

The path ran up a hill. "Seem like there is chains about my feet, time I get this far," she said, in the voice of argument old people keep to use with themselves. "Something always take a hold on this hill—pleads I should stay."

After she got to the top she turned and gave a full, severe look behind her where she had come. "Up through pines," she said at length. "Now down through oaks."

Her eyes opened their widest and she started down gently. But before she got to the bottom of the hill a bush caught her dress.

Her fingers were busy and intent, but her skirts were full and long, so that before she could pull them free in one place they were caught in another. It was not possible to allow the dress to tear. "I in the thorny bush," she said. "Thorns, you doing your appointed work. Never want to let folks pass—no sir. Old eyes thought you was a pretty little *green* bush."

Finally, trembling all over, she stood free, and after a moment dared to stoop for her cane.

"Sun so high!" she cried, leaning back and looking, while the thick tears went over her eyes. "The time getting all gone here."

At the foot of this hill was a place where a log was laid across the creek.

"Now comes the trial," said Phoenix.

Putting her right foot out, she mounted the log and shut her eyes. Lifting her skirt, levelling her cane fiercely before her, like a festival figure in some parade, she began to march across. Then she opened her eyes and she was safe on the other side.

"I wasn't as old as I thought," she said.

But she sat down to rest. She spread her skirts on the bank around her and folded her hands over her knees. Up above her was a tree in a pearly cloud of mistletoe. She did not dare to close her eyes, and when a little boy brought her a little plate with a slice of marble-cake on it she spoke to him. "That would be acceptable," she said. But when she went to take it there was just her own hand in the air.

So she left that tree, and had to go through a barbed-wire fence. There she had to creep and crawl, spreading her knees and stretching her fingers like a baby trying to climb the steps. But she talked loudly to herself: she could not let her dress be torn now, so late in the day, and she could not pay for having her arm or her leg sawed off if she got caught fast where she was.

At last she was safe through the fence and risen up out in the clearing. Big dead trees, like black men with one arm, were standing in the purple stalks of the withered cotton field. There sat a buzzard.

"Who you watching?"

In the furrow she made her way along.

"Glad this not the season for bulls," she said, looking sideways, "and the good Lord made his snakes to curl up and sleep in the winter. A pleasure I don't see no two-headed snake coming around that tree, where it come once. It took a while to get by him, back in the summer."

She passed through the old cotton and went into a field of dead corn. It whispered and shook, and was taller than her head. "Through the maze now," she said, for there was no path.

Then there was something tall, black, and skinny there, moving before her.

At first she took it for a man. It could have been a man dancing in the field. But she stood still and listened, and it did not make a sound. It was as silent as a ghost.

"Ghost," she said sharply, "who be you the ghost of? For I have heard of nary death close by."

But there was no answer, only the ragged dancing in the wind.

She shut her eyes, reached out her hand, and touched a sleeve. She found a coat and inside that an emptiness, cold as ice.

"You scarecrow," she said. Her face lighted. "I ought to be shut up for good," she said with laughter. "My senses is gone. I too old. I the oldest people I ever know. Dance, old scarecrow," she said, "while I dancing with you."

She kicked her foot over the furrow, and with mouth drawn down shook her head once or twice in a little strutting way. Some husks blew down and whirled in streamers about her skirts.

Then she went on, parting her way from side to side with the cane, through the whispering field. At last she came to the end, to a wagon track, where the silver grass blew between the red ruts. The quail were walking around like pullets, seeming all dainty and unseen.

"Walk pretty," she said. "This the easy place. This the easy going."

She followed the track, swaying through the quiet bare fields, through the little strings of trees silver in their dead leaves, past cabins silver from weather, with the doors and windows boarded shut, all like old women under a spell sitting there. "I walking in their sleep," she said, nodding her head vigorously.

In a ravine she went where a spring was silently flowing through a hollow log. Old Phoenix bent and drank. "Sweetgum makes the water sweet," she said, and drank more. "Nobody knows who made this well, for it was here when I was born."

The track crossed a swampy part where the moss hung as white as lace from every limb. "Sleep on, alligators, and blow your bubbles." Then the track went into the road.

Deep, deep the road went down between the high green-coloured banks. Overhead the live-oaks met, and it was as dark as a cave.

A black dog with a lolling tongue came up out of the weeds by the ditch. She was meditating, and not ready, and when he came at her she only hit him a little with her cane. Over she went in the ditch, like a little puff of milk-weed.

Down there, her senses drifted away. A dream visited her, and she reached her hand up, but nothing reached down and gave her a pull. So she lay there and presently went to talking. "Old woman," she said to herself, "that black dog come up out of the weeds to stall you off, and now there he sitting on his fine tail, smiling at you."

A white man finally came along and found her—a hunter, a young man, with his dog on a chain.

"Well, Granny!" he laughed. "What are you doing there?"

"Lying on my back like a June-bug waiting to be turned over, mister," she said, reaching up her hand.

He lifted her up, gave her a swing in the air, and set her down, "Anything broken, Granny?"

"No sir, them old dead weeds is springy enough," said Phoenix, when she had got her breath. "I thank you for your trouble."

"Where do you live, Granny?" he asked, while the two dogs were growling at each other.

"Away back yonder, sir, behind the ridge. You can't even see it from here."

"On your way home?"

"No, sir, I going to town."

"Why, that's too far! That's as far as I walk when I come out myself, and I get something for my trouble." He patted the stuffed bag he carried, and there hung down a little closed claw. It was one of the bobwhites, with its beak hooked bitterly to show it was dead. "Now you go on home, Granny!"

"I bound to go to town, mister," said Phoenix. "The time come around."

He gave another laugh, filling the whole landscape. "I know you colored people! Wouldn't miss going to town to see Santa Claus!"

But something held Old Phoenix very still. The deep lines in her face went into a fierce and different radiation. Without warning she had seen with her own eyes a flashing nickel fall out of the man's pocket on to the ground.

"How old are you, Granny?" he was saying.

"There is no telling, mister," she said, "no telling."

Then she gave a little cry and clapped her hands, and said, "Git on away from here, dog! Look! Look at that dog!" She laughed as if in admiration. "He ain't scared of nobody. He a big black dog." She whispered, "Sick him!"

"Watch me get rid of that cur," said the man. "Sick him, Pete! Sick him!"

Phoenix heard the dogs fighting and heard the man running and throwing sticks. She even heard a gunshot. But she was slowly bending forward by that time, further and further forward, the lids stretched down over her eyes, as if she were doing this in her sleep. Her chin was lowered almost to her knees. The yellow palm of her hand came out from the fold of her apron. Her fingers slid down and along the ground under the piece of money with the grace and care they would have in lifting an egg from under a sitting hen. Then she slowly straightened up, she stood erect, and the nickel was in her apron pocket. A bird flew by. Her lips moved. "God watching me the whole time. I come to stealing."

The man came back, and his own dog panted about them. "Well, I scared him off that time," he said, and then he laughed and lifted his gun and pointed it at Phoenix.

She stood straight and faced him.

"Doesn't the gun scare you?" he said, still pointing it.

"No, sir, I seen plenty go off closer by, in my day, and for less than what I done," she said, holding utterly still.

He smiled, and shouldered the gun. "Well, Granny," he said, "you must be a hundred years old, and scared of nothing. I'd give you a dime if I had any money with me. But you take my advice and stay home, and nothing will happen to you."

"I bound to go on my way, mister," said Phoenix. She inclined her head in the red rag. Then they went in different directions, but she could hear the gun shooting again and again over the hill.

She walked on. The shadows hung from the oak trees to the road like curtains. Then she smelled wood-smoke, and smelled the river, and she saw a steeple and the cabins on their steep steps. Dozens of little black children whirled around her. There ahead was Natchez shining. Bells were ringing. She walked on.

In the paved city it was Christmas time. There were red and green electric lights strung and crisscrossed everywhere, and all turned on in the daytime. Old Phoenix would have been lost if she had not distrusted her eyesight and depended on her feet to know where to take her.

She paused quietly on the sidewalk, where people were passing by. A lady came along in the crowd, carrying an armful of red-, green-, and silver-wrapped presents; she gave off perfume like the red roses in hot summer, and Phoenix stopped her.

"Please, missy, will you lace up my shoe?" She held up her foot.

"What do you want, Grandma?"

"See my shoe," said Phoenix. "Do all right for out in the country, but wouldn't look right to go in a big building."

"Stand still then, Grandma," said the lady. She put her packages down carefully on the sidewalk beside her and laced and tied both shoes tightly.

"Can't lace 'em with a cane," said Phoenix. "Thank you, missy. I doesn't mind asking a nice lady to tie up my shoe when I gets out on the street."

Moving slowly and from side to side, she went into the stone building and into a tower of steps, where she walked up and around and around until her feet knew to stop.

She entered a door, and there she saw nailed up on the wall the document that had been stamped with the gold seal and framed in the gold frame which matched the dream that was hung up in her head.

"Here I be," she said. There was a fixed and ceremonial stiffness over her body.

"A charity case, I suppose," said an attendant who sat at the desk before her.

But Phoenix only looked above her head. There was sweat on her face; the wrinkles shone like a bright net.

"Speak up, Grandma," the women said. "What's your name? We must have your history, you know. Have you been here before? What seems to be the trouble with you?"

Old Phoenix only gave a twitch to her face as if a fly were bothering her.

"Are you deaf?" cried the attendant.

But then the nurse came in.

"Oh, that's just old Aunt Phoenix," she said. "She doesn't come for herself—she has a little grandson. She makes these trips just as regular as clockwork. She lives away back off the Old Natchez Trace." She bent down. "Well, Aunt Phoenix, why don't you just take a seat? We won't keep you standing after your long trip." She pointed.

The old woman sat down, bolt upright in the chair.

"Now, how is the boy?" asked the nurse.

Old Phoenix did not speak.

"I said, how is the boy?"

But Phoenix only waited and stared straight ahead, her face very solemn and withdrawn into rigidity.

"Is his throat any better?" asked the nurse. "Aunt Phoenix, don't you hear me? Is your grandson's throat any better since the last time you came for the medicine?"

With her hands on her knees, the old woman waited, silent, erect and motionless, just as if she were in armour.

"You mustn't take up our time this way, Aunt Phoenix," the nurse said. "Tell us quickly about your grandson, and get it over. He isn't dead, is he?"

At last there came a flicker and then a flame of comprehension across her face, and she spoke.

"My grandson. It was my memory had left me. There I sat and forgot why I made my long trip."

"Forgot?" The nurse frowned. "After you came so far?"

Then Phoenix was like an old woman begging a dignified forgiveness for waking up frightened in the night. "I never did go to school—I was too old at the Surrender," she said in a soft voice. "I'm an old woman without an education. It was my memory fail me. My little grandson, he is just the same, and I forgot it in the coming."

"Throat never heals, does it?" said the nurse, speaking in a loud, sure voice to Old Phoenix. By now she had a card with something written on it, a little list. "Yes. Swallowed lye. When was it—January—two—three years ago—"

Phoenix spoke unasked now. "No, missy, he not dead, he just the same. Every little while his throat begin to close up again, and he not able to swallow. He not get his breath. He not able to help himself. So the time come around, and I go on another trip for the soothing-medicine."

"All right. The doctor said as long as you came to get it you could have it," said the nurse. "But it's an obstinate case."

"My little grandson, he sit up there in the house all wrapped up, waiting by himself," Phoenix went on. "We is the only two left in the world. He suffer and it don't seem to put him back at all. He got a sweet look. He going to last. He wear a little patch quilt and peep out, holding his mouth open like a little bird. I remembers so plain now. I not going to forget him again, no, the whole enduring time. I could tell him from all the others in creation."

"All right." The nurse was trying to hush her now. She brought her a bottle of medicine. "Charity," she said, making a check mark in a book.

Old Phoenix held the bottle close to her eyes and then carefully put it into her pocket.

"I thank you," she said.

"It's Christmas time, Grandma," said the attendant. "Could I give you a few pennies out of my purse?"

"Five pennies is a nickel," said Phoenix stiffly.

"Here's a nickel," said the attendant.

Phoenix rose carefully and held out her hand. She received the nickel and then fished the other nickel out of her pocket and laid it beside the new one. She stared at her palm closely, with her head on one side.

Then she gave a tap with her cane on the floor.

"This is what come to me to do," she said. "I going to the store and buy my child a little windmill they sells, made out of paper. He going to find it hard to believe there such a thing in the world. I'll march myself back where he waiting, holding it straight up in this hand."

She lifted her free hand, gave a little nod, turned round, and walked out of the doctor's office. Then her slow step began on the stairs, going down.

Final - SS102
Monday 4-6

test
2 long essays

read + review all short stories
know 3 or 4 stories real well (maybe 5)

2nd grow out of discussion of Huxley's religion as an objective question.

30-35% of grade

themeatic approach